*EVERYMAN, I will go with thee,*

*and be thy guide,*

*In thy most need to go by thy side*

JOHN DRYDEN   Born 1631; Westminster School, Trinity College, Cambridge. Major poet, satirist, propagandist, literary critic, translator, author of comedies, heroic plays, tragedies. Poet laureate, Historiographer Royal, member Royal Society. Non-conformist background, successively Anglican and Roman Catholic. Notable for *An Essay of Dramatic Poesy* (1668), *The Conquest of Granada* (1670–1), *Marriage à la Mode* (1673), *All for Love* (1677), *Absalom and Achitophel* (1681–2), *Macflecknoe* (1682), *Religio Laici* (1682). Died 1700.

WILLIAM WYCHERLEY   Born 1641. Studied in France, also briefly at Queen's College, Oxford, and Inner Temple, London. Military service, undistinguished poet. Playwright 1671–6: *Love in a Wood*, *The Gentleman Dancing-Master*, *The Country Wife* (his most popular play), *The Plain Dealer*. Bankrupt, imprisoned 1682–6. Died 1715.

WILLIAM CONGREVE   Born at Bardsley, near Leeds, 1670; educated Kilkenny College, Trinity College, Dublin, and briefly Middle Temple, London. Friend of Dryden; held several government appointments, prosperous. Produced poetry, literary criticism, prose fiction (*Incognita*, 1692), a masque, several very popular plays: *The Old Bachelor*, 1693; *The Double-Dealer*, 1693; *Love for Love*, 1695; *The Mourning Bride*, 1697 (his only tragedy). *The Way of the World*, 1700, was not enthusiastically received; this factor, plus ill health and financial independence, led him to retire c. 1700. Died 1729.

THOMAS OTWAY   Born 3 March 1652, at Trotton, Sussex. Winchester College, 1668–9; Christ Church, Oxford briefly. London as unsuccessful actor, then playwright; friend of Dryden. Best plays *The Orphan*, 1680 (domestic tragedy), *The Soldier's Fortune*, 1681 (comedy), *Venice Preserv'd*, 1682 (tragedy). Died n poverty 14 April 1685.

GEORGE FARQUHAR   Born Londonderry 1677; Trinity College, Dublin 1694–6. Unsuccessful actor in Dublin. To London 1697; wrote undistinguished poetry, prose and comedies. Lieutenant in army, principally as recruiter, c. 1704–6. Author of two memorable plays, *The Recruiting Officer*, 1706, and *The Beaux Stratagem*, 1707. Died c. 20 May 1707 (of tuberculosis).

SIR JOHN VANBRUGH   Born 24 January 1664 in London. France 1683–5, studied architecture. Military career 1686–96; imprisoned in France 1688–92. Playwright, principally 1696–8 (*The Relapse* and *The Provok'd Wife* are his only original plays); subsequent dramatic adaptations, and briefly manager of Haymarket Theatre (1705), which he had built. Professional architect from c. 1700, most notably Castle Howard and Blenheim Palace. Knighted 1714; married 1719. Died 26 March 1726.

SIR GEORGE ETHEREGE   Born c. 1635. Perhaps studied at Cambridge University; briefly apprenticed to an attorney. Wrote two popular plays, *The Comical Revenge* (1664), *She Would If She Could* (1668). Secretary to English ambassador to Turkey 1668–1671. *The Man of Mode* (1676) was a third successful play. Knighted and married a wealthy widow 1679. Envoy to Ratisbon (Bavaria) 1685–9. Died in Paris c. 1691.

# Restoration Plays

Introduction and notes by
ROBERT G. LAWRENCE
*Associate Professor of English,*
*University of Victoria,*
*Victoria, British Columbia*

Dent London Melbourne Toronto
EVERYMAN'S LIBRARY
Dutton New York

© Introductions, notes and textual revisions
J. M. Dent & Sons Ltd, 1976

Printed in Great Britain
by
Biddles Ltd, Guildford, Surrey
for
J. M. DENT & SONS LTD
Aldine House, 33 Welbeck St, London

First included in Everyman's Library 1912
Augmented edition, including *The Man of Mode*, 1932
This revised edition, including re-edited text
of *The Provok'd Wife*, 1976
Published in the U.S.A. by arrangement with
J. M. Dent & Sons Ltd

Reprinted 1980

No 604 Hardback ISBN 0 460 00604 5
No 1604 Paperback ISBN 0 460 01604 0

# CONTENTS

# NOTE TO 1976 EDITION

The present edition represents a reworking of an earlier Everyman collection of these plays. Economic considerations made it impossible to provide revised texts for all the plays; however, *The Provok'd Wife* has been newly edited, with some textual revision of the other plays, and new introductions and end notes have been provided throughout. The editor acknowledges a debt of gratitude to the Canada Council and the University of Victoria for a research fellowship and study leave.

1976                                    ROBERT G. LAWRENCE.

# INTRODUCTION

The five comedies and two tragedies in this volume are a representative sampling of the most interesting and enduring plays of the Restoration period (1660–c. 1710). Between the Puritan closing of the theatres in 1642 and the accession of Charles II in 1660, in the interregnum dominated by Oliver Cromwell, dramatic activity almost ceased. The restoration of the monarchy was enthusiastically welcomed, but both social and theatrical conditions had changed during the eighteen-year period of turmoil. Society was in search of new values to replace the rejected Puritan ethos, and almost all the pre-Civil War theatres had been destroyed. The two new theatres permitted to open were wholly controlled by the Court and catered almost exclusively to aristocratic tastes and audiences. The proscenium arch, painted scenery and the appearance of women in female roles were distinctive features of Restoration drama.

Theatrical activity in the early 1660s consisted largely of adaptations and revivals (Shakespeare, Beaumont, Fletcher, Shirley, Brome, etc.); however after the interruption caused by the Plague and Fire (1665 and 1666) the types of drama characteristic of the Restoration period firmly established themselves: the comedy of manners, tragedy and heroic plays.[1] Wycherley's *Country Wife* (1675) and Etherege's *Man of Mode* (1676) are attractive examples of the early comedy of manners, whilst Vanbrugh's *Provok'd Wife* (1697), Congreve's *Way of the World* (1700) and Farquhar's *Beaux Stratagem* (1707) represent a developing and climaxing sophistication in this form; Dryden's *All for Love* (1677) and Otway's *Venice Preserv'd* (1682) are tragedies of sufficient interest and power to be revived occasionally on stage in the twentieth century.

The 'comedy of manners', which dominates the period, is a term of convenience encompassing many aspects of form and style. The most important element in common in these plays is their authors' interest in contemporary social customs, conventions and relationships, almost invariably with a realistic urban—

---

[1] The melodramatic extravagances of heroic drama—such as Dryden's *Conquest of Granada* (1670–1), Lee's *Sophonisba* (1675) and Rowe's *Fair Penitent* (1703)—did not long survive their own period, and this type of play is not included in this anthology.

i.e. London—setting. Here were the Court, the aristocracy and the major audiences. The chief preoccupations of playwrights and audiences of the comedies were aspects of love, courtship and marriage. Few plays previous to this period had offered as sustained an analysis (or dissection) of marital relationships as these comedies of manners. (Marriage is also an important subject in the two tragedies in this collection.) The comedies put in sharp contrast the marriages arranged for dynastic or mercenary reasons (the existing Pinchwife, Sullen and Fainall unions and the proposed wedding of Young Bellair and Harriet, for example) and marriages based on genuine affection, such as those of Mirabell and Millamant, Aimwell and Dorinda, Young Bellair and Emilia. Intimately related to these topics centring on love or marriage are those of money, property, dowries, and the pleasures (or occasionally criticisms) of a dilettante, irresponsible, libertine way of life, made possible by wealth. Inevitably then, where money is lacking or the possession of it threatened, dramatic tensions are created.[1]

Some comedies of manners combine information and entertainment, being largely uncritical, perhaps bemused, depictions of the *mores* of upper-class society (like *The Man of Mode*); others have a stronger satiric emphasis, on the disjunctions between appearance and reality, on the distinctions between true wits and false wits, or on the less attractive human traits: affectation, hypocrisy, selfishness, vanity, sexual aggressiveness. Many of these plays show the indirect influence of Thomas Hobbes, who saw laughter as a symptom of superiority. Façades are important, and the mask is a frequent satiric symbol or image. Remarkably, considering the interest in both political and religious affairs evident in poetry and prose of the day, references in Restoration comedy to these topics are rare.

[1] The popular subjects of Restoration comedy suggest the pervasive influence of earlier plays like Shakespeare's *Much Ado about Nothing* and *As You Like It*, Jonson's *Volpone*, Middleton's *Trick to Catch the Old One*, Fletcher's *Wild-Goose Chase*, Shirley's *Hyde Park*, and Brome's *Jovial Crew*. A particularly enduring Elizabethan character type who lived on into the Restoration was the cuckold; Jack Pinchwife, Sir John Brute, Fainall and other men in the comedies worry about this matter, without, as usual, much sympathy from their creators. The *précieux* tradition appeared occasionally in Restoration comedy, notably in the plays of Etherege and Congreve; deriving ultimately from the Platonic sighing, unrequited lover, the convention of *préciosité* influenced late seventeenth-century comedy in the direction of extravagances (sometimes satirized) in fashion and in courtship behaviour and speech. Although Molière (1622–73) wrote many comedies dealing with love and marriage, he was not a major influence on Restoration comedy; however, it is evident that all the English playwrights of the period knew his work.

Like other early comedies of manners, *The Country Wife* and *The Man of Mode* mix description and analysis. Wycherley was surprisingly tolerant of his ambivalent hero, Horner, the pretended eunuch, and criticized the frauds more severely: Lady Fidget and her hypocritical friends, Sparkish, an unperceptive ass, and Pinchwife, a cruel, suspicious sensualist. Etherege has a comparable hero, a genuine man of mode, another sexual athlete who moves aggressively through society seeking and taking pleasure. The anathema of the playwright is the false man of mode, Sir Fopling Flutter, who symbolizes the worst affectations of Paris, from the tips of his Piccat shoes to his Chedreaux periwig.

Many elements of Vanbrugh's *Provok'd Wife* are similar; Sir John Brute is a lineal descendant of Jack Pinchwife, the much provoked Lady Brute is as likeable and intelligent a character as Alithea in *The Country Wife* or Harriet in *The Man of Mode*, and Lady Fanciful owes a small debt to Lady Fidget. The distinctive quality of Vanbrugh's play rests in his social sensitivity. Sir John and Lady Brute's *mariage de convenance* has endured uneasily for two years, punctuated regularly with quarrels aggravated by his habitual drunkenness. The play includes much discussion of divorce, which was then extremely difficult to obtain, but concludes with no resolution of the problem. The further development of the serious or analytical side of the comedy of manners is well illustrated in *The Beaux Stratagem*, which has the same marital problem, solved with a formal separation, by mutual agreement, between an incompatible husband and wife.

Chronologically *The Provok'd Wife* and *The Beaux Stratagem* are separated by Congreve's *Way of the World*. In one respect this play is a reversion to the traditional witty comedy of manners, with its concentration on the wooing of Millamant by the reformed libertine Mirabell, accompanied by conventional premarital complications of rivalries, coquetry, misunderstandings and financial considerations. In another respect *The Way of the World* is 'modern', through the seriousness with which the subject of marriage is considered. In earlier comedies of manners falling genuinely in love was regarded as a disgrace and matrimony was treated with considerable flippancy. Although Congreve was a life-long bachelor, his characters in *The Way of the World* are more articulate on the subject of matrimony than any others in contemporary comedies.

Changing trends are also illustrated by reference to two scenes dealing with sexual intercourse; the 'china scene' in *The Country*

*Wife* (1675) is charged with vigorous sexual innuendo, whereas
the 'proviso scene' of *The Way of the World* (1700) treats similar
material with much greater refinement. Despite an admirable
balancing of Congreve's evident goodwill towards several of his
characters and his contempt for fools like Petulant and Witwoud,
*The Way of the World* was too subtle or had too sharp a satiric
edge to be popular in 1700. Since then, however, no comedy of the
period has been revived as often, a tribute to its universality of
theme, sparkle, rapid pace and brilliant dialogue.

English theatregoers and readers have always demanded more
of a play than observing its characters take pleasure in life and
sharing vicariously in that pleasure. The supposed indecencies,
marital infidelities and ambiguous moral attitudes in several
comedies of manners have distressed successive generations of
critics and viewers. In particular they have reacted uneasily to
equivocal heroes—Horner, Dorimant, Mirabell, Archer and
Aimwell—who are deficient in virtue and show an unconvincing
final repentance, and to multi-faceted heroines—Margery
Pinchwife, Millamant, Mrs Sullen, Lady Brute, Harriet Woodvil
—who display an unladylike shrewdness or ruthlessness.

In its own century Restoration comedy was often attacked for
encouraging immorality, most notoriously by the Reverend
Jeremy Collier in *A Short View of the Immorality and Profaneness
of the English Stage* (1698).[1] He and other contemporary reviewers
contributed significantly to the eclipse of Restoration drama, as
did important changes in theatre audiences. The court coterie
which had given both comedy and tragedy so much impetus
disintegrated after the death of King Charles II in 1685. James II
and his successor, Mary II, reigned for too short a time to leave
any real mark on English culture, and Mary's co-regent, the
dour William III, had no interest in the theatre. As the middle
class grew in wealth and power the wives of merchants and
gentry became by the end of the seventeenth century the principal

---

[1] Collier was only one of the first amongst many critics of Restoration
comedy; for example, Sir Richard Steele devoted the whole of *Spectator*
65 (15 May 1711) to a sharp criticism of *The Man of Mode* (an anony-
mous reply, written in fact by John Dennis, *A Defense of Sir Fopling
Flutter*, appeared in 1722); Thomas Babington Macaulay, the distinguished historian-critic, a disciple of Collier, fulminated against the
indecencies of Wycherley and Congreve in 'Comic Dramatists of the
Restoration' (written in 1841, available in *Works*, 1898, vol. ix, pp. 335–
393). Detractors from and defenders of Restoration comedy have been
active in the twentieth century, the former represented by L. C. Knights
(*Explorations*, 1946) and John Wain (in *Essays in Criticism*, VI, 1956),
the latter by F. W. Bateson (in *Essays in Criticism*, VII, 1957) and
others (see Bibliography).

theatregoers and arbiters of taste and moral attitudes. They approved of the sentimental comedy produced by playwrights like Colley Cibber (*Love's Last Shift*, 1696) and Sir Richard Steele (*The Conscious Lovers*, 1722); this kind of drama was indebted to the comedy of manners, as were subsequently the plays of Sheridan and Goldsmith, who, reacting against the sentimental excesses of the drama of the first half of the eighteenth century, looked back for inspiration to the Restoration period.

Tragedy of the Restoration period was sternly moral and retributive in its emphasis. It leaned heavily on the past for plots and techniques, although more domestic in nature than earlier English tragedy. Restoration tragedies were written either in old-fashioned rhyme or in generally sententious blank verse. Both *All for Love* and *Venice Preserv'd* reveal some influences of heroic drama, but they are less rhetorical and sensational than most tragedies of the period; however, critics have been doubtful about Dryden's sentimental introduction of Octavia and her children and of Otway's inclusion of the Nicky-Nacky scenes and the bloody apparitions of Jaffeir and Pierre. The tragic impact of these and other contemporary dramas was eroded by the emphasis on emotion. Yet the ethical and moral problems which *All for Love* and *Venice Preserv'd* raise are still relevant. Both plays accentuate the conflict between duty and inclination in domestic contexts, human frailty being the primary cause of the tragic outcome. The fact that fewer than one quarter of the new plays written during the Restoration period were tragedies indicates that contemporary tastes ran more towards heroic drama and comedy.

Any survey of Restoration drama impresses one with its vitality. Both tragedy and comedy are full of dynamic people, actively, even obsessively, pursuing their objectives and creating conflicts and harmonious relationships, often in the form of the witty love game or duel, in passionate, sophisticated dialogue.[1] Restoration comedy especially has contributed several unforgettably vital characters to a permanent gallery of English fictional figures: Lady Wishfort, Millamant, Mirabell, Sir Fopling Flutter, Jack Pinchwife, Mrs Sullen, Aimwell and Archer, amongst others. The characters of Restoration drama are mirrors of the ways of their world, vividly revealing three centuries later the tastes and

[1] The action of each of the seven plays in this volume takes place in a little less or a little more than a single day, illustrating the pace of the action and echoing, at a distance, the classical 'unities'.

attitudes of the times, with, in the case of the tragedies, the extra
dimension of glimpses into an earlier past as seen through
Restoration eyes.

These plays deal both with immediate problems or values and
with timeless issues—many-dimensioned considerations of love,
marriage, wealth, social aggrandizement, and, in the tragedies,
political problems and ambitions; hence the plays have a distinct
intellectual appeal. It is the analysis of relationships between men
and women, inside and outside of marriage, and the tentative
movements towards feminine emancipation from traditional
restrictions that perhaps bring these plays closest to comparable
preoccupations of the twentieth century.[1]

## ALL FOR LOVE (1677) BY JOHN DRYDEN

In a consideration of this play some reference to *Antony and
Cleopatra* (1607) is inevitable, since Dryden specifically acknowledged his indebtedness to Shakespeare. *All for Love* was influenced
as well by Samuel Daniel's *Tragedy of Cleopatra* (c. 1593), other
dramatic versions of the story, and Plutarch's *Lives of Noble
Grecians and Romans*.

Roman historians were under some pressure to depict Antony
and Cleopatra unsympathetically; thus it is now impossible
accurately to reconstruct their careers in detail. Cleopatra was
Julius Caesar's mistress in 48 and 47 B.C., and attracted Antony
in 41 B.C., when he was about forty-two and she twenty-eight.
After his third wife, Fulvia, died in 40 B.C., Antony returned
briefly to Rome to marry the recently widowed Octavia, the
sister of Octavius Caesar. Antony's divorce of Octavia in 32 B.C.
angered Octavius, who defeated Antony at Actium in 31 B.C.
Within a year Antony and Cleopatra were under siege in Alexandria. All that is factually known of their last days is Antony's
receipt of a false message informing him of Cleopatra's suicide; he
killed himself, and Cleopatra brought her life to an end a few days
later.

*All for Love* is commendably economical. It has only a dozen
characters, no subplot, and, in keeping with the revived neo-
classical dramatic unities, the action is limited to the last day in

---

[1] Modern readers may not be aware that 'Mrs' (i.e. 'Mistress') was
used in the seventeenth century as a courtesy title for both married and
unmarried ladies.

the lives of Antony and Cleopatra. Such a concentration allows one almost to forget that the romance endured for more than ten years. Antony's days of glory and the idyllic time of the 'transcendent passion' now seem long past, and the play might logically have more funereal than triumphant overtones.

Triumphant it is though, within Dryden's essential philosophy here of *amor vincit omnia*. The first four acts balance conflicting forces: Antony's rejection of political, military and marital responsibilities in opposition to Cleopatra's immediate magnetism. In the final act she wins, a victory that Dryden makes more convincing through the treachery which drives Antony towards her and away from the Roman world of duty, rivalry and jealousy.

*All for Love* centres more on Antony, his dilemmas and conflicts, than on Cleopatra. Antony is a 'shadow of an emperor', and there is much pathos in watching his universe contract act by act as, despite repeatedly revived noble intentions, he withdraws further into a private world. Misunderstanding and betrayal ultimately drive him to the besieged mausoleum, having been earlier separated from Cleopatra by his conviction of her infidelity with Dolabella. This scene in Act IV closely echoes Othello's belief in an *affaire de cœur* between Desdemona and Cassio (*Othello*, III, iii, 94 ff.).

Although Dryden gave Cleopatra some of his best lines and a considerable dynamism, she lacks the intensity and sexuality of Shakespeare's queen. The earlier playwright would hardly have allowed a sentimental Cleopatra seriously to describe herself as 'a silly, harmless, household dove'. Whatever weaknesses she may have, however, Dryden's Cleopatra is unquestionably more desirable than her rival, the cold and virtuous Octavia. Dryden brought her, without historical justification, from Rome to Alexandria to remind Antony of responsibility and to make possible a dramatic confrontation with Cleopatra.

The 'perjured villain' Alexas—significantly a eunuch—acting with an Iago-like self-interest, aggravates the situation near the end of the lovers' careers with a lie about Cleopatra's suicide. (In Shakespeare's play the report was initiated jointly by Charmian and Cleopatra.) Part of the tragedy associated with Antony's circumstances and his death is transferred to Cleopatra, who demonstrates the ultimate loyalty: to die, like a true Roman, beside her betrayed lover. A sense of futility—'What should I fight for now?'—justifies, within the sentimental framework of the play, Antony's suicide.

Dryden prepared the way for Antony's choice by making the world that he gives up one which is well lost. The foil characters—Ventidius, Dolabella, Octavia—contribute to this end, as does Octavius Caesar. Unseen, but constantly in the background. he is a continuing reminder to Antony of the sternest side of that Roman empire which ambition had once drawn him to share. From the beginning of the drama, one is torn between compassion for Antony and impatience with his self-indulgent and Herculean posturing.

Dryden stressed morality and compassion as the foundations of tragic drama, influenced by Thomas Rymer, René Le Bossu and René Rapin. In *All for Love* Dryden utilized blank verse for the first time as a playwright, adding thereby to the realism, lyric beauty and natural flow. He had not Shakespeare's mastery of sustained image patterns, but was able to use skilfully many images relating to the sea, jewellery, childhood, ruin, jealousy and the passage of time.

*All for Love* is Dryden's best play, a concise, well-organized retelling, with an appeal to Restoration sentiment, of a story that has fascinated for centuries. The drama has penetrating psychological insights and moments of grandeur in language and action. It is a moving commentary on the power of emotion to direct destiny; *All for Love* has a particular appeal in this century, which is distinguished by its growing tolerance for a man such as Antony, torn between love and duty.

## THE COUNTRY WIFE (1675)
### BY WILLIAM WYCHERLEY

Our sisters and daughters, like usurers' money, are safest when put out; but our wives, like their writings,[1] never safe, but in our closets under lock and key.

Pinchwife's words in Act V summarize well Wycherley's social and marital satire. The play has humour and elements of farce, but there is less of comedy than of criticism. Wycherley included in his play very few admirable characters. Surnames provide some direction for attitudes: Harry Horner, the supposed eunuch, is a creator of cuckolds, that is, men with horns; Pinchwife is a cruel,

---

[1] i.e. usurers' documents.

contemptible husband; Sir Jasper and Lady Fidget are unstable
representatives of Restoration London society; the Squeamish
ladies are only superficially fastidious; a doctor named Quack pro-
vides the confirmation for Horner's disability; Alithea is 'truth'.

The men are busy wenching, displaying their wit, making
money, and guarding their wives from the attentions of the
sparks of the Town. The women are shrewd and sexually alert,
the sophisticated 'bigots in honour' hypocritical about their
interest in sex until their drunken self-revelations. One man and
one woman provide a partial counterpoise to Wycherley's largely
negative characterization of both sexes. Alithea and Harcourt
are, by their directness and honesty, evidently 'meant for each
other'; a substantial aspect of the action centres on the hind-
rances to their union. These two people are more complete or
normal than anyone else in the play; a metaphorical impotence
hinders the fulfilment of all the other characters.

Wycherley vitalized and unified both plot and characterization
by his skilful use of metaphorical and actual disguise, a device for
irony that invariably pleases theatre audiences. Horner opens the
play in his cynical role of eunuch; Lady Fidget and her friends are
intensely concerned with the appearances of respectability and
honour, but are evidently delighted to learn privately that there
is no truth in the report of Horner's condition. The most important
physical disguises are those adopted by Margery Pinchwife; they
make it possible for her to escape, at least temporarily, from her
husband and to throw herself into Horner's arms, unaware of his
pose as a eunuch.

The play is full of ironic sexual innuendo, in particular the
notable 'china scene' (IV, iii). Lady Fidget, worried, as always,
about her 'dear, dear honour', visits Horner in his rooms, subsequent to his having confided to her that he has no sexual disability. They are interrupted by her husband and her unmarried
female friends (who are her rivals for Horner's attentions). The
*double entendres* concerning the 'china' which she hopes to have
from Horner contribute much to the ironic comedy. There is,
moreover, a larger dimension to the scene, illustrating as it does
relationships as brittle and fragile as china. 'China' and 'honour'
are inextricably interwoven in this scene and others. The play
illustrates a timeless sexual game: both men and women un-
abashedly seeking sexual pleasure, the one where it may most
effortlessly be found, the other where it will not compromise
social or marital security.

A related major theme in *The Country Wife* is marriage

illustrated principally in the unsatisfactory unions between Sir Jasper and Lady Fidget (who may owe something to Sir Politic and Lady Wouldbe of Jonson's *Volpone*, 1607) and Jack and Margery Pinchwife. The causes of their marital friction will sound familiar even today. Sir Jasper, importantly rushing off to a council meeting, repeatedly urges the supposedly harmless Horner to entertain his wife, for whom business leaves Sir Jasper no time. Pinchwife has, at forty-nine, lately given up whoring for the security of marriage, but he must now work hard to protect his artless young wife from the cuckold-makers of sophisticated London.

A third marriage, that of Sparkish and Alithea, is in the offing, but it has really no greater potential for happiness than the existing two. Sparkish's pride in his wit and his naïve generosity (similar to that of Sir Jasper) in pushing his fiancée in the direction of Harcourt make him ludicrous, and no one regrets the disintegration of this betrothal and the substitution of a more admirable husband for Alithea.[1] Frank Harcourt may be an imperfect husband, but this marriage, with no over-emphasis on sex, is as far as Wycherley was willing to go towards drawing an explicit moral in *The Country Wife*. At the end of the play the other two marriages remain in their far from satisfactory states, and Horner is left free, thanks to some fast-moving perjury, cheerfully to pursue his amorous dalliance as long as it suits him, and to expose or ridicule hypocrisy and affectation.

Wycherley's alleged immorality, in particular his failure to expose Horner's deception, has offended many critics through two centuries.[2] Allowing Horner to go wholly unpunished adds realism to the play, Wycherley's clear-eyed commentary on the way of the world.

The style clearly reflects the themes of the play: repeated images of sexual corruption are evident, as are several actual and metaphorical allusions to masks. In his blunt, lively dialogue Wycherley frequently used aphorisms and maxims. He cannot be said to be a wholly original playwright, but in *The Country Wife* the author owes only a general indebtedness to Terence (*Eunuchus*, 162 B.C.), Molière (*L'École des Maris*, 1661, *L'École des*

---

[1] Sparkish's prompt acceptance of Pinchwife's inaccurate account of Alithea's unfaithfulness and subsequent rejection of her leave Alithea free to accept Harcourt, with no question of immoral behaviour (V, iii).

[2] In *The Plain Dealer* (1677) Wycherley felt obliged obliquely to defend *The Country Wife* against accusations of vulgarity. William Archer later described *The Country Wife* as 'the most bestial play in all literature' (*The Old Drama and the New*, 1929, p. 193).

*Femmes*, 1662), Thomas Duffett (*The Spanish Rogue*, 1674), and a few other seventeenth-century dramatists.

*The Country Wife*, the third of Wycherley's four plays, was immediately popular and held the boards until 1766, when it was supplanted by David Garrick's bowdlerized, sentimental adaptation, *The Country Girl*. The original version has been revived many times in the twentieth century, certainly achieving its renewed popularity in part as the result of its criticism of growing commercialism and its exposure of sexual and social hypocrisy.

## THE WAY OF THE WORLD (1700)
## BY WILLIAM CONGREVE

Of the seven plays in this volume, *The Way of the World* has had the most consistent stage popularity in this century. This eminence has been achieved slowly, since the play was received with reservations by Congreve's contemporaries and later sentimental or moralistic theatregoers.

The involved interrelationships and amours create a complex plot. Even in the theatre *The Way of the World* demands the close attention of the audience, although they are aided by Congreve's early introduction of the complications and rivalries, by the rapid pace of the action (which encompasses little more than a single afternoon), and by the presentation of characters in pairs.

The play opens with two contrasting men on stage; during their flippant, cynical dialogue they refer to, and arouse interest in, all the important characters who will appear later. Lady Wishfort does not enter until III, i, but she is alluded to on almost every page to that point; Mrs Millamant is introduced long before she appears in II, v, 'full sail, with her fan spread and streamers out'. A theatre audience is quickly caught up in the scintillating dialogue and the rapid movement of people on and off stage. The names of Congreve's people create attitudes: 'Millamant' and 'Mirabell' approbation, 'Fainall' and 'Marwood' distrust. This comedy of manners has rather fewer *double entendres* than earlier plays of the type.

In *The Way of the World* Congreve used matrimony as a timelessly interesting focal point for both plot and theme; in fact, only a few minor servants remain uninvolved in the marital game. One existing marriage and two under negotiation occupy

central positions. The Fainall union had been entered into for the
most pragmatic of reasons: Mrs Fainall needed a 'cover' for her
*affaire de cœur* with Mirabell, and Mr Fainall needed his
wife's money. The prospective second marriage of Lady
Wishfort, 'full of the vigour of fifty-five', also involves sex and
money.

The essential subject of the play is, however, the courtship of
Mirabell and Millamant. It is beset with obstacles, amongst
them the suggestion that the hero is a libertine (during Acts I and
II he is still conducting his affair with Mrs Fainall) and the heroine
a coquette.[1] These flaws turn out to be only superficial, and the
playwright stresses the sincerity and depth of feeling of which
both Mirabell and Millamant are capable, in particular how his
genuine love for her is the primary motivation for Mirabell's
seemingly ruthless deception of Lady Wishfort.

Congreve effectively unites the serious and the frivolous by
approaching this marriage via the apparently ridiculous exchange
of conditions (IV, v). The 'odious provisos' must not be taken
too seriously; the lovers have already determined to have each
other, and seek only to explore degrees of mutual tolerance,
centring on forms of address, the right to privacy, and the
avoidance of affectations. It must be remembered that marriage
was then an almost irrevocable step for a woman, and Millamant
displays beneath her banter a serious concern for her future. She
can hardly be called a liberated woman, but her conditions represent a gesture towards independence. With them she tests Mirabell's character and is much relieved by his conciliatory tone and
willingness to counter in kind. It is probable that the part of
Millamant was written for the first actress to play the role, Anne
Bracegirdle, for whom Congreve had much affection.

Mirabell and Millamant are guilty of affectation, a subject
which Congreve regarded seriously in *The Way of the World*.
Unlike other affected characters, such as Petulant and Witwoud,
the lovers rise above this failing. It is a major source of Lady
Wishfort's difficulties, reaching as far back as the preposterous
pseudo-moral education she provided for her daughter, Mrs
Fainall. One would hardly expect either woman to read habitually
or to profit much from the works of Bunyan, Prynne and Quarles.

Lady Wishfort's pretentiousness is brilliantly illustrated in the
scene during which she is wooed by Sir Rowland, whom the

[1] Small weaknesses in the plotting are Mrs Fainall's willingness to
yield Mirabell to Millamant and to allow him to trick her mother, Lady
Wishfort.

audience know to be a servant posing as an aristocrat. This episode is carefully prepared for by Lady Wishfort's affectations in her dressing-room: her fretting over cosmetics (a long-standing symbol of artificiality), ordering the brandy bottle to be hidden under the table, and practising effective poses to impress Sir Rowland.

Congreve's brilliant portrait of Lady Wishfort is not wholly unsympathetic, despite his satire of her vanity, credulity and sexuality. His characterization includes elements of pathos, as in the acknowledgment of the distressing processes of ageing ('I look like an old peeled wall'), a tolerance of her whims and something akin to admiration of her buoyancy and vitality.

The author seemed in general to accept the formal, carefully structured society he depicted in the play. It is the exaggerations, the deviations from the norm, the threats to social stability, as portrayed by Fainall and Marwood, that concerned the playwright most. The unsatisfactory marriage of Mr and Mrs Fainall and the unreal courtship of Lady Wishfort are ultimately left behind; the final memory of the play is a prospect of happiness in the marriage of Mirabell and Millamant.

Significantly, it is Fainall who represents and repeatedly refers to the way of the world. Congreve believed that this way was not immutable, but capable of improvement, as the marriage of Mirabell and Millamant illustrates. Twentieth-century taste may now be impatient with the complex plotting and contrived denouement of *The Way of the World*, but the play is undated in its perceptive exploration of social ambition and pretension, of marriage and money.

*The Way of the World* reveals few specific influences. It inevitably echoes any number of plays and narratives about marriage, the battle of the sexes, and sophisticated society. Congreve may have been influenced by earlier plays dealing with a search for a spouse, especially those involving hesitations and tests. The playwright seems to have been familiar with Shakespeare's *Much Ado about Nothing* (1600), Jonson's *Epicoene* (1609), and Otway's *Soldier's Fortune* (1681). Lady Wishfort may owe something to Lady Woodvil in Etherege's *Man of Mode* (1676), Lady Fantast in Thomas Shadwell's *Bury Fair* (1689), and Lady Wishwell in Thomas Southerne's *The Maid's Last Prayer* (1693).

This edition of *The Way of the World* is based on the 1710 edition as revised by the author from the original edition of 1700. In the later edition he deleted a few phrases and short lines of

dialogue, and added scene divisions in the French dramatic
convention then in vogue, to indicate every entrance and departure of a character.


## VENICE PRESERV'D (1682) BY THOMAS OTWAY

*Venice Preserv'd* has enjoyed two centuries of vitality on the
stage, evidence of a continuing appeal to the varied tastes of many
audiences. The tragedy incorporates several dilemma situations,
which raise challenging questions about duty and friendship,
parent-child relationships, loyalty towards even a corrupt,
oppressive state, and the sanctity of an oath.

From the beginning one is aware of corruption amongst the
present rulers of Venice and of weaknesses in the reformers.
Pierre is a naïve idealist, the shallow Jaffeir can be persuaded to
break a solemn oath, and the sensuous, opportunistic Renault
attempts to rape Jaffeir's wife, Belvidera. Otway implies that
Venice would not be significantly better off after a rebel victory.
The character or quality of the Venetian establishment is sym-
bolized by the unattractive senators Priuli and Antonio, perhaps
intended to ridicule earlier Whig enthusiasm for Venice as a
model republic.

The dilemma motif is complexly developed in individual terms
primarily through Jaffeir, who is torn apart by conflicting
loyalties: to Belvidera and to his dearest friend, Pierre. Should
Jaffeir remain loyal to his revolutionary comrade who wishes to
see every senator of Venice dead or, by betraying Pierre and his
associates, preserve the life of Senator Priuli, Jaffeir's father-in-
law, whom he has personal reasons to hate?

Out of this problem others evolve: Belvidera must choose
between husband and father, Pierre must choose between
denunciation of Renault and a show of unity amongst the conspirators, old Renault is divided between his passions and his
loyalty to Pierre. These dilemmas and others create the dramatic
tensions from which the tragedies of the three principals grow.

For the scholar or historian, however, *Venice Preserv'd* is
puzzling when seen as political allegory. Thomas Otway's Tory
and royalist sympathies were well known; thus it is plausible to
recognize a parallel between the Venice of the play, threatened by
rebellion, and England of the early 1680s, under attack by Whig
dissidents. (*Venice Preserv'd* was first performed in February1682.)

The major contemporary political tensions in England centred on the succession to the throne. Charles II had no legitimate offspring; there was, therefore, every likelihood that he would be succeeded by his brother, James, Duke of York, a practising Catholic. This prospect dismayed many Englishmen, creating, basically, a division between Tory supporters of Charles II (or heir-apparent James) and Whig promoters—led by the ruthless first Earl of Shaftesbury—of James, Duke of Monmouth, an illegitimate, though Protestant, son of King Charles.[1]

In both the dramatized seventeenth-century Venice and the real England of 1681–2 the rebellious forces were defeated. Amongst the rebels of the play Otway included old Renault, described in the Prologue as 'Turbulent, subtle, mischievous and bold, . . . Loves fumbling with a wench . . .', words that echo Dryden's character study of Achitophel, i.e. the Earl of Shaftesbury, in *Absalom and Achitophel* (Part I, lines 150–213 ff.).

Although this oblique allusion and other references make it easy to see Renault as an allegorical picture of Shaftesbury, the playwright complicated his allegory by compelling one also to identify Senator Antonio with Shaftesbury, through obvious suggestions and parallels in the first Prologue and the play. Antonio is, however, not one of the dissidents, like Renault, but a notable senator, a member of the ruling clique, which at the end of the play endures, though chastened. The play therefore creates the extraordinary situation of Renault (representing Shaftesbury) plotting assiduously to overthrow Antonio (who also represents Shaftesbury).

It has been plausibly suggested [2] that Senator Antonio was a late addition to the play, representing no more than Otway's effort late in 1681 to capitalize on a *cause célèbre* (the downfall of Shaftesbury) and to bring up to date a play that had already been constructed around a *general* political allegory. Many eighteenth-century productions of *Venice Preserv'd* omitted Antonio's 'Nicky-Nacky' scenes (III, i and part of V, i).

Otway had to avoid drawing too critical a portrait of either the establishment, the source of his own well-being, or the rebels; clearly, despite the satiric characterization of Renault, Otway wished audiences to sympathize with the revolutionaries for the most part, since from them he drew his three tragic figures. He

[1] See Dryden's *Absalom and Achitophel* (1681), on the same subject, published only a few months before *Venice Preserv'd* reached the stage.
[2] Aline Mackenzie, '*Venice Preserv'd* Reconsidered', *Tulane Studies in English*, I (1949), 81–118.

emphasized their private motivations for attempting to destroy
the senate rather than a political justification, which might,
dangerously, identify them too closely with the Whigs.

A confusion of loyalties and self-interest in everyone in the
tragedy leads to the destruction of idealistic hopes of bringing
to an end a decadent government. Pierre draws sympathy to
himself by determining to die rather than suffer the ignominy of
chains and public derision. This decision makes a redemption
possible for Jaffeir, and Belvidera's awareness of her responsibility for the imminent deaths of both men unhinges her mind.
In part through the influence of Restoration heroic plays, the
tone of tragedy was changing, not only by the incorporation of a
sentimental, melodramatic quality, reinforced by high rhetoric,
but by a modification of the traditional elements of pity, fear and
catharsis. At the end of this tragedy nothing has changed as the
result of the heroes' efforts; the tragic impact of the play derives
from the destruction of characters who have struggled passionately with conflicting interests, ultimately to achieve self-
recognition. The idealism that is a pervasive part of the theme is
in sharp contrast to the sordidness of the comic scenes, the
violence of the main action and the ugliness of the imagery.

Otway's principal source was a novel, based on fact, by César
Vischard, L'Abbé de Saint-Réal, *A Conspiracy of the Spaniards
against the State of Venice* (1674, second edition in English 1679);
the playwright magnified and modified the roles of Jaffeir, Pierre
and Renault to suit his dramatic purposes, and created Belvidera
to provide motivations with less of a political emphasis than those
of Saint-Réal.

## THE BEAUX STRATAGEM (1707)
### BY GEORGE FARQUHAR

This play is one of the few Restoration comedies set outside
London. Although the action takes place in Lichfield, London is a
significant part of the background. The young fortune-hunters,
Aimwell and Archer, left the metropolis with nearly empty
pockets and brought to Lichfield their hard-headed city values;
when Mrs Sullen would punish her uncouth, insensitive husband
she wishes that she had him in London to teach him how husbands

should behave. Farquhar's intention was not primarily to set up contrasts or parallels between Lichfield and London, nor to draw a satiric portrait of society in either, but to offer a lively, realistic commentary on human nature. *The Beaux Stratagem*, despite some conventional elements, is thus less a comedy of manners than earlier comedies of the period.

Hypocrisy dominates the stratagems of Archer and Aimwell as well as the marital problems of Squire and Mrs Sullen. Disguise is a major theme from the beginning, as the two opportunistic young men hide their poverty behind the joint arrogance of a wealthy aristocrat and his servant. They share responsibility for fraudulence by an agreement to exchange roles as they move from town to town seeking a fortune.

Their questionable Lichfield exploits begin with Aimwell's seemingly virtuous appearance in church; his real motivation is to create a favourable impression, particularly on any wealthy, susceptible girl. At the same time Archer's scheme to seduce Cherry, the inn-keeper's pretty daughter, is in action; to this end he uses flattery, insincere romantic words and a statement (ironically, a true one) that he is an aristocratic younger brother in reduced circumstances. Even the inn is ambivalent in nature. It seems to offer genuine hospitality, but is in reality the headquarters of Boniface's gang of thieves.

In his portrayal of Squire and Mrs Sullen, Farquhar seriously analysed the hypocrisy of holding together an unsuccessful marriage. A woman was then almost wholly dependent on the goodwill of her husband, as both *The Beaux Stratagem* and its partial dramatic source, Vanbrugh's *Provok'd Wife* (1697), illustrate. It was possible to obtain a formal marital separation through the ecclesiastical courts, but a divorce could be arranged only by a rare act of Parliament, accompanied by much expense and publicity.

The playwright drew sympathy towards Mrs Sullen from her first appearance; the compassion of the audience seems, however, to diminish as Mrs Sullen plans an *affaire d'amour* with Count Bellaïr (II, i), but Farquhar makes it evident that she does so only to stir her obtuse husband into taking a greater interest in her. The morality of Mrs Sullen's subsequent interest in Archer is similar. She is certainly attracted to him, as a result of her dissatisfaction with life and marriage; however, when Archer boldly proposes an inspection of her bedroom, she demurs, guided by a sense of honour considerably more genuine than that of Lady Fidget and her associates in *The Country Wife*. Mrs Sullen's brief

temptation towards sexual infidelity contributes to the realism of
*The Beaux Stratagem*, as does of course, the shrewd scheming,
both sexual and financial, of Archer and Aimwell.

The subject of marriage is of great concern to Mrs Sullen's
young unmarried sister-in-law, Dorinda; her wooing by Aimwell
parallels chronologically the wrangles between the Sullens,
creating contrasts and ironies. The lovemaking of Aimwell and
Archer reveals Farquhar's careful differentiation between the
men. The former is more intense and somewhat more sincere in all
his relationships, the latter more interested in selfishly casual
sexual liaisons.

Aimwell conventionally proposes marriage to Dorinda (V, iv) in
the guise of the rich Viscount Aimwell (in fact, his elder brother),
but immediately is impelled by conscience to confess his imposture. The remarkably opportune death in London of the true
Viscount Aimwell is essentially romantic or sentimental in spirit,
arranged to make Aimwell, now a truly wealthy heir, worthy of
Dorinda. Farquhar did not yield to the temptation to provide an
equally romantic ending to Archer's tentative affair with Mrs
Sullen. Indeed, the author left the conclusion to this phase of the
play quite ambiguous.

In the final moments of Act V, Archer leads Mrs Sullen into a
dance. This gesture may imply an extension of Archer's relationship with the lady, now divorced in spirit, if not in fact, from her
husband. A few minutes earlier, however, Archer had urged
Aimwell to persuade Dorinda to employ Cherry. One may therefore imagine Archer, the eternal playboy, continuing indefinitely
his efforts to seduce these two women.

Farquhar's language is distinguished by its naturalism and
realism. There is little of the witty repartee that characterized
many earlier Restoration comedies, *The Way of the World* (1700),
for example. Farquhar's play includes several down-to-earth
people with Elizabethan antecedents: Boniface, Cherry, Gibbet
and Hounslow. They contribute much to the lively action and the
development of several humorous situations.

Autobiographical elements probably influenced the situations
and themes of *The Beaux Stratagem*. Farquhar spent some time
in Lichfield and Shrewsbury; his military duties in the latter city
inspired *The Recruiting Officer*, 1706. The author's interest in the
difficulties of bringing a marital union to an end may have been
prompted by his own marriage about 1703. The inference that it
was unhappy is based on the tradition that his wife led him to
believe she had a substantial private income. John Milton's

*Doctrine and Discipline of Divorce*, 1643, contributed many phrases and ideas to this play.[1]

The popularity of *The Beaux Stratagem* throughout most of the eighteenth century was due in large part to David Garrick's having played the role of Archer approximately ninety-seven times between 1742 and 1776; he also acted the part of Scrub five times.[2] (The play was a major influence on Goldsmith's *She Stoops to Conquer*, 1776.) The most notable recent revival of *The Beaux Stratagem* was at the National Theatre, London, in 1970, with Maggie Smith as Mrs Sullen. (The actress has since stated that this is her favourite role.)

*The Beaux Stratagem* was first produced on 8 March 1707, and was subsequently modified. A 1728 edition, published, like the first edition of 1707, by Bernard Lintot, incorporates a footnote (III, iii, p. 45) stating that the part of Bellair was deleted after the first night's performance. Several references to him remained, but his small contribution to III, iii, was omitted and his speeches in V, iv, rewritten and given to Foigard. It cannot be proved that the dying Farquhar was responsible for these revisions, although Bellair is included in no eighteenth-century cast lists after the first night.[3] The revised lines from V, iv, as published in 1728 are printed as Appendix A below.

## THE PROVOK'D WIFE (1697)
### BY SIR JOHN VANBRUGH

Vanbrugh's second and last original play reveals a tentativeness in plot and theme which suggests that he never progressed beyond a dramatic apprenticeship. The plot of this play is somewhat disjointed and incorporates many commonplace, predictable elements, but it is distinguished for its vigour, pace and a few memorable character sketches. Amongst the conventional characters are an attractive, unmarried girl of considerable fortune, Belinda, and a handsome young man, significantly named Heartfree, who in the beginning of the action is 'a professed woman-hater'. The union of these two is as inevitable

[1] Martin A. Larson, 'The Influence of Milton's Divorce Tracts on Farquhar's *Beaux Stratagem*', *PMLA*, XXXIX (March 1924), 174–8.
[2] *The London Stage*, ed. W. Van Lennep *et al.*, Carbondale, Ill., 1960–3, Part 3, vol. ii—Part 4, vol. iii.
[3] *London Stage*, Part 2, vol. i—Part 5, vol. iii.

as is the downfall of Belinda's rival, Lady Fanciful. She is an
exaggerated, though believable, illustration of the worst of
female vanity, malice and affectation. Lady Fanciful's over-
anxiety to capture Heartfree is self-defeating; Heartfree's
cynicism evaporates as his love for Belinda grows, and at the
end of the drama they anticipate an idyllic marriage. Both
relationships are, somewhat clumsily, set in contrast to an
existing marriage which is the centre of the play, that of Sir John
and Lady Brute.

Neither the unhappy bonds of wedlock nor the union of an
uncouth husband and a virtuous wife was new to English drama.[1]
Lady Brute is, however, not a commonplace heroine, but is very
likeable and convincingly real in her impatience and vitality. It is
characteristic of her high spirits that despite Sir John's uniform
unpleasantness, she can tease and aggravate him, as she does in
III, i. Notwithstanding such occasional diversions and the
pleasure Lady Brute has in Constant's devotion, her life is
miserable, as shown in the three occasions when Sir John offers
physical roughness or violence towards her (III, i; IV, i; IV, vi).
Lady Brute's circumstances reinforce a familiar theme in the
comedies of the Restoration period: the disadvantageous position
of the woman in marriage. Some women found consolation in one
or more lovers, but Lady Brute has too strong a sense of virtue to
yield to the importunities of Constant (as in IV, i).

Drunk or sober, Sir John is one of the most vital boors in
English literature. Understandably, David Garrick was attracted
to the part and played it with enthusiasm for ninety-three
performances between 1744 and 1776.[2] With typical forthright-
ness Sir John gives his reasons for entering into this unsatisfactory marriage: 'I had a mind to lie with her, and she would not
let me.' Neither could he seduce her without having 'hedg'd'
myself into forty quarrels with her relations, besides buying my
pardon' (II, i). It gradually becomes even more evident that Sir
John Brute is both a bully and a coward; thus, even though late
in Act V he is convinced of his wife's infidelity with Constant,
thanks to Razor's fraudulent report, Sir John determines to
pocket his horns—'if I don't, that goat there, that stallion, is
ready to whip me through the guts'.

It is a major disappointment that Vanbrugh found no solution

---

[1] Vanbrugh's conception of the Brutes may have been influenced by
Etherege's *She Would if She Could* (1668) and Otway's *Soldier's Fortune*
(1681).
[2] The play has been occasionally revived in the twentieth century.

to Lady Brute's problem. Indeed, he avoided the issue by filling
much of Act V with the entertaining distractions of the Belinda-
Heartfree romance and the implausible efforts of Lady Fanciful
and Razor to frustrate it. Remarkably, all of Sir John and Lady
Brute's dialogue in the denouement concerns Belinda and
Heartfree's problems; an ambiguous contrition in Sir John
appears only in a line or two:

> Surly I may be, stubborn I am not.
> For I have both forgiven and forgot.

Words like these suggest that Sir John is fundamentally unchanged and that Lady Brute's unhappy martyrdom will continue, with a partial consolation in the loyalty of Constant.

It must be appreciated, however, that Vanbrugh's choices were
limited. He would have been false to Lady Brute's character,
which he had developed in depth, to allow her simply to leave Sir
John and turn to the waiting Constant. Divorce was then obtain-
able, but only with great difficulty, and although a formal separation was possible, it was not a satisfactory solution for a woman
without independent means.[1] A husband could be compelled to
contribute to his separated wife's support, but Sir John was
unlikely to fulfil such an obligation. George Farquhar, who
created a similar dramatic situation ten years later in *The Beaux
Stratagem*, arranged a mutually agreed separation between Squire
and Mrs Sullen, accompanied by the return of her substantial
dowry.

*The Provok'd Wife* has much variety in its dialogue. Sir
John communicates invariably with a rough vigour that includes frequent oaths, but surprisingly few sexual allusions;
Lady Fanciful and Madamoiselle amusingly convey their affectations and pseudo-fastidiousness in a mixture of French and
English; the language of the lovers has inevitably romantic overtones—'I'm afraid he's too cold to warm himself by my fire'.

The realistic tone of much of the play is reflected in the paucity
and simplicity of the figures of speech. There are intermittent
similes and metaphors, several of them illustrative of Sir John's
character: Lady Brute refers to him as 'a fiery dragon', he himself uses a few military images, as when he charges the watch,
and several metaphors are based on the cuckoldry motif. Razor's
metaphor in Act V, as he is about to reveal secrets to Madamoiselle, is the most ingenious: 'The news is that cuckoldom in folio

[1] Lady Brute had married Sir John for money (I, i).

is newly printed, and matrimony in quarto is just going into the press. Will you buy any books, Madamoiselle?'

*The Provok'd Wife* was immediately popular and held the stage through much of the eighteenth century, undergoing repeated alterations, including the incorporation of additional songs. A study of successive editions of the period reveals a progressive bowdlerizing of Vanbrugh's text, to soften the cynical overtones and to eliminate much of the vulgarity. Perhaps the most entertaining of the later editions is that of Mrs Elizabeth Inchbald, in *The British Theatre; or a Collection of Plays . . .* (1808).

Sir John Vanbrugh contributed two substantial modifications to the text. The episodes with a drunken Sir John Brute dressed in a clergyman's cassock (IV, i and iii) were evidently thought to ridicule the clergy; hence, apparently shortly before his death in 1726, the playwright conciliated popular taste by rewriting these scenes, first printed in a Dublin edition of 1743. In the revised version of IV, i, Sir John dons a gown belonging to his wife; in IV, iii, as modified, he appears drunkenly before the same obtuse justice and offers some commonplaces of anti-feminist satire; this transvestite scene is longer and more implausible than the original. The revisions appear as Appendix B below.

## THE MAN OF MODE (1676)
### BY SIR GEORGE ETHEREGE

*The Man of Mode* does not mark the beginning of the vogue for the comedy of manners in England, but Etherge's last play is one of the best of the early examples. The word 'mode' helps to define the genre, for in this play two young men, Dorimant and Fopling, variously exhibit a consciousness of style—in their dress, their ways of speaking, and their relationships with girls. Although Sir Fopling Flutter is the man of mode in Etherege's alternative title, he contributes only peripherally to the plot; his principal *raison d'être* is to illustrate excesses of affectation. Significantly, clothes are the centre of Fopling's life, to Dorimant they are incidental; the former lacks discrimination, the latter does not.

Dorimant is both an exponent of manners and the major force behind the entire action. His interest in four young women, Loveit, Emilia, Belinda and Harriet, brings out varied aspects of his personality and creates the fundamental tensions of the play.

At the same time an almost unrelated plot is working itself out
through two unmannered (i.e. natural) characters, Young
Bellair and Emilia, who are unaffectedly in love and anxious to
marry. The two plots are casually linked by the lively and independent Harriet, whom Old Bellair has commanded his son to
marry; Young Bellair is, however, already secretly betrothed to
Emilia.

Although the threads of the plots are not closely knit together,
Etherege effectively used the device of anticipation. In every
scene the playwright prepares the audience for a later situation
or character revelation. The opening episode, for example, intro-
duces a mysterious masked girl (later identified as Belinda),
announces the unexpected, ominous arrival of Old Bellair, and
refers repeatedly to Sir Fopling Flutter, who does not appear
until III, ii.

Young Bellair's 'romances' are in sharp contrast to the
libertine *affaires d'amour* of Dorimant, who is trying, at one and
the same time, to break off with the vain and passionate Loveit,
to seduce Belinda, and to offer himself as a serious lover to
Harriet. (He also has a casual interest in Emilia.) There are
obviously several unattractive aspects of Dorimant's character
which would seem to qualify his being the hero of this comedy;
however, Etherege gives to Dorimant some sincerity, tolerance
and good nature, as well as much self-interest. Dorimant's
positive and negative qualities are in balance throughout most of
the play—the combination giving him rather more realism than
most heroes of Restoration drama possess—but near the end,
as Dorimant gradually removes the obstacles to his capture of
Harriet, he must muster up all the sincerity he can to make
convincing his promises of fidelity.[1] Here Etherege is less than
persuasive, because he includes within Dorimant's protestations
of devotion the candid aside to Loveit of an intention to marry in
order 'to repair the ruins of my estate'; as well, Etherege ends the
play with Dorimant both betrothed to Harriet and on good terms
with two of his former girlfriends.

Further, the audience may be conscious that Dorimant was at
first willing to marry Harriet only because he was not able to
seduce her; Young Bellair warns him: 'You had best not think of
Mrs Harriet too much; without church security, there's no taking
up there' (IV, ii). It is not possible to assume that Dorimant and
Harriet will 'live happily ever after'; Etherege hints that

---

[1] In IV, i, Dorimant had abruptly terminated his enthusiastic wooing
of Harriet in order to fulfil an assignation made earlier with Belinda.

Dorimant may be incapable of wholly renouncing his former self.
'Easy Etherege' conveys his own tolerance of human nature in his
kindly handling of characters like Dorimant and Sir Fopling
Flutter, about whom there is potentially much to criticize.

The play includes several other characters of much interest.
Medley is a professional gossip—'a flea or a maggot is not made
more monstrous by a magnifying glass than a story is by his
telling it'—and perky Old Bellair bounces through his scenes
with his verbal eccentricities; he has a degree of affectation,
illustrated in his naïve ambition to marry, at the age of fifty-five,
the girl whom his son intends to wed. Old Bellair and the two
aristocratic ladies on the fringes of the action provide the traditional conflict of generations.

*The Man of Mode* is, as suggested, a play about appearances.
The frequent references to mirrors, cosmetics, masks and masquerades are oblique reminders of reality disguised in the background. One fine example of make-believe is Harriet and Young
Bellair's pretended wooing to deceive 'the grave people', her
mother and his father.[1] The greatest number of metaphors and
similes echo the artificiality or unreality; most have reference
directly or indirectly to Dorimant: gaming, commerce, religion
(used in a tongue-in-cheek manner), and in particular his
role as devil. His own words sum up the theme of façades: 'Love
gilds us over and makes us show fine things to one another for a
time, but soon the gold wears off, and then the native brass
appears.'

The imagery contributes significantly to the wit and sparkle of
the play, much of it conveyed in colloquial dialogue. The sophisticated interchanges, especially those between Dorimant and
Fopling, anticipate the scintillating style of *The Way of the World*.

Specific influences on *The Man of Mode* are difficult to
isolate. The play includes some reminders of Molière, and there is
a cousinship between Dorimant and Horner (the hero of
Wycherley's *Country Wife*, 1675). It is tempting to think that
Etherege modelled characters in *The Man of Mode* on individuals
whom he knew in London society, but there is little convincing
evidence that this was so. Undoubtedly the playwright drew upon
the aristocratic society with which he was familiar, and the careers
of some of the Restoration beaux and fops, like Sir George Hewitt,
Sir Car Scroope, and John Wilmot, second Earl of Rochester,
would indicate that little dramatic heightening was necessary.

---

[1] The relationship between Young Bellair and Harriet is echoed in
Goldsmith's *She Stoops to Conquer*.

# SELECT BIBLIOGRAPHY

## GENERAL

G. S. Alleman, *Matrimonial Law and the Materials of Restoration Comedy*. Philadelphia, 1942.

N. Holland, *The First Modern Comedies; the Significance of Etherege, Wycherley, and Congreve*. Cambridge, Mass., 1959.

J. R. Brown and B. Harris (eds.), *Restoration Theatre*. Stratford-upon-Avon Studies, 6, 1965.

J. Loftis (ed.), *Restoration Drama: Modern Essays in Criticism*. New York, 1966.

E. Rothstein, *Restoration Tragedy; Form and Process of Change*. Madison, Wis., 1967.

J. H. Wilson, *A Preface to Restoration Drama*. Cambridge, Mass., 1968.

K. Muir, *The Comedy of Manners*. London, 1970.

V. Birdsall, *Wild Civility, the English Comic Spirit on the Restoration Stage*. Bloomington, Ind., 1970.

## DRYDEN

Ruth Wallerstein, 'Dryden and the Analysis of Shakespeare's Techniques'. *Review of English Studies*, XIX (1943), 165–85.

John Winterbottom, 'The Development of the Hero in Dryden's Tragedies'. *Journal of English and Germanic Philology*, LII (1953), 161–73.

C. E. Ward, *The Life of John Dryden*. Chapel Hill, N.C., 1961.

E. M. Waith, *The Herculean Hero in Marlowe, Chapman, Shakespeare and Dryden*. London, 1962.

B. N. Schilling (ed.), *Dryden: a Collection of Critical Essays*. 20th Century Views Series. Englewood Cliffs, N.J., 1963 and London, 1964.

G. R. Wasserman, *John Dryden*. New York, 1964.

J. M. Osborn, *John Dryden: some Biographical Facts and Problems*. New York, revised ed., 1965.

Bruce King (ed.), *Dryden's 'All For Love'*. 20th Century Interpretations Series. London and Englewood Cliffs, N.J., 1968.

William Myers, *Dryden*. London, 1973.

## WYCHERLEY

W. C. Connely, *Brawny Wycherley*. London, 1930.

P. F. Vernon, *William Wycherley*. Writers and their Work Series. London, 1965.

R. Zimbardo, *Wycherley's Drama: a Link in the Development of English Satire*. New Haven, 1965.

S. Mukherjee, 'Marriage as Punishment in the Plays of Wycherley'. *Review of English Literature*, VII (October 1966), 61–4.

W. Freedman, 'Impotence and Self-destruction in *The Country Wife*' *English Studies*, LIII (October 1972), 421–31.

K. A. Rogers, *William Wycherley*. New York, 1972.

Wallace Jackson, '*The Country Wife*: the Premises of Love and Lust'. *South Atlantic Quarterly*, LXXII (Autumn 1973), 540–6.

## CONGREVE

J. C. Hodges, *William Congreve, the Man*. New York, 1941.

E. L. Avery, *Congreve's Plays on the Eighteenth-Century Stage*. New York, 1951.

P. and M. Mueschke, *A New View of Congreve's 'Way of the World'*. Ann Arbor, 1958.

J. Gagen, 'Congreve's Mirabell and the Ideal of a Gentleman'. *PMLA*, LXXIX (September 1964), 422–7.
H. Teyssandier, 'Congreve's "Way of the World": Decorum and Morality'. *English Studies*, LII (April 1971), 124–31.
M. E. Novak, *William Congreve*. N.Y., 1971.
B. Morris (ed.), *William Congreve*. Mermaid Critical Commentaries. London, 1972.
A. Kaufman, 'Language and Character in Congreve's *Way of the World*'. *Texas Studies in Literature and Language*, XV (Fall 1973), 411–27.

## OTWAY

R. G. Ham, *Otway and Lee*. New Haven, 1931.
A. M. Taylor, *Next to Shakespeare; Otway's 'Venice Preserv'd' and 'The Orphan' and their History on the London Stage*. Durham, N.C., 1950.
D. R. Hauser, 'Otway Preserved: Theme and Form in *Venice Preserv'd*'. *Studies in Philology*, LV (July 1958), 481–93.
W. H. McBurney, 'Otway's Tragic Muse Debauched: Sensuality in *Venice Preserv'd*'. *Journal of English and Germanic Philology*, LVIII (July 1959), 380–99.
R. Berman, 'Nature in *Venice Preserv'd*'. *English Literary History*, XXXVI (September 1969), 529–43.
D. W. Hughes, 'A New Look at *Venice Preserv'd*'. *Studies in English Literature*, XI (Summer 1971), 437–57.

## FARQUHAR

W. C. Connely, *Young George Farquhar*. London, 1949.
R. Berman, 'The Comedy of Reason'. *Texas Studies in Literature and Language*, VII (Summer 1965), 161–8.
G. Farmer, *George Farquhar*. Writers and their Work Series. London, 1966.
E. Rothstein, *George Farquhar*. N.Y., 1967.
E. N. James, *The Development of George Farquhar as a Comic Dramatist*. The Hague, 1972.

## VANBRUGH

P. Mueschke and J. Fleisher, 'A Re-evaluation of Vanbrugh'. *PMLA*, XLIX (September 1934), 848.
A. Rosenberg, 'New Light on Vanbrugh'. *Philological Quarterly*, XLV (July 1966), 603–13.
F. Patterson, 'Revised Scenes in *The Provok'd Wife*'. *English Language Notes*, IV (September 1966), 19–23.
B. Harris, *Sir John Vanbrugh*. Writers and their Work Series. London, 1967.
M. Bingham, *Masks and Façades: Sir John Vanbrugh, the Man in his Setting*. London, 1974.

## ETHEREGE

F. Tinker, *Sir George Etherege: a Study in Restoration Comedy*. London, 1931.
D. Underwood, *Etherege and the Seventeenth-century Comedy of Manners*. New Haven, 1957.
C. Cecil, 'Libertine and *Précieux* Elements in Restoration Comedy'. *Essays in Criticism*, IX (1959), 239–53.
P. C. Davies, 'The State of Nature and the State of War: a Reconsideration of *The Man of Mode*'. *University of Toronto Quarterly*, XXXIX (October 1969), 53–62.
J. Hayman, 'Dorimant and the Comedy of *The Man of Mode*'. *Modern Language Quarterly*, XXX (June 1969), 183–97.

# ALL FOR LOVE

## OR THE WORLD WELL LOST

### A TRAGEDY

TO THE RIGHT HONOURABLE

## THOMAS, EARL OF DANBY

*Viscount Latimer, and Baron Osborne of Kiveton,'in Yorkshire;
Lord High Treasurer of England, one of His Majesty's Most
Honourable Privy Council, and Knight of the Most Noble Order
of the Garter.*

MY LORD,—The gratitude of poets is so troublesome a virtue
to great men, that you are often in danger of your own benefits:
for you are threatened with some epistle, and not suffered to do
good in quiet, or to compound for their silence whom you have
obliged. Yet, I confess, I neither am nor ought to be surprised
at this indulgence; for your lordship has the same right to favour
poetry, which the great and noble have ever had—

> *Carmen amat, quisquis carmine digna gerit.*

There is somewhat of a tie in nature betwixt those who are
born for worthy actions, and those who can transmit them to
posterity; and though ours be much the inferior part, it comes
at least within the verge of alliance; nor are we unprofitable
members of the commonwealth, when we animate others to
those virtues, which we copy and describe from you.

It is indeed their interest, who endeavour the subversion of
governments, to discourage poets and historians; for the best
which can happen to them, is to be forgotten. But such who,
under kings, are the fathers of their country, and by a just and
prudent ordering of affairs preserve it, have the same reason to
cherish the chroniclers of their actions, as they have to lay up
in safety the deeds and evidences of their estates; for such
records are their undoubted titles to the love and reverence of
after ages. Your lordship's administration has already taken
up a considerable part of the English annals; and many of its

I

most happy years are owing to it. His Majesty, the most knowing judge of men, and the best master, has acknowledged the ease and benefit he receives in the incomes of his treasury, which you found not only disordered, but exhausted. All things were in the confusion of a chaos, without form or method, if not reduced beyond it, even to annihilation; so that you had not only to separate the jarring elements, but (if that boldness of expression might be allowed me) to create them. Your enemies had so embroiled the management of your office, that they looked on your advancement as the instrument of your ruin. And as if the clogging of the revenue, and the confusion of accounts, which you found in your entrance, were not sufficient, they added their own weight of malice to the public calamity, by forestalling the credit which should cure it. Your friends on the other side were only capable of pitying, but not of aiding you; no further help or counsel was remaining to you, but what was founded on yourself; and that indeed was your security; for your diligence, your constancy, and your prudence, wrought more surely within, when they were not disturbed by any outward motion. The highest virtue is best to be trusted with itself; for assistance only can be given by a genius superior to that which it assists; and it is the noblest kind of debt, when we are only obliged to God and nature. This then, my lord, is your just commendation, that you have wrought out yourself a way to glory, by those very means that were designed for your destruction. You have not only restored but advanced the revenues of your master, without grievance to the subject; and, as if that were little yet, the debts of the exchequer, which lay heaviest both on the crown, and on private persons, have by your conduct been established in a certainty of satisfaction. An action so much the more great and honourable, because the case was without the ordinary relief of laws; above the hopes of the afflicted and beyond the narrowness of the treasury to redress, had it been managed by a less able hand. It is certainly the happiest, and most unenvied part of all your fortune, to do good to many, while you do injury to none; to receive at once the prayers of the subject, and the praises of the prince; and, by the care of your conduct, to give him means of exerting the chiefest (if any be the chiefest) of his royal virtues, his distributive justice to the deserving, and his bounty and compassion to the wanting. The disposition of princes towards their people cannot better be discovered than in the choice of their ministers; who, like the animal spirits betwixt the soul and body, participate somewhat of both natures, and make the communication which is betwixt them. A king, who is just and moderate in his nature, who rules according to the laws, whom God made happy by forming the temper of his soul to the constitution of his government, and who makes us happy, by assuming over us no other sovereignty than that wherein our welfare and liberty consists; a prince, I say, of so excellent a character, and so suitable to the wishes of all good men, could not better have conveyed himself into his people's apprehensions, than in your lordship's person; who so lively express the same virtues, that you seem not so much a copy, as an emanation of him. Moderation is doubtless an establishment of greatness; but there is a steadiness of temper which is likewise requisite in a minister of state; so equal a mixture of both virtues, that he may stand like an isthmus betwixt the two encroaching seas of arbitrary power, and lawless anarchy. The undertaking would be difficult to any but an extraordinary genius, to stand at the line, and to divide the limits; to pay what is due to the great representative of the nation, and neither to enhance, nor to yield up, the undoubted prerogatives of the crown. These, my lord, are the proper virtues of a noble Englishman, as indeed they are properly English virtues; no people in the world being capable of using them, but we who have the happiness to be born under so equal, and so well-poised a government;—a government which has all the advantages of liberty beyond a commonwealth, and all the marks of kingly sovereignty, without the danger of a tyranny. Both my nature, as I am an Englishman, and my reason, as I am a man, have bred in me a loathing to that specious name of a republic; that mock appearance of a liberty, where all who have not part in the government, are slaves; and slaves they are of a viler note, than such as are subjects to an absolute dominion. For no Christian monarchy is so absolute, but it is circumscribed with laws; but when the executive power is in the law-makers, there is no further check upon them; and the people must suffer without a remedy, because they are oppressed by their representatives. If I must serve, the number of my masters, who were born my equals, would but add to the ignominy of my bondage. The nature of our government, above all others, is exactly suited both to the situation of our country, and the temper of the natives; an island being more proper for commerce and for defence, than for extending its dominions on the Continent; for what the valour of its inhabitants might gain, by reason of its remoteness, and the casualties of the seas, it could not so easily preserve. And, therefore, neither the arbitrary power of One, in a monarchy, nor of Many, in a commonwealth, could make us greater than we are. It is true, that vaster and more frequent taxes might be gathered, when the consent of the people was not asked or needed; but this were only by conquering abroad, to be poor at home; and the examples of our neighbours teach us, that they are not always the happiest subjects, whose kings extend their dominions farthest. Since therefore we cannot win by an offensive war, at least a land war, the model of our government seems naturally contrived for the defensive part; and the consent of a people is easily obtained to contribute to that power which must protect it. *Felices nimium, bona si sua nôrint, Angligenæ!* And yet there are not wanting malcontents amongst us, who, surfeiting themselves on too much happiness, would persuade the people that they might be happier by a change. It was indeed the policy of their old forefather, when himself was fallen from the station of glory, to seduce mankind into the same rebellion with him, by telling him he might yet be freer than he was; that is, more free than his nature would allow, or, if I may so say, than God could make him. We have already all the liberty which freeborn subjects can enjoy, and all beyond it is but licence. But if it be liberty of conscience which they pretend, the moderation of our church is such, that its practice extends not to the severity of persecution; and its discipline is withal so easy, that it allows more freedom to dissenters than any of the sects would allow to it. In the meantime, what right can be pretended by these men to attempt innovations in church or state? Who made them the trustees, or to speak a little nearer their own language, the keepers of the liberty of England? If their call be extraordinary, let them convince us by working miracles; for ordinary vocation they can have none, to disturb the government under which they were born, and which protects them. He who has often changed his party, and always has made his interest the rule of it, gives little evidence of his sincerity for the public good; it is manifest he changes but for himself, and takes the people for tools to work his fortune. Yet the experience of all ages might let him know, that they who trouble the waters first, have seldom the benefit of the fishing; as they who began the late rebellion enjoyed not the fruit of their undertaking, but were crushed themselves by the usurpation of their own instrument. Neither is it enough for them to answer, that they only intend a reformation of the government, but not the subversion of it; on such pretences all insurrections have been founded; it is striking at the root of power, which is obedience. Every remonstrance of private men has the seed of treason in it; and discourses, which are couched in ambiguous terms, are therefore the more dangerous, because they do all the mischief of open sedition, yet are safe from the punishment of the laws. These, my lord, are considerations, which I should not pass so lightly over, had I room to manage them as they deserve; for no man can be so inconsiderable in a nation, as not to have a share in the welfare of it; and if he be a true Englishman, he must at the same time be fired with indignation, and revenge himself as he can on the disturbers of his country. And to whom could I more fitly apply myself than to your lordship, who have not only an inborn, but an hereditary loyalty? The memorable constancy and sufferings of your father, almost to the ruin of his estate, for the royal cause, were an earnest of that which such a parent and such an institution would produce in the person of a son. But so unhappy an occasion of manifesting your own zeal, in suffering for his present majesty, the providence of God, and the prudence of your administration, will, I hope, prevent; that, as your father's fortune waited on the unhappiness of his sovereign, so your own may participate of the better fate which attends his son. The relation which you have by alliance to the noble family of your lady, serves to confirm to you both this happy augury. For what can deserve a greater place in the English chronicle, than the loyalty and courage, the actions and death, of the general of an army, fighting for his prince and country? The honour and gallantry of the Earl of Lindsey is so illustrious a subject, that it is fit to adorn an heroic poem; for he was the proto-martyr of the cause, and the type of his unfortunate royal master.

Yet after all, my lord, if I may speak my thoughts, you are happy rather to us than to yourself; for the multiplicity, the cares, and the vexations of your employment, have betrayed you from yourself, and given you up into the possession of the public. You are robbed of your privacy and friends, and scarce any hour of your life you can call your own. Those who envy your fortune, if they wanted not good-nature, might more justly pity it; and when they see you watched by a crowd of suitors, whose importunity it is impossible to avoid, would conclude, with reason, that you have lost much more in true content, than you have gained by dignity; and that a private gentleman is better attended by a single servant, than your lordship with so clamorous a train. Pardon me, my lord, if I speak like a philosopher on this subject; the fortune which makes a man uneasy, cannot make him happy; and a wise man must think himself uneasy, when few of his actions are in his choice.

This last consideration has brought me to another, and a very seasonable one for your relief; which is, that while I pity your want of leisure, I have impertinently detained you so long a time. I have put off my own business, which was my dedication, till it is so late, that I am now ashamed to begin it; and therefore I will say nothing of the poem, which I present to you, because I know not if you are like to have an hour, which, with a good conscience, you may throw away in perusing it; and for the author, I have only to beg the continuance of your protection to him, who is, my lord, your lordship's most obliged, most humble, and most obedient servant,

JOHN. DRYDEN.

# PREFACE

THE death of Antony and Cleopatra is a subject which has been treated by the greatest wits of our nation, after Shakespeare; and by all so variously, that their example has given me the confidence to try myself in this bow of Ulysses amongst the crowd of suitors; and, withal, to take my own measures, in aiming at the mark. I doubt not but the same motive has prevailed with all of us in this attempt; I mean the excellency of the moral. For the chief persons represented were famous patterns of unlawful love; and their end accordingly was unfortunate. All reasonable men have long since concluded, that the hero of the poem ought not to be a character of perfect virtue, for then he could not, without injustice, be made unhappy; nor yet altogether wicked, because he could not then be pitied. I have therefore steered the middle course; and have drawn the character of Antony as favourably as Plutarch, Appian, and Dion Cassius would give me leave; the like I have observed in Cleopatra. That which is wanting to work up the pity to a greater height, was not afforded me by the story; for the crimes of love, which they both committed, were not occasioned by any necessity, or fatal ignorance, but were wholly voluntary; since our passions are, or ought to be, within our power. The fabric of the play is regular enough, as to the inferior parts of it; and the unities of time, place, and action, more exactly observed, than perhaps the English theatre requires. Particularly, the action is so much one, that it is the only of the kind without episode, or underplot; every scene in the tragedy conducing to the main design, and every act concluding with a turn of it. The greatest error in the contrivance seems to be in the person of Octavia; for, though I might use the privilege of a poet, to introduce her into Alexandria, yet I had not enough considered, that the compassion she moved to herself and children was destructive to that which I reserved for Antony and Cleopatra; whose mutual love being founded upon vice, must lessen the favour of the audience to them, when virtue and innocence were oppressed by it. And, though I justified Antony in some measure, by making Octavia's departure to proceed wholly from herself; yet the force of the first machine still remained; and the dividing of pity, like the cutting of a river into many channels, abated the strength of the natural stream. But this is an objection which none of my critics have urged against me; and therefore I might have let it pass, if I could have resolved to

have been partial to myself. The faults my enemies have found
are rather cavils concerning little and not essential decencies;
which a master of the ceremonies may decide betwixt us. The
French poets, I confess, are strict observers of these punctilios.
They would not, for example, have suffered Cleopatra and
Octavia to have met; or, if they had met, there must have only
passed betwixt them some cold civilities, but no eagerness of
repartee, for fear of offending against the greatness of their
characters, and the modesty of their sex. This objection I fore-
saw, and at the same time contemned; for I judged it both
natural and probable, that Octavia, proud of her new-gained
conquest, would search out Cleopatra to triumph over her; and
that Cleopatra, thus attacked, was not of a spirit to shun the
encounter. And it is not unlikely, that two exasperated rivals
should use such satire as I have put into their mouths; for,
after all, though the one were a Roman, and the other a queen,
they were both women. It is true, some actions, though natural,
are not fit to be represented; and broad obscenities in words
ought in good manners to be avoided: expressions therefore are
a modest clothing of our thoughts, as breeches and petticoats
are of our bodies. If I have kept myself within the bounds of
modesty, all beyond, it is but nicety and affectation; which is
no more but modesty depraved into a vice. They betray themselves who are too quick of apprehension in such cases, and
leave all reasonable men to imagine worse of them, than of the
poet.

Honest Montaigne goes yet further: *Nous ne sommes que
cérémonie ; la cérémonie nous emporte, et laissons la substance des
choses. Nous nous tenons aux branches, et abandonnons le tronc
et le corps. Nous avons appris aux dames de rougir, oyans
seulement nommer ce qu'elles ne craignent aucunement à faire :
Nous n'osons appeller à droit nos membres, et ne craignons pas de
les employer à toute sorte de débauche. La cérémonie nous defend
d'exprimer par paroles les choses licites et naturelles, et nous l'en
croyons ; la raison nous défend de n'en faire point d'illicites et
mauvaises, et personne ne l'en croit.* My comfort is, that by this
opinion my enemies are but sucking critics, who would fain be
nibbling ere their teeth are come.

Yet, in this nicety of manners does the excellency of French
poetry consist. Their heroes are the most civil people breathing;
but their good breeding seldom extends to a word of sense; all
their wit is in their ceremony; they want the genius which
animates our stage; and therefore it is but necessary, when they
cannot please, that they should take care not to offend. But
as the civilest man in the company is commonly the dullest, so
these authors, while they are afraid to make you laugh or cry,
out of pure good manners make you sleep. They are so careful
not to exasperate a critic, that they never leave him any work;
so busy with the broom, and make so clean a riddance that there

is little left either for censure or for praise. For no part of a
poem is worth our discommending, where the whole is insipid;
as when we have once tasted of palled wine, we stay not to
examine it glass by glass. But while they affect to shine in
trifles, they are often careless in essentials. Thus, their Hippolytus is so scrupulous in point of decency, that he will rather
expose himself to death, than accuse his stepmother to his father;
and my critics I am sure will commend him for it. But we of
grosser apprehensions are apt to think that this excess of
generosity is not practicable, but with fools and madmen. This
was good manners with a vengeance; and the audience is like to
be much concerned at the misfortunes of this admirable hero.
But take Hippolytus out of his poetic fit, and I suppose he would
think it a wiser part to set the saddle on the right horse, and
choose rather to live with the reputation of a plain-spoken,
honest man, than to die with the infamy of an incestuous villain.
In the meantime we may take notice, that where the poet ought
to have preserved the character as it was delivered to us by
antiquity, when he should have given us the picture of a rough
young man, of the Amazonian strain, a jolly huntsman, and
both by his profession and his early rising a mortal enemy to
love, he has chosen to give him the turn of gallantry, sent him
to travel from Athens to Paris, taught him to make love, and
transformed the Hippolytus of Euripides into Monsieur Hippo-
lyte. I should not have troubled myself thus far with French
poets, but that I find our *Chedreux* critics wholly form their
judgments by them. But for my part, I desire to be tried by
the laws of my own country; for it seems unjust to me, that the
French should prescribe here, till they have conquered. Our
little sonneteers, who follow them, have too narrow souls to
judge of poetry. Poets themselves are the most proper, though
I conclude not the only critics. But till some genius, as universal
as Aristotle, shall arise, one who can penetrate into all arts and
sciences, without the practice of them, I shall think it reasonable,
that the judgment of an artificer in his own art should be
preferable to the opinion of another man; at least where he is
not bribed by interest, or prejudiced by malice. And this, I
suppose, is manifest by plain induction. For, first, the crowd
cannot be presumed to have more than a gross instinct, of what
pleases or displeases them. Every man will grant me this; but
then, by a particular kindness to himself, he draws his own
stake first, and will be distinguished from the multitude, of
which other men may think him one. But, if I come closer
to those who are allowed for witty men, either by the advantage
of their quality, or by common fame, and affirm that neither
are they qualified to decide sovereignly concerning poetry, I
shall yet have a strong party of my opinion; for most of them
severally will exclude the rest, either from the number of witty
men, or at least of able judges. But here again they are all

indulgent to themselves; and every one who believes himself a
wit, that is, every man, will pretend at the same time to a right
of judging.  But to press it yet further, there are many witty
men, but few poets; neither have all poets a taste of tragedy.
And this is the rock on which they are daily splitting.  Poetry,
which is a picture of nature, must generally please; but it is not
to be understood that all parts of it must please every man;
therefore is not tragedy to be judged by a witty man, whose
taste is only confined to comedy.  Nor is every man, who loves
tragedy, a sufficient judge of it; he must understand the
excellencies of it too, or he will only prove a blind admirer, not
a critic.  From hence it comes that so many satires on poets,
and censures of their writings, fly abroad.  Men of pleasant
conversation (at least esteemed so), and endued with a trifling
kind of fancy, perhaps helped out with some smattering of Latin,
are ambitious to distinguish themselves from the herd of gentlemen, by their poetry—

> *Rarus enim fermè sensus communis in illâ*
> *Fortunâ.*

And is not this a wretched affectation, not to be contented
with what fortune has done for them, and sit down quietly with
their estates, but they must call their wits in question, and
needlessly expose their nakedness to public view?  Not considering that they are not to expect the same approbation from
sober men, which they have found from their flatterers after the
third bottle.  If a little glittering in discourse has passed them
on us for witty men, where was the necessity of undeceiving the
world?  Would a man who has an ill title to an estate, but yet
is in possession of it; would he bring it of his own accord, to be
tried at Westminster?  We who write, if we want the talent,
yet have the excuse that we do it for a poor subsistence; but
what can be urged in their defence, who, not having the vocation
of poverty to scribble, out of mere wantonness take pains to
make themselves ridiculous?  Horace was certainly in the right
where he said, " That no man is satisfied with his own condition."
A poet is not pleased, because he is not rich; and the rich are
discontented, because the poets will not admit them of their
number.  Thus the case is hard with writers.  If they succeed
not, they must starve; and if they do, some malicious satire is
prepared to level them, for daring to please without their leave.
But while they are so eager to destroy the fame of others, their
ambition is manifest in their concernment; some poem of their
own is to be produced, and the slaves are to be laid flat with
their faces on the ground, that the monarch may appear in the
greater majesty.
Dionysius and Nero had the same longings, but with all their
power they could never bring their business well about.  'Tis
true, they proclaimed themselves poets by sound of trumpet;

and poets they were, upon pain of death to any man who durst
call them otherwise. The audience had a fine time on't, you
may imagine; they sat in a bodily fear, and looked as demurely
as they could: for it was a hanging matter to laugh unseasonably;
and the tyrants were suspicious, as they had reason, that their
subjects had them in the wind; so, every man, in his own defence,
set as good a face upon the business as he could. It was known
beforehand that the monarchs were to be crowned laureates;
but when the show was over, and an honest man was suffered
to depart quietly, he took out his laughter which he had stifled,
with a firm resolution never more to see an emperor's play,
though he had been ten years a-making it. In the meantime
the true poets were they who made the best markets: for they had
wit enough to yield the prize with a good grace, and not contend
with him who had thirty legions. They were sure to be rewarded,
if they confessed themselves bad writers, and that was somewhat
better than to be martyrs for their reputation. Lucan's example
was enough to teach them manners; and after he was put to
death, for overcoming Nero, the emperor carried it without
dispute for the best poet in his dominions. No man was
ambitious of that grinning honour; for if he heard the malicious
trumpeter proclaiming his name before his betters, he knew there
was but one way with him. Mæcenas took another course, and
we know he was more than a great man, for he was witty too:
but finding himself far gone in poetry, which Seneca assures us
was not his talent, he thought it his best way to be well with
Virgil and with Horace; that at least he might be a poet at the
second hand; and we see how happily it has succeeded with
him; for his own bad poetry is forgotten, and their panegyrics
of him still remain. But they who should be our patrons are
for no such expensive ways to fame; they have much of the
poetry of Mæcenas, but little of his liberality. They are for
persecuting Horace and Virgil, in the persons of their successors;
for such is every man who has any part of their soul and fire,
though in a less degree. Some of their little zanies yet go
further; for they are persecutors even of Horace himself, as far
as they are able, by their ignorant and vile imitations of him;
by making an unjust use of his authority, and turning his
artillery against his friends. But how would he disdain to be
copied by such hands! I dare answer for him, he would be more
uneasy in their company, than he was with Crispinus, their
forefather, in the Holy Way; and would no more have allowed
them a place amongst the critics, than he would Demetrius the
mimic, and Tigellius the buffoon;

> —— *Demetri, teque, Tigelli,*
> *Discipulorum inter jubeo plorare cathedras.*

With what scorn would he look down on such miserable trans-
lators, who make doggerel of his Latin, mistake his meaning,

misapply his censures, and often contradict their own? He is fixed as a landmark to set out the bounds of poetry—

> ―――― *Saxum antiquum, ingens,* ―
> *Limes agro positus, litem ut discerneret arvis.*

But other arms than theirs, and other sinews are required, to raise the weight of such an author; and when they would toss him against their enemies—

> *Genua labant, gelidus concrevit frigore sanguis.*
> *Tum lapis ipse viri, vacuum per inane volatus,*
> *Nec spatium evasit totum, nec pertulit ictum.*

For my part, I would wish no other revenge, either for myself, or the rest of the poets, from this rhyming judge of the twelve-penny gallery, this legitimate son of Sternhold, than that he would subscribe his name to his censure, or (not to tax him beyond his learning) set his mark. For, should he own himself publicly, and come from behind the lion's skin, they whom he condemns would be thankful to him, they whom he praises would choose to be condemned; and the magistrates, whom he has elected, would modestly withdraw from their employment, to avoid the scandal of his nomination. The sharpness of his satire, next to himself, falls most heavily on his friends, and they ought never to forgive him for commending them perpetually the wrong way, and sometimes by contraries. If he have a friend, whose hastiness in writing is his greatest fault, Horace would have taught him to have minced the matter, and to have called it readiness of thought, and a flowing fancy; for friendship will allow a man to christen an imperfection by the name of some neighbour virtue—

> *Vellem in amicitiá sic erraremus ; et isti*
> *Errori nomen virtus posuisset honestum.*

But he would never have allowed him to have called a slow man hasty, or a hasty writer a slow drudge, as Juvenal explains it—

> ―――― *Canibus pigris, scabieque vetustá*
> *Lævibus, et siccæ lambentibus ora lucernæ,*
> *Nomen erit, Pardus, Tigris, Leo ; si quid adhus est*
> *Quod fremit in terris violentius.*

Yet Lucretius laughs at a foolish lover, even for excusing the imperfections of his mistress—

> *Nigra* μελίχροos *est, immunda et fœtida* ἄκοσμος.
> *Balba loqui non quit,* τραυλίζει; *muta pudens est,* etc.

But to drive it *ad Æthiopem cygnum* is not to be endured. I leave him to interpret this by the benefit of his French version on the other side, and without further considering him, than I have the rest of my illiterate censors, whom I have disdained to answer, because they are not qualified for judges. It remains

that I acquaint the reader, that I have endeavoured in this play
to follow the practice of the ancients, who, as Mr. Rymer has
judiciously observed, are and ought to be our masters. Horace
likewise gives it for a rule in his art of poetry—

> ———— *Vos exemplaria Græca*
> *Nocturnâ versate manu, versate diurnâ.*

Yet, though their models are regular, they are too little for
English tragedy; which requires to be built in a larger compass.
I could give an instance in the *Œdipus Tyrannus*, which was the
masterpiece of Sophocles; but I reserve it for a more fit occasion,
which I hope to have hereafter. In my style, I have professed
to imitate the divine Shakespeare; which that I might perform
more freely, I have disencumbered myself from rhyme. Not
that I condemn my former way, but that this is more proper to
my present purpose. I hope I need not to explain myself, that
I have not copied my author servilely. Words and phrases must
of necessity receive a change in succeeding ages; but it is almost
a miracle that much of his language remains so pure; and that
he who began dramatic poetry amongst us, untaught by any,
and as Ben Jonson tells us, without learning, should by the
force of his own genius perform so much, that in a manner he
has left no praise for any who come after him. The occasion is
fair, and the subject would be pleasant to handle the difference of
styles betwixt him and Fletcher, and wherein, and how far they
are both to be imitated. But since I must not be over-confident
of my own performance after him, it will be prudence in me to
be silent. Yet, I hope, I may affirm, and without vanity, that,
by imitating him, I have excelled myself throughout the play;
and particularly, that I prefer the scene betwixt Antony and
Ventidius in the first act, to anything which I have written in
this kind.

# PROLOGUE

WHAT flocks of critics hover here to-day,
As vultures wait on armies for their prey,
All gaping for the carcase of a play!
With croaking notes they bode some dire event,
And follow dying poets by the scent.
Ours gives himself for gone; y' have watched your time:
He fights this day unarmed,—without his rhyme;—
And brings a tale which often has been told;
As sad as Dido's; and almost as old.
His hero, whom you wits his bully call,
Bates of his mettle, and scarce rants at all:
He's somewhat lewd; but a well-meaning mind;
Weeps much; fights little; but is wond'rous kind.
In short, a pattern, and companion fit,
For all the keeping Tonies of the pit.
I could name more: a wife, and mistress too;
Both (to be plain) too good for most of you:
The wife well-natured, and the mistress true.
   Now, poets, if your fame has been his care,
Allow him all the candour you can spare.
A brave man scorns to quarrel once a day;
Like Hectors, in at every petty fray.
Let those find fault whose wit's so very small,
They've need to show that they can think at all;
Errors, like straws, upon the surface flow;
He who would search for pearls, must dive below.
Fops may have leave to level all they can;
As pigmies would be glad to lop a man.
Half-wits are fleas; so little and so light,
We scarce could know they live, but that they bite.
But, as the rich, when tired with daily feasts,
For change, become their next poor tenant's guests;
Drink hearty draughts of ale from plain brown bowls,
And snatch the homely rasher from the coals:
So you, retiring from much better cheer,
For once, may venture to do penance here.
And since that plenteous autumn now is past,
Whose grapes and peaches have indulged your taste,
Take in good part, from our poor poet's board,
Such rivelled fruits as winter can afford.

# DRAMATIS PERSONÆ

MARK ANTONY.
VENTIDIUS, his General.
DOLABELLA, his Friend.
ALEXAS, the Queen's Eunuch.
SERAPION, Priest of Isis.
MYRIS, another Priest.
Servants to Antony.

CLEOPATRA, Queen of Egypt.
OCTAVIA, Antony's Wife.
CHARMION, } Cleopatra's Maids.
IRAS,
Antony's two little Daughters.

SCENE—ALEXANDRIA.

# ACT I

*Enter* SERAPION, MYRIS, Priests of Isis.

*Serap.* Portents and prodigies are grown so frequent,
That they have lost their name.  Our fruitful Nile
Flowed ere the wonted season, with a torrent
So unexpected, and so wondrous fierce,
That the wild deluge overtook the haste
Even of the hinds that watched it:  Men and beasts
Were borne above the tops of trees, that grew
On the utmost margin of the water-mark.
Then, with so swift an ebb the flood drove backward,
It slipt from underneath the scaly herd:
Here monstrous phocæ panted on the shore;
Forsaken dolphins there with their broad tails,
Lay lashing the departing waves:  hard by them,
Sea horses floundering in the slimy mud,
Tossed up their heads, and dashed the ooze about them.

*Enter* ALEXAS *behind them.*

*Myr.* Avert these omens, Heaven!
*Serap.* Last night, between the hours of twelve and one,
In a lone aisle of the temple while I walked,
A whirlwind rose, that, with a violent blast,
Shook all the dome:  the doors around me clapt;
The iron wicket  that defends the vault,
Where the long race of Ptolemies is laid,
Burst open, and disclosed the mighty dead.
From out each monument, in order placed,
An armed ghost starts up:  the boy-king last
Reared his inglorious head.   A peal of groans
Then followed, and a lamentable voice
Cried, Egypt is no more!   My blood ran back,
My shaking knees against each other knocked;
On the cold pavement down I fell entranced,
And so unfinished left the horrid scene.

*Alex.* And dreamed you this?  or did invent the story,
                                        [*Showing himself.*
To frighten our Egyptian boys withal,
And train them up, betimes, in fear of priesthood?
*Serap.* My lord, I saw you not,

17

Nor meant my words should reach your ears; but what
I uttered was most true.

 *Alex.* A foolish dream,
Bred from the fumes of indigested feasts,
And holy luxury.

 *Serap.* I know my duty:
This goes no further.

 *Alex.* 'Tis not fit it should;
Nor would the times now bear it, were it true.
All southern, from yon hills, the Roman camp
Hangs o'er us black and threatening, like a storm
Just breaking on our heads.

 *Serap.* Our faint Egyptians pray for Antony;
But in their servile hearts they own Octavius.

 *Myr.* Why then does Antony dream out his hours,
And tempts not fortune for a noble day,
Which might redeem what Actium lost?

 *Alex.* He thinks 'tis past recovery.

 *Serap.* Yet the foe
Seems not to press the siege.

 *Alex.* Oh, there's the wonder.
Mæcenas and Agrippa, who can most
With Cæsar, are his foes. His wife Octavia,
Driven from his house, solicits her revenge;
And Dolabella, who was once his friend,
Upon some private grudge, now seeks his ruin:
Yet still war seems on either side to sleep.

 *Serap.* 'Tis strange that Antony, for some days past,
Has not beheld the face of Cleopatra;
But here, in Isis' temple, lives retired,
And makes his heart a prey to black despair.

 *Alex.* 'Tis true; and we much fear he hopes by absence
To cure his mind of love.

 *Serap.* If he be vanquished,
Or make his peace, Egypt is doomed to be
A Roman province; and our plenteous harvests
Must then redeem the scarceness of their soil.
While Antony stood firm, our Alexandria
Rivalled proud Rome (dominion's other seat),
And Fortune striding, like a vast Colossus,
Could fix an equal foot of empire here.

 *Alex.* Had I my wish, these tyrants of all nature,
Who lord it o'er mankind, should perish,—perish,
Each by the other's sword; but, since our will
Is lamely followed by our power, we must
Depend on one; with him to rise or fall.

 *Serap.* How stands the queen affected?

 *Alex.* Oh, she dotes,
She dotes, Serapion, on this vanquished man,

And winds herself about his mighty ruins;
Whom would she yet forsake, yet yield him up,
This hunted prey, to his pursuer's hands,
She might preserve us all: but 'tis in vain—
This changes my designs, this blasts my counsels,
And makes me use all means to keep him here,
Whom I could wish divided from her arms,
Far as the earth's deep centre.   Well, you know
The state of things; no more of your ill omens
And black prognostics; labour to confirm
The people's hearts.

*Enter* VENTIDIUS, *talking aside with a* Gentleman *of* ANTONY'S.

    *Serap.* These Romans will o'erhear us.
But, who's that stranger?   By his warlike port,
His fierce demeanour, and erected look,
He's of no vulgar note.
    *Alex.* Oh 'tis Ventidius,
Our emperor's great lieutenant in the East,
Who first showed Rome that Parthia could be conquered.
When Antony returned from Syria last,
He left this man to guard the Roman frontiers.
    *Serap.* You seem to know him well.
    *Alex.* Too well.   I saw him at Cilicia first,
When Cleopatra there met Antony:
A mortal foe he was to us, and Egypt.
But,—let me witness to the worth I hate,—
A braver Roman never drew a sword;
Firm to his prince, but as a friend, not slave.
He ne'er was of his pleasures; but presides
O'er all his cooler hours, and morning counsels:
In short the plainness, fierceness, rugged virtue,
Of an old true-stampt Roman lives in him.
His coming bodes I know not what of ill
To our affairs.   Withdraw to mark him better;
And I'll acquaint you why I sought you here,
And what's our present work.
[*They withdraw to a corner of the stage; and* VENTIDIUS,
      *with the other, comes forward to the front.*
    *Vent.* Not see him, say you?
I say, I must, and will.
    *Gent.* He has commanded,
On pain of death, none should approach his presence.
    *Vent.* I bring him news will raise his drooping spirits,
Give him new life.
    *Gent.* He sees not Cleopatra.
    *Vent.* Would he had never seen her!
    *Gent.* He eats not, drinks not, sleeps not, has no use

Of anything, but thought; or if he talks,
'Tis to himself, and then 'tis perfect raving:
Then he defies the world, and bids it pass;
Sometimes he gnaws his lip, and curses loud
The boy Octavius; then he draws his mouth
Into a scornful smile, and cries, " Take all,
The world's not worth my care."

    *Vent.* Just, just his nature.
Virtue's his path; but sometimes 'tis too narrow
For his vast soul; and then he starts out wide,
And bounds into a vice, that bears him far
From his first course, and plunges him in ills:
But, when his danger makes him find his fault,
Quick to observe, and full of sharp remorse,
He censures eagerly his own misdeeds,
Judging himself with malice to himself,
And not forgiving what as man he did,
Because his other parts are more than man.—
He must not thus be lost.

                [ALEXAS *and the* Priests *come forward.*

    *Alex.* You have your full instructions, now advance;
Proclaim your orders loudly.

    *Serap.* Romans, Egyptians, hear the queen's command.
Thus Cleopatra bids: Let labour cease;
To pomp and triumphs give this happy day,
That gave the world a lord: 'tis Antony's.
Live, Antony; and Cleopatra live!
Be this the general voice sent up to heaven,
And every public place repeat this echo.

    *Vent.* Fine pageantry!               [*Aside.*

    *Serap.* Set out before your doors
The images of all your sleeping fathers,
With laurels crowned; with laurels wreathe your posts,
And strew with flowers the pavement; let the priests
Do present sacrifice; pour out the wine,
And call the gods to join with you in gladness.

    *Vent.* Curse on the tongue that bids this general joy!
Can they be friends of Antony, who revel
When Antony's in danger? Hide, for shame,
You Romans, your great grandsires' images,
For fear their souls should animate their marbles,
To blush at their degenerate progeny.

    *Alex.* A love, which knows no bounds, to Antony,
Would mark the day with honours, when all heaven
Laboured for him, when each propitious star
Stood wakeful in his orb, to watch that hour,
And shed his better influence. Her own birthday
Our queen neglected like a vulgar fate,
That passed obscurely by.

*Vent.* Would it had slept,
Divided far from this; till some remote
And future age had called it out, to ruin
Some other prince, not him!
    *Alex.* Your emperor,
Though grown unkind, would be more gentle, than
To upbraid my queen for loving him too well.
    *Vent.* Does the mute sacrifice upbraid the priest?
He knows him not his executioner.
Oh, she has decked his ruin with her love,
Led him in golden bands to gaudy slaughter,
And made perdition pleasing: She has left him
The blank of what he was.
I tell thee, eunuch, she has quite unmanned him.
Can any Roman see, and know him now,
Thus altered from the lord of half mankind,
Unbent, unsinewed, made a woman's toy,
Shrunk from the vast extent of all his honours,
And crampt within a corner of the world?
O Antony!
Thou bravest soldier, and thou best of friends!
Bounteous as nature; next to nature's God!
Couldst thou but make new worlds, so wouldst thou give them,
As bounty were thy being! rough in battle,
As the first Romans when they went to war;
Yet after victory more pitiful
Than all their praying virgins left at home!
    *Alex.* Would you could add, to those more shining virtues,
His truth to her who loves him.
    *Vent.* Would I could not!
But wherefore waste I precious hours with thee!
Thou art her darling mischief, her chief engine,
Antony's other fate. Go, tell thy queen,
Ventidius is arrived, to end her charms.
Let your Egyptian timbrels play alone,
Nor mix effeminate sounds with Roman trumpets.
You dare not fight for Antony; go pray,
And keep your cowards' holiday in temples.
                [*Exeunt* ALEXAS, SERAPION.

*Enter a second* Gentleman *of* M. ANTONY.

    *2 Gent.* The emperor approaches, and commands,
On pain of death, that none presume to stay.
    *1 Gent.* I dare not disobey him.     [*Going out with the other.*
    *Vent.* Well, I dare.
But I'll observe him first unseen, and find
Which way his humour drives: The rest I'll venture.
                    [*Withdraws.*

*Enter* ANTONY, *walking with a disturbed motion before*
*he speaks.*

*Ant.* They tell me, 'tis my birthday, and I'll keep it
With double pomp of sadness.
'Tis what the day deserves, which gave me breath.
Why was I raised the meteor of the world,
Hung in the skies, and blazing as I travelled,
Till all my fires were spent; and then cast downward,
To be trod out by Cæsar?
    *Vent.* [*aside*]. On my soul,
'Tis mournful, wondrous mournful!
    *Ant.* Count thy gains.
Now, Antony, wouldst thou be born for this?
Glutton of fortune, thy devouring youth
Has starved thy wanting age.
    *Vent.* How sorrow shakes him!                    [*Aside.*
So, now the tempest tears him up by the roots,
And on the ground extends the noble ruin.
                    [ANTONY *having thrown himself down.*
Lie there, thou shadow of an emperor;
The place thou pressest on thy mother earth
Is all thy empire now: now it contains thee;
Some few days hence, and then 'twill be too large,
When thou'rt contracted in thy narrow urn,
Shrunk to a few cold ashes; then Octavia
(For Cleopatra will not live to see it),
Octavia then will have thee all her own,
And bear thee in her widowed hand to Cæsar;
Cæsar will weep, the crocodile will weep,
To see his rival of the universe
Lie still and peaceful there. I'll think no more on't.
    *Ant.* Give me some music: look that it be sad:
I'll soothe my melancholy, till I swell,
And burst myself with sighing.—            [*Soft music.*
'Tis somewhat to my humour: stay, I fancy
I'm now turned wild, a commoner of nature;
Of all forsaken, and forsaking all;
Live in a shady forest's sylvan scene,
Stretched at my length beneath some blasted oak,
I lean my head upon the mossy bark,
And look just of a piece as I grew from it;
My uncombed locks, matted like mistletoe,
Hang o'er my hoary face; a murmuring brook
Runs at my foot.
    *Vent.* Methinks I fancy
Myself there too.
    *Ant.* The herd come jumping by me,
And, fearless, quench their thirst, while I look on,

And take me for their fellow-citizen.
More of this image, more; it lulls my thoughts.

[*Soft music again.*

*Vent.* I must disturb him; I can hold no longer.

[*Stands before him.*

*Ant.* [*starting up*]. Art thou Ventidius?
*Vent.* Are you Antony?
I'm liker what I was, than you to him
I left you last.
*Ant.* I'm angry.
*Vent.* So am I.
*Ant.* I would be private: leave me.
*Vent.* Sir, I love you,
And therefore will not leave you.
*Ant.* Will not leave me!
Where have you learnt that answer? Who am I?
*Vent.* My emperor; the man I love next Heaven:
If I said more, I think 'twere scarce a sin:
You're all that's good, and god-like.
*Ant.* All that's wretched.
You will not leave me then?
*Vent.* 'Twas too presuming
To say I would not; but I dare not leave you:
And, 'tis unkind in you to chide me hence
So soon, when I so far have come to see you.
*Ant.* Now thou hast seen me, art thou satisfied?
For, if a friend, thou hast beheld enough;
And, if a foe, too much.
*Vent.* Look, emperor, this is no common dew.  [*Weeping*
I have not wept this forty years; but now
My mother comes afresh into my eyes;
I cannot help her softness.
*Ant.* By heaven, he weeps! poor good old man, he weeps!
The big round drops course one another down
The furrows of his cheeks.—Stop them, Ventidius,
Or I shall blush to death: they set my shame,
That caused them, full before me.
*Vent.* I'll do my best.
*Ant.* Sure there's contagion in the tears of friends:
See, I have caught it too. Believe me, 'tis not
For my own griefs, but thine.—Nay, father!
*Vent.* Emperor.
*Ant.* Emperor! Why, that's the style of victory;
The conqu'ring soldier, red with unfelt wounds,
Salutes his general so: but never more
Shall that sound reach my ears.
*Vent.* I warrant you.
*Ant.* Actium, Actium! Oh!——
*Vent.* It sits too near you.

*Ant.* Here, here it lies; a lump of lead by day,
And, in my short, distracted, nightly slumbers,
The hag that rides my dreams.——
   *Vent.* Out with it; give it vent.
   *Ant.* Urge not my shame.
I lost a battle,——
   *Vent.* So has Julius done.
   *Ant.* Thou favour'st me, and speak'st not half thou think'st;
For Julius fought it out, and lost it fairly:
But Antony——
   *Vent.* Nay, stop not.
   *Ant.* Antony,—
Well, thou wilt have it—like a coward, fled,
Fled while his soldiers fought; fled first, Ventidius.
Thou long'st to curse me, and I give thee leave.
I know thou cam'st prepared to rail.
   *Vent.* I did.
   *Ant.* I'll help thee.—I have been a man, Ventidius.
   *Vent.* Yes, and a brave one; but——
   *Ant.* I know thy meaning.
But I have lost my reason, have disgraced
The name of soldier, with inglorious ease.
In the full vintage of my flowing honours,
Sat still, and saw it prest by other hands.
Fortune came smiling to my youth, and wooed it,
And purple greatness met my ripened years.
When first I came to empire, I was borne
On tides of people, crowding to my triumphs;
The wish of nations, and the willing world
Received me as its pledge of future peace;
I was so great, so happy, so beloved,
Fate could not ruin me; till I took pains,
And worked against my fortune, chid her from me,
And turned her loose; yet still she came again.
My careless days, and my luxurious nights,
At length have wearied her, and now she's gone,
Gone, gone, divorced for ever.  Help me, soldier,
To curse this madman, this industrious fool,
Who laboured to be wretched: Pr'ythee, curse me.
   *Vent.* No.
   *Ant.* Why?
   *Vent.* You are too sensible already
Of what you've done, too conscious of your failings;
And, like a scorpion, whipt by others first
To fury, sting yourself in mad revenge.
I would bring balm, and pour it in your wounds,
Cure your distempered mind, and heal your fortunes.
   *Ant.* I know thou would'st.
   *Vent.* I will.

*Ant.* Ha, ha, ha, ha!

*Vent.* You laugh.

*Ant.* I do, to see officious love
Give cordials to the dead.

*Vent.* You would be lost, then?

*Ant.* I am.

*Vent.* I say you are not. Try your fortune.

*Ant.* I have, to the utmost. Dost thou think me desperate,
Without just cause? No, when I found all lost
Beyond repair, I hid me from the world,
And learnt to scorn it here; which now I do
So heartily, I think it is not worth
The cost of keeping.

*Vent.* Cæsar thinks not so;
He'll thank you for the gift he could not take.
You would be killed like Tully, would you? do,
Hold out your throat to Cæsar, and die tamely.

*Ant.* No, I can kill myself; and so resolve.

*Vent.* I can die with you too, when time shall serve;
But fortune calls upon us now to live,
To fight, to conquer.

*Ant.* Sure thou dream'st, Ventidius.

*Vent.* No; 'tis you dream; you sleep away your hours
In desperate sloth, miscalled philosophy.
Up, up, for honour's sake; twelve legions wait you,
And long to call you chief: By painful journeys
I led them, patient both of heat and hunger,
Down from the Parthian marches to the Nile.
'Twill do you good to see their sunburnt faces,
Their scarred cheeks, and chopt hands: there's virtue in
   them.
They'll sell those mangled limbs at dearer rates
Than yon trim bands can buy.

*Ant.* Where left you them?

*Vent.* I said in Lower Syria.

*Ant.* Bring them hither;
There may be life in these.

*Vent.* They will not come.

*Ant.* Why didst thou mock my hopes with promised
   aids,
To double my despair? They're mutinous.

*Vent.* Most firm and loyal.

*Ant.* Yet they will not march
To succour me. O trifler!

*Vent.* They petition
You would make haste to head them.

*Ant.* I'm besieged.

*Vent.* There's but one way shut up: How came I hither?

*Ant.* I will not stir.

*Vent.* They would perhaps desire
A better reason.
    *Ant.* I have never used
My soldiers to demand a reason of
My actions.   Why did they refuse to march?
    *Vent.* They said they would not fight for Cleopatra.
    *Ant.* What was't they said?
    *Vent.* They said they would not fight for Cleopatra.
Why should they fight indeed, to make her conquer,
And make you more a slave? to gain you kingdoms,
Which, for a kiss, at your next midnight feast,
You'll sell to her?   Then she new-names her jewels,
And calls this diamond such or such a tax;
Each pendant in her ear shall be a province.
    *Ant.* Ventidius, I allow your tongue free licence
On all my other faults;  but, on your life,
No word of Cleopatra: she deserves
More worlds than I can lose.
    *Vent.* Behold, you Powers,
To whom you have intrusted humankind!
See Europe, Afric, Asia, put in balance,
And all weighed down by one light, worthless woman!
I think the gods are Antonies, and give,
Like prodigals, this nether world away
To none but wasteful hands.
    *Ant.* You grow presumptuous.
    *Vent.* I take the privilege of plain love to speak.
    *Ant.* Plain love! plain arrogance, plain insolence!
Thy men are cowards;  thou, an envious traitor;
Who, under seeming honesty, hast vented
The burden of thy rank, o'erflowing gall.
O that thou wert my equal;  great in arms
As the first Cæsar was, that I might kill thee
Without a stain to honour!
    *Vent.* You may kill me;
You have done more already,—called me traitor.
    *Ant.* Art thou not one?
    *Vent.* For showing you yourself,
Which none else durst have done?  but had I been
That name, which I disdain to speak again,
I needed not have sought your abject fortunes,
Come to partake your fate, to die with you.
What hindered me to have led my conquering eagles
To fill Octavius' bands?   I could have been
A traitor then, a glorious, happy traitor,
And not have been so called.
    *Ant.* Forgive me, soldier;
I've been too passionate.
    *Vent.* You thought me false;

Thought my old age betrayed you: Kill me, sir,
Pray, kill me; yet you need not, your unkindness
Has left your sword no work.
    *Ant.* I did not think so;
I said it in my rage: Pr'ythee, forgive me.
Why didst thou tempt my anger, by discovery
Of what I would not hear?
    *Vent.* No prince but you
Could merit that sincerity I used,
Nor durst another man have ventured it;
But you, ere love misled your wandering eyes,
Were sure the chief and best of human race,
Framed in the very pride and boast of nature;
So perfect, that the gods, who formed you, wondered
At their own skill, and cried—A lucky hit
Has mended our design. Their envy hindered,
Else you had been immortal, and a pattern,
When Heaven would work for ostentation's sake
To copy out again.
    *Ant.* But Cleopatra—
Go on; for I can bear it now.
    *Vent.* No more.
    *Ant.* Thou dar'st not trust my passion, but thou may'st;
Thou only lov'st, the rest have flattered me.
    *Vent.* Heaven's blessing on your heart for that kind word!
May I believe you love me? Speak again.
    *Ant.* Indeed I do. Speak this, and this, and this.
                               *[Hugging him.*
Thy praises were unjust; but, I'll deserve them,
And yet mend all. Do with me what thou wilt;
Lead me to victory! thou know'st the way.
    *Vent.* And, will you leave this——
    *Ant.* Pr'ythee, do not curse her,
And I will leave her; though, Heaven knows, I love
Beyond life, conquest, empire, all, but honour;
But I will leave her.
    *Vent.* That's my royal master;
And, shall we fight?
    *Ant.* I warrant thee, old soldier.
Thou shalt behold me once again in iron;
And at the head of our old troops, that beat
The Parthians, cry aloud—Come, follow me!
    *Vent.* Oh, now I hear my emperor! in that word
Octavius fell. Gods, let me see that day,
And, if I have ten years behind, take all:
I'll thank you for the exchange.
    *Ant.* O Cleopatra!
    *Vent.* Again?
    *Ant.* I've done: In that last sigh she went.

Cæsar shall know what 'tis to force a lover
From all he holds most dear.
   *Vent.* Methinks, you breathe
Another soul: Your looks are more divine;
You speak a hero, and you move a god.
   *Ant.* Oh, thou hast fired me; my soul's up in arms,
And mans each part about me: Once again,
That noble eagerness of fight has seized me;
That eagerness with which I darted upward
To Cassius' camp: In vain the steepy hill
Opposed my way; in vain a war of spears
Sung round my head, and planted all my shield;
I won the trenches, while my foremost men
Lagged on the plain below.
   *Vent.* Ye gods, ye gods,
For such another hour!
   *Ant.* Come on, my soldier!
Our hearts and arms are still the same: I long
Once more to meet our foes; that thou and I,
Like Time and Death, marching before our troops,
May taste fate to them; mow them out a passage,
And, entering where the foremost squadrons yield,
Begin the noble harvest of the field.      [*Exeunt.*

# ACT II

## SCENE I

*Enter* CLEOPATRA, IRAS, *and* ALEXAS.

   *Cleo.* What shall I do, or whither shall I turn?
Ventidius has o'ercome, and he will go.
   *Alex.* He goes to fight for you.
   *Cleo.* Then he would see me, ere he went to fight:
Flatter me not: If once he goes, he's lost,
And all my hopes destroyed.
   *Alex.* Does this weak passion
Become a mighty queen?
   *Cleo.* I am no queen:
Is this to be a queen, to be besieged
By yon insulting Roman, and to wait
Each hour the victor's chain? These ills are small;
For Antony is lost, and I can mourn
For nothing else but him. Now come, Octavius,
I have no more to lose! prepare thy bands;
I'm fit to be a captive: Antony
Has taught my mind the fortune of a slave.

*Iras.* Call reason to assist you.

*Cleo.* I have none,
And none would have: My love's a noble madness,
Which shows the cause deserved it.  Moderate sorrow
Fits vulgar love, and for a vulgar man:
But I have loved with such transcendent passion,
I soared, at first, quite out of reason's view,
And now am lost above it.  No, I'm proud
'Tis thus: Would Antony could see me now
Think you he would not sigh, though he must leave me?
Sure he would sigh; for he is noble-natured,
And bears a tender heart: I know him well.
Ah, no, I know him not; I knew him once,
But now 'tis past.

*Iras.* Let it be past with you:
Forget him, madam.

*Cleo.* Never, never, Iras.
He once was mine; and once, though now 'tis gone,
Leaves a faint image of possession still.

*Alex.* Think him inconstant, cruel, and ungrateful.

*Cleo.* I cannot: If I could, those thoughts were vain.
Faithless, ungrateful, cruel, though he be,
I still must love him.

*Enter* CHARMION.

Now, what news, my Charmion?
Will he be kind? and will he not forsake me?
Am I to live, or die?—nay, do I live?
Or am I dead? for when he gave his answer,
Fate took the word, and then I lived or died.

*Char.* I found him, madam——

*Cleo.* A long speech preparing?
If thou bring'st comfort, haste, and give it me,
For never was more need.

*Iras.* I know he loves you.

*Cleo.* Had he been kind, her eyes had told me so,
Before her tongue could speak it: Now she studies,
To soften what he said; but give me death,
Just as he sent it, Charmion, undisguised,
And in the words he spoke.

*Char.* I found him, then,
Encompassed round, I think, with iron statues;
So mute, so motionless his soldiers stood,
While awfully he cast his eyes about,
And every leader's hopes or fears surveyed:
Methought he looked resolved, and yet not pleased.
When he beheld me struggling in the crowd,
He blushed, and bade make way.

*Alex.* There's comfort yet.

*Char.* Ventidius fixed his eyes upon my passage
Severely, as he meant to frown me back,
And sullenly gave place: I told my message,
Just as you gave it, broken and disordered;
I numbered in it all your sighs and tears,
And while I moved your pitiful request,
That you but only begged a last farewell,
He fetched an inward groan; and every time
I named you, sighed, as if his heart were breaking,
But shunned my eyes, and guiltily looked down;
He seemed not now that awful Antony,
Who shook an armed assembly with his nod;
But, making show as he would rub his eyes,
Disguised and blotted out a falling tear.

*Cleo.* Did he then weep? And was I worth a tear?
If what thou hast to say be not as pleasing,
Tell me no more, but let me die contented.

*Char.* He bid me say,—He knew himself so well,
He could deny you nothing, if he saw you;
And therefore——

*Cleo.* Thou wouldst say, he would not see me?

*Char.* And therefore begged you not to use a power,
Which he could ill resist; yet he should ever
Respect you, as he ought.

*Cleo.* Is that a word
For Antony to use to Cleopatra?
O that faint word, *respect!* how I disdain it!
Disdain myself, for loving after it!
He should have kept that word for cold Octavia.
Respect is for a wife: Am I that thing,
That dull, insipid lump, without desires,
And without power to give them?

*Alex.* You misjudge;
You see through love, and that deludes your sight;
As, what is straight, seems crooked through the water:
But I, who bear my reason undisturbed,
Can see this Antony, this dreaded man,
A fearful slave, who fain would run away,
And shuns his master's eyes: If you pursue him,
My life on't, he still drags a chain along
That needs must clog his flight.

*Cleo.* Could I believe thee!—

*Alex.* By every circumstance I know he loves.
True, he's hard prest, by interest and by honour;
Yet he but doubts, and parleys, and casts out
Many a long look for succour.

*Cleo.* He sends word,
He fears to see my face.

*Alex.* And would you more?

He shows his weakness who declines the combat,
And you must urge your fortune.   Could he speak
More plainly?   To my ears, the message sounds—
Come to my rescue, Cleopatra, come;
Come, free me from Ventidius; from my tyrant:
See me, and give me a pretence to leave him!—
I hear his trumpets.   This way he must pass.
Please you, retire a while; I'll work him first,
That he may bend more easy.
   *Cleo.* You shall rule me;
But all, I fear, in vain.           [*Exit with* CHARMION *and* IRAS.
   *Alex.* I fear so too;
Though I concealed my thoughts, to make her bold;
But 'tis our utmost means, and fate befriend it!  [*Withdraws.*

*Enter* Lictors *with Fasces; one bearing the Eagle; then enter*
ANTONY *with* VENTIDIUS, *followed by other* Commanders.

   *Ant.* Octavius is the minion of blind chance,
But holds from virtue nothing.
   *Vent.* Has he courage?
   *Ant.* But just enough to season him from coward.
Oh, 'tis the coldest youth upon a charge,
The most deliberate fighter! if he ventures
(As in Illyria once, they say, he did,
To storm a town), 'tis when he cannot choose;
When all the world have fixt their eyes upon him;
And then he lives on that for seven years after;
But, at a close revenge he never fails.
   *Vent.* I heard you challenged him.
   *Ant.* I did, Ventidius.
What think'st thou was his answer?   'Twas so tame!—
He said, he had more ways than one to die;
I had not.
   *Vent.* Poor!
   *Ant.* He has more ways than one;
But he would choose them all before that one.
   *Vent.* He first would choose an ague, or a fever.
   *Ant.* No; it must be an ague, not a fever;
He has not warmth enough to die by that.
   *Vent.* Or old age and a bed.
   *Ant.* Ay, there's his choice,
He would live, like a lamp, to the last wink,
And crawl upon the utmost verge of life.
O Hercules!  Why should a man like this,
Who dares not trust his fate for one great action,
Be all the care of Heaven?   Why should he lord it
O'er fourscore thousand men, of whom each one
Is braver than himself?
   *Vent.* You conquered for him:

Philippi knows it; there you shared with him
That empire, which your sword made all your own.

*Ant.* Fool that I was, upon my eagle's wings
I bore this wren, till I was tired with soaring,
And now he mounts above me.
Good heavens, is this—is this the man who braves me?
Who bids my age make way? Drives me before him,
To the world's ridge, and sweeps me off like rubbish?

*Vent.* Sir, we lose time; the troops are mounted all.

*Ant.* Then give the word to march:
I long to leave this prison of a town,
To join thy legions; and, in open field,
Once more to show my face. Lead, my deliverer.

*Enter* ALEXAS.

*Alex.* Great emperor,
In mighty arms renowned above mankind,
But, in soft pity to the opprest, a god;
This message sends the mournful Cleopatra
To her departing lord.

*Vent.* Smooth sycophant!

*Alex.* A thousand wishes, and ten thousand prayers,
Millions of blessings wait you to the wars;
Millions of sighs and tears she sends you too,
And would have sent
As many dear embraces to your arms,
As many parting kisses to your lips;
But those, she fears, have wearied you already.

*Vent.* [*aside*]. False crocodile!

*Alex.* And yet she begs not now, you would not leave her;
That were a wish too mighty for her hopes,
Too presuming
For her low fortune, and your ebbing love;
That were a wish for her more prosperous days,
Her blooming beauty, and your growing kindness.

*Ant.* [*aside*]. Well, I must man it out:—What would the
          queen?

*Alex.* First, to these noble warriors, who attend
Your daring courage in the chase of fame,—
Too daring, and too dangerous for her quiet,—
She humbly recommends all she holds dear,
All her own cares and fears,—the care of you.

*Vent.* Yes, witness Actium.

*Ant.* Let him speak, Ventidius.

*Alex.* You, when his matchless valour bears him forward,
With ardour too heroic, on his foes,
Fall down, as she would do, before his feet;
Lie in his way, and stop the paths of death:
Tell him, this god is not invulnerable;

That absent Cleopatra bleeds in him;
And, that you may remember her petition,
She begs you wear these trifles, as a pawn,
Which, at your wished return, she will redeem
                 [*Gives jewels to the* Commanders.
With all the wealth of Egypt:
This to the great Ventidius she presents,
Whom she can never count her enemy,
Because he loves her lord.
   *Vent.* Tell her, I'll none on't;
I'm not ashamed of honest poverty;
Not all the diamonds of the east can bribe
Ventidius from his faith. I hope to see
These and the rest of all her sparkling store,
Where they shall more deservingly be placed.
   *Ant.* And who must wear them then?
   *Vent.* The wronged Octavia.
   *Ant.* You might have spared that word
   *Vent.* And he that bribe.
   *Ant.* But have I no remembrance?
   *Alex.* Yes, a dear one;
Your slave the queen——
   *Ant.* My mistress.
   *Alex.* Then your mistress;
Your mistress would, she says, have sent her soul,
But that you had long since; she humbly begs
This ruby bracelet, set with bleeding hearts,
The emblems of her own, may bind your arm.
                 [*Presenting a bracelet.*
   *Vent.* Now, my best lord,—in honour's name, I ask you,
For manhood's sake, and for your own dear safety,—
Touch not these poisoned gifts,
Infected by the sender; touch them not;
Myriads of bluest plagues lie underneath them,
And more than aconite has dipt the silk.
   *Ant.* Nay, now you grow too cynical, Ventidius:
A lady's favours may be worn with honour.
What, to refuse her bracelet! On my soul,
When I lie pensive in my tent alone,
'Twill pass the wakeful hours of winter nights,
To tell these pretty beads upon my arm,
To count for every one a soft embrace,
A melting kiss at such and such a time:
And now and then the fury of her love,
When——And what harm's in this?
   *Alex.* None, none, my lord,
But what's to her, that now 'tis past for ever.
   *Ant.* [*going to tie it*]. We soldiers are so awkward—help
    me tie it.

*Alex.* In faith, my lord, we courtiers too are awkward
In these affairs: so are all men indeed:
Even I, who am not one.    But shall I speak?
   *Ant.* Yes, freely.
   *Alex.* Then, my lord, fair hands alone
Are fit to tie it; she who sent it can.
   *Vent.* Hell, death! this eunuch pander ruins you.
You will not see her?

               [ALEXAS *whispers an* Attendant, *who goes out.*
   *Ant.* But to take my leave.
   *Vent.* Then I have washed an Æthiop.   You're undone;
Y' are in the toils; y' are taken; y' are destroyed:
Her eyes do Cæsar's work.
   *Ant.* You fear too soon.
I'm constant to myself: I know my strength;
And yet she shall not think me barbarous neither,
Born in the depths of Afric: I am a Roman,
Bred to the rules of soft humanity.
A guest, and kindly used, should bid farewell.
   *Vent.* You do not know
How weak you are to her, how much an infant:
You are not proof against a smile, or glance;
A sigh will quite disarm you.
   *Ant.* See, she comes!
Now you shall find your error.—Gods, I thank you:
I formed the danger greater than it was,
And now 'tis near, 'tis lessened.
   *Vent.* Mark the end yet.

### *Enter* CLEOPATRA, CHARMION, *and* IRAS.

   *Ant.* Well, madam, we are met.
   *Cleo.* Is this a meeting?
Then, we must part?
   *Ant.* We must.
   *Cleo.* Who says we must?
   *Ant.* Our own hard fates.
   *Cleo.* We make those fates ourselves.
   *Ant.* Yes, we have made them; we have loved each other,
Into our mutual ruin.
   *Cleo.* The gods have seen my joys with envious eyes;
I have no friends in heaven; and all the world,
As 'twere the business of mankind to part us,
Is armed against my love: even you yourself
Join with the rest; you, you are armed against me.
   *Ant.* I will be justified in all I do
To late posterity, and therefore hear me.
If I mix a lie
With any truth, reproach me freely with it;
Else, favour me with silence.

*Cleo.* You command me,
And I am dumb.

*Vent.* I like this well; he shows authority.

*Ant.* That I derive my ruin
From you alone——

*Cleo.* O heavens! I ruin you!

*Ant.* You promised me your silence, and you break it
Ere I have scarce begun.

*Cleo.* Well, I obey you.

*Ant.* When I beheld you first, it was in Egypt,
Ere Cæsar saw your eyes; you gave me love,
And were too young to know it; that I settled
Your father in his throne, was for your sake;
I left the acknowledgment for time to ripen.
Cæsar stept in, and, with a greedy hand,
Plucked the green fruit, ere the first blush of red,
Yet cleaving to the bough. He was my lord,
And was, beside, too great for me to rival;
But, I deserved you first, though he enjoyed you.
When, after, I beheld you in Cilicia,
An enemy to Rome, I pardoned you.

*Cleo.* I cleared myself——

*Ant.* Again you break your promise.
I loved you still, and took your weak excuses,
Took you into my bosom, stained by Cæsar,
And not half mine: I went to Egypt with you,
And hid me from the business of the world,
Shut out inquiring nations from my sight,
To give whole years to you.

*Vent.* Yes, to your shame be't spoken.          [*Aside.*

*Ant.* How I loved.
Witness, ye days and nights, and all your hours,
That danced away with down upon your feet,
As all your business were to count my passion!
One day passed by, and nothing saw but love;
Another came, and still 'twas only love:
The suns were wearied out with looking on,
And I untired with loving.
I saw you every day, and all the day;
And every day was still but as the first,
So eager was I still to see you more.

*Vent.* 'Tis all too true.

*Ant.* Fulvia, my wife, grew jealous
(As she indeed had reason), raised a war
In Italy, to call me back.

*Vent.* But yet
You went not.

*Ant.* While within your arms I lay,
The world fell mouldering from my hands each hour,

And left me scarce a grasp—I thank your love for't.
   *Vent.* Well pushed: that last was home.
   *Cleo.* Yet may I speak?
   *Ant.* If I have urged a falsehood, yes; else, not.
Your silence says, I have not.   Fulvia died
(Pardon, you gods, with my unkindness died);
To set the world at peace, I took Octavia,
This Cæsar's sister; in her pride of youth,
And flower of beauty, did I wed that lady,
Whom blushing I must praise, because I left her.
You called; my love obeyed the fatal summons:
This raised the Roman arms; the cause was yours.
I would have fought by land, where I was stronger;
You hindered it: yet, when I fought at sea,
Forsook me fighting; and (O stain to honour!
O lasting shame!) I knew not that I fled;
But fled to follow you.
   *Vent.* What haste she made to hoist her purple sails!
And, to appear magnificent in flight,
Drew half our strength away.
   *Ant.* All this you caused.
And, would you multiply more ruins on me?
This honest man, my best, my only friend,
Has gathered up the shipwreck of my fortunes;
Twelve legions I have left, my last recruits.
And you have watched the news, and bring your eyes
To seize them too.   If you have aught to answer,
Now speak, you have free leave.
   *Alex.* [*aside*]. She stands confounded:
Despair is in her eyes.
   *Vent.* Now lay a sigh in the way to stop his passage:
Prepare a tear, and bid it for his legions;
'Tis like they shall be sold.
   *Cleo.* How shall I plead my cause, when you, my judge,
Already have condemned me?   Shall I bring
The love you bore me for my advocate?
That now is turned against me, that destroys me;
For love, once past, is, at the best, forgotten;
But oftener sours to hate: 'twill please my lord
To ruin me, and therefore I'll be guilty.
But, could I once have thought it would have pleased you,
That you would pry, with narrow searching eyes,
Into my faults, severe to my destruction,
And watching all advantages with care,
That serve to make me wretched?   Speak, my lord,
For I end here.   Though I deserved this usage,
Was it like you to give it?
   *Ant.* Oh, you wrong me,
To think I sought this parting, or desired

To accuse you more than what will clear myself,
And justify this breach.

   *Cleo.* Thus low I thank you;
And, since my innocence will not offend,
I shall not blush to own it.

   *Vent.* After this,
I think she'll blush at nothing.

   *Cleo.* You seemed grieved
(And therein you are kind), that Cæsar first
Enjoyed my love, though you deserved it better:
I grieve for that, my lord, much more than you;
For, had I first been yours, it would have saved
My second choice: I never had been his,
And ne'er had been but yours. But Cæsar first,
You say, possessed my love. Not so, my lord:
He first possessed my person; you, my love:
Cæsar loved me; but I loved Antony.
If I endured him after, 'twas because
I judged it due to the first name of men;
And, half constrained, I gave, as to a tyrant,
What he would take by force.

   *Vent.* O Siren! Siren!
Yet grant that all the love she boasts were true,
Has she not ruined you? I still urge that,
The fatal consequence.

   *Cleo.* The consequence indeed,
For I dare challenge him, my greatest foe,
To say it was designed: 'tis true, I loved you,
And kept you far from an uneasy wife,—
Such Fulvia was.
Yes, but he'll say, you left Octavia for me;—
And, can you blame me to receive that love,
Which quitted such desert, for worthless me?
How often have I wished some other Cæsar,
Great as the first, and as the second young,
Would court my love, to be refused for you!

   *Vent.* Words, words; but Actium, sir; remember Actium.

   *Cleo.* Even there, I dare his malice. True, I counselled
To fight at sea; but I betrayed you not.
I fled, but not to the enemy. 'Twas fear;
Would I had been a man, not to have feared!
For none would then have envied me your friendship,
Who envy me your love.

   *Ant.* We are both unhappy:
If nothing else, yet our ill fortune parts us.
Speak: would you have me perish by my stay?

   *Cleo.* If, as a friend, you ask my judgment, go;
If, as a lover, stay. If you must perish——
'Tis a hard word—but stay.

*Vent.* See now the effects of her so boasted love!
She strives to drag you down to ruin with her;
But, could she 'scape without you, oh, how soon
Would she let go her hold, and haste to shore,
And never look behind!

   *Cleo.* Then judge my love by this.   [*Giving* ANTONY *a writing.*
Could I have borne
A life or death, a happiness or woe,
From yours divided, this had given me means.

   *Ant.* By Hercules, the writing of Octavius!
I know it well: 'tis that proscribing hand,
Young as it was, that led the way to mine,
And left me but the second place in murder.—
See, see, Ventidius! here he offers Egypt,
And joins all Syria to it, as a present;
So, in requital, she forsake my fortunes,
And join her arms with his.

   *Cleo.* And yet you leave me!
You leave me, Antony; and yet I love you,
Indeed I do: I have refused a kingdom;
That is a trifle;
For I could part with life, with anything,
But only you. Oh, let me die but with you!
Is that a hard request?

   *Ant.* Next living with you,
'Tis all that Heaven can give.

   *Alex.* He melts; we conquer.        [*Aside.*

   *Cleo.* No; you shall go: your interest calls you hence;
Yes; your dear interest pulls too strong, for these
Weak arms to hold you here.        [*Takes his hand.*
Go; leave me, soldier
(For you're no more a lover): leave me dying:
Push me, all pale and panting, from your bosom,
And, when your march begins, let one run after,
Breathless almost for joy, and cry—She's dead.
The soldiers shout; you then, perhaps, may sigh,
And muster all your Roman gravity:
Ventidius chides; and straight your brow clears up,
As I had never been.

   *Ant.* Gods, 'tis too much; too much for man to bear.

   *Cleo.* What is't for me then,
A weak, forsaken woman, and a lover?—
Here let me breathe my last: envy me not
This minute in your arms: I'll die apace,
As fast as e'er I can, and end your trouble.

   *Ant.* Die! rather let me perish; loosened nature
Leap from its hinges, sink the props of heaven,
And fall the skies, to crush the nether world!
My eyes, my soul, my all!        [*Embraces her.*

*Vent.* And what's this toy,
In balance with your fortune, honour, fame?
   *Ant.* What is't, Ventidius?—it outweighs them all;
Why, we have more than conquered Cæsar now:
My queen's not only innocent, but loves me.
This, this is she, who drags me down to ruin!
" But, could she 'scape without me, with what haste
Would she let slip her hold, and make to shore,
And never look behind! "
Down on thy knees, blasphemer as thou art,
And ask forgiveness of wronged innocence.
   *Vent.* I'll rather die, than take it. Will you go?
   *Ant.* Go! whither? Go from all that's excellent?
Faith, honour, virtue, all good things forbid,
That I should go from her, who sets my love
Above the price of kingdoms! Give, you gods,
Give to your boy, your Cæsar,
This rattle of a globe to play withal,
This gewgaw world, and put him cheaply off: ·
I'll not be pleased with less than Cleopatra.
   *Cleo.* She's wholly yours. My heart's so full of joy,
That I shall do some wild extravagance
Of love, in public; and the foolish world,
Which knows not tenderness, will think me mad.
   *Vent.* O women! women! women! all the gods
Have not such power of doing good to man,
As you of doing harm.      [*Exit.*
   *Ant.* Our men are armed:—
Unbar the gate that looks to Cæsar's camp:
I would revenge the treachery he meant me:
And long security makes conquest easy.
I'm eager to return before I go;
For, all the pleasures I have known beat thick
On my remembrance.—How I long for night!
   That both the sweets of mutual love may try,
   And triumph once o'er Cæsar ere we die.    [*Exeunt.*

## ACT III

### SCENE I

*At one door enter* CLEOPATRA, CHARMION, IRAS, *and* ALEXAS, *a
Train of* Egyptians: *at the other* ANTONY *and* Romans.
*The entrance on both sides is prepared by music; the trumpets
first sounding on* ANTONY's *part: then answered by timbrels,
etc., on* CLEOPATRA's. CHARMION *and* IRAS *hold a laurel
wreath betwixt them. A Dance of* Egyptians. *After the
ceremony,* CLEOPATRA *crowns* ANTONY.

    *Ant.* I thought how those white arms would fold me in,
And strain me close, and melt me into love;
So pleased with that sweet image, I sprung forwards,
And added all my strength to every blow.
    *Cleo.* Come to me, come, my soldier, to my arms!
You've been too long away from my embraces;
But, when I have you fast, and all my own,
With broken murmurs, and with amorous sighs,
I'll say, you were unkind, and punish you,
And mark you red with many an eager kiss.
    *Ant.* My brighter Venus!
    *Cleo.* O my greater Mars!
    *Ant.* Thou join'st us well, my love!
Suppose me come from the Phlegræan plains,
Where gasping giants lay, cleft by my sword,
And mountain-tops pared off each other blow,
To bury those I slew.   Receive me, goddess!
Let Cæsar spread his subtle nets, like Vulcan;
In thy embraces I would be beheld
By heaven and earth at once;
And make their envy what they meant their sport.
Let those, who took us, blush; I would love on,
With awful state, regardless of their frowns,
As their superior god.
There's no satiety of love in thee:
Enjoyed, thou still art new; perpetual spring
Is in thy arms; the ripened fruit but falls,
And blossoms rise to fill its empty place;
And I grow rich by giving.

*Enter* VENTIDIUS, *and stands apart.*

    *Alex.* Oh, now the danger's past, your general comes!
He joins not in your joys, nor minds your triumphs;
But, with contracted brows, looks frowning on,
As envying your success.

*Ant.* Now, on my soul, he loves me; truly loves me:
He never flattered me in any vice,
But awes me with his virtue: even this minute,
Methinks, he has a right of chiding me.
Lead to the temple: I'll avoid his presence;
It checks too strong upon me.	[*Exeunt the rest.*

   [*As* ANTONY *is going,* VENTIDIUS *pulls him by the robe.*
*Vent.* Emperor!
*Ant.* 'Tis the old argument; I pr'ythee, spare me.
                              [*Looking back.*

*Vent.* But this one hearing, emperor.
*Ant.* Let go
My robe; or, by my father Hercules——
*Vent.* By Hercules' father, that's yet greater,
I bring you somewhat you would wish to know.
*Ant.* Thou see'st we are observed; attend me here,
And I'll return.	[*Exit.*
   *Vent.* I am waning in his favour, yet I love him;
I love this man, who runs to meet his ruin;
And sure the gods, like me, are fond of him:
His virtues lie so mingled with his crimes,
As would confound their choice to punish one,
And not reward the other.


          *Enter* ANTONY.

   *Ant.* We can conquer,
You see, without your aid.
We have dislodged their troops;
They look on us at distance, and, like curs
'Scaped from the lion's paws, they bay far off,
And lick their wounds, and faintly threaten war.
Five thousand Romans, with their faces upward,
Lie breathless on the plain.
   *Vent.* 'Tis well; and he,
Who lost them, could have spared ten thousand more.
Yet if, by this advantage, you could gain
An easier peace, while Cæsar doubts the chance
Of arms——
   *Ant.* Oh, think not on't, Ventidius!
The boy pursues my ruin, he'll no peace;
His malice is considerate in advantage.
Oh, he's the coolest murderer! so staunch,
He kills, and keeps his temper.
   *Vent.* Have you no friend
In all his army, who has power to move him?
Mæcenas, or Agrippa, might do much.
   *Ant.* They're both too deep in Cæsar's interests.
We'll work it out by dint of sword, or perish.

*Vent.* Fain I would find some other.
    *Ant.* Thank thy love.
Some four or five such victories as this
Will save thy further pains.
    *Vent.* Expect no more; Cæsar is on his guard:
I know, sir, you have conquered against odds;
But still you draw supplies from one poor town,
And of Egyptians: he has all the world,
And, at his beck, nations come pouring in,
To fill the gaps you make.  Pray, think again.
    *Ant.* Why dost thou drive me from myself, to search
For foreign aids?—to hunt my memory,
And range all o'er a waste and barren place,
To find a friend?  The wretched have no friends.
Yet I had one, the bravest youth of Rome,
Whom Cæsar loves beyond the love of women:
He could resolve his mind, as fire does wax,
From that hard rugged image melt him down,
And mould him in what softer form he pleased.
    *Vent.* Him would I see; that man, of all the world;
Just such a one we want.
    *Ant.* He loved me too;
I was his soul; he lived not but in me:
We were so closed within each other's breasts,
The rivets were not found, that joined us first.
That does not reach us yet: we were so mixt,
As meeting streams, both to ourselves were lost;
We were one mass; we could not give or take,
But from the same; for he was I, I he.
    *Vent.* He moves as I would wish him.       *[Aside.*
    *Ant.* After this,
I need not tell his name;—'twas Dolabella.
    *Vent.* He's now in Cæsar's camp.
    *Ant.* No matter where,
Since he's no longer mine.  He took unkindly,
That I forbade him Cleopatra's sight,
Because I feared he loved her: he confessed,
He had a warmth, which, for my sake, he stifled;
For 'twere impossible that two, so one,
Should not have loved the same.  When he departed,
He took no leave; and that confirmed my thoughts.
    *Vent.* It argues, that he loved you more than her,
Else he had stayed; but he perceived you jealous,
And would not grieve his friend: I know he loves you.
    *Ant.* I should have seen him, then, ere now.
    *Vent.* Perhaps
He has thus long been labouring for your peace.
    *Ant.* Would he were here!
    *Vent.* Would you believe he loved you?

I read your answer in your eyes, you would.
Not to conceal it longer, he has sent
A messenger from Cæsar's camp, with letters.

　　*Ant.* Let him appear.
　　*Vent.* I'll bring him instantly.

[*Exit* VENTIDIUS, *and re-enters immediately with* DOLABELLA.

　　*Ant.* 'Tis he himself! himself, by holy friendship!

　　　　　　　　　　　　　　　[*Runs to embrace him.*

Art thou returned at last, my better half?
Come, give me all myself!
Let me not live,
If the young bridegroom, longing for his night,
Was ever half so fond.

　　*Dola.* I must be silent, for my soul is busy
About a nobler work: she's new come home,
Like a long-absent man, and wanders o'er
Each room, a stranger to her own, to look
If all be safe.

　　*Ant.* Thou hast what's left of me;
For I am now so sunk from what I was,
Thou find'st me at my lowest water-mark.
The rivers that ran in, and raised my fortunes,
Are all dried up, or take another course:
What I have left is from my native spring;
I've still a heart that swells, in scorn of fate,
And lifts me to my banks.

　　*Dola.* Still you are lord of all the world to me.

　　*Ant.* Why, then I yet am so; for thou art all.
If I had any joy when thou wert absent,
I grudged it to myself; methought I robbed
Thee of thy part.　But, O my Dolabella!
Thou hast beheld me other than I am.
Hast thou not seen my morning chambers filled
With sceptred slaves, who waited to salute me?
With eastern monarchs, who forgot the sun,
To worship my uprising?—menial kings
Ran coursing up and down my palace-yard,
Stood silent in my presence, watched my eyes,
And, at my least command, all started out,
Like racers to the goal.

　　*Dola.* Slaves to your fortune.

　　*Ant.* Fortune is Cæsar's now; and what am I?

　　*Vent.* What you have made yourself; I will not flatter.

　　*Ant.* Is this friendly done?

　　*Dola.* Yes; when his end is so, I must join with him;
Indeed I must, and yet you must not chide;
Why am I else your friend?

　　*Ant.* Take heed, young man,
How thou upbraid'st my love: The queen has eyes,

And thou too hast a soul. Canst thou remember,
When, swelled with hatred, thou beheld'st her first,
As accessory to thy brother's death?
 *Dola.* Spare my remembrance; 'twas a guilty day,
And still the blush hangs here.
 *Ant.* To clear herself,
For sending him no aid, she came from Egypt.
Her galley down the silver Cydnus rowed,
The tackling silk, the streamers waved with gold;
The gentle winds were lodged in purple sails:
Her nymphs, like Nereids, round her couch were placed;
Where she, another sea-born Venus, lay.
 *Dola.* No more; I would not hear it.
 *Ant.* Oh, you must!
She lay, and leant her cheek upon her hand,
And cast a look so languishingly sweet,
As if, secure of all beholders' hearts,
Neglecting, she could take them: boys, like Cupids,
Stood fanning, with their painted wings, the winds,
That played about her face. But if she smiled,
A darting glory seemed to blaze abroad,
That men's desiring eyes were never wearied,
But hung upon the object: To soft flutes
The silver oars kept time; and while they played,
The hearing gave new pleasure to the sight;
And both to thought. 'Twas heaven, or somewhat more:
For she so charmed all hearts, that gazing crowds
Stood panting on the shore, and wanted breath
To give their welcome voice.
Then, Dolabella, where was then thy soul?
Was not thy fury quite disarmed with wonder?
Didst thou not shrink behind me from those eyes
And whisper in my ear—Oh, tell her not
That I accused her of my brother's death?
 *Dola.* And should my weakness be a plea for yours?
Mine was an age when love might be excused,
When kindly warmth, and when my springing youth
Made it a debt to nature. Yours——
 *Vent.* Speak boldly.
Yours, he would say, in your declining age,
When no more heat was left but what you forced,
When all the sap was needful for the trunk,
When it went down, then you constrained the course,
And robbed from nature, to supply desire;
In you (I would not use so harsh a word)
'Tis but plain dotage.
 *Ant.* Ha!
 *Dola.* 'Twas urged too home.—
But yet the loss was private, that I made;

'Twas but myself I lost: I lost no legions;
I had no world to lose, no people's love.
   *Ant.* This from a friend?
   *Dola.* Yes, Antony, a true one;
A friend so tender, that each word I speak
Stabs my own heart, before it reach your ear.
Oh, judge me not less kind, because I chide!
To Cæsar I excuse you.
   *Ant.* O ye gods!
Have I then lived to be excused to Cæsar?
   *Dola.* As to your equal.
   *Ant.* Well, he's but my equal:
While I wear this he never shall be more.
   *Dola.* I bring conditions from him.
   *Ant.* Are they noble?
Methinks thou shouldst not bring them else; yet he
Is full of deep dissembling; knows no honour
Divided from his interest.    Fate mistook him;
For nature meant him for an usurer:
He's fit indeed to buy, not conquer kingdoms.
   *Vent.* Then, granting this,
What power was theirs, who wrought so hard a temper
To honourable terms?
   *Ant.* It was my Dolabella, or some god.
   *Dola.* Nor I, nor yet Mæcenas, nor Agrippa:
They were your enemies; and I, a friend,
Too weak alone; yet 'twas a Roman's deed.
   *Ant.* 'Twas like a Roman done: show me that man,
Who has preserved my life, my love, my honour;
Let me but see his face.
   *Vent.* That task is mine,
And, Heaven, thou know'st how pleasing.    [*Exit* VENTIDIUS.
   *Dola.* You'll remember
To whom you stand obliged?
   *Ant.* When I forget it,
Be thou unkind, and that's my greatest curse.
My queen shall thank him too.
   *Dola.* I fear she will not.
   *Ant.* But she shall do it: The queen, my Dolabella!
Hast thou not still some grudgings of thy fever?
   *Dola.* I would not see her lost.
   *Ant.* When I forsake her,
Leave me, my better stars! for she has truth
Beyond her beauty.    Cæsar tempted her,
At no less price than kingdoms, to betray me;
But she resisted all: and yet though chidest me
For loving her too well.    Could I do so?
   *Dola.* Yes; there's my reason.

*Re-enter* VENTIDIUS, *with* OCTAVIA, *leading* ANTONY'S
*two little* Daughters.

*Ant.* Where?—Octavia there!　　　　　　[*Starting back.*
　*Vent.* What, is she poison to you?—a disease?
Look on her, view her well, and those she brings:
Are they all strangers to your eyes? has nature
No secret call, no whisper they are yours?
　*Dola.* For shame, my lord, if not for love, receive them
With kinder eyes. If you confess a man,
Meet them, embrace them, bid them welcome to you.
Your arms should open, even without your knowledge,
To clasp them in; your feet should turn to wings,
To bear you to them; and your eyes dart out
And aim a kiss, ere you could reach the lips.
　*Ant.* I stood amazed, to think how they came hither.
　*Vent.* I sent for them; I brought them in unknown
To Cleopatra's guards.
　*Dola.* Yet, are you cold?
　*Octav.* Thus long I have attended for my welcome;
Which, as a stranger, sure I might expect.
Who am I?
　*Ant.* Cæsar's sister.
　*Octav.* That's unkind.
Had I been nothing more than Cæsar's sister,
Know, I had still remained in Cæsar's camp:
But your Octavia, your much injured wife,
Though banished from your bed, driven from your house,
In spite of Cæsar's sister, still is yours.
'Tis true, I have a heart disdains your coldness,
And prompts me not to seek what you should offer;
But a wife's virtue still surmounts that pride.
I come to claim you as my own; to show
My duty first; to ask, nay beg, your kindness:
Your hand, my lord; 'tis mine, and I will have it.
　　　　　　　　　　　　　　[*Taking his hand.*
　*Vent.* Do, take it; thou deserv'st it.
　*Dola.* On my soul,
And so she does: she's neither too submissive,
Nor yet too haughty; but so just a mean
Shows, as it ought, a wife, and Roman too.
　*Ant.* I fear, Octavia, you have begged my life.
　*Octav.* Begged it, my lord?
　*Ant.* Yes, begged it, my ambassadress!
Poorly and basely begged it of your brother.
　*Octav.* Poorly and basely I could never beg:
Nor could my brother grant.
　*Ant.* Shall I, who, to my kneeling slave, could say,
Rise up, and be a king; shall I fall down

And cry,—Forgive me, Cæsar! Shall I set
A man, my equal, in the place of Jove,
As he could give me being? No; that word,
Forgive, would choke me up,
And die upon my tongue.
   *Dola.* You shall not need it.
   *Ant.* I will not need it. Come, you've all betrayed me,—
My friend too!—to receive some vile conditions.
My wife has bought me, with her prayers and tears;
And now I must become her branded slave.
In every peevish mood, she will upbraid
The life she gave: if I but look awry,
She cries—I'll tell my brother.
   *Octav.* My hard fortune
Subjects me still to your unkind mistakes.
But the conditions I have brought are such,
You need not blush to take: I love your honour,
Because 'tis mine; it never shall be said,
Octavia's husband was her brother's slave.
Sir, you are free; free, even from her you loathe;
For, though my brother bargains for your love,
Makes me the price and cement of your peace,
I have a soul like yours; I cannot take
Your love as alms, nor beg what I deserve.
I'll tell my brother we are reconciled;
He shall draw back his troops, and you shall march
To rule the East: I may be dropt at Athens;
No matter where. I never will complain,
But only keep the barren name of wife,
And rid you of the trouble.

   *Vent.* Was ever such a strife of sullen honour!
Both scorn to be obliged.
   *Dola.* Oh, she has touched him in the tenderest part;
See how he reddens with despite and shame,     }*Apart.*
To be outdone in generosity!
   *Vent.* See how he winks! how he dries up a tear,
That fain would fall!
   *Ant.* Octavia, I have heard you, and must praise
The greatness of your soul;
But cannot yield to what you have proposed:
For I can ne'er be conquered but by love;
And you do all for duty. You would free me,
And would be dropt at Athens; was't not so?
   *Octav.* It was, my lord.
   *Ant.* Then I must be obliged
To one who loves me not; who, to herself,
May call me thankless and ungrateful man:—
I'll not endure it; no.
   *Vent.* I am glad it pinches there.       [*Aside.*

*Octav.* Would you triumph o'er poor Octavia's virtue?
That pride was all I had to bear me up;
That you might think you owed me for your life,
And owed it to my duty, not my love.
I have been injured, and my haughty soul
Could brook but ill the man who slights my bed.
   *Ant.* Therefore you love me not.
   *Octav.* Therefore, my lord,
I should not love you.
   *Ant.* Therefore you would leave me?
   *Octav.* And therefore I should leave you—if I could.
   *Dola.* Her soul's too great, after such injuries,
To say she loves; and yet she lets you see it.
Her modesty and silence plead her cause.
   *Ant.* O Dolabella, which way shall I turn?
I find a secret yielding in my soul;
But Cleopatra, who would die with me,
Must she be left? Pity pleads for Octavia;
But does it not plead more for Cleopatra?
   *Vent.* Justice and pity both plead for Octavia;
For Cleopatra, neither.
One would be ruined with you; but she first
Had ruined you: The other, you have ruined,
And yet she would preserve you.
In everything their merits are unequal.
   *Ant.* O my distracted soul!
   *Octav.* Sweet Heaven compose it!—
Come, come, my lord, if I can pardon you,
Methinks you should accept it. Look on these;
Are they not yours? or stand they thus neglected,
As they are mine? Go to him, children, go;
Kneel to him, take him by the hand, speak to him;
For you may speak, and he may own you too,
Without a blush; and so he cannot all
His children: go, I say, and pull him to me,
And pull him to yourselves, from that bad woman.
You, Agrippina, hang upon his arms;
And you, Antonia, clasp about his waist:
If he will shake you off, if he will dash you
Against the pavement, you must bear it, children;
For you are mine, and I was born to suffer.
           [*Here the* Children *go to him, etc.*
   *Vent.* Was ever sight so moving?—Emperor!
   *Dola.* Friend!
   *Octav.* Husband!
   *Both Child.* Father!
   *Ant.* I am vanquished: take me,
Octavia; take me, children; share me all. [*Embracing them.*
I've been a thriftless debtor to your loves,

And run out much, in riot, from your stock;
But all shall be amended.
 *Octav.* O blest hour!
 *Dola.* O happy change!
 *Vent.* My joy stops at my tongue;
But it has found two channels here for one,
And bubbles out above.
 *Ant.* [*to* OCTAV.]. This is thy triumph; lead me where thou
  wilt;
Even to thy brother's camp.
 *Octav.* All there are yours.

*Enter* ALEXAS *hastily.*

 *Alex.* The queen, my mistress, sir, and yours——
 *Ant.* 'Tis past.——
Octavia, you shall stay this night: To-morrow,
Cæsar and we are one.
  [*Exit leading* OCTAVIA; DOLABELLA *and the* Children *follow.*
 *Vent.* There's news for you; run, my officious eunuch,
Be sure to be the first; haste forward:
Haste, my dear eunuch, haste.     [*Exit.*
 *Alex.* This downright fighting fool, this thick-skulled hero,
This blunt, unthinking instrument of death,
With plain dull virtue has outgone my wit.
Pleasure forsook my earliest infancy;
The luxury of others robbed my cradle,
And ravished thence the promise of a man.
Cast out from nature, disinherited
Of what her meanest children claim by kind,
Yet greatness kept me from contempt: that's gone.
Had Cleopatra followed my advice,
Then he had been betrayed who now forsakes.
She dies for love; but she has known its joys:
Gods, is this just, that I, who know no joys,
Must die, because she loves?

*Enter* CLEOPATRA, CHARMION, IRAS, *and Train.*

O madam, I have seen what blasts my eyes!
Octavia's here.
 *Cleo.* Peace with that raven's note.
I know it too; and now am in
The pangs of death.
 *Alex.* You are no more a queen;
Egypt is lost.
 *Cleo.* What tell'st thou me of Egypt?
My life, my soul is lost! Octavia has him!—
O fatal name to Cleopatra's love!
My kisses, my embraces now are hers;
While I——But thou hast seen my rival; speak,

Does she deserve this blessing? Is she fair?
Bright as a goddess? and is all perfection
Confined to her? It is. Poor I was made
Of that coarse matter, which, when she was finished,
The gods threw by for rubbish.

    *Alex.* She is indeed a very miracle.

    *Cleo.* Death to my hopes, a miracle!

    *Alex.* A miracle;                                   [*Bowing.*
I mean of goodness; for in beauty, madam,
You make all wonders cease.

    *Cleo.* I was too rash:
Take this in part of recompense. But, oh!        [*Giving a ring.*
I fear thou flatterest me.

    *Char.* She comes! she's here!

    *Iras.* Fly, madam, Cæsar's sister!

    *Cleo.* Were she the sister of the thunderer Jove,
And bore her brother's lightning in her eyes,
Thus would I face my rival.

    [*Meets* OCTAVIA *with* VENTIDIUS. OCTAVIA *bears up to her.*
       *Their Trains come up on either side.*

    *Octav.* I need not ask if you are Cleopatra;
Your haughty carriage——

    *Cleo.* Shows I am a queen:
Nor need I ask you, who you are.

    *Octav.* A Roman:
A name that makes and can unmake a queen.

    *Cleo.* Your lord, the man who serves me, is a Roman.

    *Octav.* He was a Roman, till he lost that name,
To be a slave in Egypt; but I come
To free him thence.

    *Cleo.* Peace, peace, my lover's Juno.
When he grew weary of that household clog,
He chose my easier bonds.

    *Octav.* I wonder not
Your bonds are easy: you have long been practised
In that lascivious art: He's not the first
For whom you spread your snares: Let Cæsar witness.

    *Cleo.* I loved not Cæsar; 'twas but gratitude
I paid his love: The worst your malice can,
Is but to say the greatest of mankind
Has been my slave. The next, but far above him
In my esteem, is he whom law calls yours,
But whom his love made mine.

    *Octav.* I would view nearer        [*Coming up close to her.*
That face, which has so long usurped my right,
To find the inevitable charms, that catch
Mankind so sure, that ruined my dear lord.

    *Cleo.* Oh, you do well to search; for had you known
But half these charms, you had not lost his heart.

*Octav.* Far be their knowledge from a Roman lady,
Far from a modest wife! Shame of our sex,
Dost thou not blush to own those black endearments,
That make sin pleasing?
　*Cleo.* You may blush, who want them.
If bounteous nature, if indulgent Heaven
Have given me charms to please the bravest man,
Should I not thank them? Should I be ashamed,
And not be proud? I am, that he has loved me;
And, when I love not him, Heaven change this face
For one like that.
　*Octav.* Thou lov'st him not so well.
　*Cleo.* I love him better, and deserve him more.
　*Octav.* You do not; cannot: You have been his ruin.
Who made him cheap at Rome, but Cleopatra?
Who made him scorned abroad, but Cleopatra?
At Actium, who betrayed him? Cleopatra.
Who made his children orphans, and poor me
A wretched widow? only Cleopatra.
　*Cleo.* Yet she, who loves him best, is Cleopatra.
If you have suffered, I have suffered more.
You bear the specious title of a wife,
To gild your cause, and draw the pitying world
To favour it: the world condemns poor me.
For I have lost my honour, lost my fame,
And stained the glory of my royal house,
And all to bear the branded name of mistress.
There wants but life, and that too I would lose
For him I love.
　*Octav.* Be't so, then; take thy wish. [*Exit with her Train.*
　*Cleo.* And 'tis my wish,
Now he is lost for whom alone I lived.
My sight grows dim, and every object dances,
And swims before me, in the maze of death.
My spirits, while they were opposed, kept up;
They could not sink beneath a rival's scorn!
But now she's gone, they faint.
　*Alex.* Mine have had leisure
To recollect their strength, and furnish counsel,
To ruin her, who else must ruin you.
　*Cleo.* Vain promiser!
Lead me, my Charmion; nay, your hand too, Iras.
My grief has weight enough to sink you both,
Conduct me to some solitary chamber,
And draw the curtains round;
Then leave me to myself, to take alone
My fill of grief:
　There I till death will his unkindness weep;
　As harmless infants moan themselves asleep. [*Exeunt.*

# ACT IV

## SCENE I

### *Enter* ANTONY *and* DOLABELLA.

*Dola.* Why would you shift it from yourself on me?
Can you not tell her, you must part?
    *Ant.* I cannot.
I could pull out an eye, and bid it go,
And t'other should not weep.   O Dolabella,
How many deaths are in this word, *Depart!*
I dare not trust my tongue to tell her so:
One look of hers would thaw me into tears,
And I should melt, till I were lost again.
    *Dola.* Then let Ventidius;
He's rough by nature.
    *Ant.* Oh, he'll speak too harshly;
He'll kill her with the news: Thou, only thou.
    *Dola.* Nature has cast me in so soft a mould,
That but to hear a story, feigned for pleasure,
Of some sad lover's death, moistens my eyes,
And robs me of my manhood.   I should speak
So faintly, with such fear to grieve her heart,
She'd not believe it earnest.
    *Ant.* Therefore,—therefore
Thou only, thou art fit: Think thyself me;
And when thou speak'st (but let it first be long),
Take off the edge from every sharper sound,
And let our parting be as gently made,
As other loves begin: Wilt thou do this?
    *Dola.* What you have said so sinks into my soul,
That, if I must speak, I shall speak just so.
    *Ant.* I leave you then to your sad task: Farewell.
I sent her word to meet you. [*Goes to the door, and comes back.*
I forgot;
Let her be told, I'll make her peace with mine:
Her crown and dignity shall be preserved,
If I have power with Cæsar.——Oh, be sure
To think on that.
    *Dola.* Fear not, I will remember.
            [ANTONY *goes again to the door, and comes back.*
    *Ant.* And tell her, too, how much I was constrained;
I did not this, but with extremest force:
Desire her not to hate my memory,
For I still cherish hers;——insist on that.
    *Dola.* Trust me, I'll not forget it.

*Ant.* Then that's all.          [*Goes out, and returns again.*
Wilt thou forgive my fondness this once more?
Tell her, though we shall never meet again,
If I should hear she took another love,
The news would break my heart.—Now I must go;
For every time I have returned, I feel
My soul more tender; and· my next command
Would be, to bid her stay, and ruin both.          [*Exit.*
  *Dola.* Men are but children of a larger growth;
Our appetites as apt to change as theirs,
And full as craving too, and full as vain;
And yet the soul, shut up in her dark room,
Viewing so clear abroad, at home sees nothing;
But, like a mole in earth, busy and blind,
Works all her folly up, and casts it outward
To the world's open view: Thus I discovered,
And blamed the love of ruined Antony;
Yet wish that I were he, to be so ruined.

*Enter* VENTIDIUS *above.*

  *Vent.* Alone, and talking to himself? concerned too?
Perhaps my guess is right; he loved her once,
·And may pursue it still.
  *Dola.* O friendship! friendship!
Ill canst thou answer this; and reason, worse:
Unfaithful in the attempt; hopeless to win;
And if I win, undone: mere madness all.
And yet the occasion's fair.   What injury
To him, to wear the robe which he throws by!
  *Vent.* None, none at all.   This happens as I wish,
To ruin her yet more with Antony.

*Enter* CLEOPATRA, *talking with* ALEXAS;  CHARMION,
          IRAS *on the other side.*

  *Dola.* She comes!   What charms have sorrow on that face!
Sorrow seems pleased to dwell with so much sweetness;
Yet, now and then, a melancholy smile
Breaks loose, like lightning in a winter's night,
And shows a moment's day.
  *Vent.* If she should love him too! her eunuch there?
That porc'pisce bodes ill weather.   Draw, draw nearer,
Sweet devil, that I may bear.
  *Alex.* Believe me; try
          [DOLABELLA *goes over to* CHARMION *and* IRAS;  *seems to
          talk with them.*
To make him jealous; jealousy is like
A polished glass held to the lips when life's in doubt;
If there be breath, 'twill catch the damp, and show it.

*Cleo.*  I grant you, jealousy's a proof of love,
But 'tis a weak and unavailing medicine;
It puts out the disease, and makes it show,
But has no power to cure.

*Alex.*  'Tis your last remedy, and strongest too:
And then this Dolabella, who so fit
To practise on?  He's handsome, valiant, young,
And looks as he were laid for nature's bait,
To catch weak women's eyes.
He stands already more than half suspected
Of loving you:  the least kind word or glance
You give this youth, will kindle him with love:
Then, like a burning vessel set adrift,
You'll send him down amain before the wind,
To fire the heart of jealous Antony.

*Cleo.*  Can I do this?  Ah, no; my love's so true,
That I can neither hide it where it is,
Nor show it where it is not.  Nature meant me
A wife; a silly, harmless, household dove,
Fond without art, and kind without deceit;
But Fortune, that has made a mistress of me,
Has thrust me out to the wide world, unfurnished
Of falsehood to be happy.

*Alex.*  Force yourself.
The event will be, your lover will return,
Doubly desirous to possess the good
Which once he feared to lose.

*Cleo.*  I must attempt it;
But oh, with what regret!

                    [*Exit* ALEXAS.  *She comes up to* DOLABELLA.

*Vent.*  So, now the scene draws near; they're in my reach.

*Cleo.* [*to* DOL.].  Discoursing with my women! might not I
Share in your entertainment?

*Char.*  You have been
The subject of it, madam.

*Cleo.*  How! and how?

*Iras.*  Such praises of your beauty!

*Cleo.*  Mere poetry.
Your Roman wits, your Gallus and Tibullus,
Have taught you this from Cytheris and Delia.

*Dola.*  Those Roman wits have never been in Egypt;
Cytheris and Delia else had been unsung:
I, who have seen——had I been born a poet,
Should choose a nobler name.

*Cleo.*  You flatter me.
But, 'tis your nation's vice:  All of your country
Are flatterers, and all false.  Your friend's like you.
I'm sure  he sent you not to speak these words.

*Dola.*  No, madam; yet he sent me——

*Cleo.* Well, he sent you——

*Dola.* Of a less pleasing errand.

*Cleo.* How less pleasing?
Less to yourself, or me?

*Dola.* Madam, to both;
For you must mourn, and I must grieve to cause it.

*Cleo.* You, Charmion, and your fellow, stand at distance.—
Hold up, my spirits. [*Aside*]——Well, now your mournful
    matter!
For I'm prepared, perhaps can guess it too.

*Dola.* I wish you would; for 'tis a thankless office,
To tell ill news; And I, of all your sex,
Most fear displeasing you.

*Cleo.* Of all your sex,
I soonest could forgive you, if you should.

*Vent.* Most delicate advances! Woman! woman!
Dear, damned, inconstant sex!

*Cleo.* In the first place,
I am to be forsaken; is't not so?

*Dola.* I wish I could not answer to that question.

*Cleo.* Then pass it o'er, because it troubles you:
I should have been more grieved another time.
Next, I'm to lose my kingdom——Farewell, Egypt!
Yet, is there any more?

*Dola.* Madam, I fear
Your too deep sense of grief has turned your reason.

*Cleo.* No, no, I'm not run mad; I can bear fortune:
And love may be expelled by other love,
As poisons are by poisons.

*Dola.* You o'erjoy me, madam,
To find your griefs so moderately borne.
You've heard the worst; all are not false like him.

*Cleo.* No; Heaven forbid they should.

*Dola.* Some men are constant.

*Cleo.* And constancy deserves reward, that's certain.

*Dola.* Deserves it not; but give it leave to hope.

*Vent.* I'll swear, thou hast my leave. I have enough:
But how to manage this! Well, I'll consider.            [*Exit.*

*Dola.* I came prepared
To tell you heavy news; news, which I thought
Would fright the blood from your pale cheeks to hear:
But you have met it with a cheerfulness,
That makes my task more easy; and my tongue,
Which on another's message was employed,
Would gladly speak its own.

*Cleo.* Hold, Dolabella.
First tell me, were you chosen by my lord?
Or sought you this employment?

*Dola.* He picked me out; and, as his bosom friend,

He charged me with his words.

*Cleo.* The message then
I know was tender, and each accent smooth,
To mollify that rugged word, *Depart.*

*Dola.* Oh, you mistake: He chose the harshest words;
With fiery eyes, and with contracted brows,
He coined his face in the severest stamp;
And fury shook his fabric, like an earthquake;
He heaved for vent, and burst like bellowing Ætna,
In sounds scarce human—"Hence away for ever,
Let her begone, the blot of my renown,
And bane of all my hopes!"

> [*All the time of this speech,* CLEOPATRA *seems more and
> more concerned, till she sinks quite down.*

"Let her be driven, as far as men can think,
From man's commerce! she'll poison to the centre."

*Cleo.* Oh, I can bear no more!

*Dola.* Help, help!—O wretch! O cursed, cursed wretch!
What have I done?

*Char.* Help, chafe her temples, Iras.

*Iras.* Bend, bend her forward quickly.

*Char.* Heaven be praised,
She comes again.

*Cleo.* Oh, let him not approach me.
Why have you brought me back to this loathed being,
The abode of falsehood, violated vows,
And injured love? For pity, let me go;
For, if there be a place of long repose,
I'm sure I want it. My disdainful lord
Can never break that quiet; nor awake
The sleeping soul, with hollowing in my tomb
Such words as fright her hence.—Unkind, unkind!

*Dola.* Believe me, 'tis against myself I speak;     [*Kneeling.*
That sure desires belief; I injured him:
My friend ne'er spoke those words. Oh, had you seen
How often he came back, and every time
With something more obliging and more kind,
To add to what he said; what dear farewells;
How almost vanquished by his love he parted,
And leaned to what unwillingly he left!
I, traitor as I was, for love of you
(But what can you not do, who made me false?)
I forged that lie; for whose forgiveness kneels
This self-accused, self-punished criminal.

*Cleo.* With how much ease believe we what we wish!
Rise, Dolabella; if you have been guilty,
I have contributed, and too much love
Has made me guilty too.
The advance of kindness, which I made, was feigned,

To call back fleeting love by jealousy;
But 'twould not last.  Oh, rather let me lose,
Than so ignobly trifle with his heart.
  *Dola.* I find your breast fenced round from human reach,
Transparent as a rock of solid crystal;
Seen through, but never pierced.  My friend, my friend,
What endless treasure hast thou thrown away;
And scattered, like an infant, in the ocean,
Vain sums of wealth, which none can gather thence!
  *Cleo.* Could you not beg
An hour's admittance to his private ear?
Like one who wanders through long barren wilds
And yet foreknows no hospitable inn
Is near to succour hunger, eats his fill,
Before his painful march;
So would I feed a while my famished eyes
Before we part; for I have far to go,
If death be far, and never must return.

VENTIDIUS *with* OCTAVIA, *behind.*

  *Vent.* From hence you may discover—oh, sweet, sweet!
Would you indeed?  The pretty hand in earnest?
  *Dola.* I will, for this reward.          [*Takes her hand.*
Draw it not back.
'Tis all I e'er will beg.
  *Vent.* They turn upon us.
  *Octav.* What quick eyes has guilt!
  *Vent.* Seem not to have observed them, and go on.

*They enter.*

  *Dola.* Saw you the emperor, Ventidius?
  *Vent.* No.
I sought him; but I heard that he was private,
None with him but Hipparchus, his freedman.
  *Dola.* Know you his business?
  *Vent.* Giving him instructions,
And letters to his brother Cæsar.
  *Dola.* Well,
He must be found.          [*Exeunt* DOLABELLA *and* CLEOPATRA.
  *Octav.* Most glorious impudence!
  *Vent.* She looked, methought,
As she would say—Take your old man, Octavia;
Thank you, I'm better here.—
Well, but what use
Make we of this discovery?
  *Octav.* Let it die.
  *Vent.* I pity Dolabella; but she's dangerous;

Her eyes have power beyond Thessalian charms,
To draw the moon from heaven; for eloquence,
The sea-green sirens taught her voice their flattery;
And, while she speaks, night steals upon the day,
Unmarked of those that hear: Then she's so charming,
Age buds at sight of her, and swells to youth:
The holy priests gaze on her when she smiles;
And with heaved hands, forgetting gravity,
They bless her wanton eyes: Even I, who hate her,
With a malignant joy behold such beauty;
And, while I curse, desire it.   Antony
Must needs have some remains of passion still,
Which may ferment into a worse relapse,
If now not fully cured.   I know, this minute,
With Cæsar he's endeavouring her peace.
   *Octav.* You have prevailed:——But for a further purpose
                                             *[Walks off.*
I'll prove how he will relish this discovery.
What, make a strumpet's peace! it swells my heart:
It must not, shall not be.
   *Vent.* His guards appear.
Let me begin, and you shall second me.

#### *Enter* ANTONY.

   *Ant.* Octavia, I was looking you, my love:
What, are your letters ready?   I have given
My last instructions.
   *Octav.* Mine, my lord, are written.
   *Ant.* Ventidius.              *[Drawing him aside.*
   *Vent.* My lord?
   *Ant.* A word in private.—
When saw you Dolabella?
   *Vent.* Now, my lord,
He parted hence; and Cleopatra with him.
   *Ant.* Speak softly.—'Twas by my command he went,
To bear my last farewell.
   *Vent.* It looked indeed        *[Aloud.*
Like your farewell.
   *Ant.* More softly.—My farewell?
What secret meaning have you in those words
Of—My farewell?   He did it by my order.
   *Vent.* Then he obeyed your order.   I suppose   *[Aloud.*
You bid him do it with all gentleness,
All kindness, and all——love.
   *Ant.* How she mourned,
The poor forsaken creature!
   *Vent.* She took it as she ought; she bore your parting
As she did Cæsar's, as she would another's,

Were a new love to come.

 *Ant.* Thou dost belie her;      *[Aloud.*

Most basely and maliciously belie her.

 *Vent.* I thought not to displease you; I have done.

 *Octav.* You seemed disturbed, my lord.  *[Coming up.*

 *Ant.* A very trifle.

Retire, my love.

 *Vent.* It was indeed a trifle.

He sent——

 *Ant.* No more.  Look how thou disobey'st me; *[Angrily.*

Thy life shall answer it.

 *Octav.* Then 'tis no trifle.

 *Vent.* [*to* Octav.]. 'Tis less; a very nothing: You too saw it,

As well as I, and therefore 'tis no secret.

 *Ant.* She saw it!

 *Vent.* Yes: She saw young Dolabella——

 *Ant.* Young Dolabella!

 *Vent.* Young, I think him young,

And handsome too; and so do others think him.

But what of that?  He went by your command,

Indeed 'tis probable, with some kind message;

For she received it graciously; she smiled;

And then he grew familiar with her hand,

Squeezed it, and worried it with ravenous kisses;

She blushed, and sighed, and smiled, and blushed again;

At last she took occasion to talk softly,

And brought her cheek up close, and leaned on his;

At which, he whispered kisses back on hers;

And then she cried aloud—That constancy

Should be rewarded.

 *Octav.* This I saw and heard.

 *Ant.* What woman was it, whom you heard and saw

So playful with my friend?

Not Cleopatra?

 *Vent.* Even she, my lord.

 *Ant.* My Cleopatra?

 *Vent.* Your Cleopatra;

Dolabella's Cleopatra; every man's Cleopatra.

 *Ant.* Thou liest.

 *Vent.* I do not lie, my lord.

Is this so strange?  Should mistresses be left,

And not provide against a time of change?

You know she's not much used to lonely nights.

 *Ant.* I'll think no more on't.

I know 'tis false, and see the plot betwixt you.—

You needed not have gone this way, Octavia.

What harms it you that Cleopatra's just?

She's mine no more.  I see, and I forgive:

Urge it no further, love.

*Octav.* Are you concerned,
That she's found false?

*Ant.* I should be, were it so;
For, though 'tis past, I would not that the world
Should tax my former choice, that I loved one
Of so light note; but I forgive you both.

*Vent.* What has my age deserved, that you should think
I would abuse your ears with perjury?
If Heaven be true, she's false.

*Ant.* Though heaven and earth
Should witness it, I'll not believe her tainted.

*Vent.* I'll bring you, then, a witness
From hell, to prove her so.—Nay, go not back;
          [*Seeing* ALEXAS *just entering, and starting back.*
For stay you must and shall.

*Alex.* What means my lord?

*Vent.* To make you do what most you hate,—speak truth.
You are of Cleopatra's private counsel,
Of her bed-counsel, her lascivious hours;
Are conscious of each nightly change she makes,
And watch her, as Chaldeans do the moon,
Can tell what signs she passes through, what day.

*Alex.* My noble lord!

*Vent.* My most illustrious pander,
No fine set speech, no cadence, no turned periods,
But a plain homespun truth, is what I ask:
I did, myself, o'erhear your queen make love
To Dolabella. Speak; for I will know,
By your confession, what more passed betwixt them;
How near the business draws to your employment;
And when the happy hour.

*Ant.* Speak truth, Alexas; whether it offend
Or please Ventidius, care not: Justify
Thy injured queen from malice: Dare his worst.

*Octav.* [*aside*]. See how he gives him courage! how he fears
To find her false! and shuts his eyes to truth,
Willing to be misled!

*Alex.* As far as love may plead for woman's frailty,
Urged by desert and greatness of the lover,
So far, divine Octavia, may my queen
Stand even excused to you for loving him
Who is your lord: so far, from brave Ventidius,
May her past actions hope a fair report.

*Ant.* 'Tis well, and truly spoken: mark, Ventidius.

*Alex.* To you, most noble emperor, her strong passion
Stands not excused, but wholly justified.
Her beauty's charms alone, without her crown,
From Ind and Meroe drew the distant vows
Of sighing kings; and at her feet were laid

The sceptres of the earth, exposed on heaps,
To choose where she would reign:
She thought a Roman only could deserve her,
And, of all Romans, only Antony;
And, to be less than wife to you, disdained
Their lawful passion.

*Ant.* 'Tis but truth.

*Alex.* And yet, though love, and your unmatched desert,
Have drawn her from the due regard of honour,
At last Heaven opened her unwilling eyes
To see the wrongs she offered fair Octavia,
Whose holy bed she lawlessly usurped.
The sad effects of this improsperous war
Confirmed those pious thoughts.

*Vent. [aside].* Oh, wheel you there?
Observe him now; the man begins to mend,
And talk substantial reason.—Fear not, eunuch;
The emperor has given thee leave to speak.

*Alex.* Else had I never dared to offend his ears
With what the last necessity has urged
On my forsaken mistress; yet I must not
Presume to say, her heart is wholly altered.

*Ant.* No, dare not for thy life, I charge thee dare not
Pronounce that fatal word!

*Octav.* Must I bear this? Good Heaven, afford me patience.
　　　　　　　　　　　　　　　　　　　　*[Aside.*

*Vent.* On, sweet eunuch; my dear half-man, proceed.

*Alex.* Yet Dolabella
Has loved her long; he, next my god-like lord,
Deserves her best; and should she meet his passion,
Rejected, as she is, by him she loved——

*Ant.* Hence from my sight! for I can bear no more:
Let furies drag thee quick to hell; let all
The longer damned have rest; each torturing hand
Do thou employ, till Cleopatra comes;
Then join thou too, and help to torture her!
　　　　　　　　*[Exit* ALEXAS, *thrust out by* ANTONY.

*Octav.* 'Tis not well,
Indeed, my lord, 'tis much unkind to me,
To show this passion, this extreme concernment,
For an abandoned, faithless prostitute.

*Ant.* Octavia, leave me; I am much disordered:
Leave me, I say.

*Octav.* My lord!

*Ant.* I bid you leave me.

*Vent.* Obey him, madam: best withdraw a while,
And see how this will work.

*Octav.* Wherein have I offended you, my lord,
That I am bid to leave you? Am I false,

Or infamous? Am I a Cleopatra?
Were I she,
Base as she is, you would not bid me leave you;
But hang upon my neck, take slight excuses,
And fawn upon my falsehood.
    *Ant.* 'Tis too much.
Too much, Octavia; I am pressed with sorrows
Too heavy to be borne; and you add more:
I would retire, and recollect what's left
Of man within, to aid me.
    *Octav.* You would mourn,
In private, for your love, who has betrayed you.
You did but half return to me: your kindness
Lingered behind with her. I hear, my lord,
You make conditions for her,
And would include her treaty. Wondrous proofs
Of love to me!
    *Ant.* Are you my friend, Ventidius?
Or are you turned a Dolabella too,
And let this fury loose?
    *Vent.* Oh, be advised,
Sweet madam, and retire.
    *Octav.* Yes, I will go; but never to return.
You shall no more be haunted with this Fury.
My lord, my lord, love will not always last,
When urged with long unkindness and disdain:
Take her again, whom you prefer to me;
She stays but to be called. Poor cozened man!
Let a feigned parting give her back your heart,
Which a feigned love first got; for injured me,
Though my just sense of wrongs forbid my stay,
My duty shall be yours.
To the dear pledges of our former love
My tenderness and care shall be transferred,
And they shall cheer, by turns, my widowed nights:
So, take my last farewell; for I despair
To have you whole, and scorn to take you half.    [*Exit.*
    *Vent.* I combat Heaven, which blasts my best designs:
My last attempt must be to win her back;
But oh! I fear in vain.    [*Exit.*
    *Ant.* Why was I framed with this plain, honest heart,
Which knows not to disguise its griefs and weakness,
But bears its workings outward to the world?
I should have kept the mighty anguish in,
And forced a smile at Cleopatra's falsehood:
Octavia had believed it, and had stayed.
But I am made a shallow-forded stream,
Seen to the bottom: all my clearness scorned,
And all my faults exposed.—See where he comes,

*Enter* DOLABELLA.

Who has profaned the sacred name of friend,
And worn it into vileness!
With how secure a brow, and specious form
He gilds the secret villain!   Sure that face
Was meant for honesty; but Heaven mismatched it,
And furnished treason out with nature's pomp,
To make its work more easy.
    *Dola.* O my friend!
    *Ant.* Well, Dolabella, you performed my message?
    *Dola.* I did, unwillingly.
    *Ant.* Unwillingly?
Was it so hard for you to bear our parting?
You should have wished it.
    *Dola.* Why?
    *Ant.* Because you love me.
And she received my message with as true,
With as unfeigned a sorrow as you brought it?
    *Dola.* She loves you, even to madness.
    *Ant.* Oh, I know it.
You, Dolabella, do not better know
How much she loves me.   And should I
Forsake this beauty?   This all-perfect creature?
    *Dola.* I could not, were she mine.
    *Ant.* And yet you first
Persuaded me: How come you altered since?
    *Dola.* I said at first I was not fit to go:
I could not hear her sighs, and see her tears,
But pity must prevail: And so, perhaps,
It may again with you; for I have promised,
That she should take her last farewell: And, see,
She comes to claim my word.

*Enter* CLEOPATRA.

    *Ant.* False Dolabella!
    *Dola.* What's false, my lord?
    *Ant.* Why, Dolabella's false,
And Cleopatra's false; both false and faithless.
Draw near, you well-joined wickedness, you serpents,
Whom I have in my kindly bosom warmed,
Till I am stung to death.
    *Dola.* My lord, have I
Deserved to be thus used?
    *Cleo.* Can Heaven prepare
A newer torment?   Can it find a curse
Beyond our separation?
    *Ant.* Yes, if fate

Be just, much greater: Heaven should be ingenious
In punishing such crimes. The rolling stone
And gnawing vulture were slight pains, invented
When Jove was young, and no examples known
Of mighty ills; but you have ripened sin,
To such a monstrous growth, 'twill pose the gods
To find an equal torture. Two, two such!—
Oh, there's no further name,—two such! to me,
To me, who locked my soul within your breasts,
Had no desires, no joys, no life, but you;
When half the globe was mine, I gave it you
In dowry with my heart; I had no use,
No fruit of all, but you: A friend and mistress
Was what the world could give. O Cleopatra!
O Dolabella! how could you betray
This tender heart, which with an infant fondness
Lay lulled betwixt your bosoms, and there slept,
Secure of injured faith?
  *Dola.* If she has wronged you,
Heaven, hell, and you revenge it.
  *Ant.* If she has wronged me!
Thou wouldst evade thy part of guilt; but swear
Thou lov'st not her.
  *Dola.* Not so as I love you.
  *Ant.* Not so? Swear, swear, I say, thou dost not love her.
  *Dola.* No more than friendship will allow.
  *Ant.* No more?
Friendship allows thee nothing: Thou art perjured—
And yet thou didst not swear thou lov'st her not;
But not so much, no more. O trifling hypocrite,
Who dar'st not own to her, thou dost not love,
Nor own to me, thou dost! Ventidius heard it;
Octavia saw it.
  *Cleo.* They are enemies.
  *Ant.* Alexas is not so: He, he confessed it;
He, who, next hell, best knew it, he avowed it.
Why do I seek a proof beyond yourself?   [*To* DOLABELLA.
You, whom I sent to bear my last farewell,
Returned, to plead her stay.
  *Dola.* What shall I answer?
If to have loved be guilt, then I have sinned;
But if to have repented of that love
Can wash away my crime, I have repented.
Yet, if I have offended past forgiveness,
Let not her suffer: She is innocent.
  *Cleo.* Ah, what will not a woman do, who loves?
What means will she refuse, to keep that heart,
Where all her joys are placed? 'Twas I encouraged,

'Twas I blew up the fire that scorched his soul,
To make you jealous, and by that regain you.
But all in vain; I could not counterfeit:
In spite of all the dams my love broke o'er,
And drowned my heart again: fate took the occasion;
And thus one minute's feigning has destroyed
My whole life's truth.
    *Ant.* Thin cobweb arts of falsehood;
Seen, and broke through at first.
    *Dola.* Forgive your mistress.
    *Cleo.* Forgive your friend.
    *Ant.* You have convinced yourselves.
You plead each other's cause: What witness have you,
That you but meant to raise my jealousy?
    *Cleo.* Ourselves, and Heaven.
    *Ant.* Guilt witnesses for guilt. Hence, love and friendship!
You have no longer place in human breasts,
These two have driven you out: Avoid my sight!
I would not kill the man whom I have loved,
And cannot hurt the woman; but avoid me:
I do not know how long I can be tame;
For, if I stay one minute more, to think
How I am wronged, my justice and revenge
Will cry so loud within me, that my pity
Will not be heard for either.
    *Dola.* Heaven has but
Our sorrow for our sins; and then delights
To pardon erring man: Sweet mercy seems
Its darling attribute, which limits justice;
As if there were degrees in infinite,
And infinite would rather want perfection
Than punish to extent.
    *Ant.* I can forgive
A foe; but not a mistress and a friend.
Treason is there in its most horrid shape,
Where trust is greatest; and the soul resigned,
Is stabbed by its own guards: I'll hear no more;
Hence from my sight for ever!
    *Cleo.* How? for ever!
I cannot go one moment from your sight,
And must I go for ever?
My joys, my only joys, are centred here:
What place have I to go to? My own kingdom?
That I have lost for you: Or to the Romans?
They hate me for your sake: Or must I wander
The wide world o'er, a helpless, banished woman,
Banished for love of you; banished from you?
Ay, there's the banishment! Oh, hear me; hear me,
With strictest justice: For I beg no favour;

And if I have offended you, then kill me,
But do not banish me.
   *Ant.* I must not hear you.
I have a fool within me takes your part;
But honour stops my ears.
   *Cleo.* For pity hear me!
Would you cast off a slave who followed you?
Who crouched beneath your spurn?—He has no pity!
See, if he gives one tear to my departure;
One look, one kind farewell: O iron-heart!
Let all the gods look down, and judge betwixt us,
If he did ever love!
   *Ant.* No more: Alexas!
   *Dola.* A perjured villain!
   *Ant.* [*to* CLEO.]. Your Alexas; yours.
   *Cleo.* Oh, 'twas his plot; his ruinous design,
To engage you in my love by jealousy.
Hear him; confront him with me; let him speak.
   *Ant.* I have; I have.
   *Cleo.* And if he clear me not——
   *Ant.* Your creature! one who hangs upon your smiles!
Watches your eye, to say or to unsay,
Whate'er you please! I am not to be moved.
   *Cleo.* Then must we part? Farewell, my cruel lord!
The appearance is against me; and I go,
Unjustified, for ever from your sight.
How I have loved, you know; how yet I love,
My only comfort is, I know myself:
I love you more, even now you are unkind,
Than when you loved me most; so well, so truly
I'll never strive against it; but die pleased,
To think you once were mine.
   *Ant.* Good heaven, they weep at parting!
Must I weep too? that calls them innocent.
I must not weep; and yet I must, to think
That I must not forgive.——
Live, but live wretched; 'tis but just you should,
Who made me so: Live from each other's sight:
Let me not hear you meet. Set all the earth,
And all the seas, betwixt your sundered loves:
View nothing common but the sun and skies.
Now, all take several ways;
   And each your own sad fate, with mine, deplore;
   That you were false, and I could trust no more.
                  [*Exeunt severally.*

# ACT V

## SCENE I

*Enter* CLEOPATRA, CHARMION, *and* IRAS.

*Char.* Be juster, Heaven; such virtue punished thus,
Will make us think that chance rules all above,
And shuffles, with a random hand, the lots
Which man is forced to draw.
    *Cleo.* I could tear out these eyes that gained his heart,
And had not power to keep it.  O the curse
Of doting on, even when I find it dotage!
Bear witness, gods, you heard him bid me go;
You, whom he mocked with imprecating vows
Of promised faith!——I'll die; I will not bear it.
You may hold me——
              [*She pulls out her dagger, and they hold her.*
But I can keep my breath; I can die inward,
And choke this love.

### *Enter* ALEXAS.

    *Iras.* Help, O Alexas, help!
The queen grows desperate; her soul struggles in her
With all the agonies of love and rage,
And strives to force its passage.
    *Cleo.* Let me go.
Art thou there, traitor!—O,
O for a little breath, to vent my rage,
Give, give me way, and let me loose upon him.
    *Alex.* Yes, I deserve it, for my ill-timed truth.
Was it for me to prop
The ruins of a falling majesty?
To place myself beneath the mighty flaw,
Thus to be crushed, and pounded into atoms,
By its o'erwhelming weight?  'Tis too presuming
For subjects to preserve that wilful power,
Which courts its own destruction.
    *Cleo.* I would reason
More calmly with you.  Did not you o'errule,
And force my plain, direct, and open love,
Into these crooked paths of jealousy?
Now, what's the event?  Octavia is removed;
But Cleopatra's banished.  Thou, thou villain,
Hast pushed my boat to open sea; to prove,
At my sad cost, if thou canst steer it back.

It cannot be; I'm lost too far; I'm ruined:
Hence, thou impostor, traitor, monster, devil!—
I can no more: Thou, and my griefs, have sunk
Me down so low, that I want voice to curse thee.
    *Alex.* Suppose some shipwrecked seaman near the shore,
Dropping and faint with climbing up the cliff,
If, from above, some charitable hand
Pull him to safety, hazarding himself,
To draw the other's weight; would he look back,
And curse him for his pains? The case is yours;
But one step more, and you have gained the height.
    *Cleo.* Sunk, never more to rise.
    *Alex.* Octavia's gone, and Dolabella banished.
Believe me, madam, Antony is yours.
His heart was never lost, but started off
To jealousy, love's last retreat and covert;
Where it lies hid in shades, watchful in silence,
And listening for the sound that calls it back.
Some other, any man ('tis so advanced),
May perfect this unfinished work, which I
(Unhappy only to myself) have left
So easy to his hand.
    *Cleo.* Look well thou do't; else——
    *Alex.* Else, what your silence threatens.—Antony
Is mounted up the Pharos; from whose turret,
He stands surveying our Egyptian galleys,
Engaged with Cæsar's fleet. Now death or conquest!
If the first happen, fate acquits my promise;
If we o'ercome, the conqueror is yours. [*A distant shout within.*
    *Char.* Have comfort, madam: Did you mark that shout?
                        [*Second shout nearer.*
    *Iras.* Hark! they redouble it.
    *Alex.* 'Tis from the port.
The loudness shows it near: Good news, kind heavens!
    *Cleo.* Osiris make it so!

*Enter* SERAPION.

    *Serap.* Where, where's the queen?
    *Alex.* How frightfully the holy coward stares
As if not yet recovered of the assault,
When all his gods, and, what's more dear to him,
His offerings, were at stake.
    *Serap.* O horror, horror!
Egypt has been; our latest hour has come:
The queen of nations, from her ancient seat,
Is sunk for ever in the dark abyss:
Time has unrolled her glories to the last,
And now closed up the volume.

*Cleo.* Be more plain:
Say, whence thou comest; though fate is in thy face,
Which from thy haggard eyes looks wildly out,
And threatens ere thou speakest.
     *Serap.* I came from Pharos;
From viewing (spare me, and imagine it)
Our land's last hope, your navy——
     *Cleo.* Vanquished?
     *Serap.* No:
They fought not.
     *Cleo.* Then they fled.
     *Serap.* Nor that.   I saw,
With Antony, your well-appointed fleet
Row out; and thrice he waved his hand on high,
And thrice with cheerful cries they shouted back:
'Twas then false Fortune, like a fawning strumpet,
About to leave the bankrupt prodigal,
With a dissembled smile would kiss at parting,
And flatter to the last; the well-timed oars,
Now dipt from every bank, now smoothly run
To meet the foe; and soon indeed they met,
But not as foes.   In few, we saw their caps
On either side thrown up; the Egyptian galleys,
Received like friends, passed through, and fell behind
The Roman rear:  And now, they all come forward,
And ride within the port.
     *Cleo.* Enough, Serapion:
I've heard my doom.—This needed not, you gods:
When I lost Antony, your work was done;
'Tis but superfluous malice.—Where's my lord?
How bears he this last blow?
     *Serap.* His fury cannot be expressed by words:
Thrice he attempted headlong to have fallen
Full on his foes, and aimed at Cæsar's galley:
Withheld, he raves on you; cries, he's betrayed.
Should he now find you——
     *Alex.* Shun him; seek your safety,
Till you can clear your innocence.
     *Cleo.* I'll stay.
     *Alex.* You must not; haste you to your monument,
While I make speed to Cæsar.
     *Cleo.* Cæsar!  No,
I have no business with him.
     *Alex.* I can work him
To spare your life, and let this madman perish.
     *Cleo.* Base fawning wretch! wouldst thou betray him, too?
Hence from my sight! I will not hear a traitor;
'Twas thy design brought all this ruin on us.—

Serapion, thou art honest; counsel me:
But haste, each moment's precious.

*Serap.* Retire; you must not yet see Antony.
He who began this mischief,
'Tis just he tempt the danger; let him clear you:
And, since he offered you his servile tongue,
To gain a poor precarious life from Cæsar,
Let him expose that fawning eloquence,
And speak to Antony.

*Alex.* O heavens! I dare not;
I meet my certain death.

*Cleo.* Slave, thou deservest it.—
Not that I fear my lord, will I avoid him;
I know him noble: when he banished me,
And thought me false, he scorned to take my life;
But I'll be justified, and then die with him.

*Alex.* O pity me, and let me follow you.

*Cleo.* To death, if thou stir hence. Speak, if thou canst,
Now for thy life, which basely thou wouldst save;
While mine I prize at—this! Come, good Serapion.

[*Exeunt* CLEOPATRA, SERAPION, CHARMION, *and* IRAS.

*Alex.* O that I less could fear to lose this being,
Which, like a snowball in my coward hand,
The more 'tis grasped, the faster melts away.
Poor reason! what a wretched aid art thou!
For still, in spite of thee,
These two long lovers, soul and body, dread
Their final separation. Let me think:
What can I say, to save myself from death?
No matter what becomes of Cleopatra.

*Ant.* Which way? where?          [*Within.*
*Vent.* This leads to the monument.     [*Within.*

*Alex.* Ah me! I hear him; yet I'm unprepared:
My gift of lying's gone;
And this court-devil, which I so oft have raised,
Forsakes me at my need. I dare not stay;
Yet cannot far go hence.          [*Exit.*

### Enter ANTONY *and* VENTIDIUS.

*Ant.* O happy Cæsar! thou hast men to lead:
Think not 'tis thou hast conquered Antony;
But Rome has conquered Egypt. I'm betrayed.

*Vent.* Curse on this treacherous train!
Their soil and heaven infect them all with baseness:
And their young souls come tainted to the world
With the first breath they draw.

*Ant.* The original villain sure no god created;
He was a bastard of the sun, by Nile,

Aped into man; with all his mother's mud
Crusted about his soul.

*Vent.* The nation is
One universal traitor; and their queen
The very spirit and extract of them all.

*Ant.* Is there yet left
A possibility of aid from valour?
Is there one god unsworn to my destruction?
The least unmortgaged hope? for, if there be,
Methinks I cannot fall beneath the fate
Of such a boy as Cæsar.
The world's one half is yet in Antony;
And from each limb of it that's hewed away,
The soul comes back to me.

*Vent.* There yet remain
Three legions in the town. The last assault
Lopt off the rest; if death be your design,—
As I must wish it now,—these are sufficient
To make a heap about us of dead foes,
An honest pile for burial.

*Ant.* They are enough.
We'll not divide our stars; but, side by side,
Fight emulous, and with malicious eyes
Survey each other's acts: So every death
Thou giv'st, I'll take on me, as a just debt,
And pay thee back a soul.

*Vent.* Now you shall see I love you. Not a word
Of chiding more. By my few hours of life,
I am so pleased with this brave Roman fate,
That I would not be Cæsar, to outlive you.
When we put off this flesh, and mount together,
I shall be shown to all the ethereal crowd,—
Lo, this is he who died with Antony!

*Ant.* Who knows, but we may pierce through all their troops,
And reach my veterans yet? 'tis worth the 'tempting,
To o'erleap this gulf of fate,
And leave our wond'ring destinies behind.

*Enter* ALEXAS, *trembling.*

*Vent.* See, see, that villain!
See Cleopatra stamped upon that face,
With all her cunning, all her arts of falsehood!
How she looks out through those dissembling eyes!
How he has set his countenance for deceit,
And promises a lie, before he speaks!
Let me despatch him first.       [*Drawing.*

*Alex.* O spare me, spare me!

*Ant.* Hold; he's not worth your killing.—On thy life,
Which thou may'st keep, because I scorn to take it,

No syllable to justify thy queen;
Save thy base tongue its office.
 *Alex.* Sir, she is gone,
Where she shall never be molested more
By love, or you.
 *Ant.* Fled to her Dolabella!
Die, traitor! I revoke my promise! die! [*Going to kill him.*
 *Alex.* O hold! she is not fled.
 *Ant.* She is: my eyes
Are open to her falsehood; my whole life
Has been a golden dream of love and friendship;
But, now I wake, I'm like a merchant, roused
From soft repose, to see his vessel sinking,
And all his wealth cast over.   Ungrateful woman!
Who followed me, but as the swallow summer,
Hatching her young ones in my kindly beams,
Singing her flatteries to my morning wake:
But, now my winter comes, she spreads her wings,
And seeks the spring of Cæsar.
 *Alex.* Think not so:
Her fortunes have, in all things, mixed with yours.
Had she betrayed her naval force to Rome,
How easily might she have gone to Cæsar,
Secure by such a bribe!
 *Vent.* She sent it first,
To be more welcome after.
 *Ant.* 'Tis too plain;
Else would she have appeared, to clear herself.
 *Alex.* Too fatally she has: she could not bear
To be accused by you; but shut herself
Within her monument; looked down and sighed;
While, from her unchanged face, the silent tears
Dropt, as they had not leave, but stole their parting.
Some indistinguished words she inly murmured;
At last, she raised her eyes; and, with such looks
As dying Lucrece cast——
 *Ant.* My heart forebodes——
 *Vent.* All for the best:—Go on.
 *Alex.* She snatched her poniard,
And, ere we could prevent the fatal blow,
Plunged it within her breast; then turned to me:
Go, bear my lord, said she, my last farewell;
And ask him, if he yet suspect my faith.
More she was saying, but death rushed betwixt.
She half pronounced your name with her last breath,
And buried half within her.
 *Vent.* Heaven be praised!
 *Ant.* Then art thou innocent, my poor dear love,
And art thou dead?

O those two words! their sound should be divided:
Hadst thou been false, and died; or hadst thou lived,
And hadst been true—But innocence and death!
This shows not well above. Then what am I,
The murderer of this truth, this innocence!
Thoughts cannot form themselves in words so horrid
As can express my guilt!

*Vent.* Is't come to this? The gods have been too gracious;
And thus you thank them for it!

*Ant.* [*to* ALEX.]. Why stayest thou here?
Is it for thee to spy upon my soul,
And see its inward mourning? Get thee hence;
Thou art not worthy to behold, what now
Becomes a Roman emperor to perform.

*Alex.* He loves her still:
His grief betrays it. Good! the joy to find
She's yet alive, completes the reconcilement.
I've saved myself, and her. But, oh! the Romans!
Fate comes too fast upon my wit,
Hunts me too hard, and meets me at each double.
[*Aside. Exit.*

*Vent.* Would she had died a little sooner, though!
Before Octavia went, you might have treated:
Now 'twill look tame, and would not be received.
Come, rouse yourself, and let's die warm together.

*Ant.* I will not fight: there's no more work for war.
The business of my angry hours is done.

*Vent.* Cæsar is at your gates.

*Ant.* Why, let him enter;
He's welcome now.

*Vent.* What lethargy has crept into your soul?

*Ant.* 'Tis but a scorn of life, and just desire
To free myself from bondage.

*Vent.* Do it bravely.

*Ant.* I will; but not by fighting. O Ventidius!
What should I fight for now?—my queen is dead.
I was but great for her; my power, my empire,
Were but my merchandise to buy her love;
And conquered kings, my factors. Now she's dead,
Let Cæsar take the world,—
An empty circle, since the jewel's gone
Which made it worth my strife: my being's nauseous;
For all the bribes of life are gone away.

*Vent.* Would you be taken?

*Ant.* Yes, I would be taken;
But, as a Roman ought,—dead, my Ventidius:
For I'll convey my soul from Cæsar's reach,
And lay down life myself. 'Tis time the world
Should have a lord, and know whom to obey.

We two have kept its homage in suspense,
And bent the globe, on whose each side we trod,
Till it was dented inwards.    Let him walk
Alone upon't: I'm weary of my part.
My torch is out; and the world stands before me,
Like a black desert at the approach of night:
I'll lay me down, and stray no farther on.

    *Vent.* I could be grieved,
But that I'll not outlive you: choose your death;
For, I have seen him in such various shapes,
I care not which I take: I'm only troubled,
The life I bear is worn to such a rag,
'Tis scarce worth giving.    I could wish, indeed,
We threw it from us with a better grace;
That, like two lions taken in the toils,
We might at least thrust out our paws, and wound
The hunters that enclose us.

    *Ant.* I have thought on it.
Ventidius, you must live.

    *Vent.* I must not, sir.

    *Ant.* Wilt thou not live, to speak some good of me?
To stand by my fair fame, and guard the approaches
From the ill tongues of men?

    *Vent.* Who shall guard mine,
For living after you?

    *Ant.* Say, I command it.

    *Vent.* If we die well, our deaths will speak themselves
And need no living witness.

    *Ant.* Thou hast loved me,
And fain I would reward thee.    I must die;
Kill me, and take the merit of my death,
To make thee friends with Cæsar.

    *Vent.* Thank your kindness.
You said I loved you; and in recompense,
You bid me turn a traitor: Did I think
You would have used me thus?—that I should die
With a hard thought of you?

    *Ant.* Forgive me, Roman.
Since I have heard of Cleopatra's death,
My reason bears no rule upon my tongue,
But lets my thoughts break all at random out.
I've thought better; do not deny me twice.

    *Vent.* By Heaven I will not.
Let it not be to outlive you.

    *Ant.* Kill me first,
And then die thou; for 'tis but just thou serve
Thy friend before thyself.

    *Vent.* Give me your hand.
We soon shall meet again.    Now, farewell, emperor!—[*Embrace.*

Methinks that word's too cold to be my last:
Since death sweeps all distinctions, farewell, friend!
That's all——
I will not make a business of a trifle;
And yet I cannot look on you, and kill you;
Pray turn your face.
   *Ant.* I do: strike home, be sure.
   *Vent.* Home as my sword will reach.     [*Kills himself.*
   *Ant.* Oh, thou mistak'st;
That wound was none of thine; give it me back;
Thou robb'st me of my death.
   *Vent.* I do indeed;
But think 'tis the first time I e'er deceived you,
If that may plead my pardon.—And you, gods,
Forgive me, if you will; for I die perjured,
Rather than kill my friend.     [*Dies.*
   *Ant.* Farewell! Ever my leader, even in death!
My queen and thou have got the start of me,
And I'm the lag of honour.—Gone so soon?
Is Death no more? he used him carelessly,
With a familiar kindness: ere he knocked,
Ran to the door, and took him in his arms,
As who should say—You're welcome at all hours,
A friend need give no warning. Books had spoiled him;
For all the learned are cowards by profession.
'Tis not worth
My further thought; for death, for aught I know,
Is but to think no more. Here's to be satisfied.
     [*Falls on his sword.*
I've missed my heart. O unperforming hand!
Thou never couldst have erred in a worse time.
My fortune jades me to the last; and death,
Like a great man, takes state, and makes me wait
For my admittance.——     [*Trampling within.*
Some, perhaps, from Cæsar:
If he should find me living, and suspect
That I played booty with my life! I'l mend
My work, ere they can reach me.     [*Rises upon his knees.*

*Enter* CLEOPATRA, CHARMION, *and* IRAS.

   *Cleo.* Where is my lord? where is he?
   *Char.* There he lies,
And dead Ventidius by him.
   *Cleo.* My fears were prophets; I am come too late.
O that accursed Alexas!     [*Runs to him.*
   *Ant.* Art thou living?
Or am I dead before I knew, and thou
The first kind ghost that meets me?

*Cleo.* Help me seat him.
Send quickly, send for help!    [*They place him in a chair.*
   *Ant.* I am answered.
We live both.   Sit thee down, my Cleopatra:
I'll make the most I can of life, to stay
A moment more with thee.
   *Cleo.* How is it with you?
   *Ant.* 'Tis as with a man
Removing in a hurry; all packed up,
But one dear jewel that his haste forgot;
And he, for that, returns upon the spur:
So I come back for thee.
   *Cleo.* Too long, ye heavens, you have been cruel to me:
Now show your mended faith, and give me back
His fleeting life!
   *Ant.* It will not be, my love;
I keep my soul by force.
Say but, thou art not false.
   *Cleo.* 'Tis now too late
To say I'm true: I'll prove it, and die with you.
Unknown to me, Alexas feigned my death:
Which, when I knew, I hasted to prevent
This fatal conseqence.   My fleet betrayed
Both you and me.
   *Ant.* And Dolabella——
   *Cleo.* Scarce
Esteemed before he loved; but hated now.
   *Ant.* Enough: my life's not long enough for more.
Thou say'st, thou wilt come after: I believe thee;
For I can now believe whate'er thou sayest,
That we may part more kindly.
   *Cleo.* I will come:
Doubt not, my life, I'll come, and quickly too:
Cæsar shall triumph o'er no part of thee.
   *Ant.* But grieve not, while thou stayest,
My last disastrous times:
Think we have had a clear and glorious day
And Heaven did kindly to delay the storm,
Just till our close of evening.   Ten years' love,
And not a moment lost, but all improved
To the utmost joys,—what ages have we lived?
And now to die each other's; and, so dying,
While hand in hand we walk in groves below,
Whole troops of lovers' ghosts shall flock about us,
And all the train be ours.
   *Cleo.* Your words are like the notes of dying swans,
Too sweet to last.   Were there so many hours
For your unkindness, and not one for love?
   *Ant.* No, not a minute.—This one kiss—more worth

[*Dies.*

Than all I leave to Cæsar.

*Cleo.* O tell me so again,
And take ten thousand kisses for that word.
My lord, my lord! speak, if you yet have being;
Sign to me, if you cannot speak; or cast
One look! Do anything that shows you live.

*Iras.* He's gone too far to hear you;
And this you see, a lump of senseless clay,
The leavings of a soul.

*Char.* Remember, madam,
He charged you not to grieve.

*Cleo.* And I'll obey him.
I have not loved a Roman, not to know
What should become his wife; his wife, my Charmion!
For 'tis to that high title I aspire;
And now I'll not die less. Let dull Octavia
Survive, to mourn him dead! My nobler fate
Shall knit our spousals with a tie too strong
For Roman laws to break.

*Iras.* Will you then die?

*Cleo.* Why shouldst thou make that question?

*Iras.* Cæsar is merciful.

*Cleo.* Let him be so
To those that want his mercy: My poor lord
Made no such covenant with him, to spare me
When he was dead. Yield me to Cæsar's pride?
What! to be led in triumph through the streets,
A spectacle to base plebeian eyes;
While some dejected friend of Antony's,
Close in a corner, shakes his head, and mutters
A secret curse on her who ruined him!
I'll none of that.

*Char.* Whatever you resolve,
I'll follow, even to death.

*Iras.* I only feared
For you; but more should fear to live without you.

*Cleo.* Why, now, 'tis as it should be. Quick, my friends,
Despatch; ere this, the town's in Cæsar's hands:
My lord looks down concerned, and fears my stay,
Lest I should be surprised;
Keep him not waiting for his love too long.
You, Charmion, bring my crown and richest jewels;
With them, the wreath of victory I made
(Vain augury!) for him, who now lies dead:
You, Iras, bring the cure of all our ills.

*Iras.* The aspics, madam?

*Cleo.* Must I bid you twice?     [*Exit* CHARMION *and* IRAS.
'Tis sweet to die, when they would force life on me,
To rush into the dark abode of death,

And seize him first; if he be like my love,
He is not frightful, sure.
We're now alone, in secrecy and silence;
And is not this like lovers? I may kiss
These pale, cold lips; Octavia does not see me:
And, oh! 'tis better far to have him thus,
Than see him in her arms.—Oh, welcome, welcome!

*Enter* CHARMION *and* IRAS.

*Char.* What must be done?
*Cleo.* Short ceremony, friends;
But yet it must be decent. First, this laurel
Shall crown my hero's head: he fell not basely,
Nor left his shield behind him.—Only thou
Couldst triumph o'er thyself; and thou alone
Wert worthy so to triumph.
*Char.* To what end
These ensigns of your pomp and royalty?
*Cleo.* Dull, that thou art! why 'tis to meet my love;
As when I saw him first, on Cydnus' bank,
All sparkling, like a goddess: so adorned,
I'll find him once again; my second spousals
Shall match my first in glory. Haste, haste, both,
And dress the bride of Antony.
*Char.* 'Tis done.
*Cleo.* Now seat me by my lord. I claim this place;
For I must conquer Cæsar too, like him,
And win my share of the world.—Hail, you dear relics
Of my immortal love!
O let no impious hand remove you hence:
But rest for ever here! Let Egypt give
His death that peace, which it denied his life.—
Reach me the casket.
*Iras.* Underneath the fruit
The aspic lies.
*Cleo.* Welcome, thou kind deceiver! [*Putting aside the leaves.*
Thou best of thieves; who, with an easy key,
Dost open life, and, unperceived by us,
Even steal us from ourselves; discharging so
Death's dreadful office, better than himself;
Touching our limbs so gently into slumber,
That Death stands by, deceived by his own image,
And thinks himself but sleep.
*Serap.* The queen, where is she?       [*Within.*
The town is yielded, Cæsar's at the gates.
*Cleo.* He comes too late to invade the rights of death.
Haste, bare my arm, and rouse the serpent's fury.
           [*Holds out her arm, and draws it back.*

Coward flesh,
Wouldst thou conspire with Cæsar to betray me,
As thou wert none of mine?   I'll force thee to it,
And not be sent by him,
But bring, myself, my soul to Antony.
                    [*Turns aside, and then shows her arm bloody.*
Take hence; the work is done.
  *Serap.* Break ope the door,                    [*Within.*
And guard the traitor well.
  *Char.* The next is ours.
  *Iras.* Now, Charmion, to be worthy
Of our great queen and mistress.    [*They apply the aspics.*
  *Cleo.* Already, death, I feel thee in my veins:
I go with such a will to find my lord,
That we shall quickly meet.
A heavy numbness creeps through every limb,
And now 'tis at my head: My eyelids fall
And my dear love is vanish'd in a mist.
Where shall I find him, where?   O turn me to him,
And lay me on his breast!—Cæsar, thy worst;
Now part us, if thou canst.                    [*Dies.*
        [IRAS *sinks down at her feet, and dies;* CHARMION
            *stands behind her chair, as dressing her head.*


*Enter* SERAPION, *two* Priests, ALEXAS *bound,* Egyptians.

  *Priest.* Behold, Serapion,
What havoc death has made!
  *Serap.* 'Twas what I feared.—
Charmion, is this well done?
  *Char.* Yes, 'tis well done, and like a queen, the last
Of her great race: I follow her.        [*Sinks down: dies.*
  *Alex.* 'Tis true,
She has done well: Much better thus to die,
Than live to make a holiday in Rome.
  *Serap.* See, see how the lovers sit in state together,
As they were giving laws to half mankind!
The impression of a smile, left in her face,
Shows she died pleased with him for whom she lived,
And went to charm him in another world.
Cæsar's just entering: grief has now no leisure.
Secure that villain, as our pledge of safety,
To grace the imperial triumph.—Sleep, blest pair,
Secure from human chance, long ages out,
While all the storms of fate fly o'er your tomb;
    And fame to late posterity shall tell,
    No lovers lived so great, or died so well.        [*Exeunt.*

# EPILOGUE

POETS, like disputants, when reasons fail,
Have one sure refuge left—and that's to rail.
Fop, coxcomb, fool, are thundered through the pit;
And this is all their equipage of wit.
We wonder how the devil this difference grows,
Betwixt our fools in verse, and yours in prose:
For, 'faith, the quarrel rightly understood,
'Tis civil war with their own flesh and blood.
The threadbare author hates the gaudy coat;
And swears at the gilt coach, but swears afoot:
For 'tis observed of every scribbling man,
He grows a fop as fast as e'er he can;
Prunes up, and asks his oracle, the glass,
If pink or purple best become his face.
For our poor wretch, he neither rails nor prays;
Nor likes your wit just as you like his plays;
He has not yet so much of Mr. Bayes.
He does his best; and if he cannot please,
Would quietly sue out his *writ of ease.*
Yet, if he might his own grand jury call,
By the fair sex he begs to stand or fall.
Let Cæsar's power the men's ambition move,
But grace you him who lost the world for love!
Yet if some antiquated lady say,
The last age is not copied in his play;
Heaven help the man who for that face must drudge,
Which only has the wrinkles of a judge.
Let not the young and beauteous join with those;
For should you raise such numerous hosts of foes,
Young wits and sparks he to his aid must call;
'Tis more than one man's work to please you all.

# THE COUNTRY WIFE

# DRAMATIS PERSONÆ

Mr. HORNER.
Mr. HARCOURT.
Mr. DORILANT.
Mr. PINCHWIFE.
Mr. SPARKISH.
Sir JASPER FIDGET.
A Boy.
A Quack.
Waiters, Servants, and Attendants.

Mrs. MARGERY PINCHWIFE.
ALITHEA, Sister of Pinchwife.
Lady FIDGET.
Mrs. DAINTY FIDGET, Sister of Sir Jasper.
Mrs. SQUEAMISH.
Old Lady SQUEAMISH.
LUCY, Alithea's Maid.

SCENE—LONDON.

# PROLOGUE

SPOKEN BY MR. HART

POETS, like cudgelled bullies, never do
At first or second blow submit to you;
But will provoke you still, and ne'er have done,
Till you are weary first with laying on.
The late so baffled scribbler of this day,
Though he stands trembling, bids me boldly say,
What we before most plays are used to do,
For poets out of fear first draw on you;
In a fierce prologue the still pit defy,
And, ere you speak, like Castril give the lie.
But though our Bayes's battles oft I've fought,
And with bruised knuckles their dear conquests bought;
Nay, never yet feared odds upon the stage,
In prologue dare not hector with the age;
But would take quarter from your saving hands,
Though Bayes within all yielding countermands,
Says, you confederate wits no quarter give,
Therefore his play shan't ask your leave to live.
Well, let the vain rash fop, by huffing so,
Think to obtain the better terms of you;
But we, the actors, humbly will submit,
Now, and at any time, to a full pit;
Nay, often we anticipate your rage,
And murder poets for you on our stage:
We set no guards upon our tiring-room,
But when with flying colours there you come,
We patiently, you see, give up to you
Our poets, virgins, nay, our matrons too.

# THE COUNTRY WIFE

## ACT I

### SCENE I.—HORNER's *Lodging*

*Enter* HORNER, *and* Quack *following him at a distance.*

*Horn.* [*aside*]. A quack is as fit for a pimp, as a midwife for a bawd; they are still but in their way, both helpers of nature.— [*Aloud.*] Well, my dear doctor, hast thou done what I desired?

*Quack.* I have undone you for ever with the women, and reported you throughout the whole town as bad as an eunuch, with as much trouble as if I had made you one in earnest.

*Horn.* But have you told all the midwives you know, the orange wenches at the playhouses, the city husbands, and old fumbling keepers of this end of the town? for they'll be the readiest to report it.

*Quack.* I have told all the chambermaids, waiting-women, tire-women, and old women of my acquaintance; nay, and whispered it as a secret to 'em, and to the whisperers of Whitehall; so that you need not doubt 'twill spread, and you will be as odious to the handsome young women as——

*Horn.* As the small-pox. Well——

*Quack.* And to the married women of this end of the town, as——

*Horn.* As the great ones; nay, as their own husbands.

*Quack.* And to the city dames, as aniseed Robin, of filthy and contemptible memory; and they will frighten their children with your name, especially their females.

*Horn.* And cry, Horner's coming to carry you away. I am only afraid 'twill not be believed. You told 'em it was by an English-French disaster, and an English-French surgeon, who has given me at once not only a cure, but an antidote for the future against that damned malady, and that worse distemper, love, and all other women's evils?

*Quack.* Your late journey into France has made it the more credible, and your being here a fortnight before you appeared in public, looks as if you apprehended the shame, which I wonder you do not. Well, I have been hired by young gallants to belie 'em t'other way; but you are the first would be thought a man unfit for women.

*Horn.* Dear Mr. Doctor, let vain rogues be contented only to be thought abler men than they are, generally 'tis all the pleasure they have; but mine lies another way.

*Quack.* You take, methinks, a very preposterous way to it, and as ridiculous as if we operators in physic should put forth bills to disparage our medicaments, with hopes to gain customers.

*Horn.* Doctor, there are quacks in love as well as physic, who get but the fewer and worse patients for their boasting; a good name is seldom got by giving it one's self; and women, no more than honour, are compassed by bragging. Come, come, Doctor, the wisest lawyer never discovers the merits of his cause till the trial; the wealthiest man conceals his riches, and the cunning gamester his play. Shy husbands and keepers, like old rooks, are not to be cheated but by a new unpractised trick: false friendship will pass now no more than false dice upon 'em; no, not in the city.

*Enter* Boy.

*Boy.* There are two ladies and a gentleman coming up. [*Exit.*
*Horn.* A pox! some unbelieving sisters of my former acquaintance, who, I am afraid, expect their sense should be satisfied of the falsity of the report. No—this formal fool and women!

*Enter* Sir JASPER FIDGET, Lady FIDGET, *and* Mrs. DAINTY FIDGET.

*Quack.* His wife and sister.
*Sir Jasp.* My coach breaking just now before your door, sir, I look upon as an occasional reprimand to me, sir, for not kissing your hands, sir, since your coming out of France, sir; and so my disaster, sir, has been my good fortune, sir; and this is my wife and sister, sir.

*Horn.* What then, sir?
*Sir Jasp.* My lady, and sister, sir.—Wife, this is Master Horner.
*Lady Fid.* Master Horner, husband!
*Sir Jasp.* My lady, my Lady Fidget, sir.
*Horn.* So, sir.
*Sir Jasp.* Won't you be acquainted with her, sir?—[*Aside.*] So, the report is true, I find, by his coldness or aversion to the sex; but I'll play the wag with him.—[*Aloud.*] Pray salute my wife, my lady, sir.

*Horn.* I will kiss no man's wife, sir, for him, sir; I have taken my eternal leave, sir, of the sex already, sir.

*Sir Jasp.* [*aside*]. Ha! ha! ha! I'll plague him yet.—[*Aloud.*] Not know my wife, sir?

*Horn.* I do know your wife, sir; she's a woman, sir, and consequently a monster, sir, a greater monster than a husband, sir.

*Sir Jasp.* A husband! how, sir?

*Horn.* So, sir; but I make no more cuckolds, sir.

[*Makes horns.*

*Sir Jasp.* Ha! ha! ha! Mercury! Mercury!

*Lady Fid.* Pray, Sir Jasper, let us be gone from this rude fellow.

*Mrs. Dain.* Who, by his breeding, would think he had ever been in France?

*Lady Fid.* Foh! he's but too much a French fellow, such as hate women of quality and virtue for their love to their husbands, Sir Jasper; a woman is hated by 'em as much for loving her husband as for loving their money. But pray let's be gone.

*Horn.* You do well, madam; for I have nothing that you came for. I have brought over not so much as a bawdy picture, new postures, nor the second part of the *Ecole des Filles;* nor——

*Quack.* Hold, for shame, sir! what d'ye mean? you'll ruin yourself for ever with the sex——     [*Apart to* HORNER.

*Sir Jasp.* Ha! ha! ha! he hates women perfectly, I find.

*Mrs Dain.* What pity 'tis he should!

*Lady Fid.* Ay, he's a base, rude fellow for't. But affectation makes not a woman more odious to them than virtue.

*Horn.* Because your virtue is your greatest affectation, madam.

*Lady Fid.* How, you saucy fellow! would you wrong my honour?

*Horn.* If I could.

*Lady Fid.* How d'ye mean, sir?

*Sir Jasp.* Ha! ha! ha! no, he can't wrong your ladyship's honour, upon my honour. He, poor man—hark you in your ear—a mere eunuch.     [*Whispers.*

*Lady Fid.* O filthy French beast! foh! foh! why do we stay? let's be gone: I can't endure the sight of him.

*Sir Jasp.* Stay but till the chairs come; they'll be here presently.

*Lady Fid.* No, no.

*Sir Jasp.* Nor can I stay longer. 'Tis, let me see, a quarter and half quarter of a minute past eleven. The council will be sat; I must away. Business must be preferred always before love and ceremony with the wise, Mr. Horner.

*Horn.* And the impotent, Sir Jasper.

*Sir Jasp.* Ay, ay, the impotent, Master Horner: hah! hah! hah!

*Lady Fid.* What, leave us with a filthy man alone in his lodgings?

*Sir Jasp.* He's an innocent man now, you know. Pray stay, I'll hasten the chairs to you.—Mr. Horner, your servant; I should be glad to see you at my house. Pray come and dine with me, and play at cards with my wife after dinner; you are fit for women at that game yet, ha! ha!—[*Aside.*] 'Tis as much a husband's prudence to provide innocent diversion for a wife as to hinder her unlawful pleasures; and he had better employ her than let her employ herself.—[*Aloud.*] Farewell.

*Horn.* Your servant, Sir Jasper.        [*Exit* Sir JASPER.

*Lady Fid.* I will not stay with him, foh!——

*Horn.* Nay, madam, I beseech you stay, if it be but to see I can be as civil to ladies yet as they would desire.

*Lady Fid.* No, no, foh! you cannot be civil to ladies.

*Mrs. Dain.* You as civil as ladies would desire?

*Lady Fid.* No, no, no, foh! foh! foh!

[*Exeunt* Lady FIDGET *and* Mrs. DAINTY FIDGET.

*Quack.* Now, I think, I, or you yourself, rather, have done your business with the women.

*Horn.* Thou art an ass. Don't you see already, upon the report, and my carriage, this grave man of business leaves his wife in my lodgings, invites me to his house and wife, who before would not be acquainted with me out of jealousy?

*Quack.* Nay, by this means you may be the more acquainted with the husbands, but the less with the wives.

*Horn.* Let me alone; if I can but abuse the husbands, I'll soon disabuse the wives. Stay—I'll reckon you up the advantages I am like to have by my stratagem. First, I shall be rid of all my old acquaintances, the most insatiable sorts of duns, that invade our lodgings in a morning; and next to the pleasure of making a new mistress is that of being rid of an old one, and of all old debts. Love, when it comes to be so, is paid the most unwillingly.

*Quack.* Well, you may be so rid of your old acquaintances; but how will you get any new ones?

*Horn.* Doctor, thou wilt never make a good chemist, thou art so incredulous and impatient. Ask but all the young fellows of the town if they do not lose more time, like huntsmen, in starting the game, than in running it down. One knows not where to find 'em; who will or will not. Women of quality are so civil, you can hardly distinguish love from good breeding, and a man is often mistaken: but now I can be sure she that shows an aversion to me loves the sport, as those women that are gone, whom I warrant to be right. And then the next thing is, your women of honour, as you call 'em, are only chary of their reputations, not their persons; and 'tis scandal they would avoid, not men. Now may I have, by the reputation of an eunuch, the privileges of one, and be seen in a lady's chamber in a morning as early as her husband; kiss virgins before their parents or lovers; and may be, in short, the *passe-partout* of the town. Now, doctor.

*Quack.* Nay, now you shall be the doctor; and your process is so new that we do not know but it may succeed.

*Horn.* Not so new neither; *probatum est*, doctor.

*Quack.* Well, I wish you luck, and many patients, whilst I go to mine.        [*Exit.*

*Enter* HARCOURT *and* DORILANT.

*Har.* Come, your appearance at the play yesterday has, I hope, hardened you for the future against the women's contempt, and the men's raillery; and now you'll abroad as you were wont.

*Horn.* Did I not bear it bravely?

*Dor.* With a most theatrical impudence, nay, more than the orange-wenches show there, or a drunken vizard-mask, or a great-bellied actress; nay, or the most impudent of creatures, an ill poet; or what is yet more impudent, a second-hand critic.

*Horn.* But what say the ladies? have they no pity?

*Har.* What ladies? The vizard-masks, you know, never pity a man when all's gone, though in their service.

*Dor.* And for the women in the boxes, you'd never pity them when 'twas in your power.

*Har.* They say 'tis pity but all that deal with common women should be served so.

*Dor.* Nay, I dare swear they won't admit you to play at cards with them, go to plays with 'em, or do the little duties which other shadows of men are wont to do for 'em.

*Horn.* Who do you call shadows of men?

*Dor.* Half-men.

*Horn.* What, boys?

*Dor.* Ay, your old boys, old *beaux garçons*, who, like super-annuated stallions, are suffered to run, feed, and whinny with the mares as long as they live, though they can do nothing else.

*Horn.* Well, a pox on love and wenching! Women serve but to keep a man from better company. Though I can't enjoy them, I shall you the more. Good fellowship and friendship are lasting, rational, and manly pleasures.

*Har.* For all that, give me some of those pleasures you call effeminate too; they help to relish one another.

*Horn.* They disturb one another.

*Har.* No, mistresses are like books. If you pore upon them too much, they doze you, and make you unfit for company; but if used discreetly, you are the fitter for conversation by 'em.

*Dor.* A mistress should be like a little country retreat near the town; not to dwell in constantly, but only for a night and away, to taste the town the better when a man returns.

*Horn.* I tell you, 'tis as hard to be a good fellow, a good friend, and a lover of women, as 'tis to be a good fellow, a good friend, and a lover of money. You cannot follow both, then choose your side. Wine gives you liberty, love takes it away.

*Dor.* Gad, he's in the right on't.

*Horn.* Wine gives you joy; love, grief and tortures, besides the surgeon. Wine makes us witty; love, only sots. Wine makes us sleep; love breaks it.

*Dor.* By the world he has reason, Harcourt.

*Horn.* Wine makes——

*Dor.* Ay, wine makes us—makes us princes; love makes us beggars, poor rogues, egad—and wine——

*Horn.* So, there's one converted.—No, no, love and wine, oil and vinegar.

*Har.* I grant it; love will still be uppermost.

*Horn.* Come, for my part, I will have only those glorious manly pleasures of being very drunk and very slovenly.

*Enter* Boy.

*Boy.* Mr. Sparkish is below, sir. [*Exit.*

*Har.* What, my dear friend! a rogue that is fond of me only, I think, for abusing him.

*Dor.* No, he can no more think the men laugh at him than that women jilt him; his opinion of himself is so good.

*Horn.* Well, there's another pleasure by drinking I thought not of,—I shall lose his acquaintance, because he cannot drink: and you know 'tis a very hard thing to be rid of him; for he's one of those nauseous offerers at wit, who, like the worst fiddlers, run themselves into all companies.

*Har.* One that, by being in the company of men of sense, would pass for one.

*Horn.* And may so to the short-sighted world; as a false jewel amongst true ones is not discerned at a distance. His company is as troublesome to us as a cuckold's when you have a mind to his wife's.

*Har.* No, the rogue will· not let us enjoy one another, but ravishes our conversation; though he signifies no more to't than Sir Martin Mar-all's gaping, and awkward thrumming upon the lute, does to his man's voice and music.

*Dor.* And to pass for a wit in town shows himself a fool every night to us, that are guilty of the plot.

*Horn.* Such wits as he are, to a company of reasonable men, like rooks to the gamesters; who only fill a room at the table, but are so far from contributing to the play, that they only serve to spoil the fancy of those that do.

*Dor.* Nay, they are used like rooks too, snubbed, checked, and abused; yet the rogues will hang on.

*Horn.* A pox on 'em, and all that force nature, and would be still what she forbids 'em! Affectation is her greatest monster.

*Har.* Most men are the contraries to that they would seem. Your bully, you see, is a coward with a long sword; the little humbly-fawning physician, with his ebony cane, is he that destroys men.

*Dor.* The usurer, a poor rogue, possessed of mouldy bonds and mortgages; and we they call spendthrifts, are only wealthy, who lay out his money upon daily new purchases of pleasure.

*Horn.* Ay, your arrantest cheat is your trustee or executor; your jealous man, the greatest cuckold; your churchman the greatest atheist; and your noisy pert rogue of a wit, the greatest fop, dullest ass, and worst company, as you shall see; for here he comes.

*Enter* SPARKISH.

*Spark.* How is't, sparks? how is't? Well, faith, Harry, I must rally thee a little, ha! ha! ha! upon the report in town of thee, ha! ha! ha! I can't hold i'faith; shall I speak?

*Horn.* Yes; but you'll be so bitter then.

*Spark.* Honest Dick and Frank here shall answer for me; I will not be extreme bitter, by the universe.

*Har.* We will be bound in a ten thousand pound bond, he shall not be bitter at all.

*Dor.* Nor sharp, nor sweet.

*Horn.* What, not downright insipid?

*Spark.* Nay then, since you are so brisk, and provoke me, take what follows. You must know, I was discoursing and rallying with some ladies yesterday, and they happened to talk of the fine new signs in town——

*Horn.* Very fine ladies, I believe.

*Spark.* Said I, I know where the best new sign is.—Where? says one of the ladies.—In Covent Garden, I replied.—Said another, In what street?—In Russel Street, answered I.—Lord, says another, I'm sure there was never a fine new sign there yesterday.—Yes, but there was, said I again; and it came out of France, and has been there a fortnight.

*Dor.* A pox! I can hear no more, prithee.

*Horn.* No, hear him out; let him tune his crowd a while.

*Har.* The worst music, the greatest preparation.

*Spark.* Nay, faith, I'll make you laugh.—It cannot be, says a third lady.—Yes, yes, quoth I again.—Says a fourth lady——

*Horn.* Look to't, we'll have no more ladies.

*Spark.* No—then mark, mark, now. Said I to the fourth, Did you never see Mr. Horner? he lodges in Russel Street, and he's a sign of a man, you know, since he came out of France; ha! ha! ha!

*Horn.* But the devil take me if thine be the sign of a jest.

*Spark.* With that they all fell a-laughing, till they bepissed themselves. What, but it does not move you, methinks? Well, I see one had as good go to law without a witness, as break a jest without a laugher on one's side.—Come, come, sparks, but where do we dine? I have left at Whitehall an earl, to dine with you.

*Dor.* Why, I thought thou hadst loved a man with a title, better than a suit with a French trimming to't.

*Har.* Go to him again.

*Spark.* No, sir, a wit to me is the greatest title in the world.

*Horn.* But go dine with your earl, sir; he may be exceptious. We are your friends, and will not take it ill to be left, I do assure you.

*Har.* Nay, faith, he shall go to him.

*Spark.* Nay, pray, gentlemen.

*Dor.* We'll thrust you out, if you won't; what, disappoint anybody for us?

*Spark.* Nay, dear gentlemen, hear me.

*Horn.* No, no, sir, by no means; pray go, sir.

*Spark.* Why, dear rogues——

*Dor.* No, no.        [*They all thrust him out of the room.*

*All.* Ha! ha! ha!

### *Re-enter* SPARKISH.

*Spark.* But, sparks, pray hear me. What, d'ye think I'll eat then with gay shallow fops and silent coxcombs? I think wit as necessary at dinner as a glass of good wine; and that's the reason I never have any stomach when I eat alone.—Come, but where do we dine?

*Horn.* Even where you will.

*Spark.* At Chateline's?

*Dor.* Yes, if you will.

*Spark.* Or at the Cock?

*Dor.* Yes, if you please.

*Spark.* Or at the Dog and Partridge?

*Horn.* Ay, if you have a mind to't; for we shall dine at neither.

*Spark.* Pshaw! with your fooling we shall lose the new play; and I would no more miss seeing a new play the first day, than I would miss sitting in the wit's row. Therefore I'll go fetch my mistress, and away.        [*Exit.*

### *Enter* PINCHWIFE.

*Horn.* Who have we here? Pinchwife?

*Pinch.* Gentlemen, your humble servant.

*Horn.* Well, Jack, by thy long absence from the town, the grumness of thy countenance, and the slovenliness of thy habit, I should give thee joy, should I not, of marriage?

*Pinch.* [*aside*]. Death! does he know I'm married too? I thought to have concealed it from him at least.—[*Aloud.*] My long stay in the country will excuse my dress; and I have a suit of law that brings me up to town, that puts me out of humour. Besides, I must give Sparkish to-morrow five thousand pounds to lie with my sister.

*Horn.* Nay, you country gentlemen, rather than not purchase, will buy anything; and he is a cracked title, if we may quibble. Well, but am I to give thee joy? I heard thou wert married.

*Pinch.* What then?

*Horn.* Why, the next thing that is to be heard, is, thou'rt a cuckold.

*Pinch.* Insupportable name!        [*Aside.*

*Horn.* But I did not expect marriage from such a whoremaster as you; one that knew the town so much, and women so well.

*Pinch.* Why, I have married no London wife.

*Horn.* Pshaw! that's all one. That grave circumspection in marrying a country wife is like refusing a deceitful pampered Smithfield jade, to go and be cheated by a friend in the country.

*Pinch.* [*aside*]. A pox on him and his simile!—[*Aloud.*] At least we are a little surer of the breed there, know what her keeping has been, whether foiled or unsound.

*Horn.* Come, come, I have known a clap gotten in Wales; and there are cousins, justices' clerks, and chaplains in the country, I won't say coachmen. But she's handsome and young?

*Pinch.* [*aside*]. I'll answer as I should do.—[*Aloud.*] No, no; she has no beauty but her youth, no attraction but her modesty: wholesome, homely, and huswifely; that's all.

*Dor.* He talks as like a grazier as he looks.

*Pinch.* She's too awkward, ill-favoured, and silly to bring to town.

*Har.* Then methinks you should bring her to be taught breeding.

*Pinch.* To be taught! no, sir, I thank you. Good wives and private soldiers should be ignorant—I'll keep her from your instructions, I warrant you.

*Har.* The rogue is as jealous as if his wife were not ignorant.
[*Aside.*

*Horn.* Why, if she be ill-favoured, there will be less danger here for you than by leaving her in the country. We have such variety of dainties that we are seldom hungry.

*Dor.* But they have always coarse, constant, swingeing stomachs in the country.

*Har.* Foul feeders indeed!

*Dor.* And your hospitality is great there.

*Har.* Open house; every man's welcome.

*Pinch.* So, so, gentlemen.

*Horn.* But prithee, why wouldst thou marry her? If she be ugly, ill-bred, and silly, she must be rich then.

*Pinch.* As rich as if she brought me twenty thousand pound out of this town; for she'll be as sure not to spend her moderate portion, as a London baggage would be to spend hers, let it be what it would: so 'tis all one. Then, because she's ugly, she's the likelier to be my own; and being ill-bred, she'll hate conversation; and since silly and innocent, will not know the difference betwixt a man of one-and-twenty and one of forty.

*Horn.* Nine—to my knowledge. But if she be silly, she'll expect as much from a man of forty-nine, as from him of one-and-twenty. But methinks wit is more necessary than beauty; and I think no young woman ugly that has it, and no handsome woman agreeable without it.

*Pinch.* 'Tis my maxim, he's a fool that marries; but he's a

greater that does not marry a fool.   What is wit in a wife good
for, but to make a man a cuckold?

*Horn.*   Yes, to keep it from his knowledge.

*Pinch.*   A fool cannot contrive to make her husband a cuckold.

*Horn.*   No; but she'll club with a man that can: and what is
worse, if she cannot make her husband a cuckold, she'll make
him jealous, and pass for one: and then 'tis all one.

*Pinch.*   Well, well, I'll take care for one.   My wife shall make
me no cuckold, though she had your help, Mr. Horner.   I understand the town, sir.

*Dor.*   His help!                                               [*Aside.*

*Har.*   He's come newly to town, it seems, and has not heard
how things are with him.                                        [*Aside.*

*Horn.*   But tell me, has marriage cured thee of whoring, which it
seldom does?

*Har.*   'Tis more than age can do.

*Horn.*   No, the word is, I'll marry and live honest: but a
marriage vow is like a penitent gamester's oath, and entering
into bonds and penalties to stint himself to such a particular
small sum at play for the future, which makes him but the more
eager; and not being able to hold out, loses his money again,
and his forfeit to boot.

*Dor.*   Ay, ay, a gamester will be a gamester whilst his money
lasts, and a whoremaster whilst his vigour.

*Har.*   Nay, I have known 'em, when they are broke, and can
lose no more, keep a fumbling with the box in their hands to fool
with only, and hinder other gamesters.

*Dor.*   That had wherewithal to make lusty stakes.

*Pinch.*   Well, gentlemen, you may laugh at me; but you shall
never lie with my wife: I know the town.

*Horn.*   But prithee, was not the way you were in better? is
not keeping better than marriage?

*Pinch.*   A pox on't! the jades would jilt me, I could never
keep a whore to myself.

*Horn.*   So, then you only married to keep a whore to yourself.
Well, but let me tell you, women, as you say, are like soldiers,
made constant and loyal by good pay, rather than by oaths and
covenants.   Therefore I'd advise my friends to keep rather than
marry, since too I find, by your example, it does not serve one's
turn; for I saw you yesterday in the eighteenpenny place with
a pretty country-wench.

*Pinch.*   How the devil! did he see my wife then?   I sat there
that she might not be seen.   But she shall never go to a play
again.                                                          [*Aside.*

*Horn.*   What! dost thou blush, at nine-and-forty, for having
been seen with a wench?

*Dor.*   No, faith, I warrant 'twas his wife, which he seated
there out of sight; for he's a cunning rogue, and understands
the town.

*Har.* He blushes. Then 'twas his wife; for men are now more ashamed to be seen with them in public than with a wench.

*Pinch.* Hell and damnation! I'm undone, since Horner has seen her, and they know 'twas she.                    [*Aside.*

*Horn.* But prithee, was it thy wife? She was exceeding pretty: I was in love with her at that distance.

*Pinch.* You are like never to be nearer to her. Your servant, gentlemen.                                          [*Offers to go.*

*Horn.* Nay, prithee stay.

*Pinch.* I cannot; I will not.

*Horn.* Come, you shall dine with us.

*Pinch.* I have dined already.

*Horn.* Come, I know thou hast not: I'll treat thee, dear rogue; thou sha't spend none of thy Hampshire money to-day.

*Pinch.* Treat me! So, he uses me already like his cuckold.
                                                    [*Aside.*

*Horn.* Nay, you shall not go.

*Pinch.* I must; I have business at home.            [*Exit.*

*Har.* To beat his wife. He's as jealous of her as a Cheapside husband of a Covent Garden wife.

*Horn.* Why, 'tis as hard to find an old whoremaster without jealousy and the gout, as a young one without fear, or the pox:—
As gout in age from pox in youth proceeds,
So wenching past, then jealousy succeeds;
The worst disease that love and wenching breeds.

                                                    [*Exeunt.*


# ACT II

### SCENE I.—*A Room in* PINCHWIFE'S *House*

Mrs. MARGERY PINCHWIFE *and* ALITHEA. PINCHWIFE
*peeping behind at the door.*

*Mrs. Pinch.* Pray, sister, where are the best fields and woods to walk in, in London?

*Alith.* [*aside*]. A pretty question!—[*Aloud.*] Why, sister, Mulberry Garden and St. James's Park; and, for close walks, the New Exchange.

*Mrs. Pinch.* Pray, sister, tell me why my husband looks so grum here in town, and keeps me up so close, and will not let me go a-walking, nor let me wear my best gown yesterday.

*Alith.* O, he's jealous, sister.

*Mrs. Pinch.* Jealous! what's that?

*Alith.* He's afraid you should love another man.

*Mrs. Pinch.* How should he be afraid of my loving another man, when he will not let me see any but himself?

*Alith.* Did he not carry you yesterday to a play?

*Mrs. Pinch.* Ay; but we sat amongst ugly people. He would not let me come near the gentry, who sat under us, so that I could not see 'em. He told me, none but naughty women sat there, whom they toused and moused. But I would have ventured, for all that.

*Alith.* But how did you like the play?

*Mrs. Pinch.* Indeed I was a-weary of the play; but I liked hugeously the actors. They are the goodliest, properest men, sister!

*Alith.* O, but you must not like the actors, sister.

*Mrs. Pinch.* Ay, how should I help it, sister? Pray, sister, when my husband comes in, will you ask leave for me to go a-walking?

*Alith.* A-walking! ha! ha! Lord, a country-gentlewoman's pleasure is the drudgery of a footpost; and she requires as much airing as her husband's horses.—[*Aside.*] But here comes your husband: I'll ask, though I'm sure he'll not grant it.

*Mrs. Pinch.* He says he won't let me go abroad for fear of catching the pox.

*Alith.* Fy! the small-pox you should say.

*Enter* PINCHWIFE.

*Mrs. Pinch.* O my dear, dear bud, welcome home! Why dost thou look so fropish? who has nangered thee?

*Pinch.* You're a fool. [Mrs. PINCHWIFE *goes aside, and cries.*

*Alith.* Faith, so she is, for crying for no fault, poor tender creature!

*Pinch.* What, you would have her as impudent as yourself, as arrant a jilflirt, a gadder, a magpie; and to say all, a mere notorious town-woman?

*Alith.* Brother, you are my only censurer; and the honour of your family shall sooner suffer in your wife there than in me, though I take the innocent liberty of the town.

*Pinch.* Hark you, mistress, do not talk so before my wife.— The innocent liberty of the town!

*Alith.* Why, pray, who boasts of any intrigue with me? what lampoon has made my name notorious? what ill women frequent my lodgings? I keep no company with any women of scandalous reputations.

*Pinch.* No, you keep the men of scandalous reputations company.

*Alith.* Where? would you not have me civil? answer 'em in a box at the plays, in the drawing-room at Whitehall, in St. James's Park, Mulberry Garden, or——

*Pinch.* Hold, hold! Do not teach my wife where the men are to be found: I believe she's the worse for your town-documents already. I bid you keep her in ignorance, as I do.

*Mrs. Pinch.* Indeed, be not angry with her, bud, she will tell me nothing of the town, though I ask her a thousand times a day.

*Pinch.* Then you are very inquisitive to know, I find?

*Mrs. Pinch.* Not I indeed, dear; I hate London. Our place-house in the country is worth a thousand of't: would I were there again!

*Pinch.* So you shall, I warrant. But were you not talking of plays and players when I came in?—[*To* ALITHEA.] You are her encourager in such discourses.

*Mrs. Pinch.* No, indeed, dear; she chid me just now for liking the playermen.

*Pinch.* [*aside*]. Nay, if she be so innocent as to own to me her liking them, there is no hurt in't.—[*Aloud.*] Come, my poor rogue, but thou likest none better than me?

*Mrs. Pinch.* Yes, indeed, but I do. The playermen are finer folks.

*Pinch.* But you love none better than me?

*Mrs. Pinch.* You are mine own dear bud, and I know you. I hate a stranger.

*Pinch.* Ay, my dear, you must love me only; and not be like the naughty town-women, who only hate their husbands, and love every man else; love plays, visits, fine coaches, fine clothes, fiddles, balls, treats, and so lead a wicked town-life.

*Mrs. Pinch.* Nay, if to enjoy all these things be a town-life, London is not so bad a place, dear.

*Pinch.* How! if you love me, you must hate London.

*Alith.* The fool has forbid me discovering to her the pleasures of the town, and he is now setting her agog upon them himself.
[*Aside.*

*Mrs. Pinch.* But, husband, do the town-women love the playermen too?

*Pinch.* Yes, I warrant you.

*Mrs. Pinch.* Ay, I warrant you.

*Pinch.* Why, you do not, I hope?

*Mrs. Pinch.* No, no, bud. But why have we no playermen in the country?

*Pinch.* Ha!—Mrs. Minx, ask me no more to go to a play.

*Mrs. Pinch.* Nay, why, love? I did not care for going: but when you forbid me, you make me, as 'twere, desire it.

*Alith.* So 'twill be in other things, I warrant. [*Aside.*

*Mrs. Pinch.* Pray let me go to a play, dear.

*Pinch.* Hold your peace, I wo' not.

*Mrs. Pinch.* Why, love?

*Pinch.* Why, I'll tell you.

*Alith.* Nay, if he tell her, she'll give him more cause to forbid her that place. [*Aside.*

*Mrs. Pinch.* Pray why, dear?

*Pinch.* First, you like the actors; and the gallants may like you.

*Mrs. Pinch.* What, a homely country girl! No, bud, nobody will like me.

*Pinch.* I tell you yes, they may.

*Mrs. Pinch.* No, no, you jest—I won't believe you: I will go.

*Pinch.* I tell you then, that one of the lewdest fellows in town, who saw you there, told me he was in love with you.

*Mrs. Pinch.* Indeed! who, who, pray who was't?

*Pinch.* I've gone too far, and slipped before I was aware; how overjoyed she is! [*Aside.*

*Mrs. Pinch.* Was it any Hampshire gallant, any of our neighbours? I promise you, I am beholding to him.

*Pinch.* I promise you, you lie; for he would but ruin you, as he has done hundreds. He has no other love for women but that; such as he look upon women, like basilisks, but to destroy 'em.

*Mrs. Pinch.* Ay, but if he loves me, why should he ruin me? answer me to that. Methinks he should not, I would do him no harm.

*Alith.* Ha! ha! ha!

*Pinch.* 'Tis very well; but I'll keep him from doing you any harm, or me either. But here comes company; get you in, get you in.

*Mrs. Pinch.* But, pray, husband, is he a pretty gentleman that loves me?

*Pinch.* In, baggage, in. [*Thrusts her in, and shuts the door.*

*Enter* SPARKISH *and* HARCOURT.

What, all the lewd libertines of the town brought to my lodging by this easy coxcomb! 'sdeath, I'll not suffer it.

*Spark.* Here, Harcourt, do you approve my choice?—[*To* ALITHEA.] Dear little rogue, I told you I'd bring you acquainted with all my friends, the wits and—— [HARCOURT *salutes her.*

*Pinch.* Ay, they shall know her, as well as you yourself will, I warrant you.

*Spark.* This is one of those, my pretty rogue, that are to dance at your wedding to-morrow; and him you must bid welcome ever, to what you and I have.

*Pinch.* Monstrous! [*Aside.*

*Spark.* Harcourt, how dost thou like her, faith? Nay, dear, do not look down; I should hate to have a wife of mine out of countenance at anything.

*Pinch.* Wonderful! [*Aside.*

*Spark.* Tell me, I say, Harcourt, how dost thou like her? Thou hast stared upon her enough, to resolve me.

*Har.* So infinitely well, that I could wish I had a mistress too, that might differ from her in nothing but her love and engagement to you.

*Alith.* Sir, Master Sparkish has often told me that his acquaintance were all wits and raillieurs, and now I find it.

*Spark.* No, by the universe, madam, he does not rally now; you may believe him. I do assure you, he is the honestest, worthiest, true-hearted gentleman—a man of such perfect honour, he would say nothing to a lady he does not mean.

*Pinch.* Praising another man to his mistress!    [*Aside.*

*Har.* Sir, you are so beyond expectation obliging, that——

*Spark.* Nay, egad, I am sure you do admire her extremely; I see't in your eyes.—He does admire you, madam.—By the world, don't you?

*Har.* Yes, above the world, or the most glorious part of it, her whole sex: and till now I never thought I should have envied you, or any man about to marry, but you have the best excuse for marriage I ever knew.

*Alith.* Nay, now, sir, I'm satisfied you are of the society of the wits and raillieurs, since you cannot spare your friend, even when he is but too civil to you; but the surest sign is, since you are an enemy to marriage,—for that I hear you hate as much as business or bad wine.

*Har.* Truly, madam, I never was an enemy to marriage till now, because marriage was never an enemy to me before.

*Alith.* But why, sir, is marriage an enemy to you now? because it robs you of your friend here? for you look upon a friend married, as one gone into a monastery, that is, dead to the world.

*Har.* 'Tis indeed, because you marry him; I see, madam, you can guess my meaning. I do confess heartily and openly, I wish it were in my power to break the match; by Heavens I would.

*Spark.* Poor Frank!

*Alith.* Would you be so unkind to me?

*Har.* No, no, 'tis not because I would be unkind to you.

*Spark.* Poor Frank! no, gad, 'tis only his kindness to me.

*Pinch.* Great kindness to you indeed! Insensible fop, let a man make love to his wife to his face!    [*Aside.*

*Spark.* Come, dear Frank, for all my wife there, that shall be, thou shalt enjoy me sometimes, dear rogue. By my honour, we men of wit condole for our deceased brother in marriage, as much as for one dead in earnest: I think that was prettily said of me, ha, Harcourt?—But come, Frank, be not melancholy for me.

*Har.* No; I assure you, I am not melancholy for you.

*Spark.* Prithee, Frank, dost think my wife that shall be there, a fine person?

*Har.* I could gaze upon her till I became as blind as you are.

*Spark.* How, as I am? how?

*Har.* Because you are a lover, and true lovers are blind, stock blind.

*Spark.* True, true; but by the world she has wit too, as well as beauty: go, go with her into a corner, and try if she has wit; talk to her anything, she's bashful before me.

*Har.* Indeed if a woman wants wit in a corner, she has it nowhere.

*Alith.* Sir, you dispose of me a little before your time——
                                          [*Aside to* SPARKISH.

*Spark.* Nay, nay, madam, let me have an earnest of your obedience, or—go, go, madam——
                                  [HARCOURT *courts* ALITHEA *aside.*

*Pinch.* How, sir! if you are not concerned for the honour of a wife, I am for that of a sister; he shall not debauch her. Be a pander to your own wife! bring men to her! let 'em make love before your face! thrust 'em into a corner together, then leave 'em in private! is this your town wit and conduct?

*Spark.* Ha! ha! ha! a silly wise rogue would make one laugh more than a stark fool, ha! ha! I shall burst. Nay, you shall not disturb 'em; I'll vex thee, by the world.

     [*Struggles with* PINCHWIFE *to keep him from* HARCOURT *and*
       ALITHEA.

*Alith.* The writings are drawn, sir, settlements made; 'tis too late, sir, and past all revocation.

*Har.* Then so is my death.

*Alith.* I would not be unjust to him.

*Har.* Then why to me so?

*Alith.* I have no obligation to you.

*Har.* My love.

*Alith.* I had his before.

*Har.* You never had it; he wants, you see, jealousy, the only infallible sign of it.

*Alith.* Love proceeds from esteem; he cannot distrust my virtue: besides, he loves me, or he would not marry me.

*Har.* Marrying you is no more sign of his love than bribing your woman, that he may marry you, is a sign of his generosity. Marriage is rather a sign of interest than love; and he that marries a fortune covets a mistress, not loves her. But if you take marriage for a sign of love, take it from me immediately.

*Alith.* No, now you have put a scruple in my head; but in short, sir, to end our dispute, I must marry him, my reputation would suffer in the world else.

*Har.* No; if you do marry him, with your pardon, madam, your reputation suffers in the world, and you would be thought in necessity for a cloak.

*Alith.* Nay, now you are rude, sir.—Mr. Sparkish, pray come hither, your friend here is very troublesome, and very loving.

*Har.* Hold! hold!——                          [*Aside to* ALITHEA.

*Pinch.* D'ye hear that?

*Spark.* Why, d'ye think I'll seem to be jealous, like a country bumpkin?

*Pinch.* No, rather be a cuckold, like a credulous cit.

*Har.* Madam, you would not have been so little generous as to have told him.

*Alith.* Yes, since you could be so little generous as to wrong him.

*Har.* Wrong him! no man can do't, he's beneath an injury: a bubble, a coward, a senseless idiot, a wretch so contemptible to all the world but you, that——

*Alith.* Hold, do not rail at him, for since he is like to be my husband, I am resolved to like him: nay, I think I am obliged to tell him you are not his friend.—Master Sparkish, Master Sparkish!

*Spark.* What, what?—[*To* HARCOURT.] Now, dear rogue, has not she wit?

*Har.* Not so much as I thought, and hoped she had.

[*Speaks surlily.*

*Alith.* Mr. Sparkish, do you bring people to rail at you?

*Har.* Madam——

*Spark.* How! no; but if he does rail at me, 'tis but in jest, I warrant: what we wits do for one another, and never take any notice of it.

*Alith.* He spoke so scurrilously of you, I had no patience to hear him; besides, he has been making love to me.

*Har.* True, damned tell-tale woman! [*Aside.*

*Spark.* Pshaw! to show his parts—we wits rail and make love often, but to show our parts: as we have no affections, so we have no malice, we——

*Alith.* He said you were a wretch below an injury——

*Spark.* Pshaw!

*Har.* Damned, senseless, impudent, virtuous jade! Well, since she won't let me have her, she'll do as good, she'll make me hate her. [*Aside.*

*Alith.* A common bubble——

*Spark.* Pshaw!

*Alith.* A coward——

*Spark.* Pshaw, pshaw!

*Alith.* A senseless, drivelling idiot——

*Spark.* How! did he disparage my parts? Nay, then, my honour's concerned, I can't put up that, sir, by the world—brother, help me to kill him—[*Aside*] I may draw now, since we have the odds of him:—'tis a good occasion, too, before my mistress—— [*Offers to draw.*

*Alith.* Hold, hold!

*Spark.* What, what?

*Alith.* [*aside.*] I must not let 'em kill the gentleman neither, for his kindness to me: I am so far from hating him, that I wish my gallant had his person and understanding. Nay, if my honour——

*Spark.* I'll be thy death.

*Alith.* Hold, hold! Indeed, to tell the truth, the gentleman said after all, that what he spoke was but out of friendship to you.

*Spark.* How! Say I am, I am a fool, that is, no wit, out of friendship to me?

*Alith.* Yes, to try whether I was concerned enough for you; and made love to me only to be satisfied of my virtue, for your sake.

*Har.* Kind, however. [*Aside.*

*Spark.* Nay, if it were so, my dear rogue, I ask thee pardon; but why would not you tell me so, faith?

*Har.* Because I did not think on't, faith.

*Spark.* Come, Horner does not come; Harcourt, let's be gone to the new play.—Come, madam.

*Alith.* I will not go, if you intend to leave me alone in the box, and run into the pit, as you use to do.

*Spark.* Pshaw! I'll leave Harcourt with you in the box to entertain you, and that's as good; if I sat in the box, I should be thought no judge but of trimmings.—Come away, Harcourt, lead her down. [*Exeunt* SPARKISH, HARCOURT, *and* ALITHEA.

*Pinch.* Well, go thy ways, for the flower of the true town fops, such as spend their estates before they come to 'em, and are cuckolds before they're married. But let me go look to my own freehold.—How!

*Enter Lady* FIDGET, *Mrs.* DAINTY FIDGET, *and Mrs.*
SQUEAMISH.

*Lady Fid.* Your servant, sir: where is your lady? We are come to wait upon her to the new play.

*Pinch.* New play!

*Lady Fid.* And my husband will wait upon you presently.

*Pinch.* [*aside*]. Damn your civility.—[*Aloud.*] Madam, by no means; I will not see Sir Jasper here, till I have waited upon him at home; nor shall my wife see you till she has waited upon your ladyship at your lodgings.

*Lady Fid.* Now we are here, sir?

*Pinch.* No, Madam.

*Mrs. Dain.* Pray, let us see her.

*Mrs. Squeam.* We will not stir till we see her.

*Pinch.* [*aside*]. A pox on you all!—[*Goes to the door, and returns.*] She has locked the door, and is gone abroad.

*Lady Fid.* No, you have locked the door, and she's within.

*Mrs. Dain.* They told us below she was here.

*Pinch.* [*aside*]. Will nothing do?—[*Aloud.*] Well, it must out then. To tell you the truth, ladies, which I was afraid to let you know before, lest it might endanger your lives, my wife has just now the small-pox come out upon her; do not be frightened; but pray be gone, ladies; you shall not stay here in danger of your lives; pray get you gone, ladies.

*Lady Fid.* No, no, we have all had 'em.

*Mrs. Squeam.* Alack, alack!

*Mrs. Dain.* Come, come, we must see how it goes with her; I understand the disease.

*Lady Fid.* Come!

*Pinch.* [*aside*]. Well, there is no being too hard for women at their own weapon, lying, therefore I'll quit the field.     [*Exit.*

*Mrs. Squeam.* Here's an example of jealousy!

*Lady Fid.* Indeed, as the world goes, I wonder there are no more jealous, since wives are so neglected.

*Mrs. Dain.* Pshaw! as the world goes, to what end should they be jealous?

*Lady Fid.* Foh! 'tis a nasty world.

*Mrs. Squeam.* That men of parts, great acquaintance, and quality, should take up with and spend themselves and fortunes in keeping little playhouse creatures, foh!

*Lady Fid.* Nay, that women of understanding, great acquaintance, and good quality, should fall a-keeping too of little creatures, foh!

*Mrs. Squeam.* Why, 'tis the men of quality's f ult; they never visit women of honour and reputation as they used to do; and have not so much as common civility for ladies of our rank, but use us with the same indifferency and ill-breeding as if we were all married to 'em.

*Lady Fid.* She says true; 'tis an arrant shame women of quality should be so slighted; methinks birth—birth should go for something; I have known men admired, courted, and followed for their titles only.

*Mrs. Squeam.* Ay, one would think men of honour should not love, no more than marry, out of their own rank.

*Mrs. Dain.* Fy, fy, upon 'em! they are come to think cross breeding for themselves best, as well as for their dogs and horses.

*Lady Fid.* They are dogs and horses for't.

*Mrs. Squeam.* One would think, if not for love, for vanity a little.

*Mrs. Dain.* Nay, they do satisfy their vanity upon us sometimes; and are kind to us in their report, tell all the world they lie with us.

*Lady Fid.* Damned rascals, that we should be only wronged by 'em! To report a man has had a person, when he has not had a person, is the greatest wrong in the whole world that can be done to a person.

*Mrs. Squeam.* Well, 'tis an arrant shame noble persons should be so wronged and neglected.

*Lady Fid.* But still 'tis an arranter shame for a noble person to neglect her own honour, and defame her own noble person with little inconsiderable fellows, foh!

*Mrs. Dain.* I suppose the crime against our honour is the same with a man of quality as with another.

*Lady Fid.* How! no, sure, the man of quality is likest one's husband, and therefore the fault should be the less.

*Mrs. Dain.* But then the pleasure should be the less.

*Lady Fid.* Fy, fy, fy, for shame, sister! whither shall we ramble? Be continent in your discourse, or I shall hate you.

*Mrs. Dain.* Besides, an intrigue is so much the more notorious for the man's quality.

*Mrs. Squeam.* 'Tis true nobody takes notice of a private man, and therefore with him 'tis more secret; and the crime's the less when 'tis not known.

*Lady Fid.* You say true; i'faith, I think you are in the right on't: 'tis not an injury to a husband, till it be an injury to our honours; so that a woman of honour loses no honour with a private person; and to say truth——

*Mrs. Dain.* So, the little fellow is grown a private person—— with her——                             [*Apart to* Mrs. SQUEAMISH.

*Lady Fid.* But still my dear, dear honour——

*Enter* Sir JASPER FIDGET, HORNER, *and* DORILANT.

*Sir Jasp.* Ay, my dear, dear of honour, thou hast still so much honour in thy mouth——

*Horn.* That she has none elsewhere.             [*Aside.*

*Lady Fid.* Oh, what d'ye mean to bring in these upon us?

*Mrs. Dain.* Foh! these are as bad as wits.

*Mrs. Squeam.* Foh!

*Lady Fid.* Let us leave the room.

*Sir Jasp.* Stay, stay; faith, to tell you the naked truth——

*Lady Fid.* Fy, Sir Jasper! do not use that word naked.

*Sir Jasp.* Well, well, in short I have business at Whitehall, and cannot go to the play with you, therefore would have you go——

*Lady Fid.* With those two to a play?

*Sir Jasp.* No, not with t'other, but with Mr. Horner; there can be no more scandal to go with him than with Mr. Tattle, or Master Limberham.

*Lady Fid.* With that nasty fellow! no—no.

*Sir Jasp.* Nay, prithee, dear, hear me.

                            [*Whispers to* Lady FIDGET.

*Horn.* Ladies——

       [HORNER *and* DORILANT *draw near* Mrs. SQUEAMISH
             *and* Mrs. DAINTY FIDGET.

*Mrs. Dain.* Stand off.

*Mrs. Squeam.* Do not approach us.

*Mrs. Dain.* You herd with the wits, you are obscenity all over.

*Mrs. Squeam.* And I would as soon look upon a picture of Adam and Eve, without fig-leaves, as any of you, if I could help it; therefore keep off, and do not make us sick.

*Dor.* What a devil are these?

*Horn.* Why, these are pretenders to honour, as critics to wit, only by censuring others; and as every raw, peevish, out-of-humoured, affected, dull, tea-drinking, arithmetical fop, sets up for a wit by railing at men of sense, so these for honour, by railing at the court, and ladies of as great honour as quality.

*Sir Jasp.* Come, Mr. Horner, I must desire you to go with these ladies to the play, sir.

*Horn.* I, sir?

*Sir Jasp.* Ay, ay, come, sir.

*Horn.* I must beg your pardon, sir, and theirs; I will not be seen in women's company in public again for the world.

*Sir Jasp.* Ha, ha, strange aversion!

*Mrs. Squeam.* No, he's for women's company in private.

*Sir Jasp.* He—poor man—he—ha! ha! ha!

*Mrs. Dain.* 'Tis a greater shame amongst lewd fellows to be seen in virtuous women's company, than for the women to be seen with them.

*Horn.* Indeed, madam, the time was I only hated virtuous women, but now I hate the other too; I beg your pardon, ladies.

*Lady Fid.* You are very obliging, sir, because we would not be troubled with you.

*Sir Jasp.* In sober sadness, he shall go.

*Dor.* Nay, if he wo' not, I am ready to wait upon the ladies, and I think I am the fitter man.

*Sir Jasp.* You, sir! no, I thank you for that. Master Horner is a privileged man amongst the virtuous ladies, 'twill be a great while before you are so; he! he! he! he's my wife's gallant; he! he! he! No, pray withdraw, sir, for as I take it, the virtuous ladies have no business with you.

*Dor.* And I am sure he can have none with them. 'Tis strange a man can't come amongst virtuous women now, but upon the same terms as men are admitted into the Great Turk's seraglio. But heavens keep me from being an ombre player with 'em!—But where is Pinchwife?    [*Exit.*

*Sir Jasp.* Come, come, man; what, avoid the sweet society of womankind? that sweet, soft, gentle, tame, noble creature, woman, made for man's companion——

*Horn.* So is that soft, gentle, tame, and more noble creature a spaniel, and has all their tricks; can fawn, lie down, suffer beating, and fawn the more; barks at your friends when they come to see you, makes your bed hard, gives you fleas, and the mange sometimes. And all the difference is, the spaniel's the more faithful animal, and fawns but upon one master.

*Sir Jasp.* He! he! he!

*Mrs. Squeam.* O the rude beast!

*Mrs. Dain.* Insolent brute!

*Lady Fid.* Brute! stinking, mortified, rotten French wether, to dare——

*Sir Jasp.* Hold, an't please your ladyship.—For shame, Master Horner! your mother was a woman—[*Aside*]. Now shall I never reconcile 'em.—[*Aside to* Lady FIDGET.] Hark you, madam, take my advice in your anger. You know you often want one to make up your drolling pack of ombre players, and you may cheat him easily; for he's an ill gamester, and consequently loves play. Besides, you know you have but two old civil gentlemen (with stinking breaths too) to wait upon you abroad; take in the third into your service. The other are but crazy; and a lady should have a supernumerary gentleman-usher as a supernumerary coach-horse, lest sometimes you should be forced to stay at home.

*Lady Fid.* But are you sure he loves play, and has money?

*Sir Jasp.* He loves play as much as you, and has money as much as I.

*Lady Fid.* Then I am contented to make him pay for his scurrility. Money makes up in a measure all other wants in men.—Those whom we cannot make hold for gallants, we make fine. [*Aside.*

*Sir Jasp.* [*aside*]. So, so; now to mollify, to wheedle him.—[*Aside to* HORNER.] Master Horner, will you never keep civil company? methinks 'tis time now, since you are only fit for them. Come, come, man, you must e'en fall to visiting our wives, eating at our tables, drinking tea with our virtuous relations after dinner, dealing cards to 'em, reading plays and gazettes to ,em, picking fleas out of their shocks for 'em, collecting receipts, new songs, women, pages, and footmen for 'em.

*Horn.* I hope they'll afford me better employment, sir.

*Sir Jasp.* He! he! he! 'tis fit you know your work before you come into your place. And since you are unprovided of a lady to flatter, and a good house to eat at, pray frequent mine, and call my wife mistress, and she shall call you gallant, according to the custom.

*Horn.* Who, I?

*Sir Jasp.* Faith, thou sha't for my sake; come, for my sake only.

*Horn.* For your sake——

*Sir Jasp.* Come, come, here's a gamester for you; let him be a little familiar sometimes; nay, what if a little rude? Gamesters may be rude with ladies, you know.

*Lady Fid.* Yes; losing gamesters have a privilege with women.

*Horn.* I always thought the contrary, that the winning gamester had most privilege with women; for when you have lost your money to a man, you'll lose anything you have, all you have, they say, and he may use you as he pleases.

*Sir Jasp.* He! he! he! well, win or lose, you shall have your liberty with her.

*Lady Fid.* As he behaves himself; and for your sake I'll give him admittance and freedom.

*Horn.* All sorts of freedom, madam?

*Sir Jasp.* Ay, ay, ay, all sorts of freedom thou canst take. And so go to her, begin thy new employment; wheedle her, jest with her, and be better acquainted one with another.

*Horn.* [*aside*]. I think I know her already; therefore may venture with her my secret for hers.

[HORNER *and* Lady FIDGET *whisper.*

*Sir Jasp.* Sister cuz, I have provided an innocent playfellow for you there.

*Mrs. Dain.* Who, he?

*Mrs. Squeam.* There's a playfellow, indeed!

*Sir Jasp.* Yes sure.—What, he is good enough to play at cards, blindman's-buff, or the fool with, sometimes!

*Mrs. Squeam.* Foh! we'll have no such playfellows.

*Mrs. Dain.* No, sir; you shan't choose playfellows for us, we thank you.

*Sir Jasp.* Nay, pray hear me.           [*Whispering to them.*

*Lady Fid.* But, poor gentleman, could you be so generous, so truly a man of honour, as for the sakes of us women of honour, to cause yourself to be reported no man? No man! and to suffer yourself the greatest shame that could fall upon a man, that none might fall upon us women by your conversation? but, indeed, sir, as perfectly, perfectly the same man as before your going into France, sir? as perfectly, perfectly, sir?

*Horn.* As perfectly, perfectly, madam. Nay, I scorn you should take my word; I desire to be tried only, madam.

*Lady Fid.* Well, that's spoken again like a man of honour: all men of honour desire to come to the test. But, indeed, generally you men report such things of yourselves, one does not know how or whom to believe; and it is come to that pass, we dare not take your words no more than your tailor's, without some staid servant of yours be bound with you. But I have so strong a faith in your honour, dear, dear, noble sir, that I'd forfeit mine for yours, at any time, dear sir.

*Horn.* No, madam, you should not need to forfeit it for me; I have given you security already to save you harmless, my late reputation being so well known in the world, madam.

*Lady Fid.* But if upon any future falling-out, or upon a suspicion of my taking the trust out of your hands, to employ some other, you yourself should betray your trust, dear sir? I mean, if you'll give me leave to speak obscenely, you might tell, dear sir.

*Horn.* If I did, nobody would believe me. The reputation of impotency is as hardly recovered again in the world as that of cowardice, dear madam.

*Lady Fid.* Nay, then, as one may say, you may do your worst, dear, dear sir.

*Sir Jasp.* Come, is your ladyship reconciled to him yet? have you agreed on matters? for I must be gone to Whitehall.

*Lady Fid.* Why, indeed, Sir Jasper, Master Horner is a thousand, thousand times a better man than I thought him. Cousin Squeamish, sister Dainty, I can name him now. Truly, not long ago, you know, I thought his very name obscenity; and I would as soon have lain with him as have named him.

*Sir Jasp.* Very likely, poor madam.

*Mrs. Dain.* I believe it.

*Mrs. Squeam.* No doubt on't.

*Sir Jasp.* Well, well—that your ladyship is as virtuous as any she, I know, and him all the town knows—he! he! he! therefore now you like him, get you gone to your business together, go, go to your business, I say, pleasure, whilst I go to my pleasure, business.

*Lady Fid.* Come, then, dear gallant.

*Horn.* Come away, my dearest mistress.

*Sir Jasp.* So, so; why, 'tis as I'd have it. [*Exit.*

*Horn.* And as I'd have it.

*Lady Fid.* Who for his business from his wife will run,
　　　　Takes the best care to have her business done.

[*Exeunt.*

# ACT III

### SCENE I.—*A Room in* PINCHWIFE'S *House*

#### *Enter* ALITHEA *and* Mrs. PINCHWIFE.

*Alith.* Sister, what ails you? you are grown melancholy.

*Mrs. Pinch.* Would it not make any one melancholy to see you go every day fluttering about abroad, whilst I must stay at home like a poor lonely sullen bird in a cage?

*Alith.* Ay, sister; but you came young, and just from the nest to your cage: so that I thought you liked it, and could be as cheerful in't as others that took their flight themselves early, and are hopping abroad in the open air.

*Mrs. Pinch.* Nay, I confess I was quiet enough till my husband told me what pure lives the London ladies live abroad, with their dancing, meetings, and junketings, and dressed every day in their best gowns; and I warrant you, play at nine-pins every day of the week, so they do.

#### *Enter* PINCHWIFE.

*Pinch.* Come, what's here to do? you are putting the town-pleasures in her head, and setting her a-longing.

*Alith.* Yes, after nine-pins. You suffer none to give her those longings you mean but yourself.

*Pinch.* I tell her of the vanities of the town like a confessor.

*Alith.* A confessor! just such a confessor as he that, by forbidding a silly ostler to grease the horse's teeth, taught him to do't.

*Pinch.* Come, Mrs. Flippant, good precepts are lost when bad examples are still before us: the liberty you take abroad makes her hanker after it, and out of humour at home. Poor wretch! she desired not to come to London; I would bring her.

*Alith.* Very well.

*Pinch.* She has been this week in town, and never desired till this afternoon to go abroad.

*Alith.* Was she not at a play yesterday?

*Pinch.* Yes; but she ne'er asked me; I was myself the cause of her going.

*Alith.* Then if she ask you again, you are the cause of her asking, and not my example.

*Pinch.* Well, to-morrow night I shall be rid of you; and the next day, before 'tis light, she and I'll be rid of the town, and my dreadful apprehensions.—Come, be not melancholy; for thou sha't go into the country after to-morrow, dearest.

*Alith.* Great comfort!

*Mrs. Pinch.* Pish! what d'ye tell me of the country for?

*Pinch.* How's this! what, pish at the country?

*Mrs. Pinch.* Let me alone; I am not well.

*Pinch.* O, if that be all—what ails my dearest?

*Mrs. Pinch.* Truly, I don't know: but I have not been well since you told me there was a gallant at the play in love with me.

*Pinch.* Ha!——

*Alith.* That's by my example too!

*Pinch.* Nay, if you are not well, but are so concerned, because a lewd fellow chanced to lie, and say he liked you, you'll make me sick too.

*Mrs. Pinch.* Of what sickness?

*Pinch.* O, of that which is worse than the plague, jealousy.

*Mrs. Pinch.* Pish, you jeer! I'm sure there's no such disease in our receipt-book at home.

*Pinch.* No, thou never met'st with it, poor innocent.—Well, if thou cuckold me, 'twill be my own fault—for cuckolds and bastards are generally makers of their own fortune.     [*Aside.*

*Mrs. Pinch.* Well, but pray, bud, let's go to a play to-night.

*Pinch.* 'Tis just done, she comes from it. But why are you so eager to see a play?

*Mrs. Pinch.* Faith, dear, not that I care one pin for their talk there; but I like to look upon the player-men, and would see, if I could, the gallant you say loves me: that's all, dear bud.

*Pinch.* Is that all, dear bud?

*Alith.* This proceeds from my example!

*Mrs. Pinch.* But if the play be done, let's go abroad, however, dear bud.

*Pinch.* Come, have a little patience and thou shalt go into the country on Friday.

*Mrs. Pinch.* Therefore I would see first some sights to tell my neighbours of. Nay, I will go abroad, that's once.

*Alith.* I'm the cause of this desire too!

*Pinch.* But now I think on't, who was the cause of Horner's coming to my lodgings to-day? That was you.

*Alith.* No, you, because you would not let him see your handsome wife out of your lodging.

*Mrs. Pinch.* Why, O Lord! did the gentleman come hither to see me indeed?

*Pinch.* No, no.—You are not the cause of that damned question too, Mistress Alithea?—[*Aside.*] Well, she's in the right of it. He is in love with my wife—and comes after her—'tis so—but I'll nip his love in the bud; lest he should follow us into the country, and break his chariot-wheel near our house, on purpose for an excuse to come to't. But I think I know the town.

*Mrs. Pinch.* Come, pray, bud, let's go abroad before 'tis late; for I will go, that's flat and plain.

*Pinch.* [*aside*]. So! the obstinacy already of the town-wife; and I must, whilst she's here, humour her like one.—[*Aloud.*] Sister, how shall we do, that she may not be seen or known?

*Alith.* Let her put on her mask.

*Pinch.* Pshaw! a mask makes people but the more inquisitive, and is as ridiculous a disguise as a stage-beard: her shape, stature, habit will be known. And if we should meet with Horner, he would be sure to take acquaintance with us, must wish her joy, kiss her, talk to her, leer upon her, and the devil and all. No, I'll not use her to a mask, 'tis dangerous; for masks have made more cuckolds than the best faces that ever were known.

*Alith.* How will you do then?

*Mrs. Pinch.* Nay, shall we go? The Exchange will be shut, and I have a mind to see that.

*Pinch.* So—I have it—I'll dress her up in the suit we are to carry down to her brother, little Sir James; nay, I understand the town-tricks. Come, let's go dress her. A mask! no—a woman masked, like a covered dish, gives a man curiosity and appetite; when, it may be, uncovered, 'twould turn his stomach: no, no.

*Alith.* Indeed your comparison is something a greasy one: but I had a gentle gallant used to say, A beauty masked, like the sun in eclipse, gathers together more gazers than if it shined out.

[*Exeunt.*

## SCENE II.—*The New Exchange*

*Enter* HORNER, HARCOURT, *and* DORILANT.

*Dor.* Engaged to women, and not sup with us!

*Horn.* Ay, a pox on 'em all!

*Har.* You were much a more reasonable man in the morning, and had as noble resolutions against 'em as a widower of a week's liberty.

*Dor.* Did I ever think to see you keep company with women in vain?

*Horn.* In vain: no—'tis since I can't love 'em, to be revenged on 'em.

*Har.* Now your sting is gone, you looked in the box amongst all those women like a drone in the hive; all upon you, shoved and ill-used by 'em all, and thrust from one side to t'other.

*Dor.* Yet he must be buzzing amongst 'em still, like other old beetle-headed liquorish drones. Avoid 'em, and hate 'em, as they hate you.

*Horn.* Because I do hate 'em, and would hate 'em yet more, I'll frequent 'em. You may see by marriage, nothing makes a man hate a woman more than her constant conversation. In short, I converse with 'em, as you do with rich fools, to laugh at 'em and use 'em ill.

*Dor.* But I would no more sup with women, unless I could lie with 'em, than sup with a rich coxcomb, unless I could cheat him.

*Horn.* Yes, I have known thee sup with a fool for his drinking; if he could set out your hand that way only, you were satisfied, and if he were a wine-swallowing mouth, 'twas enough.

*Har.* Yes, a man drinks often with a fool, as he tosses with a marker, only to keep his hand in ure. But do the ladies drink?

*Horn.* Yes, sir; and I shall have the pleasure at least of laying 'em flat with a bottle, and bring as much scandal that way upon 'em as formerly t'other.

*Har.* Perhaps you may prove as weak a brother amongst 'em that way as t'other.

*Dor.* Foh! drinking with women is as unnatural as scolding with 'em. But 'tis a pleasure of decayed fornicators, and the basest way of quenching love.

*Har.* Nay, 'tis drowning love, instead of quenching it. But leave us for civil women too!

*Dor.* Ay, when he can't be the better for 'em. We hardly pardon a man that leaves his friend for a wench, and that's a pretty lawful call.

*Horn.* Faith, I would not leave you for 'em, if they would not drink.

*Dor.* Who would disappoint his company at Lewis's for a gossiping?

*Har.* Foh! Wine and women, good apart, together as nauseous as sack and sugar. But hark you, sir, before you go, a little of your advice; an old maimed general, when unfit for action, is fittest for counsel. I have other designs upon women than eating and drinking with them; I am in love with Sparkish's mistress, whom he is to marry to-morrow: now how shall I get her?

*Enter* SPARKISH, *looking about.*

*Horn.* Why, here comes one will help you to her.

*Har.* He! he, I tell you, is my rival, and will hinder my love.

*Horn.* No; a foolish rival and a jealous husband assist their rival's designs; for they are sure to make their women hate them, which is the first step to their love for another man.

*Har.* But I cannot come near his mistress but in his company.

*Horn.* Still the better for you; for fools are most easily cheated when they themselves are accessories: and he is to be bubbled of his mistress as of his money, the common mistress, by keeping him company.

*Spark.* Who is that that is to be bubbled? Faith, let me snack; I han't met with a bubble since Christmas. 'Gad, I think bubbles are like their brother woodcocks, go out with the cold weather.

*Har.* A pox! he did not hear all, I hope. [*Apart to* HORNER.

*Spark.* Come, you bubbling rogues you, where do we sup?— Oh, Harcourt, my mistress tells me you have been making fierce love to her all the play long: ha! ha! —But I——

*Har.* I make love to her!

*Spark.* Nay, I forgive thee, for I think I know thee, and I know her; but I am sure I know myself.

*Har.* Did she tell you so? I see all women are like these of the Exchange; who, to enhance the price of their commodities, report to their fond customers offers which were never made 'em.

*Horn.* Ay, women are as apt to tell before the intrigue, as men after it, and so show themselves the vainer sex. But hast thou a mistress, Sparkish? 'Tis as hard for me to believe it, as that thou ever hadst a bubble, as you bragged just now.

*Spark.* O, your servant, sir: are you at your raillery, sir? But we were some of us beforehand with you to-day at the play. The wits were something bold with you, sir; did you not hear us laugh?

*Horn.* Yes; but I thought you had gone to plays, to laugh at the poet's wit, not at your own.

*Spark.* Your servant, sir: no, I thank you. 'Gad, I go to a play as to a country treat; I carry my own wine to one, and my own wit to t'other, or else I'm sure I should not be merry at either. And the reason why we are so often louder than the players, is, because we think we speak more wit, and so become the poet's rivals in his audience: for to tell you the truth, we hate the silly rogues; nay, so much, that we find fault even with their bawdy upon the stage, whilst we talk nothing else in the pit as loud.

*Horn.* But why shouldst thou hate the silly poets? Thou hast too much wit to be one; and they, like whores, are only hated by each other: and thou dost scorn writing, I'm sure.

*Spark.* Yes; I'd have you to know I scorn writing: but women, women, that make men do all foolish things, make 'em write songs too. Everybody does it. 'Tis even as common with lovers, as playing with fans; and you can no more help rhyming to your Phillis, than drinking to your Phillis.

*Har.* Nay, poetry in love is no more to be avoided than jealousy.

*Dor.* But the poets damned your songs, did they?

*Spark.* Damn the poets! they turned 'em into burlesque, as they call it. That burlesque is a hocus-pocus trick they have got, which, by the virtue of *Hictius doctius topsy turvy*, they make a wise and witty man in the world, a fool upon the stage you know not how: and 'tis therefore I hate 'em too, for I know not but it may be my own case; for they'll put a man into a play for looking asquint. Their predecessors were contented to make serving-men only their stage-fools: but these rogues must have gentlemen, with a pox to 'em, nay, knights; and, indeed, you shall hardly see a fool upon the stage but he's a knight. And to tell you the truth, they have kept me these six years from being a knight in earnest, for fear of being knighted in a play, and dubbed a fool.

*Dor.* Blame 'em not, they must follow their copy, the age.

*Har.* But why shouldst thou be afraid of being in a play, who expose yourself every day in the play-houses, and as public places?

*Hor.* 'Tis but being on the stage, instead of standing on a bench in the pit.

*Dor.* Don't you give money to painters to draw you like? and are you afraid of your pictures at length in a playhouse, where all your mistresses may see you?

*Spark.* A pox! painters don't draw the small-pox or pimples in one's face. Come, damn all your silly authors whatever, all books and booksellers, by the world; and all readers, courteous or uncourteous!

*Har.* But who comes here, Sparkish?

*Enter* PINCHWIFE *and* Mrs. PINCHWIFE *in man's clothes,*
ALITHEA *and* LUCY.

*Spark.* Oh, hide me! There's my mistress too.

      [SPARKISH *hides himself behind* HARCOURT.

*Har.* She sees you.

*Spark.* But I will not see her. 'Tis time to go to Whitehall, and I must not fail the drawing-room.

*Har.* Pray, first carry me, and reconcile me to her.

*Spark.* Another time. Faith, the king will have supped.

*Har.* Not with the worse stomach for thy absence. Thou art one of those fools that think their attendance at the king's meals as necessary as his physicians, when you are more trouble-some to him than his doctors or his dogs.

*Spark.* Pshaw! I know my interest, sir. Prithee hide me.

*Horn.* Your servant, Pinchwife.—What, he knows us not!

*Pinch.* Come along.       [*To his* Wife *aside.*

*Mrs. Pinch.* Pray, have you any ballads? give me sixpenny worth.

*Bookseller.* We have no ballads.

*Mrs. Pinch.* Then give me " Covent Garden Drollery," and a play or two—Oh, here's " Tarugo's Wiles," and " The Slighted Maiden ";[1] I'll have them.

*Pinch.* No; plays are not for your reading. Come along; will you discover yourself ? [*Apart to her.*

*Horn.* Who is that pretty youth with him, Sparkish ?

*Spark.* I believe his wife's brother, because he's something like her: but I never saw her but once.

*Horn.* Extremely handsome; I have seen a face like it too. Let us follow 'em.

[*Exeunt* Pinchwife, Mrs. Pinchwife, Alithea, *and* Lucy; Horner *and* Dorilant *following them.*

*Har.* Come, Sparkish, your mistress saw you, and will be angry you go not to her. Besides, I would fain be reconciled to her, which none but you can do, dear friend.

*Spark.* Well, that's a better reason, dear friend. I would not go near her now for her's or my own sake; but I can deny you nothing: for though I have known thee a great while, never go, if I do not love thee as well as a new acquaintance.

*Har.* I am obliged to you indeed, dear friend. I would be well with her, only to be well with thee still; for these ties to wives usually dissolve all ties to friends. I would be contented she should enjoy you a-nights, but I would have you to myself a-days as I have had, dear friend.

*Spark.* And thou shalt enjoy me a-days, dear, dear friend, never stir: and I'll be divorced from her, sooner than from thee. Come along.

*Har.* [*aside*]. So, we are hard put to't, when we make our rival our procurer; but neither she nor her brother would let me come near her now. When all's done, a rival is the best cloak to steal to a mistress under, without suspicion; and when we have once got to her as we desire, we throw him off like other cloaks. [*Exit* Sparkish, Harcourt *following him.*

*Re-enter* Pinchwife *and* Mrs. Pinchwife.

*Pinch.* [*to* Alithea]. Sister, if you will not go, we must leave you.—[*Aside.*] The fool her gallant and she will muster up all the young saunterers of this place, and they will leave their dear sempstresses to follow us. What a swarm of cuckolds and cuckold-makers are here!—Come, let's be gone, Mistress Margery.

---

[1] " Covent Garden Drolery, Or a Colection of all the Choice Songs, Poems, Prologues, and Epilogues (Sung and Spoken at Courts and Theaters) never in Print before. Written by the refined'st Witts of the Age. And Collected by R[ichard] B[rome] Servant to His Majestie. London, Printed for James Magnes neer the Piazza in Russel-Street, 1672."—*Tarugo's Wiles, or the Coffee House ;* a comedy by Sir Thomas St. Serle, produced in 1668.—*The Slighted Maid,* a comedy by Sir Robert Stapleton, produced in 1663.

*Mrs. Pinch.* Don't you believe that; I han't half my bellyfull of sights yet.

*Pinch.* Then walk this way.

*Mrs. Pinch.* Lord, what a power of brave signs are here! stay —the Bull's-Head, the Ram's-Head, and the Stag's-Head, dear——

*Pinch.* Nay, if every husband's proper sign here were visible, they would be all alike.

*Mrs. Pinch.* What d'ye mean by that, bud?

*Pinch.* 'Tis no matter—no matter, bud.

*Mrs. Pinch.* Pray tell me: nay, I will know.

*Pinch.* They would be all Bulls, Stags, and Rams-heads.

[*Exeunt* PINCHWIFE *and* Mrs. PINCHWIFE.

*Re-enter* SPARKISH, HARCOURT, ALITHEA, *and* LUCY,
*at the other side.*

*Spark.* Come, dear madam, for my sake you shall be reconciled to him.

*Alith.* For your sake I hate him.

*Har.* That's something too cruel, madam, to hate me for his sake.

*Spark.* Ay indeed, madam, too, too cruel to me, to hate my friend for my sake.

*Alith.* I hate him because he is your enemy; and you ought to hate him too, for making love to me, if you love me.

*Spark.* That's a good one! I hate a man for loving you! If he did love you, 'tis but what he can't help; and 'tis your fault, not his, if he admires you. I hate a man for being of my opinion! I'll n'er do't, by the world.

*Alith.* Is it for your honour, or mine, to suffer a man to make love to me, who am to marry you to-morrow?

*Spark.* Is it for your honour, or mine, to have me jealous? That makes love to you, is a sign you are handsome; and that I am not jealous, is a sign you are virtuous. That I think is for your honour.

*Alith.* But 'tis your honour too I am concerned for.

*Har.* But why, dearest madam, will you be more concerned for his honour than he is himself? Let his honour alone, for my sake and his. He! he has no honour——

*Spark.* How's that?

*Har.* But what my dear friend can guard himself.

*Spark.* O ho—that's right again.

*Har.* Your care of his honour argues his neglect of it, which is no honour to my dear friend here. Therefore once more, let his honour go which way it will, dear madam.

*Spark.* Ay, ay; were it for my honour to marry a woman whose virtue I suspected, and could not trust her in a friend's hands?

*Alith.* Are you not afraid to lose me?

*Har.* He afraid to lose you, madam! No, no—you may see how the most estimable and most glorious creature in the world is valued by him. Will you not see it?

*Spark.* Right, honest Frank, I have that noble value for her that I cannot be jealous of her.

*Alith.* You mistake him. He means, you care not for me, nor who has me,

*Spark.* Lord, madam, I see you are jealous! Will you wrest a poor man's meaning from his words?

*Alith.* You astonish me, sir, with your want of jealousy.

*Spark.* And you make me giddy, madam, with your jealousy and fears, and virtue and honour. 'Gad, I see virtue makes a woman as troublesome as a little reading or learning.

*Alith.* Monstrous!

*Lucy.* Well, to see what easy husbands these women of quality can meet with! a poor chambermaid can never have such lady-like luck. Besides, he's thrown away upon her. She'll make no use of her fortune, her blessing, none to a gentleman, for a pure cuckold; for it requires good breeding to be a cuckold. [*Aside.*

*Alith.* I tell you then plainly, he pursues me to marry me.

*Spark.* Pshaw!

*Har.* Come, madam, you see you strive in vain to make him jealous of me. My dear friend is the kindest creature in the world to me.

*Spark.* Poor fellow!

*Har.* But his kindness only is not enough for me, without your favour, your good opinion, dear madam: 'tis that must perfect my happiness. Good gentleman, he believes all I say: would you would do so! Jealous of me! I would not wrong him nor you for the world.

*Spark.* Look you there. Hear him, hear him, and do not walk away so. [ALITHEA *walks carelessly to and fro.*

*Har.* I love you, madam, so——

*Spark.* How's that? Nay, now you begin to go too far indeed.

*Har.* So much, I confess, I say, I love you, that I would not have you miserable, and cast yourself away upon so unworthy and inconsiderable a thing as what you see here.

[*Clapping his hand on his breast, points at* SPARKISH.

*Spark.* No, faith, I believe thou wouldst not: now his meaning is plain; but I knew before thou wouldst not wrong me, nor her.

*Har.* No, no, Heavens forbid the glory of her sex should fall so low, as into the embraces of such a contemptible wretch, the least of mankind—my friend here—I injure him!

[*Embracing* SPARKISH.

*Alith.* Very well.

*Spark.* No, no, dear friend, I knew it.—Madam, you see he will rather wrong himself than me, in giving himself such names.

*Alith.* Do not you understand him yet?

*Spark.* Yes: how modestly he speaks of himself, poor fellow!

*Alith.* Methinks he speaks impudently of yourself, since—
before yourself too; insomuch that I can no longer suffer his
scurrilous abusiveness to you, no more than his love to me.

[*Offers to go.*

*Spark.* Nay, nay, madam, pray stay—his love to you! Lord,
madam, has he not spoke yet plain enough?

*Alith.* Yes, indeed, I should think so.

*Spark.* Well, then, by the world, a man can't speak civilly to a
woman now, but presently she says, he makes love to her. Nay,
madam, you shall stay, with your pardon, since you have not
yet understood him, till he has made an eclaircissement of his
love to you, that is, what kind of love it is. Answer to thy
catechism, friend; do you love my mistress here?

*Har.* Yes, I wish she would not doubt it.

*Spark.* But how do you love her?

*Har.* With all my soul.

*Alith.* I thank him, methinks he speaks plain enough now.

*Spark.* [*to* ALITHEA]. You are out still.—But with what kind
of love, Harcourt?

*Har.* With the best and truest love in the world.

*Spark.* Look you there then, that is with no matrimonial love,
I'm sure.

*Alith.* How's that? do you say matrimonial love is not best?

*Spark.* 'Gad, I went too far ere I was aware. But speak for
thyself, Harcourt, you said you would not wrong me nor her.

*Har.* No, no, madam, e'en take him for Heaven's sake.

*Spark.* Look you there, madam.

*Har.* Who should in all justice be yours, he that loves you
most.                      [*Claps his hand on his breast.*

*Alith.* Look you there, Mr. Sparkish, who's that?

*Spark.* Who should it be?—Go on, Harcourt.

*Har.* Who loves you more than women titles, or fortune fools.

[*Points at* SPARKISH.

*Spark.* Look you there, he means me still, for he points at me.

*Alith.* Ridiculous!

*Har.* Who can only match your faith and constancy in love.

*Spark.* Ay.

*Har.* Who knows, if it be possible, how to value so much beauty
and virtue.

*Spark.* Ay.

*Har.* Whose love can no more be equalled in the world, than
that heavenly form of yours.

*Spark.* No.

*Har.* Who could no more suffer a rival, than your absence,
and yet could no more suspect your virtue, than his own constancy
in his love to you.

*Spark.* No.

*Har.* Who, in fine, loves you better than his eyes, that first
made him love you.

*Spark.* Ay—Nay, madam, faith, you shan't go till——

*Alith.* Have a care, lest you make me stay too long.

*Spark.* But till he has saluted you; that I may be assured you are friends, after his honest advice and declaration. Come, pray, madam, be friends with him.

*Re-enter* PINCHWIFE *and* Mrs. PINCHWIFE.

*Alith.* You must pardon me, sir, that I am not yet so obedient to you.

*Pinch.* What, invite your wife to kiss men? Monstrous! are you not ashamed? I will never forgive you.

*Spark.* Are you not ashamed, that I should have more confidence in the chastity of your family than you have? You must not teach me, I am a man of honour, sir, though I am frank and free; I am frank, sir——

*Pinch.* Very frank, sir, to share your wife with your friends.

*Spark.* He is an humble, menial friend, such as reconciles the differences of the marriage bed; you know man and wife do not always agree; I design him for that use, therefore would have him well with my wife.

*Pinch.* A menial friend!—you will get a great many menial friends, by showing your wife as you do.

*Spark.* What then? It may be I have a pleasure in't, as I have to show fine clothes at a play-house, the first day, and count money before poor rogues.

*Pinch.* He that shows his wife or money will be in danger of having them borrowed sometimes.

*Spark.* I love to be envied, and would not marry a wife that I alone could love; loving alone is as dull as eating alone. Is it not a frank age? and I am a frank person; and to tell you the truth, it may be, I love to have rivals in a wife, they make her seem to a man still but as a kept mistress; and so good night, for I must to Whitehall.—Madam, I hope you are now reconciled to my friend; and so I wish you a good night, madam, and sleep if you can: for to-morrow you know I must visit you early with a canonical gentleman. Good night, dear Harcourt.      [*Exit.*

*Har.* Madam, I hope you will not refuse my visit to-morrow, if it should be earlier with a canonical gentleman than Mr. Sparkish's.

*Pinch.* This gentlewoman is yet under my care, therefore you must yet forbear your freedom with her, sir.

[*Coming between* ALITHEA *and* HARCOURT.

*Har.* Must, sir?

*Pinch.* Yes, sir, she is my sister.

*Har.* 'Tis well she is, sir—for I must be her servant, sir.— Madam——

*Pinch.* Come away, sister, we had been gone, if it had not been for you, and so avoided these lewd rake-hells, who seem to haunt us.

*Re-enter* HORNER *and* DORILANT.

*Horn.* How now, Pinchwife!

*Pinch.* Your servant.

*Horn.* What! I see a little time in the country makes a man turn wild and unsociable, and only fit to converse with his horses, dogs, and his herds.

*Pinch.* I have business, sir, and must mind it; your business is pleasure, therefore you and I must go different ways.

*Horn.* Well, you may go on, but this pretty young gentle-man—— [*Takes hold of* Mrs. PINCHWIFE.

*Har.* The lady——

*Dor.* And the maid——

*Horn.* Shall stay with us; for I suppose their business is the same with ours, pleasure.

*Pinch.* 'Sdeath, he knows her, she carries it so sillily! yet if he does not, I should be more silly to discover it first.    [*Aside.*

*Alith.* Pray, let us go, sir.

*Pinch.* Come, come——

*Horn.* [*to* Mrs. PINCHWIFE]. Had you not rather stay with us? —Prithee, Pinchwife, who is this pretty young gentleman?

*Pinch.* One to whom I'm a guardian.—[*Aside.*] I wish I could keep her out of your hands.

*Horn.* Who is he? I never saw anything so pretty in all my life.

*Pinch.* Pshaw! do not look upon him so much, he's a poor bashful youth, you'll put him out of countenance.—Come away, brother.                      [*Offers to take her away.*

*Horn.* O, your brother!

*Pinch.* Yes, my wife's brother.—Come, come, she'll stay supper for us.

*Horn.* I thought so, for he is very like her I saw you at the play with, whom I told you I was in love with.

*Mrs. Pinch.* [*aside*]. O jeminy! is this he that was in love with me? I am glad on't, I vow, for he's a curious fine gentleman, and I love him already, too.—[*To* PINCHWIFE.] Is this he, bud?

*Pinch.* Come away, come away.                [*To his* Wife.

*Horn.* Why, what haste are you in? why won't you let me talk with him?

*Pinch.* Because you'll debauch him; he's yet young and innocent, and I would not have him debauched for anything in the world.—[*Aside.*] How she gazes on him! the devil!

*Horn.* Harcourt, Dorilant, look you here, this is the likeness of that dowdy he told us of, his wife; did you ever see a lovelier creature? The rogue has reason to be jealous of his wife, since she is like him, for she would make all that see her in love with her.

*Har.* And, as I remember now, she is as like him here as can be.

*Dor.* She is indeed very pretty, if she be like him.

*Horn.* Very pretty? a very pretty commendation!—she is a glorious creature, beautiful beyond all things I ever beheld.

*Pinch.* So, so.

*Har.* More beautiful than a poet's first mistress of imagination.

*Horn.* Or another man's last mistress of flesh and blood.

*Mrs. Pinch.* Nay, now you jeer, sir; pray don't jeer me.

*Pinch.* Come, come.—[*Aside.*] By Heavens, she'll discover herself!

*Horn.* I speak of your sister, sir.

*Pinch.* Ay, but saying she was handsome, if like him, made him blush.—[*Aside.*] I am upon a rack!

*Horn.* Methinks he is so handsome he should not be a man.

*Pinch.* [*aside*]. O, there 'tis out! he has discovered her! I am not able to suffer any longer.— [*To his* Wife.] Come, come away, I say.

*Horn.* Nay, by your leave, sir, he shall not go yet.—[*Aside to them.*] Harcourt, Dorilant, let us torment this jealous rogue a little.

*Har. Dor.* How?

*Horn.* I'll show you.

*Pinch.* Come, pray let him go, I cannot stay fooling any longer; I tell you his sister stays supper for us.

*Horn.* Does she? Come then, we'll all go to sup with her and thee.

*Pinch.* No, now I think on't, having stayed so long for us, I warrant she's gone to bed.—[*Aside.*] I wish she and I were well out of their hands.—[*To his* Wife.] Come, I must rise early to-morrow, come.

*Horn.* Well then, if she be gone to bed, I wish her and you a good night. But pray, young gentleman, present my humble service to her.

*Mrs. Pinch.* Thank you heartily, sir.

*Pinch.* [*aside*]. 'Sdeath, she will discover herself yet in spite of me.—[*Aloud.*] He is something more civil to you, for your kindness to his sister, than I am, it seems.

*Horn.* Tell her, dear sweet little gentleman, for all your brother there, that you have revived the love I had for her at first sight in the playhouse.

*Mrs. Pinch.* But did you love her indeed, and indeed?

*Pinch.* [*aside*]. So, so.—[*Aloud.*] Away, I say.

*Horn.* Nay, stay.—Yes, indeed, and indeed, pray do you tell her so, and give her this kiss from me.          [*Kisses her.*

*Pinch.* [*aside*]. O Heavens! what do I suffer? Now 'tis too plain he knows her, and yet——

*Horn.* And this, and this——          [*Kisses her again.*

*Mrs. Pinch.* What do you kiss me for? I am no woman.

*Pinch.* [*aside*]. So, there, 'tis out.—[*Aloud.*] Come, I cannot, nor will stay any longer.

*Horn.* Nay, they shall send your lady a kiss too. Here, Harcourt, Dorilant, will you not?          [*They kiss her.*

*Pinch.* [*aside*]. How! do I suffer this? Was I not accusing another just now for this rascally patience, in permitting his wife to be kissed before his face? Ten thousand ulcers gnaw away their lips.—[*Aloud.*] Come, come.

*Horn.* Good night, dear little gentleman; madam, good night; farewell, Pinchwife.—[*Apart to* HARCOURT *and* DORILANT.] Did not I tell you I would raise his jealous gall?

[*Exeunt* HORNER, HARCOURT, *and* DORILANT.

*Pinch.* So, they are gone at last; stay, let me see first if the coach be at this door. [*Exit.*

*Re-enter* HORNER, HARCOURT, *and* DORILANT.

*Horn.* What, not gone yet? Will you be sure to do as I desired you, sweet sir?

*Mrs. Pinch.* Sweet sir, but what will you give me then?

*Horn.* Anything. Come away into the next walk.

[*Exit, haling away* Mrs. PINCHWIFE.

*Alith.* Hold! hold! what d'ye do?

*Lucy.* Stay, stay, hold——

*Har.* Hold, madam, hold, let him present him—he'll come presently; nay, I will never let you go till you answer my question.

*Lucy.* For God's sake, sir, I must follow 'em.

[ALITHEA *and* LUCY, *struggling with* HARCOURT *and* DORILANT.

*Dor.* No, I have something to present you with too, you shan't follow them.

*Re-enter* PINCHWIFE.

*Pinch.* Where?—how—what's become of?—gone!—whither?

*Lucy.* He's only gone with the gentleman, who will give him something, an't please your worship.

*Pinch.* Something!—give him something, with a pox!—where are they?

*Alith.* In the next walk only, brother.

*Pinch.* Only, only! where, where?

[*Exit and returns presently, then goes out again.*

*Har.* What's the matter with him? why so much concerned? But, dearest madam——

*Alith.* Pray let me go, sir; I have said and suffered enough already.

*Har.* Then you will not look upon, nor pity, my sufferings?

*Alith.* To look upon 'em, when I cannot help 'em, were cruelty, not pity; therefore, I will never see you more.

*Har.* Let me then, madam, have my privilege of a banished lover, complaining or railing, and giving you but a farewell reason why, if you cannot condescend to marry me, you should not take that wretch, my rival.

*Alith.* He only, not you, since my honour is engaged so far to

him, can give me a reason why I should not marry him; but if
he be true, and what I think him to me, I must be so to him.
Your servant, sir.

*Har.* Have women only constancy when 'tis a vice, and are, like
Fortune, only true to fools?

*Dor.* Thou sha't not stir, thou robust creature; you see I can
deal with you, therefore you should stay the rather, and be kind.

[*To* LUCY, *who struggles to get from him.*

### Re-enter PINCHWIFE.

*Pinch.* Gone, gone, not to be found! quite gone! ten thousand
plagues go with 'em! Which way went they?

*Alith.* But into t'other walk, brother.

*Lucy.* Their business will be done presently sure, an't please
your worship; it can't be long in doing, I'm sure on't.

*Alith.* Are they not there?

*Pinch.* No, you know where they are, you infamous wretch,
eternal shame of your family, which you do not dishonour enough
yourself you think, but you must help her to do it too, thou
legion of bawds!

*Alith.* Good brother——

*Pinch.* Damned, damned sister!

*Alith.* Look you here, she's coming.

### Re-enter Mrs. PINCHWIFE *running, with her hat full of oranges and dried fruit under her arm,* HORNER *following.*

*Mrs. Pinch.* O dear bud, look you here what I have got, see!

*Pinch.* And what I have got here too, which you can't see.

[*Aside, rubbing his forehead.*

*Mrs. Pinch.* The fine gentleman has given me better things
yet.

*Pinch.* Has he so?—[*Aside.*] Out of breath and coloured!—
I must hold yet.

*Horn.* I have only given your little brother an orange, sir.

*Pinch.* [*to* HORNER]. Thank you, sir.—[*Aside.*] You have
only squeezed my orange, I suppose, and given it me again; yet
I must have a city patience.—[*To his* Wife.] Come, come away.

*Mrs. Pinch.* Stay, till I have put up my fine things, bud.

### Enter Sir JASPER FIDGET.

*Sir Jasp.* O, Master Horner, come, come, the ladies stay for
you; your mistress, my wife, wonders you make not more haste
to her.

*Horn.* I have stayed this half hour for you here, and 'tis your
fault I am not now with your wife.

*Sir Jasp.* But, pray, don't let her know so much; the truth
on't is, I was advancing a certain project to his majesty about—
I'll tell you.

*Horn.* No, let's go, and hear it at your house. Good night, sweet little gentleman; one kiss more, you'll remember me now, I hope. [*Kisses her.*

*Dor.* What, Sir Jasper, will you separate friends? He promised to sup with us, and if you take him to your house, you'll be in danger of our company too.

*Sir Jasp.* Alas! gentlemen, my house is not fit for you; there are none but civil women there, which are not for your turn. He, you know, can bear with the society of civil women now, ha! ha! ha! besides, he's one of my family—he's—he! he! he!

*Dor.* What is he?

*Sir Jasp.* Faith, my eunuch, since you'll have it; he! he! he!
[*Exeunt* Sir JASPER FIDGET *and* HORNER.

*Dor.* I rather wish thou wert his or my cuckold. Harcourt, what a good cuckold is lost there for want of a man to make him one? Thee and I cannot have Horner's privilege, who can make use of it.

*Har.* Ay, to poor Horner 'tis like coming to an estate at threescore, when a man can't be the better for't.

*Pinch.* Come.

*Mrs. Pinch.* Presently, bud.

*Dor.* Come, let us go too.—[*To* ALITHEA.] Madam, your servant.—[*To* LUCY.] Good night, strapper.

*Har.* Madam, though you will not let me have a good day or night, I wish you one; but dare not name the other half of my wish.

*Alith.* Good night, sir, for ever.

*Mrs. Pinch.* I don't know where to put this here, dear bud, you shall eat it; nay, you shall have part of the fine gentleman's good things, or treat, as you call it, when we come home.

*Pinch.* Indeed, I deserve it, since I furnished the best part of it.
[*Strikes away the orange.*

The gallant treats presents, and gives the ball;
But 'tis the absent cuckold pays for all. [*Exeunt.*


## ACT IV

### SCENE I.—PINCHWIFE'S *House in the morning*

*Enter* ALITHEA *dressed in new clothes, and* LUCY.

*Lucy.* Well—madam, now have I dressed you, and set you out with so many ornaments, and spent upon you ounces of essence and pulvillio; and all this for no other purpose but as people adorn and perfume a corpse for a stinking second-hand grave: such, or as bad, I think Master Sparkish's bed.

*Alith.* Hold your peace.

*Lucy.* Nay, madam, I will ask you the reason why you would banish poor Master Harcourt for ever from your sight; how could you be so hard-hearted?

*Alith.* 'Twas because I was not hard-hearted.

*Lucy.* No, no; 'twas stark love and kindness, I warrant.

*Alith.* It was so; I would see him no more because I love him.

*Lucy.* Hey day, a very pretty reason!

*Alith.* You do not understand me.

*Lucy.* I wish you may yourself.

*Alith.* I was engaged to marry, you see, another man, whom my justice will not suffer me to deceive or injure.

*Lucy.* Can there be a greater cheat or wrong done to a man than to give him your person without your heart? I should make a conscience of it.

*Alith.* I'll retrieve it for him after I am married a while.

*Lucy.* The woman that marries to love better, will be as much mistaken as the wencher that marries to live better. No, madam, marrying to increase love is like gaming to become rich; alas! you only lose what little stock you had before.

*Alith.* I find by your rhetoric you have been bribed to betray me.

*Lucy.* Only by his merit, that has bribed your heart, you see, against your word and rigid honour. But what a devil is this honour! 'tis sure a disease in the head, like the megrim or falling-sickness, that always hurries people away to do themselves mischief. Men lose their lives by it; women, what's dearer to 'em, their love, the life of life.

*Alith.* Come, pray talk you no more of honour, nor Master Harcourt; I wish the other would come to secure my fidelity to him and his right in me.

*Lucy.* You will marry him then?

*Alith.* Certainly, I have given him already my word, and will my hand too, to make it good, when he comes.

*Lucy.* Well, I wish I may never stick pin more, if he be not an arrant natural, to t'other fine gentleman.

*Alith.* I own he wants the wit of Harcourt, which I will dispense withal for another want he has, which is want of jealousy, which men of wit seldom want.

*Lucy.* Lord, madam, what should you do with a fool to your husband? You intend to be honest, don't you? then that husbandly virtue, credulity, is thrown away upon you.

*Alith.* He only that could suspect my virtue should have cause to do it; 'tis Sparkish's confidence in my truth that obliges me to be so faithful to him.

*Lucy.* You are not sure his opinion may last.

*Alith.* I am satisfied, 'tis impossible for him to be jealous after the proofs I have had of him. Jealousy in a husband—Heaven defend me from it! it begets a thousand plagues to a poor woman, the loss of her honour, her quiet, and her——

*Lucy.* And her pleasure.

*Alith.* What d'ye mean, impertinent?

*Lucy.* Liberty is a great pleasure, madam.

*Alith.* I say, loss of her honour, her quiet, nay, her life sometimes; and what's as bad almost, the loss of this town; that is,
she is sent into the country, which is the last ill-usage of a
husband to a wife, I think.

*Lucy* [*aside*]. O, does the wind lie there?—[*Aloud.*] Then of
necessity, madam, you think a man must carry his wife into the
country, if he be wise. The country is as terrible, I find, to our
young English ladies, as a monastery to those abroad; and on
my virginity, I think they would rather marry a London jailer,
than a high sheriff of a county, since neither can stir from his
employment. Formerly women of wit married fools for a great
estate, a fine seat, or the like; but now 'tis for a pretty seat
only in Lincoln's Inn Fields, St. James's Fields, or the Pall Mall.

*Enter* SPARKISH, *and* HARCOURT, *dressed like a* Parson.

*Spark.* Madam, your humble servant, a happy day to you,
and to us all.

*Har.* Amen.

*Alith.* Who have we here?

*Spark.* My chaplain, faith—O madam, poor Harcourt remembers his humble service to you; and, in obedience to your last
commands, refrains coming into your sight.

*Alith.* Is not that he?

*Spark.* No, fy, no; but to show that he ne'er intended to
hinder our match, has sent his brother here to join our hands.
When I get me a wife, I must get her a chaplain, according to the
custom; this is his brother, and my chaplain.

*Alith.* His brother!

*Lucy.* And your chaplain, to preach in your pulpit then——
[*Aside.*

*Alith.* His brother!

*Spark.* Nay, I knew you would not believe it.—I told you, sir,
she would take you for your brother Frank.

*Alith.* Believe it!

*Lucy.* His brother! ha! ha! he! he has a trick left still, it
seems. [*Aside.*

*Spark.* Come, my dearest, pray let us go to church before the
canonical hour is past.

*Alith.* For shame, you are abused still.

*Spark.* By the world, 'tis strange now you are so incredulous.

*Alith.* 'Tis strange you are so credulous.

*Spark.* Dearest of my life, hear me. I tell you this is Ned
Harcourt of Cambridge, by the world; you see he has a sneaking
college look. 'Tis true he's something like his brother Frank;
and they differ from each other no more than in their age, for
they were twins.

*Lucy.* Ha! ha! ha!

*Alith.* Your servant, sir; I cannot be so deceived, though you are. But come, let's hear, how do you know what you affirm so confidently?

*Spark.* Why I'll tell you all. Frank Harcourt coming to me this morning to wish me joy, and present his service to you, I asked him if he could help me to a parson. Whereupon he told me, he had a brother in town who was in orders; and he went straight away, and sent him you see there to me.

*Alith.* Yes, Frank goes and puts on a black coat, then tells you he is Ned; that's all you have for't.

*Spark.* Pshaw! pshaw! I tell you, by the same token, the midwife put her garter about Frank's neck, to know 'em asunder, they were so like.

*Alith.* Frank tells you this too?

*Spark.* Ay, and Ned there too: nay, they are both in a story.

*Alith.* So, so; very foolish.

*Spark.* Lord, if you won't believe one, you had best try him by your chambermaid there; for chambermaids must needs know chaplains from other men, they are so used to 'em.

*Lucy.* Let's see: nay, I'll be sworn he has the canonical smirk, and the filthy clammy palm of a chaplain.

*Alith.* Well, most reverend doctor, pray let us make an end of this fooling.

*Har.* With all my soul, divine heavenly creature, when you please.

*Alith.* He speaks like a chaplain indeed.

*Spark.* Why, was there not soul, divine, heavenly, in what he said?

*Alith.* Once more, most impertinent black coat, cease your persecution, and let us have a conclusion of this ridiculous love.

*Har.* I had forgot, I must suit my style to my coat, or I wear it in vain.        [*Aside.*

*Alith.* I have no more patience left; let us make once an end of this troublesome love, I say.

*Har.* So be it, seraphic lady, when your honour shall think it meet and convenient so to do.

*Spark.* 'Gad, I'm sure none but a chaplain could speak so, I think.

*Alith.* Let me tell you, sir, this dull trick will not serve your turn; though you delay our marriage, you shall not hinder it.

*Har.* Far be it from me, munificent patroness, to delay your marriage; I desire nothing more than to marry you presently, which I might do, if you yourself would; for my noble, good-natured, and thrice generous patron here would not hinder it.

*Spark.* No, poor man, not I, faith.

*Har.* And now, madam, let me tell you plainly nobody else shall marry you; by Heavens! I'll die first, for I'm sure I should die after it.

*Lucy.* How his love has made him forget his function, as I have seen it in real parsons!

*Alith.* That was spoken like a chaplain too? now you understand him, I hope.

*Spark.* Poor man, he takes it heinously to be refused; I can't blame him, 'tis putting an indignity upon him, not to be suffered; but you'll pardon me, madam, it shan't be; he shall marry us; come away, pray, madam.

*Lucy.* Ha! ha! he! more ado! 'tis late.

*Alith.* Invincible stupidity! I tell you, he would marry me as your rival, not as your chaplain.

*Spark.* Come, come, madam. [*Pulling her away.*

*Lucy.* I pray, madam, do not refuse this reverend divine the honour and satisfaction of marrying you; for I dare say, he has set his heart upon't, good doctor.

*Alith.* What can you hope or design by this?

*Har.* I could answer her, a reprieve for a day only, often revokes a hasty doom. At worst, if she will not take mercy on me, and let me marry her, I have at least the lover's second pleasure, hindering my rival's enjoyment, though but for a time.
[*Aside.*

*Spark.* Come, madam, 'tis e'en twelve o'clock, and my mother charged me never to be married out of the canonical hours. Come, come; Lord, here's such a deal of modesty, I warrant, the first day.

*Lucy.* Yes, an't please your worship, married women show all their modesty the first day, because married men show all their love the first day. [*Exeunt.*


## SCENE II.—*A Bedchamber in* PINCHWIFE'S *House*

PINCHWIFE *and* Mrs. PINCHWIFE *discovered.*

*Pinch.* Come, tell me, I say.

*Mrs. Pinch.* Lord! han't I told it an hundred times over?

*Pinch.* [*aside*]. I would try, if in the repetition of the ungrateful tale, I could find her altering it in the least circumstance; for if her story be false, she is so too.—[*Aloud.*] Come, how was't, baggage?

*Mrs. Pinch.* Lord, what pleasure you take to hear it sure!

*Pinch.* No, you take more in telling it I find; but speak, how was't?

*Mrs. Pinch.* He carried me up into the house next to the Exchange.

*Pinch.* So, and you two were only in the room!

*Mrs. Pinch.* Yes, for he sent away a youth that was there, for some dried fruit, and China oranges.

*Pinch.* Did he so? Damn him for it—and for——

*Mrs. Pinch.* But presently came up the gentlewoman of the house.

*Pinch.* O, 'twas well she did; but what did he do whilst the fruit came?

*Mrs. Pinch.* He kissed me an hundred times, and told me he fancied he kissed my fine sister, meaning me, you know, whom he said he loved with all his soul, and bid me be sure to tell her so, and to desire her to be at her window, by eleven of the clock this morning, and he would walk under it at that time.

*Pinch.* And he was as good as his word, very punctual; a pox reward him for't.                                        [*Aside.*

*Mrs. Pinch.* Well, and he said if you were not within, he would come up to her, meaning me, you know, bud, still.

*Pinch.* [*aside*]. So—he knew her certainly; but for this confession, I am obliged to her simplicity.—[*Aloud.*] But what, you stood very still when he kissed you?

*Mrs. Pinch.* Yes, I warrant you; would you have had me discovered myself?

*Pinch.* But you told me he did some beastliness to you, as you called it; what was't?

*Mrs. Pinch.* Why, he put——

*Pinch.* What?

*Mrs. Pinch.* Why, he put the tip of his tongue between my lips, and so mousled me—and I said, I'd bite it.

*Pinch.* An eternal canker seize it, for a dog!

*Mrs. Pinch.* Nay, you need not be so angry with him neither, for to say truth, he has the sweetest breath I ever knew.

*Pinch.* The devil! you were satisfied with it then, and would do it again?

*Mrs. Pinch.* Not unless he should force me.

*Pinch.* Force you, changeling! I tell you, no woman can be forced.

*Mrs. Pinch.* Yes, but she may sure, by such a one as he, for he's a proper, goodly, strong man; 'tis hard, let me tell you, to resist him.

*Pinch.* [*aside*]. So, 'tis plain she loves him, yet she has not love enough to make her conceal it from me; but the sight of him will increase her aversion for me and love for him; and that love instruct her how to deceive me and satisfy him, all idiot as she is. Love! 'twas he gave women first their craft, their art of deluding. Out of Nature's hands they came plain, open, silly, and fit for slaves, as she and Heaven intended 'em; but damned Love—well—I must strangle that little monster whilst I can deal with him.—[*Aloud.*] Go fetch pen, ink, and paper out of the next room.

*Mrs. Pinch.* Yes, bud.                                        [*Exit.*

*Pinch.* Why should women have more invention in love than men? It can only be, because they have more desires, more soliciting passions, more lust, and more of the devil.

*Re-enter* Mrs. PINCHWIFE.

Come, minx, sit down and write.

*Mrs. Pinch.* Ay, dear bud, but I can't do't very well.

*Pinch.* I wish you could not at all.

*Mrs. Pinch.* But what should I write for?

*Pinch.* I'll have you write a letter to your lover.

*Mrs. Pinch.* O Lord, to the fine gentleman a letter!

*Pinch.* Yes, to the fine gentleman.

*Mrs. Pinch.* Lord, you do but jeer: sure you jest.

*Pinch.* I am not so merry: come, write as I bid you.

*Mrs. Pinch.* What, do you think I am a fool?

*Pinch.* [*aside*]. She's afraid I would not dictate any love to him, therefore she's unwilling.—[*Aloud.*] But you had best begin.

*Mrs. Pinch.* Indeed, and indeed, but I won't, so I won't.

*Pinch.* Why?

*Mrs. Pinch.* Because he's in town; you may send for him if you will.

*Pinch.* Very well, you would have him brought to you; is it come to this? I say, take the pen and write, or you'll provoke me.

*Mrs. Pinch.* Lord, what d'ye make a fool of me for? Don't I know that letters are never writ but from the country to London, and from London into the country? Now he's in town, and I am in town too; therefore I can't write to him, you know.

*Pinch.* [*aside*]. So, I am glad it is no worse; she is innocent enough yet.—[*Aloud.*] Yes, you may, when your husband bids you, write letters to people that are in town.

*Mrs. Pinch.* O, may I so? then I'm satisfied.

*Pinch.* Come, begin:—" Sir "——　　　　　　[*Dictates.*

*Mrs. Pinch.* Shan't I say, " Dear Sir? "—You know one says always something more than bare " Sir."

*Pinch.* Write as I bid you, or I will write whore with this penknife in your face.

*Mrs. Pinch.* Nay, good bud—" Sir "——　　　　[*Writes.*

*Pinch.* " Though I suffered last night your nauseous, loathed kisses and embraces "—Write!

*Mrs. Pinch.* Nay, why should I say so? You know I told you he had a sweet breath.

*Pinch.* Write!

*Mrs. Pinch.* Let me but put out " loathed."

*Pinch.* Write, I say!

*Mrs. Pinch.* Well then.　　　　　　　　　　　[*Writes.*

*Pinch.* Let's see, what have you writ?—[*Takes the paper and reads.*] " Though I suffered last night your kisses and embraces "—Thou impudent creature! where is " nauseous " and " loathed? "

*Mrs. Pinch.* I can't abide to write such filthy words.

*Pinch.* Once more write as I'd have you, and question it not, or I will spoil thy writing with this. I will stab out those eyes that cause my mischief.          [*Holds up the penknife.*

*Mrs. Pinch.* O Lord! I will.

*Pinch.* So—so—let's see now.—[*Reads.*] " Though I suffered last night your nauseous, loathed kisses and embraces "—go on—" yet I would not have you presume that you shall ever repeat them "—so——          [*She writes.*

*Mrs. Pinch.* I have writ it.

*Pinch.* On, then—" I then concealed myself from your knowledge, to avoid your insolencies."——       [*She writes.*

*Mrs. Pinch.* So——

*Pinch.* " The same reason, now I am out of your hands "——
         [*She writes.*

*Mrs. Pinch.* So——

*Pinch.* " Makes me own to you my unfortunate, though innocent frolic, of being in man's clothes "——     [*She writes.*

*Mrs. Pinch.* So——

*Pinch.* " That you may for evermore cease to pursue her, who hates and detests you "——          [*She writes on.*

*Mrs. Pinch.* So—heigh!          [*Sighs.*

*Pinch.* What, do you sigh?—" detests you—as much as she loves her husband and her honour."

*Mrs. Pinch.* I vow, husband, he'll ne'er believe I should write such a letter.

*Pinch.* What, he'd expect a kinder from you? Come, now your name only.

*Mrs. Pinch.* What, shan't I say " Your most faithful humble servant till death? "

*Pinch.* No, tormenting fiend!—[*Aside.*] Her style, I find, would be very soft.—[*Aloud.*] Come, wrap it up now, whilst I go fetch wax and a candle; and write on the backside, " For Mr. Horner."          [*Exit.*

*Mrs. Pinch.* " For Mr. Horner."—So, I am glad he has told me his name. Dear Mr. Horner! but why should I send him such a letter that will vex thee, and make thee angry with me?—Well, I will not send it.—Ay, but then my husband will kill me—for I see plainly he won't let me love Mr. Horner—but what care I for my husband?—I won't, so I won't, send poor Mr. Horner such a letter—But then my husband—but oh, what if I writ at bottom my husband made me write it?—Ay, but then my husband would see't—Can one have no shift? ah, a London woman would have had a hundred presently. Stay—what if I should write a letter, and wrap it up like this, and write upon't too? Ay, but then my husband would see't—I don't know what to do.—But yet evads I'll try, so I will—for I will not send this letter to poor Mr. Horner, come what will on't.

" Dear, sweet Mr. Horner "—[*Writes and repeats what she writes.*]—so—" my husband would have me send you a base,

rude, unmannerly letter; but I won't "—so—" and would have
me forbid you loving me; but I won't "—so—" and would have
me say to you, I hate you, poor Mr. Horner; but I won't tell a
lie for him "—there—" for I'm sure if you and I were in the
country at cards together "—so—" I could not help treading on
your toe under the table "—so—" or rubbing knees with you,
and staring in your face, till you saw me "—very well—" and
then looking down, and blushing for an hour together "—so—
" but I must make haste before my husband comes: and now
he has taught me to write letters, you shall have longer ones
from me, who am, dear, dear, poor, dear Mr. Horner, your most
humble friend, and servant to command till death,—Margery
Pinchwife."

Stay, I must give him a hint at bottom—so—now wrap it up
just like t'other—so—now write " For Mr. Horner "—But oh
now, what shall I do with it? for here comes my husband.

*Re-enter* PINCHWIFE.

*Pinch.* [*aside*]. I have been detained by a sparkish coxcomb,
who pretended a visit to me; but I fear 'twas to my wife—
[*Aloud.*] What, have you done?

*Mrs. Pinch.* Ay, ay, bud, just now.

*Pinch.* Let's see't: what d'ye tremble for? what, you would
not have it go?

*Mrs. Pinch.* Here—[*aside.*] No, I must not give him that:
so I had been served if I had given him this.

[*He opens and reads the first letter.*

*Pinch.* Come, where's the wax and seal?

*Mrs. Pinch.* [*aside*]. Lord, what shall I do now? Nay, then
I have it—[*aloud.*] Pray let me see't. Lord, you think me so
arrant a fool, I cannot seal a letter; I will do't, so I will.

[*Snatches the letter from him, changes it for the other, seals it,
and delivers it to him.*

*Pinch.* Nay, I believe you will learn that, and other things
too, which I would not have you.

*Mrs. Pinch.* So, han't I done it curiously?—[*Aside.*] I think
I have; there's my letter going to Mr. Horner, since he'll needs
have me send letters to folks.

*Pinch.* 'Tis very well; but I warrant, you would not have it
go now?

*Mrs. Pinch.* Yes, indeed, but I would, bud, now.

*Pinch.* Well, you are a good girl then. Come, let me lock you
up in your chamber, till I come back; and be sure you come not
within three strides of the window when I am gone, for I have a
spy in the street.—[*Exit* Mrs. PINCHWIFE, PINCHWIFE *locks the
door.*] At least, 'tis fit she think so. If we do not cheat women,
they'll cheat us, and fraud may be justly used with secret
enemies, of which a wife is the most dangerous; and he that has

a handsome one to keep, and a frontier town, must provide
against treachery, rather than open force.   Now I have secured
all within, I'll deal with the foe without, with false intelligence.
                                    [*Holds up the letter.   Exit.*


SCENE III.—HORNER'S *Lodging*

*Enter* HORNER *and* Quack.

*Quack.* Well, sir, how fadges the new design? have you not
the luck of all your brother projectors, to deceive only yourself
at last?

*Horn.* No, good domine doctor, I deceive you, it seems, and
others too; for the grave matrons, and old, rigid husbands think
me as unfit for love as they are; but their wives, sisters, and
daughters know, some of 'em, better things already.

*Quack.* Already!

*Horn.* Already, I say.   Last night I was drunk with half-a-
dozen of your civil persons, as you call 'em, and people of honour,
and so was made free of their society and dressing-rooms for
ever hereafter; and am already come to the privileges of sleeping
upon their pallets, warming smocks, tying shoes and garters, and
the like, doctor, already, already, doctor.

*Quack.* You have made use of your time, sir.

*Horn.* I tell thee, I am now no more interruption to 'em, when
they sing, or talk bawdy, than a little squab French page who
speaks no English.

*Quack.* But do civil persons and women of honour drink, and
sing bawdy songs?

*Horn.* O, amongst friends, amongst friends.   For your bigots
in honour are just like those in religion; they fear the eye of the
world more than the eye of Heaven; and think there is no
virtue, but railing at vice, and no sin, but giving scandal.   They
rail at a poor, little, kept player, and keep themselves some
young, modest pulpit comedian to be privy to their sins in their
closets, not to tell 'em of them in their chapels.

*Quack.* Nay, the truth on't is, priests, amongst the women
now, have quite got the better of us lay-confessors, physicians.

*Horn.* And they are rather their patients; but——

*Enter* Lady FIDGET, *looking about her.*

Now we talk of women of honour, here comes one.   Step behind
the screen there, and but observe, if I have not particular
privileges with the women of reputation already, doctor, already.
                                    [*Quack retires.*

*Lady Fid.* Well, Horner, am not I a woman of honour? you
see, I'm as good as my word.

*Horn.* And you shall see, madam, I'll not be behind-hand with you in honour; and I'll be as good as my word too, if you please but to withdraw into the next room.

*Lady Fid.* But first, my dear sir, you must promise to have a care of my dear honour.

*Horn.* If you talk a word more of your honour, you'll make me incapable to wrong it. To talk of honour in the mysteries of love, is like talking of Heaven or the Deity, in an operation of witchcraft, just when you are employing the devil: it makes the charm impotent.

*Lady Fid.* Nay, fy! let us not be smutty. But you talk of mysteries and bewitching to me; I don't understand you.

*Horn.* I tell you, madam, the word money in a mistress's mouth, at such a nick of time, is not a more disheartening sound to a younger brother, than that of honour to an eager lover like myself.

*Lady Fid.* But you can't blame a lady of my reputation to be chary.

*Horn.* Chary! I have been chary of it already, by the report I have caused of myself.

*Lady Fid.* Ay, but if you should ever let other women know that dear secret, it would come out. Nay, you must have a great care of your conduct; for my acquaintance are so censorious (oh, 'tis a wicked, censorious world, Mr. Horner!), I say, are so censorious, and detracting, that perhaps they'll talk to the prejudice of my honour, though you should not let them know the dear secret.

*Horn.* Nay, madam, rather than they shall prejudice your honour, I'll prejudice theirs; and, to serve you, I'll lie with 'em all, make the secret their own, and then they'll keep it. I am a Machiavel in love, madam.

*Lady Fid.* O, no, sir, not that way.

*Horn.* Nay, the devil take me, if censorious women are to be silenced any other way.

*Lady Fid.* A secret is better kept, I hope, by a single person than a multitude; therefore pray do not trust anybody else with it, dear, dear Mr. Horner.      [*Embracing him.*

*Enter* Sir JASPER FIDGET.

*Sir Jasp.* How now!

*Lady Fid.* [*aside*]. O my husband!—prevented—and what's almost as bad, found with my arms about another man—that will appear too much—what shall I say?—[*Aloud.*] Sir Jasper, come hither: I am trying if Mr. Horner were ticklish, and he's as ticklish as can be. I love to torment the confounded toad; let you and I tickle him.

*Sir Jasp.* No, your ladyship will tickle him better without me, I suppose. But is this your buying china? I thought you had been at the china-house.

*Horn. [aside].* China-house! that's my cue, I must take it.—
[*Aloud.*] A pox! can't you keep your impertinent wives at
home? Some men are troubled with the husbands, but I with
the wives; but I'd have you to know, since I cannot be your
journeyman by night, I will not be your drudge by day, to
squire your wife about, and be your man of straw, or scarecrow
only to pies and jays, that would be nibbling at your forbidden
fruit; I shall be shortly the hackney gentleman-usher of the
town.

*Sir Jasp. [aside].* He! he! he! poor fellow, he's in the right
on't, faith. To squire women about for other folks is as ungrateful an employment as to tell money for other folks.—
[*Aloud.*] He! he! he! be'n't angry, Horner.

*Lady Fid.* No, 'tis I have more reason to be angry, who am
left by you, to go abroad indecently alone; or, what is more
indecent, to pin myself upon such ill-bred people of your
acquaintance as this is.

*Sir Jasp.* Nay, prithee, what has he done?

*Lady Fid.* Nay, he has done nothing.

*Sir Jasp.* But what d'ye take ill, if he has done nothing?

*Lady Fid.* Ha! ha! ha! faith, I can't but laugh however; why,
d'ye think the unmannerly toad would not come down to me to
the coach? I was fain to come up to fetch him, or go without
him, which I was resolved not to do; for he knows china very
well, and has himself very good, but will not let me see it, lest
I should beg some; but I will find it out, and have what I came
for yet.

*Horn. [apart to* Lady Fidget, *as he follows her to the door].*
Lock the door, madam.—[*Exit Lady* Fidget, *and locks the door.*]
—[*Aloud.*] So, she has got into my chamber and locked me out.
Oh the impertinency of woman-kind! Well, Sir Jasper, plain-
dealing is a jewel; if ever you suffer your wife to trouble me
again here, she shall carry you home a pair of horns; by my
lord mayor she shall; though I cannot furnish you myself, you
are sure, yet I'll find a way.

*Sir Jasp.* Ha! ha! he!—[*Aside.*] At my first coming in,
and finding her arms about him, tickling him it seems, I was
half jealous, but now I see my folly.—[*Aloud.*] He! he! he!
poor Horner.

*Horn.* Nay, though you laugh now, 'twill be my turn ere long.
Oh women, more impertinent, more cunning, and more mischievous than their monkeys, and to me almost as ugly!—Now
is she throwing my things about and rifling all I have; but I'll
get in to her the back way, and so rifle her for it.

*Sir Jasp.* Ha! ha! ha! poor angry Horner.

*Horn.* Stay here a little, I'll ferret her out to you presently,
I warrant.                                  [*Exit at the other door.*

[Sir Jasper *talks through the door to his* Wife, *she answers
from within*

*Sir Jasp.* Wife! my Lady Fidget! wife! he is coming in to you the back way.

*Lady Fid.* Let him come, and welcome, which way he will.

*Sir Jasp.* He'll catch you, and use you roughly, and be too strong for you.

*Lady Fid.* Don't you trouble yourself, let him if he can.

*Quack.* [*aside*]. This indeed I could not have believed from him, nor any but my own eyes.

*Enter* Mrs. SQUEAMISH.

*Mrs. Squeam.* Where's this woman-hater, this toad, this ugly, greasy, dirty sloven?

*Sir Jasp.* [*aside*]. So, the women all will have him ugly: methinks he is a comely person, but his wants make his form contemptible to 'em; and 'tis e'en as my wife said yesterday, talking of him, that a proper handsome eunuch was as ridiculous a thing as a gigantic coward.

*Mrs. Squeam.* Sir Jasper, your servant: where is the odious beast?

*Sir Jasp.* He's within in his chamber, with my wife; she's playing the wag with him.

*Mrs. Squeam.* Is she so? and he's a clownish beast, he'll give her no quarter, he'll play the wag with her again, let me tell you: come, let's go help her.—What, the door's locked?

*Sir Jasp.* Ay, my wife locked it.

*Mrs. Squeam.* Did she so? let's break it open then.

*Sir Jasp.* No, no, he'll do her no hurt.

*Mrs. Squeam.* No. [*aside*]. But is there no other way to get in to 'em? whither goes this? I will disturb 'em.

[*Exit at another door.*

*Enter* Old Lady SQUEAMISH.

*Lady Squeam.* Where is this harlotry, this impudent baggage, this rambling tomrigg? O Sir Jasper, I'm glad to see you here; did you not see my vile grandchild come in hither just now?

*Sir Jasp.* Yes.

*Lady Squeam.* Ay, but where is she then? where is she? Lord, Sir Jasper, I have e'en rattled myself to pieces in pursuit of her: but can you tell what she makes here? they say below, no woman lodges here.

*Sir Jasp.* No.

*Lady Squeam.* No! what does she here then? say, if it be not a woman's lodging, what makes she here? But are you sure no woman lodges here?

*Sir Jasp.* No, nor no man neither, this is Mr. Horner's lodging.

*Lady Squeam.* Is it so, are you sure?

*Sir Jasp.* Yes, yes.

*Lady Squeam.* So; then there's no hurt in't, I hope. But where is he?

*Sir Jasp.* He's in the next room with my wife.

*Lady Squeam.* Nay, if you trust him with your wife, I may with my Biddy. They say, he's a merry harmless man now, e'en as harmless a man as ever came out of Italy with a good voice, and as pretty, harmless company for a lady, as a snake without his teeth.

*Sir Jasp.* Ay, ay, poor man.

### *Re-enter* Mrs. SQUEAMISH.

*Mrs. Squeam.* I can't find 'em.—Oh, are you here, grand-mother? I followed, you must know, my Lady Fidget hither; 'tis the prettiest lodging, and I have been staring on the prettiest pictures——

### *Re-enter* Lady FIDGET *with a piece of china in her hand, and* HORNER *following.*

*Lady Fid.* And I have been toiling and moiling for the prettiest piece of china, my dear.

*Horn.* Nay, she has been too hard for me, do what I could.

*Mrs. Squeam.* Oh, lord, I'll have some china too. Good Mr. Horner, don't think to give other people china, and me none; come in with me too.'

*Horn.* Upon my honour, I have none left now.

*Mrs. Squeam.* Nay, nay, I have known you deny your china before now, but you shan't put me off so. Come.

*Horn.* This lady had the last there.

*Lady Fid.* Yes indeed, madam, to my certain knowledge, he has no more left.

*Mrs. Squeam.* O, but it may be he may have some you could not find.

*Lady Fid.* What, d'ye think if he had had any left, I would not have had it too? for we women of quality never think we have china enough.

*Horn.* Do not take it ill, I cannot make china for you all, but I will have a roll-waggon for you too, another time.

*Mrs. Squeam.* Thank you, dear toad.

*Lady Fid.* What do you mean by that promise?

[*Aside to* HORNER.

*Horn.* Alas, she has an innocent, literal understanding.

[*Aside to* Lady FIDGET.

*Lady Squeam.* Poor Mr. Horner! he has enough to do to please you all, I see.

*Horn.* Ay, madam, you see how they use me.

*Lady Squeam.* Poor gentleman, I pity you.

*Horn.* I thank you, madam: I could never find pity, but from such reverend ladies as you are; the young ones will never spare a man.

*Mrs. Squeam.* Come, come, beast, and go dine with us; for we shall want a man at ombre after dinner.

*Horn.* That's all their use of me, madam, you see.

*Mrs. Squeam.* Come, sloven, I'll lead you, to be sure of you.

[*Pulls him by the cravat.*

*Lady Squeam.* Alas, poor man, how she tugs him! Kiss, kiss her; that's the way to make such nice women quiet.

*Horn.* No, madam, that remedy is worse than the torment; they know I dare suffer anything rather than do it.

*Lady Squeam.* Prithee kiss her, and I'll give you her picture in little, that you admired so last night; prithee do.

*Horn.* Well, nothing but that could bribe me: I love a woman only in effigy, and good painting as much as I hate them.—I'll do't, for I could adore the devil well painted.

[*Kisses Mrs.* SQUEAMISH.

*Mrs. Squeam.* Foh, you filthy toad! nay, now I've done jesting.

*Lady Squeam.* Ha! ha! ha! I told you so.

*Mrs. Squeam.* Foh! a kiss of his——

*Sir Jasp.* Has no more hurt in't than one of my spaniel's.

*Mrs. Squeam.* Nor no more good neither.

*Quack.* I will now believe anything he tells me.     [*Aside.*

### Enter PINCHWIFE.

*Lady Fid.* O lord, here's a man! Sir Jasper, my mask, my mask! I would not be seen here for the world.

*Sir Jasp.* What, not when I am with you?

*Lady Fid.* No, no, my honour—let's be gone.

*Mrs. Squeam.* Oh grandmother, let's be gone; make haste, make haste, I know not how he may censure us.

*Lady Fid.* Be found in the lodging of anything like a man!— Away.

[*Exeunt* Sir JASPER FIDGET, Lady FIDGET, Old Lady SQUEAMISH, *and* Mrs. SQUEAMISH.

*Quack.* What's here? another cuckold? he looks like one, and none else sure have any business with him.     [*Aside.*

*Horn.* Well, what brings my dear friend hither?

*Pinch.* Your impertinency.

*Horn.* My impertinency!—why, you gentlemen that have got handsome wives think you have a privilege of saying anything to your friends, and are as brutish as if you were our creditors.

*Pinch.* No, sir, I'll ne'er trust you any way.

*Horn.* But why not, dear Jack? why diffide in me thou know'st so well?

*Pinch.* Because I do know you so well.

*Horn.* Han't I been always thy friend, honest Jack, always

ready to serve thee, in love or battle, before thou wert married, and am so still?

*Pinch.* I believe so, you would be my second now, indeed.

*Horn.* Well then, dear Jack, why so unkind, so grum, so strange to me? Come, prithee kiss me, dear rogue: gad, I was always, I say, and am still as much thy servant as——

*Pinch.* As I am yours, sir. What, you would send a kiss to my wife, is that it?

*Horn.* So, there 'tis—a man can't show his friendship to a married man, but presently he talks of his wife to you. Prithee, let thy wife alone, and let thee and I be all one, as we were wont. What, thou art as shy of my kindness as a Lombard Street alderman of a courtier's civility at Locket's!

*Pinch.* But you are over-kind to me, as kind as if I were your cuckold already; yet I must confess you ought to be kind and civil to me, since I am so kind, so civil to you, as to bring you this: look you there, sir. [*Delivers him a letter.*

*Horn.* What is't?

*Pinch.* Only a love-letter, sir.

*Horn.* From whom?—how! this is from your wife—hum—and hum—— [*Reads.*

*Pinch.* Even from my wife, sir: am I not wondrous kind and civil to you now too?—[*Aside.*] But you'll not think her so.

*Horn.* Ha! is this a trick of his or hers? [*Aside.*

*Pinch.* The gentleman's surprised I find.—What, you expected a kinder letter?

*Horn.* No faith, not I, how could I?

*Pinch.* Yes, yes, I'm sure you did. A man so well made as you are, must needs be disappointed, if the women declare not their passion at first sight or opportunity.

*Horn.* [*aside*]. But what should this mean? Stay, the post-script.—[*Reads aside.*] " Be sure you love me, whatsoever my husband says to the contrary, and let him not see this, lest he should come home and pinch me, or kill my squirrel."—It seems he knows not what the letter contains.

*Pinch.* Come, ne'er wonder at it so much.

*Horn.* Faith, I can't help it.

*Pinch.* Now, I think I have deserved your infinite friendship and kindness, and have showed myself sufficiently an obliging kind friend and husband; am I not so, to bring a letter from my wife to her gallant?

*Horn.* Ay, the devil take me, art thou, the most obliging, kind friend and husband in the world, ha! ha!

*Pinch.* Well, you may be merry, sir; but in short I must tell you, sir, my honour will suffer no jesting.

*Horn.* What dost thou mean?

*Pinch.* Does the letter want a comment? Then, know, sir, though I have been so civil a husband, as to bring you a letter from my wife, to let you kiss and court her to my face, I will not be a cuckold, sir, I will not.

*Horn.* Thou art mad with jealousy. I never saw thy wife in my life but at the play yesterday, and I know not if it were she or no. I court her, kiss her!

*Pinch.* I will not be a cuckold, I say; there will be danger in making me a cuckold.

*Horn.* Why, wert thou not well cured of thy last clap?

*Pinch.* I wear a sword.

*Horn.* It should be taken from thee, lest thou shouldst do thyself a mischief with it; thou art mad, man.

*Pinch.* As mad as I am, and as merry as you are, I must have more reason from you ere we part. I say again, though you kissed and courted last night my wife in man's clothes, as she confesses in her letter——

*Horn.* Ha!                                              [*Aside.*

*Pinch.* Both she and I say, you must not design it again, for you have mistaken your woman, as you have done your man.

*Horn.* [*aside*]. O—I understand something now—[*Aloud.*] Was that thy wife! Why wouldst thou not tell me 'twas she? Faith, my freedom with her was your fault, not mine.

*Pinch.* Faith, so 'twas.                                [*Aside.*

*Horn.* Fy! I'd never do't to a woman before her husband's face, sure.

*Pinch.* But I had rather you should do't to my wife before my face, than behind my back; and that you shall never do.

*Horn.* No—you will hinder me.

*Pinch.* If I would not hinder you, you see by her letter she would.

*Horn.* Well, I must e'en acquiesce then, and be contented with what she writes.

*Pinch.* I'll assure you 'twas voluntarily writ; I had no hand in't you may believe me.

*Horn.* I do believe thee, faith.

*Pinch.* And believe her too, for she's an innocent creature, has no dissembling in her: and so fare you well, sir.

*Horn.* Pray, however, present my humble service to her, and tell her, I will obey her letter to a tittle, and fulfil her desires, be what they will, or with what difficulty soever I do't; and you shall be no more jealous of me, I warrant her, and you.

*Pinch.* Well then, fare you well; and play with any man's honour but mine, kiss any man's wife but mine, and welcome.

[*Exit.*

*Horn.* Ha! ha! ha! doctor.

*Quack.* It seems, he has not heard the report of you, or does not believe it.

*Horn.* Ha! ha!—now, doctor, what think you?

*Quack.* Pray let's see the letter—hum—" for—dear—love you——"                                         [*Reads the letter.*

*Horn.* I wonder how she could contrive it! What say'st thou to't? 'tis an original.

*Quack.* So are your cuckolds too originals: for they are like no other common cuckolds, and I will henceforth believe it not impossible for you to cuckold the Grand Signior amidst his guards of eunuchs, that I say.

*Horn.* And I say for the letter, 'tis the first love-letter that ever was without flames, darts, fates, destinies, lying and dissembling in't.

*Enter* SPARKISH *pulling in* PINCHWIFE.

*Spark.* Come back, you are a pretty brother-in-law, neither go to church nor to dinner with your sister bride!

*Pinch.* My sister denies her marriage, and you see is gone away from you dissatisfied.

*Spark.* Pshaw! upon a foolish scruple, that our parson was not in lawful orders, and did not say all the common-prayer; but 'tis her modesty only I believe. But let women be never so modest the first day, they'll be sure to come to themselves by night, and I shall have enough of her then. In the meantime, Harry Horner, you must dine with me: I keep my wedding at my aunt's in the Piazza.

*Horn.* Thy wedding! what stale maid has lived to despair of a husband, or what young one of a gallant?

*Spark.* O, your servant, sir—this gentleman's sister then,—no stale maid.

*Horn.* I'm sorry for't.

*Pinch.* How comes he so concerned for her?      [*Aside.*

*Spark.* You sorry for't? why, do you know any ill by her?

*Horn.* No, I know none but by thee; 'tis for her sake, not yours, and another man's sake that might have hoped, I thought.

*Spark.* Another man! another man! what is his name?

*Horn.* Nay, since 'tis past, he shall be nameless.—[*Aside.*] Poor Harcourt! I am sorry thou hast missed her.

*Pinch.* He seems to be much troubled at the match.      [*Aside.*

*Spark.* Prithee, tell me—Nay, you shan't go, brother.

*Pinch.* I must of necessity, but I'll come to you to dinner.

[*Exit.*

*Spark.* But, Harry, what, have I a rival in my wife already? But with all my heart, for he may be of use to me hereafter; for though my hunger is now my sauce, and I can fall on heartily without, but the time will come when a rival will be as good sauce for a married man to a wife, as an orange to veal.

*Horn.* O thou damned rogue! thou hast set my teeth on edge with thy orange.

*Spark.* Then let's to dinner—there I was with you again. Come.

*Horn.* But who dines with thee?

*Spark.* My friends and relations, my brother Pinchwife, you see, of your acquaintance.

*Horn.* And his wife?

*Spark.* No, 'gad, he'll ne'er let her come amongst us good fellows; your stingy country coxcomb keeps his wife from his friends, as he does his little firkin of ale, for his own drinking, and a gentleman can't get a smack on't; but his servants, when his back is turned, broach it at their pleasures, and dust it away, ha! ha! ha!—'Gad, I am witty, I think, considering I was married to-day, by the world; but come——

*Horn.* No, I will not dine with you, unless you can fetch her too.

*Spark.* Pshaw! what pleasure canst thou have with women now, Harry?

*Horn.* My eyes are not gone; I love a good prospect yet, and will not dine with you unless she does too; go fetch her, therefore, but do not tell her husband 'tis for my sake.

*Spark.* Well, I'll go try what I can do; in the meantime, come away to my aunt's lodging, 'tis in the way to Pinchwife's.

*Horn.* The poor woman has called for aid, and stretched forth her hand, doctor; I cannot but help her over the pale out of the briars. [*Exeunt.*

## SCENE IV.—*A Room in* PINCHWIFE'S *House*

Mrs. PINCHWIFE *alone, leaning on her elbow.—A table, pen, ink, and paper.*

*Mrs. Pinch.* Well, 'tis e'en so, I have got the London disease they call love; I am sick of my husband, and for my gallant. I have heard this distemper called a fever, but methinks 'tis liker an ague; for when I think of my husband, I tremble, and am in a cold sweat, and have inclinations to vomit; but when I think of my gallant, dear Mr. Horner, my hot fit comes, and I am all in a fever indeed; and, as in other fevers, my own chamber is tedious to me, and I would fain be removed to his, and then methinks I should be well. Ah, poor Mr. Horner! Well, I cannot, will not stay here; therefore I'll make an end of my letter to him, which shall be a finer letter than my last, because I have studied it like anything. Oh sick, sick!

[*Takes the pen and writes.*

*Enter* PINCHWIFE, *who seeing her writing, steals softly behind her and looking over her shoulder, snatches the paper from her.*

*Pinch.* What, writing more letters?

*Mrs. Pinch.* O Lord, bud, why d'ye fright me so?

[*She offers to run out; he stops her, and reads.*

*Pinch.* How's this? nay, you shall not stir, madam:—" Dear, dear, dear Mr. Horner"—very well—I have taught you to write letters to good purpose—but let us see't. "First, I am to beg your pardon for my boldness in writing to you, which I'd have you to know I would not have done, had not you said first you loved me so extremely, which if you do, you will never suffer me to lie in the arms of another man whom I loathe, nauseate, and detest."—Now you can write these filthy words. But what follows?—"Therefore, I hope you will speedily find some way to free me from this unfortunate match, which was never, I assure you, of my choice, but I'm afraid 'tis already too far gone; however, if you love me, as I do you, you will try what you can do; but you must help me away before to-morrow, or else, alas! I shall be for ever out of your reach, for I can defer no longer our— our——" what is to follow "our"?—speak, what—our journey into the country I suppose—Oh woman, damned woman! and Love, damned Love, their old tempter! for this is one of his miracles; in a moment he can make those blind that could see, and those see that were blind, those dumb that could speak, and those prattle who were dumb before; nay, what is more than all, make these dough-baked, senseless, indocile animals, women, too hard for us, their politic lords and rulers, in a moment. But make an end of your letter, and then I'll make an end of you thus, and all my plagues together. [*Draws his sword.*

*Mrs. Pinch.* O Lord, O Lord, you are such a passionate man, bud!

*Enter* SPARKISH.

*Spark.* How now, what's here to do?
*Pinch.* This fool here now!
*Spark.* What! drawn upon your wife? You should never do that, but at night in the dark, when you can't hurt her. This is my sister-in-law, is it not? ay, faith, e'en our country Margery [*pulls aside her handkerchief*]; one may know her. Come, and you must go dine with me; dinner's ready, come. But where's my wife? is she not come home yet? where is she?
*Pinch.* Making you a cuckold; 'tis that they all do, as soon as they can.
*Spark.* What, the wedding-day? no, a wife that designs to make a cully of her husband will be sure to let him win the first stake of love, by the world. But come, they stay dinner for us: come, I'll lead down our Margery.
*Pinch.* No—sir, go, we'll follow you.
*Spark.* I will not wag without you.
*Pinch.* This coxcomb is a sensible torment to me amidst the greatest in the world. [*Aside.*
*Spark.* Come, come, Madam Margery.
*Pinch.* No; I'll lead her my way: what, would you treat your friends with mine, for want of your own wife?—[*Leads her to the other door, and locks her in and returns.*] I am contented my rage should take breath—— [*Aside.*

*Spark.* I told Horner this.

*Pinch.* Come now.

*Spark.* Lord, how shy you are of your wife! but let me tell you, brother, we men of wit have amongst us a saying, that cuckolding, like the small-pox, comes with a fear; and you may keep your wife as much as you will out of danger of infection, but if her constitution incline her to't, she'll have it sooner or later, by the world, say they.

*Pinch.* [*aside*]. What a thing is a cuckold, that every fool can make him ridiculous!—[*Aloud.*] Well, sir—but let me advise you, now you are come to be concerned, because you suspect the danger, not to neglect the means to prevent it, especially when the greatest share of the malady will light upon your own head, for

> Hows'e'er the kind wife's belly comes to swell,
> The husband breeds for her, and first is ill.

[*Exeunt.*

# 'ACT V

### SCENE I.—Pinchwife's *House*

*Enter* Pinchwife *and* Mrs. Pinchwife.    *A table and candle.*

*Pinch.* Come, take the pen and make an end of the letter, just as you intended; if you are false in a tittle, I shall soon perceive it, and punish you with this as you deserve.—[*Lays his hand on his sword.*] Write what was to follow—let's see—" You must make haste, and help me away before to-morrow, or else I shall be for ever out of your reach, for I can defer no longer our"—What follows " our"?

*Mrs. Pinch.* Must all out, then, bud?—Look you there, then.
                    [Mrs. Pinchwife *takes the pen and writes.*

*Pinch.* Let's see— "For I can defer no longer our—wedding— Your slighted Alithea."—What's the meaning of this? my sister's name to't? speak, unriddle.

*Mrs. Pinch.* Yes, indeed, bud.

*Pinch.* But why her name to't? speak—speak, I say.

*Mrs. Pinch.* Ay, but you'll tell her then again.  If you would not tell her again——

*Pinch.* I will not:—I am stunned, my head turns round.— Speak.

*Mrs. Pinch.* Won't you tell her, indeed, and indeed?

*Pinch.* No; speak, I say.

*Mrs. Pinch.* She'll be angry with me; but I had rather she should be angry with me than you, bud; and, to tell you the truth, 'twas she made me write the letter, and taught me what I should write.

*Pinch.* [*aside*]. Ha! I thought the style was somewhat better than her own.—[*Aloud.*] But how could she come to you to teach you, since I had locked you up alone?

*Mrs. Pinch.* O, through the key-hole, bud.

*Pinch.* But why should she make you write a letter for her to him, since she can write herself?

*Mrs. Pinch.* Why, she said because—for I was unwilling to do it——

*Pinch.* Because what—because?

*Mrs. Pinch.* Because, lest Mr. Horner should be cruel, and refuse her; or be vain afterwards, and show the letter, she might disown it, the hand not being hers.

*Pinch.* [*aside*]. How's this? Ha!—then I think I shall come to myself again.—This changeling could not invent this lie: but. if she could, why should she? she might think I should soon discover it.—Stay—now I think on't too, Horner said he was sorry she had married Sparkish; and her disowning her marriage to me makes me think she has evaded it for Horner's sake: yet why should she take this course? But men in love are fools; women may well be so—[*aloud.*] But hark you, madam, your sister went out in the morning, and I have not seen her within since.

*Mrs. Pinch.* Alack-a-day, she has been crying all day above, it seems, in a corner.

*Pinch.* Where is she? let me speak with her.

*Mrs. Pinch.* [*aside*]. O Lord, then she'll discover all!—[*Aloud.*] Pray hold, bud; what, d'ye mean to discover me? she'll know I have told you then. Pray, bud, let me talk with her first.

*Pinch.* I must speak with her, to know whether Horner ever made her any promise, and whether she be married to Sparkish or no.

*Mrs. Pinch.* Pray, dear bud, don't, till I have spoken with her, and told her that I have told you all; for she'll kill me else.

*Pinch.* Go then, and bid her come out to me.

*Mrs. Pinch.* Yes, yes, bud.

*Pinch.* Let me see——            [*Pausing.*

*Mrs. Pinch.* [*aside*]. I'll go, but she is not within to come to him: I have just got time to know of Lucy her maid, who first set me on work, what lie I shall tell next; for I am e'en at my wit's end.            [*Exit.*

*Pinch.* Well, I resolve it, Horner shall have her: I'd rather give him my sister than lend him my wife; and such an alliance will prevent his pretensions to my wife, sure. I'll make him of kin to her, and then he won't care for her.

*Re-enter* Mrs. PINCHWIFE.

*Mrs. Pinch.* O Lord, bud! I told you what anger you would make me with my sister.

*Pinch.* Won't she come hither?

*Mrs. Pinch.* No, no. Alack-a-day, she's ashamed to look you in the face: and she says, if you go in to her, she'll run away downstairs, and shamefully go herself to Mr. Horner, who has promised her marriage, she says; and she will have no other, so she won't.

*Pinch.* Did he so?—promise her marriage!—then she shall have no other. Go tell her so; and if she will come and discourse with me a little concerning the means, I will about it immediately. Go.—[*Exit* Mrs. PINCHWIFE.] His estate is equal to Sparkish's, and his extraction as much better than his, as his parts are; but my chief reason is, I'd rather be of kin to him by the name of brother-in-law than that of cuckold.

*Re-enter* Mrs. PINCHWIFE.

Well, what says she now?

*Mrs. Pinch.* Why, she says, she would only have you lead her to Horner's lodging; with whom she first will discourse the matter before she talks with you, which yet she cannot do; for alack, poor creature, she says she can't so much as look you in the face, therefore she'll come to you in a mask. And you must excuse her, if she make you no answer to any question of yours, till you have brought her to Mr. Horner; and if you will not chide her, nor question her, she'll come out to you immediately.

*Pinch.* Let her come: I will not speak a word to her, nor require a word from her.

*Mrs. Pinch.* Oh, I forgot: besides, she says she cannot look you in the face, though through a mask; therefore would desire you to put out the candle.

*Pinch.* I agree to all. Let her make haste.—There, 'tis out.— [*Puts out the candle.* Exit *Mrs.* PINCHWIFE.] My case is something better: I'd rather fight with Horner for not lying with my sister, than for lying with my wife; and of the two, I had rather find my sister too forward than my wife. I expected no other from her free education, as she calls it, and her passion for the town. Well, wife and sister are names which make us expect love and duty, pleasure and comfort; but we find 'em plagues and torments, and are equally, though differently, troublesome to their keeper; for we have as much ado to get people to lie with our sisters as to keep 'em from lying with our wives.

*Re-enter* Mrs. PINCHWIFE *masked, and in hoods and scarfs, and a night-gown and petticoat of* ALITHEA'S.

What, are you come, sister? let us go then.—But first, let me lock up my wife. Mrs. Margery, where are you?

*Mrs. Pinch.* Here, bud.

*Pinch.* Come hither, that I may lock you up: get you in.—
[*Locks the door.*] Come, sister, where are you now?

[Mrs. PINCHWIFE *gives him her hand ; but when he lets her
go, she steals softly on to the other side of him, and is led
away by him for his* Sister, ALITHEA.

### SCENE II.—HORNER's *Lodging*

#### HORNER *and* Quack.

*Quack.* What, all alone? not so much as one of your cuckolds
here, nor one of their wives! They use to take their turns with
you, as if they were to watch you.

*Horn.* Yes, it often happens that a cuckold is but his wife's
spy, and is more upon family duty when he is with her gallant
abroad, hindering his pleasure, than when he is at home with
her playing the gallant. But the hardest duty a married woman
imposes upon a lover is keeping her husband company always.

*Quack.* And his fondness wearies you almost as soon as hers.

*Horn.* A pox! keeping a cuckold company, after you have
had his wife, is as tiresome as the company of a country squire to
a witty fellow of the town, when he has got all his money.

*Quack.* And as at first a man makes a friend of the husband to
get the wife, so at last you are fain to fall out with the wife to
be rid of the husband.

*Horn.* Ay, most cuckold-makers are true courtiers; when once
a poor man has cracked his credit for 'em, they can't abide to
come near him.

*Quack.* But at first, to draw him in, are so sweet, so kind, so
dear! just as you are to Pinchwife. But what becomes of that
intrigue with his wife?

*Horn.* A pox! he's as surly as an alderman that has been bit;
and since he's so coy, his wife's kindness is in vain, for she's a
silly innocent.

*Quack.* Did she not send you a letter by him?

*Horn.* Yes; but that's a riddle I have not yet solved. Allow
the poor creature to be willing, she is silly too, and he keeps her
up so close——

*Quack.* Yes, so close, that he makes her but the more willing,
and adds but revenge to her love; which two, when met, seldom
fail of satisfying each other one way or other.

*Horn.* What! here's the man we are talking of, I think.

*Enter* PINCHWIFE, *leading in his* Wife *masked, muffled,
and in her* Sister's *gown.*

Pshaw!

*Quack.* Bringing his wife to you is the next thing to bringing
a love-letter from her.

*Horn.* What means this?

*Pinch.* The last time, you know, sir, I brought you a love-letter; now, you see, a mistress; I think you'll say I am a civil man to you.

*Horn.* Ay, the devil take me, will I say thou art the civilest man I ever met with; and I have known some. I fancy I understand thee now better than I did the letter. But, hark thee, in thy ear——

*Pinch.* What?

*Horn.* Nothing but the usual question, man: is she sound, on thy word?

*Pinch.* What, you take her for a wench, and me for a pimp?

*Horn.* Pshaw! wench and pimp, paw words; I know thou art an honest fellow, and hast a great acquaintance among the ladies, and perhaps hast made love for me, rather than let me make love to thy wife.

*Pinch.* Come, sir, in short, I am for no fooling.

*Horn.* Nor I neither: therefore prithee, let's see her face presently. Make her show, man: art thou sure I don't know her?

*Pinch.* I am sure you do know her.

*Horn.* A pox! why dost thou bring her to me then?

*Pinch.* Because she's a relation of mine——

*Horn.* Is she, faith, man? then thou art still more civil and obliging, dear rogue.

*Pinch.* Who desired me to bring her to you.

*Horn.* Then she is obliging, dear rogue.

*Pinch.* You'll make her welcome for my sake, I hope.

*Horn.* I hope she is handsome enough to make herself welcome. Prithee let her unmask.

*Pinch.* Do you speak to her; she would never be ruled by me.

*Horn.* Madam—— [Mrs. PINCHWIFE *whispers to* HORNER.] She says she must speak with me in private. Withdraw, prithee.

*Pinch.* [*aside*]. She's unwilling, it seems, I should know all her indecent conduct in this business.—[*Aloud.*] Well then, I'll leave you together, and hope when I am gone, you'll agree; if not, you and I shan't agree, sir.

*Horn.* What means the fool? if she and I agree 'tis no matter what you and I do.

[*Whispers to* Mrs. PINCHWIFE, *who makes signs with her hand for him to be gone.*

*Pinch.* In the meantime I'll fetch a parson, and find out Sparkish, and disabuse him. You would have me fetch a parson, would you not? Well then—now I think I am rid of her, and shall have no more trouble with her—our sisters and daughters, like usurers' money, are safest when put out; but our wives, like their writings, never safe, but in our closets under lock and key.

[*Exit.*

*Enter* Boy.

*Boy*. Sir Jasper Fidget, sir, is coming up.          [*Exit.*

*Horn*. Here's the trouble of a cuckold now we are talking of. A pox on him! has he not enough to do to hinder his wife's sport, but he must other women's too?—Step in here, madam.

[*Exit* Mrs. PINCHWIFE.

*Enter* Sir JASPER FIDGET.

*Sir Jasp*. My best and dearest friend.

*Horn*. [*aside to* Quack]. The old style, doctor.—[*Aloud.*] Well, be short, for I am busy. What would your impertinent wife have now?

*Sir Jasp*. Well guessed, i'faith; for I do come from her.

*Horn*. To invite me to supper! Tell her, I can't come: go.

*Sir Jasp*. Nay, now you are out, faith; for my lady, and the whole knot of the virtuous gang, as they call themselves, are resolved upon a frolic of coming to you to-night in a masquerade, and are all dressed already.

*Horn*. I shan't be at home.

*Sir Jasp*. [*aside*]. Lord, how churlish he is to women!— [*Aloud.*] Nay, prithee don't disappoint 'em; they'll think 'tis my fault: prithee don't. I'll send in the banquet and the fiddles. But make no noise on't; for the poor virtuous rogues would not have it known, for the world, that they go a-masquerading; and they would come to no man's ball but yours.

*Horn*. Well, well—get you gone; and tell 'em, if they come, 'twill be at the peril of their honour and yours.

*Sir Jasp*. He! he! he!—we'll trust you for that: farewell.

[*Exit.*

*Horn*. Doctor, anon you too shall be my guest,
    But now I'm going to a private feast.          [*Exeunt.*

SCENE III.—*The Piazza of Covent Garden*

*Enter* SPARKISH *with a letter in his hand,* PINCHWIFE *following.*

*Spark*. But who would have thought a woman could have been false to me? By the world, I could not have thought it.

*Pinch*. You were for giving and taking liberty: she has taken it only, sir, now you find in that letter. You are a frank person, and so is she, you see there.

*Spark*. Nay, if this be her hand—for I never saw it.

*Pinch*. 'Tis no matter whether that be her hand or no; I am sure this hand, at her desire, led her to Mr. Horner, with whom I left her just now, to go fetch a parson to 'em at their desire too, to deprive you of her for ever; for it seems yours was but a mock marriage.

*Spark.* Indeed, she would needs have it that 'twas Harcourt himself, in a parson's habit, that married us; but I'm sure he told me 'twas his brother Ned.

*Pinch.* O, there 'tis out; and you were deceived, not she: for you are such a frank person. But I must be gone.—You'll find her at Mr. Horner's. Go, and believe your eyes.    [*Exit.*

*Spark.* Nay, I'll to her, and call her as many crocodiles, sirens, harpies, and other heathenish names, as a poet would do a mistress who had refused to hear his suit, nay more, his verses on her.—But stay, is not that she following a torch at t'other end of the Piazza? and from Horner's certainly—'tis so.

*Enter* ALITHEA *following a torch, and* LUCY *behind.*

You are well met, madam, though you don't think so. What, you have made a short visit to Mr. Horner? but I suppose you'll return to him presently, by that time the parson can be with him.

*Alith.* Mr. Horner and the parson, sir!

*Spark.* Come, madam, no more dissembling, no more jilting; for I am no more a frank person.

*Alith.* How's this?

*Lucy.* So, 'twill work, I see.    [*Aside.*

*Spark.* Could you find out no easy country fool to abuse? none but me, a gentleman of wit and pleasure about the town? But it was your pride to be too hard for a man of parts, unworthy false woman! false as a friend that lends a man money to lose; false as dice, who undo those that trust all they have to 'em.

*Lucy.* He has been a great bubble, by his similes, as they say.
    [*Aside.*

*Alith.* You have been too merry, sir, at your wedding-dinner, sure.

*Spark.* What, d'ye mock me too?

*Alith.* Or you have been deluded.

*Spark.* By you.

*Alith.* Let me understand you.

*Spark.* Have you the confidence (I should call it something else, since you know your guilt) to stand my just reproaches? you did not write an impudent letter to Mr. Horner? who I find now has clubbed with you in deluding me with his aversion for women, that I might not, forsooth, suspect him for my rival.

*Lucy.* D'ye think the gentleman can be jealous now, madam?
    [*Aside.*

*Alith.* I write a letter to Mr. Horner!

*Spark.* Nay, madam, do not deny it. Your brother showed it me just now; and told me likewise, he left you at Horner's lodging to fetch a parson to marry you to him: and I wish you joy, madam, joy, joy; and to him too, much joy; and to myself more joy, for not marrying you.

*Alith.* [*aside*]. So, I find my brother would break off the match; and I can consent to't, since I see this gentleman can be made jealous.—[*Aloud.*]  O Lucy, by his rude usage and jealousy, he makes me almost afraid I am married to him.  Art thou sure 'twas Harcourt himself, and no parson, that married us?

*Spark.* No, madam, I thank you.  I suppose, that was a contrivance too of Mr. Horner's and yours, to make Harcourt play the parson; but I would as little as you have him one now, no, not for the world.  For, shall I tell you another truth?  I never had any passion for you till now, for now I hate you.  'Tis true, I might have married your portion, as other men of parts of the town do sometimes: and so, your servant.  And to show my unconcernedness, I'll come to your wedding, and resign you with as much joy, as I would a stale wench to a new cully; nay, with as much joy as I would after the first night, if I had been married to you.  There's for you; and so your servant, servant.    [*Exit.*

*Alith.* How was I deceived in a man!

*Lucy.* You'll believe then a fool may be made jealous now? for that easiness in him that suffers him to be led by a wife, will likewise permit him to be persuaded against her by others.

*Alith.* But marry Mr. Horner! my brother does not intend it, sure: if I thought he did, I would take thy advice, and Mr. Harcourt for my husband.  And now I wish, that if there be any over-wise woman of the town, who, like me, would marry a fool for fortune, liberty, or title, first, that her husband may love play, and be a cully to all the town but her, and suffer none but Fortune to be mistress of his purse; then, if for liberty, that he may send her into the country, under the conduct of some huswifely mother-in-law; and if for title, may the world give 'em none but that of cuckold.

*Lucy.* And for her greater curse, madam, may he not deserve it.

*Alith.* Away, impertinent!  Is not this my old Lady Lanterlu's?

*Lucy.* Yes, madam.—[*Aside.*]  And here I hope we shall find Mr. Harcourt.    [*Exeunt.*


SCENE IV.—HORNER's *Lodging.    A table, banquet, and bottles*

*Enter* HORNER, Lady FIDGET, Mrs. DAINTY FIDGET, *and* Mrs SQUEAMISH.

*Horn.*  A pox! they are come too soon—before I have sent back my new mistress.  All that I have now to do is to lock her in, that they may not see her.    [*Aside.*

*Lady Fid.* That we may be sure of our welcome, we have brought our entertainment with us, and are resolved to treat thee, dear toad.

*Mrs. Dain.* And that we may be merry to purpose, have left

Sir Jasper and my old Lady Squeamish quarrelling at home at backgammon.

*Mrs. Squeam.* Therefore let us make use of our time, lest they should chance to interrupt us.

*Lady Fid.* Let us sit then.

*Horn.* First, that you may be private, let me lock this door and that, and I'll wait upon you presently.

*Lady Fid.* No, sir, shut 'em only, and your lips for ever; for we must trust you as much as our women.

*Horn.* You know all vanity's killed in me; I have no occasion for talking.

*Lady Fid.* Now, ladies, supposing we had drank each of us our two bottles, let us speak the truth of our hearts.

*Mrs. Dain, and Mrs. Squeam.* Agreed.

*Lady Fid.* By this brimmer, for truth is nowhere else to be found—[*aside to Horner*] not in thy heart, false man!

*Horn.* You have found me a true man, I'm sure.

[*Aside to Lady* FIDGET.

*Lady Fid.* [*aside to* HORNER]. Not every way.—But let us sit and be merry.                                   [*Sings.*

> Why should our damned tyrants oblige us to live
> On the pittance of pleasure which they only give?
>       We must not rejoice
>       With wine and with noise:
> In vain we must wake in a dull bed alone,
> Whilst to our warm rival the bottle they're gone.
>       Then lay aside charms,
>       And take up these arms.
> 'Tis wine only gives 'em their courage and wit;
> Because we live sober, to men we submit.
>       If for beauties you'd pass,
>       Take a lick of the glass,
> 'Twill mend your complexions, and when they are gone,
>       The best red we have is the red of the grape:
> Then, sisters, lay't on,
>       And damn a good shape.

*Mrs. Dain.* Dear brimmer! Well, in token of our openness and plain-dealing, let us throw our masks over our heads.

*Horn.* So, 'twill come to the glasses anon.          [*Aside.*

*Mrs. Squeam.* Lovely brimmer! let me enjoy him first.

*Lady Fid.* No, I never part with a gallant till I've tried him. Dear brimmer! that makest our husbands short-sighted.

*Mrs. Dain.* And our bashful gallants bold.

*Mrs. Squeam.* And, for want of a gallant, the butler lovely in our eyes.—Drink, eunuch.

*Lady Fid.* Drink, thou representative of a husband.—Damn a husband!

*Mrs. Dain.* And, as it were a husband, an old keeper.

*Mrs. Squeam.* And an old grandmother.

*Horn.* And an English bawd, and a French surgeon.

*Lady Fid.* Ay, we have all reason to curse 'em.

*Horn.* For my sake, ladies?

*Lady Fid.* No, for our own; for the first spoils all young gallants' industry.

*Mrs. Dain.* And the other's art makes 'em bold only with common women.

*Mrs. Squeam.* And rather run the hazard of the vile distemper amongst them, than of a denial amongst us.

*Mrs. Dain.* The filthy toads choose mistresses now as they do stuffs, for having been fancied and worn by others.

*Mrs. Squeam.* For being common and cheap.

*Lady Fid.* Whilst women of quality, like the richest stuffs, lie untumbled, and unasked for.

*Horn.* Ay, neat, and cheap, and new, often they think best.

*Mrs. Dain.* No, sir, the beasts will be known by a mistress longer than by a suit.

*Mrs. Squeam.* And 'tis not for cheapness neither.

*Lady Fid.* No; for the vain fops will take up druggets and embroider 'em. But I wonder at the depraved appetites of witty men; they use to be out of the common road, and hate imitation. Pray tell me, beast, when you were a man, why you rather chose to club with a multitude in a common house for an entertainment, than to be the only guest at a good table.

*Horn.* Why, faith, ceremony and expectation are unsufferable to those that are sharp bent. People always eat with the best stomach at an ordinary, where every man is snatching for the best bit.

*Lady Fid.* Though he get a cut over the fingers.—But I have heard, that people eat most heartily of another man's meat, that is, what they do not pay for.

*Horn.* When they are sure of their welcome and freedom; for ceremony in love and eating is as ridiculous as in fighting: falling on briskly is all should be done on those occasions.

*Lady Fid.* Well then, let me tell you, sir, there is nowhere more freedom than in our houses; and we take freedom from a young person as a sign of good breeding; and a person may be as free as he pleases with us, as frolic, as gamesome, as wild as he will.

*Horn.* Han't I heard you all declaim against wild men?

*Lady Fid.* Yes; but for all that, we think wildness in a man as desirable a quality as in a duck or rabbit: a tame man! foh!

*Horn.* I know not, but your reputations frightened me as much as your faces invited me.

*Lady Fid.* Our reputation! Lord, why should you not think that we women make use of our reputation, as you men of yours, only to deceive the world with less suspicion? Our virtue is like the statesman's religion, the quaker's word, the gamester's oath, and the great man's honour; but to cheat those that trust us.

*Mrs. Squeam.* And that demureness, coyness, and modesty, that you see in our faces in the boxes at plays, is as much a sign of a kind woman as a vizard-mask in the pit.

*Mrs. Dain.* For, I assure you, women are least masked when they have the velvet vizard on.

*Lady Fid.* You would have found us modest women in our denials only.

*Mrs. Squeam.* Our bashfulness is only the reflection of the men's.

*Mrs. Dain.* We blush when they are shamefaced.

*Horn.* I beg your pardon, ladies, I was deceived in you devilishly. But why that mighty pretence to honour?

*Lady Fid.* We have told you; but sometimes 'twas for the same reason you men pretend business often, to avoid ill company, to enjoy the better and more privately those you love.

*Horn.* But why would you ne'er give a friend a wink then?

*Lady Fid.* Faith, your reputation frightened us, as much as ours did you, you were so notoriously lewd.

*Horn.* And you so seemingly honest.

*Lady Fid.* Was that all that deterred you?

*Horn.* And so expensive—you allow freedom, you say.

*Lady Fid.* Ay, ay.

*Horn.* That I was afraid of losing my little money, as well as my little time, both which my other pleasures required.

*Lady Fid.* Money! foh! you talk like a little fellow now: do such as we expect money?

*Horn.* I beg your pardon, madam, I must confess, I have heard that great ladies, like great merchants, set but the higher prices upon what they have, because they are not in necessity of taking the first offer.

*Mrs. Dain.* Such as we make sale of our hearts?

*Mrs. Squeam.* We bribed for our love? foh!

*Horn.* With your pardon, ladies, I know, like great men in offices, you seem to exact flattery and attendance only from your followers; but you have receivers about you, and such fees to pay, a man is afraid to pass your grants. Besides, we must let you win at cards, or we lose your hearts; and if you make an assignation, 'tis at a goldsmith's, jeweller's, or china-house; where for your honour you deposit to him, he must pawn his to the punctual cit, and so paying for what you take up, pays for what he takes up.

*Mrs. Dain.* Would you not have us assured of our gallants' love?

*Mrs. Squeam.* For love is better known by liberality than by jealousy.

*Lady Fid.* For one may be dissembled, the other not.—[*Aside.*]

But my jealousy can be no longer dissembled, and they are telling ripe.—[*Aloud.*]—Come, here's to our gallants in waiting, whom we must name, and I'll begin.   This is my false rogue.
                                          [*Claps him on the back.*

*Mrs. Squeam.* How!
*Horn.* So, all will out now.                        [*Aside.*
*Mrs. Squeam.* Did you not tell me, 'twas for my sake only you reported yourself no man?         [*Aside to* HORNER.
*Mrs. Dain.* Oh, wretch! did you not swear to me, 'twas for my love and honour you passed for that thing you do?
                                          [*Aside to* HORNER.
*Horn.* So, so.
*Lady Fid.* Come, speak, ladies: this is my false villain.
*Mrs. Squeam.* And mine too.
*Mrs. Dain.* And mine.
*Horn.* Well then, you are all three my false rogues too, and there's an end on't.
*Lady Fid.* Well then, there's no remedy; sister sharers, let us not fall out, but have a care of our honour.   Though we get no presents, no jewels of him, we are savers of our honour, the jewel of most value and use, which shines yet to the world unsuspected, though it be counterfeit.
*Horn.* Nay, and is e'en as good as if it were true, provided the world think so; for honour, like beauty now, only depends on the opinion of others.
*Lady Fid.* Well, Harry Common, I hope you can be true to three.   Swear; but 'tis to no purpose to require your oath, for you are as often forsworn as you swear to new women.
*Horn.* Come, faith, madam, let us e'en pardon one another; for all the difference I find betwixt we men and you women, we forswear ourselves at the beginning of an amour, you as long as it lasts.

*Enter* Sir JASPER FIDGET, *and* Old Lady SQUEAMISH.

*Sir Jasp.* Oh, my Lady Fidget, was this your cunning, to come to Mr. Horner without me? but you have been nowhere else, I hope.
*Lady Fid.* No, Sir Jasper.
*Lady Squeam.* And you came straight hither, Biddy?
*Mrs. Squeam.* Yes, indeed, lady grandmother.
*Sir Jasp.* 'Tis well, 'tis well; I knew when once they were thoroughly acquainted with poor Horner, they'd ne'er be from him: you may let her masquerade it with my wife and Horner, and I warrant her reputation safe.

*Enter* Boy.

*Boy.* O, sir, here's the gentleman come, whom you bid me not suffer to come up, without giving you notice, with a lady too, and other gentlemen.

*Horn.* Do you all go in there, whilst I send 'em away; and, boy, do you desire 'em to stay below till I come, which shall be immediately.

[*Exeunt* Sir JASPER FIDGET, Lady FIDGET, Lady SQUEAMISH, Mrs. SQUEAMISH, *and* Mrs. DAINTY FIDGET.

*Boy.* Yes, sir. [*Exit.*

[*Exit* HORNER *at the other door, and returns with* Mrs. PINCHWIFE.

*Horn.* You would not take my advice, to be gone home before your husband came back, he'll now discover all; yet pray, my dearest, be persuaded to go home, and leave the rest to my management; I'll let you down the back way.

*Mrs. Pinch.* I don't know the way home, so I don't.

*Horn.* My man shall wait upon you.

*Mrs. Pinch.* No, don't you believe that I'll go at all; what, are you weary of me already?

*Horn.* No, my life, 'tis that I may love you long, 'tis to secure my love, and your reputation with your husband; he'll never receive you again else.

*Mrs. Pinch.* What care I? d'ye think to frighten me with that? I don't intend to go to him again; you shall be my husband now.

*Horn.* I cannot be your husband, dearest, since you are married to him.

*Mrs. Pinch.* O, would you make me believe that? Don't I see every day at London here, women leave their first husbands, and go and live with other men as their wives? pish, pshaw! you'd make me angry, but that I love you so mainly.

*Horn.* So, they are coming up—In again, in, I hear 'em.— [*Exit* Mrs. PINCHWIFE.] Well, a silly mistress is like a weak place, soon got, soon lost, a man has scarce time for plunder; she betrays her husband first to her gallant, and then her gallant to her husband.

*Enter* PINCHWIFE, ALITHEA, HARCOURT, SPARKISH, LUCY, *and a* Parson.

*Pinch.* Come, madam, 'tis not the sudden change of your dress, the confidence of your asseverations, and your false witness there, shall persuade me I did not bring you hither just now; here's my witness, who cannot deny it, since you must be confronted.—Mr. Horner, did not I bring this lady to you just now?

*Horn.* Now must I wrong one woman for another's sake,— but that's no new thing with me, for in these cases I am still on the criminal's side against the innocent. [*Aside.*

*Alith.* Pray speak, sir.

*Horn.* It must be so. I must be impudent, and try my luck; impudence uses to be too hard for truth. [*Aside.*

*Pinch.* What, you are studying an evasion or excuse for her! Speak, sir.

*Horn.* No, faith, I am something backward only to speak in women's affairs or disputes.

*Pinch.* She bids you speak.

*Alith.* Ah, pray, sir, do, pray satisfy him.

*Horn.* Then truly, you did bring that lady to me just now.

*Pinch.* O ho!

*Alith.* How, sir?

*Har.* How, Horner?

*Alith.* What mean you, sir? I always took you for a man of honour.

*Horn.* Ay, so much a man of honour, that I must save my mistress, I thank you, come what will on't.                [*Aside.*

*Spark.* So, if I had had her, she'd have made me believe the moon had been made of a Christmas pie.

*Lucy.* Now could I speak, if I durst, and solve the riddle, who am the author of it.                [*Aside.*

*Alith.* O unfortunate woman! A combination against my honour! which most concerns me now, because you share in my disgrace, sir, and it is your censure, which I must now suffer, that troubles me, not theirs.

*Har.* Madam, then have no trouble, you shall now see 'tis possible for me to love too, without being jealous; I will not only believe your innocence myself, but make all the world believe it.—[*Aside to* HORNER.] Horner, I must now be concerned for this lady's honour.

*Horn.* And I must be concerned for a lady's honour too.

*Har.* This lady has her honour, and I will protect it.

*Horn.* My lady has not her honour, but has given it me to keep, and I will preserve it.

*Har.* I understand you not.

*Horn.* I would not have you.

*Mrs. Pinch.* What's the matter with 'em all?

[*Peeping in behind.*

*Pinch.* Come, come, Mr. Horner, no more disputing; here's the parson, I brought him not in vain.

*Har.* No, sir, I'll employ him, if this lady please.

*Pinch.* How! what d'ye mean?

*Spark.* Ay, what does he mean?

*Horn.* Why, I have resigned your sister to him, he has my consent.

*Pinch.* But he has not mine, sir; a woman's injured honour, no more than a man's, can be repaired or satisfied by any but him that first wronged it; and you shall marry her presently, or——

[*Lays his hand on his sword.*

### Re-enter Mrs. PINCHWIFE.

*Mrs. Pinch.* O Lord, they'll kill poor Mr. Horner! besides, he shan't marry her whilst I stand by, and look on; I'll not lose my second husband so.

*Pinch.* What do I see?

*Alith.* My sister in my clothes!

*Spark.* Ha!

*Mrs. Pinch.* Nay, pray now don't quarrel about finding work for the parson, he shall marry me to Mr. Horner; for now, I believe, you have enough of me.          [*To* PINCHWIFE.

*Horn.* Damned, damned loving changeling!.          [*Aside.*

*Mrs. Pinch.* Pray, sister, pardon me for telling so many lies of you.

*Horn.* I suppose the riddle is plain now.

*Lucy.* No, that must be my work.—Good sir, hear me.

          [*Kneels to* PINCHWIFE, *who stands doggedly with his hat over his eyes.*

*Pinch.* I will never hear woman again, but make 'em all silent thus——          [*Offers to draw upon his* Wife.

*Horn.* No, that must not be.

*Pinch.* You then shall go first, 'tis all one to me.

          [*Offers to draw on* HORNER, *but is stopped by* HARCOURT.

*Har.* Hold!


*Re-enter* Sir JASPER FIDGET, Lady FIDGET, Lady SQUEAMISH, Mrs. DAINTY FIDGET, *and* Mrs. SQUEAMISH.


*Sir Jasp.* What's the matter? what's the matter? pray, what's the matter, sir? I beseech you communicate, sir.

*Pinch.* Why, my wife has communicated, sir, as your wife may have done too, sir, if she knows him, sir.

*Sir Jasp.* Pshaw, with him! ha! ha! he!

*Pinch.* D'ye mock me, sir? a cuckold is a kind of a wild beast; have a care, sir.

*Sir Jasp.* No, sure, you mock me, sir. He cuckold you! it can't be, ha! ha! he! why, I'll tell you, sir——

          [*Offers to whisper.*

*Pinch.* I tell you again, he has whored my wife, and yours too, if he knows her, and all the women he comes near; 'tis not his dissembling, his hypocrisy, can wheedle me.

*Sir Jasp.* How! does he dissemble? is he an hypocrite? Nay, then—how—wife—sister, is he an hypocrite?

*Lady Squeam.* An hypocrite! a dissembler! Speak, young harlotry, speak, how?

*Sir Jasp.* Nay, then—O my head too!—O thou libidinous lady!

*Lady Squeam.* O thou harloting harlotry! hast thou done't then?

*Sir Jasp.* Speak, good Horner, art thou a dissembler, a rogue? hast thou——

*Horn.* Soh—

*Lucy.* I'll fetch you off, and her too, if she will but hold her tongue.          [*Apart to* HORNER.

*Horn.* Canst thou? I'll give thee——        [*Apart to* LUCY.

*Lucy* [*to* PINCHWIFE]. Pray have but patience to hear me, sir, who am the unfortunate cause of all this confusion. Your wife is innocent, I only culpable; for I put her upon telling you all these lies concerning my mistress, in order to the breaking off the match between Mr. Sparkish and her, to make way for Mr. Harcourt.

*Spark.* Did you so, eternal rotten tooth? Then, it seems, my mistress was not false to me, I was only deceived by you. Brother, that should have been, now man of conduct, who is a frank person now, to bring your wife to her lover, ha?

*Lucy.* I assure you, sir, she came not to Mr. Horner out of love, for she loves him no more——

*Mrs. Pinch.* Hold, I told lies for you, but you shall tell none for me, for I do love Mr. Horner with all my soul, and nobody shall say me nay; pray, don't you go to make poor Mr. Horner believe to the contrary; 'tis spitefully done of you, I'm sure.

*Horn.* Peace, dear idiot.        [*Aside to* Mrs. PINCHWIFE.

*Mrs. Pinch.* Nay, I will not peace.

*Pinch.* Not till I make you.

### *Enter* DORILANT *and* Quack.

*Dor.* Horner, your servant; I am the doctor's guest, he must excuse our intrusion.

*Quack.* But what's the matter, gentlemen? for Heaven's sake, what's the matter?

*Horn.* Oh, 'tis well you are come. 'Tis a censorious world we live in; you may have brought me a reprieve, or else I had died for a crime I never committed, and these innocent ladies had suffered with me; therefore, pray satisfy these worthy, honourable, jealous gentlemen—that——        [*Whispers.*

*Quack.* O, I understand you, is that all?—Sir Jasper, by Heavens, and upon the word of a physician, sir——
        [*Whispers to* Sir JASPER.

*Sir Jasp.* Nay, I do believe you truly.—Pardon me, my virtuous lady, and dear of honour.

*Lady Squeam.* What, then all's right again?

*Sir Jasp.* Ay, ay, and now let us satisfy him too.
        [*They whisper with* PINCHWIFE.

*Pinch.* An eunuch! Pray, no fooling with me.

*Quack.* I'll bring half the surgeons in town to swear it.

*Pinch.* They!—they'll swear a man that bled to death through his wounds died of an apoplexy.

*Quack.* Pray, hear me, sir—why, all the town has heard the report of him.

*Pinch.* But does all the town believe it?

*Quack.* Pray, inquire a little, and first of all these.

*Pinch.* I'm sure when I left the town, he was the lewdest fellow in't.

*Quack.* I tell you, sir, he has been in France since; pray, ask but these ladies and gentlemen, your friend Mr. Dorilant. Gentlemen and ladies, han't you all heard the late sad report of poor Mr. Horner?

*All the Ladies.* Ay, ay, ay.

*Dor.* Why, thou jealous fool, dost thou doubt it? he's an arrant French capon.

*Mrs. Pinch.* 'Tis false, sir, you shall not disparage poor Mr. Horner, for to my certain knowledge——

*Lucy.* O, hold!

*Mrs. Squeam.* Stop her mouth!  [*Aside to* LUCY.

*Lady Fid.* Upon my honour, sir, 'tis as true——[*To* PINCHWIFE.

*Mrs. Dain.* D'ye think we would have been seen in his company?

*Mrs. Squeam.* Trust our unspotted reputations with him?

*Lady Fid.* This you get, and we too, by trusting your secret to a fool.  [*Aside to* HORNER.

*Horn.* Peace, madam.—[*Aside to* Quack.] Well, doctor, is not this a good design, that carries a man on unsuspected, and brings him off safe?

*Pinch.* Well, if this were true—but my wife——  [*Aside.*
[DORILANT *whispers with* Mrs. PINCHWIFE.

*Alith.* Come, brother, your wife is yet innocent, you see; but have a care of too strong an imagination, lest, like an over-concerned timorous gamester, by fancying an unlucky cast, it should come. Women and fortune are truest still to those that trust 'em.

*Lucy.* And any wild thing grows but the more fierce and hungry for being kept up, and more dangerous to the keeper.

*Alith.* There's doctrine for all husbands, Mr. Harcourt.

*Har.* I edify, madam, so much, that I am impatient till I am one.

*Dor.* And I edify so much by example, I will never be one.

*Spark.* And because I will not disparage my parts, I'll ne'er be one.

*Horn.* And I, alas! can't be one. ·

*Pinch.* But I must be one—against my will to a country wife, with a country murrain to me!

*Mrs. Pinch.* And I must be a country wife still too, I find; for I can't, like a city one, be rid of my musty husband, and do what I list.  [*Aside.*

*Horn.* Now, sir, I must pronounce your wife innocent, though I blush whilst I do it; and I am the only man by her now exposed to shame, which I will straight drown in wine, as you shall your suspicion; and the ladies' troubles we'll divert with a ballad.— Doctor, where are your maskers?

*Lucy.* Indeed, she's innocent, sir, I am her witness; and her end of coming out was but to see her sister's wedding; and what she has said to your face of her love to Mr. Horner, was but the usual innocent revenge on a husband's jealousy;—was it not, madam, speak?

*Mrs. Pinch.* [*aside to* LUCY *and* HORNER]. Since you'll have me tell more lies—[*Aloud.*] Yes, indeed, bud.

    *Pinch.* For my own sake fain I would all believe;

        Cuckolds, like lovers, should themselves deceive.

        But——                       [*Sighs.*

        His honour is least safe (too late I find)

        Who trusts it with a foolish wife or friend.


### A Dance of Cuckolds.


    *Horn.* Vain fops but court and dress, and keep a pother,

        To pass for women's men with one another;

        But he who aims by women to be prized,

        First by the men, you see, must be despised.      [*Exeunt.*

# EPILOGUE

## SPOKEN BY MRS. KNEP

Now you the vigorous, who daily here
O'er vizard-mask in public domineer,
And what you'd do to her, if in place where;
Nay, have the confidence to cry, " Come out! "
Yet when she says, " Lead on! " you are not stout;
But to your well-dressed brother straight turn round,
And cry, " Pox on her, Ned, she can't be sound! "
Then slink away, a fresh one to engage,
With so much seeming heat and loving rage,
You'd frighten listening actress on the stage;
Till she at last has seen you huffing come,
And talk of keeping in the tiring-room,
Yet cannot be provoked to lead her home.
Next, you Falstaffs of fifty, who beset
Your buckram maidenheads, which your friends get;
And whilst to them you of achievements boast,
They share the booty, and laugh at your cost.
In fine, you essenced boys, both old and young,
Who would be thought so eager, brisk, and strong,
Yet do the ladies, not their husbands wrong;
Whose purses for your manhood make excuse,
And keep your Flanders mares for show not use;
Encouraged by our woman's man to-day,
A Horner's part may vainly think to play;
And may intrigues so bashfully disown,
That they may doubted be by few or none;
May kiss the cards at picquet, ombre, loo,
And so be thought to kiss the lady too;
But, gallants, have a care, faith, what you do.
The world, which to no man his due will give,
You by experience know you can deceive,
And men may still believe you vigorous,
But then we women—there's no cozening us.

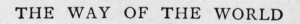

# THE WAY OF THE WORLD

# DRAMATIS PERSONÆ

FAINALL, in love with Mrs. Marwood  .  . Mr. BETTERTON.
MIRABELL, in love with Mrs. Millamant .  . Mr. VERBRUGGEN.
WITWOUD  &#125; Followers of Mrs. Millamant .  &#123; Mr. BOWEN.
PETULANT &#125;         &#123; Mr. BOWMAN.
Sir WILFULL WITWOUD, Half-brother to Wit-
 woud, and Nephew to Lady Wishfort . . Mr. UNDERHILL.
WAITWELL, Servant to Mirabell  .  .  . Mr. BRIGHT.

Lady WISHFORT, Enemy to Mirabell, for having
 falsely pretended love to her  .  .  . Mrs. LEIGH.
Mrs. MILLAMANT, a fine lady, Niece to Lady
 Wishfort, and loves Mirabell  .  .  . Mrs. BRACEGIRDLE.
Mrs. MARWOOD, Friend to Mr. Fainall, and likes
 Mirabell . . . . . . . Mrs. BARRY.
Mrs. FAINALL, Daughter to Lady Wishfort, and
 wife to Fainall, formerly friend to Mirabell . Mrs. BOWMAN.
FOIBLE, Woman to Lady Wishfort.  .  . Mrs. WILLIS.
MINCING, Woman to Mrs. Millamant  .  . Mrs. PRINCE.

Dancers, Footmen, and Attendants.

SCENE—LONDON.

*The time equal to that of the presentation.*

# RALPH, EARL OF MOUNTAGUE, &c.

My Lord,—Whether the world will arraign me of vanity, or not, that I have presumed to dedicate this comedy to your lordship, I am yet in doubt. though it may be it is some degree of vanity even to doubt of it. One who has at any time had the honour of your lordship's conversation, cannot be supposed to think very meanly of that which he would prefer to your perusal: yet it were to incur the imputation of too much sufficiency, to pretend to such a merit as might abide the test of your lordship's censure.

Whatever value may be wanting to this play while yet it is mine, will be sufficiently made up to it, when it is once become your lordship's; and it is my security, that I cannot have overrated it more by my dedication, than your lordship will dignify it by your patronage.

That it succeeded on the stage, was almost beyond my expectation; for but little of it was prepared for that general taste which seems now to be predominant in the pallats of our audience.

Those characters which are meant to be ridiculed in most of our comedies, are of fools so gross, that in my humble opinion, they should rather disturb than divert the well-natured and reflecting part of an audience; they are rather objects of charity than contempt; and instead of moving our mirth, they ought very often to excite our compassion.

This reflection moved me to design some characters, which should appear ridiculous not so much through a natural folly (which is incorrigible, and therefore not proper for the stage) as through an affected wit; a wit, which at the same time that it is affected, is also false. As there is some difficulty in the formation of a character of this nature, so there is some hazard which attends the progress of its success, upon the stage: for many come to a play, so over-charged with criticism, that they very often let fly their censure, when through their rashness they have mistaken their aim. This I had occasion lately to observe: for this play had been acted two or three days, before some of these hasty judges could find the leisure to distinguish betwixt the character of a Witwoud and a Truewit.

I must beg your lordship's pardon for this digression from the true course of this epistle; but that it may not seem altogether impertinent, I beg, that I may plead the occasion of it, in part of that excuse of which I stand in need, for recommending this comedy to your protection. It is only by the countenance of your lordship, and the *few* so qualified, that such who write with care and pains can hope to be distinguished: for the prostituted name of *poet* promiscuously levels all that bear it.

Terence, the most correct writer in the world, had a Scipio and a Lelius, if not to assist him, at least to support him in his reputation: and notwithstanding his extraordinary merit, it may be, their countenance was not more than necessary.

The purity of his style, the delicacy of his turns, and the justness of his characters, were all of them beauties, which the greater part of his audience were incapable of tasting: some of the coarsest strokes of Plautus, so severely censured by Horace, were more likely to affect the multitude; such, who come with expectation to laugh at the last act of a play, and are better entertained with two or three unseasonable jests, than with the artful solution of the fable.

As Terence excelled in his performances, so had he great advantages to encourage his undertakings; for he built most on the foundations of Menander: his plots were generally modelled, and his characters ready drawn to his hand. He copied Menander; and Menander had no less light in the formation of his characters, from the observations of Theophrastus, of whom he was a disciple; and Theophrastus it is known was not only the disciple, but the immediate successor of Aristotle, the first and greatest judge of poetry. These were great models to design by; and the further advantage which Terence possessed, towards giving his plays the due ornaments of purity of style and justness of manners, was not less considerable, from the freedom of conversation, which was permitted him with Lelius and Scipio, two of the greatest and most polite men of his age. And indeed, the privilege of such a conversation is the only certain means of attaining to the perfection of dialogue.

If it has happened in any part of this comedy, that I have gained a turn of style, or expression more correct, or at least more corrigible than in those which I have formerly written, I must, with equal pride and gratitude, ascribe it to the honour of your lordship's admitting me into your conversation, and that of a society where everybody else was so well worthy of you, in your retirement last summer from the town: for it was immediately after, that this comedy was written. If I have failed in my performance, it is only to be regretted, where there were so many, not inferior either to a Scipio or a Lelius, that there should be one wanting, equal in capacity to a Terence.

If I am not mistaken, poetry is almost the only art which has not yet laid claim to your lordship's patronage. Architecture and painting, to the great honour of our country, have flourished under your influence and protection. In the meantime, poetry, the eldest sister of all arts, and parent of most, seems to have resigned her birthright, by having neglected to pay her duty to your lordship; and by permitting others of a later extraction to prepossess that place in your esteem, to which none can pretend a better title. Poetry, in its nature, is sacred to the good and great; the relation between them is reciprocal, and they are ever propitious to it. It is the privilege of poetry to address to them, and it is their prerogative alone to give it protection.

This received maxim is a general apology for all writers who consecrate their labours to great men: but I could wish, at this time, that this address were exempted from the common pretence of all dedications; and that as I can distinguish your lordship even among the most deserving, so this offering might become remarkable by some particular instance of respect, which should assure your lordship that I am, with all due sense of your extreme worthiness and humanity, my lord, your lordship's most obedient and most obliged humble servant,

WILL. CONGREVE.

# PROLOGUE

## SPOKEN BY MR. BETTERTON

Of those few fools, who with ill stars are curst,
Sure scribling fools, called poets, fare the worst:
For they're a sort of fools which Fortune makes,
And after she has made 'em fools, forsakes.
With Nature's oafs 'tis quite a diff'rent case,
For Fortune favours all her Idiot-race:
In her own nest the Cuckow-eggs we find,
O'er which she broods to hatch the Changling-kind.
No portion for her own she has to spare,
So much she doats on her adopted care.

    Poets are bubbles, by the town drawn in,
Suffered at first some trifling stakes to win:
But what unequal hazards do they run!
Each time they write they venture all they've won: }
The squire that's buttered still, is sure to be undone. }
This author, heretofore, has found your favour,
But pleads no merit from his past behaviour.
To build on that might prove a vain presumption,
Should grants to poets made, admit resumption:
And in Parnassus he must lose his seat,
If that be found a forfeited estate.

    He owns, with toil, he wrought the following scenes,
But if they're naught ne'er spare him for his pains:
Damn him the more; have no commiseration
For dulness on mature deliberation.
He swears he'll not resent one hissed-off scene,
Nor, like those peevish wits, his play maintain,
Who, to assert their sense, your taste arraign.
Some plot we think he has, and some new thought;
Some humour too, no farce; but that's a fault.
Satire, he thinks, you ought not to expect;
For so reformed a town, who dares correct?
To please, this time, has been his sole pretence,
He'll not instruct, lest it should give offence.
Should he by chance a knave or fool expose,
That hurts none here, sure here are none of those.
In short, our play shall (with your leave to shew it)
Give you one instance of a passive poet.
Who to your judgments yields all resignation;
So save or damn, after your own discretion.

# THE WAY OF THE WORLD

## ACT I

### SCENE I.—*A Chocolate-house*

MIRABELL *and* FAINALL [*rising from Cards*], BETTY *waiting*.

*Mira.* You are a fortunate man, Mr. Fainall.

*Fain.* Have we done?

*Mira.* What you please. I'll play on to entertain you.

*Fain.* No, I'll give you your revenge another time, when you are not so indifferent; you are thinking of something else now, and play too negligently; the coldness of a losing gamester lessens the pleasure of the winner. I'd no more play with a man that slighted his ill fortune, than I'd make love to a woman who undervalued the loss of her reputation.

*Mira.* You have a taste extremely delicate, and are for refining on your pleasures.

*Fain.* Prithee, why so reserved? Something has put you out of humour.

*Mira.* Not at all: I happen to be grave to-day; and you are gay; that's all.

*Fain.* Confess, Millamant and you quarrelled last night, after I left you; my fair cousin has some humours that would tempt the patience of a Stoick. What, some coxcomb came in, and was well received by her, while you were by.

*Mira.* Witwoud and Petulant; and what was worse, her aunt, your wife's mother, my evil genius; or to sum up all in her own name, my old Lady Wishfort came in——

*Fain.* O there it is then—she has a lasting passion for you, and with reason.—What, then my wife was there?

*Mira.* Yes, and Mrs. Marwood and three or four more, whom I never saw before; seeing me, they all put on their grave faces, whispered one another, then complained aloud of the vapours, and after fell into a profound silence.

*Fain.* They had a mind to be rid of you.

*Mira.* For which reason I resolved not to stir. At last the good old lady broke through her painful taciturnity, with an invective against long visits. I would not have understood her, but Millamant joining in the argument, I rose and with a constrained smile told her I thought nothing was so easy as to know when a visit began to be troublesome; she redened and I with-drew, without expecting her reply.

*Fain.* You were to blame to resent what she spoke only in compliance with her aunt.

*Mira.* She is more mistress of herself, than to be under the necessity of such a resignation.

*Fain.* What? though half her fortune depends upon her marrying with my lady's approbation?

*Mira.* I was then in such a humour, that I should have been better pleased if she had been less discreet.

*Fain.* Now I remember, I wonder not they were weary of you; last night was one of their cabal-nights; they have 'em three times a week, and meet by turns, at one another's apartments, where they come together like the coroner's inquest, to sit upon the murdered reputations of the week. You and I are excluded; and it was once proposed that all the male sex should be excepted; but somebody moved that to avoid scandal there might be one man of the community; upon which motion Witwoud and Petulant were enrolled members.

*Mira.* And who may have been the foundress of this sect? My Lady Wishfort, I warrant, who publishes her detestation of mankind; and full of the vigour of fifty-five, declares for a friend and ratafia; and let posterity shift for itself, she'll breed no more.

*Fain.* The discovery of your sham addresses to her, to conceal your love to her niece, has provoked this separation: had you dissembled better, things might have continued in the state of nature.

*Mira.* I did as much as man could, with any reasonable conscience; I proceeded to the very last act of flattery with her, and was guilty of a song in her commendation. Nay, I got a friend to put her into a lampoon, and compliment her with the imputation of an affair with a young fellow, which I carried so far, that I told her the malicious town took notice that she was grown fat of a sudden; and when she lay in of a dropsy, persuaded her she was reported to be in labour. The devil's in't, if an old woman is to be flattered further, unless a man should endeavour downright personally to debauch her; and that my vertue forbad me. But for the discovery of this amour, I am indebted to your friend, or your wife's friend, Mrs. Marwood.

*Fain.* What should provoke her to be your enemy, unless she has made you advances, which you have slighted? Women do not easily forgive omissions of that nature.

*Mira.* She was always civil to me, 'till of late; I confess I am not one of those coxcombs who are apt to interpret a woman's good manners to her prejudice; and think that she who does not refuse 'em everything, can refuse 'em nothing.

*Fain.* You are a gallant man, Mirabell; and though you may have cruelty enough, not to satisfy a lady's longing; you have too much generosity, not to be tender of her honour. Yet you speak with an indifference which seems to be affected; and confesses you are conscious of a negligence.

*Mira.* You pursue the argument with a distrust that seems to be unaffected, and confesses you are conscious of a concern for which the lady is more indebted to you, than is your wife.

*Fain.* Fie, fie, friend, if you grow censorious I must leave you;—I'll look upon the gamesters in the next room.

*Mira.* Who are they?

*Fain.* Petulant and Witwoud.—Bring me some chocolate.

*Mira.* Betty, what says your clock?

*Bet.* Turned of the last canonical hour, sir.

*Mira.* How pertinently the jade answers me! Ha! almost one a clock! [*Looking on his watch.*] O, y'are come——

## SCENE II

### MIRABELL *and* Footman.

*Mira.* Well, is the grand affair over? You have been something tedious.

*Serv.* Sir, there's such coupling at Pancras, that they stand behind one another, as 'twere in a country dance. Ours was the last couple to lead up; and no hopes appearing of dispatch, besides, the parson growing hoarse, we were afraid his lungs would have failed before it came to our turn; so we drove round to Duke's Place; and there they were riveted in a trice.

*Mira.* So, so, you are sure they are married.

*Serv.* Married and bedded, sir: I am witness.

*Mira.* Have you the certificate?

*Serv.* Here it is, sir.

*Mira.* Has the tailor brought Waitwell's cloaths home, and the new liveries?

*Serv.* Yes, sir.

*Mira.* That's well. Do you go home again, d'ye hear, and adjourn the consummation 'till farther order; bid Waitwell shake his ears, and Dame Partlet rustle up her feathers, and meet me at one a clock by Rosamond's Pond; that I may see her before she returns to her lady: and as you tender your ears be secret.

## SCENE III

### MIRABELL, FAINALL, BETTY.

*Fain.* Joy of your success, Mirabell; you look pleased.

*Mira.* Ay; I have been engaged in a matter of some sort of mirth, which is not yet ripe for discovery. I am glad this is not a cabal-night. I wonder, Fainall, that you who are married, and of consequence should be discreet, will suffer your wife to be of such a party.

*Fain.* Faith, I am not jealous. Besides, most who are en-gaged are women and relations; and for the men, they are of a kind too contemptible to give scandal.

*Mira.* I am of another opinion. The greater the coxcomb, always the more the scandal: for a woman who is not a fool, can have but one reason for associating with a man who is one.

*Fain.* Are you jealous as often as you see Witwoud enter-tained by Millamant?

*Mira.* Of her understanding I am, if not of her person.

*Fain.* You do her wrong; for to give her her due, she has wit.

*Mira.* She has beauty enough to make any man think so; and complaisance enough not to contradict him who shall tell her so.

*Fain.* For a passionate lover, methinks you are a man some-what too discerning in the failings of your mistress.

*Mira.* And for a discerning man, somewhat too passionate a lover; for I like her with all her faults; nay, like her for her faults. Her follies are so natural, or so artful, that they become her; and those affectations which in another woman would be odious, serve but to make her more agreeable. I'll tell thee, Fainall, she once used me with that insolence, that in revenge I took her to pieces; sifted her, and separated her failings; I studied 'em, and got 'em by rote. The catalogue was so large, that I was not without hopes, one day or other, to hate her heartily: to which end I so used myself to think of 'em, that at length, contrary to my design and expectation, they gave me every hour less and less disturbance; 'till in a few days it became habitual to me, to remember 'em without being dis-pleased. They are now grown as familiar to me as my own frailties; and in all probability in a little time longer I shall like 'em as well.

*Fain.* Marry her, marry her; be half as well acquainted with her charms, as you are with her defects, and my life on't, you are your own man again.

*Mira.* Say you so?

*Fain.* I, I, I have experience: I have a wife, and so forth.


### SCENE IV

*[To them]* Messenger.

*Mess.* Is one Squire Witwoud here?

*Bet.* Yes; what's your business?

*Mess.* I have a letter for him, from his brother, Sir Wilfull, which I am charged to deliver into his own hands.

*Bet.* He's in the next room, friend—that way.

## SCENE V

### MIRABELL, FAINALL, BETTY.

*Mira.* What, is the chief of that noble family in town, Sir Wilfull Witwoud?

*Fain.* He is expected to-day. Do you know him?

*Mira.* I have seen him, he promises to be an extraordinary person; I think you have the honour to be related to him.

*Fain.* Yes; he is half-brother to this Witwoud by a former wife, who was sister to my Lady Wishfort, my wife's mother. If you marry Millamant, you must call cousins too.

*Mira.* I had rather be his relation than his acquaintance.

*Fain.* He comes to town in order to equip himself for travel.

*Mira.* For travel! Why the man that I mean is above forty.

*Fain.* No matter for that; 'tis for the honour of England, that all Europe should know we have blockheads of all ages.

*Mira.* I wonder there is not an act of parliament to save the credit of the nation, and prohibit the exportation of fools.

*Fain.* By no means, 'tis better as 'tis; 'tis better to trade with a little loss, than to be quite eaten up, with being over-stocked.

*Mira.* Pray, are the follies of this knight-errant, and those of the squire his brother, anything related?

*Fain.* Not at all; Witwoud grows by the knight, like a medlar grafted on a crab. One will melt in your mouth, and t'other set your teeth on edge; one is all pulp, and the other all core.

*Mira.* So one will be rotten before he be ripe, and the other will be rotten without ever being ripe at all.

*Fain.* Sir Wilfull is an odd mixture of bashfulness and obstinacy.—But when he's drunk, he's as loving as the monster in the "Tempest;" and much after the same manner. To give t'other his due, he has something of good nature, and does not always want wit.

*Mira.* Not always; but as often as his memory fails him, and his commonplace of comparisons. He is a fool with a good memory, and some few scraps of other folks' wit. He is one whose conversation can never be approved, yet it is now and then to be endured. He has indeed one good quality, he is not exceptious; for he so passionately affects the reputation of understanding raillery, that he will construe an affront into a jest; and call downright rudeness and ill language, satire and fire.

*Fain.* If you have a mind to finish his picture, you have an opportunity to do it at full length. Behold the original.

## SCENE VI

### [*To them*] WITWOUD.

*Wit.* Afford me your compassion, my dears; pity me, Fainall, Mirabell, pity me.

*Mira.* I do from my soul.

*Fain.* Why, what's the matter?

*Wit.* No letters for me, Betty?

*Bet.* Did not a messenger bring you one but now, sir?

*Wit.* Ay, but no other?

*Bet.* No, sir.

*Wit.* That's hard, that's very hard;—a messenger, a mule, a beast of burden, he has brought me a letter from the fool my brother, as heavy as a panegyrick in a funeral sermon, or a copy of commendatory verses from one poet to another. And what's worse, 'tis as sure a forerunner of the author, as an epistle dedicatory.

*Mira.* A fool, and your brother, Witwoud!

*Wit.* Ay, ay, my half-brother. My half-brother he is, no nearer, upon honour.

*Mira.* Then 'tis possible he may be but half a fool.

*Wit.* Good, good, Mirabell, *le drole!* Good, good, hang him, don't let's talk of him;—Fainall, how does your lady? Gad! I say anything in the world to get this fellow out of my head. I beg pardon that I should ask a man of pleasure, and the town, a question at once so foreign and domestick. But I talk like an old maid at a marriage, I don't know what I say: but she's the best woman in the world.

*Fain.* 'Tis well you don't know what you say, or else your commendation would go near to make me either vain or jealous.

*Wit.* No man in town lives well with a wife but Fainall. Your judgment, Mirabell?

*Mira.* You had better step and ask his wife, if you would be credibly informed.

*Wit.* Mirabell.

*Mira.* Ay.

*Wit.* My dear, I ask ten thousand pardons;—Gad I have forgot what I was going to say to you.

*Mira.* I thank you heartily, heartily.

*Wit.* No, but prithee excuse me,—my memory is such a memory.

*Mira.* Have a care of such apologies, Witwoud;—for I never knew a fool but he affected to complain, either of the spleen or his memory.

*Fain.* What have you done with Petulant?

*Wit.* He's reckoning his money,—my money it was—I have no luck to-day.

*Fain.* You may allow him to win of you at play;—for you are sure to be too hard for him at repartee: since you monopolise the wit that is between you, the fortune must be his of course.

*Mira.* I don't find that Petulant confesses the superiority of wit to be your talent, Witwoud.

*Wit.* Come, come, you are malicious now, and would breed debates—Petulant's my friend, and a very honest fellow, and a very pretty fellow, and has a smattering—faith and troth a pretty deal of an odd sort of a small wit: Nay, I'll do him justice. I'm his friend, I won't wrong him.—And if he had any judgment in the world,—he would not be altogether contemptible. Come, come, don't detract from the merits of my friend.

*Fain.* You don't take your friend to be over-nicely bred.

*Wit.* No, no, hang him, the rogue has no manners at all, that I must own—no more breeding than a bum-baily, that I grant you.—'Tis pity; the fellow has fire and life.

*Mira.* What, courage?

*Wit.* Hum, faith I don't know as to that,—I can't say as to that.—Yes, faith, in a controversy he'll contradict anybody.

*Mira.* Though 'twere a man whom he feared, or a woman whom he loved.

*Wit.* Well, well, he does not always think before he speaks;—We have all our failings; you are too hard upon him, you are, faith. Let me excuse him,—I can defend most of his faults, except one or two; one he has, that's the truth on't, if he were my brother, I could not acquit him—that indeed I could wish were otherwise.

*Mira.* Ay marry, what's that, Witwoud?

*Wit.* O pardon me—expose the infirmities of my friend.—No, my dear, excuse me there.

*Fain.* What I warrant he's unsincere, or 'tis some such trifle.

*Wit.* No, no, what if he be? 'Tis no matter for that, his wit will excuse that: a wit should no more be sincere, than a woman constant; one argues a decay of parts, as t'other of beauty.

*Mira.* Maybe you think him too positive?

*Wit.* No, no, his being positive is an incentive to argument, and keeps up conversation.

*Fain.* Too illiterate.

*Wit.* That! that's his happiness—his want of learning gives him the more opportunities to shew his natural parts.

*Mira.* He wants words.

*Wit.* Ay; but I like him for that now; for his want of words gives me the pleasure very often to explain his meaning.

*Fain.* He's impudent.

*Wit.* No, that's not it.

*Mira.* Vain.

*Wit.* No.

*Mira.* What, he speaks unseasonable truths sometimes, because he has not wit enough to invent an evasion.

*Wit.* Truths! Ha, ha, ha! No, no, since you will have it,— I mean, he never speaks truth at all,—that's all. He will lie like a chambermaid, or a woman of quality's porter. Now that is a fault.

## SCENE VII

### [*To them*] Coachman.

*Coach.* Is Master Petulant here, mistress?

*Bet.* Yes.

*Coach.* Three gentlewomen in a coach would speak with him.

*Fain.* O brave Petulant, three!

*Bet.* I'll tell him.

*Coach.* You must bring two dishes of chocolate and a glass of cinnamon-water.

## SCENE VIII

### MIRABELL, FAINALL, WITWOUD.

*Wit.* That should be for two fasting strumpets, and a bawd troubled with wind. Now you may know what the three are.

*Mira.* You are very free with your friend's acquaintance.

*Wit.* Ay, ay, friendship without freedom is as dull as love without enjoyment, or wine without toasting; but to tell you a secret, these are trulls whom he allows coach-hire, and something more by the week, to call on him once a day at publick places.

*Mira.* How!

*Wit.* You shall see he won't go to 'em because there's no more company here to take notice of him—Why this is nothing to what he used to do;—before he found out this way, I have known him call for himself——

*Fain.* Call for himself? What dost thou mean?

*Wit.* Mean, why he would slip you out of this chocolate-house, just when you had been talking to him—as soon as your back was turned—whip he was gone;—then trip to his lodging, clap on a hood and scarf, and a mask, slap into a hackney-coach, and drive hither to the door again in a trice; where he would send in for himself, that I mean, call for himself, wait for himself, nay and what's more, not finding himself, sometimes leave a letter for himself.

*Mira.* I confess this is something extraordinary—I believe he waits for himself now, he is so long a coming; O I ask his pardon.

## SCENE IX

PETULANT, MIRABELL, FAINALL, WITWOUD, BETTY.

*Bet.* Sir, the coach stays.

*Pet.* Well, well; I come.—'Sbud a man had as good be a professed midwife, as a professed whoremaster, at this rate; to be knocked up and raised at all hours, and in all places. Pox on 'em, I won't come—D'ye hear, tell 'em I won't come.— Let 'em snivel and cry their hearts out.

*Fain.* You are very cruel, Petulant.

*Pet.* All's one, let it pass—I have a humour to be cruel.

*Mira.* I hope they are not persons of condition that you use at this rate.

*Pet.* Condition, condition's a dried fig, if I am not in humour. —By this hand, if they were your—a—a—your what-dee-call- 'ems themselves, they must wait or rub off, if I want appetite.

*Mira.* What-dee-call-'ems!  What are they, Witwoud?

*Wit.* Empresses, my dear—by your what-dee-call-'ems he means sultana queens.

*Pet.* Ay, Roxolanas.

*Mira.* Cry you mercy.

*Fain.* Witwoud says they are——

*Pet.* What does he say th'are?

*Wit.* I; fine ladies I say.

*Pet.* Pass on, Witwoud—Harkee, by this light his relations— two co-heiresses his cousins, and an old aunt, who loves catter- wauling better than a conventicle.

*Wit.* Ha, ha, ha; I had a mind to see how the rogue would come off.—Ha, ha, ha; Gad I can't be angry with him, if he had said they were my mother and my sisters.

*Mira.* No!

*Wit.* No; the rogue's wit and readiness of invention charm me, dear Petulant.

*Bet.* They are gone, sir, in great anger.

*Pet.* Enough, let 'em trundel.  Anger helps complexion, saves paint.

*Fain.* This continence is all dissembled; this is in order to have something to brag of the next time he makes court to Millamant, and swear he has abandoned the whole sex for her sake.

*Mira.* Have you not left off your impudent pretensions there yet?  I shall cut your throat, sometime or other, Petulant, about that business.

*Pet.* Ay, ay, let that pass—there are other throats to be cut.—

*Mira.* Meaning mine, sir?

*Pet.* Not I—I mean nobody—I know nothing.—But there are

uncles and nephews in the world—and they may be rivals—
What then? All's one for that——

*Mira.* How! Harkee, Petulant, come hither—Explain, or I
shall call your interpreter.

*Pet.* Explain; I know nothing.—Why you have an uncle,
have you not, lately come to town, and lodges by my Lady
Wishfort's?

*Mira.* True.

*Pet.* Why that's enough—you and he are not friends; and if
he should marry and have a child, you may be disinherited, ha?

*Mira.* Where hast thou stumbled upon all this truth?

*Pet.* All's one for that; why then say I know something.

*Mira.* Come, thou art an honest fellow, Petulant, and shalt
make love to my mistress, thou shalt, faith. What hast thou
heard of my uncle?

*Pet.* I, nothing I. If throats are to be cut, let swords clash;
snug's the word, I shrug and am silent.

*Mira.* O raillery, raillery. Come, I know thou art in the
women's secrets.—What you're a cabalist, I know you staid at
Millamant's last night, after I went. Was there any mention
made of my uncle or me? Tell me; if thou hadst but good
nature equal to thy wit, Petulant, Tony Witwoud, who is now
thy competitor in fame, would shew as dim by thee as a dead
whiting's eye by a pearl of Orient; he would no more be seen
by thee, than Mercury is by the sun: Come, I'm sure thou wo't
tell me.

*Pet.* If I do, will you grant me common sense then, for the
future?

*Mira.* Faith I'll do what I can for thee, and I'll pray that
Heaven may grant it thee in the meantime.

*Pet.* Well, harkee.

*Fain.* Petulant and you both will find Mirabell as warm a
rival as a lover.

*Wit.* Pshaw, pshaw, that she laughs at Petulant is plain.
And for my part—but that it is almost a fashion to admire her,
I should—harkee—to tell you a secret, but let it go no further—
between friends, I shall never break my heart for her.

*Fain.* How!

*Wit.* She's handsome; but she's a sort of an uncertain woman.

*Fain.* I thought you had died for her.

*Wit.* Umh—no——

*Fain.* She has wit.

*Wit.* 'Tis what she will hardly allow anybody else—Now,
demme, I should hate that, if she were as handsome as Cleopatra.
Mirabell is not so sure of her as he thinks for.

*Fain.* Why do you think so?

*Wit.* We staid pretty late there last night; and heard something of an uncle to Mirabell, who is lately come to town,—and
is between him and the best part of his estate; Mirabell and he

are at some distance, as my Lady Wishfort has been told; and you know she hates Mirabell, worse than a Quaker hates a parrot, or than a fishmonger hates a hard frost. Whether this uncle has seen Mrs. Millamant or not, I cannot say; but there were items of such a treaty being in embrio; and if it should come to life, poor Mirabell would be in some sort unfortunately fobbed i'faith.

*Fain.* 'Tis impossible Millamant should harken to it.

*Wit.* Faith, my dear, I can't tell; she's a woman and a kind of a humorist.

*Mira.* And this is the sum of what you could collect last night.

*Pet.* The quintessence. Maybe Witwoud knows more, he stayed longer.—Besides they never mind him; they say anything before him.

*Mira.* I thought you had been the greatest favourite.

*Pet.* Ay, *tête à tête*; but not in publick, because I make remarks.

*Mira.* You do?

*Pet.* Ay, ay, pox I'm malicious, man. Now he's soft, you know, they are not in awe of him—the fellow's well bred, he's what you call a—what-d'ye-call-'em. A fine gentleman, but he's silly withal.

*Mira.* I thank you, I know as much as my curiosity requires. Fainall, are you for the Mall?

*Fain.* Ay, I'll take a turn before dinner.

*Wit.* Ay, we'll all walk in the Park, the ladies talked of being there.

*Mira.* I thought you were obliged to watch for your brother Sir Wilfull's arrival.

*Wit.* No, no, he comes to his aunt's, my Lady Wishfort; pox on him, I shall be troubled with him too; what shall I do with the fool?

*Pet.* Beg him for his estate; that I may beg you afterwards; and so have but one trouble with you both.

*Wit.* O rare Petulant; thou art as quick as fire in a frosty morning; thou shalt to the Mall with us; and we'll be very severe.

*Pet.* Enough, I'm in a humour to be severe.

*Mira.* Are you? Pray then walk by yourselves,—let not us be accessory to your putting the ladies out of countenance, with your senseless ribaldry; which you roar out aloud as often as they pass by you; and when you have made a handsome woman blush, then you think you have been severe.

*Pet.* What, what? Then let 'em either shew their innocence by not understanding what they hear, or else shew their discretion by not hearing what they would not be thought to understand.

*Mira.* But hast not thou then sense enough to know that thou ought'st to be most ashamed of thyself, when thou hast put another out of countenance?

*Pet.* Not I, by this hand—I always take blushing either for a sign of guilt, or ill breeding.

*Mira.* I confess you ought to think so. You are in the right, that you may plead the error of your judgment in defence of your practice.

> Where modesty's ill manners, 'tis but fit
> That impudence and malice pass for wit.

# ACT II

## SCENE I.—*St. James's Park*

### Mrs. FAINALL *and* Mrs. MARWOOD.

*Mrs. Fain.* Ay, ay, dear Marwood, if we will be happy, we must find the means in ourselves, and among ourselves. Men are ever in extremes; either doating, or averse. While they are lovers, if they have fire and sense, their jealousies are insupportable: and when they cease to love (we ought to think at least) they loath; they look upon us with horror and distaste; they meet us like the ghosts of what we were, and as from such, fly from us.

*Mrs. Mar.* True, 'tis an unhappy circumstance of life, that love should ever die before us; and that the man so often should outlive the lover. But say what you will, 'tis better to be left, than never to have been loved. To pass our youth in dull indifference, to refuse the sweets of life because they once must leave us, is as preposterous as to wish to have been born old, because we one day must be old. For my part, my youth may wear and waste, but it shall never rust in my possession.

*Mrs. Fain.* Then it seems you dissemble an aversion to mankind, only in compliance to my mother's humour.

*Mrs. Mar.* Certainly. To be free; I have no taste of those insipid dry discourses, with which our sex of force must entertain themselves, apart from men. We may affect endearments to each other, profess eternal friendships, and seem to dote like lovers; but 'tis not in our natures long to persevere. Love will resume his empire in our breasts, and every heart, or soon or late, receive and readmit him as its lawful tyrant.

*Mrs. Fain.* Bless me, how have I been deceived! Why you profess a libertine.

*Mrs. Mar.* You see my friendship by my freedom.   Come, be as sincere, acknowledge that your sentiments agree with mine.

*Mrs. Fain.* Never.

*Mrs. Mar.* You hate mankind?

*Mrs. Fain.* Heartily, inveterately.

*Mrs. Mar.* Your husband?

*Mrs. Fain.* Most transcendently; ay, though I say it, meritoriously.

*Mrs. Mar.* Give me your hand upon it.

*Mrs. Fain.* There.

*Mrs. Mar.* I join with you; what I have said has been to try you.

*Mrs. Fain.* Is it possible?   Dost thou hate those vipers men?

*Mrs. Mar.* I have done hating 'em, and am now come to despise 'em; the next thing I have to do, is eternally to forget 'em.

*Mrs. Fain.* There spoke the spirit of an Amazon, a Penthesilea.

*Mrs. Mar.* And yet I am thinking sometimes to carry my aversion further.

*Mrs. Fain.* How?

*Mrs. Mar.* Faith by marrying; if I could but find one that loved me very well, and would be thoroughly sensible of ill usage, I think I should do myself the violence of undergoing the ceremony.

*Mrs. Fain.* You would not make him a cuckold?

*Mrs. Mar.* No; but I'd make him believe I did, and that's as bad.

*Mrs. Fain.* Why had not you as good do it?

*Mrs. Mar.* O if he should ever discover it, he would then know the worst, and be out of his pain; but I would have him ever to continue upon the rack of fear and jealousy.

*Mrs. Fain.* Ingenious mischief! Would thou wert married to Mirabell.

*Mrs. Mar.* Would I were.

*Mrs. Fain.* You change colour.

*Mrs. Mar.* Because I hate him.

*Mrs. Fain.* So do I; but I can hear him named.   But what reason have you to hate him in particular?

*Mrs. Mar.* I never loved him; he is, and always was, insufferably proud.

*Mrs. Fain.* By the reason you give for your aversion, one would think it dissembled; for you have laid a fault to his charge of which his enemies must acquit him.

*Mrs. Mar.* O then it seems you are one of his favourable enemies.   Methinks you look a little pale, and now you flush again.

*Mrs. Fain.* Do I?   I think I am a little sick o' the sudden.

*Mrs. Mar.* What ails you?

*Mrs. Fain.* My husband. Don't you see him? He turned short upon me unawares, and has almost overcome me.

## SCENE II

### [*To them*] FAINALL *and* MIRABELL.

*Mrs. Mar.* Ha, ha, ha; he comes opportunely for you.

*Mrs. Fain.* For you, for he has brought Mirabell with him.

*Fain.* My dear.

*Mrs. Fain.* My soul.

*Fain.* You don't look well to-day, child.

*Mrs. Fain.* D'ye think so?

*Mira.* He is the only man that does, madam.

*Mrs. Fain.* The only man that would tell me so at least; and the only man from whom I could hear it without mortification.

*Fain.* O my dear, I am satisfied of your tenderness; I know you cannot resent anything from me; especially what is an effect of my concern.

*Mrs. Fain.* Mr. Mirabell, my mother interrupted you in a pleasant relation last night: I would fain hear it out.

*Mira.* The persons concerned in that affair have yet a tolerable reputation.—I am afraid Mr. Fainall will be censorious.

*Mrs. Fain.* He has a humour more prevailing than his curiosity, and will willingly dispense with the hearing of one scandalous story, to avoid giving an occasion to make another by being seen to walk with his wife. This way, Mr. Mirabell, and I dare promise you will oblige us both.

## SCENE III

### FAINALL, Mrs. MARWOOD.

*Fain.* Excellent creature! Well, sure if I should live to be rid of my wife, I should be a miserable man.

*Mrs. Mar.* Ay!

*Fain.* For having only that one hope, the accomplishment of it, of consequence must put an end to all my hopes; and what a wretch is he who must survive his hopes! Nothing remains when that day comes, but to  it down and weep like Alexander, when he wanted other worlds to conquer.

*Mrs. Mar.* Will you not follow 'em?

*Fain.* Faith, I think not.

*Mrs. Mar.* Pray let us; I have a reason.

*Fain.* You are not jealous?

*Mrs. Mar.* Of whom?

*Fain.* Of Mirabell.

*Mrs. Mar.* If I am, is it inconsistent with my love to you that I am tender of your honour?

*Fain.* You would intimate then, as if there were a fellow-feeling between my wife and him.

*Mrs. Mar.* I think she does not hate him to that degree she would be thought.

*Fain.* But he, I fear, is too insensible.

*Mrs. Mar.* It may be you are deceived.

*Fain.* It may be so. I do now begin to apprehend it.

*Mrs. Mar.* What?

*Fain.* That I have been deceived, madam, and you are false.

*Mrs. Mar.* That I am false! What mean you?

*Fain.* To let you know I see through all your little arts—Come, you both love him; and both have equally dissembled your aversion. Your mutual jealousies of one another, have made you clash 'till you have both struck fire. I have seen the warm confession reddening on your cheeks, and sparkling from your eyes.

*Mrs. Mar.* You do me wrong.

*Fain.* I do not—'twas for my ease to oversee and wilfully neglect the gross advances made him by my wife; that by permitting her to be engaged, I might continue unsuspected in my pleasures; and take you oftener to my arms in full security. But could you think, because the nodding husband would not wake, that e'er the watchful lover slept?

*Mrs. Mar.* And wherewithal can you reproach me?

*Fain.* With infidelity, with loving another, with love of Mirabell.

*Mrs. Mar.* 'Tis false. I challenge you to shew an instance that can confirm your groundless accusation. I hate him.

*Fain.* And wherefore do you hate him? He is insensible, and your resentment follows his neglect. An instance! The injuries you have done him are a proof: your interposing in his love. What cause had you to make discoveries of his pretended passion? To undeceive the credulous aunt, and be the officious obstacle of his match with Millamant?

*Mrs. Mar.* My obligations to my lady urged me: I had professed a friendship to her; and could not see her easy nature so abused by that dissembler.

*Fain.* What, was it conscience then? Professed a friendship! O the pious friendships of the female sex!

*Mrs. Mar.* More tender, more sincere, and more enduring, than all the vain and empty vows of men, whether professing love to us, or mutual faith to one another.

*Fain.* Ha, ha, ha; you are my wife's friend too.

*Mrs. Mar.* Shame and ingratitude! Do you reproach me! You, you upbraid me! Have I been false to her, through strict fidelity to you, and sacrificed my friendship to keep my love inviolate? And have you the baseness to charge me with the guilt, unmindful of the merit! To you it should be meritorious, that I have been vicious: And do you reflect that guilt upon me‘ which should lie buried in your bosom?

*Fain.* You misinterpret my reproof. I meant but to remind you of the slight account you once could make of strictest ties, when set in competition with your love to me.

*Mrs. Mar.* 'Tis false, you urged it with deliberate malice— 'twas spoke in scorn, and I never will forgive it.

*Fain.* Your guilt, not your resentment, begets your rage. If yet you loved, you could forgive a jealousy: but you are stung to find you are discovered.

*Mrs. Mar.* It shall be all discovered. You too shall be discovered; be sure you shall. I can but be exposed—if I do it myself I shall prevent your baseness.

*Fain.* Why, what will you do?

*Mrs. Mar.* Disclose it to your wife; own what has past between us.

*Fain.* Frenzy!

*Mrs. Mar.* By all my wrongs I'll do't—I'll publish to the world the injuries you have done me, both in my fame and fortune: With both I trusted you, you bankrupt in honour, as indigent of wealth.

*Fain.* Your fame I have preserved. Your fortune has been bestowed as the prodigality of your love would have it, in pleasures which we both have shared. Yet, had not you been false, I had e'er this repaid it—'Tis true—had you permitted Mirabell with Millamant to have stollen their marriage, my lady had been incensed beyond all means of reconcilement: Millamant had forfeited the moiety of her fortune; which then would have descended to my wife;—And wherefore did I marry, but to make lawful prize of a rich widow's wealth, and squander it on love and you?

*Mrs. Mar.* Deceit and frivolous pretence.

*Fain.* Death, am I not married? What's pretence? Am I not imprisoned, fettered? Have I not a wife? Nay, a wife that was a widow, a young widow, a handsome widow; and would be again a widow, but that I have a heart of proof, and something of a constitution to bustle through the ways of wedlock and this world. Will you yet be reconciled to truth and me?

*Mrs. Mar.* Impossible. Truth and you are inconsistent—I hate you, and shall for ever.

*Fain.* For loving you?

*Mrs. Mar.* I loath the name of love after such usage; and next to the guilt with which you would asperse me, I scorn you most. Farewell.

*Fain.* Nay, we must not part thus.

*Mrs. Mar.* Let me go.

*Fain.* Come, I'm sorry.

*Mrs. Mar.* I care not—let me go—break my hands, do—I'd leave 'em to get loose.

*Fain.* I would not hurt you for the world.  Have I no other hold to keep you here?

*Mrs. Mar.* Well, I have deserved it all.

*Fain.* You know I love you.

*Mrs. Mar.* Poor dissembling!—O that—Well, it is not yet——

*Fain.* What?  What is it not?  What is it not yet?  It is not yet too late——

*Mrs. Mar.* No, it is not yet too late—I have that comfort.

*Fain.* It is, to love another.

*Mrs. Mar.* But not to loath, detest, abhor mankind, myself and the whole treacherous world.

*Fain.* Nay, this is extravagance.—Come, I ask your pardon—no tears—I was to blame, I could not love you and be easy in my doubts—pray forbear—I believe you; I'm convinced I've done you wrong; and any way, every way will make amends;—I'll hate my wife yet more, damn her, I'll part with her, rob her of all she's worth, and we'll retire somewhere, anywhere, to another world.  I'll marry thee—be pacified.—'Sdeath, they come, hide your face, your tears—you have a mask, wear it a moment.  This way, this way, be persuaded.


SCENE IV

MIRABELL *and* Mrs. FAINALL.

*Mrs. Fain.* They are here yet.

*Mira.* They are turning into the other walk.

*Mrs. Fain.* While I only hated my husband, I could bear to see him; but since I have despised him, he's too offensive.

*Mira.* O you should hate with prudence.

*Mrs. Fain.* Yes, for I have loved with indiscretion.

*Mira.* You should have just so much disgust for your husband as may be sufficient to make you relish your lover.

*Mrs. Fain.* You have been the cause that I have loved without bounds, and would you set limits to that aversion, of which you have been the occasion?  Why did you make me marry this man?

*Mira.* Why do we daily commit disagreeable and dangerous actions?  To save that idol reputation.  If the familiarities of our loves had produced that consequence, of which you were apprehensive, where could you have fixed a father's name with credit, but on a husband?  I knew Fainall to be a man lavish

of his morals, an interested and professing friend, a false and a
designing lover; yet one whose wit and outward fair behaviour
have gained a reputation with the town, enough to make that
woman stand excused, who has suffered herself to be won by
his addresses.   A better man ought not to have been sacrificed
to the occasion; a worse had not answered to the purpose.   When
you are weary of him, you know your remedy.

*Mrs. Fain.* I ought to stand in some degree of credit with
you, Mirabell.

*Mira.* In justice to you, I have made you privy to my whole
design, and put it in your power to ruin or advance my fortune.

*Mrs. Fain.* Whom have you instructed to represent your
pretended uncle ?

*Mira.* Waitwell, my servant.

*Mrs. Fain.* He is an humble servant to Foible, my mother's
woman, and may win her to your interest.

*Mira.* Care is taken for that—she is won and worn by this time.
They were married this morning.

*Mrs. Fain.* Who ?

*Mira.* Waitwell and Foible.   I would not tempt my servant
to betray me by trusting him too far.   If your mother, in hopes
to ruin me, should consent to marry my pretended uncle, he
might, like Mosca in the " Fox," stand upon terms; so I made him
sure before-hand.

*Mrs. Fain.* So, if my poor mother is caught in a contract, you
will discover the imposture betimes; and release her by produc-
ing a certificate of her gallant's former marriage.

*Mira.* Yes, upon condition that she consent to my marriage
with her niece, and surrender the moiety of her fortune in her
possession.

*Mrs. Fain.* She talked last night of endeavouring at a match
between Millamant and your uncle.

*Mira.* That was by Foible's direction, and my instruction, that
she might seem to carry it more privately.

*Mrs. Fain.* Well, I have an opinion of your success; for I
believe my lady will do anything to get an husband; and when
she has this, which you have provided for her, I suppose she will
submit to anything to get rid of him.

*Mira.* Yes, I think the good lady would marry anything that
resembled a man, though 'twere no more than what a butler
could pinch out of a napkin.

*Mrs. Fain.* Female frailty!   We must all come to it, if we
live to be old, and feel the craving of a false appetite when the
true is decayed.

*Mira.* An old woman's appetite is depraved like that of a
girl—'tis the green-sickness of a second childhood; and like the
faint offer of a latter spring, serves but to usher in the fall; and
withers in an affected bloom.

*Mrs. Fain.* Here's your mistress.

## SCENE V

[*To them*] Mrs. MILLAMANT, WITWOUD, MINCING.

*Mira.* Here she comes i'faith full sail, with her fan spread and streamers out, and a shoal of fools for tenders—Ha, no, I cry her mercy.

*Mrs. Fain.* I see but one poor empty sculler; and he tows her woman after him.

*Mira.* You seem to be unattended, madam,—you used to have the *beau-mond* throng after you; and a flock of gay fine perukes hovering round you.

*Wit.* Like moths about a candle—I had like to have lost my comparison for want of breath.

*Milla.* O I have denied myself airs to-day. I have walked as fast through the croud——

*Wit.* As a favourite just disgraced; and with as few followers.

*Milla.* Dear Mr. Witwoud, truce with your similitudes: for I am as sick of 'em——

*Wit.* As a physician of a good air—I cannot help it, madam, though 'tis against myself.

*Milla.* Yet again! Mincing, stand between me and his wit.

*Wit.* Do, Mrs. Mincing, like a skreen before a great fire. I confess I do blaze to-day, I am too bright.

*Mrs. Fain.* But, dear Millamant, why were you so long?

*Milla.* Long! Lord, have I not made violent haste? I have asked every living thing I met for you; I have enquired after you, as after a new fashion.

*Wit.* Madam, truce with your similitudes—No, you met her husband, and did not ask him for her.

*Mira.* By your leave, Witwoud, that were like enquiring after an old fashion, to ask a husband for his wife.

*Wit.* Hum, a hit, a hit, a palpable hit, I confess it.

*Mrs. Fain.* You were dressed before I came abroad.

*Milla.* Ay, that's true—O but then I had—Mincing, what had I? Why was I so long?

*Minc.* O mem, your laship staid to peruse a pecquet of letters.

*Milla.* O ay, letters—I had letters—I am persecuted with letters—I hate letters—nobody knows how to write letters; and yet one has 'em, one does not know why—they serve one to pin up one's hair.

*Wit.* Is that the way? Pray, madam, do you pin up your hair with all your letters? I find I must keep copies.

*Milla.* Only with those in verse, Mr. Witwoud. I never pin up my hair with prose. I think I tried once, Mincing.

*Minc.* O mem, I shall never forget it.

*Milla.* Ay, poor Mincing tift and tift all the morning.

*Minc.* 'Till I had the cremp in my fingers, I'll vow, mem. And all to no purpose. But when your laship pins it up with poetry, it sits so pleasant the next day as anything, and is so pure and so crips.

*Wit.* Indeed, so crips?

*Minc.* You're such a critick, Mr. Witwoud.

*Milla.* Mirabell, did you take exceptions last night? O ay, and went away—Now I think on't I'm angry—no, now I think on't I'm pleased—for I believe I gave you some pain.

*Mira.* Does that please you?

*Milla.* Infinitely; I love to give pain.

*Mira.* You would affect a cruelty which is not in your nature; your true vanity is in the power of pleasing.

*Milla.* O I ask your pardon for that—one's cruelty is one's power, and when one parts with one's cruelty, one parts with one's power; and when one has parted with that, I fancy one's old and ugly.

*Mira.* Ay, ay, suffer your cruelty to ruin the object of your power, to destroy your lover—and then how vain, how lost a thing you'll be? Nay, 'tis true: you are no longer handsome when you've lost your lover; your beauty dies upon the instant: For beauty is the lover's gift; 'tis he bestows your charms—your glass is all a cheat. The ugly and the old, whom the look-ing-glass mortifies, yet after commendation can be flattered by it, and discover beauties in it: for that reflects our praises, rather than your face.

*Milla.* O the vanity of these men! Fainall, d'ye hear him? If they did not commend us, we were not handsome! Now you must know they could not commend one, if one was not hand-some. Beauty the lover's gift—Lord, what is a lover, that it can give? Why one makes lovers as fast as one pleases, and they live as long as one pleases, and they die as soon as one pleases: and then if one pleases one makes more.

*Wit.* Very pretty. Why you make no more of making of lovers, madam, than of making so many card-matches.

*Milla.* One no more owes one's beauty to a lover, than one's wit to an eccho: they can but reflect what we look and say; vain empty things if we are silent or unseen, and want a being.

*Mira.* Yet, to those two vain empty things, you owe two [of] the greatest pleasures of your life.

*Milla.* How so?

*Mira.* To your lover you owe the pleasure of hearing your-selves praised; and to an eccho the pleasure of hearing yourselves talk.

*Wit.* But I know a lady that loves talking so incessantly, she won't give an eccho fair play; she has that everlasting rotation of tongue, that an eccho must wait 'till she dies, before it can catch her last words.

*Milla.* O fiction; Fainall, let us leave these men.

*Mira.* Draw off Witwoud. [*Aside to* Mrs. FAINALL.
*Mrs. Fain.* Immediately; I have a word or two for Mr. Witwoud.

## SCENE VI

### MILLAMANT, MIRABELL, MINCING.

*Mira.* I would beg a little private audience too—you had the tyranny to deny me last night; though you knew I came to impart a secret to you that concerned my love.

*Milla.* You saw I was engaged.

*Mira.* Unkind. You had the leisure to entertain a herd of fools; things who visit you from their excessive idleness; bestowing on your easiness that time, which is the incumbrance of their lives. How can you find delight in such society? It is impossible they should admire you, they are not capable: or if they were, it should be to you as a mortification; for sure to please a fool is some degree of folly.

*Milla.* I please myself—besides, sometimes to converse with fools is for my health.

*Mira.* Your health! Is there a worse disease than the conversation of fools?

*Milla.* Yes, the vapours; fools are physick for it, next to *assa-fœtida.*

*Mira.* You are not in a course of fools?

*Milla.* Mirabell, if you persist in this offensive freedom, you'll displease me—I think I must resolve after all, not to have you—we shan't agree.

*Mira.* Not in our physick it may be.

*Milla.* And yet our distemper in all likelihood will be the same; for we shall be sick of one another. I shan't endure to be reprimanded, nor instructed; 'tis so dull to act always by advice, and so tedious to be told of one's faults—I can't bear it. Well, I won't have you, Mirabell—I'm resolved—I think—You may go—ha, ha, ha. What would you give, that you could help loving me?

*Mira.* I would give something that you did not know, I could not help it.

*Milla.* Come, don't look grave then. Well, what do you say to me?

*Mira.* I say that a man may as soon make a friend by his wit, or a fortune by his honesty, as win a woman with plain-dealing and sincerity.

*Milla.* Sententious Mirabell! Prithee don't look with that violent and inflexible wise face, like Solomon at the dividing of the child in an old tapestry hanging.

*Mira.* You are merry, madam, but I would persuade you for a moment to be serious.

*Milla.* What, with that face? No, if you keep your countenance, 'tis impossible I should hold mine. Well, after all, there
is something very moving in a lovesick face. Ha, ha, ha—Well
I won't laugh, don't be peevish—Heigho! Now I'll be melancholy, as melancholy as a watch-light. Well, Mirabell, if ever
you will win me woo me now—Nay, if you are so tedious, fare
you well;—I see they are walking away.

*Mira.* Can you not find in the variety of your disposition one
moment——

*Milla.* To hear you tell me Foible's married, and your plot
like to speed.—No.

*Mira.* But how you came to know it——

*Milla.* Without the help of the devil, you can't imagine;
unless she should tell me herself. Which of the two it may have
been, I will leave you to consider; and when you have done
thinking of that, think of me.


## SCENE VII

### MIRABELL *alone.*

*Mira.* I have something more—Gone—think of you! To
think of a whirlwind, though 'twere in a whirlwind, were a case
of more steady contemplation; a very tranquility of mind and
mansion. A fellow that lives in a windmill, has not a more
whimsical dwelling than the heart of a man that is lodged in a
woman. There is no point of the compass to which they cannot
turn, and by which they are not turned; and by one as well as
another; for motion not method is their occupation. To know
this, and yet continue to be in love, is to be made wise from the
dictates of reason, and yet persevere to play the fool by the force
of instinct.—O here come my pair of turtles.—what, billing so
sweetly! Is not Valentine's Day over with you yet?


## SCENE VIII

### [*To him*] WAITWELL, FOIBLE.

*Mira.* Sirrah, Waitwell, why sure you think you were married
for your own recreation, and not for my conveniency.

*Wait.* Your pardon, sir. With submission, we have indeed
been solacing in lawful delights; but still with an eye to business.
sir. I have instructed her as well as I could. If she can take
your directions as readily as my instructions, sir, your affairs
are in a prosperous way.

*Mira.* Give you joy, Mrs. Foible.

*Foib.* O-las, sir, I'm so ashamed—I'm afraid my lady has been in a thousand inquietudes for me. But I protest, sir, I made as much haste as I could.

*Wait.* That she did indeed, sir. It was my fault that she did not make more.

*Mira.* That I believe.

*Foib.* But I told my lady as you instructed me, sir. That I had a prospect of seeing Sir Rowland your uncle; and that I would put her ladyship's picture in my pocket to shew him; which I'll be sure to say has made him so enamoured of her beauty, that he burns with impatience to lie at her ladyship's feet and worship the original.

*Mira.* Excellent Foible! Matrimony has made you eloquent in love.

*Wait.* I think she has profited, sir. I think so.

*Foib.* You have seen Madam Millamant, sir?

*Mira.* Yes.

*Foib.* I told her, sir, because I did not know that you might find an opportunity; she had so much company last night.

*Mira.* Your diligence will merit more—In the meantime——

[*Gives money.*

*Foib.* O dear sir, your humble servant.

*Wait.* Spouse.

*Mira.* Stand off, sir, not a penny.—Go on and prosper, Foible —the lease shall be made good and the farm stocked, if we succeed.

*Foib.* I don't question your generosity, sir: and you need not doubt of success. If you have no more commands, sir, I'll be gone; I'm sure my lady is at her toilet, and can't dress 'till I come.—O dear, I'm sure that [*looking out*] was Mrs. Marwood that went by in a mask; if she has seen me with you I'm sure she'll tell my lady. I'll make haste home and prevent her. Your servant, sir. B'w'y, Waitwell.


## SCENE IX

### MIRABELL, WAITWELL.

*Wait.* Sir Rowland if you please. The jade's so pert upon her preferment she forgets herself.

*Mira.* Come, sir, will you endeavour to forget yourself—and transform into Sir Rowland.

*Wait.* Why, sir; it will be impossible I should remember myself—married, knighted and attended all in one day! 'Tis enough to make any man forget himself. The difficulty will be how to recover my acquaintance and familiarity with my former self; and fall from my transformation to a reformation into

Waitwell.   Nay, I shan't be quite the same Waitwell neither—
for now I remember me, I'm married, and can't be my own
man again.

> Ay there's my grief;  that's the sad change of life;
> To lose my title, and yet keep my wife.

# ACT III

### SCENE I.—*A Room in* Lady WISHFORT'S *House.*

#### Lady WISHFORT *at her toilet,* PEG *waiting.*

*Lady.*  Merciful, no news of Foible yet?

*Peg.*  No, madam.

*Lady.*  I have no more patience—if I have not fretted myself
'till I am pale again, there's no veracity in me.  Fetch me the
red—the red, do you hear, sweetheart?  An arrant ash colour,
as I'm a person.  Look you how this wench stirs!  Why dost
thou not fetch me a little red?  Didst thou not hear me, mopus?

*Peg.*  The red ratafia does your ladyship mean, or the cherry-
brandy?

*Lady.*  Ratafia, fool.  No, fool.  Not the ratafia, fool—grant
me patience!  I mean the Spanish paper, idiot, complexion
darling.  Paint, paint, paint, dost thou understand that,
changeling, dangling thy hands like bobbins before thee?  Why
dost thou not stir, puppet?  thou wooden thing upon wires.

*Peg.*  Lord, madam, your ladyship is so impatient—I cannot
come at the paint, madam, Mrs. Foible has locked it up, and
carried the key with her.

*Lady.*  A pox take you both—fetch me the cherry-brandy then.

### SCENE II

#### Lady WISHFORT.

I'm as pale and as faint, I look like Mrs. Qualmsick the curate's
wife, that's always breeding—Wench, come, come, wench, what
art thou doing, sipping? tasting?  Save thee, dost thou not
know the bottle?

### SCENE III

#### Lady WISHFORT, PEG *with a bottle and china cup.*

*Peg.*  Madam, I was looking for a cup.

*Lady.*  A cup, save thee, and what a cup hast thou brought !

Dost thou take me for a fairy, to drink out of an acorn? Why didst thou not bring thy thimble? Hast thou ne'er a brass thimble clinking in thy pocket with a bit of nutmeg? I warrant thee. Come, fill, fill.—So—again. See who that is.—[*One knocks.*] Set down the bottle first. Here, here, under the table—What, wouldst thou go with the bottle in thy hand like a tapster. As I'm a person, this wench has lived in an inn upon the road, before she came to me, like Maritornes the Asturian in *Don Quixote.* No Foible yet?

*Peg.* No, madam, Mrs. Marwood.

*Lady.* O Marwood, let her come in. Come in, good Marwood.


## SCENE IV

### [*To them*] Mrs. MARWOOD.

*Mrs. Mar.* I'm surprized to find your ladyship in *dishabillé* at this time of day.

*Lady.* Foible's a lost thing; has been abroad since morning, and never heard of since.

*Mrs. Mar.* I saw her but now, as I came masked through the Park, in conference with Mirabell.

*Lady.* With Mirabell! You call my blood into my face, with mentioning that traitor. She durst not have the confidence. I sent her to negotiate an affair, in which if I'm detected I'm undone. If that wheadling villain has wrought upon Foible to detect me, I'm ruined. Oh my dear friend, I'm a wretch of wretches if I'm detected.

*Mrs. Mar.* O madam, you cannot suspect Mrs. Foible's integrity.

*Lady.* O, he carries poison in his tongue that would corrupt integrity itself. If she has given him an opportunity, she has as good as put her integrity into his hands. Ah, dear Marwood, what's integrity to an opportunity?—Hark! I hear her.—Dear friend, retire into my closet, that I may examine her with more freedom—You'll pardon me, dear friend, I can make bold with you—There are books over the chimney—Quarles and Prynne, and the *Short View of the Stage*, with Bunyan's works to entertain you.—Go, you thing, and send her in. [*To* PEG.


## SCENE V

### Lady WISHFORT, FOIBLE.

*Lady.* O Foible, where hast thou been? what hast thou been doing?

*Foib.* Madam, I have seen the party.

*Lady.* But what hast thou done?

*Foib.* Nay, 'tis your ladyship has done, and are to do; I have

only promised. But a man so enamoured—so transported!
Well, if worshipping of pictures be a sin—poor Sir Rowland, I say.

*Lady.* The miniature has been counted true—But hast thou not
betrayed me, Foible? Hast thou not detected me to that faithless Mirabell?—What hadst thou to do with him in the Park?
Answer me, has he got nothing out of thee?

*Foib.* So, the devil has been beforehand with me, what shall
I say?—Alas, madam, could I help it, if I met that confident
thing? Was I in fault? If you had heard how he used me,
and all upon your ladyship's account, I'm sure you would not
suspect my fidelity. Nay, if that had been the worst I could
have borne: but he had a fling at your ladyship too; and then I
could not hold: but i'faith I gave him his own.

*Lady.* Me? What did the filthy fellow say?

*Foib.* O madam; 'tis a shame to say what he said—with his
taunts and his fleers, tossing up his nose. Humh (says he), what
you are a hatching some plot (says he), you are so early abroad,
or catering (says he), ferreting for some disbanded officer, I
warrant—half pay is but thin subsistance (says he)—Well, what
pension does your lady propose? Let me see (says he), what
she must come down pretty deep now, she's superannuated
(says he) and——

*Lady.* Ods my life, I'll have him, I'll have him murdered.
I'll have him poisoned. Where does he eat? I'll marry a
drawer to have him poisoned in his wine. I'll send for Robin
from Lockets—immediately.

*Foib.* Poison him? Poisoning's too good for him. Starve
him, madam, starve him; marry Sir Rowland, and get him
disinherited. O you would bless yourself, to hear what he said.

*Lady.* A villain, superannuated!

*Foib.* Humh (says he), I hear you are laying designs against
me too (says he), and Mrs. Millamant is to marry my uncle (he
does not suspect a word of your ladyship); but (says he) I'll fit
you for that, I warrant you (says he), I'll hamper you for that
(says he), you and your old frippery too (says he), I'll handle
you——

*Lady.* Audacious villain! handle me, would he durst—
Frippery? old frippery! Was there ever such a foul-mouthed
fellow? I'll be married to-morrow, I'll be contracted to-night..

*Foib.* The sooner the better, madam.

*Lady.* Will Sir Rowland be here, say'st thou? when, Foible?

*Foib.* Incontinently, madam. No new sheriff's wife expects
the return of her husband after knighthood, with that impatience
in which Sir Rowland burns for the dear hour of kissing your
ladyship's hand after dinner.

*Lady.* Frippery! superannuated frippery! I'll frippery the
villain; I'll reduce him to frippery and rags: a tatterdemallion
—I hope to see him hung with tatters, like a Long-Lane penthouse, or a gibbet-thief. A slander-mouthed railer: I warrant

the spendthrift prodigal's in debt as much as the million lottery, or the whole court upon a birthday. I'll spoil his credit with his tailor. Yes, he shall have my niece with her fortune, he shall.

*Foib.* He! I hope to see him lodge in Ludgate first, and angle into Black-Fryars for brass farthings, with an old mitten.

*Lady.* Ay, dear Foible; thank thee for that, dear Foible. He has put me out of all patience. I shall never recompose my features to receive Sir Rowland with any oeconomy of face. This wretch has fretted me that I am absolutely decayed. Look, Foible.

*Foib.* Your ladyship has frowned a little too rashly, indeed, madam. There are some cracks discernible in the white vernish.

*Lady.* Let me see the glass—Cracks, say'st thou? Why, I am arrantly flayed—I look like an old peeled wall. Thou must repair me, Foible, before Sir Rowland comes; or I shall never keep up to my picture.

*Foib.* I warrant you, madam; a little art once made your picture like you; and now a little of the same art must make you like your picture. Your picture must sit for you, madam.

*Lady.* But art thou sure Sir Rowland will not fail to come? Or will a not fail when he does come? Will he be importunate, Foible, and push? For if he should not be importunate—I shall never break decorums—I shall die with confusion, if I am forced to advance—Oh no, I can never advance—I shall swoon if he should expect advances. No, I hope Sir Rowland is better bred, than to put a lady to the necessity of breaking her forms. I won't be too coy neither.—I won't give him despair—but a little disdain is not amiss; a little scorn is alluring.

*Foib.* A little scorn becomes your ladyship.

*Lady.* Yes, but tenderness becomes me best—a sort of a dyingness—You see that picture has a sort of a—Ha, Foible? A swimmingness in the eyes—Yes, I'll look so—my niece affects it; but she wants features. Is Sir Rowland handsome? Let my toilet be removed—I'll dress above. I'll receive Sir Rowland here. Is he handsome? Don't answer me. I won't know: I'll be surprized. I'll be taken by surprize.

*Foib.* By storm, madam. Sir Rowland's a brisk man.

*Lady.* Is he! O then he'll importune, if he's a brisk man. I shall save decorums if Sir Rowland importunes. I have a mortal terror at the apprehension of offending against decorums. O I'm glad he's a brisk man. Let my things be removed, good Foible.

## SCENE VI

### Mrs. FAINALL, FOIBLE.

*Mrs. Fain.* O Foible, I have been in a fright, lest I should come too late. That devil, Marwood, saw you in the Park with Mirabell, and I'm afraid will discover it to my lady.

*Foib.* Discover what, madam?

*Mrs. Fain.* Nay, nay, put not on that strange face. I am privy to the whole design, and know that Waitwell, to whom thou wert this morning married, is to personate Mirabell's uncle, and as such, winning my lady, to involve her in those difficulties from which Mirabell only must release her, by his making his conditions to have my cousin and her fortune left to her own disposal.

*Foib.* O dear madam, I beg your pardon. It was not my confidence in your ladyship that was deficient; but I thought the former good correspondence between your ladyship and Mr. Mirabell, might have hindered his communicating this secret.

*Mrs. Fain.* Dear Foible, forget that.

*Foib.* O dear madam, Mr. Mirabell is such a sweet winning gentleman—But your ladyship is the pattern of generosity.— Sweet lady, to be so good! Mr. Mirabell cannot chuse but be grateful. I find your ladyship has his heart still. Now, madam, I can safely tell your ladyship our success, Mrs. Marwood had told my lady; but I warrant I managed myself. I turned it all for the better. I told my lady that Mr. Mirabell railed at her. I laid horrid things to his charge, I'll vow; and my lady is so incensed, that she'll be contracted to Sir Rowland to-night, she says;—I warrant I worked her up, that he may have her for asking for, as they say of a Welsh maiden-head.

*Mrs. Fain.* O rare Foible!

*Foib.* Madam, I beg your ladyship to acquaint Mr. Mirabell of his success. I would be seen as little as possible to speak to him—besides, I believe Madam Marwood watches me.—She has a month's mind; but I know Mr. Mirabell can't abide her.— [*Calls.*] John—remove my lady's toilet. Madam, your servant. My lady is so impatient, I fear she'll come for me, if I stay.

*Mrs. Fain.* I'll go with you up the back stairs, lest I should meet her.

## SCENE VII

### MRS. MARWOOD *alone.*

*Mrs. Mar.* Indeed, Mrs. Engine, is it thus with you? Are you become a go-between of this importance? Yes, I shall watch you. Why this wench is the *pass-par-toute*, a very master-key to everybody's strong box. My friend Fainall, have you carried it so swimmingly? I thought there was something in it; but it seems it's over with you. Your loathing is not from a want of appetite then, but from a surfeit. Else you could never be so cool to fall from a principal to be an assistant; to procure for him! A pattern of generosity, that I confess. Well, Mr. Fainall, you have met with your match.— O man, man! Woman, woman! The devil's an ass: if I were

a painter, I would draw him like an idiot, a driveler with a bib
and bells. Man should have his head and horns, and woman
the rest of him. Poor simple fiend! Madam Marwood has a
month's mind, but he can't abide her—'Twere better for him you
had not been his confessor in that affair; without you could have
kept his counsel closer. I shall not prove another pattern of
generosity—he has not obliged me to that with those excesses
of himself; and now I'll have none of him. Here comes the
good lady, panting ripe; with a heart full of hope, and a head
full of care, like any chymist upon the day of projection.

## SCENE VIII

### [*To her*] Lady WISHFORT.

*Lady.* O dear Marwood, what shall I say for this rude forgetfulness—but my dear friend is all goodness.

*Mrs. Mar.* No apologies, dear madam. I have been very
well entertained.

*Lady.* As I'm a person I am in a very chaos to think I should
so forget myself—but I have such an olio of affairs really I
know not what to do.—[*Calls*]—Foible—I expect my nephew
Sir Wilfull every moment too:—Why, Foible—He means to travel
for improvement.

*Mrs. Mar.* Methinks Sir Wilfull should rather think of marrying than travelling at his years. I hear he is turned of forty.

*Lady.* O he's in less danger of being spoiled by his travels—I
am against my nephew's marrying too young. It will be time
enough when he comes back, and has acquired discretion to
chuse for himself.

*Mrs. Mar.* Methinks Mrs. Millamant and he would make a
very fit match. He may travel afterwards. 'Tis a thing very
usual with young gentlemen.

*Lady.* I promise you I have thought on't—and since 'tis your
judgment, I'll think on't again. I assure you I will; I value
your judgment extremely. On my word I'll propose it.

## SCENE IX

### [*To them*] FOIBLE.

*Lady.* Come, come, Foible—I had forgot my nephew will be
here before dinner—I must make haste.

*Foib.* Mr. Witwoud and Mr. Petulant are come to dine with
your ladyship.

*Lady.* O dear, I can't appear 'till I am dressed. Dear Marwood, shall I be free with you again, and beg you to entertain 'em. I'll make all imaginable haste. Dear friend, excuse me.

### SCENE X

#### Mrs. Marwood, Mrs. Millamant, Mincing.

*Milla.* Sure never anything was so unbred as that odious man.—Marwood, your servant.

*Mrs. Mar.* You have a colour, what's the matter?

*Milla.* That horrid fellow Petulant has provoked me into a flame—I have broke my fan—Mincing, lend me yours;—Is not all the powder out of my hair?

*Mrs. Mar.* No. What has he done?

*Milla.* Nay, he has done nothing; he has only talked—Nay, he has said nothing neither; but he has contradicted everything that has been said. For my part, I thought Witwoud and he would have quarrelled.

*Minc.* I vow, mem, I thought once they would have fit.

*Milla.* Well, 'tis a lamentable thing I swear, that one has not the liberty of chusing one's acquaintance as one does one's cloaths.

*Mrs. Mar.* If we had that liberty, we should be as weary of one set of acquaintance, though never so good, as we are of one suit, though never so fine. A fool and a doily stuff would now and then find days of grace, and be worn for variety.

*Milla.* I could consent to wear 'em, if they would wear alike; but fools never wear out—they are such *drap-de-berry* things! Without one could give 'em to one's chambermaid after a day or two.

*Mrs. Mar.* 'Twere better so indeed. Or what think you of the play-house? A fine gay glossy fool should be given there, like a new masking habit, after the masquerade is over, and we have done with the disguise. For a fool's visit is always a disguise; and never admitted by a woman of wit, but to blind her affair with a lover of sense. If you would but appear barefaced now, and own Mirabell; you might as easily put off Petulant and Witwoud, as your hood and scarf. And indeed 'tis time, for the town has found it: the secret is grown too big for the pretence: 'tis like Mrs. Primly's great belly; she may lace it down before, but it burnishes on her hips. Indeed, Millamant, you can no more conceal it, than my Lady Strammel can her face, that goodly face, which in defiance of her Rhenish-wine tea, will not be comprehended in a mask.

*Milla.* I'll take my death, Marwood, you are more censorious than a decayed beauty, or a discarded toast; Mincing, tell the men they may come up. My aunt is not dressing here; their folly is less provoking than your malice.

## SCENE XI

### MILLAMANT, MARWOOD.

*Milla.* The town has found it. What has it found? That Mirabell loves me is no more a secret, than it is a secret that you discovered it to my aunt, or than the reason why you discovered it is a secret.

*Mrs. Mar.* You are nettled.

*Milla.* You're mistaken. Ridiculous!

*Mrs. Mar.* Indeed, my dear, you'll tear another fan, if you don't mitigate those violent airs.

*Milla.* O silly! Ha, ha, ha. I could laugh immoderately. Poor Mirabell! His constancy to me has quite destroyed his complaisance for all the world beside. I swear, I never enjoined it him, to be so coy—If I had the vanity to think he would obey me, I would command him to shew more gallantry—'tis hardly well bred to be so particular on one hand, and so insensible on the other. But I despair to prevail, and so let him follow his own way. Ha, ha, ha. Pardon me, dear creature, I must laugh, ha, ha, ha; though I grant you 'tis a little barbarous, ha, ha, ha.

*Mrs. Mar.* What pity 'tis, so much fine railery, and delivered with so significant gesture, should be so unhappily directed to miscarry.

*Milla.* Hæ! Dear creature, I ask your pardon—I swear I did not mind you.

*Mrs. Mar.* Mr. Mirabell and you both may think it a thing impossible, when I shall tell him by telling you——

*Milla.* O dear, what? for it is the same thing, if I hear it—ha, ha, ha.

*Mrs. Mar.* That I detest him, hate him, madam.

*Milla.* O madam, why so do I—and yet the creature loves me, ha, ha, ha. How can one forbear laughing to think of it—I am a Sybil if I am not amazed to think what he can see in me. I'll take my death, I think you are handsomer—and within a year or two as young.—If you could but stay for me, I should overtake you—but that cannot be—Well, that thought makes me melancholick—now I'll be sad.

*Mrs. Mar.* Your merry note may be changed sooner than you think.

*Milla.* D'ye say so? Then I'm resolved I'll have a song to keep up my spirits.

## SCENE XII

### [*To them*] MINCING.

*Minc.* The gentlemen stay but to comb, madam; and will wait on you.

*Milla.* Desire Mrs. —— that is in the next room to sing the song I would have learnt yesterday. You shall hear it, madam —Not that there's any great matter in it—but 'tis agreeable to my humour.

## SONG

### *Set by Mr. John Eccles.*

I

Love's but the frailty of the mind,
When 'tis not with ambition joined;
A sickly flame, which if not fed expires;
And feeding, wastes in self-consuming fires.

II

'Tis not to wound a wanton boy
Or am'rous youth, that gives the joy;
But 'tis the glory to have pierced a swain,
For whom inferior beauties sighed in vain.

III

Then I alone the conquest prize,
When I insult a rival's eyes:
If there's delight in love, 'tis when I see
That heart which others bleed for, bleed for me.

## SCENE XIII

### [*To them*] PETULANT, WITWOUD.

*Milla.* Is your animosity composed, gentlemen?

*Wit.* Raillery, raillery, madam, we have no animosity—we hit off a little wit now and then, but no animosity—The falling out of wits is like the falling out of lovers—We agree in the main, like treble and base. Ha, Petulant!

*Pet.* Ay, in the main—but when I have a humour to contradict——

*Wit.* Ay, when he has a humour to contradict, then I contradict too. What, I know my cue. Then we contradict one another like two battledores; for contradictions beget one another like Jews.

*Pet.* If he says black's black—if I have a humour to say 'tis blue—let that pass—all's one for that. If I have a humour to prove it, it must be granted.

*Wit.* Not positively must—but it may—it may.

*Pet.* Yes, it positively must, upon proof positive.

*Wit.* Ay, upon proof positive it must; but upon proof presumptive it only may. That's a logical distinction now, madam.

*Mrs. Mar.* I perceive your debates are of importance, and very learnedly handled.

*Pet.* Importance is one thing, and learning's another; but a debate's a debate, that I assert.

*Wit.* Petulant's an enemy to learning; he relies altogether on his parts.

*Pet.* No, I'm no enemy to learning; it hurts not me.

*Mrs. Mar.* That's a sign indeed it's no enemy to you.

*Pet.* No, no, it's no enemy to anybody, but them that have it.

*Milla.* Well, an illiterate man's my aversion, I wonder at the impudence of any illiterate man, to offer to make love.

*Wit.* That I confess I wonder at too.

*Milla.* Ah! to marry an ignorant! that can hardly read or write.

*Pet.* Why should a man be any further from being married though he can't read, than he is from being hanged? The ordinary's paid for setting the psalm, and the parish-priest for reading the ceremony. And for the rest which is to follow in both cases, a man may do it without book—so all's one for that.

*Milla.* D'ye hear the creature? Lord, here's company, I'll be gone.

## SCENE XIV

### Sir WILFULL WITWOUD *in a riding dress*, Mrs. MARWOOD, PETULANT, WITWOUD, Footman.

*Wit.* In the name of Bartlemew and his fair, what have we here?

*Mrs. Mar.* 'Tis your brother, I fancy. Don't you know him?

*Wit.* Not I—Yes, I think it is he—I've almost forgot him; I have not seen him since the Revolution.

*Foot.* Sir, my lady's dressing. Here's company; if you please to walk in, in the meantime.

*Sir Wil.* Dressing! What, it's but morning here I warrant with you in London; we should count it towards afternoon in

our parts, down in Shropshire.—Why then belike my aunt han't
dined yet—ha, friend?

*Foot.* Your aunt, sir?

*Sir Wil.* My aunt, sir, yes, my aunt, sir, and you: lady, sir;
your lady is my aunt, sir—Why, what do'st thou not know me,
friend? Why then send somebody hither that does. How
long hast thou lived with thy lady, fellow, ha?

*Foot.* A week, sir; longer than anybody in the house, except
my lady's woman.

*Sir Wil.* Why then belike thou dost not know thy lady, if
thou see'st her, ha, friend?

*Foot.* Why truly, sir, I cannot safely swear to her face in a
morning, before she is dressed. 'Tis like I may give a shrewd
guess at her by this time.

*Sir Wil.* Well, prithee try what thou canst do; if thou canst
not guess, enquire her out, do'st hear, fellow? And tell her, her
nephew, Sir Wilfull Witwoud, is in the house.

*Foot.* I shall, sir.

*Sir Wil.* Hold ye, hear me, friend; a word with you in your
ear, prithee who are these gallants?

*Foot.* Really, sir, I can't tell; here come so many here, 'tis
hard to know 'em all.


SCENE XV

Sir WILFULL WITWOUD, PETULANT, WITWOUD,
Mrs. MARWOOD.


*Sir Wil.* Oons this fellow knows less than a starling; I don't
think a' knows his own name.

*Mrs. Mar.* Mr. Witwoud, your brother is not behind-hand in
forgetfulness—I fancy he has forgot you too.

*Wit.* I hope so—the devil take him that remembers first, I say.

*Sir Wil.* Save you, gentlemen and lady.

*Mrs. Mar.* For shame, Mr. Witwoud; why won't you speak
to him?—And you, sir.

*Wit.* Petulant, speak.

*Pet.* And you, sir.

*Sir Wil.* No offence, I hope.          [*Salutes* MARWOOD.

*Mrs. Mar.* No, sure, sir.

*Wit.* This is a vile dog, I see that already. No offence! Ha,
ha, ha, to him; to him, Petulant, smoke him.

*Pet.* It seems as if you had come a journey, sir; hem, hem.
                                        [*Surveying him round.*

*Sir Wil.* Very likely, sir, that it may seem so.

*Pet.* No offence, I hope, sir.

*Wit.* Smoke the boots, the boots; Petulant, the boots; ha,
ha, ha.

*Sir Wil.* Maybe not, sir; thereafter as 'tis meant, sir.

*Pet.* Sir, I presume upon the information of your boots.

*Sir Wil.* Why, 'tis like you may, sir: if you are not satisfied with the information of my boots, sir, if you will step to the stable, you may enquire further of my horse, sir.

*Pet.* Your horse, sir! Your horse is an ass, sir!

*Sir Wil.* Do you speak by way of offence, sir?

*Mrs. Mar.* The gentleman's merry, that's all, sir.—S'life, we shall have a quarrel betwixt an horse and an ass, before they find one another out. You must not take anything amiss from your friends, sir. You are among your friends here, though it may be you don't know it.—If I am not mistaken, you are Sir Wilfull Witwoud.

*Sir Wil.* Right, lady; I am Sir Wilfull Witwoud, so I write myself; no offence to anybody, I hope; and nephew to the Lady Wishfort of this mansion.

*Mrs. Mar.* Don't you know this gentleman, sir?

*Sir Wil.* Hum! What, sure 'tis not—Yea, by'r lady, but 'tis —'Sheart, I know not whether 'tis or no—Yea, but 'tis, by the Rekin. Brother Antony! What, Tony, i'faith! What do'st thou not know me? By'r Lady, nor I thee, thou art so be-cravated, and so beperriwiged—'Sheart, why do'st not speak? Art thou o'erjoyed?

*Wit.* Odso, brother, is it you? Your servant, brother.

*Sir Wil.* Your servant! Why yours, sir. Your servant again—'Sheart, and your friend and servant to that—And a— (*puff*) and a flap dragon for your service, sir: and a hare's foot, and a hare's scut for your service, sir; an you be so cold and so courtly!

*Wit.* No offence, I hope, brother.

*Sir Wil.* 'Sheart, sir, but there is, and much offence.—A pox, is this your Inns o' Court breeding, not to know your friends and your relations, your elders, and your betters?

*Wit.* Why, brother Wilfull of Salop, you may be as short as a Shrewsbury cake, if you please. But I tell you 'tis not modish to know relations in town. You think you're in the country, where great lubberly brothers slabber and kiss one another when they meet, like a call of serjeants—'Tis not the fashion here; 'tis not indeed, dear brother.

*Sir Wil.* The fashion's a fool; and you're a fop, dear brother. 'Sheart, I've suspected this—By'r Lady I conjectured you were a fop, since you began to change the style of your letters, and write in a scrap of paper gilt round the edges, no bigger than a subpæna. I might expect this when you left off Honoured Brother; and hoping you are in good health, and so forth—to begin with a Rat me, knight, I'm so sick of a last night's debauch —O'ds heart, and then tell a familiar tale of a cock and a bull, and a whore and a bottle, and so conclude—You could write news before you were out of your time, when you lived with honest Pumple-Nose, the attorney of Furnival's Inn—You could intreat to be remembered then to your friends round the Rekin. We could have Gazettes then, and Dawks's Letter, and the Weekly Bill, 'till of late days.

*Pet.* 'Slife, Witwoud, were you ever an attorney's clerk? Of the family of the Furnivals. Ha, ha, ha!

*Wit.* Ay, ay, but that was but for a while. Not long, not long; pshaw, I was not in my own power then. An orphan, and this fellow was my guardian; ay, ay, I was glad to consent to that man to come to London. He had the disposal of me then. If I had not agreed to that, I might have been bound prentice to a felt-maker in Shrewsbury; this fellow would have bound me to a maker of felts.

*Sir Wil.* 'Sheart, and better than to be bound to a maker of fops; where, I suppose, you have served your time; and now you may set up for yourself.

*Mrs. Mar.* You intend to travel, sir, as I'm informed.

*Sir Wil.* Belike I may, madam. I may chance to sail upon the salt seas, if my mind hold.

*Pet.* And the wind serve.

*Sir Wil.* Serve or not serve, I shan't ask license of you, sir; nor the weather-cock your companion. I direct my discourse to the lady, sir. 'Tis like my aunt may have told you, madam— Yes, I have settled my concerns, I may say now, and am minded to see foreign parts. If an how that the peace holds, whereby that is taxes abate.

*Mrs. Mar.* I thought you had designed for France at all adventures.

*Sir Wil.* I can't tell that; 'tis like I may, and 'tis like I may not. I am somewhat dainty in making a resolution,—because when I make it I keep it. I don't stand shill I, shall I, then; if I say't, I'll do't: But I have thoughts to tarry a small matter in town, to learn somewhat of your lingo first, before I cross the seas. I'd gladly have a spice of your French as they say, whereby to hold discourse in foreign countries.

*Mrs. Mar.* Here's an academy in town for that use.

*Sir Wil.* There is? 'Tis like there may.

*Mrs. Mar.* No doubt you will return very much improved.

*Wit.* Yes, refined like a Dutch skipper from a whale-fishing.

### SCENE XVI

#### [*To them*] Lady WISHFORT *and* FAINALL.

*Lady.* Nephew, you are welcome.

*Sir Wil.* Aunt, your servant.

*Fain.* Sir Wilfull, your most faithful servant.

*Sir Wil.* Cousin Fainall, give me your hand.

*Lady.* Cousin Witwoud, your servant; Mr. Petulant, your servant—nephew, you are welcome again. Will you drink anything after your journey, nephew, before you eat? Dinner's almost ready.

*Sir Wil.* I'm very well I thank you, aunt—however, I thank you for your courteous offer. 'Sheart, I was afraid you would have been in the fashion too, and have remembered to have forgot your relations. Here's your Cousin Tony, belike, I mayn't call him brother for fear of offence.

*Lady.* O he's a rallier, nephew—my cousin's a wit; and your great wits always rally their best friends to chuse. When you have been abroad, nephew, you'll understand raillery better.

[FAIN. *and* Mrs. MARWOOD *talk apart.*

*Sir Wil.* Why then let him hold his tongue in the meantime; and rail when that day comes.

## SCENE XVII

### [*To them*] MINCING.

*Minc.* Mem, I come to acquaint your laship that dinner is impatient.

*Sir Wil.* Impatient? Why then belike it won't stay 'till I pull off my boots. Sweetheart, can you help me to a pair of slippers?—My man's with his horses, I warrant.

*Lady.* Fie, fie, nephew, you would not pull off your boots here—go down into the hall—dinner shall stay for you.—My nephew's a little unbred, you'll pardon him, madam—Gentlemen, will you walk? Marwood?

*Mrs. Mar.* I'll follow you, madame,—before Sir Wilfull is ready.

## SCENE XVIII

### MARWOOD, FAINALL.

*Fain.* Why then Foible's a bawd, an arrant, rank, matchmaking bawd. And I, it seems, am a husband, a rank-husband; and my wife a very arrant, rank-wife,—all in the way of the world. 'Sdeath, to be a cuckold by anticipation, a cuckold in embrio? Sure I was born with budding antlers like a young satyr, or a citizen's child. 'Sdeath, to be outwitted, to be outjilted—out-matrimonied—If I had kept my speed like a stag, 'twere somewhat—but to crawl after, with my horns like a snail, and be outstripped by my wife—'tis scurvy wedlock.

*Mrs. Mar.* Then shake it off, you have often wished for an opportunity to part;—and now you have it. But first prevent their plot,—the half of Millamant's fortune is too considerable to be parted with, to a foe, to Mirabell.

*Fain.* Damn him, that had been mine, had you not made that fond discovery—that had been forfeited, had they been married. My wife had added lustre to my horns, by that increase of fortune, I could have worn 'em tipt with gold, though my forehead had been furnished like a deputy-lieutenant's hall.

*Mrs. Mar.* They may prove a cap of maintenance to you still, if you can away with your wife. And she's no worse than when you had her—I dare swear she had given up her game, before she was married.

*Fain.* Hum! That may be——

*Mrs. Mar.* You married her to keep you: and if you can contrive to have her keep you better than you expected, why should you not keep her longer than you intended?

*Fain.* The means, the means.

*Mrs. Mar.* Discover to my lady your wife's conduct; threaten to part with her—my lady loves her, and will come to any composition to save her reputation. Take the opportunity of breaking it, just upon the discovery of this imposture. My lady will be enraged beyond bounds, and sacrifice niece, and fortune, and all at that conjuncture. And let me alone to keep her warm; if she should flag in her part, I will not fail to prompt her.

*Fain.* Faith, this has an appearance.

*Mrs. Mar.* I'm sorry I hinted to my lady to endeavour a match between Millamant and Sir Wilfull, that may be an obstacle.

*Fain.* O for that matter leave me to manage him; I'll disable him for that, he will drink like a Dane: after dinner, I'll set his hand in.

*Mrs. Mar.* Well, how do you stand affected towards your lady?

*Fain.* Why faith I'm thinking of it.—Let me see—I am married already; so that's over—My wife has plaid the jade with me—well, that's over too—I never loved her, or if I had, why that would have been over too by this time—Jealous of her I cannot be, for I am certain; so there's an end of jealousy. Weary of her, I am and shall be—No, there's no end of that; no, no, that were too much to hope. Thus far concerning my repose. Now for my reputation—As to my own, I married not for it; so that's out of the question.—And as to my part in my wife's—why she had parted with hers before; so bringing none to me, she can take none from me; 'tis against all rule of play, that I should lose to one who has not wherewithal to stake.

*Mrs. Mar.* Besides, you forget, marriage is honourable.

*Fain.* Hum! Faith and that's well thought on; marriage is honourable, as you say; and if so, wherefore should cuckoldom be a discredit, being derived from so honourable a root?

*Mrs. Mar.* Nay, I know not; if the root be honourable, why not the branches?

*Fain.* So, so, why this point's clear.—Well, how do we proceed?

*Mrs. Mar.* I will contrive a letter which shall be delivered to my lady at the time when that rascal who is to act Sir Rowland is with her. It shall come as from an unknown hand—for the less I appear to know of the truth, the better I can play the incendiary. Besides, I would not have Foible provoked if I could help it,—because you know she knows some passages—nay, I expect all will come out—but let the mine be sprung first, and then I care not if I am discovered.

*Fain.* If the worst come to the worst, I'll turn my wife to grass—I have already a deed of settlement of the best part of her estate; which I wheadled out of her; and that you shall partake at least.

*Mrs. Mar.* I hope you are convinced that I hate Mirabell now: you'll be no more jealous?

*Fain.* Jealous, no,—by this kiss—let husbands be jealous; but let the lover still believe: or if he doubt, let it be only to endear his pleasure, and prepare the joy that follows, when he proves his mistress true. But let husbands' doubts convert to endless jealousy; or if they have belief, let it corrupt to superstition, and blind credulity. I am single, and will herd no more with 'em. True, I wear the badge, but I'll disown the order. And since I take my leave of 'em, I care not if I leave 'em a common motto to their common crest.

All husbands must, or pain, or shame, endure;
The wise too jealous are, fools too secure.

## ACT IV

### SCENE I.—[*Scene continues*]

#### Lady WISHFORT *and* FOIBLE.

*Lady.* Is Sir Rowland coming, say'st thou, Foible? and are things in order?

*Foib.* Yes, madam. I have put wax-lights in the sconces; and placed the footmen in a row in the hall, in their best liveries, with the coachman and postilion to fill up the equipage.

*Lady.* Have you pullvilled the coachman and postilion, that they may not stink of the stable, when Sir Rowland comes by?

*Foib.* Yes, madam.

*Lady.* And are the dancers and the music ready, that he may be entertained in all points with correspondence to his passion?

*Foib.* All is ready, madam.

*Lady.* And—well—and how do I look, Foible?

*Foib.* Most killing well, madam.

*Lady.* Well, and how shall I receive him? In what figure shall I give his heart the first impression? There is a great deal in the first impression. Shall I sit?—No, I won't sit—I'll walk —ay, I'll walk from the door upon his entrance; and then turn full upon him—No, that will be too sudden. I'll lie—ay, I'll lie down—I'll receive him in my little dressing-room, there's a couch—yes, yes, I'll give the first impression on a couch—I won't lie neither, but loll and lean upon one elbow; with one foot a little dangling off, jogging in a thoughtful way—yes— and then as soon as he appears, start, ay, start and be surprised, and rise to meet him in a pretty disorder—yes—O, nothing is more alluring than a levee from a couch in some confusion— it shews the foot to advantage, and furnishes with blushes, and re-composing airs beyond comparison. Hark! There's a coach.

*Foib.* 'Tis he, madam.

*Lady.* O dear, has my nephew made his addresses to Millamant? I ordered him.

*Foib.* Sir Wilfull is set in to drinking, madam, in the parlour.

*Lady.* Ods my life, I'll send him to her. Call her down, Foible; bring her hither. I'll send him as I go—When they are together, then come to me, Foible, that I may not be too long alone with Sir Rowland.


SCENE II

Mrs. MILLAMANT, Mrs. FAINALL, FOIBLE.

*Foib.* Madam, I stayed here, to tell your ladyship that Mr. Mirabell has waited this half-hour for an opportunity to talk with you. Though my lady's orders were to leave you and Sir Wilfull together. Shall I tell Mr. Mirabell that you are at leisure?

*Milla.* No—What would the dear man have? I am thought-ful, and would amuse myself,—bid him come another time.

> There never yet was woman made,
> Nor shall, but to be cursed.
>
> [*Repeating and walking about.*

That's hard!

*Mrs. Fain.* You are very fond of Sir John Suckling to-day, Millamant, and the poets.

*Milla.* He? Ay, and filthy verses—so I am.

*Foib.* Sir Wilfull is coming, madam. Shall I send Mr. Mirabell away?

*Milla.* Ay, if you please, Foible, send him away,—or send him hither,—just as you will, dear Foible.—I think I'll see him—Shall I? Ay, let the wretch come.

Thyrsis, a youth of the inspired train.   [*Repeating.*
Dear Fainall, entertain Sir Wilfull—thou hast philosophy to undergo a fool, thou art married and hast patience—I would confer with my own thoughts.

*Mrs. Fain.* I am obliged to you, that you would make me your proxy in this affair; but I have business of my own.


### SCENE III

[*To them*] Sir WILFULL.

*Mrs. Fain.* O Sir Wilfull; you are come at the critical instant. There's your mistress up to the ears in love and contemplation, pursue your point, now or never.

*Sir Wil.* Yes; my aunt will have it so,—I would gladly have been encouraged with a bottle or two, because I'm somewhat wary at first, before I am acquainted—[*This while* MILLA. *walks about repeating to herself.*] But I hope, after a time, I shall break my mind—that is upon further acquaintance.—So for the present, cousin, I'll take my leave—if so be you'll be so kind to make my excuse, I'll return to my company——

*Mrs. Fain.* O fie, Sir Wilfull! What, you must not be daunted.

*Sir Wil.* Daunted, no, that's not it, it is not so much for that —for if so be that I set on't, I'll do't.   But only for the present, 'tis sufficient 'till further acquaintance, that's all—your servant.

*Mrs. Fain.* Nay, I'll swear you shall never lose so favourable an opportunity, if I can help it.   I'll leave you together, and lock the door.


### SCENE IV

Sir WILFULL, MILLAMANT.

*Sir Wil.* Nay, nay, cousin,—I have forgot my gloves.—What d'ye do?  'Sheart, a' has locked the door indeed, I think—Nay, Cousin Fainall, open the door—Pshaw, what a vixen trick is this?—Nay, now a' has seen me too—cousin, I made bold to pass through as it were—I think this door's inchanted——

*Milla.* [*repeating*].

> I prithee spare me, gentle boy,
> Press me no more for that slight toy.

*Sir. Wil.* Anan? Cousin, your servant.
*Milla.*      That foolish trifle of a heart——
Sir Wilfull!

*Sir Wil.* Yes—your servant.   No offence, I hope, cousin.

*Milla.* [*repeating.*]

> I swear it will not do its part,
> Though thou dost thine, employ'st thy power and art.

Natural, easy Suckling!

*Sir Wil.* Anan?   Suckling?   No such suckling neither, cousin nor stripling: I thank Heaven, I'm no minor.

*Milla.* Ah, rustick, ruder than Gothick.

*Sir Wil.* Well, well, I shall understand your lingo one of these days, cousin, in the meanwhile I must answer in plain English.

*Milla.* Have you any business with me, Sir Wilfull?

*Sir Wil.* Not at present, cousin.—Yes, I made bold to see, to come and know if that how you were disposed to fetch a walk this evening, if so be that I might not be troublesome, I would have fought a walk with you.

*Milla.* A walk?   What then?

*Sir Wil.* Nay, nothing—only for the walk's sake, that's all——

*Milla.* I nauseate walking; 'tis a country diversion, I loath the country and everything that relates to it.

*Sir Wil.* Indeed!   Hah!   Look ye, look ye, you do?   Nay, 'tis like you may—Here are choice of pastimes here in town, as plays and the like, that must be confessed indeed——

*Milla.* Ah *l'etourdie!* I hate the town too.

*Sir Wil.* Dear heart, that's much—Hah! that you should hate 'em both!   Hah! 'tis like you may; there are some can't relish the town, and others can't away with the country,—'tis like you may be one of those, cousin.

*Milla.* Ha, ha, ha.   Yes, 'tis like I may.—You have nothing further to say to me?

*Sir Wil.* Not at present, cousin.—'Tis like when I have an opportunity to be more private, I may break my mind in some measure—I conjecture you partly guess—However, that's as time shall try,—but spare to speak and spare to speed, as they say.

*Milla.* If it is of no great importance, Sir Wilfull, you will oblige me to leave me: I have just now a little business——

*Sir Wil.* Enough, enough, cousin: yes, yes, all a case—when you're disposed, when you're disposed.   Now's as well as another time; and another time as well as now.   All's one for that.—Yes, yes, if your concerns call you, there's no haste; it will keep cold as they say—Cousin, your servant.—I think this door's locked.

*Milla.* You may go this way, sir.

*Sir Wil.* Your servant, then with your leave I'll return to my company.

*Milla.* Ay, ay; ha, ha, ha.

> Like Phœbus sung the no less am'rous boy.

## SCENE V

### MILLAMANT, MIRABELL.

*Mira.*        Like Daphne she, as lovely and as coy.
Do you lock yourself up from me, to make my search more
curious? Or is this pretty artifice contrived, to signify that
here the chase must end, and my pursuit be crowned, for you
can fly no further?

*Milla.* Vanity! No—I'll fly and be followed to the last
moment, though I am upon the very verge of matrimony, I
expect you should sollicit me as much as if I were wavering at
the grate of a monastery, with one foot over the threshold. I'll
be sollicited to the very last, nay and afterwards.

*Mira.* What, after the last?

*Milla.* O, I should think I was poor and had nothing to
bestow, if I were reduced to an inglorious ease, and freed from
the agreeable fatigues of sollicitation.

*Mira.* But do not you know, that when favours are conferred
upon instant and tedious sollicitation, that they diminish in
their value, and that both the giver loses the grace, and the
receiver lessens his pleasure?

*Milla.* It may be in things of common application; but never
sure in love. O, I hate a lover that can dare to think he draws
a moment's air, independent on the bounty of his mistress.
There is not so impudent a thing in nature, as the sawcy look of
an assured man, confident of success. The pedantick arrogance
of a very husband has not so pragmatical an air. Ah! I'll
never marry, unless I am first made sure of my will and pleasure.

*Mira.* Would you have 'em both before marriage? Or will
you be contented with the first now, and stay for the other 'till
after grace?

*Milla.* Ah, don't be impertinent—My dear liberty, shall I
leave thee? My faithful solitude, my darling contemplation,
must I bid you then adieu? Ay-h, adieu—my morning thoughts,
agreeable wakings, indolent slumbers, all ye *douceurs*, ye *someils
du matin*, adieu—I can't do't, 'tis more than impossible—
Positively, Mirabell, I'll lie abed in a morning as long as I please.

*Mira.* Then I'll get up in a morning as early as I please.

*Milla.* Ah! Idle creature, get up when you will—And d'ye
hear, I won't be called names after I'm married; positively I
won't be called names.

*Mira.* Names!

*Milla.* Ay, as wife, spouse, my dear, joy, jewel, love, sweetheart, and the rest of that nauseous cant, in which men and their
wives are so fulsomly familiar—I shall never bear that—Good
Mirabell, don't let us be familiar or fond, nor kiss before folks,
like my Lady Fadler and Sir Francis: nor go to Hyde Park

together the first Sunday in a new chariot, to provoke eyes and whispers; and then never be seen there together again; as if we were proud of one another the first week, and ashamed of one another ever after. Let us never visit together, nor go to a play together, but let us be very strange and well bred: let us be as strange as if we had been married a great while; and as well bred as if we were not married at all.

*Mira.* Have you any more conditions to offer? Hitherto your demands are pretty reasonable.

*Milla.* Trifles,—as liberty to pay and receive visits to and from whom I please; to write and receive letters, without interrogatories or wry faces on your part; to wear what I please; and chuse conversation with regard only to my own taste; to have no obligation upon me to converse with wits that I don't like, because they are your acquaintance; or to be intimate with fools because they may be your relations. Come to dinner when I please, dine in my dressing-room when I'm out of humour, without giving a reason. To have my closet inviolate; to be sole empress of my tea-table, which you must never presume to approach without first asking leave. And lastly, wherever I am, you shall always knock at the door before you come in. These articles subscribed, if I continue to endure you a little longer, I may by degrees dwindle into a wife.

*Mira.* Your bill of fare is something advanced in this latter account. Well, have I liberty to offer conditions—that when you are dwindled into a wife, I may not be beyond measure enlarged into a husband?

*Milla.* You have free leave, propose your utmost, speak and spare not.

*Mira.* I thank you. *Inprimis* then, I covenant that your acquaintance be general; that you admit no sworn confidante, or intimate of your own sex; no she friend to skreen her affairs under your countenance, and tempt you to make trial of a mutual secrecy. No decoy-duck to wheadle you a *fop—scrambling* to the play in a mask—then bring you home in a pretended fright, when you think you shall be found out—and rail at me for missing the play, and disappointing the frolick which you had to pick me up and prove my constancy.

*Milla.* Detestable *inprimis!* I go to the play in a mask!

*Mira. Item,* I article, that you continue to like your own face as long as I shall: and while it passes current with me, that you endeavour not to new coin it. To which end, together with all vizards for the day, I prohibit all masks for the night, made of oiled-skins and I know not what—hog's bones, hare's gall, pig water, and the marrow of a roasted cat. In short, I forbid all commerce with the gentlewoman in *what-d'ye-call-it* Court. *Item,* I shut my doors against all bauds with baskets, and pennyworths of *muslin, china, fans, atlasses,* etc.—*Item,* when you shall be breeding——

*Milla.* Ah! name it not.

*Mira.* Which may be presumed, with a blessing on our endeavours——

*Milla.* Odious endeavours!

*Mira.* I denounce against all strait lacing, squeezing for a shape, 'till you mould my boy's head like a sugar-loaf; and instead of a man-child, make me father to a crooked-billet. Lastly, to the dominion of the *tea-table* I submit.—But with *proviso*, that you exceed not in your province; but restrain yourself to native and simple *tea-table* drinks, as *tea, chocolate,* and *coffee.* As likewise to genuine and authorised *tea-table* talk—such as mending of fashions, spoiling reputations, railing at absent friends, and so forth—but that on no account you encroach upon the men's prerogative, and presume to drink healths, or toast fellows; for prevention of which, I banish all *foreign forces,* all auxiliaries to the *tea-table,* as *orange-brandy,* all *anniseed, cinamon, citron* and *Barbado's-waters,* together with *ratafia* and the most noble spirit of *clary.*—But for *couslip-wine, poppy-water,* and all *dormitives,* those I allow.—These *provisos* admitted, in other things I may prove a tractable and complying husband.

*Milla.* O horrid *provisos!* filthy strong waters! I toast fellows, odious men! I hate your odious *provisos.*

*Mira.* Then we're agreed. Shall I kiss your hand upon the contract? and here comes one to be a witness to the sealing of the deed.


### SCENE VI

#### [*To them*] Mrs. FAINALL.

*Milla.* Fainall, what shall I do? Shall I have him? I think I must have him.

*Mrs. Fain.* Ay, ay, take him, take him, what should you do?

*Milla.* Well then—I'll take my death I'm in a horrid fright— Fainall, I shall never say it—Well—I think—I'll endure you.

*Mrs. Fain.* Fy, fy, have him, have him, and tell him so in plain terms: for I am sure you have a mind to him.

*Milla.* Are you? I think I have—and the horrid man looks as if he thought so too—Well, you ridiculous thing you, I'll have you—I won't be kissed, nor I won't be thanked—Here, kiss my hand though—so, hold your tongue now, don't say a word.

*Mrs. Fain.* Mirabell, there's a necessity for your obedience; —you have neither time to talk nor stay. My mother is coming; and in my conscience, if she should see you, would fall into fits, and maybe not recover time enough to return to Sir Rowland; who, as Foible tells me, is in a fair way to succeed. Therefore spare your ecstasies for another occasion, and slip down the back stairs, where Foible waits to consult you.

*Milla.* Ay, go, go. In the meantime I suppose you have said something to please me.

*Mira.* I am all obedience.


### SCENE VII

#### MILLAMANT, Mrs. FAINALL.

*Mrs. Fain.* Yonder Sir Wilfull's drunk; and so noisy that my mother has been forced to leave Sir Rowland to appease him; but he answers her only with singing and drinking— What they may have done by this time I know not; but Petulant and he were upon quarrelling as I came by.

*Milla.* Well, if Mirabell should not make a good husband, I am a lost thing; for I find I love him violently.

*Mrs. Fain.* So it seems; for you mind not what's said to you. —If you doubt him, you had best take up with Sir Wilfull.

*Milla.* How can you name that superannuated lubber? foh!


### SCENE VIII

#### [*To them*] WITWOUD *from drinking.*

*Mrs. Fain.* So, is the fray made up, that you have left 'em?

*Wit.* Left 'em? I could stay no longer—I have laughed like ten christnings—I am tipsy with laughing—if I had staid any longer I should have burst,—I must have been let out and pieced in the sides like an unsized camlet—Yes, yes, the fray is composed; my lady came in like a *noli prosequi*, and stopt the proceedings.

*Milla.* What was the dispute?

*Wit.* That's the jest; there was no dispute. They could neither of 'em speak for rage; and so fell a sputtering at one another like two roasting apples.


### SCENE IX

#### [*To them*] PETULANT *drunk.*

*Wit.* Now, Petulant? all's over, all's well? Gad, my head begins to whim it about—Why dost thou not speak? thou art both as drunk and as mute as a fish.

*Pet.* Look you, Mrs. Millamant—if you can love me, dear nymph—say it—and that's the conclusion—pass on, or pass off,—that's all.

*Wit.* Thou hast uttered volumes, folios, in less than *decimo sexto,* my dear Lacedemonian. Sirrah, Petulant, thou art an epitomiser of words.

*Pet.* Witwoud—you are an annihilator of sense.

*Wit.* Thou art a retailer of phrases; and dost deal in remnants of remnants, like a maker of pincushions—thou art in truth (metaphorically speaking) a speaker of shorthand.

*Pet.* Thou art (without a figure) just one half of an ass, and Baldwin yonder, thy half-brother, is the rest—a gemini of asses split, would make just four of you.

*Wit.* Thou dost bite, my dear mustard-seed; kiss me for that.

*Pet.* Stand off—I'll kiss no more males,—I have kissed your *twin* yonder in a humour of reconciliation, 'till he (*hiccup*) rises upon my stomach like a radish.

*Milla.* Eh! filthy creature—what was the quarrel?

*Pet.* There was no quarrel—there might have been a quarrel.

*Wit.* If there had been words enow between 'em to have expressed provocation, they had gone together by the ears like a pair of castanets.

*Pet.* You were the quarrel.

*Milla.* Me!

*Pet.* If I have a humour to quarrel, I can make less matters conclude premises.—If you are not handsom, what then; if I have a humour to prove it?—If I shall have my reward, say so; if not, fight for your face the next time yourself—I'll go sleep.

*Wit.* Do, wrap thyself up like a woodlouse, and dream revenge—and hear me, if thou canst learn to write by to-morrow morning, pen me a challenge—I'll carry it for thee.

*Pet.* Carry your mistress's monkey a spider,—go flea dogs, and read romances—I'll go to bed to my maid.

*Mrs. Fain.* He's horridly drunk—how came you all in this pickle?

*Wit.* A plot, a plot, to get rid of the knight,—your husband's advice; but he sneaked off.


## SCENE X

### Sir Wilfull *drunk,* Lady Wishfort, Witwoud, Millamant, Mrs. Fainall.

*Lady.* Out upon't, out upon't, at years of discretion, and comport yourself at this rantipole rate.

*Sir Wil.* No offence, aunt.

*Lady.* Offence? As I'm a person, I'm ashamed of you—Fogh! how you stink of wine! D'ye think my niece will ever endure such a *borachio!* you're an absolute *borachio.*

*Sir Wil.* Borachio!

*Lady.* At a time when you should commence an amour, and put your best foot foremost——

*Sir Wil.* 'Sheart, an you grutch me your liquor, make a bill—give me more drink, and take my purse.     [*Sings.*

> Prithee fill me the glass
> 'Till it laugh in my face,
> With ale that is potent and mellow;
> He that whines for a lass
> Is an ignorant ass,
> For a *bumper* has not its fellow.

But if you would have me marry my cousin, say the word, and I'll do't—Wilfull will do't, that's the word—Wilfull will do't, that's my crest—my motto I have forgot.

*Lady.* My nephew's a little overtaken, cousin—but 'tis with drinking your health—O' my word you are obliged to him——

*Sir Wil.* *In vino veritas*, aunt:—If I drunk your health to-day, cousin, I am a *borachio*. But if you have a mind to be married say the word, and send for the piper, Wilfull will do't. If not, dust it away, and let's have t'other round—Tony, 'odsheart, where's Tony—Tony's an honest fellow, but he spits after a bumper, and that's a fault.     [*Sings.*

> We'll drink and we'll never ha' done, boys,
> Put the glass then around with the sun, boys,
> Let Apollo's example invite us;
> For he's drunk every night,
> And that makes him so bright,
> That he's able next morning to light us.

The sun's a good pimple, an honest soaker, he has a cellar at your Antipodes. If I travel, aunt, I touch at your Antipodes—your Antipodes are a good rascally sort of topsie-turvy fellows—if I had a bumper I'd stand upon my head and drink a health to 'em—A match or no match, cousin, with the hard name—aunt, Wilfull will do't. If she has her maidenhead let her look to't; if she has not, let her keep her own counsel in the mean-time, and cry out at the nine months' end.

*Milla.* Your pardon, madam, I can stay no longer—Sir Wilfull grows very powerful. Egh! how he smells! I shall be overcome if I stay. Come, cousin.

### SCENE XI

#### Lady WISHFORT, Sir WILFULL WITWOUD, Mr. WITWOUD, FOIBLE.

*Lady.* Smells! he would poison a tallow-chandler and his family. Beastly creature, I know not what to do with him.—Travel, quoth a; ay travel, travel, get thee gone, get thee but far enough, to the Saracens, or the Tartars, or the Turks—for thou art not fit to live in a Christian commonwealth, thou beastly pagan.

*Sir Wil.* Turks, no; no Turks, aunt: your Turks are infidels, and believe not in the grape. Your Mahometan, your Mussulman is a dry stinkard—no offence, aunt. My map says that your Turk is not so honest a man as your Christian—I cannot find by the map that your mufti is orthodox—whereby it is a plain case, that orthodox is a hard word, aunt, and (*hiccup*) Greek for claret. [*Sings.*

> To drink is a Christian diversion
> Unknown to the Turk or the Persian:
>    Let Mahometan fools
>    Live by heathenish rules
> And be damned over tea-cups and coffee.
>    But let British lads sing,
>    Crown a health to the king,
> And a fig for your sultan and Sophy.

Ah, Tony! [FOIBLE *whispers* Lady WISHFORT.

*Lady.* Sir Rowland impatient? Good lack! what shall I do with this beastly tumbril?—Go lie down and sleep, you sot—or as I'm a person, I'll have you bastinadoed with broom-sticks. Call up the wenches with broom-sticks.

*Sir Wil.* Ahey? Wenches, where are the wenches?

*Lady.* Dear Cousin Witwoud, get him away, and you will bind me to you inviolably. I have an affair of moment that invades me with some precipitation.—You will oblige me to all futurity.

*Wit.* Come, knight—pox on him, I don't know what to say to him—will you go to a cock-match?

*Sir Wil.* With a wench, Tony? Is she a shake-bag, sirrah? Let me bite your cheek for that.

*Wit.* Horrible! He has a breath like a bagpipe—Ay, ay, come, will you march, my Salopian?

*Sir Wil.* Lead on, little Tony—I'll follow thee, my Anthony, my Tantony. Sirrah, thou shalt be my Tantony, and I'll be thy pig.

—And a fig for your sultan and Sophy.

*Lady.* This will never do. It will never make a match—at least before he has been abroad.

## SCENE XII

Lady WISHFORT, WAITWELL *disguised as for* Sir ROWLAND.

*Lady.* Dear Sir Rowland, I am confounded with confusion at the retrospection of my own rudeness,—I have more pardons to ask than the pope distributes in the year of jubilee. But I hope where there is likely to be so near an alliance, we may unbend the severity of decorum, and dispense with a little ceremony.

*Wait.* My impatience, madam, is the effect of my transport;—and 'till I have the possession of your adorable person, I am tantalised on the rack; and do but hang, madam, on the tenter of expectation.

*Lady.* You have excess of gallantry, Sir Rowland; and press things to a conclusion, with a most prevailing vehemence.—But a day or two for decency of marriage——

*Wait.* For decency of funeral, madam. The delay will break my heart—or if that should fail, I shall be poisoned. My nephew will get an inkling of my designs, and poison me,—and I would willingly starve him before I die—I would gladly go out of the world with that satisfaction.—That would be some comfort to me, if I could but live so long as to be revenged on that unnatural viper.

*Lady.* Is he so unnatural, say you? Truly I would contribute much both to the saving of your life, and the accomplishment of your revenge—not that I respect myself; though he has been a perfidious wretch to me.

*Wait.* Perfidious to you!

*Lady.* O Sir Rowland, the hours that he has died away at my feet, the tears that he has shed, the oaths that he has sworn, the palpitations that he has felt, the trances and the tremblings, the ardors and the ecstasies, the kneelings, and the risings, the heart-heavings and the hand-gripings, the pangs and the pathetick regards of his protesting eyes! Oh, no memory can register.

*Wait.* What, my rival! Is the rebel my rival? a' dies.

*Lady.* No, don't kill him at once, Sir Rowland, starve him gradually inch by inch.

*Wait.* I'll do't. In three weeks he shall be bare-foot; in a month out at knees with begging an alms,—he shall starve upward and upward, 'till he has nothing living but his head, and then go out in a stink like a candle's end upon a save-all.

*Lady.* Well, Sir Rowland, you have the way,—you are no novice in the labyrinth of love—you have the clue—But as I am a person, Sir Rowland, you must not attribute my yielding to any sinister appetite, or indigestion of widow-hood; nor impute my complacency to any lethargy of continence—I hope you do not think me prone to any iteration of nuptials——

*Wait.* Far be it from me——

*Lady.* If you do, I protest I must recede—or think that I have made a prostitution of decorums, but in the vehemence of compassion, and to save the life of a person of so much importance——

*Wait.* I esteem it so——

*Lady.* Or else you wrong my condescension——

*Wait.* I do not, I do not——
*Lady.* Indeed you do.
*Wait.* I do not, fair shrine of virtue.
*Lady.* If you think the least scruple of carnality was an ingredient——
*Wait.* Dear madam, no.  You are all camphire and frankincense, all chastity and odour.
*Lady.* Or that——

## SCENE XIII

### [*To them*] FOIBLE.

*Foib.* Madam, the dancers are ready, and there's one with a letter, who must deliver it into your own hands.
*Lady.* Sir Rowland, will you give me leave?  Think favourably, judge candidly, and conclude you have found a person who would suffer racks in honour's cause, dear Sir Rowland, and will wait on you incessantly.

## SCENE XIV

### WAITWELL, FOIBLE.

*Wait.* Fie, fie!—What a slavery have I undergone; spouse, hast thou any cordial, I want spirits.
*Foib.* What a washy rogue art thou, to pant thus for a quarter of an hour's lying and swearing to a fine lady?
*Wait.* O, she is the antidote to desire.  Spouse, thou wilt fare the worse for't—I shall have no appetite to iteration of nuptials this eight and forty hours—By this hand I'd rather be a chairman in the dog-days, than act Sir Rowland 'till this time to-morrow.

## SCENE XV

### [*To them*] Lady *with a letter.*

*Lady.* Call in the dancers;—Sir Rowland, we'll sit, if you please, and see the entertainment.              [*Dance.*
Now with your permission, Sir Rowland, I will peruse my letter—I would open it in your presence, because I would not make you uneasy.  If it should make you uneasy I would burn it—speak if it does—but you may see, the superscription is like a woman's hand.
*Foib.* By heaven!  Mrs. Marwood's, I know it,—my heart aches—get it from her——              [*To him.*

*Wait.* A woman's hand? No, madam, that's no woman's hand, I see that already. That's somebody whose throat must be cut.

*Lady.* Nay, Sir Rowland, since you give me a proof of your passion by your jealousy, I promise you I'll make a return, by a frank communication—You shall see it—we'll open it together —look you here.

[*Reads.*] " Madam, though unknown to you,"—Look you there, 'tis from nobody that I know—" I have that honour for your character, that I think myself obliged to let you know you are abused. He who pretends to be Sir Rowland is a cheat and a rascal——" Oh heavens! what's this?

*Foib.* Unfortunate, all's ruined.

*Wait.* How, how, let me see, let me see [*reading*], " A rascal and disguised, and suborned for that imposture,"—O villany! O villany!—" by the contrivance of——"

*Lady.* I shall faint, I shall die, oh!

*Foib.* Say 'tis your nephew's hand.—Quickly, his plot, swear, swear it.       [*To him.*

*Wait.* Here's a villain! Madam, don't you perceive it, don't you see it?

*Lady.* Too well, too well. I have seen too much.

*Wait.* I told you at first I knew the hand—A woman's hand? The rascal writes a sort of a large hand; your Roman hand—I saw there was a throat to be cut presently. If he were my son, as he is my nephew, I'd pistol him——

*Foib.* O treachery! But are you sure, Sir Rowland, it is his writing?

*Wait.* Sure? Am I here? do I live? do I love this pearl of India? I have twenty letters in my pocket from him, in the same character.

*Lady.* How!

*Foib.* O what luck it is, Sir Rowland, that you were present at this juncture! This was the business that brought Mr. Mirabell disguised to Madam Millamant this afternoon. I thought something was contriving, when he stole by me and would have hid his face.

*Lady.* How, how!—I heard the villain was in the house indeed; and now I remember, my niece went away abruptly, when Sir Wilfull was to have made his addresses.

*Foib.* Then, then, madam, Mr. Mirabell waited for her in her chamber; but I would not tell your ladyship to discompose you when you were to receive Sir Rowland.

*Wait.* Enough, his date is short.

*Foib.* No, good Sir Rowland, don't incur the law.

*Wait.* Law! I care not for law. I can but die, and 'tis in a good cause—my lady shall be satisfied of my truth and innocence, though it cost me my life.

*Lady.* No, dear Sir Rowland, don't fight, if you should be

killed I must never shew my face; or hanged—O consider my
reputation, Sir Rowland—No, you shan't fight.—I'll go in and
examine my niece; I'll make her confess. I conjure you, Sir
Rowland, by all your love, not to fight.

*Wait.* I am charmed, madam, I obey. But some proof you
must let me give you;—I'll go for a black box, which contains
the writings of my whole estate, and deliver that into your hands.

*Lady.* Ay, dear Sir Rowland, that will be some comfort, bring
the black box.

*Wait.* And may I presume to bring a contract to be signed
this night? May I hope so far?

*Lady.* Bring what you will; but come alive, pray come alive.
O this is a happy discovery.

*Wait.* Dead or alive I'll come—and married we will be in
spight of treachery; ay, and get an heir that shall defeat the
last remaining glimpse of hope in my abandoned nephew.
Come, my buxom widow:

> E'er long you shall substantial proof receive
> That I'm an arrant knight——

*Foib.* Or arrant knave.


# ACT V

## SCENE I.—[*Scene continues*]

### Lady WISHFORT *and* FOIBLE.

*Lady.* Out of my house, out of my house, thou viper, thou
serpent, that I have fostered; thou bosom traitress, that I raised
from nothing—begone, begone, begone, go, go,—that I took
from washing of old gauze and weaving of dead hair, with a
bleak blue nose, over a chafing-dish of starved embers, and
dining behind a traverse rag, in a shop no bigger than a bird-
cage,—go, go, starve again, do, do.

*Foib.* Dear madam, I'll beg pardon on my knees.

*Lady.* Away, out, out, go set up for yourself again—do, drive
a trade, do, with your threepenny-worth of small ware, flaunting
upon a packthread, under a brandy-seller's bulk, or against a
dead wall by a ballad-monger. Go, hang out an old frisoneer-
gorget with a yard of yellow colberteen again; do; an old gnawed
mask, two rows of pins and a child's fiddle; a glass necklace
with the beads broken, and a quilted nightcap with one ear.
Go, go, drive a trade.—These were your commodities, you
treacherous trull, this was the merchandize you dealt in, when

I took you into my house, placed you next myself, and made you governante of my whole family. You have forgot this, have you, now you have feathered your nest?

*Foib.* No, no, dear madam. Do but hear me, have but a moment's patience—I'll confess all. Mr. Mirabell seduced me; I am not the first that he has wheadled with his dissembling tongue; your ladyship's own wisdom has been deluded by him, then how should I, a poor ignorant, defend myself? O madam, if you knew but what he promised me, and how he assured me your ladyship should come to no damage—or else the wealth of the Indies should not have bribed me to conspire against so good, so sweet, so kind a lady as you have been to me.

*Lady.* No damage? What, to betray me, to marry me to a cast-serving-man; to make me a receptacle, an hospital for a decayed pimp? No damage? O thou frontless impudence, more than a big-bellied actress.

*Foib.* Pray do but hear me, madam, he could not marry your ladyship, madam—no indeed, his marriage was to have been void in law; for he was married to me first, to secure your adyship. He could not have bedded your ladyship; for if he had consummated with your ladyship, he must have run the risk of the law, and been put upon his clergy—Yes indeed, I enquired of the law in that case before I would meddle or make.

*Lady.* What, then I have been your property, have I? I have been convenient to you, it seems,—while you were catering for Mirabell; I have been broaker for you? What, have you made a passive bawd of me?—This exceeds all precedent; I am brought to fine uses, to become a botcher of second-hand marriages between Abigails and Andrews! I'll couple you. Yes, I'll baste you together, you and your Philander. I'll Duke's Place you, as I'm a person. Your turtle is in custody already: you shall coo in the same cage, if there be constable or warrant in the parish.

*Foib.* O that ever I was born, O that I was ever married,— a bride, ay, I shall be a Bridewell-bride. Oh!

## SCENE II

### Mrs FAINALL, FOIBLE.

*Mrs. Fain.* Poor Foible, what's the matter?

*Foib.* O madam, my lady's gone for a constable; I shall be had to a justice, and put to Bridewell to beat hemp; poor Waitwell's gone to prison already.

*Mrs. Fain.* Have a good heart, Foible, Mirabell's gone to give security for him. This is all Marwood's and my husband's doing.

*Foib.* Yes, yes; I know it, madam; she was in my lady's

closet, and overheard all that you said to me before dinner.
She sent the letter to my lady; and that missing effect, Mr.
Fainall laid this plot to arrest Waitwell, when he pretended to
go for the papers; and in the meantime Mrs. Marwood declared
all to my lady.

*Mrs. Fain.* Was there no mention made of me in the letter?
—My mother does not suspect my being in the confederacy?
I fancy Marwood has not told her, though she has told my
husband.

*Foib.* Yes, madam; but my lady did not see that part: we
stifled the letter before she read so far. Has that mischievous
devil told Mr. Fainall of your ladyship then?

*Mrs. Fain.* Ay, all's out, my affair with Mirabell, everything
discovered. This is the last day of our living together, that's
my comfort.

*Foib.* Indeed, madam, and so 'tis a comfort if you knew all,—
he has been even with your ladyship; which I could have told
you long enough since, but I love to keep peace and quietness
by my good will: I had rather bring friends together than set
'em at distance. But Mrs. Marwood and he are nearer related
than ever their parents thought for.

*Mrs. Fain.* Say'st thou so, Foible? Canst thou prove this?

*Foib.* I can take my oath of it, madam, so can Mrs. Mincing;
we have had many a fair word from Madam Marwood, to conceal
something that passed in our chamber one evening when you
were at Hyde Park;—and we were thought to have gone a walking: but we went up unawares,—though we were sworn to
secrecy too; Madam Marwood took a book and swore us upon
it: but it was but a book of poems,—so long as it was not a
Bible-oath, we may break it with a safe conscience.

*Mrs. Fain.* This discovery is the most opportune thing I
could wish. Now Mincing?

## SCENE III

*[To them]* MINCING.

*Minc.* My lady would speak with Mrs. Foible, mem. Mr.
Mirabell is with her; he has set your spouse at liberty, Mrs.
Foible, and would have you hide yourself in my lady's closet,
'till my old lady's anger is abated. O, my old lady is in a
perilous passion at something Mr. Fainall has said; he swears,
and my old lady cries. There's a fearful hurricane I vow.
He says, mem, how that he'll have my lady's fortune made
over to him, or he'll be divorced.

*Mrs. Fain.* Does your lady or Mirabell know that?

*Minc.* Yes, mem, they have sent me to see if Sir Wilfull be
sober, and to bring him to them. My lady is resolved to have

him I think, rather than lose such a vast sum as six thousand
pound. O, come, Mrs. Foible, I hear my old lady.

*Mrs. Fain.* Foible, you must tell Mincing that she must
prepare to vouch when I call her.

*Foib.* Yes, yes, madam.

*Minc.* O yes, mem, I'll vouch anything for your ladyship's
service, be what it will.


## SCENE IV

### Mrs. Fainall, Lady Wishfort, Marwood.

*Lady.* O my dear friend, how can I enumerate the benefits
that I have received from your goodness? To you I owe the
timely discovery of the false vows of Mirabell; to you I owe the
detection of the impostor Sir Rowland. And now you are
become an intercessor with my son-in-law, to save the honour
of my house, and compound for the frailties of my daughter.
Well, friend, you are enough to reconcile me to the bad world, or
else I would retire to deserts and solitudes; and feed harmless
sheep by groves and purling streams. Dear Marwood, let us
leave the world, and retire by ourselves and be shepherdesses.

*Mrs. Mar.* Let us first dispatch the affair in hand, madam.
We shall have leisure to think of retirement afterwards. Here
is one who is concerned in the treaty.

*Lady.* O daughter, daughter, is it possible thou should'st be
my child, bone of my bone, and flesh of my flesh, and as I may
say, another me, and yet transgress the most minute particle of
severe virtue? Is it possible you should lean aside to iniquity,
who have been cast in the direct mold of virtue? I have not
only been a mold but a pattern for you, and a model for you,
after you were brought into the world.

*Mrs. Fain.* I don't understand your ladyship.

*Lady.* Not understand? Why, have you not been naught?
Have you not been sophisticated? Not understand? Here I
am ruined to compound for your caprices and your cuckoldoms.
I must pawn my plate and my jewels, and ruin my niece, and
all little enough——

*Mrs. Fain.* I am wronged and abused, and so are you. 'Tis
a false accusation, as false as hell, as false as your friend there,
ay, or your friend's friend, my false husband.

*Mrs. Mar.* My friend, Mrs. Fainall? Your husband my
friend, what do you mean?

*Mrs. Fain.* I know what I mean, madam, and so do you;
and so shall the world at a time convenient.

*Mrs. Mar.* I am sorry to see you so passionate, madam.
More temper would look more like innocence. But I have done.
I am sorry my zeal to serve your ladyship and family should

admit of misconstruction, or make me liable to affronts. You
will pardon me, madam, if I meddle no more with an affair in
which I am not personally concerned.

*Lady.* O dear friend, I am so ashamed that you should meet
with such returns—You ought to ask pardon on your knees,
ungrateful creature; she deserves more from you, than all your
life can accomplish—O don't leave me destitute in this per-
plexity;—no, stick to me, my good genius.

*Mrs. Fain.* I tell you, madam, you're abused—Stick to you?
ay, like a leach, to suck your best blood—she'll drop off when
she's full. Madam, you shan't pawn a bodkin, nor part with a
brass counter, in composition for me. I defy 'em all. Let 'em
prove their aspersions: I know my own innocence, and dare
stand a trial.

## SCENE V

### Lady WISHFORT, MARWOOD.

*Lady.* Why, if she should be innocent, if she should be wronged
after all, ha? I don't know what to think,—and I promise you,
her education has been unexceptionable—I may say it; for I
chiefly made it my own care to initiate her very infancy in the
rudiments of virtue, and to impress upon her tender years a
young odium and aversion to the very sight of men,—ay, friend,
she would ha' shrieked if she had but seen a man, 'till she was in
her teens. As I'm a person 'tis true.—She was never suffered
to play with a male-child, though but in coats; nay, her very
babies were of the feminine gender,—O, she never looked a man
in the face but her own father, or the chaplain, and him we
made a shift to put upon her for a woman, by the help of his
long garments, and his sleek face; 'till she was going in her
fifteen.

*Mrs. Mar.* 'Twas much she should be deceived so long.

*Lady.* I warrant you, or she would never have borne to have
been catechised by him; and have heard his long lectures
against singing and dancing, and such debaucheries; and going
to filthy plays; and profane musick-meetings, where the lewd
trebles squeek nothing but bawdy, and the bases roar blasphemy.
O, she would have swooned at the sight or name of an obscene
play-book—and can I think after all this, that my daughter can
be naught? What, a whore? And thought it excommunica-
tion to set her foot within the door of a play-house. O dear
friend, I can't believe it, no, no; as she says, let him prove it,
let him prove it.

*Mrs Mar.* Prove it, madam? What, and have your name
prostituted in a publick court; yours and your daughter's
reputation worried at the bar by a pack of bawling lawyers?

To be ushered in with an *Oyez* of scandal; and have your case opened by an old fumbling lecher in a quoif like a man midwife, to bring your daughter's infamy to light; to be a theme for legal punsters, and quiblers by the statute; and become a jest, against a rule of court, where there is no precedent for a jest in any record; not even in Doomsday Book: to discompose the gravity of the bench, and provoke naughty interrogatories in more naughty law Latin; while the good judge, tickled with the proceeding, simpers under a grey beard, and fidges off and on his cushion as if he had swallowed cantharides, or sate upon cow-itch.

*Lady.* O, 'tis very hard!

*Mrs. Mar.* And then to have my young revellers of the Temple take notes, like prentices at a conventicle; and after talk it over again in Commons, or before drawers in an eating-house.

*Lady.* Worse and worse.

*Mrs. Mar.* Nay, this is nothing; if it would end here 'twere well. But it must after this be consigned by the shorthand writers to the publick press; and from thence be transferred to the hands, nay, into the throats and lungs of hawkers, with voices more licentious than the loud flounder-man's: and this you must hear 'till you are stunned; nay, you must hear nothing else for some days.

*Lady.* O, 'tis insupportable. No, no, dear friend, make it up, make it up; ay, ay, I'll compound. I'll give up all, myself and my all, my niece and her all—anything, everything for composition.

*Mrs. Mar.* Nay, madam, I advise nothing, I only lay before you, as a friend, the inconveniencies which perhaps you have overseen. Here comes Mr. Fainall, if he will be satisfied to huddle up all in silence, I shall be glad. You must think I would rather congratulate than condole with you.

## SCENE VI

### FAINALL, Lady WISHFORT, Mrs. MARWOOD.

*Lady.* Ay, ay, I do not doubt it, dear Marwood: no, no, I do not doubt it.

*Fain.* Well, madam; I have suffered myself to be overcome by the importunity of this lady your friend; and am content you shall enjoy your own proper estate during life; on condition you oblige yourself never to marry, under such penalty as I think convenient.

*Lady.* Never to marry?

*Fain.* No more Sir Rowlands,—the next imposture may not be so timely detected.

*Mrs. Mar.* That condition, I dare answer, my lady will consent to, without difficulty; she has already but too much experienced the perfidiousness of men. Besides, madam, when we retire to our pastoral solitude we shall bid adieu to all other thoughts.

*Lady.* Ay, that's true; but in case of necessity; as of health, or some such emergency——

*Fain.* O, if you are prescribed marriage, you shall be considered; I will only reserve to myself the power to chuse for you. If your physick be wholsome, it matters not who is your apothecary. Next, my wife shall settle on me the remainder of her fortune, not made over already; and for her maintenance depend entirely on my discretion.

*Lady.* This is most inhumanly savage; exceeding the barbarity of a Muscovite husband.

*Fain.* I learned it from his czarish majesty's retinue, in a winter evening's conference over brandy and pepper, amongst other secrets of matrimony and policy, as they are at present practised in the northern hemisphere. But this must be agreed unto, and that positively. Lastly, I will be endowed, in right of my wife, with that six thousand pound, which is the moiety of Mrs. Millamant's fortune in your possession; and which she has forfeited (as will appear by the last will and testament of your deceased husband, Sir Jonathan Wishfort) by her disobedience in contracting herself against your consent or knowledge; and by refusing the offered match with Sir Wilfull Witwoud, which you, like a careful aunt, had provided for her.

*Lady.* My nephew was *non compos ;* and could not make his addresses.

*Fain.* I come to make demands—I'll hear no objections.

*Lady.* You will grant me time to consider?

*Fain.* Yes, while the instrument is drawing, to which you must set your hand 'till more sufficient deeds can be perfected: which I will take care shall be done with all possible speed. In the meanwhile I will go for the said instrument, and 'till my return you may ballance this matter in your own discretion.


## SCENE VII

### Lady WISHFORT, Mrs. MARWOOD.

*Lady.* This insolence is beyond all precedent, all parallel; must I be subject to this merciless villain?

*Mrs. Mar.* 'Tis severe indeed, madam, that you should smart for your daughter's wantonness.

*Lady.* 'Twas against my consent that she married this barbarian, but she would have him, though her year was not out.—Ah! her first husband, my son Languish, would not have carried it thus.  Well, that was my choice, this is hers; she is matched now with a witness—I shall be mad, dear friend, is there no comfort for me?  Must I live to be confiscated at this rebel-rate?—Here come two more of my Egyptian plagues too.

### SCENE VIII

#### *To them*] MILLAMANT, Sir WILFULL.

*Sir Wil.*  Aunt, your servant.

*Lady.*  Out, caterpillar, call not me aunt; I know thee not.

*Sir Wil.*  I confess I have been a little in disguise, as they say —'Sheart! and I'm sorry for't.  What would you have?  I hope I committed no offence, aunt—and if I did I am willing to make satisfaction; and what can a man say fairer?  If I have broke anything I'll pay for't, an it cost a pound.  And so let that content for what's past, and make no more words.  For what's to come, to pleasure you I'm willing to marry my cousin. So pray let's all be friends, she and I are agreed upon the matter before a witness.

*Lady.*  How's this, dear niece?  Have I any comfort?  Can this be true?

*Milla.*  I am content to be a sacrifice to your repose, madam; and to convince you that I had no hand in the plot, as you were misinformed, I have laid my commands on Mirabell to come in person, and be a witness that I give my hand to this flower of knighthood; and for the contract that passed between Mirabell and me, I have obliged him to make a resignation of it in your ladyship's presence;—he is without, and waits your leave for admittance.

*Lady.*  Well, I'll swear I am something revived at this testimony of your obedience; but I cannot admit that traitor,—I fear I cannot fortify myself to support his appearance.  He is as terrible to me as a Gorgon; if I see him I fear I shall turn to stone, petrify incessantly.

*Milla.*  If you disoblige him he may resent your refusal, and insist upon the contract still.  Then 'tis the last time he will be offensive to you.

*Lady.*  Are you sure it will be the last time?—If I were sure of that—shall I never see him again?

*Milla.*  Sir Wilfull, you and he are to travel together, are you not?

*Sir Wil.*  'Sheart, the gentleman's a civil gentleman. aunt, let him come in; why, we are sworn brothers and fellow-travellers. —We are to be Pylades and Orestes, he and I—he is to be my interpreter in foreign parts.  He has been over-seas once already;

and with proviso that I marry my cousin, will cross 'em once again, only to bear me company.—'Sheart, I'll call him in,—an I set on't once, he shall come in; and see who'll hinder him.

[*Goes to the door and hems.*

*Mrs. Mar.* This is precious fooling, if it would pass; but I'll know the bottom of it.

*Lady.* O dear Marwood, you are not going?

*Mar.* Not far, madam; I'll return immediately.

## SCENE IX

Lady WISHFORT, MILLAMANT, Sir WILFULL, MIRABELL.

*Sir Wil.* Look up, man, I'll stand by you, 'sbud, an she do frown, she can't kill you;—besides—harkee, she dare not frown desperately, because her face is none of her own; 'sheart, and she should her forehead would wrinkle like the coat of a cream-cheese; but mum for that, fellow-traveller.

*Mira.* If a deep sense of the many injuries I have offered to so good a lady, with a sincere remorse, and a hearty contrition, can but obtain the least glance of compassion, I am too happy —Ah, madam, there was a time—but let it be forgotten—I confess I have deservedly forfeited the high place I once held, of sighing at your feet; nay, kill me not, by turning from me in disdain—I come not to plead for favour;—nay, not for pardon; I am a suppliant only for pity—I am going where I never shall behold you more——

*Sir Wil.* How, fellow-traveller!—You shall go by yourself then.

*Mira.* Let me be pitied first; and afterwards forgotten—I ask no more.

*Sir Wil.* By'r Lady, a very reasonable request, and will cost you nothing, aunt.—Come, come, forgive and forget, aunt, why you must an you are a Christian.

*Mira.* Consider, madam, in reality, you could not receive much prejudice; it was an innocent device; though I confess it had a face of guiltiness, it was at most an artifice which love contrived—and errors which love produces have ever been accounted venial. At least think it is punishment enough, that I have lost what in my heart I hold most dear, that to your cruel indignation I have offered up this beauty, and with her my peace and quiet; nay, all my hopes of future comfort.

*Sir Wil.* An he does not move me, would I may never be o' the quorum,—an it were not as good a deed as to drink, to give her to him again, I would I might never take shipping— Aunt, if you don't forgive quickly, I shall melt, I can tell you that. My contract went no farther than a little mouth-glue, and that's hardly dry;—one doleful sigh more from my fellow-traveller and 'tis dissolved.

*Lady.* Well, nephew, upon your account—Ah, he has a false insinuating tongue—Well, sir, I will stifle my just resentment at my nephew's request.—I will endeavour what I can to forget,—but on proviso that you resign the contract with my niece immediately.

*Mira.* It is in writing and with papers of concern; but I have sent my servant for it, and will deliver it to you, with all acknowledgments for your transcendent goodness.

*Lady.* Oh, he has witchcraft in his eyes and tongue;—when I did not see him I could have bribed a villain to his assassination; but his appearance rakes the embers which have so long lain smothered in my breast.—— [*Aside.*


SCENE X

[*To them*] FAINALL, Mrs. MARWOOD.

*Fain.* Your date of deliberation, madam, is expired. Here is the instrument, are you prepared to sign?

*Lady.* If I were prepared, I am not impowered. My niece exerts a lawful claim, having matched herself by my direction to Sir Wilfull.

*Fain.* That sham is too gross to pass on me—though 'tis imposed on you, madam.

*Milla.* Sir, I have given my consent.

*Mira.* And, sir, I have resigned my pretensions.

*Sir Wil.* And, sir, I assert my right; and will maintain it in defiance of you, sir, and of your instrument. 'Sheart, an you talk of an instrument, sir, I have an old fox by my thigh shall hack your instrument of ram vellum to shreds, sir. It shall not be sufficient for a mittimus or a tailor's measure; therefore withdraw your instrument, sir, or by'r Lady I shall draw mine.

*Lady.* Hold, nephew, hold.

*Milla.* Good Sir Wilfull, respite your valour.

*Fain.* Indeed? Are you provided of your guard, with your single beef-eater there? But I'm prepared for you; and insist upon my first proposal. You shall submit your own estate to my management, and absolutely make over my wife's to my sole use; as pursuant to the purport and tenor of this other covenant.—I suppose, madam, your consent is not requisite in this case; nor, Mr. Mirabell, your resignation; nor, Sir Wilfull, your right—you may draw your fox if you please sir, and make a bear-garden flourish somewhere else; for here it will not avail. This, my Lady Wishfort, must be subscribed, or your darling daughter's turned adrift, like a leaky hulk to sink or swim, as she and the current of this lewd town can agree.

*Lady.* Is there no means, no remedy, to stop my ruin? Ungrateful wretch! dost thou not owe thy being, thy subsistence, to my daughter's fortune?

*Fain.* I'll answer you when I have the rest of it in my possession.

*Mira.* But that you would not accept of a remedy from my hands—I own I have not deserved you should owe any obligation to me; or else perhaps I could advise——

*Lady.* O what? what? to save me and my child from ruin, from want, I'll forgive all that's past; nay, I'll consent to anything to come, to be delivered from this tyranny.

*Mira.* Ay, madam; but that is too late, my reward is intercepted. You have disposed of her, who only could have made me a compensation for all my services;—but be it as it may, I am resolved I'll serve you, you shall not be wronged in this savage manner.

*Lady.* How! Dear Mr. Mirabell, can you be so generous at last! But it is not possible. Harkee, I'll break my nephew's match, you shall have my niece yet, and all her fortune, if you can but save me from this imminent danger.

*Mira.* Will you? I take you at your word. I ask no more. I must have leave for two criminals to appear.

*Lady.* Ay, ay, anybody, anybody.

*Mira.* Foible is one, and a penitent.


### SCENE XI

[*To them*] Mrs. FAINALL, FOIBLE, MINCING.

MIRA. *and* Lady *go to* Mrs. FAIN. *and* FOIBLE.

*Mrs. Mar.* O my shame! these corrupt things are brought hither to expose me. [*To* FAIN.

*Fain.* If it must all come out, why let 'em know it, 'tis but *the way of the world.* That shall not urge me to relinquish or abate one tittle of my terms, no, I will insist the more.

*Foib.* Yes indeed, madam, I'll take my Bible-oath of it.

*Minc.* And so will I, mem.

*Lady.* O Marwood, Marwood, art thou false? my friend deceive me? Hast thou been a wicked accomplice with that profligate man?

*Mrs. Mar.* Have you so much ingratitude and injustice, to give credit against your friend, to the aspersions of two such mercenary truls?

*Minc.* Mercenary, mem? I scorn your words. 'Tis true we found you and Mr. Fainall in the blue garret; by the same token, you swore us to secrecy upon Messalinas's poems. Mercenary? No, if we would have been mercenary, we should have held our tongues; you would have bribed us sufficiently.

*Fain.* Go, you are an insignificant thing.—Well, what are you the better for this!. Is this Mr. Mirabell's expedient? I'll be put off no longer—You, thing, that was a wife, shall smart for this. I will not leave thee wherewithal to hide thy shame: your body shall be naked as your reputation.

*Mrs. Fain.* I despise you, and defy your malice—you have aspersed me wrongfully—I have proved your falsehood—go you and your treacherous—I will not name it, but starve together—perish.

*Fain.* Not while you are worth a groat, indeed, my dear. Madam, I'll be fooled no longer.

*Lady.* Ah, Mr. Mirabell, this is small comfort, the detection of this affair.

*Mira.* O in good time—Your leave for the other offender and penitent to appear, madam.


### SCENE XII

*[To them]* WAITWELL *with a box of writings.*

*Lady.* O Sir Rowland—Well, rascal.

*Wait.* What your ladyship pleases.—I have brought the black box at last, madam.

*Mira.* Give it me.   Madam, you remember your promise.

*Lady.* Ay, dear sir.

*Mira.* Where are the gentlemen?

*Wait.* At hand, sir, rubbing their eyes,—just risen from sleep.

*Fain.* S'death, what's this to me?   I'll not wait your private concerns.


### SCENE XIII

*[To them]* PETULANT, WITWOUD.

*Pet.* How now? what's the matter? whose hand's out?

*Wit.* Hey day! what, are you all got together, like players at the end of the last act?

*Mira.* You may remember, gentlemen, I once requested your hands as witnesses to a certain parchment.

*Wit.* Ay, I do, my hand I remember—Petulant set his mark.

*Mira.* You wrong him, his name is fairly written, as shall appear—You do not remember, gentlemen, anything of what that parchment contained?                    [*Undoing the box.*

*Wit.* No.

*Pet.* Not I.   I writ, I read nothing.

*Mira.* Very well, now you shall know—Madam, your promise.

*Lady.* Ay, ay, sir, upon my honour.

*Mira.* Mr. Fainall, it is now time that you should know that your lady, while she was at her own disposal, and before you had by your insinuations wheadled her out of a pretended settlement of the greatest part of her fortune——

*Fain.* Sir! pretended!

*Mira.* Yes, sir. I say that this lady while a widow, having it seems received some cautions respecting your inconstancy and tyranny of temper, which from her own partial opinion and fondness of you she could never have suspected—she did, I say, by the wholesome advice of friends and of sages learned in the laws of this land, deliver this same as her act and deed to me in trust, and to the uses within mentioned. You may read if you please—[*holding out the parchment*] though perhaps what is written on the back may serve your occasions.

*Fain.* Very likely, sir. What's here? Damnation!

[*Reads.*] "A deed of conveyance of the whole estate real of Arabella Languish, widow, in trust to Edward Mirabell."— Confusion!

*Mira.* Even so, sir, 'tis *the way of the world*, sir; of the widows of the world. I suppose this deed may bear an elder date than what you have obtained from your lady.

*Fain.* Perfidious fiend! then thus I'll be revenged.——

[*Offers to run at* Mrs. FAIN.

*Sir Wil.* Hold, sir, now you may make your bear-garden flourish somewhere else, sir.

*Fain.* Mirabell, you shall hear of this, sir, be sure you shall.— Let me pass, oaf.

*Mrs. Fain.* Madam, you seem to stifle your resentment: you had better give it vent.

*Mrs. Mar.* Yes, it shall have vent—and to your confusion, or I'll perish in the attempt.


## SCENE XIV (THE LAST)

Lady WISHFORT, MILLAMANT, MIRABELL, Mrs. FAINALL, Sir WILFULL, PETULANT, WITWOUD, FOIBLE, MINCING, WAITWELL.

*Lady.* O daughter, daughter, 'tis plain thou hast inherited thy mother's prudence.

*Mrs. Fain.* Thank Mr. Mirabell, a cautious friend, to whose advice all is owing.

*Lady.* Well, Mr. Mirabell, you have kept your promise—and I must perform mine.—First I pardon for your sake Sir Rowland there and Foible—the next thing is to break the matter to my nephew—and how to do that——

*Mira.* For that, madam, give yourself no trouble,—let me have your consent—Sir Wilfull is my friend; he has had compassion upon lovers, and generously engaged a volunteer in this action, for our service; and now designs to prosecute his travels.

*Sir Wil.* 'Sheart, aunt, I have no mind to marry. My cousin's a fine lady, and the gentleman loves her, and she loves him, and they deserve one another; my resolution is to see foreign parts—I have set on't—and when I'm set on't, I must do't. And if these two gentlemen would travel too, I think they may be spared.

*Pet.* For my part, I say little—I think things are best off or on.

*Wit.* I gad, I understand nothing of the matter,—I'm in a maze yet, like a dog in a dancing-school.

*Lady.* Well, sir, take her, and with her all the joy I can give you.

*Milla.* Why does not the man take me? Would you have me give myself to you over again?

*Mira.* Ay, and over and over again.—[*Kisses her hand.*] I would have you as often as possibly I can. Well, Heaven grant I love you not too well, that's all my fear.

*Sir Wil.* 'Sheart, you'll have time enough to toy after you're married; or if you will toy now, let us have a dance in the meantime; that we who are not lovers may have some other employment, besides looking on.

*Mira.* With all my heart, dear Sir Wilfull. What shall we do for musick?

*Foib.* O sir, some that were provided for Sir Rowland's entertainment are yet within call.          [*A dance.*

*Lady.* As I am a person I can hold out no longer;—I have wasted my spirits so to-day already, that I am ready to sink under the fatigue; and I cannot but have some fears upon me yet, that my son Fainall will pursue some desperate course.

*Mira.* Madam, disquiet not yourself on that account; to my knowledge his circumstances are such, he must of force comply. For my part, I will contribute all that in me lies to a reunion; in the meantime, madam [*to* Mrs. FAIN.], let me before these witnesses restore to you this deed of trust; it may be a means, well managed, to make you live easily together.

> From hence let those be warned, who mean to wed;
> Lest mutual falshood stain the bridal-bed:
> For each deceiver to his cost may find,
> That marriage frauds too oft are paid in kind.
>
>                                        [*Exeunt omnes.*

# EPILOGUE

AFTER our epilogue this crowd dismisses,
I'm thinking how this play'll be pulled to pieces.
But pray consider, e'er you doom its fall,
How hard a thing 'twould be, to please you all.
There are some criticks so with spleen diseased,
They scarcely come inclining to be pleased:
And sure he must have more than mortal skill,
Who pleases any one against his will.
Then, all bad poets we are sure are foes,
And how their number's swelled the town well knows:
In shoals, I've marked 'em judging in the pit; ⎫
Though they're on no pretence for judgment fit, ⎬
But that they have been damned for want of wit. ⎭
Since when, they by their own offences taught,
Set up for spies on plays, and finding fault.
Others there are whose malice we'd prevent; ⎫
Such, who watch plays, with scurrilous intent ⎬
To mark out who by Characters are meant. ⎭
And though no perfect likeness they can trace;
Yet each pretends to know the Copied Face.
These, with false glosses feed their own ill-nature,
And turn to Libel, what was meant a Satire.
May such malicious Fops this fortune find,
To think themselves alone the Fools designed:
If any are so arrogantly vain, ⎫
To think they singly can support a Scene, ⎬
And furnish Fool enough to entertain. ⎭
For well the learned and the judicious know, ⎫
That Satire scorns to stoop so meanly low, ⎬
As any one abstracted Fop to show. ⎭
For, as when painters form a matchless face,
They from each Fair one catch some different grace;
And shining features in one portrait blend,
To which no single beauty must pretend:
So poets oft, do in one piece expose
Whole *belles assemblées* of *cocquets* and *beaux*.

235

# VENICE PRESERVED

# DRAMATIS PERSONÆ

DUKE OF VENICE.
PRIULI, Father to Belvidera, a Senator.
ANTONIO, a Fine Speaker in the Senate.

JAFFEIR
PIERRE
RENAULT
BEDAMAR
SPINOSA
THEODORE
ELIOT
REVILLIDO      } Conspirators.
DURAND
MEZZANA
BRAMVEIL
TERNON
BRABE
RETROSI

BELVIDERA.
AQUILINA.

Two Women, Attendants on Belvidera.
Two Women, Servants to Aquilina.
The Council of Ten.
Officer.
Guards.
Friar.
Executioner and Rabble.

## EPISTLE DEDICATORY

TO HER GRACE

## THE DUCHESS OF PORTSMOUTH

MADAM,—Were it possible for me to let the world know how entirely your Grace's goodness has devoted a poor man to your service; were there words enough in speech to express the mighty sense I have of your great bounty towards me; surely I should write and talk of it for ever: but your Grace has given me so large a theme, and laid so very vast a foundation, that imagination wants stock to build upon it. I am as one dumb when I would speak of it, and when I strive to write, I want a scale of thought sufficient to comprehend the height of it. Forgive me, then, madam, if (as a poor peasant once made a present of an apple to an emperor) I bring this small tribute, the humble growth of my little garden, and lay it at your feet. Believe it is paid you with the utmost gratitude, believe that so long as I have thought to remember how very much I owe your generous nature, I will ever have a heart that shall be grateful for it too: Your grace, next Heaven, deserves it amply from me; that gave me life, but on a hard condition, till your extended favour taught me to prize the gift, and took the heavy burthen it was clogged with from me: I mean hard fortune: when I had enemies, that with malicious power kept back and shaded me from those royal beams, whose warmth is all I have, or hope to live by; your noble pity and compassion found me, where I was far cast backward from my blessing; down in the rear of Fortune, called me up, placed me in the shine, and I have felt its comfort. You have in that restored me to my native right, for a steady faith, and loyalty to my prince, was all the inheritance my father left me, and however hardly my ill-fortune deal with me, 'tis what I prize so well that I ne'er pawned it yet, and hope I ne'er shall part with it. Nature and Fortune were certainly in league when you were born, and as the first took care to give you beauty enough to enslave the hearts of all the world, so the other resolved to do its merit justice, that none but a monarch, fit to rule that world, should e'er possess it, and in it he had an empire. The young prince you have given him, by his blooming virtues, early declares the mighty stock he came from; and as you have taken all the pious care of a dear mother and a prudent guardian to give him a noble and generous education may it succeed according to his merits and your wishes: may he grow up to be a bulwark to his illustrious father, and a patron to his loyal subjects, with wisdom and learning to assist him, whenever called to his councils, to defend his right against the encroachments of republicans in his senates, to cherish such men as shall be able to vindicate the royal cause, that good and fit servants to the crown may never be lost for want of a protector. May he have courage and conduct, fit to fight his battles abroad, and terrify his rebels at home; and that all these may be yet more sure, may he never, during the spring-time of his years, when these growing virtues ought with care to be cherished, in order to their ripening; may he never meet with vicious natures, or the tongues of faithless, sordid, insipid flatterers, to blast 'em. To conclude; may he be as great as the hand of Fortune (with his honour) shall be able to make him: and may your grace, who are so good a mistress, and so noble a patroness, never meet with a less grateful servant than, madam, your grace's entirely devoted creature,

THOMAS OTWAY.

# PROLOGUE

In these distracted times, when each man dreads
The bloody stratagems of busy heads;
When we have feared three years we know not what,
Till witnesses begin to die o' th' rot,
What made our poet meddle with a plot?
Was't that he fancied, for the very sake
And name of plot, his trifling play might take?
For there's not in't one inch-board evidence,
But 'tis, he says, to reason plain and sense,
And that he thinks a plausible defence.
Were Truth by Sense and Reason to be tried,
Sure all our swearers might be laid aside:
No, of such tools our author has no need,
To make his plot, or make his play succeed;
He of black Bills, has no prodigious tales,
Or Spanish pilgrims cast ashore in Wales;
Here's not one murther'd magistrate at least,
Kept rank like ven'son for a city feast,
Grown four days stiff, the better to prepare
And fit his pliant limbs to ride in chair:
Yet here's an army raised, though under ground,
But no man seen, nor one commission found;
Here is a traitor too, that's very old,
Turbulent, subtle, mischievous, and bold,
Bloody, revengeful, and to crown his part,
Loves fumbling with a wench, with all his heart;
Till after having many changes passed,
In spite of age (thanks heaven) is hanged at last:
Next is a senator that keeps a whore,
In Venice none a higher office bore;
To lewdness every night the letcher ran,
Show me, all London, such another man,
Match him at Mother Creswold's if you can.
O Poland, Poland! had it been thy lot,
T' have heard in time of this Venetian plot,
Thou surely chosen hadst one king from thence,
And honoured them as thou hast England since.

# VENICE PRESERVED

## OR, A PLOT DISCOVERED

## ACT I

### SCENE I

*Enter* Priuli *and* Jaffeir.

*Priu.* No more! I'll hear no more; begone and leave.
*Jaff.* Not hear me! by my sufferings but you shall!
My lord, my lord! I'm not that abject wretch
You think me: Patience! where's the distance throws
Me back so far, but I may boldly speak
In right, though proud oppression will not hear me!
  *Priu.* Have you not wrong'd me?
  *Jaff.*                 Could my nature e'er
Have brook'd injustice or the doing wrongs,
I need not now thus low have bent myself
To gain a hearing from a cruel father!
Wronged you?
  *Priu.*       Yes! wronged me, in the nicest point:
The honour of my house; you have done me wrong;
You may remember (for I now will speak,
And urge its baseness): when you first came home
From travel, with such hopes as made you looked on
By all men's eyes, a youth of expectation;
Pleased with your growing virtue, I received you:
Courted, and sought to raise you to your merits:
My house, my table, nay my fortune too,
My very self, was yours; you might have used me
To your best service; like an open friend,
I treated, trusted you, and thought you mine;
When in requital of my best endeavours,
You treacherously practised to undo me,
Seduced the weakness of my age's darling,
My only child, and stole her from my bosom:
O Belvidera!
  *Jaff.*       'Tis to me you owe her,
Childless you had been else, and in the grave,
Your name extinct, nor no more Priuli heard of.

You may remember, scarce five years are past,
Since in your brigandine you sailed to see
The Adriatic wedded by our Duke,
And I was with you: your unskilful pilot
Dashed us upon a rock; when to your boat
You made for safety; entered first yourself;
The affrighted Belvidera following next,
As she stood trembling on the vessel side,
Was by a wave washed off into the deep,
When instantly I plunged into the sea,
And buffeting the billows to her rescue,
Redeemed her life with half the loss of mine:
Like a rich conquest in one hand I bore her,
And with the other dashed the saucy waves,
That thronged and pressed to rob me of my prize:
I brought her, gave her to your despairing arms:
Indeed you thanked me; but a nobler gratitude
Rose in her soul: for from that hour she loved me,
Till for her life she paid me with herself.
   *Priu.* You stole her from me, like a thief you stole her,
At dead of night; that curséd hour you chose
To rifle me of all my heart held dear.
May all your joys in her prove false like mine;
A sterile fortune and a barren bed,
Attend you both; continual discord make
Your days and nights bitter and grievous: still
May the hard hand of a vexatious need
Oppress, and grind you; till at last you find
The curse of disobedience all your portion.
   *Jaff.* Half of your curse you have bestowed in vain,
Heaven has already crowned our faithful loves
With a young boy, sweet as his mother's beauty.
May he live to prove more gentle than his grandsire,
And happier than his father!
   *Priu.*                Rather live
To bait thee for his bread, and din your ears
With hungry cries: whilst his unhappy mother
Sits down and weeps in bitterness of want.
   *Jaff.* You talk as if 'twould please you.
   *Priu.*               'Twould, by Heaven.
Once she was dear indeed; the drops that fell
From my sad heart, when she forgot her duty,
The fountain of my life was not so precious:
But she is gone, and if I am a man
I will forget her.
   *Jaff.* Would I were in my grave!
   *Priu.*             And she too with thee;
For, living here, you're but my cursed remembrancers
I once was happy.

*Jaff.* You use me thus, because you know my soul
Is fond of Belvidera: you perceive
My life feeds on her, therefore thus you treat me·
Oh! could my soul ever have known satiety:
Were I that thief, the doer of such wrongs
As you upbraid me with, what hinders me,
But I might send her back to you with contumely,
And court my fortune where she would be kinder!

*Priu.* You dare not do't——

*Jaff.*                    Indeed, my lord, I dare not.
My heart that awes me is too much my master:
Three years are past since first our vows were plighted,
During which time, the world must bear me witness,
I have treated Belvidera like your daughter,
The daughter of a senator of Venice;
Distinction, place, attendance, and observance,
Due to her birth, she always has commanded;
Out of my little fortune I have done this;
Because (though hopeless e'er to win your nature)
The world might see, I loved her for herself,
Not as the heiress of the great Priuli——

*Priu.* No more!

*Jaff.*            Yes! all, and then adieu for ever.
There's not a wretch that lives on common charity
But's happier than me: for I have known
The luscious sweets of plenty; every night
Have slept with soft content about my head,
And never waked but to a joyful morning;
Yet now must fall like a full ear of corn,
Whose blossom scaped, yet's withered in the ripening.

*Priu.* Home and be humble, study to retrench;
Discharge the lazy vermin of thy hall,
Those pageants of thy folly,
Reduce the glittering trappings of thy wife
To humble weeds, fit for thy little state;
Then to some suburb cottage both retire;
Drudge, to feed loathsome life: get brats, and starve——
Home, home, I say.——            [*Exit* PRIULI.

*Jaff.*            Yes, if my heart would let me—
This proud, this swelling heart: home I would go,
But that my doors are hateful to my eyes,
Filled and dammed up with gaping creditors,
Watchful as fowlers when their game will spring;
I have now not fifty ducats in the world,
Yet still I am in love, and pleased with ruin.
O Belvidera! oh, she is my wife—
And we will bear our wayward fate together,
But ne'er know comfort more.

*Enter* PIERRE.

*Pierr.*　　　　　　　　　　My friend, good morrow!
How fares the honest partner of my heart?
What, melancholy! not a word to spare me?
　　*Jaff.* I'm thinking, Pierre, how that damned starving quality
Called Honesty got footing in the world.
　　*Pierr.* Why, powerful Villainy first set it up,
For its own ease and safety: honest men
Are the soft easy cushions on which knaves
Repose and fatten: were all mankind villains,
They'd starve each other; lawyers would want practice,
Cut-throats rewards: each man would kill his brother
Himself, none would be paid or hanged for murder:
Honesty was a cheat invented first
To bind the hands of bold deserving rogues,
That fools and cowards might sit safe in power,
And lord it uncontrolled above their betters.
　　*Jaff.* Then Honesty is but a notion.
　　*Pierr.*　　　　　　　　　　Nothing else,
Like wit, much talked of, not to be defined:
He that pretends to most, too, has least share in't;
'Tis a ragged virtue: Honesty! no more on't.
　　*Jaff.* Sure thou art honest?
　　*Pierr.*　　　　　　　So indeed men think me.
But they're mistaken, Jaffeir; I am a rogue
As well as they;
A fine gay bold-faced villain, as thou seest me;
'Tis true, I pay my debts when they're contracted;
I steal from no man; would not cut a throat
To gain admission to a great man's purse,
Or a whore's bed; I'd not betray my friend,
To get his place or fortune: I scorn to flatter
A blown-up fool above me, or crush the wretch beneath me,
Yet, Jaffeir, for all this, I am a villain!
　　*Jaff.* A villain——
　　*Pierr.*　　　　　　Yes, a most notorious villain:
To see the suff'rings of my fellow-creatures,
And own myself a man: to see our senators
Cheat the deluded people with a show
Of Liberty, which yet they ne'er must taste of;
They say, by them our hands are free from fetters,
Yet whom they please they lay in basest bonds;
Bring whom they please to Infamy and Sorrow;
Drive us like wracks down the rough tide of power,
Whilst no hold's left to save us from destruction;
All that bear this are villains; and I one,
Not to rouse up at the great call of nature,
And check the growth of these domestic spoilers,

That make us slaves and tell us 'tis our charter.
    *Jaff.* O Aquilina!   Friend, to lose such beauty,
The dearest purchase of thy noble labours;
She was thy right by conquest, as by love.
    *Pierr.* O Jaffeir!   I'd so fixed my heart upon her,
That wheresoe'er I framed a scheme of life
For time to come, she was my only joy
With which I wished to sweeten future cares;
I fancied pleasures, none but one that loves
And dotes as I did can imagine like 'em:
When in the extremity of all these hopes,
In the most charming hour of expectation,
Then when our eager wishes soar the highest,
Ready to stoop and grasp the lovely game,
A haggard owl, a worthless kite of prey,
With his foul wings sailed in and spoiled my quarry.
    *Jaff.* I know the wretch, and scorn him as thou hat'st him.
    *Pierr.* Curse on the common good that's so protected!
Where every slave that heaps up wealth enough
To do much wrong becomes a lord of right:
I, who believed no ill could e'er come near me,
Found in the embraces of my Aquilina
A wretched old but itching senator;
A wealthy fool, that had bought my title,
A rogue, that uses beauty like a lambskin,
Barely to keep him warm: that filthy cuckoo too
Was in my absence crept into my nest,
And spoiling all my brood of noble pleasure.
    *Jaff.* Didst thou not chase him thence?
    *Pierr.*                                    I did, and drove.
The rank old bearded Hirco stinking home:
The matter was complained of in the Senate,
I summoned to appear, and censured basely,
For violating something they call *privilege*—
This was the recompense of my service:
Would I'd been rather beaten by a coward!
A soldier's mistress, Jaffeir, 's his religion,
When that's profaned, all other ties are broken;
That even dissolves all former bonds of service,
And from that hour I think myself as free
To be the foe as e'er the friend of Venice.—
Nay, dear Revenge, whene'er thou call'st I'm ready.
    *Jaff.* I think no safety can be here for virtue,
And grieve, my friend, as much as thou to live
In such a wretched state as this of Venice;
Where all agree to spoil the public good,
And villains fatten with the brave man's labours.
    *Pierr.* We have neither safety, unity, nor peace,
For the foundation's lost of common good.

Justice is lame as well as blind amongst us;
The laws (corrupted to their ends that make 'em)
Serve but for instruments of some new tyranny,
That every day starts up to enslave us deeper:
Now could this glorious cause but find out friends
To do it right! O Jaffeir! then might'st thou
Not wear these seals of woe upon thy face.
The proud Priuli should be taught humanity,
And learn to value such a son as thou art.
I dare not speak! But my heart bleeds this moment!

   *Jaff.* Cursed be the cause, though I thy friend be part on't:
Let me partake the troubles of thy bosom,
For I am used to misery, and perhaps
May find a way to sweeten 't to thy spirit.

   *Pierr.* Too soon it will reach thy knowledge——
   *Jaff.*                     Then from thee
Let it proceed. There's virtue in thy friendship
Would make the saddest tale of sorrow pleasing,
Strengthen my constancy, and welcome ruin.

   *Pierr.* Then thou art ruined!
   *Jaff.*                That I long since knew;
I and ill-fortune have been long acquaintance.

   *Pierr.* I passed this very moment by thy doors,
And found them guarded by a troop of villains;
The sons of public rapine were destroying:
They told me, by the sentence of the law
They had commission to seize all thy fortune,
Nay more, Priuli's cruel hand hath signed it.
Here stood a ruffian with a horrid face
Lording it o'er a pile of massy plate,
Tumbled into a heap for public sale:
There was another making villainous jests
At thy undoing; he had ta'en possession
Of all thy ancient most domestic ornaments,
Rich hangings, intermixed and wrought with gold;
The very bed, which on thy wedding-night
Received thee to the arms of Belvidera,
The scene of all thy joys, was violated
By the coarse hands of filthy dungeon villains,
And thrown amongst the common lumber.

   *Jaff.* Now, thanks Heaven——
   *Pierr.* Thank Heaven! for what?
   *Jaff.*              That I am not worth a ducat.

   *Pierr.* Curse thy dull stars, and the worse fate of Venice,
Where brothers, friends, and fathers, all are false;
Where there's no trust, no truth; where Innocence
Stoops under vile Oppression, and Vice lords it:
Hadst thou but seen, as I did, how at last
Thy beauteous Belvidera, like a wretch

That's doomed to banishment, came weeping forth,
Shining through tears, like April suns in showers
That labour to o'ercome the cloud that loads 'em,
Whilst two young virgins, on whose arms she leaned,
Kindly looked up, and at her grief grew sad,
As if they catched the sorrows that fell from her:
Even the lewd rabble that were gathered round
To see the sight, stood mute when they beheld her;
Governed their roaring throats and grumbled pity:
I could have hugged the greasy rogues: they pleased me.

    *Jaff.* I thank thee for this story, from my soul,
Since now I know the worst that can befall me:
Ah, Pierre! I have a heart, that could have borne
The roughest wrong my fortune could have done me:
But when I think what Belvidera feels,
The bitterness her tender spirit tastes of,
I own myself a coward: bear my weakness,
If throwing thus my arms about thy neck,
I play the boy, and blubber in thy bosom.
Oh! I shall drown thee with my sorrows!

    *Pierr.*                            Burn!
First burn, and level Venice to thy ruin.
What! starve like beggars' brats in frosty weather,
Under a hedge, and whine ourselves to death!
Thou, or thy cause, shall never want assistance,
Whilst I have blood or fortune fit to serve thee;
Command my heart: thou art every way its master.

    *Jaff.* No: there's a secret pride in bravely dying.

    *Pierr.* Rats die in holes and corners, dogs run mad;
Man knows a braver remedy for sorrow:
Revenge! the attribute of gods, they stamped it
With their great image on our natures; die!
Consider well the cause that calls upon thee:
And if thou'rt base enough, die then: remember
Thy Belvidera suffers: Belvidera!
Die!—damn first!—what! be decently interred
In a churchyard, and mingle thy brave dust
With stinking rogues that rot in dirty winding-sheets,
Surfeit-slain fools, the common dung o' th' soil.

    *Jaff.* Oh!

    *Pierr.*       Well said, out with't, swear a little——

    *Jaff.*                            Swear!
By sea and air! by earth, by heaven and hell.
I will revenge my Belvidera's tears!
Hark thee, my friend—Priuli—is—a Senator!

    *Pierr.* A dog!

    *Jaff.*          Agreed.

    *Pierr.*             Shoot him.

    *Jaff.*                       With all my heart.

No more: where shall we meet at night?
   *Pierr.*                      I'll tell thee;
On the *Rialto* every night at twelve
I take my evening's walk of meditation,
There we two will meet, and talk of precious
Mischief——
   *Jaff.*         Farewell.
   *Pierr.*               At twelve.
   *Jaff.*                  At any hour, my plagues
Will keep me waking.               [*Exit* PIERRE.
Tell me why, good Heaven,
Thou mad'st me what I am, with all the spirit,
Aspiring thoughts and elegant desires
That fill the happiest man? Ah! rather why
Didst thou not form me sordid as my fate,
Base-minded, dull, and fit to carry burdens?
Why have I sense to know the curse that's on me?
Is this just dealing, Nature? Belvidera!


               *Enter* BELVIDERA.

Poor Belvidera!
   *Belv.* Lead me, lead me, my virgins,
To that kind voice. My lord, my love, my refuge!
Happy my eyes, when they behold thy face:
My heavy heart will leave its doleful beating
At sight of thee, and bound with sprightful joys.
O smile, as when our loves were in their spring,
And cheer my fainting soul.
   *Jaff.*               As when our loves
Were in their spring? has then my fortune changed?
Art thou not Belvidera, still the same,
Kind, good, and tender, as my arms first found thee?
If thou art altered, where shall I have harbour?
Where ease my loaded heart? Oh! where complain?
   *Belv.* Does this appear like change, or love decaying?
When thus I throw myself into thy bosom,
With all the resolution of a strong truth:
Beats not my heart, as 'twould alarum thine
To a new charge of bliss; I joy more in thee,
Than did thy mother when she hugged thee first,
And blessed the gods for all her travail past.
   *Jaff.* Can there in woman be such glorious faith?
Sure all ill stories of thy sex are false.
O woman! lovely woman! Nature made thee
To temper man: we had been brutes without you:
Angels are painted fair, to look like you;
There's in you all that we believe of heaven,
Amazing brightness, purity and truth,

Eternal joy, and everlasting love.

    *Belv.* If love be treasure, we'll be wondrous rich;
I have so much, my heart will surely break with 't;
Vows cannot express it; when I would declare
How great's my joy, I am dumb with the big thought;
I swell, and sigh, and labour with my longing.
O lead me to some desert wide and wild,
Barren as our misfortunes, where my soul
May have its vent: where I may tell aloud
To the high heavens, and ever-list'ning planet,
With what a boundless stock my bosom's fraught!
Where I may throw my eager arms about thee,
Give loose to love with kisses, kindling joy,
And let off all the fire that's in my heart.

    *Jaff.* O Belvidera! double I'm a beggar,
Undone by fortune, and in debt to thee;
Want! worldly Want! that hungry meagre fiend
Is at my heels, and chases me in view;
Canst thou bear cold and hunger? can these limbs,
Framed for the tender offices of love,
Endure the bitter gripes of smarting poverty?
When banished by our miseries abroad
(As suddenly we shall be), to seek out
(In some far climate where our names are strangers)
For charitable succour; wilt thou then,
When in a bed of straw we shrink together,
And the bleak winds shall whistle round our heads,
Wilt thou then talk thus to me? Wilt thou then
Hush my cares thus, and shelter me with love?

    *Belv.* Oh, I will love thee, even in madness love thee.
Though my distracted senses should forsake me,
I'd find some intervals, when my poor heart
Should 'suage itself and be let loose to thine.
Though the bare earth be all our resting-place,
Its roots our food, some clift our habitation,
I'll make this arm a pillow for thy head;
As thou sighing liest, and swelled with sorrow,
Creep to thy bosom, pour the balm of love
Into thy soul, and kiss thee to thy rest;
Then praise our God, and watch thee till the morning.

    *Jaff.* Hear this, you heavens, and wonder how you made her!
Reign, reign, ye monarchs that divide the world,
Busy rebellion ne'er will let you know
Tranquillity and happiness like mine;
Like gaudy ships, th' obsequious billows fall
And rise again, to lift you in your pride;
They wait but for a storm and then devour you:
I, in my private bark, already wrecked,
Like a poor merchant driven on unknown land,

That had by chance packed up his choicest treasure
In one dear casket, and saved only that:

> Since I must wander further on the shore,
> Thus hug my little, but my precious store;
> Resolved to scorn, and trust my fate no more.

[*Exeunt.*

## ACT II

### [SCENE I]

#### *Enter* PIERRE *and* AQUILINA.

*Aquil.* By all thy wrongs, thou'rt dearer to my arms
Than all the wealth of Venice: prithee stay,
And let us love to-night.
  *Pierr.*    No: there's fool,
There's fool about thee: when a woman sells
Her flesh to fools, her beauty's lost to me;
They leave a taint, a sully where they've past,
There's such a baneful quality about 'em,
E'en spoils complexions with their own nauseousness.
They infect all they touch; I cannot think
Of tasting anything a fool has palled.
  *Aquil.* I loathe and scorn that fool thou mean'st, as much
Or more than thou canst; but the beast has gold
That makes him necessary: power too,
To qualify my character, and poise me
Equal with peevish virtue, that beholds
My liberty with envy: in their hearts
Are loose as I am; but an ugly power
Sits in their faces, and frights pleasures from 'em.
  *Pierr.* Much good may't do you, madam, with your Senator.
  *Aquil.* My Senator! why, canst thou think that wretch
E'er filled thy Aquilina's arms with pleasure?
Think'st thou, because I sometimes give him leave
To foil himself at what he is unfit for,
Because I force myself to endure and suffer him,
Think'st thou I love him? No, by all the joys
Thou ever gav'st me, his presence is my penance;
The worst thing an old man can be's a lover,
A mere *memento mori* to poor woman.
I never lay by his decrepit side,
But all that night I pondered on my grave.
  *Pierr.* Would he were well sent thither!

*Aquil.*                              That's my wish too:
For then, my Pierre, I might have cause with pleasure
To play the hypocrite; oh! how I could weep
Over the dying dotard, and kiss him too,
In hopes to smother him quite; then, when the time
Was come to pay my sorrows at his funeral,
For he's already made me heir to treasures,
Would make me out-act a real widow's whining:
How could I frame my face to fit my mourning,
With wringing hands attend him to his grave,
Fall swooning on his hearse, take mad possession
Even of the dismal vault where he lay·buried,
There like the Ephesian matron dwell, till thou,
My lovely soldier, com'st to my deliverance;
Then throwing up my veil, with open arms
And laughing eyes, run to new-dawning joy.

*Pierr.* No more! I have friends to meet me here to-night,
And must be private. As you prize my friendship
Keep up your coxcomb: let him not pry nor listen
Nor fisk about the house as I have seen him,
Like a tame mumping squirrel with a bell on;
Curs will be abroad to bite him if you do.

*Aquil.* What friends to meet? may I not be of your council?

*Pierr.* How! a woman ask questions out of bed?
Go to your Senator, ask him what passes
Amongst his brethren, he'll hide nothing from you;
But pump not me for politics. No more!
Give order that whoever in my name
Comes here, receive admittance: so good-night.

*Aquil.* Must we ne'er meet again? Embrace no more?
Is love so soon and utterly forgotten?

*Pierr.* As you henceforward treat your fool, I'll think on't.

*Aquil.* Curst be all fools, and doubly curst myself,
The worst of fools—I die if he forsakes me;
And how to keep him, heaven or hell instruct me.      [*Exeunt.*


[SCENE II.]—*The Rialto*

*Enter* JAFFEIR.

*Jaff.* I am here, and thus, the shades of night around me,
I look as if all hell were in my heart,
And I in hell. Nay, surely 'tis so with me;—
For every step I tread, methinks some fiend
Knocks at my breast, and bids it not be quiet:
I've heard how desperate wretches, like myself,
Have wandered out at this dead time of night
To meet the foe of mankind in his walk:

Sure I'm so curst, that, tho' of Heaven forsaken,
No minister of darkness cares to tempt me.
Hell! hell! why sleepest thou?

#### *Enter* PIERRE.

*Pierr.*                     Sure I have stayed too long:
The clock has struck, and I may lose my proselyte.
Speak, who goes there?
*Jaff.*              A dog, that comes to howl
At yonder moon: what's he that asks the question?
*Pierr.* A friend to dogs, for they are honest creatures
And ne'er betray their masters; never fawn
On any that they love not: well met, friend:
Jaffeir!
*Jaff.* The same. O Pierre! thou art come in season,
I was just going to pray.
*Pierr.*              Ah, that's mechanic,
Priests make a trade on't, and yet starve by it too:
No praying, it spoils business, and time's precious;
Where's Belvidera?
*Jaff.*            For a day or two
I've lodged her privately, till I see further
What fortune will do with me . Prithee, friend,
If thou wouldst have me fit to hear good counsel,
Speak not of Belvidera——
*Pierr.*           Speak not of her.
*Jaff.* Oh no!
*Pierr.* Nor name her. May be I wish her well.
*Jaff.* Who well?
*Pierr.*          Thy wife, thy lovely Belvidera;
I hope a man may wish his friend's wife well,
And no harm done!
*Jaff.*        Y' are merry, Pierre!
*Pierr.*                I am so:
Thou shalt smile too, and Belvidera smile;
We'll all rejoice; here's something to buy pins,
Marriage is chargeable.
*Jaff.*        I but half wished
To see the Devil, and he's here already.
Well!
What must this buy, rebellion, murder, treason?
Tell me which way I must be damned for this.
*Pierr.* When last we parted, we had no qualms like these,
But entertained each other's thoughts like men,
Whose souls were well acquainted. Is the world
Reformed since our last meeting? what new miracles
Have happened? has Priuli's heart relented?
Can he be honest?
*Jaff.*          Kind Heaven! let heavy curses

Gall his old age; cramps, aches, rack his bones,
And bitterest disquiet wring his heart;
Oh, let him live till life become his burden!
Let him groan under't long, linger an age
In the worst agonies and pangs of death,
And find its ease, but late.

*Pierr.*                          Nay, couldst thou not
As well, my friend, have stretched the curse to all
The Senate round, as to one single villain?

*Jaff.* But curses stick not: could I kill with cursing,
By Heaven, I know not thirty heads in Venice
Should not be blasted; Senators should rot
Like dogs on dunghills; but their wives and daughters
Die of their own diseases.   Oh, for a curse
To kill with!

*Pierr.*          Daggers, daggers are much better!

*Jaff.* Ha!

*Pierr.*          Daggers.

*Jaff.*                    But where are they?

*Pierr.*                                        Oh, a thousand
May be disposed in honest hands in Venice.

*Jaff.* Thou talk'st in clouds.

*Pierr.*                    But yet a heart half wronged
As thine has been, would find the meaning, Jaffeir.

*Jaff.* A thousand daggers, all in honest hands;
And have not I a friend will stick one here?

*Pierr.* Yes, if I thought thou wert not to be cherished
To a nobler purpose, I'd be that friend.
But thou hast better friends, friends whom thy wrongs
Have made thy friends; friends worthy to be called so;
I'll trust thee with a secret: there are spirits
This hour at work.   But as thou art a man,
Whom I have picked and chosen from the world,
Swear, that thou wilt be true to what I utter,
And when I have told thee, that which only gods
And men like gods are privy to, then swear,
No chance or change shall wrest it from my bosom.

*Jaff.* When thou wouldst bind me, is there need of oaths?
(Greensickness girls lose maidenheads with such counters)
For thou'rt so near my heart, that thou mayst see
Its bottom, sound its strength and firmness to thee:
Is coward, fool, or villain, in my face?
If I seem none of these, I dare believe
Thou wouldst not use me in a little cause,
For I am fit for honour's toughest task;
Nor ever yet found fooling was my province;
And for a villainous inglorious enterprise,
I know thy heart so well, I dare lay mine
Before thee, set it to what point thou wilt.

 *Pierr.* Nay, it's a cause thou wilt be fond of, Jaffeir.
For it is founded on the noblest basis,
Our liberties, our natural inheritance;
There's no religion, no hypocrisy in't;
We'll do the business, and ne'er fast and pray for't:
Openly act a deed, the world shall gaze
With wonder at, and envy when it's done.
 *Jaff.* For liberty!
 *Pierr.*     For liberty, my friend!
Thou shalt be freed from base Priuli's tyranny,
And thy sequestered fortunes healed again.
I shall be freed from opprobrious wrongs,
That press me now, and bend my spirit downward:
All Venice free, and every growing merit
Succeed to its just right: fools shall be pulled
From Wisdom's seat; those baleful unclean birds,
Those lazy owls, who (perched near Fortune's top)
Sit only watchful with their heavy wings
To cuff down new-fledged virtues, that would rise
To nobler heights, and make the grove harmonious.
 *Jaff.* What can I do?
 *Pierr.*     Canst thou not kill a Senator?
 *Jaff.* Were there one wise or honest, I could kill him
For herding with that nest of fools and knaves;
By all my wrongs, thou talk'st as if revenge
Were to be had, and the brave story warms me.
 *Pierr.* Swear, then!
 *Jaff.*     I do, by all those glittering stars
And yond great ruling planet of the night!
By all good powers above, and ill below!
By love and friendship, dearer than my life!
No power or death shall make me false to thee.
 *Pierr.* Here we embrace, and I'll unlock my heart.
A council's held hard by, where the destruction
Of this great Empire's hatching: there I'll lead thee!
But be a man, for thou'rt to mix with men
Fit to disturb the peace of all the world,
And rule it when it's wildest——
 *Jaff.*     I give thee thanks
For this kind warning: yes, I will be a man,
And charge thee, Pierre, whene'er thou seest my fears
Betray me less, to rip this heart of mine
Out of my breast, and show it for a coward's.
Come, let's begone, for from this hour I chase
All little thoughts, all tender human follies
Out of my bosom: vengeance shall have room:
Revenge!
 *Pierr.* And liberty!
 *Jaff.*     Revenge! revenge!   *[Exeunt.*

[SCENE III.]—*The Scene changes to* AQUILINA'S *house,*
*the Greek Courtesan*

*Enter* RENAULT.

*Renault.* Why was my choice ambition  the first ground
A wretch can build on? it's indeed at distance
A good prospect, tempting to the view,
The height delights us, and the mountain top
Looks beautiful, because it's nigh to heaven,
But we ne'er think how sandy's the foundation,
What storm will batter, and what tempest shake us!
Who's there?

*Enter* SPINOSA.

*Spin.*          Renault, good morrow! for by this time
I think the scale of night has turned the balance,
And weighs up morning: has the clock struck twelve?
   *Ren.* Yes, clocks will go as they are set.   But Man,
Irregular Man's ne'er constant, never certain:
I've spent at least three precious hours of darkness
In waiting dull attendance; 'tis the curse
Of diligent virtue to be mixed like mine,
With giddy tempers, souls but half resolved.
   *Spin.* Hell seize that soul amongst us  it can frighten!
   *Ren.* What's then the cause that I am here alone?
Why are we not together?

*Enter* ELIOT.

                                        O sir, welcome!
You are an Englishman: when treason's hatching
One might have thought you'd not have been behindhand.
In what whore's lap have you been lolling?
Give but an Englishman his whore and ease,
Beef and sea-coal fire, he's yours for ever.
   *Eliot.* Frenchman, you are saucy.
   *Ren.*                                        How!

*Enter* BEDAMAR *the* Ambassador, THEODORE, BRAMVEIL, DURAND,
   BRABE, REVILLIDO, MEZZANA, TERNON, RETROSI, Conspirators.

   *Beda.*                                At difference, fie!
Is this a time for quarrels?   Thieves and rogues
Fall out and brawl: should men of your high calling,
Men separated by the choice of Providence,
From the gross heap of mankind, and set here
In this great assembly as in one great jewel,
To adorn the bravest purpose it e'er smiled on,
Should you like boys wrangle for trifles?

*Ren.*                                                    Boys!
*Beda.* Renault, thy hand!
*Ren.*                                    I thought I'd given my heart
Long since to every man that mingles here;
But grieve to find it trusted with such tempers,
That can't forgive my froward age its weakness.
  *Beda.* Eliot, thou once hadst virtue; I have seen
Thy stubborn temper bend with godlike goodness,
Not half thus courted: 'tis thy nation's glory,
To hug the foe that offers brave alliance.
Once more embrace, my friends—we'll all embrace—
United thus, we are the mighty engine
Must twist this rooted Empire from its basis!
Totters it not already?
  *Eliot.*                        Would it were tumbling!
  *Beda.* Nay, it shall down: this night we seal its ruin.

### *Enter* PIERRE.

O Pierre! thou art welcome!
Come to my breast, for by its hopes thou look'st
Lovelily dreadful, and the fate of Venice
Seems on thy sword already. O my Mars!
The poets that first feigned a god of war
Sure prophesied of thee.
  *Pierr.*                        Friends! was not Brutus
(I mean that Brutus who in open senate
Stabbed the first Cæsar that usurped the world
A gallant man?
  *Ren.*                Yes, and Catiline too;
Though story wrong his fame: for he conspired
To prop the reeling glory of his country:
His cause was good.
  *Beda.*                And ours as much above it,
As Renault thou art superior to Cethegus,
Or Pierre to Cassius.
  *Pierr.*                Then to what we aim at
When do we start? or must we talk for ever?
  *Beda.* No, Pierre, the deed's near birth: Fate seems to have
    set
The business up, and given it to our care;
I hope there's not a heart nor hand amongst us
But is firm and ready.
  *All.*                All!
We'll die with Bedamar.
  *Beda.*                O men,
Matchless, as will your glory be hereafter.
The game is for a matchless prize, if won;
If lost, disgraceful ruin.
  *Ren.*                What can lose it?

The public stock's a beggar; one Venetian
Trusts not another: look into their stores
Of general safety; empty magazines,
A tattered fleet, a murmuring unpaid army,
Bankrupt nobility, a harassed commonalty,
A factious, giddy, and divided Senate,
Is all the strength of Venice: let's destroy it;
Let's fill their magazines with arms to awe them,
Man out their fleet, and make their trade maintain it;
Let loose the murmuring army on their masters,
To pay themselves with plunder; lop their nobles
To the base roots, whence most of 'em first sprung;
Enslave the rout, whom smarting will make humble;
Turn out their droning Senate, and possess
That seat of empire which our souls were framed for.

 *Pierr.* Ten thousand men are armed at your nod,
Commanded all by leaders fit to guide
A battle for the freedom of the world;
This wretched state has starved them in its service,
And by your bounty quickened, they're resolved
To serve your glory, and revenge their own!
They've all their different quarters in this city,
Watch for th' alarm, and grumble 'tis so tardy.

 *Beda.* I doubt not, friend, but thy unwearied diligence
Has still kept waking, and it shall have ease;
After this night it is resolved we meet
No more, till Venice own us for her lords.

 *Pierr.* How lovely the Adriatic whore,
Dressed in her flames, will shine! devouring flames!
Such as shall burn her to the watery bottom
And hiss in her foundation.

 *Beda.*       Now if any
Amongst us that owns this glorious cause,
Have friends or interest he'd wish to save,
Let it be told, the general doom is sealed;
But I'd forego the hopes of a world's empire,
Rather than wound the bowels of my friend.

 *Pierr.* I must confess you there have touched my weakness,
I have a friend; hear it, such a friend!
My heart was ne'er shut to him: nay, I'll tell you,
He knows the very business of this hour;
But he rejoices in the cause, and loves it,
We've changed a vow to live and die together,
And he's at hand to ratify it here.

 *Ren.*       How! all betrayed?

 *Pierr.* No—I've dealt nobly with you;
I've brought my all into the public stock;
I had but one friend, and him I'll share amongst you!
Receive and cherish him: or if, when seen

And searched, you find him worthless, as my tongue
Has lodged this secret in his faithful breast,
To ease your fears I wear a dagger here
Shall rip it out again, and give you rest.
Come forth, thou only good I e'er could boast of.

*Enter* JAFFEIR *with a Dagger.*

*Beda.* His presence bears the show of manly virtue.
*Jaff.* I know you'll wonder all, that thus uncalled,
I dare approach this place of fatal counsels;
But I'm amongst you, and by Heaven it glads me,
To see so many virtues thus united,
To restore justice and dethrone oppression.
Command this sword, if you would have it quiet,
Into this breast; but if you think it worthy
To cut the throats of reverend rogues in robes,
Send me into the cursed assembled Senate;
It shrinks not, though I meet a father there;
Would you behold this city flaming? Here's
A hand shall bear a lighted torch at noon
To the Arsenal, and set its gates on fire.
    *Ren.* You talk this well, sir.
    *Jaff.*                              Nay—by Heaven I'll do this.
Come, come, I read distrust in all your faces;
You fear me a villain, and indeed it's odd
To hear a stranger talk thus at first meeting,
Of matters that have been so well debated;
But I come ripe with wrongs as you with counsels,
I hate this Senate, am a foe to Venice;
A friend to none but men resolved like me,
To push on mischief; oh, did you but know me,
I need not talk thus!
    *Beda.*                  Pierre! I must embrace him,
My heart beats to this man as if it knew him.
    *Ren.* I never lov'd these huggers.
    *Jaff.*                              Still I see
The cause delights me not. Your friends survey me,
As I were dangerous—but I come armed
Against all doubts, and to your trust will give
A pledge, worth more than all the world can pay for.
My Belvidera! Ho! My Belvidera!
    *Beda.* What wonder next?
    *Jaff.*                      Let me entreat you,
As I have henceforth hopes to call ye friends,
That all but the ambassador, [and] this
Grave guide of councils, with my friend that owns me,
Withdraw a while to spare a woman's blushes.

                [*Exeunt all but* BEDAMAR, RENAULT, JAFFEIR, PIERRE.

*Beda.* Pierre, whither will this ceremony lead us?
*Jaff.* My Belvidera! Belvidera!

*Enter* BELVIDERA.

*Belv.* Who calls so loud at this late peaceful hour?
That voice was wont to come in gentler whispers,
And fill my ears with the soft breath of love:
Thou hourly image of my thoughts, where art thou?
*Jaff.* Indeed 'tis late.
*Belv.*                         Oh! I have slept and dreamt,
And dreamt again: where hast thou been, thou loiterer?
Tho' my eyes closed, my arms have still been opened;
Stretched every way betwixt my broken slumbers,
To search if thou wert come to crown my rest;
There's no repose without thee: Oh, the day
Too soon will break, and wake us to our sorrow;
Come, come to bed, and bid thy cares good-night.
*Jaff.* O Belvidera! we must change the scene
In which the past delights of life were tasted:
The poor sleep little, we must learn to watch
Our labours late, and early every morning,
Midst winter frosts; then clad and fed with sparing,
Rise to our toils, and drudge away the day.
*Belv.* Alas! where am I? whither is't you lead me?
Methinks I read distraction in your face!
Something less gentle than the fate you tell me:
You shake and tremble too! your blood runs cold!
Heavens guard my love, and bless his heart with patience.
*Jaff.* That I have patience, let our fate bear witness,
Who has ordained it so, that thou and I,
(Thou the divinest Good man e'er possessed,
And I the wretched'st of the race of man)
This very hour, without one tear, must part.
*Belv.* Part! must we part? Oh! am I then forsaken?
Will my love cast me off? have my misfortunes
Offended him so highly, that he'll leave me?
Why drag you from me; whither are you going?
My dear! my life! my love!
*Jaff.*                         O friends!
*Belv.* Speak to me.
*Jaff.*                         Take her from my heart;
She'll gain such hold else, I shall ne'er get loose.
I charge thee take her, but with tender'st care
Relieve her troubles and assuage her sorrows.
*Ren.* Rise, madam! and command amongst your servants!
*Jaff.* To you, sirs, and your honours, I bequeath her,
And with her this, when I prove unworthy—     [*Gives a dagger.*
You know the rest:—then strike it to her heart;

And tell her, he, who three whole happy years
Lay in her arms, and each kind night repeated
The passionate vows of still-increasing love,
Sent that reward for all her truth and sufferings.
 *Belv.* Nay, take my life, since he has sold it cheaply;
Or send me to some distant clime your slave,
But let it be far off, lest my complainings
Should reach his guilty ears, and shake his peace.
 *Jaff.* No, Belvidera, I've contrived thy honour.
Trust to my faith, and be but fortune kind
To me, as I'll preserve that faith unbroken,
When next we meet, I'll lift thee to a height,
Shall gather all the gazing world about thee,
To wonder what strange virtue placed thee there.
But if we ne'er meet more——
   *Belv.*     O thou unkind one,
Never meet more? have I deserved this from you?
Look on me, tell me, speak, thou dear deceiver,
Why am I separated from thy love?
If I am false, accuse me; but if true,
Don't, prithee, don't in poverty forsake me,
But pity the sad heart, that's torn with parting.
Yet hear me! yet recall me——
     [*Exeunt* RENAULT, BEDAMAR, *and* BELVIDERA.
 *Jaff.*      O my eyes!
Look not that way, but turn yourselves awhile
Into my heart, and be wean'd all together.
My friend, where art thou?
 *Pierr.*     Here, my honour's brother.
 *Jaff.* Is Belvidera gone?
 *Pierr.*     Renault has led her
Back to her own apartment: but, by Heaven,
Thou must not see her more till our work's over.
 *Jaff.* No.
 *Pierr.*  Not for your life.
 *Jaff.*     O Pierre, wert thou but she,
How I could pull thee down into my heart,
Gaze on thee till my eye-strings cracked with love,
Till all my sinews with its fire extended,
Fixed me upon the rack of ardent longing;
Then swelling, sighing, raging to be blest,
Come like a panting turtle to thy breast,
On thy soft bosom, hovering, bill and play,
Confess the cause why last I fled away;
 Own 'twas a fault, but swear to give it o'er
 And never follow false ambition more.   [*Exeunt ambo.*

# ACT III

## [SCENE II]

*Enter* AQUILINA *and her* Maid.

*Aquil.* Tell him I am gone to bed: tell him I am not at home; tell him I've better company with me, or anything; tell him, in short, I will not see him, the, eternal, troublesome, vexatious fool: he's worse company than an ignorant physician—I'll not be disturbed at these unseasonable hours.

*Maid.* But madam! He's here already, just entered the doors.

*Aquil.* Turn him out again, you unnecessary, useless, giddy-brained ass! If he will not begone, set the house a-fire and burn us both: I had rather meet a toad in my dish than that old hideous animal in my chamber to-night.

## *Enter* ANTONIO.

*Anto.* Nacky, Nacky, Nacky—how dost do, Nacky? Hurry durry. I am come, little Nacky; past eleven o'clock, a late hour; time in all conscience to go to bed, Nacky—Nacky, did I say? Ay Nacky; Aquilina, lina, lina, quilina, quilina, quilina, Aquilina, Naquilina, Naquilina, Acky, Acky, Nacky, Nacky, Queen Nacky—come let's to bed—you Fubbs, you Pugg you—you little Puss—Purree Tuzzey—I am a Senator.

*Aquil.* You are a fool, I am sure.

*Anto.* May be so too, sweetheart. Never the worse Senator for all that. Come Nacky, Nacky, let's have a game at rump, Nacky.

*Aquil.* You would do well, signor, to be troublesome here no longer, but leave me to myself: be sober and go home, sir.

*Anto.* Home, Madonna!

*Aquil.* Ay, home, sir. Who am I?

*Anto.* Madonna, as I take it you are my—you are—thou art my little Nicky Nacky . . . that's all!

*Aquil.* I find you are resolved to be troublesome, and so to make short of the matter in few words, I hate you, detest you, loathe you, I am weary of you, sick of you—hang you, you are an old, silly, impertinent, impotent, solicitous coxcomb, crazy in your head, and lazy in your body, love to be meddling with everything, and if you had not money, you are good for nothing.

*Anto.* Good for nothing! Hurry durry, I'll try that presently. Sixty-one years old, and good for nothing: that's brave.—[*To the maid.*] Come, come, come, Mistress Fiddle-faddle, turn you out for a season; go turn out, I say, it is our will and pleasure

to be private some moments—out, out when you are bid to.—
[*Puts her out and locks the door.*]    Good for nothing, you say.

*Aquil.* Why, what are you good for?

*Anto.* In the first place, madam, I am old, and consequently
very wise, very wise, Madonna, d'ye mark that? in the second
place, take notice, if you please, that I am a Senator, and when
I think fit can make speeches, Madonna.    Hurry durry, I can
make a speech in the Senate-house now and then—would make
your hair stand on end, Madonna.

*Aquil.* What care I for your speeches in the Senate-house: if
you would be silent here, I should thank you.

*Anto.* Why, I can make speeches to thee too, my lovely
Madonna; for example—my cruel fair one.

[*Takes out a purse of gold and at every pause shakes it.*
Since it is my fate, that you should with your servant angry
prove; tho' late at night—I hope 'tis not too late with this to
gain reception for my love—there's for thee, my little Nicky
Nacky—take it, here take it—I say take it, or I'll throw it at your
head—how now, rebel!

*Aquil.* Truly, my illustrious Senator, I must confess your
honour is at present most profoundly eloquent indeed.

*Anto.* Very well;   come, now let's sit down and think upon't
a little—come sit I say—sit down by me a little, my Nicky
Nacky, ha !—[*Sits down.*]    Hurry durry—good for nothing——

*Aquil.* No, sir, if you please I can know my distance and
stand.

*Anto.* Stand: how?   Nacky up and I down !   Nay, then, let
me exclaim with the poet,

> Show me a case more pitiful who can,
> A standing woman, and a falling man.

Hurry durry—not sit down—see this, ye gods—You won't sit
down?

*Aquil.* No, sir.

*Anto.* Then look you now, suppose me a bull, a *basan*-bull,
the bull of bulls, or any bull.    Thus up I get and with my brows
thus bent—I broo, I say I broo, I broo, I broo.   You won't sit
down, will you?—I broo—[*Bellows like a bull, and drives her about.*

*Aquil.* Well, sir, I must endure this.   Now your [*she sits down*]
honour has been a bull, pray what beast will your worship please
to be next?

*Anto.* Now I'll be a Senator again, and thy lover, little Nicky
Nacky!   [*He sits by her.*]   Ah toad, toad, toad, toad! spit in
my face a little, Nacky—spit in my face prithee, spit in my face,
never so little: spit but a little bit—spit, spit, spit, spit, when
you are bid, I say; do prithee spit—now, now, now, spit: what,
you won't spit, will you?   Then I'll be a dog.

*Aquil.* A dog, my lord?

*Anto.* Ay, a dog—and I'll give thee this t'other purse to let

me be a dog—and to use me like a dog a little.  Hurry durry—
I will—here 'tis.                          [*Gives the purse.*

*Aquil.* Well, with all my heart.  But let me beseech your
dogship to play your tricks over as fast as you can, that you may
come to stinking the sooner, and be turned out of doors as you
deserve.

*Anto.* Ay, ay—no matter for that—that—[*He gets under the
table*]—shan't move me——Now, bow wow wow, how wow .  .  .
                                        [*Barks like a dog.*

*Aquil.* Hold, hold, hold, sir, I beseech you: what is't you do?
If curs bite, they must be kicked, sir.   Do you see, kicked thus.

*Anto.* Ay, with all my heart: do kick, kick on, now I am
under the table, kick again—kick harder—harder yet, bow wow
wow, wow, bow—'od I'll have a snap at thy shins—bow wow
wow, wow, bow—'od she kicks bravely.——

*Aquil.* Nay, then I'll go another way to work with you: and.
I think here's an instrument fit for the purpose.
                              [*Fetches a whip and bell.*
What, bite your mistress, sirrah!  out, out of doors, you dog, to
kennel and be hanged—bite your mistress by the legs, you
rogue——                             [*She whips him.*

*Anto.* Nay, prithee Nacky, now thou art too loving: Hurry
durry, 'od I'll be a dog no longer.

*Aquil.* Nay, none of your fawning and grinning: but be gone,
or here's the discipline: what, bite your mistress by the legs,
you mongrel?  out of doors—hout hout, to kennel, sirrah!  go.

*Anto.* This is very barbarous usage, Nacky, very barbarous:
look you, I will not go—I will not stir from the door, that I
resolve—hurry durry, what, shut me out?  [*She whips him out.*

*Aquil.* Ay, and if you come here any more to-night I'll have
my footmen lug you, you cur: what, bite your poor mistress
Nacky, sirrah!

*Enter* Maid.

*Maid.* Heavens, madam!  What's the matter?
                     [*He howls at the door like a dog.*
*Aquil.* Call my footmen hither presently.

*Enter two* Footmen.

*Maid.* They are here already, madam, the house is all alarmed
with a strange noise, that nobody knows what to make of.

*Aquil.* Go all of you and turn that troublesome beast in the
next room out of my house—If I ever see him within these walls
again, without my leave for his admittance, you sneaking rogues,
I'll have you poisoned all, poisoned, like rats; every corner of
the house shall stink of one of you; go, and learn hereafter to
know my pleasure.   So now for my Pierre:

> Thus when godlike lover was displeased,
> We sacrifice our fool and he's appeased.        [*Exeunt.*

## SCENE II

*Enter* BELVIDERA.

*Belv.* I'm sacrificed! I am sold! betray'd to shame!
Inevitable ruin has enclosed me!
No sooner was I to my bed repaired
To weigh, and (weeping) ponder my condition,
But the old hoary wretch, to whose false care
My peace and honour was entrusted, came
(Like Tarquin) ghastly with infernal lust.
O thou, Roman Lucrece! thou couldst find friends
To vindicate thy wrong,
I never had but one, and he's proved false;
He that should guard my virtue has betrayed it;
Left me! undone me! O that I could hate him!
Where shall I go! O whither whither wander?

*Enter* JAFFEIR.

*Jaff.* Can Belvidera want a resting place
When these poor arms are open to receive her?
Oh, 'tis in vain to struggle with desires
Strong as my love to thee; for every moment
I'm from thy sight, the heart within my bosom
Moans like a tender infant in its cradle
Whose nurse has left it; come, and with the songs
Of gentle love persuade it to its peace.
*Belv.* I fear the stubborn wanderer will not own me,
'Tis grown a rebel to be ruled no longer,
Scorns the indulgent bosom that first lulled it,
And like a disobedient child disdains
The soft authority of Belvidera.
*Jaff.* There was a time——
*Belv.*                           Yes, yes, there was a time
When Belvidera's tears, her cries, and sorrows,
Were not despised; when if she chanced to sigh,
Or look but sad—there was indeed a time
When Jaffeir would have ta'en her in his arms,
Eased her declining head upon his breast,
And never left her till he found the cause.
But let her now weep seas,
Cry, till she rend the earth; sigh till she burst
Her heart asunder; still he bears it all;
Deaf as the wind, and as the rocks unshaken.
*Jaff.* Have I been deaf? am I that rock unmoved,
Against whose root tears beat and sighs are sent?
In vain have I beheld thy sorrows calmly!

Witness against me, heavens, have I done this?
Then bear me in a whirlwind back again,
And let that angry dear one ne'er forgive me!
O thou too rashly censur'st of my love!
Couldst thou but think how I have spent this night,
Dark and alone, no pillow to my head,
Rest in my eyes, nor quiet in my heart,
Thou wouldst not, Belvidera, sure thou wouldst not
Talk to me thus, but like a pitying angel
Spreading thy wings come settle on my breast,
And hatch warm comfort there ere sorrows freeze it.

    *Belv.* Why, then, poor mourner, in what baleful corner
Hast thou been talking with that witch the night?
On what cold stone hast thou been stretched along,
Gathering the grumbling winds about thy head,
To mix with theirs the accents of thy woes!
Oh, now I find the cause my love forsakes me!
I am no longer fit to bear a share
In his concernments: my weak female virtue
Must not be trusted; 'tis too frail and tender.

    *Jaff.* O Portia! Portia! what a soul was thine!

    *Belv.* That Portia was a woman, and when Brutus,
Big with the fate of Rome (Heaven guard thy safety!)
Concealed from her the labours of his mind,
She let him see her blood was great as his,
Flowed from a spring as noble, and a heart
Fit to partake his troubles, as his love:
Fetch, fetch that dagger back, the dreadful dower
Thou gav'st last night in parting with me; strike it
Here to my heart; and as the blood flows from it
Judge if it run not pure as Cato's daughter's.

    *Jaff.* Thou art too good, and I indeed unworthy,
Unworthy so much virtue: teach me how
I may deserve such matchless love as thine,
And see with what attention I'll obey thee.

    *Belv.* Do not despise me: that's the all I ask.

    *Jaff.* Despise thee! Hear me——

    *Belv.*            Oh, thy charming tongue
Is but too well acquainted with my weakness,
Knows, let it name but love, my melting heart
Dissolves within my breast; till with closed eyes
I reel into thy arms, and all's forgotten.

    *Jaff.* What shall I do?

    *Belv.*            Tell me! be just, and tell me
Why dwells that busy cloud upon thy face?
Why am I made a stranger? why that sigh,
And I not know the cause? Why, when the world
Is wrapt in rest, why chooses then my love
To wander up and down in horrid darkness

Loathing his bed, and these desiring arms?
Why are these eyes bloodshot with tedious watching?
Why starts he now? and looks as if he wished
His fate were finished? Tell me, ease my fears;
Lest when we next time meet, I want the power
To search into the sickness of thy mind,
But talk as wildly then as thou look'st now.

 *Jaff.*  O Belvidera!

 *Belv.*  Why was I last night delivered to a villain?

 *Jaff.*  Ha, a villain!

 *Belv.*  Yes! to a villain!  Why at such an hour
Meets that assembly all made up of wretches
That look as hell had drawn 'em into league?
Why, I in this hand, and in that a dagger,
Was I delivered with such dreadful ceremonies?
*" To you, sirs, and to your honour I bequeath her,*
*And with her this : whene'er I prove unworthy,*
*You know the rest, then strike it to her heart "* ?
Oh! why's that *rest* concealed from me? must I
Be made the hostage of a hellish trust?
For such I know I am; that's all my value?
But by the love and loyalty I owe thee,
I'll free thee from the bondage of these slaves,
Straight to the Senate, tell 'em all I know,
All that I think, all that my fears inform me!

 *Jaff.*  Is this the Roman virtue! this the blood
That boasts its purity with Cato's daughter's!
Would she have e'er betrayed her Brutus?

 *Belv.*           No:
For Brutus trusted her: wert thou so kind,
What would not Belvidera suffer for thee?

 *Jaff.*  I shall undo myself, and tell thee all.

 *Belv.*  Look not upon me, as I am a woman,
But as a bone, thy wife, thy friend, who long
Has had admission to thy heart, and there
Studied the virtues of thy gallant nature;
Thy constancy, thy courage and thy truth,
Have been my daily lesson: I have learnt them,
Am bold as thou, can suffer or despise
The worst of fates for thee, and with thee share them.

 *Jaff.*  O you divinest Powers! look down and hear
My prayers! instruct me to reward this virtue!
Yet think a little ere thou tempt me further:
Think I have a tale to tell, will shake thy nature,
Melt all this boasted constancy thou talk'st of
Into vile tears and despicable sorrows:
Then if thou shouldst betray me!

 *Belv.*         Shall I swear?

 *Jaff.*  No: do not swear: I would not violate

Thy tender nature with so rude a bond:
But as thou hopest to see me live my days,
And love thee long, lock this within thy breast;
I've bound myself by all the strictest sacraments
Divine and human——

    *Belv.*          Speak!
    *Jaff.*                To kill thy father——
    *Belv.* My father!
    *Jaff.*        Nay, the throats of the whole Senate
Shall bleed, my Belvidera: he amongst us
That spares his father, brother, or his friend,
Is damned: how rich and beauteous will the face
Of Ruin look, when these wide streets run blood; ˙
I and the glorious partners of my fortune
Shouting, and striding o'er the prostrate dead,
Still to new waste; whilst thou, far off in safety,
Smiling, shalt see the wonders of our daring,
And when night comes, with praise and love receive me.

    *Belv.* Oh!
    *Jaff.*    Have a care, and shrink not even in thought!
For if thou dost——
    *Belv.*          I know it, thou wilt kill me.
Do, strike thy sword into this bosom: lay me
Dead on the earth, and then thou wilt be safe:
Murder my father! tho' his cruel nature
Has persecuted me to my undoing,
Driven me to basest wants, can I behold him,
With smiles of vengeance, butchered in his age?
The sacred fountain of my life destroyed?
And canst thou shed the blood that gave me being,
Nay, be a traitor too, and sell thy country?
Can thy great heart descend so vilely low,
Mix with hired slaves, bravos, and common stabbers,
Nose-slitters, alley-lurking villains! join
With such a crew and take a ruffian's wages
To cut the throats of wretches as they sleep?

    *Jaff.* Thou wrong'st me, Belvidera! I've engaged
With men of souls: fit to reform the ills
Of all mankind: there's not a heart amongst them,
But's as stout as death, yet honest as the nature
Of man first made, ere fraud and vice were fashions.

    *Belv.* What's he, to whose curst hands last night thou gav'st me?
Was that well done? Oh! I could tell a story
Would rouse thy lion-heart out of its den
And make it rage with terrifying fury.

    *Jaff.* Speak on, I charge thee!
    *Belv.*          O my love! if e'er
Thy Belvidera's peace deserved thy care,
Remove me from this place: last night, last night——

*Jaff.* Distract me not, but give me all the truth.

*Belv.* No sooner wert thou gone, and I alone,
Left in the power of that old son of mischief;
No sooner was I lain on my sad bed,
But that vile wretch approached me; loose, unbuttoned,
Ready for violation: then my heart
Throbb'd with its fears: oh, how I wept and sighed
And shrunk and trembled; wished in vain for him
That should protect me. Thou, alas, wert gone!

*Jaff.* Patience, sweet Heaven, till I make vengeance sure!

*Belv.* He drew the hideous dagger forth thou gav'st him,
And with upbraiding smiles, he said, " *Behold it;
This is the pledge of a false husband's love :* "
And in my arms then pressed, and would have clasped me;
But with my cries I scared his coward heart,
Till he withdrew, and muttered vows to hell.
These are thy friends! with these thy life, thy honour,
Thy love, all's staked, and all will go to ruin.

*Jaff.* No more: I charge thee keep this secret close;
Clear up thy sorrows, look as if thy wrongs
Were all forgot, and treat him like a friend,
As no complaint were made. No more, retire;
Retire, my life, and doubt not of my honour;
I'll heal its failings and deserve thy love.

*Belv.* Oh, should I part with thee, I fear thou wilt
In anger leave me, and return no more.

*Jaff.* Return no more! I would not live without thee
Another night to purchase the creation.

*Belv.* When shall we meet again?

*Jaff.*                          Anon at twelve!
I'll steal myself to thy expecting arms,
Come like a travelled dove and bring thee peace.

*Belv.* Indeed!

*Jaff.*        By all our loves!

*Belv.*                          'Tis hard to part:
But sure no falsehood ever looked so fairly.
Farewell—remember twelve.        [*Exit* BELVIDERA.

*Jaff.*                    Let Heaven forget me
When I remember not thy truth, thy love.
How curst is my condition, tossed and justled,
From every corner; Fortune's common fool,
The jest of rogues, an instrumental ass
For villains to lay loads of shame upon,
And drive about just for their ease and scorn.

*Enter* PIERRE.

*Pierr.* Jaffeir!

*Jaff.*          Who calls!

*Pierr.*                    A friend, that could have wished

T' have found thee otherwise employed: what, hunt
A wife on the dull foil! sure a staunch husband
Of all hounds is the dullest? wilt thou never,
Never be weaned from caudles and confections?
What feminine tale hast thou been listening to,
Of unaired shirts; catarrhs and toothache got
By thin-soled shoes? Damnation! that a fellow
Chosen to be a sharer in the destruction
Of a whole people, should sneak thus in corners
To ease his fulsome lusts, and fool his mind.

   *Jaff.* May not a man then trifle out an hour
With a kind woman and not wrong his calling?

   *Pierr.* Not in a cause like ours.

   *Jaff.*              Then, friend, our cause
Is in a damned condition: for I'll tell thee,
That canker-worm called Lechery has touched it,
'Tis tainted vilely: wouldst thou think it, Renault
(That mortified old withered winter rogue)
Loves simple fornication like a priest;
I found him out for watering at my wife:
He visited her last night like a kind guardian:
Faith, she has some temptations, that's the truth on't.

   *Pierr.* He durst not wrong his trust!

   *Jaff.*           'Twas something late, though,
To take the freedom of a lady's chamber.

   *Pierr.* Was she in bed?

   *Jaff.*         Yes, faith, in virgin sheets
White as her bosom, Pierre, dished neatly up,
Might tempt a weaker appetite to taste.
Oh, how the old fox stunk, I warrant thee,
When the rank fit was on him!

   *Pierr.*          Patience guide me!
He used no violence?

   *Jaff.*        No, no! out on't, violence!
Played with her neck; brushed her with his grey-beard,
Struggled and towzed, tickled her till she squeaked a little
May be, or so—but not a jot of violence——

   *Pierr.* Damn him!

   *Jaff.*       Ay, so say I: but hush, no more on't—
All hitherto is well, and I believe
Myself no monster yet: though no man knows
What fate he's born to: sure 'tis near the hour
We all should meet for our concluding orders:
Will the ambassador be here in person?

   *Pierr.* No: he has sent commission to that villain, Renault,
To give the executing charge.
I'd have thee be a man, if possible,
And keep thy temper; for a brave revenge
Ne'er comes too late.

*Jaff.*                    Fear not, I'm cool as patience:
Had he completed my dishonour, rather
Than hazard the success our hopes are ripe for,
I'd bear it all with mortifying virtue.
    *Pierr.* He's yonder coming this way through the hall;
His thoughts seem full.
    *Jaff.*                    Prithee retire, and leave me
With him alone: I'll put him to some trial,
See how his rotten part will bear the touching.
    *Pierr.* Be careful, then.                    [*Exit* PIERRE.
    *Jaff.*                    Nay, never doubt, but trust me.
What, be a devil! take a damning oath
For shedding native blood! can there be a sin
In merciful repentance? O this villain!


*Enter* RENAULT.


    *Ren.* Perverse! and peevish! what a slave is Man !
To let his itching flesh thus get the better of him!
Despatch the tool her husband—that were well.
Who's there?
    *Jaff.*        A man.
    *Ren.*                    My friend, my near ally!
The hostage of your faith, my beauteous charge, is very well.
    *Jaff.* Sir, are you sure of that?
Stands she in perfect health? beats her pulse even?
Neither too hot nor cold?
    *Ren.*                    What means that question?
    *Jaff.* Oh, women have fantastic constitutions,
Inconstant as their wishes, always wavering,
And ne'er fixed; was it not boldly done
Even at first sight to trust the thing I loved
(A tempting treasure too!) with youth so fierce
And vigorous as thine? but thou art honest.
    *Ren.* Who dares accuse me?
    *Jaff.*                    Cursed be him that doubts
Thy virtue: I have tried it, and declare,
Were I to choose a guardian of my honour
I'd put it into thy keeping; for I know thee.
    *Ren.* Know me!
    *Jaff.*        Ay, know thee: there's no falsehood in thee.
Thou lookst just as thou art: let us embrace.
Now wouldst thou cut my throat or I cut thine?
    *Ren.* You dare not do't.
    *Jaff.*                    You lie, sir.
    *Ren.*                    How!
    *Jaff.*                    No more.
'Tis a base world, and must reform, that's all.

*Enter* SPINOSA, THEODORE, ELIOT, REVILLIDO, DURAND,
BRAMVEIL, *and the rest of the* Conspirators.

*Ren.* Spinosa, Theodore!
*Spin.*                    The same.
*Ren.* You are welcome!
*Spin.*                    You are trembling, sir.
*Ren.* 'Tis a cold night indeed, I am aged,
Full of decay and natural infirmities;      [PIERRE *re-enters.*
We shall be warm, my friend, I hope, to-morrow.
   *Pierr.* 'Twas not well done, thou shouldst have stroked him
And not have galled him.
   *Jaff.*                    Damn him, let him chew on't.
Heaven! where am I? beset with cursed fiends,
That wait to damn me: what a devil's man,
When he forgets his nature—hush, my heart.
   *Ren.* My friends, 'tis late: are we assembled all?
Where's Theodore?
   *Theo.*              At hand.
   *Ren.*                    Spinosa.
   *Spin.*                         Here.
   *Ren.* Bramveil.
   *Bram.*         I'm ready.
   *Ren.*                    Durand and Brabe.
   *Dur.*                              Command us,
We are both prepared!
   *Ren.*              Mezzana, Revillido,
Ternon, Retrosi; oh, you are men, I find,
Fit to behold your fate, and meet her summons.
To-morrow's rising sun must see you all
Decked in your honours! are the soldiers ready?
   *Omn.* All, all.
   *Ren.* You, Durand, with your thousand must possess
St. Mark's: you, captain, know your charge already:
'Tis to secure the ducal palace: you,
Brabe, with a hundred more must gain the Secque.
With the like number Bramveil to the Procuralie.
Be all this done with the least tumult possible,
Till in each place you post sufficient guards:
Then sheathe your swords in every breast you meet.
   *Jaff.* O reverend cruelty! damn'd bloody villain!
   *Ren.* During this execution, Durand, you
Must in the midst keep your battalia fast,
And, Theodore, be sure to plant the cannon
That may command the streets; whilst Revillido,
Mezzana, Ternon, and Retrosi, guard you.
This done, we'll give the general alarm,
Apply petards, and force the ars'nal gates;
Then fire the city round in several places,

Or with our cannon, if it dare resist,
Batter't to ruin.   But 'bove all I charge you
Shed blood enough, spare neither sex nor age,
Name nor condition; if there live a Senator
After to-morrow, tho' the dullest rogue
That e'er said nothing, we have lost our ends;
If possible, let's kill the very name
Of Senator, and bury it in blood.

*Jaff.* Merciless, horrid slave!—Ay, blood enough!
Shed blood enough, old Renault: how thou charm'st me!

*Ren.* But one thing more, and then farewell till Fate
Join us again, or separate us ever:
First, let's embrace, Heav'n knows who next shall thus
Wing ye together: but let's all remember
We wear no common cause upon our swords;
Let each man think that on his single virtue
Depends the good and fame of all the rest,
Eternal honour or perpetual infamy.
Let's remember through what dreadful hazards
Propitious Fortune hitherto has led us,
How often on the brink of some discovery
Have we stood tottering, and yet kept our ground
So well, the busiest searchers ne'er could follow
Those subtle tracks which puzzled all suspicion:
You droop, sir.

*Jaff.*         No: with a most profound attention
I've heard it all, and wonder at thy virtue.

*Ren.* Tho' there be yet few hours 'twixt them and Ruin,
Are not the Senate lulled in full security,
Quiet and satisfied, as fools are always?
Never did so profound repose forerun
Calamity so great: nay, our good fortune
Has blinded the most piercing of mankind;
Strengthened the fearful'st, charm'd the most suspectful,
Confounded the most subtle; for we live,
We live, my friends, and quickly shall our life
Prove fatal to these tyrants: let's consider
That we destroy oppression, avarice,
A people nursed up equally with vices
And loathsome lusts, which Nature most abhors,
And such as without shame she cannot suffer.

*Jaff.* O Belvidera, take me to thy arms
And show me where's my peace, for I have lost it.
                                        [*Exit* JAFFEIR.

*Ren.* Without the least remorse then let's resolve
With fire and sword t' exterminate these tyrants,
And when we shall behold those curst tribunals,
Stained by the tears and sufferings of the innocent,
Burning with flames rather from Heav'n than ours,

The raging furious and unpitying soldier
Pulling his reeking dagger from the bosoms
Of gasping wretches; death in every quarter,
With all that sad disorder can produce,
To make a spectacle of horror: then,
Then let us call to mind, my dearest friends,
That there is nothing pure upon the earth,
That the most valued things have most alloys,
And that in change of all those vile enormities,
Under whose weight this wretched country labours,
The means are only in our hands to crown them.

   *Pierr.* And may those Powers above that are propitious
To gallant minds record this cause, and bless it.

   *Ren.* Thus happy, thus secure of all we wish for,
Should there, my friends, be found amongst us one
False to this glorious enterprise, what fate,
What vengeance were enough for such a villain?

   *Eliot.* Death here without repentance, hell hereafter.

   *Ren.* Let that be my lot, if as here I stand
Lifted by Fate amongst her darling sons,
Tho' I'd one only brother, dear by all
The strictest ties of nature; tho' one hour
Had given us birth, one fortune fed our wants,
One only love, and that but of each other,
Still filled our minds: could I have such a friend
Joined in this cause, and had but ground to fear
Meant foul play; may this right hand drop from me,
If I'd not hazard all my future peace,
And stab him to the heart before you: who
Would not do less? Wouldst not thou, Pierre, the same?

   *Pierr.* You've singled me, sir, out for this hard question,
As if 'twere started only for my sake!
Am I the thing you fear? Here, here's my bosom,
Search it with all your swords! am I a traitor?

   *Ren.* No: but I fear your late commended friend
Is little less: come, sirs, 'tis now no time
To trifle with our safety. Where's this Jaffeir?

   *Spin.* He left the room just now in strange disorder.

   *Ren.* Nay, there's danger in him: I observ'd him,
During the time I took for explanation,
He was transported from most deep attention
To a confusion which he could not smother.
His looks grew full of sadness and surprise,
All which betrayed a wavering spirit in him,
That laboured with reluctancy and sorrow;
What's requisite for safety must be done
With speedy execution: he remains
Yet in our power: I for my own part wear
A dagger.

*Pierr.*    Well?
*Ren.*            And I could wish it!
*Pierr.*                        Where?
*Ren.* Buried in his heart.
*Pierr.*                Away! we're yet all friends;
No more of this, 'twill breed ill blood amongst us.
    *Spin.* Let us all draw our swords, and search the house,
Pull him from the dark hole where he sits brooding
O'er his cold fears, and each man kill his share of him.
    *Pierr.* Who talks ot killing? who's he'll shed the blood
That's dear to me? is't you? or you? or you, sir?
What, not one speak? how you stand gaping all
On your grave oracle, your wooden god there;
Yet not a word: then, sir, I'll tell you a secret,
Suspicion's but at best a coward's virtue!        [*To* RENAULT.
    *Ren.* A coward——            [*Handles his sword.*
    *Pierr.*            Put, put up the sword, old man,
Thy hand shakes at it; come, let's heal this breach,
I am too hot; we yet may live friends.
    *Spin.* Till we are safe, our friendship cannot be so.
    *Pierr.* Again: who's that?
    *Spin.*                'Twas I.
    *Theo.*                And I.
    *Revill.*                    And I.
    *Eliot.*                        And all.
    *Ren.* Who are on my side?
    *Spin.*                Every honest sword;
Let's die like men and not be sold like slaves.
    *Pierr.* One such word more, by Heav'n I'll to the Senate
And hang ye all, like dogs in clusters.
Why peep your coward swords half out their shells?
Why do you not all brandish them like mine?
You fear to die, and yet dare talk of killing?
    *Ren.* Go to thy Senate and betray us, hasten,
Secure thy wretched life, we fear to die
Less than thou dar'st be honest.
    *Pierr.*                That's rank falsehood.
Fear'st not thou death? fie, there's a knavish itch
In that salt blood, an utter foe to smarting.
Had Jaffeir's wife proved kind, he'd still been true.
Foh—how that stinks!
Thou die! thou kill my friend, or thou, or thou,
Or thou, with that lean wither'd wretched face!
Away! disperse all to your several charges,
And meet to-morrow where your honour calls you;
I'll bring that man, whose blood you so much thirst for,
And you shall see him venture for you fairly—
Hence, hence, I say.            [*Exit* RENAULT *angrily.*
    *Spin.*            I fear we've been to blame;

And done too much.

   *Theo.* 'Twas too far urged against the man you loved.

   *Revill.* Here, take our swords and crush 'em with your feet.

   *Spin.* Forgive us, gallant friend.

   *Pierr.*                   Nay, now ye've found
The way to melt and cast me as you will:
I'll fetch this friend and give him to your mercy:
Nay, he shall die if you will take him from me;
For your repose I'll quit my heart's jewel,
But would not have him torn away by villains
And spiteful villainy.

   *Spin.*           No; may you both
For ever live and fill the world with fame!

   *Pierr.* Now you are too kind. Whence rose all this discord?
Oh, what a dangerous precipice have we scaped!
How near a fall was all we had long been building!
What an eternal blot had stained our glories,
If one, the bravest and the best of men,
Had fallen a sacrifice to rash suspicion,
Butchered by those whose cause he came to cherish:
Oh, could you know him all as I have known him,
How good he is, how just, how true, how brave,
You would not leave this place till you had seen him;
Humbled yourselves before him, kissed his feet,
And gained remission for the worst of follies;
  Come but to-morrow all your doubts shall end,
  And to your loves me better recommend,
  That I've preserved your fame, and saved my friend.

                                  *[Exeunt omnes.*


# ACT IV

## [SCENE I]

### *Enter* JAFFEIR *and* BELVIDERA.

   *Jaff.* Where dost thou lead me? Every step I move,
Methinks I tread upon some mangled limb
Of a rack'd friend: O my dear charming ruin!
Where are we wandering?

   *Belv.*              To eternal honour;
To do a deed shall chronicle thy name,
Among the glorious legends of those few
That have sav'd sinking nations: thy renown
Shall be the future song of all the virgins,
Who by thy piety have been preserved

From horrid violation: every street
Shall be adorn'd with statues to thy honour,
And at thy feet this great inscription written,
*Remember him that propp'd the fall of Venice.*
 *Jaff.* Rather, remember him, who after all
The sacred bonds of oaths and holier friendship,
In fond compassion to a woman's tears
Forgot his manhood, virtue, truth and honour,
To sacrifice the bosom that relieved him.
Why wilt thou damn me?
 *Belv.*     O inconstant man!
How will you promise? how will you deceive?
Do return back, replace me in my bondage,
Tell all thy friends how dangerously thou lov'st me,
And let thy dagger do its bloody office;
O that kind dagger, Jaffeir, how 'twill look
Stuck through my heart, drench'd in my blood to th' hilts!
Whilst these poor dying eyes shall with their tears
No more torment thee, then thou wilt be free:
Or if thou think'st it nobler, let me live
Till I'm a victim to the hateful lust
Of that infernal devil, that old fiend
That's damned himself and would undo mankind:
Last night, my love——
 *Jaff.*    Name, name it not again,
It shows a beastly image to my fancy,
Will wake me into madness.  Oh, the villain!
That durst approach such purity as thine
On terms so vile: destruction, swift destruction

Fall on my coward-head, and make my name
The common scorn of fools if I forgive him;
If I forgive him, if I not revenge
With utmost rage and most unstaying fury
Thy sufferings, thou dear darling of my life, love.
 *Belv.* Delay no longer, then, but to the Senate;
And tell the dismal'st story e'er was utter'd,
Tell 'em what bloodshed, rapines, desolations,
Have been prepared, how near's the fatal hour!
Save thy poor country, save the reverend blood
Of all its nobles, which to-morrow's dawn
Must else see shed: save the poor tender lives
Of all those little infants which the swords
Of murtherers are whetting for this moment:
Think thou already hearst their dying screams,
Think that thou seest their sad distracted mothers
Kneeling before thy feet, and begging pity
With torn dishevell'd hair and streaming eyes,
Their naked mangled breasts besmear'd with blood,
And even the milk with which their fondled babes

Softly they hush'd, dropping in anguish from 'em.
Think thou seest this, and then consult thy heart.
   *Jaff.* Oh!
   *Belv.* Think too, if [that] thou lose this present minute,
What miseries the next day bring upon thee.
Imagine all the  horors of that night,
Murder and rapine, waste and desolation,
Confusedly ranging.  Think what then may prove
My lot! the ravisher may then come safe,
And midst the terror of the public ruin
Do a damn'd deed; perhaps to lay a train
May catch thy life; then where will be revenge,
The dear revenge that's due to such a wrong?
   *Jaff.* By all Heaven's powers, prophetic truth dwells in thee,
For every word thou speak'st strikes through my heart
Like a new light, and shows it how't has wandered;
Just what thou'st made me, take me, Belvidera,
And lead me to the place where I'm to say
This bitter lesson, where I must betray
My truth, my virtue, constancy and friends:
Must I betray my friends!  Ah, take me quickly,
Secure me well before that thought's renewed;
If I relapse once more, all's lost for ever.
   *Belv.* Hast thou a friend more dear than Belvidera?
   *Jaff.* No, thou'rt my soul itself; wealth, friendship, honour,
All present joys, and earnest of all future,
Are summ'd in thee: methinks when in thy arms
Thus leaning on thy breast, one minute's more
Than a long thousand years of vulgar hours.
Why was such happiness not given me pure?
Why dash'd with cruel wrongs, and bitter wantings?
Come, lead me forward now like a tame lamb
To sacrifice; thus in his fatal garlands,
Deck'd fine and pleas'd, the wanton skips and plays,
   Trots by the enticing flattering priestess' side,
   And much transported with his little pride,
   Forgets his dear companions of the plain
   Till, by her bound, he's on the altar lain,
   Yet then too hardly bleats, such pleasure's in the pain.

       *Enter* Officer *and six* Guards.

   *Offic.* Stand, who goes there?
   *Belv.* Friends.
   *Jaff.* Friends, Belvidera! hide me from my friends:
By heaven, I'd rather see the face of hell,
Than meet the man I love.
   *Offic.*             But what friends are you?
   *Belv.* Friends to the Senate and the State of Venice.
   *Offic.* My orders are to seize on all I find

At this late hour, and bring 'em to the Council,
Who now are sitting.
   *Jaff.*           Sir, you shall be obeyed.
Hold, brutes, stand off, none of your paws upon me.
Now the lot's cast, and Fate do what thou wilt!

                                   *[Exeunt guarded.*


### SCENE [II.]—*The Senate-house*

*Where appear sitting, the* Duke of VENICE, PRIULI,
ANTONIO, *and eight other* Senators.

   *Duke.* Antony, Priuli, Senators of Venice,
Speak; why are we assembled here this night?
What have you to inform us of, concerns
The State of Venice, honour, or its safety?
   *Priu.* Could words express the story I have to tell you,
Fathers, these tears were useless, these sad tears
That fall from my old eyes; but there is cause
We all should weep; tear off these purple robes,
And wrap ourselves in sackcloth, sitting down
On the sad earth, and cry aloud to Heaven.
Heaven knows if yet there be an hour to come
Ere Venice be no more.
   *All Senators.*        How!
   *Priu.*             Nay, we stand
Upon the very brink of gaping ruin.
Within this city's formed a dark conspiracy,
To massacre us all, our wives and children,
Kindred and friends, our palaces and temples
To lay in ashes: nay, the hour too, fix'd;
The swords, for aught I know, drawn e'en this moment,
And the wild waste begun: from unknown hands
I had this warning: but if we are men
Let's not be tamely butchered, but do something
That may inform the world in after ages,
Our virtue was not ruin'd though we were.   *[A noise without.*
Room, room, make room for some prisoners——
   *Second Senator.* Let's raise the city.

              *Enter* Officer *and* Guard.

   *Priu.*             Speak there, what disturbance?
   *Offic.* Two prisoners have the guard seiz'd in the streets,
Who say they come to inform this reverend Senate
About the present danger.

       *Enter* JAFFEIR *and* BELVIDERA *guarded.*

   *All.*              Give 'em entrance——
Well, who are you?

*Jaff.* A villain.

*Anto.* Short and pithy.
Th man speaks well.

*Jaff.* Would every man that hears me
Would deal so honestly. and own his title.

*Duke.* 'Tis rumour'd that a plot has been contriv'd
Against this State; that you have a share in't too.
If you're a villain, to redeem your honour,
Unfold the truth and be restored with mercy.

*Jaff.* Think not that I to save my life come hither,
I know its value better; but in pity
To all those wretches whose unhappy dooms
Are fix'd and seal'd. You see me here before you,
The sworn and covenanted foe of Venice;
But use me as my dealings may deserve
And I may prove a friend.

*Duke.* The slave capitulates;
Give him the tortures.

*Jaff.* That you dare not do,
Your fears won't let you, nor the longing itch
To hear a story which you dread the truth of,
Truth which the fear of smart shall ne'er get from me.
Cowards are scared with threat'nings; boys are whipp'd
Into confessions: but a steady mind
Acts of itself, ne'er asks the body counsel.
Give him the tortures! Name but such a thing
Again, by Heaven I'll shut these lips for ever,
Not all your racks, your engines, or your wheels
Shall force a groan away—that you may guess at.

*Anto.* A bloody-minded fellow, I'll warrant;
A damn'd bloody-minded fellow.

*Duke.* Name your conditions.

*Jaff.* For myself full pardon,
Besides the lives of two and twenty friends, [*Delivers a list.*
Whose names are here enrolled: nay, let their crimes
Be ne'er so monstrous, I must have the oaths
And sacred promise of this reverend Council,
That in a full assembly of the Senate
The thing I ask be ratified. Swear this,
And I'll unfold the secrets of your danger.

*All.* We'll swear.

*Duke.* Propose the oath.

*Jaff.* By all the hopes
Ye have of peace and happiness hereafter,
Swear.

*All.* We all swear.

*Jaff.* To grant me what I've asked,
Ye swear.

*All.* We swear.

*Jaff.*                 And as ye keep the oath,
May you and your posterity be blest
Or curst for ever.

*All.*                 Else be curst for ever.

*Jaff.* Then here's the list, and with't the full disclose
Of all that threatens you.          [*Delivers another paper.*
                   Now Fate, thou hast caught me.

*Anto.* Why, what a dreadful catalogue of cut-throats is here!
I'll warrant you not one of these fellows but has a face like a
lion.
I dare not so much as read their names over.

*Duke.* Give orders that all diligent search be made
To seize these men, their characters are public;
The paper intimates their rendezvous
To be at the house of a famed Grecian courtesan
Called Aquilina; see that place secured.

*Anto.* What, my Nicky Nacky, hurry durry, Nicky Nacky
         in the plot—I'll make a speech.    Most noble Senators,
What headlong apprehension drives you on,
Right noble, wise and truly solid senators,
To violate the laws and rights of nations?
The lady is a lady of renown.
'Tis true, she holds a house of fair reception,
And though I say't myself, as many more
Can say as well as I.

*Second Senator.*        My lord, long speeches
Are frivolous here when dangers are so near us;
We all well know your interest in that lady,
The world talks loud on't.

*Anto.*              Verily, I have done,
I say no more.

*Duke.*          But since he has declared
Himself concerned, pray, captain, take great caution
To treat the fair one as becomes her character,
And let her bed-chamber be searched with decency.
You, Jaffeir, must with patience bear till morning
To be our prisoner.

*Jaff.*          Would the chains of death
Had bound me fast ere I had known this minute.
I've done a deed will make my story hereafter
Quoted in competition with all ill ones:
The history of my wickedness shall run
Down through the low traditions of the vulgar,
And boys be taught to tell the tale of Jaffeir.

*Duke.* Captain, withdraw your prisoner.

*Jaff.*                Sir, if possible,
Lead me where my own thoughts themselves may lose me,
Where I may doze out what I've left of life,

Forget myself and this day's guilt and falsehood.
Cruel remembrance, how shall I appease thee!    [*Exit guarded.*

*Noise without.*

*Voices.* More traitors; room, room, make room there.

*Duke.* How's this? guards!
Where are our guards? shut up the gates, the treason's
Already at our doors.

*Enter* Officer.

*Offic.*                My lords, more traitors:
Seized in the very act of consultation;
Furnished with arms and instruments of mischief.
Bring in the prisoners.

*Enter* PIERRE, RENAULT, THEODORE, ELIOT, REVILLIDO,
*and other* Conspirators, *in fetters, guarded.*

*Pierr.*                You, my lords and fathers
(As you are pleased to call yourselves) of Venice;
If you sit here to guide the course of Justice,
Why these disgraceful chains upon the limbs
That have so often laboured in your service?
Are these the wreaths of triumph ye bestow
On those that bring you conquests home and honours?
*Duke.* Go on: you shall be heard, sir.
*Anto.* And be hanged too, I hope.
*Pierr.* Are these the trophies I've deserv'd for fighting
Your battles with confederated powers?
When winds and seas conspir'd to overthrow you,
And brought the fleets of Spain to your own harbours:
When you, great Duke, shrunk trembling in your palace,
And saw your wife, th' Adriatic, plough'd
Like a lewd whore by bolder prows than yours,
Stepp'd not I forth, and taught your loose Venetians
The task of honour and the way to greatness,
Rais'd you from your capitulating fears
To stipulate the terms of sued-for peace?
And this my recompense? If I'm a traitor
Produce my charge; or show the wretch that's base enough
And brave enough to tell me I'm a traitor.
*Duke.* Know you one Jaffeir?    [*All the* Conspirators *murmur.*
*Pierr.*                Yes, and know his virtue,
His justice, truth; his general worth and sufferings
From a hard father taught me first to love him.

*Enter* JAFFEIR *guarded.*

*Duke.* See him brought forth.
*Pierr.*                My friend too bound! nay then
Our fate has conquered us, and we must fall.

Why droops the man whose welfare's so much mine
They're but one thing? these reverend tyrants, Jaffeir,
Call us all traitors: art thou one, my brother?

*Jaff.* To thee I am the falsest, veriest slave
That e'er betrayed a generous trusting friend,
And gave up honour to be sure of ruin.
All our fair hopes which morning was to have crown'd
Has this curs'd tongue o'erthrown.

*Pierr.*                    So, then, all's over;
Venice has lost her freedom; I my life;
No more, farewell.

*Duke.*          Say, will you make confession
Of your vile deeds and trust the Senate's mercy?

*Pierr.* Cursed be your Senate: cursed your constitution:
The curse of growing factions and division
Still vex your councils, shake your public safety,
And make the robes of government you wear
Hateful to you, as these base chains to me.

*Duke.* Pardon or death?

*Pierr.*                    Death, honourable death!

*Ren.* Death's the best thing we ask or you can give.

*All Conspir.* No shameful bonds, but honourable death.

*Duke.* Break up the council: captain, guard your prisoners.
Jaffeir, you are free, but these must wait for judgment.
                    [*Exeunt all the* Senators.

*Pierr.* Come, where's my dungeon? lead me to my straw:
It will not be the first time I've lodged hard
To do your Senate service.

*Jaff.*                    Hold one moment.

*Pierr.* Who's he disputes the judgment of the Senate?
Presumptuous rebel—on——          [*Strikes* JAFFEIR.

*Jaff.*               By Heaven, you stir not.
I must be heard, I must have leave to speak;
Thou hast disgrac'd me, Pierre, by a vile blow:
Had not a dagger done thee nobler justice?
But use me as thou wilt, thou canst not wrong me,
For I am fallen beneath the basest injuries;
Yet look upon me with an eye of mercy,
With pity and with charity behold me;
Shut not thy heart against a friend's repentance,
But as there dwells a god-like nature in thee
Listen with mildness to my supplications.

*Pierr.* What whining monk art thou? what holy cheat,
That wouldst encroach upon my credulous ears
And cant'st thus vilely? hence. I know thee not.
Dissemble and be nasty: leave me, hypocrite.

*Jaff.* Not know me, Pierre?

*Pierr.*               No, I know thee not: what art thou?

*Jaff.* Jaffeir, thy friend, thy once loved, valued friend!

Though now deservedly scorned, and used most hardly.
   *Pierr.* Thou Jaffeir! Thou my once loved, valued friend?
By heavens, thou liest; the man, so call'd, my friend,
Was generous, honest, faithful, just and valiant,
Noble in mind, and in his person lovely,
Dear to my eyes and tender to my heart:
But thou a wretched, base, false, worthless coward,
Poor even in soul, and loathsome in thy aspect,
All eyes must shun thee, and all hearts detest thee.
Prithee avoid, nor longer cling thus round me,
Like something baneful, that my nature's chill'd at.
   *Jaff.* I have not wrong'd thee, by these tears I have not.
But still am honest, true, and hope too, valiant:
My mind still full of thee, therefore still noble;
Let not thy eyes then shun me, nor thy heart
Detest me utterly; oh, look upon me,
Look back and see my sad sincere submission!
How my heart swells, as even 'twould burst my bosom;
Fond of its gaol, and labouring to be at thee!
What shall I do? what say to make thee hear me?
   *Pierr.* Hast thou not wronged me? dar'st thou call thyself
Jaffeir, that once loved, valued friend of mine,
And swear thou hast not wronged me? whence these chains?
Whence the vile death which I may meet this moment?
Whence this dishonour, but from thee, thou false one?
   *Jaff.* All's true, yet grant one thing, and I've done asking.
   *Pierr.* What's that?
   *Jaff.*            To take thy life on such conditions
The Council have propos'd: thou and thy friends
May yet live long, and to be better treated.
   *Pierr.* Life! ask my life! confess! record myself
A villain for the privilege to breathe,
And carry up and down this cursed city
A discontented and repining spirit,
Burthensome to itself a few years longer,
To lose it, may be, at last in a lewd quarrel
For some new friend, treacherous and false as thou art
No, this vile world and I have long been jangling,
And cannot part on better terms than now,
When only men like thee are fit to live in't.
   *Jaff.* By all that's just——
   *Pierr.*               Swear by some other powers,
For thou hast broke that sacred oath too lately.
   *Jaff.* Then by that hell I merit, I'll not leave thee,
Till to thyself at least thou'rt reconciled,
However thy resentments deal with me.
   *Pierr.* Not leave me!
   *Jaff.*           No, thou shalt not force me from thee.
Use me reproachfully, and like a slave,

Tread on me, buffet me, heap wrongs on wrongs
On my poor head: ·I'll bear it all with patience,
Shall weary out thy most unfriendly cruelty,
Lie at thy feet and kiss 'em though they spurn me,
Till, wounded by my sufferings, thou relent,
And raise me to thy arms with dear forgiveness.

    *Pierr.* Art thou not——
    *Jaff.*               What?
    *Pierr.*                  A traitor?
    *Jaff.*                         Yes.
    *Pierr.*                                  A villain?
    *Jaff.* Granted. ·
    *Pierr.*          A coward, a most scandalous coward,
Spiritless, void of honour, one who has sold
Thy everlasting fame for shameless life?
    *Jaff.* All, all, and more, much more: my faults are numberless.
    *Pierr.* And wouldst thou have me live on terms like thine?
Base as thou art false——
    *Jaff.*            No, 'tis to me that's granted.
The safety of thy life was all I aim'd at,
In recompense for faith and trust so broken.
    *Pierr.* I scorn it more because preserv'd by thee.
And as when first my foolish heart took pity
On thy misfortunes, sought thee in thy miseries,
Relieved thy wants, and raised thee from thy state
Of wretchedness in which thy fate had plung'd thee,
To rank thee in my list of noble friends;
All I received in surety for thy truth,
Were unregarded oaths; and this, this dagger,
Given with a worthless pledge, thou since hast stol'n,
So I restore it back to thee again,
Swearing by all those powers which thou hast violated,
Never from this curs'd hour to hold communion,
Friendship or interest with thee, though our years
Were to exceed those limited the world.
Take it—farewell—for now I owe thee nothing.
    *Jaff.* Say thou wilt live, then.
    *Pierr.*            For my life, dispose it
Just as thou wilt, because 'tis what I'm tired with.
    *Jaff.* O Pierre!
    *Pierr.*          No more.
    *Jaff.*            My eyes won't lose the sight of thee,
But languish after thine, and ache with gazing.
    *Pierr.* Leave me—nay, then, thus, thus, I throw thee from me
And curses, great as is thy falsehood, catch thee.
    *Jaff.* Amen.
He's gone, my father, friend, preserver,
And here's the portion he has left me.      [*Holds the dagger up.*
This dagger, well remembered, with this dagger

I gave a solemn vow of dire importance,
Parted with this and Belvidera together;
Have a care, mem'ry, drive that thought no farther;
No, I'll esteem it as a friend's last legacy,
Treasure it up within this wretched bosom,
Where it may grow acquainted with my heart,
That when they meet, they start not from each other.
So; now for thinking: a blow, call'd traitor, villain,
Coward, dishonourable coward, fough!
O for a long sound sleep, and so forget it!
Down, busy devil.—

*Enter* BELVIDERA.

   *Belv.*          Whither shall I fly?
Where hide me and my miseries together?
Where's now the Roman constancy I boasted?
Sunk into trembling fears and desperation!
Not daring now to look up to that dear face
Which used to smile even on my faults, but down
Bending these miserable eyes to earth,
Must move in penance, and implore much mercy.
   *Jaff.* Mercy, kind Heaven, has surely endless stores
Hoarded for thee of blessings yet untasted;
Let wretches loaded hard with guilt as I am,
Bow [with] the weight and groan beneath the burthen,
Creep with a remnant of that strength they've left,
Before the footstool of that Heaven they've injured.
O Belvidera! I'm the wretched'st creature
E'er crawled on earth: now if thou hast virtue, help me,
Take me into thy arms, and speak the words of peace
To my divided soul, that wars within me,
And raises every sense to my confusion;
By Heav'n, I'm tottering on the very brink
Of peace; and thou art all the hold I've left.
   *Belv.* Alas! I know thy sorrows are most mighty;
I know thou'st cause to mourn; to mourn, my Jaffeir,
With endless cries, and never-ceasing wailings,
Thou'st lost——
   *Jaff.*       Oh, I have lost what can't be counted;
My friend too, Belvidera, that dear friend,
Who, next to thee, was all my health rejoiced in,
Has used me like a slave; shamefully used me;
'Twould break thy pitying heart to hear the story.
What shall I do? resentment, indignation,
Love, pity, fear and mem'ry, how I've wronged him,
Distract my quiet with the very thought on't,
And tear my heart to pieces in my bosom.
   *Belv.* What has he done?
*Jaff.*           Thou'dst hate me, should I tell thee.

*Belv.* Why?

*Jaff.* Oh, he has us'd me! yet, by Heaven, I bear it:
He has us'd me, Belvidera, but first swear
That when I've told thee, thou'lt not loathe me utterly,
Though vilest blots and stains appear upon me;
But still at least with charitable goodness,
Be near me in the pangs of my affliction,
Not scorn me, Belvidera, as he has done.

*Belv.* Have I then e'er been false that now I'm doubted?
Speak, what's the cause I'm grown into distrust,
Why thought unfit to hear my love's complainings?

*Jaff.* Oh!

*Belv.* Tell me.

*Jaff.* Bear my failings, for they are many.
O my dear angel! in that friend I've lost
All my soul's peace; for every thought of him
Strikes my sense hard, and deads it in my brains;
Wouldst thou believe it?

*Belv.* Speak!

*Jaff.* Before we parted,
Ere yet his guards had led him to his prison,
Full of severest sorrows for his suff'rings,
With eyes o'erflowing and a bleeding heart,
Humbling myself almost beneath my nature,
As at his feet I kneel'd, and sued for mercy,
Forgetting all our friendship, all the dearness,
In which we've lived so many years together,
With a reproachful hand he dashed a blow.
He struck me, Belvidera, by Heaven, he struck me,
Buffeted, called me traitor, villain, coward.
Am I a coward? am I a villain? tell me:
Thou'rt the best judge, and mad'st me, if I am so.
Damnation: coward!

*Belv.* Oh! forgive him, Jaffeir.
And if his sufferings wound thy heart already,
What will they do to-morrow?

*Jaff.* Hah!

*Belv.* To-morrow,
When thou shalt see him stretch'd in all the agonies
Of a tormenting and a shameful death,
His bleeding bowels, and his broken limbs,
Insulted o'er by a vile butchering villain;
What will thy heart do then? oh, sure 'twill stream
Like my eyes now.

*Jaff.* What means thy dreadful story?
Death, and to-morrow? broken limbs and bowels!
Insulted o'er by a vile butchering villain!
By all my fears I shall start out to madness,
With barely guessing if the truth's hid longer.

*Belv.* The faithless Senators, 'tis they've decreed it:
They say according to our friend's request,
They shall have death, and not ignoble bondage:
Declare their promised mercy all as forfeited,
False to their oaths, and deaf to intercession;
Warrants are passed for public death to-morrow.

*Jaff.* Death! doomed to die! condemned unheard! unpleaded!

*Belv.* Nay, cruell'st racks and torments are preparing,
To force confessions from their dying pangs.
Oh, do not look so terribly upon me,
How your lips shake, and all your face disordered!
What means my love?

*Jaff.* Leave me, I charge thee, leave me—strong temptations
Wake in my heart.

*Belv.*                For what?

*Jaff.*                            No more, but leave me.

*Belv.* Why?

*Jaff.* Oh! by Heaven I love you with that fondness
I would not have thee stay a moment longer,
Near these curs'd hands; are they not cold upon thee?

[*Pulls the dagger half out of his bosom and puts it back again.*

*Belv.* No, everlasting comfort's in thy arms.
To lean thus on thy breast is softer ease
Than downy pillows deck'd with leaves of roses.

*Jaff.* Alas! thou think'st not of the thorns 'tis filled with:
Fly ere they [gall] thee: there's a lurking serpent,
Ready to leap and sting thee to thy heart;
Art thou not terrified?

*Belv.*                No.

*Jaff.*                        Call to mind
What thou hast done, and whither thou hast brought me.

*Belv.* Hah!

*Jaff.* Where's my friend? my friend, thou smiling mischief?
Nay, shrink not, now 'tis too late, thou shouldst have fled
When thy guilt first had cause, for dire revenge
Is up and raging for my friend.   He groans,
Hark how he groans, his screams are in my ears
Already; see, they've fix'd him on the wheel,
And now they tear him—Murther! perjur'd Senate!
Murther—Oh!—hark thee, traitress, thou hast done this:

[*Fumbling for his dagger.*

Thanks to thy tears and false persuading love.
How her eyes speak! O thou bewitching creature!
Madness cannot hurt thee: come, thou little trembler,
Creep, even into my heart, and there lie safe:
'Tis thy own citadel—ha!—yet stand off,
Heaven must have justice, and my broken vows
Will sink me else beneath its reaching mercy;
I'll wink and then 'tis done——

*Belv.*                                    What means the lord
Of me, my life and love? what's in thy bosom,
                    [*Draws the dagger, offers to stab her.*
Thou grasp'st at so? Nay, why am I thus treated?
What wilt thou do? Ah! do not kill me, Jaffeir,
Pity these panting breasts, and trembling limbs,
That used to clasp thee when thy looks were milder,
That yet hang heavy on my unpurg'd soul,
And plunge it not into eternal darkness.

*Jaff.* No, Belvidera, when we parted last
I gave this dagger with thee as in trust
To be thy portion, if I e'er proved false.
On such condition was my truth believ'd:
But now 'tis forfeited and must be paid for.
                          [*Offers to stab her again.*

*Belv.* Oh, mercy!                         [*Kneeling.*
*Jaff.*             Nay, no struggling.
*Belv.*                          Now, then, kill me.
                [*Leaps upon his neck and kisses him.*
While thus I cling about thy cruel neck,
Kiss thy revengeful lips and die in joys
Greater than any I can guess hereafter.

*Jaff.* I am, I am a coward; witness't, heaven,·
Witness it, earth, and every being witness;
'Tis but one blow; yet, by immortal love,
I cannot longer bear a thought to harm thee;
          [*He throws away the dagger and embraces her.*
The seal of Providence is sure upon thee,
And thou wert born for yet unheard-of wonders:
Oh, thou wert either born to save or damn me!
By all the power that's given thee o'er my soul,
By thy resistless tears and conquering smiles,
By the victorious love that still waits on thee,
Fly to thy cruel father: save my friend,
Or all our future quiet's lost for ever:
Fall at his feet, cling round his reverend knees;
Speak to him with thy eyes, and with thy tears
Melt his hard heart, and wake dead nature in him;
Crush him in thy arms, and torture him with thy softness:
  Nor, till thy prayers are granted, set him free,
  But conquer him, as thou hast vanquish'd me. [*Exeunt ambo.*

# ACT V

## [SCENE I]

*Enter* PRIULI, *solus.*

*Priu.* Why, cruel Heaven, have my unhappy days
Been lengthen'd to this sad one? Oh, dishonour
And deathless infamy is fall'n upon me!
Was it my fault? Am I a traitor? No.
But then, my only child, my daughter, wedded;
There my best blood runs foul, and a disease
Incurable has seized upon my memory,
To make it rot and stink to after ages.
Cursed be the fatal minute when I got her;
Or would that I'd been anything but man,
And raised an issue which would ne'er have wrong'd me.
The miserablest creatures, man excepted,
Are not the less esteemed, though their posterity
Degenerate from the virtues of their fathers;
The vilest beasts are happy in their offsprings,
While only man gets traitors, whores and villains.
Cursed be the names, and some swift blow from Fate
Lay his head deep, where mine may be forgotten.

*Enter* BELVIDERA *in a long mourning veil.*

*Belv.* He's there, my father, my inhuman father,
That, for three years, has left an only child
Exposed to all the outrages of Fate,
And cruel ruin—oh!——
    *Priu.*              What child of sorrow
Art thou that com'st thus wrapt in weeds of sadness,
And mov'st as if thy steps were towards a grave?
    *Belv.* A wretch, who from the very top of happiness
Am fallen into the lowest depths of misery,
And want your pitying hand to raise me up again.
    *Priu.* Indeed thou talk'st as thou hadst tasted sorrows;
Would I could help thee!
    *Belv.*         'Tis greatly in your power.
The world, too, speaks you charitable, and I,
Who ne'er asked alms before, in that dear hope
Am come a-begging to you, sir.
    *Priu.*         For what?
    *Belv.* O well regard me, is this voice a strange one?
Consider, too, when beggars once pretend
A case like mine, no little will content 'em.

*Priu.* What wouldst thou beg for?

*Belv.*      Pity and forgiveness;      [*Throws up her veil.*
By the kind tender names of child and father,
Hear my complaints and take me to your love.

*Priu.* My daughter?

*Belv.*            Yes, your daughter, by a mother
Virtuous and noble, faithful to your honour,
Obedient to your will, kind to your wishes,
Dear to your arms: by all the joys she gave you,
When in her blooming years she was your treasure,
Look kindly on me; in my face behold
The lineaments of hers you've kiss'd so often,
Pleading the cause of your poor cast-off child.

*Priu.* Thou art my daughter?

*Belv.*                  Yes—and you've oft told me,
With smiles of love and chaste paternal kisses,
I'd much resemblance of my mother.

*Priu.*                  Oh!
Hadst thou inherited her matchless virtues
I'd been too bless'd.

*Belv.*            Nay, do not call to memory
My disobedience, but let pity enter
Into your heart, and quite deface the impression;
For could you think how mine's perplexed, what sadness,
Fears and despairs distract the peace within me,
Oh, you would take me in your dear, dear arms,
Hover with strong compassion o'er your young one,
To shelter me with a protecting wing,
From the black gather'd storm, that's just, just breaking.

*Priu.* Don't talk thus.

*Belv.*                  Yes, I must, and you must hear too.
I have a husband.

*Priu.*            Damn him.

*Belv.*                  Oh, do not curse him!
He would not speak so hard a word towards you,
On any terms, [howe'er] he deal with me.

*Priu.* Ha! what means my child?

*Belv.* Oh, there's but this short moment
'Twixt me and Fate, yet send me not with curses
Down to my grave, afford me one kind blessing
Before we part: just take me in your arms,
And recommend me with a prayer to Heaven,
That I may die in peace, and when I'm dead——

*Priu.* How my soul's catched!

*Belv.*                  Lay me, I beg you, lay me
By the dear ashes of my tender mother:
She would have pitied me, had Fate yet spared her.

*Priu.* By heaven, my aching heart forebodes much mischief;
Tell me thy story, for I'm still thy father.

*Belv.* No, I'm contented.
*Priu.*       Speak.
*Belv.*         No matter.
*Priu.*           Tell me.
By you, blest Heaven, my heart runs o'er with fondness.
 *Belv.* Oh!
 *Priu.*  Utter't.
 *Belv.*     O my husband, my dear husband
Carries a dagger in his once kind bosom,
To pierce the heart of your poor Belvidera.
 *Priu.* Kill thee?
 *Belv.*    Yes, kill me. When he pass'd his faith
And covenant, against your State and Senate,
He gave me up as hostage for his truth,
With me a dagger and a dire commission
Whene'er he failed, to plunge it through this bosom.
I learnt the danger, chose the hour of love
To attempt his heart, and bring it back to honour.
Great love prevail'd and bless'd me with success:
He came, confessed, betrayed his dearest friends
For promis'd mercy; now they're doomed to suffer,
Gall'd with remembrance of what then was sworn,
If they are lost, he vows to appease the gods
With this poor life, and make my blood the atonement.
 *Priu.* Heavens!
 *Belv.*   Think you saw what pass'd at our last parting;
Think you beheld him like a raging lion,
Pacing the earth and tearing up his steps,
Fate in his eyes, and roaring with the pain
Of burning fury; think you saw his one hand
Fix'd on my throat, while the extended other
Grasp'd a keen threat'ning dagger: oh, 'twas thus
We last embrac'd, when, trembling with revenge,
He dragg'd me to the ground, and at my bosom
Presented horrid death, cried out: " My friends,
Where are my friends? " swore, wept, rag'd, threaten'd, lov'd,
For he yet loved, and that dear love preserved me,
To this last trial of a father's pity.
I fear not death, but cannot bear a thought
That that dear hand should do the unfriendly office;
If I was ever then your care, now hear me;
Fly to the Senate, save the promised lives
Of his dear friends, ere mine be made the sacrifice.
 *Priu.* O my heart's comfort!
 *Belv.*     Will you not, my father?
Weep not, but answer me.
 *Priu.*     By Heaven, I will.
Not one of 'em but what shall be immortal.
Canst thou forgive me all my follies past,

I'll henceforth be indeed a father; never,
Never more thus expose, but cherish thee,
Dear as the vital warmth that feeds my life,
Dear as these eyes that weep in fondness o'er thee.
Peace to thy heart.   Farewell.
    *Belv.*                    Go, and remember
'Tis Belvidera's life her father pleads for.   [*Exeunt severally.*

*Enter* ANTONIO.

Hum, hum, ha,
Signor Priuli, my lord Priuli, my lord, my lord, my lord:
[how] we lords love to call one another by our titles! My lord,
my lord, my lord—pox on him, I am a lord as well as he; and
so let him fiddle—I'll warrant him he's gone to the Senate-house,
and I'll be there too, soon enough for somebody.   'Od, here's a
tickling speech about the plot, I'll prove there's a plot with a
vengeance—would I had it without book; let me see—
Most reverend Senators,
That there is a plot, surely by this time, no man that hath
eyes or understanding in his head will presume to doubt, 'tis as
plain as the light in the cucumber—no—hold there—cucumber
does not come in yet—'tis as plain as the light in the sun, or as
the man in the moon, even at noonday; it is indeed a pumpkin-
plot, which, just as it was mellow, we have gathered, and now we
have gathered it, prepared and dressed it, shall we throw it like
a pickled cucumber out at the window? no: that it is not only
a bloody, horrid, execrable, damnable and audacious plot, but it
is, as I may so say, a saucy plot: and we all know, most reverend
fathers, that what is sauce for a goose is sauce for a gander:
therefore, I say, as those bloodthirsty ganders of the conspiracy
would have destroyed us geese of the Senate, let us make haste
to destroy them, so I humbly move for hanging—ha! hurry
durry—I think this will do, tho' I was something out, at first,
about the sun and the cucumber.

*Enter* AQUILINA.

    *Aquil.* Good-morrow, Senator.
    *Anto.* Nacky, my dear Nacky, morrow, Nacky, 'od I am very
brisk, very merry, very pert, very jovial—ha-a-a-a-a—kiss me,
Nacky; how dost thou do, my little tory rory strumpet, kiss me,
I say, hussy, kiss me.
    *Aquil.* Kiss me, Nacky, hang you, sir, coxcomb, hang you, sir.
    *Anto.* Hayty, tayty, is it so indeed, with all my heart, faith—
*hey then up go we,* faith—*hey then up go we,* dum dum derum
dump.                                  [*Sings.*
    *Aquil.* Signior.
    *Anto.* Madonna.
    *Aquil.* Do you intend to die in your bed——?

*Anto.* About threescore years hence, much may be done, my dear.

*Aquil.* You'll be hanged, signior.

*Anto.* Hanged, sweetheart? prithee be quiet! hanged quotha? that's a merry conceit, with all my heart! why thou jok'st, Nacky, thou art given to joking, I'll swear; well, I protest, Nacky, nay, I must protest, and will protest that I love joking dearly, man. And I love thee for joking, and I'll kiss thee for joking, and towse thee for joking, and 'od, I have a devilish mind to take thee aside about that business for joking too, 'od I have, and *Hey then up go we*, dum dum derum dump.          [*Sings.*

*Aquil.* See you this, sir?          [*Draws a dagger.*

*Anto.* O Laud, a dagger! O Laud! it is naturally my aversion, I cannot endure the sight on't, hide it for Heaven's sake, I cannot look that way till it be gone—hide it, hide it, oh, oh, hide it!

*Aquil.* Yes, in your heart I'll hide it.

*Anto.* My heart; what, hide a dagger in my heart's blood?

*Aquil.* Yes, in thy heart, thy throat, thou pampered devil; Thou hast help'd to spoil my peace, and I'll have vengeance On thy cursed life, for all the bloody Senate, The perjur'd faithless Senate: where's my lord, My happiness, my love, my god, my hero, Doom'd by thy accursed tongue, amongst the rest, T' a shameful wrack? By all the rage that's in me I'll be whole years in murthering thee.

*Anto.*                              Why, Nacky, Wherefore so passionate? what have I done? what's the matter, my dear Nacky? am not I thy love, thy happiness, thy lord, thy hero, thy Senator, and everything in the world, Nacky?

*Aquil.* Thou! think'st thou, thou art fit to meet my joys; To bear the eager clasps of my embraces? Give me my Pierre, or——

*Anto.* Why, he's to be hang'd, little Nacky, Trussed up for treason, and so forth, child.

*Aquil.* Thou liest: stop down thy throat that hellish sentence, Or 'tis thy last: swear that my love shall live, Or thou art dead.

*Anto.*                    Ah-h-h-h.

*Aquil.*                              Swear to recall his doom, Swear at my feet, and tremble at my fury.

*Anto.* I do. Now if she would but kick a little bit, one kick now.

Ah-h-h-h.

*Aquil.*     Swear, or——

*Anto.*                    I do, by these dear fragrant foots And little toes, sweet as, e-e-e-e my Nacky Nacky Nacky.

*Aquil.* How!

*Anto.* Nothing but untie thy shoe-string a little, faith and troth,

That's all, that's all, as I hope to live, Nacky, that's all.

*Aquil.* Nay, then——

*Anto.*                    Hold, hold, thy love, thy lord, thy hero
Shall be preserv'd and safe.

*Aquil.*                    Or may this poniard
Rust in thy heart.

*Anto.*                    With all my soul.

*Aquil.*                              Farewell——

[*Exit* AQUILINA.

*Anto.* Adieu. Why, what a bloody-minded, inveterate,
termagant strumpet have I been plagued with! Oh-h-h yet
more! nay then I die, I die—I am dead already.

[*Stretches himself out.*

### Enter JAFFEIR.

*Jaff.* Final destruction seize on all the world:
Bend down, ye heavens, and shutting round this earth,
Crush the vile globe into its first confusion;
Scorch it, with elemental flames, to one curst cinder,
And all us little creepers in't, called men,
Burn, burn to nothing: but let Venice burn
Hotter than all the rest: here kindle hell
Ne'er to extinguish, and let souls hereafter
Groan here, in all those pains which mine feels now.

### Enter BELVIDERA.

*Belv.* My life——                    [*Meeting him*
*Jaff.*          My plague——          [*Turning from her.*
*Belv.*                    Nay then I see my ruin
If I must die!

*Jaff.*          No, Death's this day too busy,
Thy father's ill-timed mercy came too late.
I thank thee for thy labours though and him too,
But all my poor betray'd unhappy friends
Have summons to prepare for Fate's black hour;
And yet I live.

*Belv.*          Then be the next my doom.
I see thou'st pass'd my sentence in thy heart,
And I'll no longer weep or plead against it,
But with the humblest, most obedient patience
Meet thy dear hands, and kiss 'em when they wound me;
Indeed I'm willing, but I beg thee do it
With some remorse, and where thou giv'st the blow,
View me with eyes of a relenting love,
And show me pity, for 'twill sweeten justice.

*Jaff.* Show pity to thee?

*Belv.*                    Yes, and when thy hands,
Charg'd with my fate, come trembling to the deed,
As thou hast done a thousand thousand dear times,

To this poor breast, when kinder rage has brought thee,
When our stinged hearts have leaped to meet each other,
And melting kisses sealed our lips together,
When joys have left me gasping in thy arms,
So let my death come now, and I'll not shrink from't.

 *Jaff.* Nay, Belvidera, do not fear my cruelty,
Nor let the thoughts of death perplex thy fancy,
But answer me to what I shall demand
With a firm temper and unshaken spirit.

 *Belv.* I will when I've done weeping——

 *Jaff.*         Fie, no more on't——
How long is't since the miserable day
We wedded first——

 *Belv.*    Oh-h-h!

 *Jaff.*       Nay, keep in thy tears,
Lest they unman me too.

 *Belv.*      Heaven knows I cannot;
The words you utter sound so very sadly
These streams will follow——

 *Jaff.*      Come, I'll kiss 'em dry, then.

 *Belv.* But was't a miserable day?

 *Jaff.*      A curs'd one.

 *Belv.* I thought it otherwise, and you've oft sworn
In the transporting hours of warmest love
When sure you spoke the truth, you've sworn you blessed it.

 *Jaff.* 'Twas a rash oath.

 *Belv.*    Then why am I not curs'd too?

 *Jaff.* No, Belvidera; by the eternal truth,
I dote with too much fondness.

 *Belv.*     Still so kind?
Still then do you love me?

 *Jaff.*     Nature, in her workings,
Inclines not with more ardour to creation,
Than I do now towards thee: man ne'er was bless'd,
Since the first pair first met, as I have been.

 *Belv.* Then sure you will not curse me.

 *Jaff.*       No, I'll bless thee.
I came on purpose, Belvidera, to bless thee.
'Tis now, I think, three years we've liv'd together.

 *Belv.* And may no fatal minute ever part us,
Till, reverend grown, for age and love, we go
Down to one grave, as our last bed, together,
There sleep in peace till an eternal morning.

 *Jaff.* When will that be?       [*Sighing.*

 *Belv.*     I hope long ages hence.

 *Jaff.* Have I not hitherto (I beg thee tell me
Thy very fears) used thee with tender'st love?
Did e'er my soul rise up in wrath against thee?
Did e'er I frown when Belvidera smiled,

Or, by the least unfriendly word, betray
A bating passion? have I ever wronged thee?
 *Belv.* No.
 *Jaff.*   Has my heart, or have my eyes e'er wandered
To any other woman?
 *Belv.*     Never, never—
I were the worst of false ones should I accuse thee;
I own I've been too happy, bless'd above
My sex's charter.
 *Jaff.* Did I not say I came to bless thee?
 *Belv.* Yes.
 *Jaff.*   Then hear me, bounteous Heaven!
Pour down your blessings on this beauteous head,
Where everlasting sweets are always springing,
With a continual giving hand: let peace,
Honour, and safety, always hover round her:
Feed her with plenty, let her eyes ne'er see
A sight of sorrow, nor her heart know mourning:
Crown all her days with joy, her nights with rest,
Harmless as her own thoughts; and prop her virtue,
To bear the loss of one that too much lov'd,
And comfort her with patience in our parting.
 *Belv.* How, parting! parting!
 *Jaff.*     Yes, for ever parting.
I have sworn, Belvidera, by yon heaven,
That best can tell how much I lose to leave thee,
We part this hour for ever.
 *Belv.*    Oh, call back
Your cruel blessings, stay with me and curse me!
 *Jaff.* No, 'tis resolv'd.
 *Belv.*    Then hear me too, just Heaven!
Pour down your curses on this wretched head
With never-ceasing vengeance: let despair,
Danger or infamy, nay, all surround me:
Starve me with wantings: let my eyes ne'er see
A sight of comfort, nor my heart know peace,
But dash my days with sorrow, nights with horrors
Wild as my own thoughts now, and let loose fury
To make me mad enough for what I lose,
If I must lose him; if I must, I will not.
O turn and hear me!
 *Jaff.*   Now hold, heart, or never.
 *Belv.* By all the tender days we've liv'd together;
By all our charming nights, and joys that crown'd 'em:
Pity my sad condition, speak, but speak.
 *Jaff.* Oh-h-h!
 *Belv.*   By these arms that now cling round thy neck:
By this dear kiss and by ten thousand more,
By these poor streaming eyes——

*Jaff.*                              Murther! unhold me:
                                *[Draws his dagger.*

By the immortal destiny that doom'd me
To this curs'd minute, I'll not live one longer.
Resolve to let me go or see me fall——
　　*Belv.* Hold, sir, be patient.
　　*Jaff.*                    Hark, the dismal bell
                                *[Passing bell tolls.*

Tolls out for death; I must attend its call too,
For my poor friend, my dying Pierre expects me:
He sent a message to require I'd see him
Before he died, and take his last forgiveness.
Farewell for ever.          *[Going out looks back at her.*
　　*Belv.*      Leave thy dagger with me.
Bequeath me something.—Not one kiss at parting?
O my poor heart, when wilt thou break?
　　*Jaff.*                              Yet stay,
We have a child, as yet a tender infant.
Be a kind mother to him when I am gone:
Breed him in virtue and the paths of honour,
But let him never know his father's story:
I charge thee guard him from the wrongs my fate
May do his future fortune or his name.
Now—nearer yet—          *[Approaching each other.*
O that my arms were riveted
Thus round thee ever! But my friends, my oath!
This and no more.                    *[Kisses her.*
　　*Belv.*          Another, sure another,
For that poor little one you've ta'en care of,
I'll give't him truly.
　　*Jaff.*          So, now farewell.
　　*Belv.*                              For ever?
　　*Jaff.* Heaven knows for ever; all good angels guard thee.
　　　　　　　　　　　　　　　　　　　　　　*[Exit.*

　　*Belv.* All ill ones sure had charge of me this moment.
Curs'd be my days, and doubly curs'd my nights,
Which I must now mourn out in widow'd tears;
Blasted be every herb and fruit and tree;
Curs'd be the rain that falls upon the earth,
And may the general curse reach man and beast;
Oh, give me daggers, fire or water!
How I could bleed, how burn, how drown, the waves
Huzzing and booming round my sinking head,
Till I descended to the peaceful bottom!
Oh, there's all quiet, here all rage and fury:
The air's too thin, and pierces my weak brain:
I long for thick substantial sleep: hell, hell,
Burst from the centre, rage and roar aloud,
If thou art half so hot, so mad as I am.

*Enter* PRIULI *and* Servants.
Who's there?                                                    [*They seize her.*
   *Priu.* Run, seize and bring her safely home.
Guard her as you would life: alas, poor creature!
   *Belv.* What? to my husband then conduct me quickly.
Are all things ready? shall we die most gloriously?
Say not a word of this to my old father.
Murmuring streams, soft shades, and springing flowers,
Lutes, laurels, seas of milk, and ships of amber.          [*Exit.*


## [SCENE II]

*Scene opening discovers a Scaffold and a Wheel prepared for the
    executing of* PIERRE, *then enter* Officers, PIERRE *and* Guards,
    a Friar, Executioner, *and a great rabble.*

   *Offic.* Room, room there—stand all by, make room for the
prisoner.
   *Pierr.* My friend not come yet?
   *Father.* Why are you so obstinate?
   *Pierr.* Why you so troublesome, that a poor wretch
Can't die in peace,
But you, like ravens, will be croaking round him?
   *Fath.* Yet, Heaven——
   *Pierr.*                          I tell thee Heaven and I are friends.
I ne'er broke peace with't yet, by cruel murthers,
Rapine or perjury, or vile deceiving,
But lived in moral justice towards all men,
Nor am a foe to the most strong believers,
Howe'er my own short-sighted faith confine me.
   *Fath.* But an all-seeing Judge——
   *Pierr.*                          You say my conscience
Must be mine accuser: I've search'd that conscience,
And find no records there of crimes that scare me.
   *Fath.* 'Tis strange you should want faith.
   *Pierr.*                          You want to lead
My reason blindfold, like a hamper'd lion,
Check'd of its nobler vigour; then, when baited
Down to obedient tameness, make it couch,
And show strange tricks, which you call signs of faith.
So silly souls are gull'd and you get money.
Away, no more: Captain, I would hereafter
This fellow write no lies of my conversion,
Because he has crept upon my troubled hours.


*Enter* JAFFEIR.

   *Jaff.* Hold: eyes, be dry!
Heart, strengthen me to bear

This hideous sight, and humble me, to take
The last forgiveness of a dying friend,
Betray'd by my vile falsehood, to his ruin.
O Pierre!
   *Pierr.*   Yet nearer.
   *Jaff.*             Crawling on my knees,
And prostrate on the earth, let me approach thee:
How shall I look up to thy injured face,
That always used to smile, with friendship on me?
It darts an air of so much manly virtue,
That I, methinks, look little in thy sight,
And stripes are fitter for me than embraces.
   *Pierr.* Dear to my arms, though thou'st undone my fame,
I cannot forget to love thee; prithee, Jaffeir,
Forgive that filthy blow my passion dealt thee;
I'm now preparing for the land of peace,
And fain would have the charitable wishes
Of all good men, like thee, to bless my journey.
   *Jaff.* Good! I am the vilest creature; worse than e'er
Suffer'd the shameful fate thou'rt going to taste of.
Why was I sent for to be used thus kindly?
Call, call me villain, as I am, describe
The foul complexion of my hateful deeds,
Lead me to the rack, and stretch me in thy stead,
I've crimes enough to give it its full load,
And do it credit. Thou wilt but spoil the use on't,
And honest men hereafter bear its figure
About 'em, as a charm from treacherous friendship.
   *Offic.* The time grows short, your friends are dead already.
   *Jaff.* Dead!
   *Pierr.*     Yes, dead, Jaffeir, they've all died like men too,
Worthy their character.
   *Jaff.*            And what must I do?
   *Pierr.* O Jaffeir!
   *Jaff.*          Speak aloud thy burthen'd soul,
And tell thy troubles to thy tortured friend.
   *Pierr.* Friend! Couldst thou yet be a friend, a generous friend,
I might hope comfort from thy noble sorrows.
Heav'n knows I want a friend.
   *Jaff.*           And I a kind one,
That would not thus scorn my repenting virtue,
Or think when he's to die, my thoughts are idle.
   *Pierr.* No! live, I charge thee, Jaffeir.
   *Jaff.*            Yes, I'll live.
But it shall be to see thy fall revenged
At such a rate, as Venice long shall groan for.
   *Pierr.* Wilt thou?
   *Jaff.*     I will, by Heav'n.
   *Pierr.*                Then still thou'rt noble,

And I forgive thee, oh—yet—shall I trust thee?
  *Jaff.* No: I've been false already.
  *Pierr.*                Dost thou love me?
  *Jaff.* Rip up my heart, and satisfy thy doubtings.
  *Pierr.* Curse on this weakness.      [*He weeps.*
  *Jaff.*           Tears! Amazement! Tears!
I never saw thee melted thus before,
And know there's something labouring in thy bosom
That must have vent: though I'm a villain, tell me.
  *Pierr.* Seest thou that engine?   [*Pointing to the Wheel.*
  *Jaff.* Why?
  *Pierr.* Is't fit a soldier, who has liv'd with honour,
Fought nations' quarrels, and been crown'd with conquest,
Be exposed a common carcase on a wheel?
  *Jaff.* Ha!
  *Pierr.*    Speak! is't fitting?
  *Jaff.*            Fitting?
  *Pierr.*              Yes, is't fitting?
  *Jaff.* What's to be done?
  *Pierr.*         I'd have thee undertake
Something that's noble, to preserve my memory
From the disgrace that's ready to attaint it.
  *Offic.* The day grows late, sir.
  *Pierr.*         I'll make haste!  O Jaffeir,
Though thou'st betray'd me, do me some way justice.
  *Jaff.* No more of that: thy wishes shall be satisfied.
I have a wife, and she shall bleed, my child too
Yield up his little throat, and all t' appease thee——
              [*Going away,* PIERRE *holds him.*
  *Pierr.* No—this—no more!     [*He whispers* JAFFEIR.
  *Jaff.*          Ha! is't then so?
  *Pierr.*            Most certainly.
  *Jaff.* I'll do't.
  *Pierr.*    Remember.
  *Offic.*        Sir.
  *Pierr.*          Come, now I'm ready.
       [*He and* JAFFEIR *ascend the scaffold.*
Captain, you should be a gentleman of honour.
Keep off the rabble, that I may have room
To entertain my fate and die with decency.
Come!  [*Takes off his gown,* Executioner *prepares to bind him.*
  *Fath.* Son!
  *Pierr.*    Hence, tempter.
  *Offic.*         Stand off, priest.
  *Pierr.* I thank you, sir.
          You'll think on't.    [*To* JAFFEIR.
  *Jaff.* 'Twon't grow stale before to-morrow.
  *Pierr.* Now, Jaffeir! now I am going.  Now;—
            [Executioner *having bound him.*

*Jaff.* Have at thee,
Thou honest heart, then—here—     [*Stabs him.*
And this is well too.     [*Then stabs himself.*
    *Fath.* Damnable deed!
    *Pierr.* Now thou hast indeed been faithful.
This was done nobly—we've deceived the Senate.
    *Jaff.* Bravely.
    *Pierr.* Ha! ha! ha!—oh! oh!——     [*Dies.*
    *Jaff.* Now, ye curs'd rulers,
Thus of the blood ye've shed I make libation,
And sprinkle it mingling: may it rest upon you,
And all your race: be henceforth peace a stranger
Within your walls; let plagues and famine waste
Your generations—O poor Belvidera!
Sir, I have a wife, bear this [*Giving dagger.*] in safety to her.
A token that with my dying breath I blessed her,
And the dear little infant left behind me.
I'm sick—I'm quiet——     [JAFFEIR *dies.*
    *Offic.* Bear this news to the Senate,
And guard their bodies till there's farther order:
Heaven grant I die so well!     [*Scene shuts upon them.*


    *Soft music.   Enter* BELVIDERA *distracted, led by two of
her women,* PRIULI *and Servants.*


    *Priu.* Strengthen her heart with patience, pitying Heaven.
    *Belv.* Come come come come come, nay, come to bed!
Prithee my love.   The winds! hark how they whistle!
And the rain beats: oh, how the weather shrinks me!
You are angry now, who cares? pish, no indeed.
Choose then, I say you shall not go, you shall not;
Whip your ill nature; get you gone then! oh,
                        [JAFFEIR's *ghost rises.*
Are you return'd?   See, father, here he's come again!
Am I to blame to love him?   O thou dear one!     [*Ghost sinks.*
Why do you fly me? are you angry still, then?
Jaffeir! where art thou?   Father, why do you do thus?
Stand off, don't hide him from me.   He's here somewhere.


    *Enter* Officer *and others.*


Stand off, I say! what, gone? remember't, Tyrant!
I may revenge myself for this trick one day.
I'll do't—I'll do't! Renault's a nasty fellow.
Hang him, hang him, hang him.
    *Priu.* News, what news?     [*Officer whispers* PRIULI.
    *Offic.* Most sad, sir.
Jaffeir, upon the scaffold, to prevent

A shameful death, stabb'd Pierre, and next himself:
Both fell together.

> [*The ghosts of* JAFFEIR *and* PIERRE *rise together, both bloody.*

*Priu.*                    Daughter.

*Belv.*                                      Ha, look there!
My husband bloody, and his friend too!   Murther!
Who has done this?  speak to me, thou sad vision,   [*Ghosts sink.*
On these poor trembling knees I beg it.   Vanish'd!
Here they went down; oh, I'll dig, dig the den up.
You shan't delude me thus.   Ho, Jaffeir, Jaffeir,
Peep up and give me but a look.   I have him!
I've got him, father: oh, how I'll smuggle him!
My love! my dear! my blessing! help me, help me!
They've hold on me, and drag me to the bottom.
Nay—now they pull so hard—farewell——        [*She dies.*

*Maid.*                              She's dead.
Breathless and dead.

*Priu.*                    Then guard me from the sight on't;
Lead me into some place that's fit for mourning;
Where the free air, light, and the cheerful sun
May never enter: hang it round with black:
Set up one taper that may last a day
As long as I've to live: and there all leave me.
    Sparing no tears when you this tale relate,
    But bid all cruel fathers dread my fate.

> [*Curtain falls.   Exeunt omnes.*

# EPILOGUE

THE text is done, and now for application,
And when that's ended pass your approbation.
Though the conspiracy's prevented here,
Methinks I see another hatching there;
And there's a certain faction fain would sway,
If they had strength enough, and damn this play,
But this the author bade me boldly say:
If any take his plainness in ill part,
He's glad on't from the bottom of his heart;
Poets in honour of the truth should write,
With the same spirit brave men for it fight;
And though against him causeless hatreds rise,
And daily where he goes of late, he spies
The scowls of sullen and revengeful eyes;
'Tis what he knows with much contempt to bear,
And serves a cause too good to let him fear:
He fears no poison from an incensed drab,
No ruffian's five-foot sword, nor rascal's stab;
Nor any other snares of mischief laid,
Not a Rose-alley cudgel-ambuscade,
From any private cause where malice reigns,
Or general pique all blockheads have to brains:
Nothing shall daunt his pen when Truth does call,
No, not the picture mangler at Guildhall.
The rebel tribe, of which that vermin's one,
Have now set forward and their course begun;
And while that Prince's figure they deface,
    As they before had massacred his name,
Durst their base fears but look him in the face,
    They'd use his Person as they've used his fame;
A face, in which such lineaments they read
Of that great Martyr's, whose rich blood they shed,
That their rebellious hate they still retain,
And in his Son would murther Him again:
With indignation then, let each brave heart
Rouse and unite to take his injured part;
Till royal love and goodness call him home,
And songs of triumph meet him as he come;
Till Heaven his honour and our peace restore,
And villains never wrong his virtue more.

305

# APPENDIX

## PROLOGUE

To His Royal Highness
Upon his first appearance at the Duke's Theatre
since his Return from Scotland

*Written by Mr. Dryden.*                    *Spoken by Mr. Smith.*

In those cold Regions which no Summers chear,
When brooding darkness covers half the year,
To hollow Caves the shivering Natives go;
Bears range abroad, and hunt in tracks of Snow:
But when the tedious Twilight wears away,
And stars grow paler at th' approach of Day,
The longing Crowds to frozen Mountains run,
Happy who first can see the glimmering Sun!
The surly Salvage Offspring disappear;
And curse the bright Successour of the year.
Yet, though rough Bears in Covert seek defence, ⎫
White Foxes stay, with seeming Innocence: ⎬
That crafty kind with daylight can dispense. ⎭
Still we are throng'd so full with Reynard's race,
That Loyal Subjects scarce can find a place:
Thus modest Truth is cast behind the Crowd:
Truth speaks too Low; Hypocrisie too Loud.
Let 'em be first, to flatter in success;
Duty can stay; but Guilt has need to press.
Once, when true Zeal the Sons of God did call,
To make their solemn show at Heaven's White-hall,
The fawning Devil appear'd among the rest,
And made as good a Courtier as the best.
The friends of Job, who rail'd at him before,
Came Cap in hand when he had three time more.
Yet late Repentance may, perhaps, be true;
Kings can forgive if Rebels can but sue:
A Tyrant's Pow'r in rigour is exprest:
The Father yearns in the true Prince's Breast.
We grant an Ore'grown Whig no grace can mend;
But most are Babes, that know not they offend.
The Crowd, to restless motion still enclin'd,
Are Clouds, that rack according to the Wind.

306

Driv'n by their Chiefs, they storms of Hailstones pour:
Then mourn, and soften to a silent showre.
O welcome to this much offending Land
The Prince that brings forgiveness in his hand!
Thus Angels on Glad Messages appear:
Their first salute commands us not to fear:
Thus Heav'n, that cou'd constrain us to obey,
(With rev'rence if we might presume to say,)
Seems to relax the rights of Sov'reign sway;
Permits to Man the choice of Good and Ill;
And makes us Happy by our own Free-will.

# THE EPILOGUE

Written by Mr. Otway to his Play call'd *Venice Preserv'd, or, A Plot Discover'd ;* spoken upon his Royal Highness the Duke of York's coming to the Theatre, Friday, April 21, 1682

WHEN too much Plenty, Luxury, and Ease,
Had surfeited this Isle to a Disease;
When noisome Blaines did its best parts orespread,
And on the rest their dire Infection shed;
Our Great Physician, who the Nature knew ⎫
Of the Distemper, and from whence it grew, ⎬
Fix't for Three Kingdoms quiet (Sir) on You: ⎭
He cast his searching Eyes o'er all the Frame,
And finding whence before one sickness came,
How once before our Mischiefs foster'd were,
Knew well Your Vertue, and apply'd You there:
Where so Your Goodness, so Your Justice sway'd,
You but appear'd, and the wild Plague was stay'd.
When from the filthy Dunghil-faction bred, ⎫
New form'd Rebellion durst rear up its head, ⎬
Answer me all: who struck the Monster dead? ⎭
  See, see, the injur'd PRINCE, and bless his Name,
Think on the Martyr from whose Loynes he came:
Think on the Blood was shed for you before,
And curse the Paricides that thirst for more.
His foes are yours, then of their wiles beware:
Lay, lay him in your Hearts, and guard him there;
Where let his Wrongs your Zeal for him Improve;
He wears a Sword will justifie your Love.
With Blood still ready for your good t' expend,
And has a Heart that ne're forgot his friend.
His Duteous Loyalty before you lay,
And learn of him, unmurm'ring to obey.
Think what he'as born, your Quiet to restore;
Repent your madness and rebell no more.
No more let Bout'feu's hope to lead Petitions,
Scriv'ners to be Treas'rures; Pedlars Politicians;
Nor ev'ry fool, whose wife has tript at Court,
Pluck up a Spirit, and turn Rebell for't.
  In Lands where Cuckolds multiply like ours,
What Prince can be too Jealous of their powers,
Or can too often think himself alarm'd?
They're male contents that ev'rywhere go arm'd:

And when the horned Herd's together got,
Nothing portends a Commonwealth like that.
   Cast, cast your Idols off, your Gods of wood,
Er'e yet Philistins fatten with your blood:
Renounce your Priests of Baal with Amen-faces,
Your Wapping Feasts and your Mile-End High-places.
Nail all your Medals on the Gallows Post,
In recompense th' Original was lost:
At these, illustrious Repentance pay,
In his kind hands your humble Offrings lay:
Let Royal Pardon be by him implor'd,
Th' Attoning Brother of your Anger'd Lord:
He only brings a medicine fit to aswage
A people's folly, and rowz'd Monarch's rage;
An Infant Prince yet lab'ring in the womb,  ⎫
Fated with wond'rous happiness to come,  ⎬
He goes to fetch the mighty blessing home:  ⎭
Send all your wishes with him, let the Ayre  ⎫
With gentle breezes waft it safely here,  ⎬
The Seas, like what they'l carry, calm and fair:  ⎭
Let the Illustrious Mother touch our Land
Mildly, as hereafter may her Son Command;
While our glad Monarch welcomes her to shore,
With kind assurance; she shall part no more.
   Be the Majestick Babe then smiling born,
And all good signs of Fate his Birth adorn,
So live and grow, a constant pledg to stand
Of Cæsar's Love to an obedient Land.

# THE BEAUX STRATAGEM

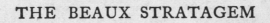

## ADVERTISEMENT

THE reader may find some faults in this play, which my illness prevented the amending of; but there is great amends made in the representation, which cannot be matched, no more than the friendly and indefatigable care of Mr. Wilks, to whom I chiefly owe the success of the play.

GEORGE FARQUHAR.

# DRAMATIS PERSONÆ

*With names of the original actors and actresses.*

| | | |
|---|---|---|
| THOMAS AIMWELL<br>FRANCIS ARCHER | Two Gentlemen of broken fortunes, the first as master, and the second as servant | Mr. MILLS.<br>Mr. WILKS. |
| Count BELLAIR . | A French Officer, prisoner at Lichfield | Mr. BOWMAN. |
| Squire SULLEN . | A country Blockhead, brutal to his Wife | Mr. VERBRUGGEN. |
| Sir CHARLES FREEMAN | A Gentleman from London, brother to Mrs. Sullen | Mr. KEEN. |
| FOIGARD . . | A Priest, Chaplain to the French Officers | Mr. BOWEN. |
| GIBBET . . | A Highwayman . . | Mr. CIBBER. |
| HOUNSLOW .<br>BAGSHOT . | } His Companions. | |
| BONIFACE . . | Landlord of the Inn . . | Mr. BULLOCK. |
| SCRUB . . | Servant to Squire Sullen . | Mr. NORRIS. |
| Lady BOUNTIFUL . | An old, civil, Country Gentlewoman, that cures all her neighbours of all distempers, and foolishly fond of her son, Squire Sullen | MRS. POWELL. |
| Mrs. SULLEN . | Her Daughter-in-law, wife to Squire Sullen | Mrs. OLDFIELD. |
| DORINDA . . | Lady Bountiful's Daughter | Mrs. BRADSHAW. |
| GIPSY . . | Maid to the Ladies . . | Mrs. MILLS. |
| CHERRY . . | The Landlord's Daughter in the Inn | Mrs. BICKNELL. |

Tapster, Coach-passengers, Countryman, Countrywoman, and Servants.

SCENE—LICHFIELD.

# PROLOGUE

SPOKEN BY MR. WILKS

WHEN strife disturbs, or sloth corrupts an age,
Keen satire is the business of the stage.
When the *Plain-Dealer* writ, he lash'd those crimes,
Which then infested most the modish times:
But now, when faction sleeps, and sloth is fled,
And all our youth in active fields are bred;
When through Great Britain's fair extensive round,
The trumps of fame, the notes of UNION sound;
When Anna's sceptre points the laws their course,
And her example gives her precepts force:
There scarce is room for satire; all our lays
Must be or songs of triumph or of praise.
But as in grounds best cultivated, tares
And poppies rise among the golden ears;
Our products so, fit for the field or school,
Must mix with nature's favourite plant—a fool:
A weed that has to twenty summers ran,
Shoots up in stalk, and vegetates to man.
Simpling our author goes from field to field,
And culls such fools as may diversion yield;
And, thanks to Nature, there's no want of those,
For rain or shine, the thriving coxcomb grows.
Follies to-night we show ne'er lash'd before,
Yet such as nature shows you every hour;
Nor can the pictures give a just offence,
For fools are made for jests to men of sense.

# THE BEAUX STRATAGEM

## ACT I

SCENE I.—*A Room in* BONIFACE'S *Inn*

*Enter* BONIFACE *running.*

*Bon.* Chamberlain! maid! Cherry! daughter Cherry! all asleep? all dead?

*Enter* CHERRY *running.*

*Cher.* Here, here! why d'ye bawl so, father? d'ye think we have no ears?

*Bon.* You deserve to have none, you young minx! The company of the Warrington coach has stood in the hall this hour, and nobody to show them to their chambers.

*Cher.* And let 'em wait farther; there's neither red-coat in the coach, nor footman behind it.

*Bon.* But they threaten to go to another inn to-night.

*Cher.* That they dare not, for fear the coachman should overturn them to-morrow.—Coming! coming!—Here's the London coach arrived.

*Enter several people with trunks, bandboxes, and other luggage, and cross the stage.*

*Bon.* Welcome, ladies!

*Cher.* Very welcome, gentlemen!—Chamberlain, show the *Lion* and the *Rose.* [*Exit with the company.*

*Enter* AIMWELL *in a riding-habit, and* ARCHER *as footman, carrying a portmantle.*

*Bon.* This way, this way, gentlemen!

*Aim.* [to ARCHER]. Set down the things; go to the stable, and see my horses well rubbed.

*Arch.* I shall, sir. [*Exit.*

*Aim.* You're my landlord, I suppose?

*Bon.* Yes, sir, I'm old Will Boniface, pretty well known upon this road, as the saying is.

*Aim.* O Mr. Boniface, your servant!

*Bon.* O sir!—What will you honour please to drink, as the saying is?

315

*Aim.* I have heard your town of Lichfield much famed for ale; I think I'll taste that.

*Bon.* Sir, I have now in my cellar ten tun of the best ale in Staffordshire; 'tis smooth as oil, sweet as milk, clear as amber, and strong as brandy; and will be just fourteen year old the fifth day of next March, old style.

*Aim.* You're very exact, I find, in the age of your ale.

*Bon.* As punctual, sir, as I am in the age of my children. I'll show you such ale!—Here, tapster [*enter* Tapster], broach number 1706, as the saying is.—Sir, you shall taste my *Anno Domini*.—I have lived in Lichfield, man and boy, above eight-and-fifty years, and, I believe, have not consumed eight-and-fifty ounces of meat.

*Aim.* At a meal, you mean, if one may guess your sense by your bulk.

*Bon.* Not in my life, sir: I have fed purely upon ale; I have eat my ale, drank my ale, and I always sleep upon ale.

*Enter* Tapster *with a bottle and glass, and exit.*

Now, sir, you shall see!—[*Filling out a glass.*] Your worship's health.—[*Drinks.*] Ha! delicious, delicious! fancy it burgundy, only fancy it, and 'tis worth ten shillings a quart.

*Aim.* [*drinks*]. 'Tis confounded strong!

*Bon.* Strong! it must be so, or how should we be strong that drink it?

*Aim.* And have you lived so long upon this ale, landlord?

*Bon.* Eight-and-fifty years, upon my credit, sir—but it killed my wife, poor woman, as the saying is.

*Aim.* How came that to pass?

*Bon.* I don't know how, sir; she would not let the ale take its natural course, sir; she was for qualifying it every now and then with a dram, as the saying is; and an honest gentleman that came this way from Ireland, made her a present of a dozen bottles of usquebaugh—but the poor woman was never well after: but, howe'er, I was obliged to the gentleman, you know.

*Aim.* Why, was it the usquebaugh that killed her?

*Bon.* My Lady Bountiful said so. She, good lady, did what could be done; she cured her of three tympanies, but the fourth carried her off. But she's happy, and I'm contented, as the saying is.

*Aim.* Who's that Lady Bountiful you mentioned?

*Bon.* Ods my life, sir, we'll drink her health.—[*Drinks.*] My Lady Bountiful is one of the best of women. Her last husband, Sir Charles Bountiful, left her worth a thousand pound a year; and, I believe, she lays out one-half on't in charitable uses for the good of her neighbours. She cures rheumatisms, ruptures, and broken shins in men; green-sickness, obstructions, and fits of the mother, in women; the king's evil, chincough, and chilblains, in children: in short, she has cured more people in and about Lichfield within ten years than the doctors have killed in twenty; and that's a bold word.

*Aim.* Has the lady been any other way useful in her generation?

*Bon.* Yes, sir; she has a daughter by Sir Charles, the finest woman in all our country, and the greatest fortune. She has a son too, by her first husband, Squire Sullen, who married a fine lady from London t'other day; if you please, sir, we'll drink his health.

*Aim.* What sort of a man is he?

*Bon.* Why, sir, the man's well enough; says little, thinks less, and does—nothing at all, faith. But he's a man of a great estate, and values nobody.

*Aim.* A sportsman, I suppose?

*Bon.* Yes, sir, he's a man of pleasure; he plays at whisk and smokes his pipe eight-and-forty hours together sometimes.

*Aim.* And married, you say?

*Bon.* Ay, and to a curious woman, sir. But he's a—he wants it here, sir.                              [*Pointing to his forehead.*

*Aim.* He has it there, you mean?

*Bon.* That's none of my business; he's my landlord, and so a man, you know, would not—But—ecod, he's no better than—Sir, my humble service to you.—[*Drinks.*] Though I value not a farthing what he can do to me; I pay him his rent at quarter-day; I have a good running-trade; I have but one daughter, and I can give her—but no matter for that.

*Aim.* You're very happy, Mr. Boniface. Pray, what other company have you in town?

*Bon.* A power of fine ladies; and then we have the French officers.

*Aim.* Oh, that's right, you have a good many of those gentlemen: pray, how do you like their company?

*Bon.* So well, as the saying is, that I could wish we had as many more of 'em; they're full of money, and pay double for everything they have. They know, sir, that we paid good round taxes for the taking of 'em, and so they are willing to reimburse us a little. One of 'em lodges in my house.

*Re-enter* ARCHER.

*Arch.* Landlord, there are some French gentlemen below that ask for you.

*Bon.* I'll wait on 'em.—[*Aside to* ARCHER.] Does your master stay long in town, as the saying is?

*Arch.* I can't tell, as the saying is.

*Bon.* Come from London?

*Arch.* No.

*Bon.* Going to London, mayhap?

*Arch.* No.

*Bon.* [*aside*]. An odd fellow this.—[*To* AIMWELL.] I beg your worship's pardon, I'll wait on you in half a minute. [*Exit.*

*Aim.* The coast's clear, I see.—Now, my dear Archer, welcome to Lichfield!

*Arch.* I thank thee, my dear brother in iniquity.

*Aim.* Iniquity! prithee, leave canting; you need not change your style with your dress.

*Arch.* Don't mistake me, Aimwell, for 'tis still my maxim, that there is no scandal like rags, nor any crime so shameful as poverty.

*Aim.* The world confesses it every day in its practice though men won't own it for their opinion. Who did that worthy lord, my brother, single out of the side-box to sup with him t'other night?

*Arch.* Jack Handicraft, a handsome, well-dressed, mannerly, sharping rogue, who keeps the best company in town.

*Aim.* Right! And, pray, who married my lady Manslaughter t'other day, the great fortune?

*Arch.* Why, Nick Marrabone, a professed pickpocket, and a good bowler; but he makes a handsome figure, and rides in his coach, that he formerly used to ride behind.

*Aim.* But did you observe poor Jack Generous in the Park last week?

*Arch.* Yes, with his autumnal periwig, shading his melancholy face, his coat older than anything but its fashion, with one hand idle in his pocket, and with the other picking his useless teeth; and, though the Mall was crowded with company, yet was poor Jack as single and solitary as a lion in a desert.

*Aim.* And as much avoided, for no crime upon earth but the want of money.

*Arch.* And that's enough. Men must not be poor; idleness is the root of all evil; the world's wide enough, let 'em bustle. Fortune has taken the weak under her protection, but men of sense are left to their industry.

*Aim.* Upon which topic we proceed, and, I think, luckily hitherto. Would not any man swear now, that I am a man of quality, and you my servant, when if our intrinsic value were known——

*Arch.* Come, come, we are the men of intrinsic value who can strike our fortunes out of ourselves, whose worth is independent of accidents in life, or revolutions in government: we have heads to get money and hearts to spend it.

*Aim.* As to our hearts, I grant ye, they are as willing tits as any within twenty degrees: but I can have no great opinion of our heads from the service they have done us hitherto, unless it be that they have brought us from London hither to Lichfield, made me a lord and you my servant.

*Arch.* That's more than you could expect already. But what money have we left?

*Aim.* But two hundred pound.

*Arch.* And our horses, clothes, rings, etc.—Why, we have very good fortunes now for moderate people; and, let me tell you, that this two hundred pound, with the experience that we are now masters of, is a better estate than the ten we have spent. —Our friends, indeed, began to suspect that our pockets were low, but we came off with flying colours, showed no signs of want either in word or deed.

*Aim.* Ay, and our going to Brussels was a good pretence enough for our sudden disappearing; and, I warrant you, our friends imagine that we are gone a-volunteering.

*Arch.* Why, faith, if this prospect fails, it must e'en come to that. I am for venturing one of the hundreds, if you will, upon this knight-errantry; but, in case it should fail, we'll reserve t'other to carry us to some counterscarp, where we may die, as we lived, in a blaze.

*Aim.* With all my heart; and we have lived justly, Archer; we can't say that we have spent our fortunes, but that we have enjoyed 'em.

*Arch.* Right! so much pleasure for so much money. We have had our pennyworths; and, had I millions, I would go to the same market again.—O London! London!—Well, we have had our share, and let us be thankful: past pleasures, for aught I know, are best, such as we are sure of; those to come may disappoint us.

*Aim.* It has often grieved the heart of me to see how some inhuman wretches murder their kind fortunes; those that, by sacrificing all to one appetite, shall starve all the rest. You shall have some that live only in their palates, and in their sense of tasting shall drown the other four: others are only epicures in appearances, such who shall starve their nights to make a figure a days, and famish their own to feed the eyes of others: a contrary sort confine their pleasures to the dark, and contract their spacious acres to the circuit of a muff-string.

*Arch.* Right! But they find the Indies in that spot where they consume 'em, and I think your kind keepers have much the best on't: for they indulge the most senses by one expense, there's the seeing, hearing, and feeling, amply gratified; and, some philosophers will tell you, that from such a commerce there arises a sixth sense, that gives infinitely more pleasure than the other five put together.

*Aim.* And to pass to the other extremity, of all keepers I think those the worst that keep their money.

*Arch.* Those are the most miserable wights in being, they destroy the rights of nature, and disappoint the blessings of Providence. Give me a man that keeps his five senses keen and bright as his sword, that has 'em always drawn out in their just order and strength, with his reason as commander at the head of 'em, that detaches 'em by turns upon whatever party of pleasure agreeably offers, and commands 'em to retreat upon the least appearance of disadvantage or danger! For my part, I can stick to my bottle while my wine, my company, and my reason, hold good; I can be charmed with Sappho's singing without falling in love with her face: I love hunting, but would not, like Actæon, be eaten up by my own dogs; I love a fine house, but let another keep it; and just so I love a fine woman.

*Aim.* In that last particular you have the better of me.

*Arch.* Ay, you're such an amorous puppy, that I'm afraid you'll spoil our sport; you can't counterfeit the passion without feeling it.

*Aim.* Though the whining part be out of doors in town, 'tis still in force with the country ladies: and let me tell you, Frank, the fool in that passion shall outdo the knave at any time.

*Arch.* Well, I won't dispute it now; you command for the day, and so I submit: at Nottingham, you know, I am to be master.

*Aim.* And at Lincoln, I again.

*Arch.* Then, at Norwich I mount, which, I think, shall be our last stage; for, if we fail there, we'll embark for Holland, bid adieu to Venus, and welcome Mars.

*Aim.* A match!—Mum!

### Re-enter BONIFACE.

*Bon.* What will your worship please to have for supper?

*Aim.* What have you got?

*Bon.* Sir, we have a delicate piece of beef in the pot, and a pig at the fire.

*Aim.* Good supper-meat, I must confess. I can't eat beef, landlord.

*Arch.* And I hate pig.

*Aim.* Hold your prating, sirrah! do you know who you are?

*Bon.* Please to bespeak something else; I have everything in the house.

*Aim.* Have you any veal?

*Bon.* Veal! sir, we had a delicate loin of veal on Wednesday last.

*Aim.* Have you got any fish or wildfowl?

*Bon.* As for fish, truly, sir, we are an inland town, and indifferently provided with fish, that's the truth on't; and then for wildfowl—we have a delicate couple of rabbits.

*Aim.* Get me the rabbits fricasseed.

*Bon.* Fricasseed! Lard, sir, they'll eat much better smothered with onions.

*Arch.* Psha! Damn your onions!

*Aim.* Again, sirrah!—Well, landlord, what you please. But hold, I have a small charge of money, and your house is so full of strangers, that I believe it may be safer in your custody than mine; for when this fellow of mine gets drunk he minds nothing. —Here, sirrah, reach me the strong-box.

*Arch.* Yes, sir.—[*Aside.*] This will give us a reputation.
[*Brings* AIMWELL *the box.*

*Aim.* Here, landlord; the locks are sealed down both for your security and mine; it holds somewhat above two hundred pound: if you doubt it, I'll count it to you after supper; but be sure you lay it where I may have it at a minute's warning; for my affairs are a little dubious at present; perhaps I may be gone in half an hour, perhaps I may be your guest till the best part of that be spent; and pray order your ostler to keep my horses always saddled. But one thing above the rest I must beg, that you would let this fellow have none of your *Anno Domini*, as you call it; for he's the most insufferable sot.—Here, sirrah, light me to my chamber.                    [*Exit, lighted by* ARCHER.

*Bon.* Cherry! daughter Cherry!

*Re-enter* CHERRY.

*Cher.* D'ye call, father?
*Bon.* Ay, child, you must lay by this box for the gentleman: 'tis full of money.
*Cher.* Money! all that money! why, sure, father, the gentleman comes to be chosen parliament-man. Who is he?
*Bon.* I don't know what to make of him; he talks of keeping his horses ready saddled, and of going perhaps at a minute's warning, or of staying perhaps till the best part of this be spent.
*Cher.* Ay, ten to one, father, he's a highwayman.
*Bon.* A highwayman! upon my life, girl, you have hit it, and this box is some new-purchased booty. Now, could we find him out, the money were ours.
*Cher.* He don't belong to our gang.
*Bon.* What horses have they?
*Cher.* The master rides upon a black.
*Bon.* A black! ten to one the man upon the black mare; and since he don't belong to our fraternity, we may betray him with a safe conscience: I don't think it lawful to harbour any rogues but my own. Look'ee, child, as the saying is, we must go cunningly to work, proofs we must have; the gentleman's servant loves drink, I'll ply him that way, and ten to one loves a wench: you must work him t'other way.
*Cher.* Father, would you have me give my secret for his?
*Bon.* Consider, child, there's two hundred pound to boot.— [*Ringing without.*] Coming! coming!—Child, mind your business.
[*Exit.*
*Cher.* What a rogue is my father! My father? I deny it. My mother was a good, generous, free-hearted woman, and I can't tell how far her good nature might have extended for the good of her children. This landlord of mine, for I think I can call him no more, would betray his guest, and debauch his daughter into the bargain—by a footman too!

*Re-enter* ARCHER.

*Arch.* What footman, pray, mistress, is so happy as to be the subject of your contemplation?

*Cher.* Whoever he is, friend, he'll be but little the better for't.

*Arch.* I hope so, for, I'm sure, you did not think of me.

*Cher.* Suppose I had?

*Arch.* Why, then, you're but even with me; for the minute I came in, I was a-considering in what manner I should make love to you.

*Cher.* Love to me, friend!

*Arch.* Yes, child.

*Cher.* Child! manners!—If you kept a little more distance, friend, it would become you much better.

*Arch.* Distance! good-night, sauce-box.    [*Going.*

*Cher.* [*aside*]. A pretty fellow! I like his pride.—[*Aloud.*] Sir, pray, sir, you see, sir [ARCHER *returns*], I have the credit to be entrusted with your master's fortune here, which sets me a degree above his footman; I hope, sir, you an't affronted?

*Arch.* Let me look you full in the face, and I'll tell you whether you can affront me or no. 'Sdeath, child, you have a pair of delicate eyes, and you don't know what to do with 'em!

*Cher.* Why, sir, don't I see everybody?

*Arch.* Ay, but if some women had 'em, they would kill everybody. Prithee, instruct me, I would fain make love to you, but I don't know what to say.

*Cher.* Why, did you never make love to anybody before?

*Arch.* Never to a person of your figure, I can assure you, madam: my addresses have been always confined to people within my own sphere, I never aspired so high before.    [*Sings.*

But you look so bright,
And are dress'd so tight,
That a man would swear you're right,
As arm was e'er laid over.
Such an air
You freely wear
To ensnare,
As makes each guest a lover!

Since then, my dear, I'm your guest,
Prithee give me of the best
Of what is ready drest:
Since then, my dear, etc.

*Cher.* [*aside*]. What can I think of this man?—[*Aloud.*] Will you give me that song, sir?

*Arch.* Ay, my dear, take it while 'tis warm.—[*Kisses her.*] Death and fire! her lips are honeycombs.

*Cher.* And I wish there had been bees too, to have stung you for your impudence.

*Arch.* There's a swarm of Cupids, my little Venus, that has done the business much better.

*Cher.* [*aside*]. This fellow is misbegotten as well as I.— [*Aloud.*] What's your name, sir?

*Arch.* [*aside*]. Name! egad, I have forgot it.—[*Aloud.*] Oh! Martin.

*Cher.* Where were you born?

*Arch.* In St. Martin's parish.

*Cher.* What was your father?

*Arch.* St. Martin's parish.

*Cher.* Then, friend, good-night.

*Arch.* I hope not.

*Cher.* You may depend upon't.

*Arch.* Upon what?

*Cher.* That you're very impudent.

*Arch.* That you're very handsome.

*Cher.* That you're a footman.

*Arch.* That you're an angel.

*Cher.* I shall be rude.

*Arch.* So shall I.

*Cher.* Let go my hand.

*Arch.* Give me a kiss.  [*Kisses her.*

[*Call without.*] Cherry! Cherry!

*Cher.* I'm—my father calls; you plaguy devil, how durst you stop my breath so? Offer to follow me one step, if you dare.

[*Exit.*

*Arch.* A fair challenge, by this light! this is a pretty fair opening of an adventure; but we are knight-errants, and so Fortune be our guide. [*Exit.*


# ACT II


### SCENE I.—*A Gallery in* Lady Bountiful's *House*


#### *Enter* Mrs. Sullen *and* Dorinda, *meeting.*

*Dor.* Morrow, my dear sister; are you for church this morning?

*Mrs. Sul.* Anywhere to pray; for Heaven alone can help me. But I think, Dorinda, there's no form of prayer in the liturgy against bad husbands.

*Dor.* But there's a form of law in Doctors-Commons; and I swear, sister Sullen, rather than see you thus continually discontented, I would advise you to apply to that: for besides the part that I bear in your vexatious broils, as being sister to the husband, and friend to the wife, your example gives me such an impression of matrimony, that I shall be. apt to condemn my person to a long vacation all its life. But supposing, madam, that you brought it to a case of separation, what can you urge against your husband? My brother is, first, the most constant man alive.

*Mrs. Sul.* The most constant husband, I grant ye.

*Dor.* He never sleeps from you.

*Mrs. Sul.* No, he always sleeps with me.

*Dor.* He allows you a maintenance suitable to your quality.

*Mrs. Sul.* A maintenance! do you take me, madam, for an hospital child, that I must sit down, and bless my benefactors for meat, drink, and clothes? As I take it, madam, I brought your brother ten thousand pound, out of which I might expect some pretty things, called pleasures.

*Dor.* You share in all the pleasures that the country affords.

*Mrs. Sul.* Country pleasures! racks and torments! Dost think, child, that my limbs were made for leaping of ditches, and clambering over stiles? or that my parents, wisely fore-seeing my future happiness in country pleasures, had early instructed me in the rural accomplishments of drinking fat ale, playing at whisk, and smoking tobacco with my husband? or of spreading of plasters, brewing of diet-drinks, and stilling rosemary-water, with the good old gentlewoman my mother-in-law?

*Dor.* I'm sorry, madam, that it is not more in our power to divert you; I could wish, indeed, that our entertainments were a little more polite, or your taste a little less refined. But, pray, madam, how came the poets and philosophers, that laboured so much in hunting after pleasure, to place it at last in a country life?

*Mrs. Sul.* Because they wanted money, child, to find out the pleasures of the town. Did you ever see a poet or philosopher worth ten thousand pound? if you can show me such a man, I'll lay you fifty pound you'll find him somewhere within the weekly bills. Not that I disapprove rural pleasures, as the poets have painted them; in their landscape, every Phillis has her Corydon, every murmuring stream and every flowery mead gives fresh alarms to love. Besides, you'll find that their couples were never married:—but yonder I see my Corydon, and a sweet swain it is, Heaven knows! Come, Dorinda, don't be angry, he's my husband, and your brother; and, between both, is he not a sad brute?

*Dor.* I have nothing to say to your part of him, you're the best judge.

*Mrs. Sul.* O sister, sister! if ever you marry, beware of a sullen, silent sot, one that's always musing, but never thinks. There's some diversion in a talking blockhead; and since a

woman must wear chains, I would have the pleasure of hearing
'em rattle a little.   Now you shall see, but take this by the way.
He came home this morning at his usual hour of four, wakened
me out of a sweet dream of something else, by tumbling over the
tea-table, which he broke all to pieces; after his man and he had
rolled about the room, like sick passengers in a storm, he comes
flounce into bed, dead as a salmon into a fishmonger's basket;
his feet cold as ice, his breath hot as a furnace, and his hands and
his face as greasy as his flannel night-cap.   O matrimony!   He
tosses up the clothes with a barbarous swing over his shoulders,
disorders the whole economy of my bed, leaves me half naked,
and my whole night's comfort is the tuneable serenade of that
wakeful nightingale, his nose!   Oh, the pleasure of counting the
melancholy clock by a snoring husband!   But now, sister, you
shall see how handsomely, being a well-bred man, he will beg
my pardon.

*Enter* Squire SULLEN.

*Squire Sul.* My head aches consumedly.
*Mrs. Sul.* Will you be pleased, my dear, to drink tea with us
this morning?  it may do your head good.
*Squire Sul.* No.
*Dor.* Coffee, brother?
*Squire Sul.* Psha!
*Mrs. Sul.* Will you please to dress, and go to church with me?
the air may help you.
*Squire Sul.* Scrub!                                           [*Calls.*

*Enter* SCRUB.

*Scrub.* Sir!
*Squire Sul.* What day o' th' week is this?
*Scrub.* Sunday, an't please your worship.
*Squire Sul.* Sunday!  bring me a dram; and d'ye hear, set
out the venison-pasty and a tankard of strong beer upon the
hall-table, I'll go to breakfast.                              [*Going.*
*Dor.* Stay, stay, brother, you shan't get off so; you were very
naught last night, and must make your wife reparation; come,
come, brother, won't you ask pardon?
*Squire Sul.* For what?
*Dor.* For being drunk last night.
*Squire Sul.* I can afford it, can't I?
*Mrs. Sul.* But I can't, sir.
*Squire Sul.* Then you may let it alone.
*Mrs. Sul.* But I must tell you, sir, that this is not to be borne.
*Squire Sul.* I'm glad on't.
*Mrs. Sul.* What is the reason, sir, that you use me thus
inhumanly?
*Squire Sul.* Scrub!
*Scrub.* Sir!

*Squire Sul.* Get things ready to shave my head.          [*Exit.*

*Mrs. Sul.* Have a care of coming near his temples, Scrub, for fear you meet something there that may turn the edge of your razor.—[*Exit* SCRUB.] Inveterate stupidity! did you ever know so hard, so obstinate a spleen as his? O sister, sister! I shall never ha' good of the beast till I get him to town; London, dear London, is the place for managing and breaking a husband.

*Dor.* And has not a husband the same opportunities there for humbling a wife?

*Mrs. Sul.* No, no, child, 'tis a standing maxim in conjugal discipline, that when a man would enslave his wife, he hurries her into the country; and when a lady would be arbitrary with her husband, she wheedles her booby up to town. A man dare not play the tyrant in London, because there are so many examples to encourage the subject to rebel. O Dorinda! Dorinda! a fine woman may do anything in London: o' my conscience, she may raise an army of forty thousand men.

*Dor.* I fancy, sister, you have a mind to be trying your power that way here in Lichfield; you have drawn the French count to your colours already.

*Mrs. Sul.* The French are a people that can't live without their gallantries.

*Dor.* And some English that I know, sister, are not averse to such amusements.

*Mrs. Sul.* Well, sister, since the truth must out, it may do as well now as hereafter; I think one way to rouse my lethargic, sottish husband is to give him a rival: security begets negligence in all people, and men must be alarmed to make 'em alert in their duty. Women are like pictures, of no value in the hands of a fool, till he hears men of sense bid high for the purchase.

*Dor.* This might do, sister, if my brother's understanding were to be convinced into a passion for you; but, I fancy, there's a natural aversion on his side; and I fancy, sister, that you don't come much behind him, if you dealt fairly.

*Mrs. Sul.* I own it, we are united contradictions, fire and water: but I could be contented, with a great many other wives, to humour the censorious mob, and give the world an appearance of living well with my husband, could I bring him but to dissemble a little kindness to keep me in countenance.

*Dor.* But how do you know, sister, but that, instead of rousing your husband by this artifice to a counterfeit kindness, he should awake in a real fury?

*Mrs. Sul.* Let him: if I can't entice him to the one, I would provoke him to the other.

*Dor.* But how must I behave myself between ye?

*Mrs. Sul.* You must assist me.

*Dor.* What, against my own brother?

*Mrs. Sul.* He's but half a brother, and I'm your entire friend. If I go a step beyond the bounds of honour, leave me; till then,

I expect you should go along with me in everything; while I trust my honour in your hands, you may trust your brother's in mine.    The count is to dine here to-day.

*Dor.* 'Tis a strange thing, sister, that I can't like that man.

*Mrs. Sul.* You like nothing; your time is not come; Love and Death have their fatalities, and strike home one time or other: you'll pay for all one day, I warrant ye.    But come, my lady's tea is ready, and 'tis almost church time.    *[Exeunt.*


### SCENE II.—*A Room in* BONIFACE'S *Inn*

*Enter* AIMWELL *dressed, and* ARCHER.

*Aim.* And was she the daughter of the house?

*Arch.* The landlord is so blind as to think so; but I dare swear she has better blood in her veins.

*Aim.* Why dost think so?

*Arch.* Because the baggage has a pert *je ne sais quoi ;* she reads plays, keeps a monkey, and is troubled with vapours.

*Aim.* By which discoveries I guess that you know more of her.

*Arch.* Not yet, faith; the lady gives herself airs; forsooth, nothing under a gentleman!

*Aim.* Let me take her in hand.

*Arch.* Say one word more o' that, and I'll declare myself, spoil your sport there, and everywhere else; look ye, Aimwell, every man in his own sphere.

*Aim.* Right; and therefore you must pimp for your master.

*Arch.* In the usual forms, good sir, after I have served myself. —But to our business.    You are so well dressed, Tom, and make so handsome a figure, that I fancy you may do execution in a country church; the exterior part strikes first, and you're in the right to make that impression favourable.

*Aim.* There's something in that which may turn to advantage. The appearance of a stranger in a country church draws as many gazers as a blazing-star; no sooner he comes into the cathedral, but a train of whispers runs buzzing round the congregation in a moment: *Who is he ?    Whence comes he ?    Do you know him ?* Then I, sir, tips me the verger with half-a-crown; he pockets the simony, and inducts me into the best pew in the church; I pull out my snuff-box, turn myself round, bow to the bishop, or the dean, if he be the commanding-officer; single out a beauty, rivet both my eyes to hers, set my nose a-bleeding by the strength of imagination, and show the whole church my concern, by my endeavouring to hide it; after the sermon, the whole town gives me to her for a lover, and by persuading the lady that I am a-dying for her, the tables are turned, and she in good earnest falls in love with me.

*Arch.* There's nothing in this, Tom, without a precedent;

but instead of riveting your eyes to a beauty, try to fix 'em upon a fortune; that's our business at present.

*Aim.* Psha! no woman can be a beauty without a fortune. Let me alone, for I am a marksman.

*Arch.* Tom!

*Aim.* Ay.

*Arch.* When were you at church before, pray?

*Aim.* Um—I was there at the coronation.

*Arch.* And how can you expect a blessing by going to church now?

*Aim.* Blessing! nay, Frank, I ask but for a wife.    [*Exit.*

*Arch.* Truly, the man is not very unreasonable in his demands.
    [*Exit at the opposite door.*

#### Enter BONIFACE *and* CHERRY.

*Bon.* Well, daughter, as the saying is, have you brought Martin to confess?

*Cher.* Pray, father, don't put me upon getting anything out of a man; I'm but young, you know, father, and I do..'t understand wheedling.

*Bon.* Young! why, you jade, as the saying is, can any woman wheedle that is not young? your mother was useless at five-and-twenty. Not wheedle! would you make your mother a whore, and me a cuckold, as the saying is? I tell you, his silence confesses it, and his master spends his money so freely, and is so much a gentleman every manner of way, that he must be a highwayman.

#### Enter GIBBET, *in a cloak.*

*Gib.* Landlord, landlord, is the coast clear?

*Bon.* O Mr. Gibbet, what's the news?

*Gib.* No matter, ask no questions, all fair and honourable.— Here, my dear Cherry.—[*Gives her a bag.*]   Two hundred sterling pounds, as good as any that ever hanged or saved a rogue; lay 'em by with the rest; and here—three wedding or mourning rings, 'tis much the same, you know—here, two silver-hilted swords; I took those from fellows that never show any part of their swords but the hilts—here is a diamond necklace which the lady hid in the privatest place in the coach, but I found it out— this gold watch I took from a pawnbroker's wife; it was left in her hands by a person of quality: there's the arms upon the case.

*Cher.* But who had you the money from?

*Gib.* Ah! poor woman! I pitied her;—from a poor lady just eloped from her husband. She had made up her cargo, and was bound for Ireland, as hard as she could drive; she told me of her husband's barbarous usage, and so I left her half-a-crown. But I had almost forgot, my dear Cherry, I have a present for you.

*Cher.* What is't?

*Gib.* A pot of ceruse, my child, that I took out of a lady's under-pocket.

*Cher.* What, Mr. Gibbet, do you think that I paint?

*Gib.* Why, you jade, your betters do; I'm sure the lady that I took it from had a coronet upon her handkerchief. Here, take my cloak, and go, secure the premises.

*Cher.* I will secure 'em.                                   [*Exit.*

*Bon.* But, hark'ee, where's Hounslow and Bagshot?

*Gib.* They'll be here to-night.

*Bon.* D'ye know of any other gentlemen o' the pad on this road?

*Gib.* No.

*Bon.* I fancy that I have two that lodge in the house just now.

*Gib.* The devil! how d'ye smoke 'em?

*Bon.* Why, the one is gone to church.

*Gib.* That's suspicious, I must confess.

*Bon.* And the other is now in his master's chamber; he pretends to be servant to the other; we'll call him out and pump him a little.

*Gib.* With all my heart.

*Bon.* Mr. Martin! Mr. Martin!                            [*Calls*

*Enter* ARCHER, *combing a periwig and singing.*

*Gib.* The roads are consumed deep, I'm as dirty as Old Brentford at Christmas.—A good pretty fellow that; whose servant are you, friend?

*Arch.* My master's.

*Gib.* Really!

*Arch.* Really.

*Gib.* That's much.—The fellow has been at the bar by his evasions.—But pray, sir, what is your master's name?

*Arch.* Tall, all, dall!—[*Sings and combs the periwig.*] This is the most obstinate curl——

*Gib.* I ask you his name?

*Arch.* Name, sir—*tall, all, dall!*—I never asked him his name in my life.—*Tall, all, dall!*

*Bon.* What think you now?                 [*Aside to* GIBBET.

*Gib.* [*aside to* BONIFACE] Plain, plain, he talks now as if he were before a judge.—[*To* ARCHER.] But pray, friend, which way does your master travel?

*Arch.* A-horseback.

*Gib.* [*aside*]. Very well again, an old offender, right.—[*To* ARCHER.] But, I mean, does he go upwards or downwards?

*Arch.* Downwards, I fear, sir.—*Tall, all!*

*Gib.* I'm afraid my fate will be a contrary way.

*Bon.* Ha! ha! ha! Mr. Martin, you're very arch. This gentleman is only travelling towards Chester, and would be glad of your company, that's all.—Come, captain, you'll stay to-night, I suppose? I'll show you a chamber—come, captain.

*Gib.* Farewell, friend!

*Arch.* Captain, your servant.—[*Exeunt* BONIFACE *and* GIBBET.]
Captain! a pretty fellow! 'Sdeath, I wonder that the officers
of the army don't conspire to beat all scoundrels in red but
their own.

*Re-enter* CHERRY.

*Cher.* [*aside*]. Gone, and Martin here! I hope he did not
listen; I would have the merit of the discovery all my own,
because I would oblige him to love me.—[*Aloud.*] Mr. Martin,
who was that man with my father?

*Arch.* Some recruiting serjeant, or whipped-out trooper, I
suppose.

*Cher.* All's safe, I find.　　　　　　　　　　　　　　[*Aside.*

*Arch.* Come, my dear, have you conned over the catechise I
taught you last night?

*Cher.* Come, question me.

*Arch.* What is love?

*Cher.* Love is I know not what, it comes I know not how, and
goes I know not when.

*Arch.* Very well, an apt scholar.—[*Chucks her under the chin.*]
Where does love enter?

*Cher.* Into the eyes.

*Arch.* And where go out?

*Cher.* I won't tell ye.

*Arch.* What are the objects of that passion?

*Cher.* Youth, beauty, and clean linen.

*Arch.* The reason?

*Cher.* The two first are fashionable in nature, and the third
at court.

*Arch.* That's my dear.—What are the signs and tokens of
that passion?

*Cher.* A stealing look, a stammering tongue, words improbable,
designs impossible, and actions impracticable.

*Arch.* That's my good child, kiss me.—What must a lover do
to obtain his mistress?

*Cher.* He must adore the person that disdains him, he must
bribe the chambermaid that betrays him, and court the footman
that laughs at him.　He must—he must——

*Arch.* Nay, child, I must whip you if you don't mind your
lesson; he must treat his——

*Cher.* Oh ay!—he must treat his enemies with respect, his
friends with indifference, and all the world with contempt; he
must suffer much, and fear more; he must desire much, and
hope little; in short, he must embrace his ruin, and throw
himself away.

*Arch.* Had ever man so hopeful a pupil as mine!—Come, my
dear, why is love called a riddle?

*Cher.* Because, being blind, he leads those that see, and, though a child, he governs a man.

*Arch.* Mighty well!—And why is Love pictured blind?

*Cher.* Because the painters out of the weakness or privilege of their art chose to hide those eyes that they could not draw.

*Arch.* That's my dear little scholar, kiss me again.—And why should Love, that's a child, govern a man?

*Cher.* Because that a child is the end of love.

*Arch.* And so ends Love's catechism.—And now, my dear, we'll go in and make my master's bed.

*Cher.* Hold, hold, Mr. Martin! You have taken a great deal of pains to instruct me, and what d'ye think I have learned by it?

*Arch.* What?

*Cher.* That your discourse and your habit are contradictions, and it would be nonsense in me to believe you a footman any longer.

*Arch.* 'Oons, what a witch it is!

*Cher.* Depend upon this, sir, nothing in this garb shall ever tempt me; for, though I was born to servitude, I hate it. Own your condition, swear you love me, and then——

*Arch.* And then we shall go make the bed?

*Cher.* Yes.

*Arch.* You must know, then, that I am born a gentleman, my education was liberal; but I went to London a younger brother, fell into the hands of sharpers, who stripped me of my money, my friends disowned me, and now my necessity brings me to what you see.

*Cher.* Then take my hand—promise to marry me before you sleep, and I'll make you master of two thousand pound.

*Arch.* How?

*Cher.* Two thousand pound that I have this minute in my own custody; so, throw off your livery this instant, and I'll go find a parson.

*Arch.* What said you? a parson!

*Cher.* What! do you scruple?

*Arch.* Scruple! no, no, but—Two thousand pound, you say?

*Cher.* And better.

*Arch.* [*aside*]. 'Sdeath, what shall I do?—[*Aloud.*] But hark'ee, child, what need you make me master of yourself and money, when you may have the same pleasure out of me, and still keep your fortune in your hands?

*Cher.* Then you won't marry me?

*Arch.* I would marry you, but——

*Cher.* O sweet sir, I'm your humble servant, you're fairly caught! Would you persuade me that any gentleman who could bear the scandal of wearing a livery would refuse two thousand pound, let the condition be what it would? no, no, sir. But I hope you'll pardon the freedom I have taken, since it was only to inform myself of the respect that I ought to pay you. [*Going.*

*Arch.* [*aside.*] Fairly bit, by Jupiter!—[*Aloud.*]　Hold! hold!
—And have you actually two thousand pound?

*Cher.* Sir, I have my secrets as well as you; when you please
to be more open I shall be more free, and be assured that I have
discoveries that will match yours, be what they will.　In the
meanwhile, be satisfied that no discovery I make shall ever hurt
you, but beware of my father!　　　　　　　　　　　[*Exit.*

*Arch.* So! we're like to have as many adventures in our inn
as Don Quixote had in his.　Let me see—two thousand pound
—if the wench would promise to die when the money were spent,
egad, one would marry her; but the fortune may go off in a year
or two, and the wife may live—Lord knows how long.　Then
an innkeeper's daughter! ay, that's the devil—there my pride
brings me off.

> For whatsoe'er the sages charge on pride,
> The angels' fall, and twenty faults beside,
> On earth, I'm sure, 'mong us of mortal calling,
> Pride saves man oft, and woman too, from falling.

　　　　　　　　　　　　　　　　　　　　　　　[*Exit.*


# ACT III

### SCENE I.—*The Gallery in* Lady BOUNTIFUL'S *House*

#### *Enter* Mrs. SULLEN *and* DORINDA.

*Mrs. Sul.* Ha! ha! ha! my dear sister, let me embrace thee!
now we are friends indeed; for I shall have a secret of yours as
a pledge for mine—now you'll be good for something, I shall
have you conversable in the subjects of the sex.

*Dor.* But do you think that I am so weak as to fall in love
with a fellow at first sight?

*Mrs. Sul.* Psha! now you spoil all; why should not we be as
free in our friendships as the men?　I warrant you, the gentleman has got to his confidant already, has avowed his passion,
toasted your health, called you ten thousand angels, has run
over your lips, eyes, neck, shape, air, and everything, in a
description that warms their mirth to a second enjoyment.

*Dor.* Your hand, sister, I an't well.

*Mrs. Sul.* So—she's breeding already—come, child, up with
it—hem a little—so—now tell me, don't you like the gentleman
that we saw at church just now?

*Dor.* The man's well enough.

*Mrs. Sul.* Well enough! is he not a demigod, a Narcissus, a
star, the man i' the moon?

*Dor.* O sister, I'm extremely ill!

*Mrs. Sul.* Shall I send to your mother, child, for a little of her cephalic plaster to put to the soles of your feet, or shall I send to the gentleman for something for you? Come, unlace your stays, unbosom yourself. The man is perfectly a pretty fellow; I saw him when he first came into church.

*Dor.* I saw him too, sister, and with an air that shone, methought, like rays about his person.

*Mrs. Sul.* Well said, up with it!

*Dor.* No forward coquette behaviour, no airs to set him off, no studied looks nor artful posture—but Nature did it all——

*Mrs. Sul.* Better and better!—one touch more—come!

*Dor.* But then his looks—did you observe his eyes?

*Mrs. Sul.* Yes, yes, I did.—His eyes, well, what of his eyes?

*Dor.* Sprightly, but not wandering; they seemed to view, but never gazed on anything but me.—And then his looks so humble were, and yet so noble, that they aimed to tell me that he could with pride die at my feet, though he scorned slavery anywhere else.

*Mrs. Sul.* The physic works purely!—How d'ye find yourself now, my dear?

*Dor.* Hem! much better, my dear.—Oh, here comes our Mercury!

*Enter* SCRUB.

Well, Scrub, what news of the gentleman?

*Scrub.* Madam, I have brought you a packet of news.

*Dor.* Open it quickly, come.

*Scrub.* In the first place I inquired who the gentleman was; they told me he was a stranger. Secondly, I asked what the gentleman was; they answered and said, that they never saw him before. Thirdly, I inquired what countryman he was; they replied, 'twas more than they knew. Fourthly, I demanded whence he came; their answer was, they could not tell. And, fifthly, I asked whither he went; and they replied, they knew nothing of the matter,—and this is all I could learn.

*Mrs. Sul.* But what do the people say? can't they guess?

*Scrub.* Why, some think he's a spy, some guess he's a mountebank, some say one thing, some another: but, for my own part, I believe he's a Jesuit.

*Dor.* A Jesuit! why a Jesuit?

*Scrub.* Because he keeps his horses always ready saddled, and his footman talks French.

*Mrs. Sul.* His footman!

*Scrub.* Ay, he and the count's footman were jabbering French like two intriguing ducks in a mill-pond; and I believe they talked of me, for they laughed consumedly.

*Dor.* What sort of livery has the footman?

*Scrub.* Livery! Lord, madam, I took him for a captain, he's so bedizzened with lace! And then he has tops to his shoes, up to his mid leg, a silver-headed cane dangling at his knuckles; he carries his hands in his pockets just so—[*walks in the French air*]—and has a fine long periwig tied up in a bag.—Lord, madam, he's clear another sort of man than I!

*Mrs. Sul.* That may easily be.—But what shall we do now, sister?

*Dor.* I have it—this fellow has a world of simplicity, and some cunning, the first hides the latter by abundance.—Scrub!

*Scrub.* Madam!

*Dor.* We have a great mind to know who this gentleman is, only for our satisfaction.

*Scrub.* Yes, madam, it would be a satisfaction, no doubt.

*Dor.* You must go and get acquainted with his footman, and invite him hither to drink a bottle of your ale because you're butler to-day.

*Scrub.* Yes, madam, I am butler every Sunday.

*Mrs. Sul.* O brave! sister, o' my conscience, you understand the mathematics already. 'Tis the best plot in the world: your mother, you know, will be gone to church, my spouse will be got to the ale-house with his scoundrels, and the house will be our own—so we drop in by accident, and ask the fellow some questions ourselves. In the country, you know, any stranger is company, and we're glad to take up with the butler in a country-dance, and happy if he'll do us the favour.

*Scrub.* O madam, you wrong me! I never refused your ladyship the favour in my life.

*Enter* GIPSY.

*Gip.* Ladies, dinner's upon table.

*Dor.* Scrub, we'll excuse your waiting—go where we ordered you.

*Scrub.* I shall. [*Exeunt.*

SCENE II.—*A Room in* BONIFACE'S *Inn*

*Enter* AIMWELL *and* ARCHER.

*Arch.* Well, Tom, I find you're a marksman.

*Aim.* A marksman! who so blind could be, as not discern a swan among the ravens?

*Arch.* Well, but hark'ee, Aimwell!

*Aim.* Aimwell! call me Oroöndates, Cesario, Amadis, all that romance can in a lover paint, and then I'll answer. O Archer! I read her thousands in her looks, she looked like Ceres in her harvest: corn, wine and oil, milk and honey, gardens, groves, and purling streams played on her plenteous face.

*Arch.* Her face! her pocket, you mean; the corn, wine, and oil lies there. In short, she has ten thousand pound, that's the English on't.

*Aim.* Her eyes——

*Arch.* Are demi-cannons, to be sure; so I won't stand their battery.                                                    [*Going.*

*Aim.* Pray excuse me, my passion must have vent.

*Arch.* Passion! what a plague, d'ye think these romantic airs will do our business? Were my temper as extravagant as yours, my adventures have something more romantic by half.

*Aim.* Your adventures!

*Arch.* Yes,

The nymph that with her twice ten hundred pounds,
With brazen engine hot, and quoif clear-starched,
Can fire the guest in warming of the bed——

There's a touch of sublime Milton for you, and the subject but an innkeeper's daughter! I can play with a girl as an angler does with his fish; he keeps it at the end of his line, runs it up the stream, and down the stream, till at last he brings it to hand, tickles the trout, and so whips it into his basket.

### *Enter* BONIFACE.

*Bon.* Mr. Martin, as the saying is—yonder's an honest fellow below, my Lady Bountiful's butler, who begs the honour that you would go home with him and see his cellar.

*Arch.* Do my *baise-mains* to the gentleman, and tell him I will do myself the honour to wait on him immediately.

[*Exit* BONIFACE.

*Aim.* What do I hear?
     Soft Orpheus play, and fair Toftida sing!

*Arch.* Psha! damn your raptures; I tell you, here's a pump going to be put into the vessel, and the ship will get into harbour, my life on't. You say, there's another lady very handsome there?

*Aim.* Yes, faith.

*Arch.* I'm in love with her already.

*Aim.* Can't you give me a bill upon Cherry in the meantime?

*Arch.* No, no, friend, all her corn, wine, and oil is ingrossed to my market. And once more I warn you, to keep your anchorage clear of mine; for if you fall foul of me, by this light you shall go to the bottom! What! make prize of my little frigate, while I am upon the cruise for you!——

*Aim.* Well, well, I won't.                              [*Exit* ARCHER.

### *Re-enter* BONIFACE.

Landlord, have you any tolerable company in the house? I don't care for dining alone.

*Bon.* Yes, sir, there's a captain below, as the saying is, that arrived about an hour ago.

*Aim.* Gentlemen of his coat are welcome everywhere; will you make him a compliment from me and tell him I should be glad of his company?

*Bon.* Who shall I tell him, sir, would——

*Aim.* [*aside*]. Ha! that stroke was well thrown in!—[*Aloud.*] I'm only a traveller, like himself, and would be glad of his company, that's all.

*Bon.* I obey your commands, as the saying is.          [*Exit.*

### Re-enter ARCHER.

*Arch.* 'Sdeath! I had forgot; what title will you give yourself?

*Aim.* My brother's, to be sure; he would never give me anything else, so I'll make bold with his honour this bout:—you know the rest of your cue.

*Arch.* Ay, ay.          [*Exit.*

### Enter GIBBET.

*Gib.* Sir, I'm yours.

*Aim.* 'Tis more than I deserve, sir, for I don't know you.

*Gib.* I don't wonder at that, sir, for you never saw me before—[*aside*] I hope.

*Aim.* And pray, sir, how came I by the honour of seeing you now?

*Gib.* Sir, I scorn to intrude upon any gentleman—but my landlord——

*Aim.* O sir, I ask your pardon, you're the captain he told me of?

*Gib.* At your service, sir.

*Aim.* What regiment, may I be so bold?

*Gib.* A marching regiment, sir, an old corps.

*Aim.* [*aside*]. Very old, if your coat be regimental.—[*Aloud.*] You have served abroad, sir?

*Gib.* Yes, sir—in the plantations, 'twas my lot to be sent into the worst service; I would have quitted it indeed, but a man of honour, you know—Besides, 'twas for the good of my country that I should be abroad:—anything for the good of one's country —I'm a Roman for that.

*Aim.* [*aside*]. One of the first; I'll lay my life.—[*Aloud.*] You found the West Indies very hot, sir?

*Gib.* Ay, sir, too hot for me.

*Aim.* Pray, sir, han't I seen your face at Will's coffee-house?

*Gib.* Yes, sir, and at White's too.

*Aim.* And where is your company now, captain?

*Gib.* They an't come yet.

*Aim.* Why, d'ye expect 'em here?

*Gib.* They'll be here to-night, sir.

*Aim.* Which way do they march?

*Gib.* Across the country.—[*Aside.*] The devil's in't, if I han't said enough to encourage him to declare! But I'm afraid he's not right; I must tack about.

*Aim.* Is your company to quarter in Lichfield?

*Gib.* In this house, sir.

*Aim.* What! all?

*Gib.* My company's but thin, ha! ha! ha! we are but three, ha! ha! ha!

*Aim.* You're merry, sir.

*Gib.* Ay, sir, you must excuse me, sir; I understand the world, especially the art of travelling: I don't care, sir, for answering questions directly upon the road—for I generally ride with a charge about me.

*Aim.* Three or four, I believe.                    [*Aside.*

*Gib.* I am credibly informed that there are highwaymen upon this quarter; not, sir, that I could suspect a gentleman of your figure—but truly, sir, I have got such a way of evasion upon the road, that I don't care for speaking truth to any man.

*Aim.* [*aside*]. Your caution may be necessary.—[*Aloud.*] Then I presume you're no captain?

*Gib.* Not I, sir; captain is a good travelling name, and so I take it; it stops a great many foolish inquiries that are generally made about gentlemen that travel, it gives a man an air of something, and makes the drawers obedient:—and thus far I am a captain, and no farther.

*Aim.* And pray, sir, what is your true profession?

*Gib.* O sir, you must excuse me!—upon my word, sir, I don't think it safe to tell ye.

*Aim.* Ha! ha! ha! upon my word I commend you.

*Re-enter* BONIFACE.

Well, Mr. Boniface, what's the news?

*Bon.* There's another gentleman below, as the saying is, that hearing you were but two, would be glad to make the third man, if you would give him leave.

*Aim.* What is he?

*Bon.* A clergyman, as the saying is.

*Aim.* A clergyman! is he really a clergyman? or is it only his travelling name, as my friend the captain has it?

*Bon.* O sir, he's a priest, and chaplain to the French officers in town.

*Aim.* Is he a Frenchman?

*Bon.* Yes, sir, born at Brussels.

*Gib.* A Frenchman, and a priest! I won't be seen in his company, sir; I have a value for my reputation, sir.

*Aim.* Nay, but, captain, since we are by ourselves—can he speak English, landlord?

*Bon.* Very well, sir; you may know him, as the saying is, to be a foreigner by his accent, and that's all.

*Aim.* Then he has been in England before?

*Bon.* Never, sir; but he's a master of languages, as the saying is; he talks Latin—it does me good to hear him talk Latin.

*Aim.* Then you understand Latin, Mr. Boniface?

*Bon.* Not I, sir, as the saying is; but he talks it so very fast, that I'm sure it must be good.

*Aim.* Pray, desire him to walk up.

*Bon.* Here he is, as the saying is.

### Enter FOIGARD.

*Foi.* Save you, gentlemen, both.

*Aim.* [*aside*]. A Frenchman!—[*To Foigard.*] Sir, your most humble servant.

*Foi.* Och, dear joy, I am your most faithful shervant, and yours alsho.

*Gib.* Doctor, you talk very good English, but you have a mighty twang of the foreigner.

*Foi.* My English is very vell for the vords, but we foreigners, you know, cannot bring our tongues about the pronunciation so soon.

*Aim.* [*aside*]. A foreigner! a downright Teague, by this light!—[*Aloud.*] Were you born in France, doctor?

*Foi.* I was educated in France, but I was borned at Brussels; I am a subject of the King of Spain, joy.

*Gib.* What King of Spain, sir? speak;

*Foi.* Upon my shoul, joy, I cannot tell you as yet.

*Aim.* Nay, captain, that was too hard upon the doctor; he's a stranger.

*Foi.* Oh, let him alone, dear joy; I am of a nation that is not easily put out of countenance.

*Aim.* Come, gentlemen, I'll end the dispute.—Here, landlord, is dinner ready?

*Bon.* Upon the table, as the saying is.

*Aim.* Gentlemen—pray—that door——

*Foi.* No, no, fait, the captain must lead.

*Aim.* No, doctor, the church is our guide.

*Gib.* Ay, ay, so it is.

[*Exit* FOIGARD *foremost, the others following.*

### SCENE III.—*The Gallery in* Lady BOUNTIFUL'S *House*

*Enter* ARCHER *and* SCRUB *singing, and hugging one another, the latter with a tankard in his hand.* GIPSY *listening at a distance.*

*Scrub.* Tall, all, dall!—Come, my dear boy, let's have that song once more.

*Arch.* No, no, we shall disturb the family.—But will you be sure to keep the secret?

*Scrub.* Pho! upon my honour, as I'm a gentleman.

*Arch.* 'Tis enough. You must know, then, that my master is the Lord Viscount Aimwell; he fought a duel t'other day in London, wounded his man so dangerously that he thinks fit to withdraw till he hears whether the gentleman's wounds be mortal or not. He never was in this part of England before, so he chose to retire to this place, that's all.

*Gip.* And that's enough for me.          [*Exit.*

*Scrub.* And where were you when your master fought?

*Arch.* We never know of our masters' quarrels.

*Scrub.* No! if our masters in the country here receive a challenge, the first thing they do is to tell their wives; the wife tells the servants, the servants alarm the tenants, and in half an hour you shall have the whole county in arms.

*Arch.* To hinder two men from doing what they have no mind for.—But if you should chance to talk now of my business?

*Scrub.* Talk! ay, sir, had I not learned the knack of holding my tongue, I had never lived so long in a great family.

*Arch.* Ay, ay, to be sure there are secrets in all families.

*Scrub.* Secrets! ay;—but I'll say no more. Come, sit down, we'll make an end of our tankard: here——

                    [*Gives* ARCHER *the tankard.*

*Arch.* With all my heart; who knows but you and I may come to be better acquainted, eh? Here's your ladies' healths; you have three, I think, and to be sure there must be secrets among 'em.          [*Drinks.*

*Scrub.* Secrets! ay, friend.—I wish I had a friend!

*Arch.* Am not I your friend? come, you and I will be sworn brothers.

*Scrub.* Shall we?

*Arch.* From this minute. Give me a kiss:—and now, brother Scrub——

*Scrub.* And now, brother Martin, I will tell you a secret that will make your hair stand on end. You must know that I am consumedly in love.

*Arch.* That's a terrible secret, that's the truth on't.

*Scrub.* That jade, Gipsy, that was with us just now in the cellar, is the arrantest whore that ever wore a petticoat; and I'm dying for love of her.

*Arch.* Ha! ha! ha!—Are you in love with her person or her virtue, brother Scrub?

*Scrub.* I should like virtue best, because it is more durable than beauty: for virtue holds good with some women long, and many a day after they have lost it.

*Arch.* In the country, I grant ye, where no woman's virtue is lost, till a bastard be found.

*Scrub.* Ay, could I bring her to a bastard, I should have her all to myself; but I dare not put it upon that lay, for fear of being sent for a soldier. Pray, brother, how do you gentlemen in London like that same Pressing Act?

*Arch.* Very ill, brother Scrub; 'tis the worst that ever was made for us. Formerly I remember the good days, when we could dun our masters for our wages, and if they refused to pay us, we could have a warrant to carry 'em before a Justice: but now if we talk of eating, they have a warrant for us, and carry us before three Justices.

*Scrub.* And to be sure we go, if we talk of eating; for the Justices won't give their own servants a bad example. Now this is my misfortune—I dare not speak in the house, while that jade Gipsy dings about like a fury.—Once I had the better end of the staff.

*Arch.* And how comes the change now?

*Scrub.* Why, the mother of all this mischief is a priest.

*Arch.* A priest!

*Scrub.* Ay, a damned son of a whore of Babylon, that came over hither to say grace to the French officers, and eat up our provisions. There's not a day goes over his head without a dinner or supper in this house.

*Arch.* How came he so familiar in the family?

*Scrub.* Because he speaks English as if he had lived here all his life, and tells lies as if he had been a traveller from his cradle.

*Arch.* And this priest, I'm afraid, has converted the affections of your Gipsy?

*Scrub.* Converted! ay, and perverted, my dear friend: for, I'm afraid, he has made her a whore and a papist! But this is not all; there's the French count and Mrs. Sullen, they're in the confederacy, and for some private ends of their own, to be sure.

*Arch.* A very hopeful family yours, brother Scrub! I suppose the maiden lady has her lover too?

*Scrub.* Not that I know: she's the best on 'em, that's the truth on't: but they take care to prevent my curiosity, by giving me so much business, that I'm a perfect slave. What d'ye think is my place in this family?

*Arch.* Butler, I suppose.

*Scrub.* Ah, Lord help you! I'll tell you. Of a Monday I drive the coach, of a Tuesday I drive the plough, on Wednesday I follow the hounds, a Thursday I dun the tenants, on Friday I go to market, on Saturday I draw warrants, and a Sunday I draw beer.

*Arch.* Ha! ha! ha! if variety be a pleasure in life, you have enough on't, my dear brother. But what ladies are those?

*Scrub.* Ours, ours; that upon the right hand is Mrs. Sullen, and the other is Mrs. Dorinda. Don't mind 'em; sit still, man.

### *Enter* Mrs. SULLEN *and* DORINDA.

*Mrs. Sul.* I have heard my brother talk of my Lord Aimwell; but they say that his brother is the finer gentleman.

*Dor.* That's impossible, sister.

*Mrs. Sul.* He's vastly rich, but very close, they say.

*Dor.* No matter for that; if I can creep into his heart, I'll open his breast, I warrant him: I have heard say, that people may be guessed at by the behaviour of their servants; I could wish we might talk to that fellow.

*Mrs. Sul.* So do I; for I think he's a very pretty fellow. Come this way, I'll throw out a lure for him presently.

> [DORINDA *and* Mrs. SULLEN *walk a turn towards the opposite side of the stage.*

*Arch.* [*aside*]. Corn, wine, and oil indeed!—But, I think, the wife has the greatest plenty of flesh and blood; she should be my choice.—Ay, ay, say you so!—[Mrs. SULLEN *drops her glove,* ARCHER *runs, takes it up and gives to her.*] Madam—your ladyship's glove.

*Mrs. Sul.* O sir, I thank you!—[*To* DORINDA.] What a handsome bow the fellow has!

*Dor.* Bow! why, I have known several footmen come down from London set up here for dancing-masters, and carry off the best fortunes in the country.

*Arch.* [*aside*]. That project, for aught I know, had been better than ours.—[*To* SCRUB.] Brother Scrub, why don't you introduce me?

*Scrub.* Ladies, this is the strange gentleman's servant that you saw at church to-day; I understood he came from London, and so I invited him to the cellar, that he might show me the newest flourish in whetting my knives.

*Dor.* And I hope you have made much of him?

*Arch.* Oh yes, madam, but the strength of your ladyship's liquor is a little too potent for the constitution of your humble servant.

*Mrs. Sul.* What, then you don't usually drink ale?

*Arch.* No, madam; my constant drink is tea, or a little wine and water. 'Tis prescribed me by the physician for a remedy against the spleen.

*Scrub.* Oh la! Oh la! a footman have the spleen!

*Mrs. Sul.* I thought that distemper had been only proper to people of quality?

*Arch.* Madam, like all other fashions it wears out, and so descends to their servants; though in a great many of us, I believe, it proceeds from some melancholy particles in the blood, occasioned by the stagnation of wages.

*Dor.* [*aside to* Mrs. SULLEN]. How affectedly the fellow talks! —[*To* ARCHER.] How long, pray, have you served your present master?

*Arch.* Not long; my life has been mostly spent in the service of the ladies.

*Mrs. Sul.* And pray, which service do you like best?

*Arch.* Madam, the ladies pay best; the honour of serving them is sufficient wages; there is a charm in their looks that delivers a pleasure with their commands, and gives our duty the wings of inclination.

*Mrs. Sul.* [*aside*]. That flight was above the pitch of a livery. —[*Aloud.*] And, sir, would not you be satisfied to serve a lady again?

*Arch.* As a groom of the chamber, madam, but not as a footman.

*Mrs. Sul.* I suppose you served as footman before?

*Arch.* For that reason I would not serve in that post again; for my memory is too weak for the load of messages that the ladies lay upon their servants in London. My Lady Howd'ye, the last mistress I served, called me up one morning, and told me, "Martin, go to my Lady Allnight with my humble service; tell her I was to wait on her ladyship yesterday, and left word with Mrs. Rebecca, that the preliminaries of the affair she knows of are stopped till we know the concurrence of the person that I know of, for which there are circumstances wanting which we shall accommodate at the old place; but that in the meantime there is a person about her ladyship, that from several hints and surmises, was accessory at a certain time to the disappointments that naturally attend things, that to her knowledge are of more importance——"

*Mrs. Sul., Dor.* Ha! ha! ha! where are you going, sir?

*Arch.* Why, I han't half done!—The whole howd'ye was about half an hour long; so I happened to misplace two syllables, and was turned off, and rendered incapable.

*Dor.* [*aside to* Mrs. Sullen]. The pleasantest fellow, sister, I ever saw!—[*To* Archer.] But, friend, if your master be married, I presume you still serve a lady?

*Arch.* No, madam, I take care never to come into a married family! the commands of the master and mistress are always so contrary, that 'tis impossible to please both.

*Dor.* There's a main point gained: my lord is not married, I find.                                                              [*Aside.*

*Mrs. Sul.* But I wonder, friend, that in so many good services, you had not a better provision made for you.

*Arch.* I don't know how, madam. I had a lieutenancy offered me three or four times; but that is not bread, madam— I live much better as I do.

*Scrub.* Madam, he sings rarely! I was thought to do pretty well here in the country till he came; but alack a day, I'm nothing to my brother Martin!

*Dor.* Does he?—Pray, sir, will you oblige us with a song?

*Arch.* Are you for passion or humour?

*Scrub.* Oh le! he has the purest ballad about a trifle——

*Mrs. Sul.* A trifle! pray, sir, let's have it.

*Arch.* I'm ashamed to offer you a trifle, madam; but since you command me—

[*Sings to the tune of "Sir Simon the King."*

A trifling song you shall hear,
Begun with a trifle and ended:
All trifling people draw near,
And I shall be nobly attended.

Were it not for trifles, a few,
That lately have come into play;
The men would want something to do,
And the women want something to say.

What makes men trifle in dressing?
Because the ladies (they know)
Admire, by often possessing,
That eminent trifle, a beau.

When the lover his moments has trifled,
The trifle of trifles to gain:
No sooner the virgin is rifled,
But a trifle shall part 'em again.

What mortal man would be able
At White's half an hour to sit?
Or who could bear a tea-table,
Without talking of trifles for wit?

The court is from trifles secure,
Gold keys are no trifles, we see:
White rods are no trifles, I'm sure,
Whatever their bearers may be.

But if you will go to the place,
Where trifles abundantly breed,
The levee will show you His Grace
Makes promises trifles indeed.

A coach with six footmen behind,
I count neither trifle nor sin:
But, ye gods! how oft do we find
A scandalous trifle within.

A flask of champagne, people think it
A trifle, or something as bad:
But if you'll contrive how to drink it,
You'll find it no trifle, egad!

A parson's a trifle at sea,
A widow's a trifle in sorrow:
A peace is a trifle to-day,
Who knows what may happen to-morrow?

A black coat a trifle may cloak,
Or to hide it, the red may endeavour:
But if once the army is broke,
We shall have more trifles than ever.

The stage is a trifle, they say,
The reason, pray carry along,
Because at every new play,
The house they with trifles so throng.

But with people's malice to trifle,
And to set us all on a foot:
The author of this is a trifle,
And his song is a trifle to boot.

*Mrs. Sul.* Very well, sir, we're obliged to you.—Something for a pair of gloves. [*Offering him money.*

*Arch.* I humbly beg leave to be excused: my master, madam, pays me; nor dare I take money from any other hand, without injuring his honour, and disobeying his commands.

[*Exit* ARCHER *and* SCRUB.

*Dor.* This is surprising! Did you ever see so pretty a well-bred fellow?

*Mrs. Sul.* The devil take him for wearing that livery!

*Dor.* I fancy, sister, he may be some gentleman, a friend of my lord's, that his lordship has pitched upon for his courage, fidelity, and discretion, to bear him company in this dress, and who ten to one was his second too.

*Mrs. Sul.* It is so, it must be so, and it shall be so!—for I like him.

*Dor.* What! better than the Count?

*Mrs. Sul.* The Count happened to be the most agreeable man upon the place; and so I chose him to serve me in my design upon my husband. But I should like this fellow better in a design upon myself.

*Dor.* But now, sister, for an interview with this lord and this gentleman; how shall we bring that about?

*Mrs. Sul.* Patience! you country ladies give no quarter if once you be entered. Would you prevent their desires, and give the fellows no wishing-time? Look'ee, Dorinda, if my Lord Aimwell loves you or deserves you, he'll find a way to see you, and there we must leave it. My business comes now upon the tapis. Have you prepared your brother?

*Dor.* Yes, yes.

*Mrs. Sul.* And how did he relish it?

*Dor.* He said little, mumbled something to himself, promised to be guided by me—but here he comes.

*Enter* Squire SULLEN.

*Squire Sul.* What singing was that I heard just now?

*Mrs. Sul.* The singing in your head, my dear; you complained of it all day.

*Squire Sul.* You're impertinent.

*Mrs. Sul.* I was ever so, since I became one flesh with you.

*Squire Sul.* One flesh! rather two carcasses joined unnaturally together.

*Mrs. Sul.* Or rather a living soul coupled to a dead body.

*Dor.* So, this is fine encouragement for me!

*Squire Sul.* Yes, my wife shows you what you must do.

*Mrs. Sul.* And my husband shows you what you must suffer.

*Squire Sul.* 'Sdeath, why can't you be silent?

*Mrs. Sul.* 'Sdeath, why can't you talk?

*Squire Sul.* Do you talk to any purpose?

*Mrs. Sul.* Do you think to any purpose?

*Squire Sul.* Sister, hark'ee!—[*Whispers.*] I shan't be home till it be late.   [*Exit.*

*Mrs. Sul.* What did he whisper to ye?

*Dor.* That he would go round the back way, come into the closet, and listen as I directed him. But let me beg you once more, dear sister, to drop this project; for as I told you before, instead of awaking him to kindness, you may provoke him to a rage; and then who knows how far his brutality may carry him?

*Mrs. Sul.* I'm provided to receive him, I warrant you. But here comes the Count: vanish!   [*Exit* DORINDA.

*Enter* Count BELLAIR.

Don't you wonder, Monsieur le Count, that I was not at church this afternoon?

*Count Bel.* I more wonder, madam, that you go dere at all, or how you dare to lift those eyes to heaven that are guilty of so much killing.

*Mrs. Sul.* If Heaven, sir, has given to my eyes with the power of killing the virtue of making a cure, I hope the one may atone for the other.

*Count Bel.* Oh, largely, madam, would your ladyship be as ready to apply the remedy as to give the wound. Consider, madam, I am doubly a prisoner; first to the arms of your general, then to your more conquering eyes. My first chains are easy—there a ransom may redeem me; but from your fetters I never shall get free.

*Mrs. Sul.* Alas, sir! why should you complain to me of your captivity, who am in chains myself? You know, sir, that I am bound, nay, must be tied up in that particular that might give you ease: I am like you, a prisoner of war—of war, indeed—I have given my parole of honour! would you break yours to gain your liberty?

*Count Bel.* Most certainly I would, were I a prisoner among the Turks; dis is your case, you're a slave, madam, slave to the worst of Turks, a husband.

*Mrs. Sul.* There lies my foible, I confess; no fortifications, no courage, conduct, nor vigilancy, can pretend to defend a place where the cruelty of the governor forces the garrison to mutiny.

*Count Bel.* And where de besieger is resolved to die before de place.—Here will I fix [*kneels*]:—with tears, vows, and prayers assault your heart and never rise till you surrender; or if I must storm—Love and St. Michael!—And so I begin the attack.

*Mrs. Sul.* Stand off!—[*Aside.*] .Sure he hears me not!—And I could almost wish he did not!—The fellow makes love very prettily.—[*Aloud*.] But, sir, why should you put such a value upon my person, when you see it despised by one that knows it so much better?

*Count Bel*. He knows it not, though he possesses it; if he but knew the value of the jewel he is master of he would always wear it next his heart, and sleep with it in his arms.

*Mrs. Sul*. But since he throws me unregarded from him——

*Count Bel*. And one that knows your value well comes by and takes you up, is it not justice?          [*Goes to lay hold of her*.

*Enter* Squire SULLEN *with his sword drawn*.

*Squire Sul*. Hold, villain, hold!

*Mrs. Sul*. [*presenting a pistol*]. Do you hold!

*Squire Sul*. What! murder your husband, to defend your bully?

*Mrs. Sul*. Bully! for shame, Mr. Sullen, bullies wear long swords, the gentleman has none; he's a prisoner, you know. I was aware of your outrage, and prepared this to receive your violence; and, if occasion were, to preserve myself against the force of this other gentleman.

*Count Bel*. O madam, your eyes be bettre firearms than your pistol; they nevre miss.

*Squire Sul*. What! court my wife to my face?

*Mrs. Sul*. Pray, Mr. Sullen, put up; suspend your fury for a minute.

*Squire Sul*. To give you time to invent an excuse!

*Mrs. Sul*. I need none.

*Squire Sul*. No, for I heard every syllable of your discourse.

*Count Bel*. Ah! and begar, I tink the dialogue was vera pretty.

*Mrs. Sul*. Then I suppose, sir, you heard something of your own barbarity?

*Squire Sul*. Barbarity! 'oons, what does the woman call barbarity? Do I ever meddle with you?

*Mrs. Sul*. No.

*Squire Sul*. As for you, sir, I shall take another time.

*Count Bel*. Ah, begar, and so must I.

*Squire Sul*. Look'ee, madam, don't think that my anger proceeds from any concern I have for your honour, but for my own, and if you can contrive any way of being a whore without making me a cuckold, do it and welcome.

*Mrs. Sul*. Sir, I thank you kindly, you would allow me the sin but rob me of the pleasure. No, no, I'm resolved never to venture upon the crime without the satisfaction of seeing you punished for't.

*Squire Sul*. Then will you grant me this, my dear? Let anybody else do you the favour but that Frenchman, for I mortally hate his whole generation.          [*Exit*.

*Count Bel*. Ah, sir, that be ungrateful, for begar, I love some of yours.—Madam——          [*Approaching her*.

*Mrs. Sul.* No, sir.

*Count Bel.* No, sir!· garzoon, madam, I am not your husband.

*Mrs. Sul.* 'Tis time to undeceive you, sir. I believed your addresses to me were no more than an amusement, and I hope you will think the same of my complaisance; and to convince you that you ought, you must know that I brought you hither only to make you instrumental in setting me right with my husband, for he was planted to listen by my appointment.

*Count Bel.* By your appointment?

*Mrs. Sul.* Certainly.

*Count Bel.* And so, madam, while I was telling twenty stories to part you from your husband, begar, I was bringing you together all the while?

*Mrs. Sul.* I ask your pardon, sir, but I hope this will give you a taste of the virtue of the English ladies.

*Count Bel.* Begar, madam, your virtue be vera great, but garzoon, your honeste be vera little.

### *Re-enter* DORINDA.

*Mrs. Sul.* Nay, now, you're angry, sir.

*Count Bel.* Angry!—*Fair Dorinda* [*Sings "Fair Dorinda," the opera tune, and addresses* DORINDA.] Madam, when your ladyship want a fool, send for me. *Fair Dorinda, Revenge, etc.*
[*Exit singing.*

*Mrs. Sul.* There goes the true humour of his nation—resentment with good manners, and the height of anger in a song! Well, sister, you must be judge, for you have heard the trial.

*Dor.* And I bring in my brother guilty.

*Mrs. Sul.* But I must bear the punishment. 'Tis hard, sister.

*Dor.* I own it; but you must have patience.

*Mrs. Sul.* Patience! the cant of custom—Providence sends no evil without a remedy. Should I lie groaning under a yoke I can shake off, I were accessory to my ruin, and my patience were no better than self-murder.

*Dor.* But how can you shake off the yoke? your divisions don't come within the reach of the law for a divorce.

*Mrs. Sul.* Law! what law can search into the remote abyss of nature? what evidence can prove the unaccountable disaffections of wedlock? Can a jury sum up the endless aversions that are rooted in our souls, or can a bench give judgment upon antipathies?

*Dor.* They never pretended, sister; they never meddle, but in case of uncleanness.

*Mrs. Sul.* Uncleanness! O sister! casual violation is a transient injury, and may possibly be repaired, but can radical hatreds be ever reconciled? No, no, sister, nature is the first lawgiver, and when she has set tempers opposite, not all the golden links of wedlock nor iron manacles of law can keep 'em fast.

Wedlock we own ordain'd by Heaven's decree,
But such as Heaven ordain'd it first to be;—
Concurring tempers in the man and wife
As mutual helps to draw the load of life.
View all the works of Providence above,
The stars with harmony and concord move;
View all the works of Providence below,
The fire, the water, earth, and air, we know,
All in one plant agree to make it grow.
Must man, the chiefest work of art divine,
Be doom'd in endless discord to repine?
No, we should injure Heaven by that surmise,
Omnipotence is just, were man but wise.    [*Exeunt.*

## ACT IV

### SCENE I.—*The Gallery in* Lady BOUNTIFUL'S *House*

#### Mrs. SULLEN *discovered alone.*

*Mrs. Sul.* Were I born an humble Turk, where women have
no soul nor property, there I must sit contented. But in
England, a country whose women are its glory, must women be
abused? where women rule, must women be enslaved? Nay,
cheated into slavery, mocked by a promise of comfortable
society into a wilderness of solitude! I dare not keep the
thought about me. Oh, here comes something to divert me.

#### *Enter a* Countrywoman.

*Wom.* I come, an't please your ladyship—you're my Lady
Bountiful, an't ye?

*Mrs. Sul.* Well, good woman, go on.

*Wom.* I have come seventeen long mail to have a cure for my
husband's sore leg.

*Mrs. Sul.* Your husband! what, woman, cure your husband!

*Wom.* Ay, poor man, for his sore leg won't let him stir from
home.

*Mrs. Sul.* There, I confess, you have given me a reason.
Well, good woman, I'll tell you what you must do. You must
lay your husband's leg upon a table, and with a chopping-knife
you must lay it open as broad as you can, then you must take
out the bone, and beat the flesh soundly with a rolling-pin, then
take salt, pepper, cloves, mace, and ginger, some sweet-herbs,
and season it very well, then roll it up like brawn, and put it
into the oven for two hours.

*Wom.* Heavens reward your ladyship!—I have two little babies too that are piteous bad with the graips, an't please ye.

*Mrs. Sul.* Put a little pepper and salt in their bellies, good woman.

*Enter* Lady BOUNTIFUL.

I beg your ladyship's pardon for taking your business out of your hands; I have been a-tampering here a little with one of your patients.

*Lady Boun.* Come, good woman, don't mind this mad creature; I am the person that you want, I suppose. What would you have, woman?

*Mrs. Sul.* She wants something for her husband's sore leg.

*Lady Boun.* What's the matter with his leg, goody?

*Wom.* It come first, as one might say, with a sort of dizziness in his foot, then he had a kind of laziness in his joints, and then his leg broke out, and then it swelled, and then it closed again, and then it broke out again, and then it festered, and then it grew better, and then it grew worse again.

*Mrs. Sul.* Ha! ha! ha!

*Lady Boun.* How can you be merry with the misfortunes of other people?

*Mrs. Sul.* Because my own make me sad, madam.

*Lady Boun.* The worst reason in the world, daughter; your own misfortunes should teach you to pity others.

*Mrs. Sul.* But the woman's misfortunes and mine are nothing alike; her husband is sick, and mine, alas! is in health.

*Lady Boun.* What! would you wish your husband sick?

*Mrs. Sul.* Not of a sore leg, of all things.

*Lady Boun.* Well, good woman, go to the pantry, get your bellyful of victuals, then I'll give you a receipt of diet-drink for your husband. But d'ye hear, goody, you must not let your husband move too much .

*Wom.* No, no, madam, the poor man's inclinable enough to lie still.                    [*Exit.*

*Lady Boun.* Well, daughter Sullen, though you laugh, I have done miracles about the country here with my receipts.

*Mrs. Sul.* Miracles indeed, if they have cured anybody; but I believe, madam, the patient's faith goes farther toward the miracle than your prescription.

*Lady Boun.* Fancy helps in some cases; but there's your husband, who has as little fancy as anybody, I brought him from death's door.

*Mrs. Sul.* I suppose, madam, you made him drink plentifully of ass's milk.

*Enter* DORINDA, *who runs to* Mrs. SULLEN.

*Dor.* News, dear sister! news! news!

*Enter* ARCHER, *running.*

*Arch.* Where, where is my Lady Bountiful?—Pray, which is
the old lady of you three?

*Lady Boun.* I am.

*Arch.* O madam, the fame of your ladyship's charity, goodness, benevolence, skill and ability, have drawn me hither to
implore your ladyship's help in behalf of my unfortunate master,
who is this moment breathing his last.

*Lady Boun.* Your master! where is he?

*Arch.* At your gate, madam. Drawn by the appearance of
your handsome house to view it nearer, and walking up the
avenue within five paces of the court-yard, he was taken ill of a
sudden with a sort of I-know-not-what, but down he fell, and
there he lies.

*Lady Boun.* Here, Scrub! Gipsy! all run, get my easy-chair
down stairs, put the gentleman in it, and bring him in quickly!
quickly!

*Arch.* Heaven will reward your ladyship for this charitable act.

*Lady Boun.* Is your master used to these fits?

*Arch.* O yes, madam, frequently: I have known him have
five or six of a night.

*Lady Boun.* What's his name?

*Arch.* Lord, madam, he's a-dying! a minute's care or neglect
may save or destroy his life.

*Lady Boun.* Ah, poor gentleman!—Come, friend, show me
the way; I'll see him brought in myself.     [*Exit with* ARCHER.

*Dor.* O sister, my heart flutters about strangely! I can
hardly forbear running to his assistance.

*Mrs. Sul.* And I'll lay my life he deserves your assistance
more than he wants it. Did not I tell you that my lord would
find a way to come at you? Love's his distemper, and you
must be the physician; put on all your charms, summon all
your fire into your eyes, plant the whole artillery of your looks
against his breast, and down with him.

*Dor.* O sister! I'm but a young gunner; I shall be afraid to
shoot, for fear the piece should recoil, and hurt myself.

*Mrs. Sul.* Never fear, you shall see me shoot before you, if
you will.

*Dor.* No, no, dear sister; you have missed your mark so
unfortunately, that I shan't care for being instructed by you.

*Enter* AIMWELL *in a chair carried by* ARCHER *and* SCRUB, *and
counterfeiting a swoon;* Lady BOUNTIFUL *and* GIPSY *following.*

*Lady Boun.* Here, here, let's see the hartshorn drops.—
Gipsy, a glass of fair water! His fit's very strong.—Bless me,
how his hands are clinched!

*Arch.* For shame, ladies, what d'ye do? why don't you help
us?—[*To* DORINDA.] Pray, madam, take his hand, and open

it, if you can, whilst I hold his head.   [DORINDA *takes his hand.*

*Dor.* Poor gentleman!—Oh!—he has got my hand within his, and squeezes it unmercifully——

*Lady Boun.* 'Tis the violence of his convulsion, child.

*Arch.* Oh, madam, he's perfectly possessed in these cases—he'll bite if you don't have a care.

*Dor.* Oh, my hand! my hand!

*Lady Boun.* What's the matter with the foolish girl? I have got his hand open, you see, with a great deal of ease.

*Arch.* Ay, but, madam, your daughter's hand is somewhat warmer than your ladyship's, and the heat of it draws the force of the spirits that way.

*Mrs. Sul.* I find, friend, you're very learned in these sorts of fits.

*Arch.* 'Tis no wonder, madam, for I'm often troubled with them myself; I find myself extremely ill at this minute.

[*Looking hard at* Mrs. SULLEN.

*Mrs. Sul.* I fancy I could find a way to cure you.   [*Aside.*

*Lady Boun.* His fit holds him very long.

*Arch.* Longer than usual, madam.—Pray, young lady, open his breast and give him air.

*Lady Boun.* Where did his illness take him first, pray?

*Arch.* To-day at church, madam.

*Lady Boun.* In what manner was he taken?

*Arch.* Very strangely, my lady. He was of a sudden touched with something in his eyes, which, at the first, he only felt, but could not tell whether 'twas pain or pleasure.

*Lady Boun.* Wind, nothing but wind!

*Arch.* By soft degrees it grew and mounted to his brain, there his fancy caught it; there formed it so beautiful, and dressed it up in such gay, pleasing colours, that his transported appetite seized the fair idea, and straight conveyed it to his heart. That hospitable seat of life sent all its sanguine spirits forth to meet, and opened all its sluicy gates to take the stranger in.

*Lady Boun.* Your master should never go without a bottle to smell to.—Oh—he recovers! The lavender-water—some feathers to burn under his nose—Hungary water to rub his temples.—Oh, he comes to himself!—Hem a little, sir, hem.—Gipsy! bring the cordial-water.

[AIMWELL *seems to awake in amaze.*

*Dor.* How d'ye, sir?

*Aim.* Where am I?                                    [*Rising.*

Sure I have pass'd the gulf of silent death,
And now I land on the Elysian shore!—
Behold the goddess of those happy plains,
Fair Proserpine—let me adore thy bright divinity.

[*Kneels to* DORINDA, *and kisses her hand.*

*Mrs. Sul.* So, so, so! I knew where the fit would end!

*Aim.* Eurydice perhaps—

> How could thy Orpheus keep his word,
> And not look back upon thee?
> No treasure but thyself could sure have bribed him
> To look one minute off thee.

*Lady Boun.* Delirious, poor gentleman!
*Arch.* Very delirious, madam, very delirious.
*Aim.* Martin's voice, I think.
*Arch.* Yes, my lord.—How does your lordship?
*Lady Boun.* Lord! did you mind that, girls?
[Aside to Mrs. SULLEN and DORINDA.

*Aim.* Where am I?
*Arch.* In very good hands, sir. You were taken just now with one of your old fits, under the trees, just by this good lady's house; her ladyship had you taken in, and has miraculously brought you to yourself, as you see.
*Aim.* I am so confounded with shame, madam, that I can now only beg pardon; and refer my acknowledgments for your ladyship's care till an opportunity offers of making some amends. I dare be no longer troublesome.—Martin! give two guineas to the servants. [*Going.*
*Dor.* Sir, you may catch cold by going so soon into the air; you don't look, sir, as if you were perfectly recovered.

[*Here* ARCHER *talks to* Lady BOUNTIFUL *in dumb show.*
*Aim.* That I shall never be, madam; my present illness is so rooted that I must expect to carry it to my grave.
*Mrs. Sul.* Don't despair, sir; I have known several in your distemper shake it off with a fortnight's physic.
*Lady Boun.* Come, sir, your servant has been telling me that you're apt to relapse if you go into the air: your good manners shan't get the better of ours—you shall sit down again, sir. Come, sir, we don't mind ceremonies in the country—here, sir, my service t'ye.—You shall taste my water; 'tis a cordial I can assure you, and of my own making—drink it off, sir.—[AIMWELL *drinks.*] And how d'ye find yourself now, sir?
*Aim.* Somewhat better—though very faint still.
*Lady Boun.* Ay, ay, people are always faint after these fits.—Come, girls, you shall show the gentleman the house.—'Tis but an old family building, sir; but you had better walk about, and cool by degrees, than venture immediately into the air. You'll find some tolerable pictures.—Dorinda, show the gentleman the way. I must go to the poor woman below. [*Exit.*
*Dor.* This way, sir.
*Aim.* Ladies, shall I beg leave for my servant to wait on you, for he understands pictures very well?
*Mrs. Sul.* Sir, we understand originals as well as he does pictures, so he may come along.

[*Exeunt all but* SCRUB, AIMWELL *leading* DORINDA.

*Enter* FOIGARD.

*Foi.* Save you, Master Scrub!

*Scrub.* Sir, I won't be saved your way—I hate a priest, I abhor the French, and I defy the devil. Sir, I'm a bold Briton, and will spill the last drop of my blood to keep out popery and slavery.

*Foi.* Master Scrub, you would put me down in politics, and so I would be speaking with Mrs. Shipsy.

*Scrub.* Good Mr. Priest, you can't speak with her; she's sick, sir, she's gone abroad, sir, she's—dead two months ago, sir.

*Re-enter* GIPSY.

*Gip.* How now, impudence! how dare you talk so saucily to the doctor?—Pray, sir, don't take it ill; for the common people of England are not so civil to strangers, as——

*Scrub.* You lie! you lie! 'tis the common people that are civilest to strangers.

*Gip.* Sirrah, I have a good mind to—get you out, I say!

*Scrub.* I won't.

*Gip.* You won't, sauce-box!—Pray, doctor, what is the captain's name that came to your inn last night?

*Scrub.* [*aside*]. The captain! ah, the devil, there she hampers me again; the captain has me on one side and the priest on t'other: so between the gown and the sword, I have a fine time on't.—But, *Cedunt arma togæ.*          [*Going.*

*Gip.* What, sirrah, won't you march?

*Scrub.* No, my dear, I won't march—but I'll walk.—[*Aside.*] And I'll make bold to listen a little too.

                    [*Goes behind the side-scene and listens.*

*Gip.* Indeed, doctor, the Count has been barbarously treated, that's the truth on't.

*Foi.* Ah, Mrs. Gipsy, upon my shoul, now, gra, his complainings would mollify the marrow in your bones, and move the bowels of your commiseration! He veeps, and he dances, and he fistles, and he swears, and he laughs, and he stamps, and he sings; in conclusion, joy, he's afflicted *à-la-Française,* and a stranger would not know whider to cry or to laugh with him.

*Gip.* What would you have me do, doctor?

*Foi.* Noting, joy, but only hide the Count in Mrs. Sullen's closet when it is dark.

*Gip.* Nothing! is that nothing? it would be both a sin and a shame, doctor.

*Foi.* Here is twenty louis-d'ors, joy, for your shame; and I will give you an absolution for the shin.

*Gip.* But won't that money look like a bribe?

*Foi.* Dat is according as you shall tauk it. If you receive the money beforehand, 'twill be *logicè,* a bribe; but if you stay till afterwards, 'twill be only a gratification.

*Gip.* Well, doctor, I'll take it *logicè*. But what must I do with my conscience, sir?

*Foi.* Leave dat wid me, joy; I am your priest, gra; and your conscience is under my hands.

*Gip.* But should I put the Count into the closet——

*Foi.* Vel, is dere any shin for a man's being in a closhet? one may go to prayers in a closhet.

*Gip.* But if the lady should come into her chamber, and go to bed?

*Foi.* Vel, and is dere any shin in going to bed, joy?

*Gip.* Ay, but if the parties should meet, doctor?

*Foi.* Vel den—the parties must be responsible. Do you be gone after putting the Count into the closhet; and leave the shins wid themselves. I will come with the Count to instruct you in your chamber.

*Gip.* Well, doctor, your religion is so pure! Methinks I'm so easy after an absolution, and can sin afresh with so much security, that I'm resolved to die a martyr to't. Here's the key of the garden door, come in the back way when 'tis late, I'll be ready to receive you; but don't so much as whisper, only take hold of my hand; I'll lead you, and do you lead the Count, and follow me.                                                               [*Exeunt.*

*Scrub* [*coming forward*]. What witchcraft now have these two imps of the devil been a-hatching here? " There's twenty louis-d'ors "; I heard that, and saw the purse.—But I must give room to my betters.                                                     [*Exit.*

*Re-enter* AIMWELL, *leading* DORINDA, *and making love in dumb show ;* MRS. SULLEN *and* ARCHER *following.*

*Mrs. Sul.* [*to* ARCHER]. Pray, sir, how d'ye like that piece?

*Arch.* Oh, 'tis Leda! You find, madam, how Jupiter comes disguised to make love——

*Mrs. Sul.* But what think you there of Alexander's battles?

*Arch.* We only want a Le Brun, madam, to draw greater battles, and a greater general of our own. The Danube, madam, would make a greater figure in a picture than the Granicus; and we have our Ramillies to match their Arbela.

*Mrs. Sul.* Pray, sir, what head is that in the corner there?

*Arch.* O madam, 'tis poor Ovid in his exile.

*Mrs. Sul.* What was he banished for?

*Arch.* His ambitious love, madam.—[*Bowing.*] His misfortune touches me.

*Mrs. Sul.* Was he successful in his amours?

*Arch.* There he has left us in the dark. He was too much a gentleman to tell.

*Mrs. Sul.* If he were secret, I pity him.

*Arch.* And if he were successful, I envy him.

*Mrs. Sul.* How d'ye like that Venus over the chimney?

*Arch.* Venus! I protest, madam, I took it for your picture; but now I look again, 'tis not handsome enough.

*Mrs. Sul.* Oh, what a charm is flattery! If you would see my picture, there it is over that cabinet. How d'ye like it?

*Arch.* I must admire anything, madam, that has the least resemblance of you. But, methinks, madam—[*He looks at the picture and* Mrs. SULLEN *three or four times, by turns.*] Pray, madam, who drew it?

*Mrs. Sul.* A famous hand, sir.

[*Here* AIMWELL *and* DORINDA *go off.*

*Arch.* A famous hand, madam!—Your eyes, indeed, are featured there; but where's the sparking moisture, shining fluid, in which they swim? The picture, indeed, has your dimples; but where's the swarm of killing Cupids that should ambush there? The lips too are figured out; but where's the carnation dew, the pouting ripeness that tempts the taste in the original?

*Mrs. Sul.* Had it been my lot to have matched with such a man!                       [*Aside.*

*Arch.* Your breasts too—presumptuous man! what, paint Heaven!—Apropos, madam, in the very next picture is Salmoneus, that was struck dead with lightning, for offering to imitate Jove's thunder; I hope you served the painter so, madam?

*Mrs. Sul.* Had my eyes the power of thunder, they should employ their lightning better.

*Arch.* There's the finest bed in that room, madam! I suppose 'tis your ladyship's bedchamber.

*Mrs. Sul.* And what then, sir?

*Arch.* I think the quilt is the richest that ever I saw. I can't at this distance, madam, distinguish the figures of the embroidery; will you give me leave, madam?

*Mrs. Sul.* [*aside*]. The devil take his impudence!—Sure, if I gave him an opportunity, he durst not offer it?—I have a great mind to try.—[*Going : returns.*] 'Sdeath, what am I doing?—And alone, too!—Sister! sister!            [*Runs out.*

*Arch.* I'll follow her close—

For where a Frenchman durst attempt to storm,
A Briton sure may well the work perform.       [*Going.*

### *Re-enter* SCRUB.

*Scrub.* Martin! brother Martin!

*Arch.* O brother Scrub, I beg your pardon, I was not a-going: here's a guinea my master ordered you.

*Scrub.* A guinea! hi! hi! hi! a guinea! eh—by this light it is a guinea! But I suppose you expect one-and-twenty shillings in change?

*Arch.* Not at all; I have another for Gipsy.

*Scrub.* A guinea for her! faggot and fire for the witch! Sir, give me that guinea, and I'll discover a plot.

*Arch.* A plot!

*Scrub.* Ay, sir, a plot, and a horrid plot! First, it must be a plot, because there's a woman in't: secondly, it must be a plot, because there's a priest in't: thirdly, it must be a plot, because there's French gold in't: and fourthly, it must be a plot, because I don't know what to make on't.

*Arch.* Nor anybody else, I'm afraid, brother Scrub.

*Scrub.* Truly, I'm afraid so too; for where there's a priest and a woman, there's always a mystery and a riddle. This I know, that here has been the doctor with a temptation in one hand and an absolution in the other, and Gipsy has sold herself to the devil; I saw the price paid down, my eyes shall take their oath on't.

*Arch.* And is all this bustle about Gipsy?

*Scrub.* That's not all; I could hear but a word here and there; but I remember they mentioned a Count, a closet, a back-door, and a key.

*Arch.* The Count!—Did you hear nothing of Mrs. Sullen?

*Scrub.* I did hear some word that sounded that way; but whether it was Sullen or Dorinda, I could not distinguish.

*Arch.* You have told this matter to nobody, brother?

*Scrub.* Told! no, sir, I thank you for that; I'm resolved never to speak one word *pro* nor *con*, till we have a peace.

*Arch.* You're i' the right, brother Scrub. Here's a treaty afoot between the Count and the lady: the priest and the chambermaid are the plenipotentiaries. It shall go hard but I find a way to be included in the treaty.—Where's the doctor now?

*Scrub.* He and Gipsy are this moment devouring my lady's marmalade in the closet.

*Aim.* [*from without*]. Martin! Martin!

*Arch.* I come, sir, I come.

*Scrub.* But you forget the other guinea, brother Martin.

*Arch.* Here, I give it with all my heart.

*Scrub.* And I take it with all my soul.—[*Exit* ARCHER.] Ecod, I'll spoil your plotting, Mrs. Gipsy! and if you should set the captain upon me, these two guineas will buy me off.    [*Exit.*

*Re-enter* Mrs. SULLEN *and* DORINDA, *meeting.*

*Mrs. Sul.* Well, sister!

*Dor.* And well, sister!

*Mrs. Sul.* What's become of my lord?

*Dor.* What's become of his servant?

*Mrs. Sul.* Servant! he's a prettier fellow, and a finer gentleman by fifty degrees, than his master.

*Dor.* O' my conscience, I fancy you could beg that fellow at the gallows-foot!

*Mrs. Sul.* O' my conscience I could, provided I could put a friend of yours in his room.

*Dor.* You desired me, sister, to leave you, when you transgressed the bounds of honour.

*Mrs. Sul.* Thou dear censorious country girl! what dost mean? You can't think of the man without the bedfellow, I find.

*Dor.* I don't find anything unnatural in that thought: while the mind is conversant with flesh and blood, it must conform to the humours of the company.

*Mrs. Sul.* How a little love and good company improves a woman! Why, child, you begin to live—you never spoke before.

*Dor.* Because I was never spoke to.—My lord has told me that I have more wit and beauty than any of my sex; and truly I begin to think the man is sincere.

*Mrs. Sul.* You're in the right, Dorinda; pride is the life of a woman, and flattery is our daily bread; and she's a fool that won't believe a man there, as much as she that believes him in anything else. But I'll lay you a guinea that I had finer things said to me than you had.

*Dor.* Done! What did your fellow say to ye?

*Mrs. Sul.* My fellow took the picture of Venus for mine.

*Dor.* But my lover took me for Venus herself.

*Mrs. Sul.* Common cant! Had my spark called me a Venus directly, I should have believed him a footman in good earnest.

*Dor.* But my lover was upon his knees to me.

*Mrs. Sul.* And mine was upon his tiptoes to me.

*Dor.* Mine vowed to die for me.

*Mrs. Sul.* Mine swore to die with me.

*Dor.* Mine spoke the softest moving things.

*Mrs. Sul.* Mine had his moving things too.

*Dor.* Mine kissed my hand ten thousand times.

*Mrs. Sul.* Mine has all that pleasure to come.

*Dor.* Mine offered marriage.

*Mrs. Sul.* O Lard! d'ye call that a moving thing?

*Dor.* The sharpest arrow in his quiver, my dear sister! Why, my ten thousand pounds may lie brooding here this seven years, and hatch nothing at last but some ill-natured clown like yours. Whereas, if I marry my Lord Aimwell, there will be title, place, and precedence, the Park, the play, and the drawing-room, splendour, equipage, noise, and flambeaux.—*Hey, my Lady Aimwell's servants there!—Lights, lights to the stairs!—My Lady Aimwell's coach put forward!—Stand by, make room for her ladyship!*—Are not these things moving?—What! melancholy of a sudden?

*Mrs. Sul.* Happy, happy sister! your angel has been watchful for your happiness, whilst mine has slept regardless of his charge. Long smiling years of circling joys for you, but not one hour for me!                    [*Weeps.*

*Dor.* Come, my dear, we'll talk of something else.

*Mrs. Sul.* O Dorinda! I own myself a woman, full of my sex, a gentle, generous soul, easy and yielding to soft desires; a spacious heart, where love and all his train might lodge. And must the fair apartment of my breast be made a stable for a brute to lie in?

*Dor.* Meaning your husband, I suppose?

*Mrs. Sul.* Husband! no; even husband is too soft a name the him.—But, come, I expect my brother here to-night or to-morrow; he was abroad when my father married me; perhaps he'll find a way to make me easy.

*Dor.* Will you promise not to make yourself easy in the meantime with my lord's friend?

*Mrs. Sul.* You mistake me, sister. It happens with us as among the men, the greatest talkers are the greatest cowards? and there's a reason for it; those spirits evaporate in prattle, which might do more mischief if they took another course.— Though, to confess the truth, I do love that fellow;—and if I met him dressed as he should be, and I undressed as I should be —look'ee, sister, I have no supernatural gifts—I can't swear I could resist the temptation; though I can safely promise to avoid it; and that's as much as the best of us can do. [*Exeunt.*

SCENE II.—*A Room in* BONIFACE'S *Inn*

*Enter* AIMWELL *and* ARCHER *laughing.*

*Arch.* And the awkward kindness of the good motherly old gentlewoman——

*Aim.* And the coming easiness of the young one—'Sdeath, 'tis pity to deceive her!

*Arch.* Nay, if you adhere to these principles, stop where you are.

*Aim.* I can't stop; for I love her to distraction.

*Arch.* 'Sdeath, if you love her a hair's-breadth beyond dis-cretion, you must go no further.

*Aim.* Well, well, anything to deliver us from sauntering away our idle evenings at White's, Tom's, or Will's, and be stinted to bare looking at our old acquaintance, the cards; because our impotent pockets can't afford us a guinea for the mercenary drabs.

*Arch.* Or be obliged to some purse-proud coxcomb for a scandalous bottle, where we must not pretend to our share of the discourse, because we can't pay our club o' th' reckoning.— Damn it, I had rather sponge upon Morris, and sup upon a dish of bohea scored behind the door!

*Aim.* And there expose our want of sense by talking criticisms, as we should our want of money by railing at the government.

*Arch.* Or be obliged to sneak into the side-box, and between both houses steal two acts of a play, and because we han't money to see the other three, we come away discontented, and damn the whole five.

*Aim.* And ten thousand such rascally tricks—had we outlived our fortunes among our acquaintance.—But now——

*Arch.* Ay, now is the time to prevent all this:—strike while the iron is hot.—This priest is the luckiest part of our adventure; he shall marry you, and pimp for me.

*Aim.* But I should not like a woman that can be so fond of a Frenchman.

*Arch.* Alas, sir! Necessity has no law. The lady may be in distress; perhaps she has a confounded husband, and her revenge may carry her farther than her love. Egad, I have so good an opinion of her, and of myself, that I begin to fancy strange things: and we must say this for the honour of our women, and indeed of ourselves, that they do stick to their men as they do to their *Magna Charta*. If the plot lies as I suspect, I must put on the gentleman.—But here comes the doctor—I shall be ready.                                                                        [*Exit.*

### Enter FOIGARD.

*Foi.* Sauve you, noble friend.

*Aim.* O sir, your servant! Pray, doctor, may I crave your name?

*Foi.* Fat naam is upon me? My naam is Foigard, joy.

*Aim.* Foigard! a very good name for a clergyman. Pray, Doctor Foigard, were you ever in Ireland?

*Foi.* Ireland! no, joy. Fat sort of plaace is dat saam Ireland? Dey say de people are catched dere when dey are young.

*Aim.* And some of 'em when they are old:—as for example.— [*Takes* FOIGARD *by the shoulder.*] Sir, I arrest you as a traitor against the government; you're a subject of England, and this morning showed me a commission, by which you served as chaplain in the French army. This is death by our law, and your reverence must hang for it.

*Foi.* Upon my shoul, noble friend, dis is strange news you tell me! Fader Foigard a subject of England! de son of a burgo-master of Brussels, a subject of England! ubooboo——

*Aim.* The son of a bog-trotter in Ireland! Sir, your tongue will condemn you before any bench in the kingdom.

*Foi.* And is my tongue all your evidensh, joy?

*Aim.* That's enough.

*Foi.* No, no, joy, for I vill never spake English no more.

*Aim.* Sir, I have other evidence.—Here, Martin!

### Re-enter ARCHER.

You know this fellow?

*Arch.* [*in a brogue*]. Saave you, my dear cussen, how does your health?

*Foi.* [*aside*]. Ah! upon my shoul dere is my countryman, and his brogue will hang mine.—[*To* ARCHER.] *Mynheer, Ick wet neat watt hey zacht, Ick universton ewe neat, sacramant!*

*Aim.* Altering your language won't do, sir; this fellow knows your person, and will swear to your face.

*Foi.* Faash! fey, is dere a brogue upon my faash too?

*Arch.* Upon my soulvation dere ish, joy!—But cussen Mackshane, vil you not put a remembrance upon me?

*Foi.* Mackshane! by St. Paatrick, dat ish my naam shure enough!                                                                    [*Aside.*

*Aim.* I fancy, Archer, you have it.          [*Aside to* ARCHER.

*Foi.* The devil hang you, joy! by fat acquaintance are you my cussen?

*Arch.* Oh, de devil hang yourshelf, joy! you know we were little boys togeder upon de school, and your foster-moder's son was married upon my nurse's chister, joy, and so we are Irish cussens.

*Foi.* De devil taake de relation! vel, joy, and fat school was it?

*Arch.* I tinks it vas—aay—'twas Tipperary.

*Foi.* No, no, joy; it vas Kilkenny.

*Aim.* That's enough for us—self-confession,—come, sir, we must deliver you into the hands of the next magistrate.

*Arch.* He sends you to gaol, you're tried next assizes, and away you go swing into purgatory.

*Foi.* And is it so wid you, cussen?

*Arch.* It vil be sho wid you, cussen, if you don't immediately confess the secret between you and Mrs. Gipsy. Look'ee, sir, the gallows or the secret, take your choice.

*Foi.* The gallows! upon my shoul I hate that saam gallow, for it is a diseash dat is fatal to our family. Vel, den, dere is nothing, shentlemens, but Mrs. Shullen would spaak wid the Count in her chamber at midnight, and dere is no haarm, joy, for I am to conduct the Count to the plash, myshelf.

*Arch.* As I guessed.—Have you communicated the matter to the Count?

*Foi.* I have not sheen him since.

*Arch.* Right again! Why then, doctor—you shall conduct me to the lady instead of the Count.

*Foi.* Fat, my cussen to the lady! upon my shoul, gra, dat is too much upon the brogue.

*Arch.* Come, come, doctor; consider we have got a rope about your neck, and if you offer to squeak, we'll stop your windpipe, most certainly: we shall have another job for you in a day or two, I hope.

*Aim.* Here's company coming this way; let's into my chamber and there concert our affairs farther.

*Arch.* Come, my dear cussen, come along.          [*Exeunt.*

*Enter* BONIFACE, HOUNSLOW, *and* BAGSHOT *at one door,* GIBBET *at the opposite.*

*Gib.* Well, gentlemen, 'tis a fine night for our enterprise.

*Houn.* Dark as hell.

*Bag.* And blows like the devil; our landlord here has showed us the window where we must break in, and tells us the plate stands in the wainscot cupboard in the parlour.

*Bon.* Ay, ay, Mr. Bagshot, as the saying is, knives and forks, and cups and cans, and tumblers and tankards. There's one tankard, as the saying is, that's near upon as big as me; it was a present to the squire from his godmother, and smells of nutmeg and toast like an East-India ship.

*Houn.* Then you say we must divide at the stairhead?

*Bon.* Yes, Mr. Hounslow, as the saying is. At one end of that gallery lies my Lady Bountiful and her daughter, and at the other Mrs. Sullen. As for the squire——

*Gib.* He's safe enough, I have fairly entered him, and he's more than half seas over already. But such a parcel of scoundrels are got about him now, that, egad, I was ashamed to be seen in their company.

*Bon.* 'Tis now twelve, as the saying is—gentlemen, you must set out at one.

*Gib.* Hounslow, do you and Bagshot see our arms fixed, and I'll come to you presently.

*Houn., Bag.* We will. [*Exeunt.*

*Gib.* Well, my dear Bonny, you assure me that Scrub is a coward?

*Bon.* A chicken, as the saying is. You'll have no creature to deal with but the ladies.

*Gib.* And I can assure you, friend, there's a great deal of address and good manners in robbing a lady; I am the most a gentleman that way that ever travelled the road.—But, my dear Bonny, this prize will be a galleon, a Vigo business.—I warrant you we shall bring off three or four thousand pounds.

*Bon.* In plate, jewels, and money, as the saying is, you may.

*Gib.* Why then, Tyburn, I defy thee! I'll get up to town, sell off my horse and arms, buy myself some pretty employment in the household, and be as snug and as honest as any courtier of 'em all.

*Bon.* And what think you then of my daughter Cherry for a wife?

*Gib.* Look'ee, my dear Bonny—Cherry *is the Goddess I adore,* as the song goes; but it is a maxim, that man and wife should never have it in their power to hang one another; for if they should, the Lord have mercy on 'um both! [*Exeunt.*

## ACT V

### SCENE I.—*A Room in* BONIFACE'S *Inn*

*Knocking without, enter* BONIFACE.

*Bon.* Coming! Coming!—A coach and six foaming horses at this time o' night! some great man, as the saying is, for he scorns to travel with other people.

#### *Enter* Sir CHARLES FREEMAN.

*Sir Chas.* What, fellow! a public house, and abed when other people sleep?

*Bon.* Sir, I an't abed, as the saying is.

*Sir Chas.* Is Mr. Sullen's family abed, think'ee?

*Bon.* All but the squire himself, sir, as the saying is; he's in the house.

*Sir Chas.* What company has he?

*Bon.* Why, sir, there's the constable, Mr. Gage the exciseman, the hunch-backed barber, and two or three other gentlemen.

*Sir Chas.* I find my sister's letters gave me the true picture of her spouse.                                    [*Aside.*

#### *Enter* Squire SULLEN, *drunk.*

*Bon.* Sir, here's the squire.

*Squire Sul.* The puppies left me asleep—Sir!

*Sir Chas.* Well, sir.

*Squire Sul.* Sir, I am an unfortunate man—I have three thousand pounds a year, and I can't get a man to drink a cup of ale with me.

*Sir Chas.* That's very hard.

*Squire Sul.* Ay, sir; and unless you have pity upon me, and smoke one pipe with me, I must e'en go home to my wife, and I had rather go to the devil by half.

*Sir Chas.* But I presume, sir, you won't see your wife to-night; she'll be gone to bed. You don't use to lie with your wife in that pickle?

*Squire Sul.* What! not lie with my wife! why, sir, do you take me for an atheist or a rake?

*Sir Chas.* If you hate her, sir, I think you had better lie from her.

*Squire Sul.* I think so too, friend. But I'm a justice of peace, and must do nothing against the law.

*Sir Chas.* Law! as I take it, Mr. Justice, nobody observes law for law's sake, only for the good of those for whom it was made.

*Squire Sul.* But, if the law orders me to send you to gaol, you must lie there, my friend.

*Sir Chas.* Not unless I commit a crime to deserve it.

*Squire Sul.* A crime? 'oons, an't I married?

*Sir Chas.* Nay, sir, if you call marriage a crime, you must disown it for a law.

*Squire Sul.* Eh! I must be acquainted with you, sir.—But, sir, I should be very glad to know the truth of this matter.

*Sir Chas.* Truth, sir, is a profound sea, and few there be that dare wade deep enough to find out the bottom on't. Besides, sir, I'm afraid the line of your understanding mayn't be long enough.

*Squire Sul.* Look'ee, sir, I have nothing to say to your sea of truth, but, if a good parcel of land can entitle a man to a little truth, I have as much as any He in the country.

*Bon.* I never heard your worship, as the saying is, talk so much before.

*Squire Sul.* Because I never met with a man that I liked before.

*Bon.* Pray, sir, as the saying is, let me ask you one question: are not man and wife one flesh?

*Sir Chas.* You and your wife, Mr. Guts, may be one flesh, because ye are nothing else; but rational creatures have minds that must be united.

*Squire Sul.* Minds!

*Sir Chas.* Ay, minds, sir; don't you think that the mind takes place of the body?

*Squire Sul.* In some people.

*Sir Chas.* Then the interest of the master must be consulted before that of his servant.

*Squire Sul.* Sir, you shall dine with me to-morrow!—'Oons, I always thought that we were naturally one.

*Sir Chas.* Sir, I know that my two hands are naturally one, because they love one another, kiss one another, help one another in all the actions of life; but I could not say so much if they were always at cuffs.

*Squire Sul.* Then 'tis plain that we are two.

*Sir Chas.* Why don't you part with her, sir?

*Squire Sul.* Will you take her, sir?

*Sir Chas.* With all my heart.

*Squire Sul.* You shall have her to-morrow morning, and a venison-pasty into the bargain.

*Sir Chas.* You'll let me have her fortune too?

*Squire Sul.* Fortune! why, sir, I have no quarrel at her fortune: I only hate the woman, sir, and none but the woman shall go.

*Sir Chas.* But her fortune, sir——

*Squire Sul.* Can you play at whisk, sir?

*Sir Chas.* No, truly, sir.

*Squire Sul.* Nor at all-fours?

*Sir Chas.* Neither.

*Squire Sul.* [*aside*]. 'Oons! where was this man bred?—
[*Aloud.*] Burn me, sir! I can't go home, 'tis but two o'clock.

*Sir Chas.* For half an hour, sir, if you please; but you must
consider 'tis late.

*Squire Sul.* Late! that's the reason I can't go to bed.—
Come, sir!                                            [*Exeunt.*

*Enter* CHERRY, *runs across the stage, and knocks at* AIMWELL'S
*chamber door. Enter* AIMWELL *in his nightcap and gown.*

*Aim.* What's the matter? you tremble, child; you're frighted.

*Cher.* No wonder, sir—But, in short, sir, this very minute a
gang of rogues are gone to rob my Lady Bountiful's house.

*Aim.* How!

*Cher.* I dogged 'em to the very door, and left 'em breaking in.

*Aim.* Have you alarmed anybody else with the news?

*Cher.* No, no, sir, I wanted to have discovered the whole plot,
and twenty other things, to your man Martin; but I have
searched the whole house, and can't find him: where is he?

*Aim.* No matter, child; will you guide me immediately to
the house?

*Cher.* With all my heart, sir; my Lady Bountiful is my
godmother, and I love Mrs. Dorinda so well——

*Aim.* Dorinda! the name inspires me, the glory and the
danger shall be all my own.—Come, my life, let me but get my
sword.                                               [*Exeunt.*

SCENE II.—*A Bedchamber in* Lady BOUNTIFUL'S *House*

Mrs. SULLEN *and* DORINDA *discovered undressed;
a table and lights.*

*Dor.* 'Tis very late, sister, no news of your spouse yet?

*Mrs. Sul.* No, I'm condemned to be alone till towards four,
and then perhaps I may be executed with his company.

*Dor.* Well, my dear, I'll leave you to your rest; you'll go
directly to bed, I suppose?

*Mrs. Sul.* I don't know what to do.—Heigh-ho!

*Dor.* That's a desiring sigh, sister.

*Mrs. Sul.* This is a languishing hour, sister.

*Dor.* And might prove a critical minute if the pretty fellow
were here.

*Mrs. Sul.* Here! what, in my bedchamber at two o'clock
o' th' morning, I undressed, the family asleep, my hated husband
abroad, and my lovely fellow at my feet!—O gad, sister!

*Dor.* Thoughts are free, sister, and them I allow you.—So,
my dear, good night.

*Mrs. Sul.* A good rest to my dear Dorinda!—[*Exit* DORINDA.]
Thoughts free! are they so? Why, then suppose him here,
dressed like a youthful, gay, and burning bridegroom,
                    [*Here* ARCHER *steals out of a closet behind.*
with tongue enchanting, eyes bewitching, knees imploring.—
[*Turns a little on one side and sees* ARCHER *in the posture she
describes.*]—Ah!—[*Shrieks, and runs to the other side of the stage.*]
Have my thoughts raised a spirit?—What are you, sir, a man
or a devil?

*Arch.* A man, a man, madam.                    [*Rising.*
*Mrs. Sul.* How shall I be sure of it?
*Arch.* Madam, I'll give you demonstration this minute.
                    [*Takes her hand.*
*Mrs. Sul.* What, sir! do you intend to be rude?
*Arch.* Yes, madam, if you please.
*Mrs. Sul.* In the name of wonder, whence came ye?
*Arch.* From the skies, madam—I'm a Jupiter in love, and you
shall be my Alcmena.
*Mrs. Sul.* How came you in?
*Arch.* I flew in at the window, madam; your cousin Cupid
lent me his wings, and your sister Venus opened the casement.
*Mrs. Sul.* I'm struck dumb with admiration!
*Arch.* And I—with wonder!        [*Looks passionately at her.*
*Mrs. Sul.* What will become of me?
*Arch.* How beautiful she looks!—The teeming jolly Spring
smiles in her blooming face, and, when she was conceived, her
mother smelt to roses, looked on lilies—

Lilies unfold their white, their fragrant charms,
When the warm sun thus darts into their arms.

                    [*Runs to her.*
*Mrs. Sul.* Ah!                    [*Shrieks.*
*Arch.* 'Oons, madam, what d'ye mean? you'll raise the
house.
*Mrs. Sul.* Sir, I'll wake the dead before I bear this!—What!
approach me with the freedom of a keeper! I'm glad on't, your
impudence has cured me.
*Arch.* If this be impudence—[*Kneels.*] I leave to your partial
self; no panting pilgrim, after a tedious, painful voyage, e'er
bowed before his saint with more devotion.
*Mrs. Sul.* [*aside*]. Now, now, I'm ruined if he kneels!—
[*Aloud.*] Rise, thou prostrate engineer, not all thy undermining
skill shall reach my heart.—Rise, and know I am a woman
without my sex; I can love to all the tenderness of wishes, sighs,
and tears—but go no farther.—Still, to convince you that I'm
more than woman, I can speak my frailty, confess my weakness
even for you, but——
*Arch.* For me!                    [*Going to lay hold on her.*
*Mrs. Sul.* Hold, sir! build not upon that; for my most mortal

hatred follows if you disobey what I command you now.—
Leave me this minute.—[*Aside.*] If he denies I'm lost.

*Arch.* Then you'll promise——

*Mrs. Sul.* Anything another time.

*Arch.* When shall I come?

*Mrs. Sul.* To-morrow—when you will.

*Arch.* Your lips must seal the promise.

*Mrs. Sul.* Psha!

*Arch.* They must! they must!—[*Kisses her.*] Raptures and
paradise!—And why not now, my angel? the time, the place,
silence, and secrecy, all conspire. And the now conscious stars
have preordained this moment for my happiness.

[*Takes her in his arms.*

*Mrs. Sul.* You will not! cannot, sure!

*Arch.* If the sun rides fast, and disappoints not mortals of
to-morrow's dawn, this night shall crown my joys.

*Mrs. Sul.* My sex's pride assist me!

*Arch.* My sex's strength help me!

*Mrs. Sul.* You shall kill me first!

*Arch.* I'll die with you. [*Carrying her off.*

*Mrs. Sul.* Thieves! thieves! murder!

*Enter* SCRUB *in his breeches, and one shoe.*

*Scrub.* Thieves! thieves! murder! popery!

*Arch.* Ha! the very timorous stag will kill in rutting time.

[*Draws, and offers to stab* SCRUB.

*Scrub* [*kneeling*]. O pray, sir, spare all I have, and take my life!

*Mrs. Sul.* [*holding* ARCHER's *hand*]. What does the fellow
mean?

*Scrub.* O madam, down upon your knees, your marrow-bones!
—he's one of 'um.

*Arch.* Of whom?

*Scrub.* One of the rogues—I beg your pardon, one of the
honest gentlemen that just now are broke into the house.

*Arch.* How!

*Mrs. Sul.* I hope you did not come to rob me?

*Arch.* Indeed I did, madam, but I would have taken nothing
but what you might ha' spared; but your crying "Thieves"
has waked this dreaming fool, and so he takes 'em for granted.

*Scrub.* Granted! 'tis granted, sir; take all we have.

*Mrs. Sul.* The fellow looks as if he were broke out of Bedlam.

*Scrub.* 'Oons, madam, they're broke into the house with fire
and sword! I saw them, heard them; they'll be here this
minute.

*Arch.* What, thieves!

*Scrub.* Under favour, sir, I think so.

*Mrs. Sul.* What shall we do, sir?

*Arch.* Madam, I wish your ladyship a good night.

*Mrs. Sul.* Will you leave me?

*Arch.* Leave you! Lord, madam, did not you command me to be gone just now, upon pain of your immortal hatred?

*Mrs. Sul.* Nay, but pray, sir——        [*Takes hold of him.*

*Arch.* Ha! ha! ha! now comes my turn to be ravished.— You see now, madam, you must use men one way or other; but take this by the way, good madam, that none but a fool will give you the benefit of his courage, unless you'll take his love along with it.—How are they armed, friend?

*Scrub.* With sword and pistol, sir.

*Arch.* Hush!—I see a dark lantern coming through the gallery.—Madam, be assured I will protect you, or lose my life.

*Mrs. Sul.* Your life! no, sir, they can rob me of nothing that I value half so much; therefore now, sir, let me entreat you to be gone.

*Arch.* No, madam, I'll consult my own safety for the sake of yours; I'll work by stratagem. Have you courage enough to stand the appearance of 'em?

*Mrs. Sul.* Yes, yes, since I have 'scaped your hands, I can face anything.

*Arch.* Come hither, brother Scrub! don't you know me?

*Scrub.* Eh, my dear brother, let me kiss thee.

[*Kisses* ARCHER.

*Arch.* This way—here——

[ARCHER *and* SCRUB *hide behind the bed.*

*Enter* GIBBET, *with a dark lantern in one hand, and a pistol in the other.*

*Gib.* Ay, ay, this is the chamber, and the lady alone.

*Mrs. Sul.* Who are you, sir? what would you have? d'ye come to rob me?

*Gib.* Rob you! alack a day, madam, I'm only a younger brother, madam; and so, madam, if you make a noise, I'll shoot you through the head; but don't be afraid, madam.— [*Laying his lantern and pistol upon the table.*] These rings, madam; don't be concerned, madam, I have a profound respect for you, madam; your keys, madam; don't be frighted, madam, I'm the most of a gentleman.—[*Searching her pockets.*] This necklace, madam; I never was rude to any lady;—I have a veneration—for this necklace——

[*Here* ARCHER *having come round, and seized the pistol, takes* GIBBET *by the collar, trips up his heels, and claps the pistol to his breast.*

*Arch.* Hold, profane villain, and take the reward of thy sacrilege!

*Gib.* Oh! pray, sir, don kill me; I an't prepared.

*Arch.* How many is there of 'em, Scrub?

*Scrub.* Five-and-forty, sir.

*Arch.* Then I must kill the villain, to have him out of the way.

*Gib.* Hold, hold, sir, we are but three, upon my honour.

*Arch.* Scrub, will you undertake to secure him?

*Scrub.* Not I, sir; kill him, kill him!

*Arch.* Run to Gipsy's chamber, there you'll find the doctor; bring him hither presently.—[*Exit* SCRUB, *running.*] Come, rogue, if you have a short prayer, say it.

*Gib.* Sir, I have no prayer at all; the government has provided a chaplain to say prayers for us on these occasions. ,

*Mrs. Sul.* Pray, sir, don't kill him: you fright me as much as him.

*Arch.* The dog shall die, madam, for being the occasion of my disappointment.—Sirrah, this moment is your last.

*Gib.* Sir, I'll give you two hundred pound to spare my life.

*Arch.* Have you no more, rascal?

*Gib.* Yes, sir, I can command four hundred, but I must reserve two of 'em to save my life at the sessions.

### *Re-enter* SCRUB *and* FOIGARD.

*Arch.* Here, doctor, I suppose Scrub and you between you may manage him. Lay hold of him, doctor.

[FOIGARD *lays hold of* GIBBET.

*Gib.* What! turned over to the priest already!—Look'ee, doctor, you come before your time; I an't condemned yet, I thank ye.

*Foi.* Come, my dear joy, I vill secure your body and your shoul too; I vill make you a good Catholic, and give you an absolution.

*Gib.* Absolution! can you procure me a pardon, doctor?

*Foi.* No, joy.

*Gib.* Then you and your absolution may go to the devil.

*Arch.* Convey him into the cellar, there bind him:—take the pistol, and if he offers to resist, shoot him through the head— and come back to us with all the speed you can.

*Scrub.* Ay, ay, come, doctor, do you hold him fast, and I'll guard him.        [*Exit* FOIGARD *with* GIBBET, SCRUB *following.*

*Mrs. Sul.* But how came the doctor——

*Arch.* In short, madam—[*Shrieking without.*] 'Sdeath! the rogues are at work with the other ladies—I'm vexed I parted with the pistol; but I must fly to their assistance.—Will you stay here, madam, or venture yourself with me?

*Mrs. Sul.* [*taking him by the arm*]. Oh, with you, dear sir, with you.        [*Exeunt.*


### SCENE III.—*Another Bedchamber in the same*

*Enter* HOUNSLOW *and* BAGSHOT, *with swords drawn, haling in* Lady BOUNTIFUL *and* DORINDA.

*Houn.* Come, come, your jewels, mistress!

*Bag.* Your keys, your keys, old gentlewoman!

*Enter* AIMWELL *and* CHERRY.

*Aim.* Turn this way, villains! I durst engage an army in such a cause.   [*He engages them both.*

*Dor.* O madam, had I but a sword to help the brave man!

*Lady Boun.* There's three or four hanging up in the hall; but they won't draw. I'll go fetch one, however.   [*Exit.*

*Enter* ARCHER *and* MRS. SULLEN.

*Arch.* Hold, hold, my lord! every man his bird, pray.

[*They engage man to man;* HOUNSLOW *and* BAGSHOT *are thrown and disarmed.*

*Cher.* [*aside*]. What! the rogues taken! then they'll impeach my father: I must give him timely notice.   [*Runs out.*

*Arch.* Shall we kill the rogues?

*Aim.* No, no, we'll bind them.

*Arch.* Ay, ay.—[*To* Mrs. SULLEN, *who stands by him.*] Here, madam, lend me your garter.

*Mrs. Sul.* [*aside*]. The devil's in this fellow! he fights, loves, and banters, all in a breath.—[*Aloud.*] Here's a cord that the rogues brought with 'em, I suppose.

*Arch.* Right, right, the rogue's destiny, a rope to hang him-self.—Come, my lord—this is but a scandalous sort of an office [*Binding the* Highwaymen *together*], if our adventures should end in this sort of hangman-work; but I hope there is something in prospect, that——

*Enter* SCRUB.

*Arch.* Well, Scrub, have you secured your Tartar?

*Scrub.* Yes, sir, I left the priest and him disputing about religion.

*Aim.* And pray carry these gentlemen to reap the benefit of the controversy.

[*Delivers the prisoners to* SCRUB, *who leads them out.*

*Mrs. Sul.* Pray, sister, how came my lord here?

*Dor.* And pray, how came the gentleman here?

*Mrs. Sul.* I'll tell you the greatest piece of villainy—

[*They talk in dumb show.*

*Aim.* I fancy, Archer, you have been more successful in your adventures than the housebreakers.

*Arch.* No matter for my adventure, yours is the principal.—Press her this minute to marry you—now while she's hurried between the palpitation of her fear and the joy of her deliverance, now while the tide of her spirits is at high-flood—throw yourself at her feet, speak some romantic nonsense or other—address her, like Alexander in the height of his victory, confound her senses, bear down her reason, and away with her.—The priest is now in the cellar, and dare not refuse to do the work.

*Re-enter* Lady BOUNTIFUL.

*Aim.* But how shall I get off without being observed?

*Arch.* You a lover, and not find a way to get off!—Let me see——

*Aim.* You bleed, Archer.

*Arch.* 'Sdeath, I'm glad on't; this wound will do the business. I'll amuse the old lady and Mrs. Sullen about dressing my wound, while you carry off Dorinda.

*Lady Boun.* Gentlemen, could we understand how you would be gratified for the services——

*Arch.* Come, come, my lady, this is no time for compliments; I'm wounded, madam.

*Lady Boun., Mrs. Sul.* How! wounded!

*Dor.* I hope, sir, you have received no hurt?

*Aim.* None but what you may cure——

[*Makes love in dumb show.*

*Lady Boun.* Let me see your arm, sir—I must have some powder-sugar to stop the blood.—O me! an ugly gash; upon my word, sir, you must go into bed.

*Arch.* Ay, my lady, a bed would do very well.—[*To* Mrs. SULLEN.] Madam, will you do me the favour to conduct me to a chamber?

*Lady Boun.* Do, do, daughter—while I get the lint and the probe and the plaster ready.

[*Runs out one way,* AIMWELL *carries off* DORINDA *another.*

*Arch.* Come, madam, why don't you obey your mother's commands?

*Mrs. Sul.* How can you, after what is passed, have the confidence to ask me?

*Arch.* And if you go to that, how can you, after what is passed, have the confidence to deny me? Was not this blood shed in your defence, and my life exposed for your protection? Look'ee, madam, I'm none of your romantic fools, that fight giants and monsters for nothing; my valour is downright Swiss; I'm a soldier of fortune, and must be paid.

*Mrs. Sul.* 'Tis ungenerous in you, sir, to upbraid me with your services!

*Arch.* 'Tis ungenerous in you, madam, not to reward 'em.

*Mrs. Sul.* How! at the expense of my honour?

*Arch.* Honour! can honour consist with ingratitude? If you would deal like a woman of honour, do like a man of honour. D'ye think I would deny you in such a case?

*Enter a* Servant.

*Serv.* Madam, my lady ordered me to tell you, that your brother is below at the gate.                    [*Exit.*

*Mrs. Sul.* My brother! Heavens be praised!—Sir, he shall thank you for your services; he has it in his power.

*Arch.* Who is your brother, madam?

*Mrs. Sul.* Sir Charles. Freeman.—You'll excuse me, sir; I must go and receive him.    [*Exit.*

*Arch.* Sir Charles Freeman! 'sdeath and hell! my old acquaintance. Now unless Aimwell has made good use of his time, all our fair machine goes souse into the sea like the Eddystone.

[*Exit.*

### SCENE IV.—*The Gallery in the same house*

#### *Enter* AIMWELL *and* DORINDA.

*Dor.* Well, well, my lord, you have conquered; your late generous action will, I hope, plead for my easy yielding; though I must own, your lordship had a friend in the fort before.

*Aim.* The sweets of Hybla dwell upon her tongue!—Here, doctor——

#### *Enter* FOIGARD, *with a book.*

*Foi.* Are you prepared boat?

*Dor.* I'm ready. But first, my lord, one word.—I have a frightful example of a hasty marriage in my own family; when I reflect upon't it shocks me. Pray, my lord, consider a little——

*Aim.* Consider! do you doubt my honour or my love?

*Dor.* Neither: I do believe you equally just as brave: and were your whole sex drawn out for me to choose, I should not cast a look upon the multitude if you were absent. But, my lord, I'm a woman; colours, concealments may hide a thousand faults in me, therefore know me better first; I hardly dare affirm I know myself in anything except my love.

*Aim.* [*aside*]. Such goodness who could injure? I find myself unequal to the task of villain; she has gained my soul, and made it honest like her own.—I cannot, cannot hurt her.—[*Aloud.*] Doctor, retire.—[*Exit* FOIGARD.] Madam, behold your lover and your proselyte, and judge of my passion by my conversion!—I'm all a lie, nor dare I give a fiction to your arms; I'm all counterfeit, except my passion.

*Dor.* Forbid it, Heaven! a counterfeit!

*Aim.* I am no lord, but a poor needy man, come with a mean, a scandalous design to prey upon your fortune; but the beauties of your mind and person have so won me from myself that, like a trusty servant, I prefer the interest of my mistress to my own.

*Dor.* Sure I have had the dream of some poor mariner, a sleepy image of a welcome port, and wake involved in storms!—Pray, sir, who are you?

*Aim.* Brother to the man whose title I usurped, but stranger to his honour or his fortune.

*Dor.* Matchless honesty!—Once I was proud, sir, of your

wealth and title, but now am prouder that you want it: now I
can show my love was justly levelled, and had no aim but love.
—Doctor, come in.

*Enter* FOIGARD *at one door,* GIPSY *at another,
who whispers* DORINDA.

[*To* FOIGARD.]   Your pardon, sir, we sha' not want you now.—
[*To* AIMWELL.]   Sir, you must excuse me—I'll wait on you
presently.                                        [*Exit with* GIPSY.
   *Foi.* Upon my shoul, now, dis is foolish.              [*Exit.*
   *Aim.* Gone! and bid the priest depart!—It has an ominous
look.

*Enter* ARCHER.

   *Arch.* Courage, Tom!—Shall I wish you joy?
   *Aim.* No.
   *Arch.* 'Oons, man, what ha' you been doing?
   *Aim.* O Archer! my honesty, I fear, has ruined me.
   *Arch.* How?
   *Aim.* I have discovered myself.
   *Arch.* Discovered! and without my consent? What! have
I embarked my small remains in the same bottom with yours,
and you dispose of all without my partnership?
   *Aim.* O Archer! I own my fault.
   *Arch.* After conviction—'tis then too late for pardon.—You
may remember, Mr. Aimwell, that you proposed this folly: as
you begun, so end it. Henceforth I'll hunt my fortune single—
so farewell!
   *Aim.* Stay, my dear Archer, but a minute.
   *Arch.* Stay! what, to be despised, exposed, and laughed at!
No, I would sooner change conditions with the worst of the
rogues we just now bound, than bear one scornful smile from
the proud knight that once I treated as my equal.
   *Aim.* What knight?
   *Arch.* Sir Charles Freeman, brother to the lady that I had
almost—but no matter for that, 'tis a cursed night's work, and
so I leave you to make the best on't.              [*Going.*
   *Aim.* Freeman!—One word, Archer. Still I have hopes;
methought she received my confession with pleasure.
   *Arch.* 'Sdeath, who doubts it?
   *Aim.* She consented after to the match; and still I dare
believe she will be just.
   *Arch.* To herself, I warrant her, as you should have been.
   *Aim.* By all my hopes she comes, and smiling comes!

*Re-enter* DORINDA, *mighty gay.*

   *Dor.* Come, my dear lord—I fly with impatience to your arms
—the minutes of my absence were a tedious year. Where's
this priest?

*Re-enter* FOIGARD.

*Arch.* 'Oons, a brave girl!

*Dor.* I suppose, my lord, this gentleman is privy to our affairs?

*Arch.* Yes, yes, madam, I'm to be your father.

*Dor.* Come, priest, do your office.

*Arch.* Make haste, make haste, couple 'em any way.—[*Takes*
AIMWELL's *hand.*] Come, madam, I'm to give you——

*Dor.* My mind's altered; I won't.

*Arch.* Eh!

*Aim.* I'm confounded!

*Foi.* Upon my shoul, and sho is myshelf.

*Arch.* What's the matter now, madam?

*Dor.* Look'ee, sir, one generous action deserves another.—
This gentleman's honour obliged him to hide nothing from me;
my justice engages me to conceal nothing from him. In short,
sir, you are the person that you thought you counterfeited; you
are the true Lord Viscount Aimwell, and I wish your Lordship
joy.—Now, priest, you may be gone; if my Lord is pleased now
with the match, let his Lordship marry me in the face of the
world.

*Aim., Arch.* What does she mean?

*Dor.* Here's a witness for my truth.

*Enter* Sir CHARLES FREEMAN *and* Mrs. SULLEN.

*Sir Chas.* My dear Lord Aimwell, I wish you joy.

*Aim.* Of what?

*Sir Chas.* Of your honour and estate. Your brother died
the day before I left London; and all your friends have writ
after you to Brussels;—among the rest I did myself the honour.

*Arch.* Hark'ee, sir knight, don't you banter now?

*Sir Chas.* 'Tis truth, upon my honour.

*Aim.* Thanks to the pregnant stars that formed this accident.

*Arch.* Thanks to the womb of time that brought it forth!—
away with it!

*Aim.* Thanks to my guardian angel that led me to the prize!
[*Taking* DORINDA'S *hand.*

*Arch.* And double thanks to the noble Sir Charles Freeman.—
My Lord, I wish you joy.—My Lady, I wish you joy.—Egad, Sir
Freeman, you're the honestest fellow living!—'Sdeath, I'm
grown strange airy upon this matter!—My Lord, how d'ye?—
A word, my Lord; don't you remember something of a previous
agreement, that entitles me to the moiety of this lady's fortune,
which I think will amount to five thousand pound?

*Aim.* Not a penny, Archer; you would ha' cut my throat
just now, because I would not deceive this lady.

*Arch.* Ay, and I'll cut your throat again, if you should deceive
her now.

*Aim.* That's what I expected; and to end the dispute, the

lady's fortune is ten thousand pound, we'll divide stakes: take the ten thousand pound or the lady.

*Dor.* How! is your Lordship so indifferent?

*Arch.* No, no, no, madam! his Lordship knows very well that I'll take the money; I leave you to his Lordship, and so we're both provided for.

*Enter* Count BELLAIR.

*Count Bel.* *Mesdames et Messieurs,* I am your servant trice humble! I hear you be rob here.

*Aim.* The ladies have been in some danger, sir.

*Count Bel.* And, begar, our inn be rob too!

*Aim.* Our inn! by whom?

*Count Bel.* By the landlord, begar!—Garzoon, he has rob himself, and run away!

*Arch.* Robbed himself!

*Count Bel.* Ay, begar, and me too of a hundre pound.

*Arch.* A hundred pound?

*Count Bel.* Yes, that I owed him.

*Aim.* Our money's gone, Frank.

*Arch.* Rot the money! my wench is gone.—[*To* Count BELLAIR.] *Savez-vous quelquechose de Mademoiselle Cherry?*

*Enter a* Countryman *with a strong-box and a letter.*

*Coun.* Is there one Martin here?

*Arch.* Ay, ay—who wants him?

*Coun.* I have a box here, and letter for him.

*Arch.* [*taking the box*]. Ha! ha! ha! what's here? Legerdemain!—By this light, my lord, our money again!—But this unfolds the riddle.—[*Opening the letter.*] Hum, hum, hum!—Oh, 'tis for the public good, and must be communicated to the company.                    [*Reads.*

" MR. MARTIN.—My father being afraid of an impeachment by the rogues that are taken to-night, is gone off; but if you can procure him a pardon, he'll make great discoveries that may be useful to the country. Could I have met you instead of your master to-night, I would have delivered myself into your hands, with a sum that much exceeds that in your strong-box, which I have sent you, with an assurance to my dear Martin that I shall ever be his most faithful friend till death.—CHERRY BONIFACE."

There's a *billet-doux* for you! As for the father, I think he ought to be encouraged; and for the daughter—pray, my Lord, persuade your bride to take her into her service instead of Gipsy.

*Aim.* I can assure you, madam, your deliverance was owing to her discovery.

*Dor.* Your command, my Lord, will do without the obligation. I'll take care of her.

*Sir Chas.* This good company meets opportunely in favour of a design I have in behalf of my unfortunate sister. I intend to part her from her husband—gentlemen, will you assist me?

*Arch.* Assist you! 'sdeath, who would not?

*Count Bel.* Assist! garzoon, we all assist!

*Enter* Squire SULLEN.

*Squire Sul.* What's all this? They tell me, spouse, that you had like to have been robbed.

*Mrs. Sul.* Truly, spouse, I was pretty near it, had not these two gentlemen interposed.

*Squire Sul.* How came these gentlemen here?

*Mrs. Sul.* That's his way of returning thanks, you must know.

*Count Bel.* Garzoon, the question be apropos for all dat.

*Sir Chas.* You promised last night, sir, that you would deliver your lady to me this morning.

*Squire Sul.* Humph!

*Arch.* Humph! what do you mean by humph? Sir, you shall deliver her—in short, sir, we have saved you and your family; and if you are not civil, we'll unbind the rogues, join with 'em, and set fire to your house. What does the man mean? not part with his wife!

*Count Bel.* Ay, garzoon, de man no understan common justice.

*Mrs. Sul.* Hold, gentlemen, all things here must move by consent, compulsion would spoil us; let my dear and I talk the matter over, and you shall judge it between us.

*Squire Sul.* Let me know first who are to be our judges. Pray, sir, who are you?

*Sir Chas.* I am Sir Charles Freeman, come to take away your wife.

*Squire Sul.* And you, good sir?

*Aim.* Thomas, Viscount Aimwell, come to take away your sister.

*Squire Sul.* And you, pray, sir?

*Arch.* Francis Archer, esquire, come——

*Squire Sul.* To take away my mother, I hope. Gentlemen, you're heartily welcome; I never met with three more obliging people since I was born!—And now, my dear, if you please, you shall have the first word.

*Arch.* And the last, for five pound!

*Mrs. Sul.* Spouse!

*Squire Sul.* Rib!

*Mrs. Sul.* How long have we been married?

*Squire Sul.* By the almanac, fourteen months; but by my account, fourteen years.

*Mrs. Sul.* 'Tis thereabout by my reckoning.

*Count Bel.* Garzoon, their account will agree.

*Mrs. Sul.* Pray, spouse, what did you marry for?

*Squire Sul.* To get an heir to my estate.

*Sir Chas.* And have you succeeded?

*Squire Sul.* No.

*Arch.* The condition fails of his side.—Pray, madam, what did you marry for?

*Mrs. Sul.* To support the weakness of my sex by the strength of his, and to enjoy the pleasures of an agreeable society.

*Sir Chas.* Are your expectations answered?

*Mrs. Sul.* No.

*Count Bel.* A clear case! a clear case!

*Sir Chas.* What are the bars to your mutual contentment?

*Mrs. Sul.* In the first place, I can't drink ale with him.

*Squire Sul.* Nor can I drink tea with her.

*Mrs. Sul.* I can't hunt with you.

*Squire Sul.* Nor can I dance with you.

*Mrs. Sul.* I hate cocking and racing.

*Squire Sul.* And I abhor ombre and piquet.

*Mrs. Sul.* Your silence is intolerable.

*Squire Sul.* Your prating is worse.

*Mrs. Sul.* Have we not been a perpetual offence to each other? a gnawing vulture at the heart?

*Squire Sul.* A frightful goblin to the sight?

*Mrs. Sul.* A porcupine to the feeling?

*Squire Sul.* Perpetual wormwood to the taste?

*Mrs. Sul.* Is there on earth a thing we could agree in?

*Squire Sul.* Yes—to part.

*Mrs. Sul.* With all my heart.

*Squire Sul.* Your hand.

*Mrs. Sul.* Here.

*Squire Sul.* These hands joined us, these shall part us.— Away!

*Mrs. Sul.* North.

*Squire Sul.* South.

*Mrs. Sul.* East.

*Squire Sul.* West—far as the poles asunder.

*Count Bel.* Begar, the ceremony be vera pretty!

*Sir Chas.* Now, Mr. Sullen, there wants only my sister's fortune to make us easy.

*Squire Sul.* Sir Charles, you love your sister, and I love her fortune; every one to his fancy.

*Arch.* Then you won't refund;

*Squire Sul.* Not a stiver.

*Arch.* Then I find, madam, you must e'en go to your prison again.

*Count Bel.* What is the portion?

*Sir Chas.* Ten thousand pound, sir.

*Count Bel.* Garzoon, I'll pay it, and she shall go home wid me.

*Arch.* Ha! ha! ha! French all over.—Do you know, sir, what ten thousand pound English is?

*Count Bel.* No, begar, not justement.

*Arch.* Why, sir, 'tis a hundred thousand livres.

*Count Bel.* A hundre tousand livres! Ah! garzoon, me canno' do't, your beauties and their fortunes are both too much for me.

*Arch.* Then I will.—This night's adventure has proved strangely lucky to us all—for Captain Gibbet in his walk had made bold, Mr. Sullen, with your study and escritoir, and had taken out all the writings of your estate, all the articles of marriage with this lady, bills, bonds, leases, receipts to an infinite value: I took 'em from him, and I deliver 'em to Sir Charles.

[*Gives* Sir CHARLES FREEMAN *a parcel of papers and parchments.*

*Squire Sul.* How, my writings!—my head aches consumedly. —Well, gentlemen, you shall have her fortune, but I can't talk. If you have a mind, Sir Charles, to be merry, and celebrate my sister's wedding and my divorce, you may command my house —but my head aches consumedly.—Scrub, bring me a dram.

*Arch.* [*to* Mrs. SULLEN]. Madam, there's a country dance to the trifle that I sung to-day; your hand, and we'll lead it up.

### Here a Dance.

'Twould be hard to guess which of these parties is the better pleased, the couple joined, or the couple parted; the one rejoicing in hopes of an untasted happiness, and the other in their deliverance from an experienced misery.

> Both happy in their several states we find,
> Those parted by consent, and those conjoined.
> Consent, if mutual, saves the lawyer's fee.
> Consent is law enough to set you free.     [*Exeunt omnes.*

# EPILOGUE

*Designed to be spoken in " The Beaux Stratagem."*

IF to our play your judgment can't be kind,
Let its expiring author pity find:
Survey his mournful case with melting eyes,
Nor let the bard be damn'd before he dies.
Forbear, you fair, on his last scene to frown,
But his true exit with a plaudit crown;
Then shall the dying poet cease to fear
The dreadful knell, while your applause he hears.
At Leuctra so the conquering Theban died,
Claim'd his friends' praises, but their tears denied:
Pleased in the pangs of death he greatly thought
Conquest with loss of life but cheaply bought.
The difference this, the Greek was one would fight,
As brave, though not so gay, as Serjeant Kite;
Ye sons of Will's, what's that to those who write?
To Thebes alone the Grecian owed his bays,
You may the bard above the hero raise,
Since yours is greater than Athenian praise.

# THE PROVOK'D WIFE

## A COMEDY IN FIVE ACTS

# DRAMATIS PERSONÆ

Constant.

Heartfree.

Sir John Brute.

Treble, a singing master.

Razor, valet de chambre to Sir John Brute.

Justice of the Peace.

Lord Rake, }
Col. Bully. } companions to Sir John Brute.

Constable and Watch.

[Tailor, Porter, Servants.]

Lady Brute.

Belinda, her niece.

Lady Fanciful.

Madamoiselle.

Cornet and Pipe, servants to Lady Fanciful.

[Lovewell, waiting woman to Lady Brute.]

# PROLOGUE

## SPOKEN BY MISTRESS BRACEGIRDLE

Since 'tis the intent and business of the stage
To copy out the follies of the age,
To hold to every man a faithful glass,
And show him of what species he's an ass,
I hope the next that teaches in the school
Will show our author he's a scribbling fool.
And that the satire may be sure to bite,
Kind Heav'n, inspire some venom'd priest to write,
And grant some ugly lady may indite.
For I would have him lash'd, by Heav'ns, I would,
Till his presumption swam away in blood.
Three plays at once proclaims a face of brass,
No matter what they are! That's not the case;
To write three plays, ev'n that's to be an ass.
But what I least forgive, he knows it too,
For to his cost he lately has known you.
Experience shows, to many a writer's smart,
You hold a court where mercy ne'er had part;
So much of the old serpent's sting you have,
You love to damn, as Heav'n delights to save.
In foreign parts let a bold volunteer
For public good upon the stage appear,
He meets ten thousand smiles to dissipate his fear.
All tickle on th'adventuring young beginner,
And only scourge th'incorrigible sinner.
They touch indeed his faults, but with a hand
So gentle that his merit still may stand;
Kindly they buoy the follies of his pen,
That he may shun 'em when he writes again.
But 'tis not so in this good-natur'd town;
All's one—an ox, a poet, or a crown,
Old England's play was always knocking down.

# THE PROVOK'D WIFE

## ACT I

### SCENE I—Sir John Brute's *house.*

*Enter* Sir John, *solus.*

*Sir John.* What cloying meat is love, when matrimony's the sauce to it. Two years' marriage has debauch'd my five senses. Everything I see, everything I hear, everything I feel, everything I smell, and everything I taste, methinks has wife in't. No boy was ever so weary of his tutor, no girl of her bib, no nun of doing penance, nor old maid of being chaste, as I am of being married. Sure there's a secret curse entail'd upon the very name of wife. My lady is a young lady, a fine lady, a witty lady, a virtuous lady, and yet I hate her. There is but one thing on earth I loathe beyond her: that's fighting. Would my courage come up but to a fourth part of my ill nature, I'd stand buff to her relations, and thrust her out of doors. But marriage has sunk me down to such an ebb of resolution, I dare not draw my sword, though even to get rid of my wife. But here she comes.

### *Enter* Lady Brute.

*Lady B.* Do you dine at home to-day, Sir John?

*Sir John.* Why, do you expect I should tell you what I don't know myself?

*Lady B.* I thought there was no harm in asking you.

*Sir John.* If thinking wrong were an excuse for impertinence, women might be justified in most things they say or do.

*Lady B.* I'm sorry I have said anything to displease you.

*Sir John.* Sorrow for things past is of as little importance to me as my dining at home or abroad ought to be to you.

*Lady B.* My inquiry was only that I might have provided what you lik'd.

*Sir John.* Six to four you had been in the wrong there again, for what I lik'd yesterday I don't like to-day, and what I like to-day, 'tis odds I mayn't like to-morrow.

*Lady B.* But if I had ask'd what you lik'd?

*Sir John.* Why then there would have been more asking about it than the thing was worth.

*Lady B.* I wish I did but know how I might please you.

*Sir John.* Ay, but that sort of knowledge is not a wife's talent.

*Lady B.* Whate'er my talent is, I'm sure my will has ever been to make you easy.

*Sir John.* If women were to have their wills, the world would be finely govern'd:

*Lady B.* What reason have I given you to use me as you do of late? It once was otherwise. You married me for love.

*Sir John.* And you me for money. So you have your reward and I have mine.

*Lady B.* What is it that disturbs you?

*Sir John.* A parson.

*Lady B.* Why, what has he done to you?

*Sir John.* He has married me.                    [*Exit.*

*Lady B.* The devil's in the fellow, I think. I was told before I married him that thus 'twould be. But I thought I had charms enough to govern him, and that where there was an estate, a woman must needs be happy. So my vanity has deceiv'd me, and my ambition has made me uneasy. But some comfort still: if one would be reveng'd of him, these are good times. A woman may have a gallant and a separate maintenance too. The surly puppy! Yet he's a fool for't. For hitherto he has been no monster; but who knows how far he may provoke me? I never lov'd him, yet I have been ever true to him, and that in spite of all the attacks of art and nature upon a poor weak woman's heart in favour of a tempting lover. Methinks so noble a defence as I have made should be rewarded with a better usage. Or who can tell? Perhaps a good part of what I suffer from my husband may be a judgment upon me for my cruelty to my lover. Lord, with what pleasure could I indulge that thought were there but a possibility of finding arguments to make it good. And how do I know but there may? Let me see. What opposes? My matrimonial vow? Why, what did I vow? I think I promis'd to be true to my husband. Well, and he promis'd to be kind to me. But he han't kept his word. Why then I'm absolv'd from mine. Ay, that seems clear to me. The argument's good between the king and the people; why not between the husband and the wife? Oh, but that condition was not express'd. No matter; 'twas understood. Well, by all I see, if I argue the matter a little longer with myself, I shan't find so many bugbears in the way as I thought I should. Lord, what fine notions of virtue do we women take up upon the credit of old foolish philosophers. Virtue's its own reward, virtue's this, virtue's that. Virtue's an ass, and a gallant's worth forty on't.

### *Enter* BELINDA.

Good morrow, dear cousin.

*Bel.* Good morrow, madam. You look pleas'd this morning.

*Lady B.* I am so.

*Bel.* With what, pray?

*Lady B.* With my husband.

*Bel.* Drown husbands! For yours is a provoking fellow. As he went out just now I pray'd him to tell me what time of day 'twas, and he ask'd me if I took him for the church clock, that was oblig'd to tell all the parish.

*Lady B.* He has been saying some good obliging things to me too. In short, Belinda, he has used me so barbarously of late that I could almost resolve to play the downright wife—and cuckold him.

*Bel.* That would be downright indeed.

*Lady B.* Why, after all there's more to be said for't than you'd imagine, child. I know according to the strict statute law of religion, I should do wrong; but if there were a Court of Chancery in Heaven, I'm sure I should cast him.

*Bel.* If there were a House of Lords you might.

*Lady B.* In either I should infallibly carry my cause. Why, he is the first aggressor, not I.

*Bel.* Ay, but you know we must return good for evil.

*Lady B.* That may be a mistake in the translation. Prithee be of my opinion, Belinda, for I'm positive I'm in the right; and if you'll keep up the prerogative of a woman, you'll likewise be positive you are in the right whenever you do anything you have a mind to. But I shall play the fool, and jest on till I make you begin to think I'm in earnest.

*Bel.* I shan't take the liberty, madam, to think of anything that you desire to keep a secret from me.

*Lady B.* Alas, my dear, I have no secrets. My heart could never yet confine my tongue.

*Bel.* Your eyes, you mean, for I am sure I have seen them gadding when your tongue has been lock'd up fast enough.

*Lady B.* My eyes gadding? Prithee after who, child?

*Bel.* Why, after one that thinks you hate him, as much as I know you love him.

*Lady B.* Constant, you mean.

*Bel.* I do so.

*Lady B.* Lord, what should put such a thing into your head?

*Bel.* That which puts things into most people's heads, observation.

*Lady B.* Why, what have you observ'd, in the name of wonder?

*Bel.* I have observ'd you blush when you meet him, force yourself away from him, and then be out of humour with everything about you. In a word, never was poor creature so spurr'd on by desire and so rein'd in with fear.

*Lady B.* How strong is fancy!

*Bel.* How weak is woman.

*Lady B.* Prithee, niece, have a better opinion of your aunt's inclinations.

*Bel.* Dear aunt, have a better opinion of your niece's understanding.

*Lady B.* You'll make me angry.

*Bel.* You'll make me laugh.

*Lady B.* Then you are resolv'd to persist?

*Bel.* Positively.

*Lady B.* And all I can say——

*Bel.* Will signify nothing.

*Lady B.* Though I should swear 'twere false——

*Bel.* I should think it true.

*Lady B.* Then let us both forgive, *Kissing her.* for we have both offended, I in making a secret, you in discovering it.

*Bel.* Good nature may do much, but you have more reason to forgive one than I have to pardon t'other.

*Lady B.* 'Tis true, Belinda, you have given me so many proofs of your friendship that my reserve has been indeed a crime. But that you may more easily forgive me, remember, child, that when our nature prompts us to a thing our honour and religion have forbid us, we would, were't possible, conceal even from the soul itself the knowledge of the body's weakness.

*Bel.* Well, I hope, to make your friend amends, you'll hide nothing from her for the future, though the body should still grow weaker and weaker.

*Lady B.* No. From this moment I have no more reserve; and for a proof of my repentance, I own, Belinda, I'm in danger. Merit and wit assault me from without, nature and love solicit me within, my husband's barbarous usage piques me to revenge, and Satan, catching at the fair occasion, throws in my way that vengeance which of all vengeance pleases women best.

*Bel.* 'Tis well Constant don't know the weakness of the fortifications, for o' my conscience he'd soon come on to the assault.

*Lady B.* Ay, and I'm afraid carry the town too. But whatever you may have observ'd, I have dissembled so well as to keep him ignorant. So you see I'm no coquette, Belinda, and if you'll follow my advice you'll never be one neither. 'Tis true, coquetry is one of the main ingredients in the natural composition of a woman, and I as well as others could be well enough pleas'd to see a crowd of young fellows ogling and glancing and watching all occasions to do forty foolish officious things; nay, should some of 'em push on, even to hanging or drowning, why, faith, if I should let pure woman alone, I should e'en be but too well pleas'd with't.

*Bel.* I'll swear 'twould tickle me strangely.

*Lady B.* But after all, 'tis a vicious practice in us to give the least encouragement but where we design to come to a conclusion. For 'tis an unreasonable thing to engage a man in a disease which we beforehand resolve we never will apply a cure to.

*Bel.* 'Tis true; but then a woman must abandon one of the supreme blessings of her life. For I am fully convinced no man has half that pleasure in possessing a mistress as a woman has in jilting a gallant.

*Lady B.* The happiest woman then on earth must be our neighbour.

*Bel.* Oh, the impertinent composition! She has vanity and affectation enough to make her a ridiculous original, in spite of all that art and nature ever furnish'd to any of her sex before her.

*Lady B.* She concludes all men her captives, and whatever course they take, it serves to confirm her in that opinion.

*Bel.* If they shun her, she thinks 'tis modesty, and takes it for a proof of their passion.

*Lady B.* And if they are rude to her, 'tis conduct, and done to prevent town talk.

*Bel.* When her folly makes em laugh, she thinks they are pleas'd with her wit.

*Lady B.* And when her impertinence makes 'em dull, concludes they are jealous of her favours.

*Bel.* All their actions and their words she takes for granted aim at her.

*Lady B.* And pities all other women because she thinks they envy her.

*Bel.* Pray, out of pity to ourselves, let us find a better subject, for I am weary of this. Do you think your husband inclin'd to jealousy?

*Lady B.* Oh no. He does not love me well enough for that. Lord, how wrong men's maxims are. They are seldom jealous of their wives unless they are very fond of 'em; whereas they ought to consider the woman's inclinations, for there depends their fate. Well, men may talk, but they are not so wise as we, that's certain.

*Bel.* At least in our affairs.

*Lady B.* Nay, I believe we should outdo 'em in the business of the state too, for methinks they do and undo, and make but mad work on't.

*Bel.* Why then don't we get into the intrigues of government as well as they?

*Lady B.* Because we have intrigues of our own that make us more sport, child. And so let's in and consider of 'em. *Exeunt.*


SCENE [II].—Lady FANCIFUL's *dressing room.*

*Enter* Lady FANCIFUL, MADAMOISELLE, *and* CORNET.

*Lady F.* How do I look this morning?

*Cor.* Your ladyship looks very ill, truly.

*Lady F.* Lard, how ill-natured thou art, Cornet, to tell me so, though the thing should be true. Don't you know that I have humility enough to be but too easily out of conceit with myself? Hold the glass. I dare swear that will have more manners than you have. Madamoiselle, let me have your opinion too.

*Madam.* My opinion pe, matam, dat your ladyship never look so well in your life.

*Lady F.* Well, the French are the prettiest obliging people. They say the most acceptable, well-mannered things, and never flatter.

*Madam.* Your ladyship say great justice inteed.

*Lady F.* Nay, everything's just in my house but Cornet. The very looking glass gives her the *dementi*. But I'm almost afraid it flatters me, it makes me look so very engaging.

*Looking affectedly in the glass.*

*Madam.* Inteed, matam, your face pe hansomer den all de looking glass in tee world, *croyez moi*.

*Lady F.* But is it possible my eyes can be so languishing, and so very full of fire?

*Madam.* Matam, if de glass was burning glass, I believe your eyes set de fire in de house.

*Lady F.* You may take that nightgown, Madamoiselle. Get out of the room, Cornet; I can't endure you. This wench methinks does look so unsufferably ugly. *Exit* CORNET.

*Madam.* Everyting look ugly, matam, dat stand by your latyship.

*Lady F.* No, really, Madamoiselle, methinks you look mighty pretty.

*Madam.* Ah, matam, de moon have no *éclat* ven de sun appear.

*Lady F.* O pretty expression! Have you ever been in love, Madamoiselle?

*Madam. Sighing. Oui*, matam.

*Lady F.* And were you belov'd again?

*Madam. Sighing.* No, matam.

*Lady F.* O ye gods, what an unfortunate creature should I be in such a case! But nature has made me nice for my own defence. I'm nice, strangely nice, Madamoiselle. I believe were the merit of whole mankind bestow'd upon one single person, I should still think the fellow wanted something to make it worth my while to take notice of him. And yet I could love, were it possible to have a thing made on purpose for me; for I'm not cruel, Madamoiselle, I'm only nice.

*Madam.* Ah, matam, I wish I was fine gentleman for your sake. I do all de ting in de world to get leetel way into your heart. I make song, I make verse, I give you de serenade, I give great many present to Madamoiselle. I no eat, I no sleep, I be lean, I be mad, I hang myself, I drown myself. Ah, *ma chère dame, que je vous aimerais*. *Embracing her*.

*Lady F.* Well, the French have strange, obliging ways with 'em. You may take those two pair of gloves, Madamoiselle.

*Madam.* Me humbly tank my sweet lady.

*Enter* CORNET.

*Cor.* Madam, here's a letter for your ladyship by the penny
post.

*Lady F.* Some new conquest, I'll warrant you. For, without
vanity, I look'd extremely clear last night when I went to the
Park. *Opens the letter.* Oh, agreeable. Here's a new song made
of me. And ready set too. O thou welcome thing! *Kissing it.*
Call Pipe hither. She shall sing it instantly.

*Enter* PIPE.

Here, sing me this new song, Pipe.

SONG

I

Fly, fly, you happy shepherds, fly,
   Avoid Philira's charms.
The rigour of her heart denies
   The heaven that's in her arms.
Ne'er hope to gaze and then retire,
   Nor yielding, to be bless'd.
Nature, who form'd her eyes of fire,
   Of ice compos'd her breast.

II

Yet, lovely maid, this once believe
   A slave whose zeal you move:
The gods, alas, your youth deceive;
   Their heaven consists in love.
In spite of all the thanks you owe,
   You may reproach 'em this,
That where they did their form bestow
   They have denied their bliss.

[*Exit* PIPE.]

*Lady F.* Well, there may be faults, Madamoiselle, but the
design is so very obliging, 'twould be a matchless ingratitude in
me to discover 'em.

*Madam.* *Ma foi*, matam, I tink de gentleman's song tell you de
trute. If you never love, you never be happy. Ah, *que j'aime
l'amour, moi.*

*Enter* SERVANT *with another letter.*

*Serv.* Madam, here's another letter for your ladyship.

*Lady F.* 'Tis thus I am importun'd every morning, Madamoiselle. Pray, how do the French ladies when they are thus
*accablées*?

*Madam.* Matam, dey never complain. *Au contraire.* When
one Frense laty have got hundred lover, den she do all she can, to
get hundred more.

*Lady F.* Well, strike me dead, I think they have *le goût bon.* For 'tis an unutterable pleasure to be ador'd by all the men and envied by all the women. Yet I'll swear I'm concerned at the torture I give 'em. Lard, why was I form'd to make the whole creation uneasy? But let me read my letter.          *Reads.* "If you have a mind to hear of your faults instead of being praised for your virtues, take the pains to walk in the Green Walk in St. James's with your woman an hour hence. You'll there meet one who hates you for some things as he could love you for others, and therefore is willing to endeavour your reformation. If you come to the place I mention, you'll know who I am; if you don't, you never shall, so take your choice." This is strangely familiar, Madamoiselle. Now have I a provoking fancy to know who this impudent fellow is.

*Madam.* Den take your scarf and your mask and go to de rendezvous. De Frense laty do *justement comme ça.*

*Lady F.* Rendezvous! What, rendezvous with a man, Madamoiselle?

*Madam.* Eh, *pourquoi non?*

*Lady F.* What, and a man perhaps I never saw in my life?

*Madam.* *Tant mieux; c'est donc quelque chose de nouveau.*

*Lady F.* Why, how do I know what designs he may have? He may intend to ravish me for aught I know.

*Madam.* Ravish? Bagatelle! I would fain see one impudent rogue ravish Madamoiselle, *oui, je le voudrais.*

*Lady F.* Oh, but my reputation, Madamoiselle, my reputation, ah, *ma chère réputation.*

*Madam.* Matam, *quand on l'a une fois perdue, on n'en est plus embarrassée.*

*Lady F.* Fie, Madamoiselle, fie! Reputation is a jewel.

*Madam. Qui coûte bien chère,* matam.

*Lady F.* Why sure, you would not sacrifice your honour to your pleasure?

*Madam. Je suis philosophe.*

*Lady F.* Bless me, how you talk! Why, what if honour be a burden, Madamoiselle, must it not be borne?

*Madam. Chaqu'un à sa façon. Quand quelque chose m'incommode, moi, je m'en défais, vite.*

*Lady F.* Get you gone, you little naughty Frenchwoman, you. I vow and swear I must turn you out of doors if you talk thus.

*Madam.* Turn me out of doors? Turn yourself out of doors, and go see what do gentleman have to say to you. *Tenez. Giving her her things hastily. Voilà votre écharpe, voilà votre coiffe, voilà votre masque, voilà tout. Calling within.* Hey, Mercure, Coquin, call one chair for matam, and one oder for me. *Va t'en vite. Turning to her lady and helping her on hastily with her things. Allons,* matam. *Dépêchez vous donc. Mon dieu, quelles scrupules!*

*Lady F.* Well, for once, Madamoiselle, I'll follow your advice,

out of the intemperate desire I have to know who this ill-bred
fellow is. But I have too much delicatesse to make a practice
on it.

*Madam.* Belle chose vraiment que la délicatesse, lorsqu'il s'agit
de se divertir. À ça, vous voilà équipée, partons. He bien,
qu'avez vous donc ?

*Lady F.* J'ai peur.

*Madam.* Je n'en ai point, moi.

*Lady F.* I dare not go.

*Madam.* Demeurez donc.

*Lady F.* Je suis poltrone.

*Madam.* Tant pis pour vous.

*Lady F.* Curiosity's a wicked devil.

*Madam.* C'est une charmante sainte.

*Lady F.* It ruin'd our first parents.

*Madam.* Elle a bien diverti leurs enfants.

*Lady F.* L'honneur est contre.

*Madam.* Le plaisir est pour.

*Lady F.* Must I then go?

*Madam.* Must you go? Must you eat, must you drink, must
you sleep, must you live? De nature bid you do one, de nature
bid you do t'oder. Vous me ferez enrager.

*Lady F.* But when reason corrects nature, Madamoiselle ?

*Madam.* Elle est donc bien insolente. C'est sa soeur aînée.

*Lady F.* Do you then prefer your nature to your reason,
Madamoiselle?

*Madam.* Oui da.

*Lady F.* Pourquoi ?

*Madam.* Because my nature make me merry, my reason make
me mad.

*Lady F.* Ah, la méchante française !

*Madam.* Ah, la belle anglaise ! *Forcing her lady off.*

# ACT II

## SCENE [I].—*St. James's Park.*

*Enter* Lady FANCIFUL *and* MADAMOISELLE.

*Lady F.* Well, I vow, Madamoiselle, I'm strangely impatient
to know who this confident fellow is.

### *Enter* HEARTFREE.

Look, there's Heartfree. But sure it can't be him, he's a profess'd woman-hater. Yet who knows what my wicked eyes may
have done ?

*Madam.* Il nous approche, madam.

*Lady F.* Yes, 'tis he. Now will he be most intolerably cavalier, though he should be in love with me.

*Heart.* Madam, I'm your humble servant. I perceive you have more humility and good nature than I thought you had.

*Lady F.* What you attribute to humility and good nature, sir, may perhaps be only due to curiosity. I had a mind to know who 'twas had ill manners enough to write that letter.

*Throwing him his letter.*

*Heart.* Well, and now I hope you are satisfied.

*Lady F.* I am so, sir. Goodbye to ye.

*Heart.* Nay, hold there. Though you have done your business, I han't done mine. By your ladyship's leave. we must have one moment's prattle together. Have you a mind to be the prettiest woman about town or not? How she stares upon me! What, this passes for an impertinent question with you now, because you think you are so already.

*Lady F.* Pray, sir, let me ask you a question in my turn. By what right do you pretend to examine me?

*Heart.* By the same right that the strong govern the weak, because I have you in my power, for you cannot get so quickly to your coach but I shall have time enough to make you hear everything I have to say to you.

*Lady F.* These are strange liberties you take, Mr. Heartfree.

*Heart.* They are so, madam, but there's no help for it; for know that I have a design upon you.

*Lady F.* Upon me, sir?

*Heart.* Yes, and one that will turn to your glory and my comfort, if you will be but a little wiser than you use to be.

*Lady F.* Very well, sir.

*Heart.* Let me see. Your vanity, madam, I take to be about some eight degrees higher than any woman's in the town, let t'other be who she will; and my indifference is naturally about the same pitch. Now could you find the way to turn this indifference into fire and flames, methinks your vanity ought to be satisfied; and this perhaps you might bring about upon pretty reasonable terms.

*Lady F.* And, pray, at what rate would this indifference be bought off, if one should have so deprav'd an appetite to desire it?

*Heart.* Why, madam, to drive a Quaker's bargain, and make but one word with you, if I do part with it, you must lay me down—your affectation.

*Lady F.* My affectation, sir?

*Heart.* Why, I ask you nothing but what you may very well spare.

*Lady F.* You grow rude, sir. Come, Madamoiselle, 'tis high time to be gone.

*Madam. Allons, allons, allons.*

*Heart. Stopping 'em.* Nay, you may as well stand still, for hear me you shall, walk which way you please.

*Lady F.* What mean you, sir?

*Heart.* I mean to tell you that you are the most ungrateful woman upon earth.

*Lady F.* Ungrateful? To who?

*Heart.* To nature.

*Lady F.* Why, what has nature done for me?

*Heart.* What you have undone by art. It made you handsome; it gave you beauty to a miracle, a shape without a fault, wit enough to make 'em relish, and so turned you loose to your own discretion, which has made such work with you that you are become the pity of our sex and the jest of your own. There is not a feature in your face but you have found the way to teach it some affected convulsion; your feet, your hands, your very fingers' ends are directed never to move without some ridiculous air or other; and your language is a suitable trumpet to draw people's eyes upon the raree-show.

*Madam. Aside. Est ce qu'on fait l'amour en Angleterre comme ça?*

*Lady F. Aside.* Now could I cry for madness, but that I know he'd laugh at me for it.

*Heart.* Now do you hate me for telling you the truth, but that's because you don't believe it is so; for were you once convinc'd of that, you'd reform for your own sake. But 'tis as hard to persuade a woman to quit anything that makes her ridiculous as 'tis to prevail with a poet to see a fault in his own play.

*Lady F.* Every circumstance of nice breeding must needs appear ridiculous to one who has so natural an antipathy to good manners.

*Heart.* But suppose I could find the means to convince you that the whole world is of my opinion, and that those who flatter and commend you do it to no other intent but to make you persevere in your folly that they may continue in their mirth.

*Lady F.* Sir, though you and all that world you talk of should be so impertinently officious as to think to persuade me I don't know how to behave myself, I should still have charity enough for my own understanding to believe myself in the right and all you in the wrong.

*Madam. Le voilà mort.*

*Exeunt* Lady FANCIFUL *and* MADAMOISELLE.

*Heart. Gazing after her.* There her single clapper has publish'd the sense of the whole sex. Well, this once I have endeavour'd to wash the blackamoor white, but henceforward I'll sooner undertake to teach sincerity to a courtier, generosity to an usurer, honesty to a lawyer, nay, humility to a divine, than discretion to a woman I see has once set her heart upon playing the fool.

*Enter* CONSTANT.

,Morrow, Constant.

*Con.* Good morrow, Jack. What are you doing here this morning?

*Heart.* Doing? Guess if thou canst. Why, I have been endeavouring to persuade my Lady Fanciful that she's the foolishest woman about town.

*Con.* A pretty endeavour truly.

*Heart.* I have told her in as plain English as I could speak both what the town says of her, and what I think of her. In short, I have us'd her as an absolute king would do magna charta.

*Con.* And how does she take it?

*Heart.* As children do pills: bite 'em, but can't swallow 'em.

*Con.* But, prithee, what has put it in your head, of all mankind, to turn reformer?

*Heart.* Why, one thing was, the morning hung upon my hands; I did not know what to do with myself. And another was, that as little as I care for women, I could not see with patience one that Heaven has taken such wondrous pains about be so very industrious to make herself the jack pudding of the creation.

*Con.* Well, now could I almost wish to see my cruel mistress make the selfsame use of what Heaven has done for her, that so I might be cur'd of a disease that makes me so very uneasy; for love, love is the devil, Heartfree.

*Heart.* And why do you let the devil govern you?

*Con.* Because I have more flesh and blood than grace and self-denial. My dear, dear mistress! 'Sdeath, that so genteel a woman should be a saint when religion's out of fashion!

*Heart.* Nay, she's much in the wrong truly, but who knows how far time and good example may prevail?

*Con.* Oh, they have play'd their parts in vain already. 'Tis now two years since that damn'd fellow her husband invited me to his wedding, and there was the first time I saw that charming woman, whom I have lov'd ever since, more than e'er a martyr did his soul. But she's cold, my friend, still cold as the northern star.

*Heart.* So are all women by nature, which makes 'em so willing to be warm'd.

*Con.* Oh, don't profane the sex. Prithee think 'em all angels for her sake, for she's virtuous even to a fault.

*Heart.* A lover's head is a good accountable thing truly; he adores his mistress for being virtuous, and yet is very angry with her because she won't be lewd.

*Con.* Well, the only relief I expect in my misery is to see thee some day or other as deeply engag'd as myself, which will force me to be merry in the midst of all my misfortunes.

*Heart.* That day will never come, be assur'd, Ned. Not but that I can pass a night with a woman, and for the time perhaps make myself as good sport as you can do. Nay, I can court a woman too, call her nymph, angel, goddess, what you please; but here's the difference 'twixt you and I: I persuade a woman she's

an angel, she persuades you she's one.    Prithee let me tell you
how I avoid falling in love; that which serves me for prevention
may chance to serve you for a cure.

*Con.* Well, use the ladies moderately then, and I'll hear you.

*Heart.* That using 'em moderately undoes us all; but I'll use
'em justly, and that you ought to be satisfied with.    I always
consider a woman, not as the tailor, the shoemaker, the tire-
woman, the sempstress, and—which is more than all that—the
poet makes her, but I consider her as pure nature has contrived
her, and that more strictly than I should have done our old
Grandmother Eve, had I seen her naked in the Garden, for I
consider her turn'd inside out.    Her heart well examin'd, I find
there pride, vanity, covetousness, indiscretion, but above all
things, malice; plots eternally aforging to destroy one another's
reputations, and as honestly to charge the levity of men's tongues
with the scandal; hourly debates how to make poor gentlemen
in love with 'em, with no other intent but to use 'em like dogs
when they have done; a constant desire of doing more mischief,
and an everlasting war wag'd against truth and good nature.

*Con.* Very well, sir, an admirable composition truly.

*Heart.* Then for her outside, I consider it merely as an outside.
She has a thin tiffany covering over just such stuff as you and I
are made on.    As for her motion, her mien, her airs, and all those
tricks, I know they affect you mightily.    If you should see your
mistress at a coronation, dragging her peacock's train, with all her
state and insolence about her, 'twould strike you with all the
awful thoughts that Heaven itself could pretend to from you;
whereas I turn the whole matter into a jest, and suppose her
strutting in the self-same stately manner with nothing on but her
stays and her scanty quilted under-petticoat.

*Con.* Hold thy profane tongue, for I'll hear no more.

*Heart.* What, you'll love on then?

*Con.* Yes, to eternity.

*Heart.* Yet have you no hopes at all?

*Con.* None.

*Heart.* Nay, the resolution may be discreet enough.    Perhaps
you have found out some new philosophy, that love's like virtue,
its own reward; so you and your mistress will be as well content
at a distance as others that have less learning are in coming
together.

*Con.* No, but if she should prove kind at last, my dear Heartfree!                                                    *Embracing him.*

*Heart.* Nay, prithee don't take me for your mistress, for lovers
are very troublesome.

*Con.* Well, who knows what time may do?

*Heart.* And just now he was sure time could do nothing.

*Con.* Yet not one kind glance in two years is somewhat strange.

*Heart.* Not strange at all.    She don't like you, that's all the
business.

*Con.* Prithee don't distract me.

*Heart.* Nay, you are a good handsome young fellow. She might use you better. Come, will you go see her? Perhaps she may have chang'd her mind. There's some hopes as long as she's a woman.

*Con.* Oh, 'tis in vain to visit her. Sometimes to get a sight of her, I visit that beast her husband, but she certainly finds some pretence to quit the room as soon as I enter.

*Heart.* It's much she don't tell him you have made love to her too, for that's another good-natured thing usual amongst women, in which they have several ends. Sometimes 'tis to recommend their virtue, that they may be lewd with the greater security. Sometimes 'tis to make their husbands fight in hopes they may be kill'd, when their affairs require it should be so. But more commonly 'tis to engage two men in a quarrel, that they may have the credit of being fought for; and if the lover's kill'd in the business, they cry, "Poor fellow, he had ill luck", and so they go to cards.

*Con.* Thy injuries to women are not to be forgiven. Look to't if ever thou dost fall into their hands.

*Heart.* They can't use me worse than they do you, that speak well of 'em. Oho! Here comes the knight.

### *Enter* Sir JOHN BRUTE.

*Heart.* Your humble servant, Sir John.

*Sir John.* Servant, sir.

*Heart.* How does all your family?

*Sir John.* Pox o' my family.

*Con.* How does your lady? I han't seen her abroad a good while.

*Sir John.* Do? I don't know how she does, not I. She was well enough yesterday; I han't been at home to-night.

*Con.* What, were you out of town?

*Sir John.* Out of town? No, I was drinking.

*Con.* You are a true Englishman, don't know your own happiness. If I were married to such a woman, I would not be from her a night for all the wine in France.

*Sir John.* Not from her? Oons, what a time should a man have of that?

*Heart.* Why, there's no division, I hope?

*Sir John.* No, but there's a conjunction, and that's worse. A pox o' the parson. Why the plague don't you two marry? I fancy I look like the devil to you.

*Heart.* Why, you don't think you have horns, do you?

*Sir John.* No. I believe my wife's religion will keep her honest.

*Heart.* And what will make her keep her religion?

*Sir John.* Persecution; and therefore she shall have it.

*Heart.* Have a care, knight; women are tender things.

*Sir John.* And yet, methinks, 'tis a hard matter to break their hearts.

*Con.* Fie, fie! You have one of the best wives in the world, and yet you seem the most uneasy husband.

*Sir John.* Best wives! The woman's well enough; she has no vice that I know of, but she's a wife, and—damn a wife! If I were married to a hogshead of claret, matrimony would make me hate it.

*Heart.* Why did you marry then? You were old enough to know your own mind.

*Sir John.* Why did I marry? I married because I had a mind to lie with her, and she would not let me.

*Heart.* Why did not you ravish her?

*Sir John.* Yes, and so have hedg'd myself into forty quarrels with her relations, besides buying my pardon. But more than all that, you must know I was afraid of being damn'd in those days, for I kept sneaking, cowardly company, fellows that went to church, said grace to their meat, and had not the least tincture of quality about 'em.

*Heart.* But I think you are got into a better gang now.

*Sir John.* Zoons, sir, my Lord Rake and I are hand and glove. I believe we may get our bones broke together to-night. Have you a mind to share a frolic?

*Con.* Not I truly. My talent lies to softer exercises.

*Sir John.* What, a down bed and a strumpet? A pox of venery, I say. Will you come and drink with me this afternoon?

*Con.* I can't drink to-day, but we'll come and sit an hour with you if you will.

*Sir John.* Phugh! Pox! Sit an hour! Why can't you drink?

*Con.* Because I'm to see my mistress.

*Sir John.* Who's that?

*Con.* Why, do you use to tell?

*Sir John.* Yes.

*Con.* So won't I.

*Sir John.* Why?

*Con.* Because 'tis a secret.

*Sir John.* Would my wife knew it, 'twould be no secret long.

*Con.* Why, do you think she can't keep a secret?

*Sir John.* No more than she can keep Lent.

*Heart.* Prithee tell it her to try, Constant.

*Sir John.* No, prithee don't, that I mayn't be plagu'd with it.

*Con.* I'll hold you a guinea you don't make her tell it you.

*Sir John.* I'll hold you a guinea I do.

*Con.* Which way?

*Sir John.* Why, I'll beg her not to tell it me.

*Heart.* Nay, if anything does it, that will.

*Con.* But do you think, sir——

*Sir John.* Oons, sir, I think a woman and a secret are the two impertinentest themes in the universe. Therefore, pray, let's hear no more of my wife nor your mistress. Damn 'em both with all my heart, and everything else that daggles a petticoat, except four generous whores, with Betty Sands at the head of 'em, who were drunk with my Lord Rake and I ten times in a fortnight.                                                    *Exit* Sir JOHN.

*Con.* Here's a dainty fellow for you. And the veriest coward too. But his usage of his wife makes me ready to stab the villain.

*Heart.* Lovers are short-sighted; all their senses run into that of feeling. This proceeding of his is the only thing on earth can make your fortune. If anything can prevail with her to accept a gallant, 'tis his ill usage of her, for women will do more for revenge than they'll do for the gospel. Prithee take heart. I have great hopes for you, and since I can't bring you quite off of her, I'll endeavour to bring you quite on, for a whining lover is the damn'd'st companion upon earth.

*Con.* My dear friend, flatter me a little more with these hopes; for whilst they prevail I have Heaven within me, and could melt with joy.

*Heart.* Pray, no melting yet. Let things go farther first. This afternoon perhaps we shall make some advance. In the meanwhile, let's go dine at Locket's, and let hope get you a stomach.                                              *Exeunt.*

### SCENE [II].—Lady FANCIFUL'S *house.*

#### *Enter* Lady FANCIFUL *and* MADAMOISELLE.

*Lady F.* Did you ever see anything so importune, Madamoiselle?

*Madam.* Inteed, matam, to say de trute, he want leetel good breeding.

*Lady F.* Good breeding? He wants to be can'd, Madamoiselle. An insolent fellow! And yet let me expose my weakness: 'tis the only man on earth I could resolve to dispense my favours on, were he but a fine gentleman. Well, did men but know how deep an impression a fine gentleman makes in a lady's heart, they would reduce all their studies to that of good breeding alone.

#### *Enter* CORNET.

*Cor.* Madam, here's Mr. Treble. He has brought home the verses your ladyship made and gave him to set.

*Lady F.* Oh, let him come in, by all means. Now, Madamoiselle, am I going to be unspeakably happy.

#### *Enter* TREBLE.

So, Mr. Treble, you have set my little dialogue?

*Treble.* Yes, Madam, and I hope your ladyship will be pleased with it.

*Lady F.* Oh, no doubt on't, for really, Mr. Treble, you set all things to a wonder. But your music is in particular heavenly when you have my words to clothe in't.

*Treble.* Your words themselves, madam, have so much music in 'em they inspire me.

*Lady F.* Nay, now you make me blush, Mr. Treble. But pray let's hear what you have done.

*Treble.* You shall, madam.

A Song to be sung between a man and a woman.

*Man.*     Ah, lovely nymph, the world's on fire;
        Veil, veil those cruel eyes.
*Woman.* The world may then in flames expire,
        And boast that so it dies.
*Man.*     But when all mortals are destroy'd,
        Who then shall sing your praise?
*Woman.* Those who are fit to be employ'd:
        The gods shall altars raise.

*Treble.* How does your ladyship like it, madam?

*Lady F.* Rapture, rapture, Mr. Treble, I'm all rapture! O wit and art, what power you have when join'd! I must needs tell you the birth of this little dialogue, Mr. Treble. Its father was a dream, and its mother was the moon. I dreamt that by an unanimous vote I was chosen queen of that pale world and that the first time I appear'd upon my throne all my subjects fell in love with me. Just then I wak'd, and seeing pen, ink and paper lie idle upon the table, I slid into my morning gown, and writ this impromptu.

*Treble.* So I guess the dialogue, madam, is suppos'd to be between your majesty and your first minister of state.

*Lady F.* Just. He as minister advises me to trouble my head about the welfare of my subjects, which I as sovereign find a very impertinent proposal. But is the town so dull, Mr. Treble, it affords us never another new song?

*Treble.* Madam, I have one in my pocket came out but yesterday, if your ladyship pleases to let Mrs. Pipe sing it.

*Lady F.* By all means. Here, Pipe. Make what music you can of this song here.

[*Enter* Mrs. PIPE].

SONG

I

Not an angel dwells above
Half so fair as her I love.
    Heaven knows how she'll receive me;
If she smiles, I'm blest indeed,
If she frowns, I'm quickly freed.
    Heaven knows she ne'er can grieve me.

II

> None can love her more than I;
> Yet she ne'er shall make me die,
>   If my flame can never warm her.
> Lasting beauty I'll adore;
> I shall never love her more,
>   Cruelty will so deform her.　　　　　　*Exit* PIPE.

*Lady F.* Very well. This is Heartfree's poetry without question.

*Treble.* Won't your ladyship please to sing yourself this morning?

*Lady F.* Oh Lord, Mr. Treble, my cold is still so barbarous to refuse me that pleasure. He, he, hem.

*Treble.* I'm very sorry for it, madam. Methinks all mankind should turn physician for the cure on't.

*Lady F.* Why truly, to give mankind their due, there's few that know me but have offer'd their remedy.

*Treble.* They have reason, madam, for I know nobody sings so near a cherubin as your ladyship.

*Lady F.* What I do I owe chiefly to your skill and care, Mr. Treble. People do flatter me indeed that I have a voice and a *je-ne-sais-quoi* in the conduct of it that will make music of anything. And truly I begin to believe so, since what happen'd t'other night. Would you think it, Mr. Treble, walking pretty late in the Park, for I often walk late in the Park, Mr. Treble, a whim took me to sing "Chevy Chase", and would you believe it, next morning I had three copies of verses and six billets-doux at my levee upon it.

*Treble.* And without all dispute you deserv'd as many more. Madam, are there any further commands for your ladyship's humble servant?

*Lady F.* Nothing more at this time, Mr. Treble. But I shall expect you here every morning for this month, to sing my little matter there to me. I'll reward you for your pains.

*Treble.* Oh Lord, madam,——

*Lady F.* Good morrow, sweet Mr. Treble.

*Treble.* Your ladyship's most obedient servant. *Exit* TREBLE.

*Enter* SERVANT.

*Serv.* Will your ladyship please to dine yet?

*Lady F.* Yes, let 'em serve.　　　　　　*Exit* SERVANT.
Sure this Heartfree has bewitch'd me, Madamoiselle. You can't imagine how oddly he mix'd himself in my thoughts during my rapture e'en now. I vow 'tis a thousand pities he is not more polish'd. Don't you think so?

*Madam.* Matam, I think it so great pity dat if I was in your ladyship place I take him home in my house. I lock him up in my closet, and I never let him go till I teach him everyting dat fine laty expect from fine gentleman.

*Lady F.* Why truly, I believe I should soon subdue his brutality, for without doubt he has a strange penchant to grow fond
of me, in spite of his aversion to the sex, else he would ne'er have
taken so much pains about me. Lord, how proud would some
poor creatures be of such a conquest? But I, alas, I don't know
how to receive as a favour what I take to be so infinitely my due.
But what shall I do to new-mould him, Madamoiselle? For till
then he's my utter aversion.

*Madam.* Matam, you must laugh at him in all de place dat you
meet him, and turn into de ridicule all he say and all he do.

*Lady F.* Why truly, satire has been ever of wondrous use to
reform ill manners. Besides 'tis my particular talent to ridicule
folks. I can be severe, strangely severe, when I will, Madamoiselle. Give me the pen and ink. I find myself whimsical.
I'll write to him. *Sitting down to write.* Or I'll let it alone and
be severe upon him that way. *Rising up again.* Yet active
severity is better than passive. *Sitting down.* 'Tis as good let
alone too, for every lash I give him, perhaps he'll take for a
favour. *Rising.* Yet 'tis a thousand pities so much satire
should be lost. *Sitting.* But if it should have a wrong effect
upon him 'twould distract me. *Rising.* Well, I must write
though after all. *Sitting.* Or I'll let it alone, which is the same
thing. *Rising.*

*Madam. La voilà determinée.*

*Exeunt.*

# ACT III

## SCENE [I].—[Sir JOHN BRUTE's *house*.]

*Scene opens.* Sir JOHN, Lady BRUTE and BELINDA *rising
from the table.*

*Sir John. To a servant.* Here, take away the things; I expect
company. But first bring me a pipe; I'll smoke.

*Lady B.* Lord, Sir John, I wonder you won't leave that nasty
custom.

*Sir John.* Prithee don't be impertinent.

*Bel. To* Lady BRUTE. I wonder who those are he expects this
afternoon.

*Lady B. To* BELINDA. I'd give the world to know. Perhaps
'tis Constant; he comes here sometimes. If it does prove him,
I'm resolved I'll share the visit.

*Bel.* We'll send for our work and sit here.

*Lady B.* He'll choke us with his tobacco.

*Bel.* Nothing will choke us when we are doing what we have a
mind to. Lovewell!

*Enter* LOVEWELL.

*Love.* Madam.

*Lady B.* Here, bring my cousin's work and mine hither.

> *Exit* LOVEWELL *and re-enters with their work.*

*Sir John.* Why, pox, can't you work somewhere else?

*Lady B.* We shall be careful not to disturb you, sir.

*Bel.* Your pipe would make you too thoughtful, uncle, if you were left alone. Our prittle-prattle will cure your spleen.

*Sir John.* Will it so, Mrs. Pert? Now I believe it will so increase it, I shall take my own house for a paper mill.

> *Sitting and smoking.*

*Lady B. To* BELINDA *aside.* Don't let's mind him; let him say what he will.

*Sir John.* A woman's tongue a cure for the spleen! Oons! *Aside:* If a man had got the headache, they'd be for applying the same remedy.

*Lady B.* You have done a great deal, Belinda, since yesterday.

*Bel.* Yes, I have worked very hard. How do you like it?

*Lady B.* Oh, 'tis the prettiest fringe in the world. Well, cousin, you have the happiest fancy. Prithee advise me about altering my crimson petticoat.

*Sir John.* A pox o' your petticoat! Here's such a prating a man can't digest his own thoughts for you.

*Lady B. Aside.* Don't answer him.—Well, what do you advise me?

*Bel.* Why, really I would not alter it at all. Methinks 'tis very pretty as it is.

*Lady B.* Ay, that's true. But you know one grows weary of the prettiest things in the world when one has had 'em long.

*Sir John.* Yes, I have taught her that.

*Bel.* Shall we provoke him a little?

*Lady B.* With all my heart. Belinda, don't you long to be married?

*Bel.* Why, there are some things in 't I could like well enough.

*Lady B.* What do you think you should dislike?

*Bel.* My husband, a hundred to one else.

*Lady B.* O ye wicked wretch! Sure you don't speak as you think.

*Bel.* Yes, I do; especially if he smok'd tobacco. *He looks earnestly at 'em.*

*Lady B.* Why, that many times takes off worse smells.

*Bel.* Then he must smell very ill indeed.

*Lady B.* So some men will, to keep their wives from coming near 'em.

*Bel.* Then those wives should cuckold 'em at a distance.

> *He rises in a fury, throws his pipe at 'em and drives 'em out.*
> *As they run off,* CONSTANT *and* HEARTFREE *enter.*
> Lady BRUTE *runs against* CONSTANT.

*Sir John.* Oons, get you gone upstairs, you confederating strumpets you, or I'll cuckold you with a vengeance.

*Lady B.* Oh Lord, he'll beat us, he'll beat us! Dear, dear Mr. Constant, save us.        *Exeunt* Lady BRUTE *and* BELINDA.

*Sir John.* I'll cuckold you, with a pox.

*Con.* Heavens, Sir John, what's the matter?

*Sir John.* Sure if woman had been already created, the devil, instead of being kick'd down into Hell, had been married.

*Heart.* Why, what new plague have you found now?

*Sir John.* Why, these two gentlewomen did but hear me say I expected you here this afternoon, upon which they presently resolv'd to take up the room, o' purpose to plague me and my friends.

*Con.* Was that all? Why, we should have been glad of their company.

*Sir John.* Then I should have been weary of yours, for I can't relish both together. They found fault with my smoking tobacco too, and said men stunk. But I have a good mind to say something.

*Con.* No, nothing against the ladies, pray.

*Sir John.* Split the ladies! Come, will you sit down? Give us wine, fellow. You won't smoke?

*Con.* No, nor drink neither, at this time. I must ask your pardon.

*Sir John.* What, this mistress of yours runs in your head. I'll warrant it's some such squeamish minx as my wife, that's grown so dainty of late she finds fault even with a dirty shirt.

*Heart.* That a woman may do, and not be very dainty neither.

*Sir John.* Pox o' the women, let's drink. Come, you shall take one glass, though I send for a box of lozenges to sweeten your mouth after it.

*Con.* Nay, if one glass will satisfy you, I'll drink it without putting you to that expense.

*Sir John.* Why, that's honest. Fill some wine, sirrah. So, here's to you, gentlemen. A wife's the devil. To your being both married. *They drink.*

*Heart.* Oh, your most humble servant, sir.

*Sir John.* Well, how do you like my wine?

*Con.* 'Tis very good indeed.

*Heart.* 'Tis admirable.

*Sir John.* Then give us t'other glass.

*Con.* No, pray excuse us now. We'll come another time and then we won't spare it.

*Sir John.* This one glass and no more. Come, it shall be your mistresses' health, and that's a great compliment from me, I assure you.

*Con.* And 'tis a very obliging one to me. So give us the glasses.

*Sir John.* So. Let her live.

*Heart.* And be kind.        Sir JOHN *coughs in the glass.*

*Con.* What's the matter? Does't go the wrong way?

*Sir John.* If I had love enough to be jealous, I should take this for an ill omen. For I never drank my wife's health in my life but I puk'd in the glass.

*Con.* Oh, she's too virtuous to make a reasonable man jealous.

*Sir John.* Pox of her virtue. If I could but catch her adulterating, I might be divorc'd from her by law.

*Heart.* And so pay her a yearly pension to be a distinguished cuckold.

### Enter SERVANT.

*Serv.* Sir, there's my Lord Rake, Colonel Bully and some other gentlemen at the Blue Posts desire your company.

*Sir John.* Cods so, we are to consult about playing the devil to-night.

*Heart.* Well, we won't hinder business.

*Sir John.* Methinks I don't know how to leave you though. But for once I must make bold. Or, look you, maybe the conference mayn't last long; so if you'll wait here half an hour or an hour—if I don't come then, why then, I won't come at all.

*Heart. To* CONSTANT *aside.* A good modest proposition truly.

*Con.* But let's accept on't however. Who knows what may happen?

*Heart.* Well, sir, to show you how fond we are of your company, we'll expect your return as long as we can.

*Sir John.* Nay, maybe I mayn't stay at all; but business, you know, must be done. So, your servant. Or, hark you, if you have a mind to take a frisk with us, I have an interest with my lord; I can easily introduce you.

*Con.* We are much beholding to you, but for my part I'm engaged another way.

*Sir John.* What? To your mistress, I'll warrant. Prithee leave your nasty punk to entertain herself with her own lewd thoughts, and make one with us to-night.

*Con.* Sir, 'tis business that is to employ me.

*Heart.* And me. And business must be done, you know.

*Sir John.* Ay, women's business, though the world were consum'd for't!                                    *Exit* Sir JOHN.

*Con.* Farewell, beast. And now, my dear friend, would my mistress be but as complaisant as some men's wives, who think it a piece of good breeding to receive the visits of their husbands' friends in his absence.

*Heart.* Why, for your sake I could forgive her, though she should be so complaisant to receive something else in his absence. But what way shall we invent to see her?

*Con.* Oh, ne'er hope it. Invention will prove as vain as wishes.

### Enter Lady BRUTE *and* BELINDA.

*Heart.* What do you think now, friend?

*Con.* I think I shall swoon.

*Heart.* I'll speak first then, whilst you fetch breath.

*Lady B.* We think ourselves oblig'd, gentlemen, to come and return you thanks for your knight-errantry. We were just upon being devour'd by the fiery dragon.

*Bel.* Did not his fumes almost knock you down, gentlemen?

*Heart.* Truly, ladies, we did undergo some hardships, and should have done more, if some greater heroes than ourselves hard by had not diverted him.

*Con.* Though I'm glad of the service you are pleased to say we have done you, yet I'm sorry we could do it no other way than by making ourselves privy to what you would perhaps have kept a secret.

*Lady B.* For Sir John's part, I suppose he design'd it no secret, since he made so much noise. And for myself, truly I am not much concern'd, since 'tis fallen only into this gentleman's hands and yours, who I have many reasons to believe will neither interpret nor report anything to my disadvantage.

*Con.* Your good opinion, madam, was what I fear'd I never could have merited.

*Lady B.* Your fears were vain then, sir, for I am just to everybody.

*Heart.* Prithee, Constant, what is't you do to get the ladies' good opinions, for I'm a novice at it?

*Bel.* Sir, will you give me leave to instruct you?

*Heart.* Yes, that I will with all my soul, madam.

*Bel.* Why then, you must never be slovenly, never be out of humour, fare well and cry roast meat, smoke tobacco, nor drink but when you are a-dry.

*Heart.* That's hard.

*Con.* Nay, if you take his bottle from him, you'll break his heart, madam.

*Bel.* Why, is it possible the gentleman can love drinking?

*Heart.* Only by way of antidote.

*Bel.* Against what, pray?

*Heart.* Against love, madam.

*Lady B.* Are you afraid of being in love, sir?

*Heart.* I should if there were any danger of it.

*Lady B.* Pray, why so?

*Heart.* Because I always had an aversion to being us'd like a dog.

*Bel.* Why truly men in love are seldom us'd better.

*Lady B.* But was you never in love, sir?

*Heart.* No, I thank Heaven, madam.

*Bel.* Pray, where got you your learning then?

*Heart.* From other people's expense.

*Bel.* That's being a sponger, sir, which is scarce honest. If you'd buy some experience with your own money, as 'twould be fairlier got, so 'twould stick longer by you.

*Enter* FOOTMAN.

*Foot.* Madam, here's my Lady Fanciful to wait upon your ladyship.

*Lady B.* Shield me, kind Heaven! What an inundation of impertinence is here coming upon us!

*Enter* Lady FANCIFUL, *who runs first to* Lady BRUTE, *then to* BELINDA, *kissing 'em.*

*Lady F.* My dear Lady Brute, and sweet Belinda! Methinks 'tis an age since I saw you.

*Lady B.* Yet 'tis but three days. Sure you have passed your time very ill, it seems so long to you.

*Lady F.* Why really, to confess the truth to you, I am so everlastingly fatigu'd with the addresses of unfortunate gentlemen, that were it not for the extravagancy of the example, I should e'en tear out these wicked eyes with my own fingers, to make both myself and mankind easy. What think you on't, Mr. Heartfree, for I take you to be my faithful adviser?

*Heart.* Why truly, madam, I think—every project that is for the good of mankind ought to be encourag'd.

*Lady F.* Then I have your consent, sir.

*Heart.* To do whatever you please, madam.

*Lady F.* You had a much more limited complaisance this morning, sir. Would you believe it, ladies? The gentleman has been so exceeding generous to tell me of above fifty faults in less time than it was well possible for me to commit two of 'em.

*Con.* Why truly, madam, my friend there is apt to be something familiar with the ladies.

*Lady F.* He is indeed, sir, but he's wondrous charitable with it; he has the goodness to design a reformation, even down to my fingers' ends. 'Twas thus, I think, sir, you would have had 'em stand. *Opening her fingers in an awkward manner.* My eyes too he did not like. How was't you would have directed 'em? Thus, I think. *Staring at him.* Then there was something amiss in my gait too; I don't know well how 'twas, but as I take it he would have had me walk like him. Pray, sir, do me the favour to take a turn or two about the room, that the company may see you. He's sullen, ladies, and won't. But, to make short, and give you as true an idea as I can of the matter, I think 'twas much about this figure in general he would have moulded me to. *She walks awkwardly about, staring and looking ungainly, then changes on a sudden to the extremity of her usual affectation.* But I was an obstinate woman, and could not resolve to make myself mistress of his heart by growing as awkward as his fancy.

*Here* CONSTANT *and* Lady BRUTE *talk together apart.*

*Heart.* Just thus women do when they think we are in love with 'em, or when they are so with us.

*Lady F.* 'Twould, however, be less vanity for me to conclude the former than you the latter, sir.

*Heart.* Madam, all I shall presume to conclude is that if I were in love, you'd find the means to make me soon weary on't.

*Lady F.* Not by over-fondness, upon my word, sir. But pray, let's stop here, for you are so much govern'd by instinct I know you'll grow brutish at last.

*Bel. Aside.* Now am I sure she's fond of him. I'll try to make her jealous.—Well, for my part, I should be glad to find somebody would be so free with me that I might know my faults and mend 'em.

*Lady F.* Then pray let me recommend this gentleman to you. I have known him for some time and will be surety for him that, upon a very limited encouragement on your side, you shall find an extended impudence on his.

*Heart.* I thank you, madam, for your recommendation. But, hating idleness, I'm unwilling to enter into a place where I believe there would be nothing to do. I was fond of serving your ladyship because I knew you'd find me constant employment.

*Lady F.* I told you he'd be rude, Belinda.

*Bel.* Oh, a little bluntness is a sign of honesty, which makes me always ready to pardon it. So, sir, if you have no other exceptions to my service but the fear of being idle in't, you may venture to list yourself. I shall find you work, I warrant you.

*Heart.* Upon those terms I engage, madam, and this, with your leave, I take for earnest. *Offering to kiss her hand.*

*Bel.* Hold there, sir, I'm none of your earnest givers. But if I'm well serv'd, I give good wages and pay punctually.

HEARTFREE *and* BELINDA *seem to continue talking familiarly.*

*Lady F. Aside.* I don't like this jesting between 'em. Methinks the fool begins to look as if he were in earnest; but then he must be a fool indeed. Lard, what a difference there is between me and her! *Looking at* BELINDA *scornfully.* How I should despise such a thing if I were a man! What a nose she has, what a chin, what a neck! Then her eyes, and the worst kissing lips in the universe. No, no, he can never like her, that's positive; yet I can't suffer 'em together any longer.—Mr. Heartfree, do you know that you and I must have no quarrel for all this? I can't forbear being a little severe now and then. But women, you know, may be allowed anything.

*Heart.* Up to a certain age, madam.

*Lady F.* Which I am not yet past, I hope.

*Heart. Aside.* Nor never will, I dare swear.

*Lady F. To* Lady BRUTE. Come, madam, will your ladyship be witness to our reconciliation?

*Lady B.* You agree then at last?

*Heart. Slightingly.* We forgive.

*Lady F. Aside.* That was a cold, ill-natured reply.

*Lady B.* Then there's no challenges sent between you?

*Heart.* Not from me, I promise.—*Aside to* CONSTANT: But

that's more than I'll do for her, for I know she can as well be damn'd as forbear writing to me.

*Con.* That I believe.   But I think we had best be going lest she should suspect something and be malicious.

*Heart.* With all my heart.

*Con.* Ladies, we are your humble servants.   I see Sir John is quite engag'd.   'Twould be in vain to expect him.   Come, Heartfree.                                          *Exit* CONSTANT.

*Heart.* Ladies, your servant.—*To* BELINDA: I hope, madam, you won't forget our bargain: I'm to say what I please to you.

*Bel.* Liberty of speech entire, sir.              *Exit* HEARTFREE.

*Lady F. Aside.* Very pretty truly.   But how the blockhead went out, languishing at her, and not a look toward me.   Well, churchmen may talk, but miracles are not ceas'd.   For 'tis more than natural such a rude fellow as he and such a little impertinent as she should be capable of making a woman of my sphere uneasy. But I can bear her sight no longer.   Methinks she's grown ten times uglier than Cornet.   I must go home and study revenge.— *To* Lady BRUTE: Madam, your humble servant.   I must take my leave.

*Lady B.* What, going already, madam?

*Lady F.* I must beg you'll excuse me this once.   For really I have eighteen visits to return this afternoon, so you see I'm importun'd by the women as well as the men.

*Bel. Aside.* And she's quits with 'em both.

*Lady F. Going.* Nay, you shan't go one step out of the room.

*Lady B.* Indeed, I'll wait upon you down.

*Lady F.* No, sweet Lady Brute; you know I swoon at ceremony.

*Lady B.* Pray give me leave.

*Lady F.* You know I won't.

*Lady B.* Indeed I must.

*Lady F.* Indeed you shan't.

*Lady B.* Indeed I will.

*Lady F.* Indeed you shan't.

*Lady B.* Indeed I will.

*Lady F.* Indeed you shan't.   Indeed, indeed, indeed you shan't.                    *Exit* Lady FANCIFUL *running.   They follow.*

*Re-enter* Lady BRUTE, *sola.*

*Lady B.* This impertinent woman has put me out of humour for a fortnight.   What an agreeable moment has her foolish visit interrupted.   Lord, how like a torrent love flows into the heart when once the sluice of desire is open'd!   Good Gods, what a pleasure there is in doing what we should not do!

*Re-enter* CONSTANT.

Ha, here again?

*Con.* Though the renewing my visit may seem a little irregular,

I hope I shall obtain your pardon for it, madam, when you know
I only left the room lest the lady who was here should have been
as malicious in her remarks as she's foolish in her conduct.

*Lady B.* He who has discretion enough to be tender of a
woman's reputation carries a virtue about him may atone for a
great many faults.

*Con.* If it has a title to atone for any, its pretensions must needs
be strongest where the crime is love. I therefore hope I shall be
forgiven the attempt I have made upon your heart, since my
enterprise has been a secret to all the world but yourself.

*Lady B.* Secrecy indeed in sins of this kind is an argument of
weight to lessen the punishment, but nothing's a plea for a
pardon entire without a sincere repentance.

*Con.* If sincerity in repentance consist in sorrow for offending,
no cloister ever enclosed so true a penitent as I should be.   But
I hope it cannot be reckon'd an offence to love where 'tis a duty to
adore.

*Lady B.* 'Tis an offence, a great one, where it would rob a
woman of all she ought to be ador'd for, her virtue.

*Con.* Virtue?  Virtue, alas, is no more like the thing that's
call'd so than 'tis like vice itself.  Virtue consists in goodness,
honour, gratitude, sincerity and pity, and not in peevish, snarling,
strait-lac'd chastity.  True virtue, wheresoe'er it moves, still
carries an intrinsic worth about it, and is in every place and in
each sex of equal value.  So is not continence, you see, that
phantom of honour, which men in every age have so condemn'd,
they have thrown it amongst the women to scrabble for.

*Lady B.* If it be a thing of so very little value, why do you so
earnestly recommend it to your wives and daughters?

*Con.* We recommend it to our wives, madam, because we would
keep 'em to ourselves.   And to our daughters, because we would
dispose of 'em to others.

*Lady B.* 'Tis then of some importance it seems, since you can't
dispose of 'em without it.

*Con.* That importance, madam, lies in the humour of the
country, not in the nature of the thing.

*Lady B.* How do you prove that, sir?

*Con.* From the wisdom of a neighb'ring nation in a contrary
practice.  In monarchies things go by whimsy, but common-
wealths weigh all things in the scale of reason.

*Lady B.* I hope we are not so very light a people to bring up
fashions without some ground.

*Con.* Pray, what does your ladyship think of a powder'd coat
for deep mourning?

*Lady B.* I think, sir, your sophistry has all the effect that you
can reasonably expect it should have: it puzzles, but don't
convince.

*Con.* I'm sorry for it.

*Lady B.* I'm sorry to hear you say so.

*Con.* Pray, why?

*Lady B.* Because if you expected more from it, you have a worse opinion of my understanding than I desire you should have.

*Con. Aside.* I comprehend her. She would have me set a value upon her chastity that I may think myself the more oblig'd to her when she makes me a present of it. *To her:* I beg you will believe I did but rally, madam. I know you judge too well of right and wrong to be deceiv'd by arguments like those. I hope you'll have so favourable an opinion of my understanding too to believe the thing call'd virtue has worth enough with me to pass for an eternal obligation where'er 'tis sacrific'd.

*Lady B.* It is, I think, so great a one as nothing can repay.

*Con.* Yes, the making the man you love your everlasting debtor.

*Lady B.* When debtors once have borrow'd all we have to lend, they are very apt to grow very shy of their creditors' company.

*Con.* That, madam, is only when they are forc'd to borrow of usurers and not of a generous friend. Let us choose our creditors, and we are seldom so ungrateful to shun 'em.

*Lady B.* What think you of Sir John, sir? I was his free choice.

*Con.* I think he's married, madam.

*Lady B.* Does marriage then exclude men from your rule of constancy?

*Con.* It does. Constancy's a brave, free, haughty, generous agent that cannot buckle to the chains of wedlock. There's a poor, sordid slavery in marriage that turns the flowing tide of honour and sinks us to the lowest ebb of infamy. 'Tis a corrupted soil; ill nature, avarice, sloth, cowardice and dirt are all its product.

*Lady B.* Have you no exceptions to this general rule, as well as to t'other?

*Con.* Yes, I would, after all, be an exception to it myself if you were free in power and will to make me so.

*Lady B.* Compliments are well plac'd where 'tis impossible to lay hold on 'em.

*Con.* I would to Heaven 'twere possible for you to lay hold on mine, that you might see it is no compliment at all. But since you are already dispos'd on beyond redemption to one who does not know the value of the jewel you have put into his hands, I hope you would not think him greatly wrong'd, though it should sometimes be look'd on by a friend who knows how to esteem it as he ought.

*Lady B.* If looking on't alone would serve his turn, the wrong perhaps might not be very great.

*Con.* Why, what if he should wear it now and then a day, so he gave good security to bring it home again at night?

*Lady B.* Small security, I fancy, might serve for that. One might venture to take his word.

*Con.* Then where's the injury to the owner?

*Lady B.* 'Tis an injury to him if he think it one. For if happiness be seated in the mind, unhappiness must be so too.

*Con.* Here I close with you, madam, and draw my conclusive argument from your own position: if the injury lie in the fancy, there needs nothing but secrecy to prevent the wrong.

*Lady B. Going.* A surer way to prevent it is to hear no more arguments in its behalf.

*Con. Following her.* But, madam,——

*Lady B.* But, sir, 'tis my turn to be discreet now, and not suffer too long a visit.

*Con. Catching her hand.* By Heaven, you shall not stir till you give me hopes that I shall see you again, at some more convenient time and place.

*Lady B.* I give you just hopes enough *Breaking from him.* to get loose from you, and that's all I can afford you at this time.

*Exit running.*

*Con. Solus.* Now by all that's great and good, she is a charming woman. In what ecstasy of joy she has left me! For she gave me hope. Did she not say she gave me hope? Hope? Ay. What hope? Enough to make me let her go. Why, that's enough in conscience. Or no matter how 'twas spoke. Hope was the word. It came from her, and it was said to me.

*Enter* HEARTFREE.

Ha, Heartfree, thou hast done me noble service in prattling to the young gentlewoman without there. Come to my arms, thou venerable bawd, and let me squeeze thee *Embracing him eagerly.* as a new pair of stays does a fat country girl when she's carried to court to stand for a maid of honour.

*Heart.* Why, what the devil's all this rapture for?

*Con.* Rapture? There's ground for rapture, man. There's hopes, my Heartfree, hopes, my friend.

*Heart.* Hopes? Of what?

*Con.* Why, hopes that my lady and I together—for 'tis more than one body's work—should make Sir John a cuckold.

*Heart.* Prithee, what did she say to thee?

*Con.* Say? What did she not say? She said that, says she, she said—Zoons, I don't know what she said. But she look'd as if she said everything I'd have her; and so if thou'lt go to the tavern, I'll treat thee with anything that gold can buy. I'll give all my silver amongst the drawers, make a bonfire before the door, say the plenipos have sign'd the peace, and the Bank of England's grown honest.    *Exeunt.*

SCENE [II].—*The Blue Posts.*

Lord RAKE, Sir JOHN, *etc., at a table drinking.*

*All.* Huzza!

*Lord Rake.* Come, boys. Charge again. So. Confusion to all order. Here's liberty of conscience!

*All.* Huzza!

*Lord Rake.* I'll sing you a song I made this morning to this purpose.

*Sir John.* 'Tis wicked, I hope.

*Col. Bully.* Don't my lord tell you he made it?

*Sir John.* Well then, let's ha't.

Lord RAKE *sings.*

I

What a pother of late
Have they kept in the state
    About setting our consciences free.
A bottle has more
Dispensation in store
    Than the king and the state can decree.

II

When my head's full of wine,
I o'erflow with design
    And know no penal laws that can curb me.
Whate'er I devise
Seems good in my eyes,
    And religion ne'er dares to disturb me.

III

No saucy remorse
Intrudes in my course,
    Nor impertinent notions of evil.
So there's claret in store,
In peace I've my whore,
    And in peace I jog on to the devil.

*All sing.* So there's claret, etc.

*Lord Rake. Repeats.* And in peace I jog on to the devil. Well, how do you like it, gentlemen?

*All.* Oh, admirable!

*Sir John.* I would not give a fig for a song that is not full of sin and impudence.

*Lord Rake.* Then my muse is to your taste. But drink away;

the night steals upon us, we shall want time to be lewd in. Hey, page, sally out, sirrah, and see what's doing in the camp; we'll beat up their quarters presently.

*Page.* I'll bring your lordship an exact account.          *Exit.*

*Lord Rake.* Now let the spirit of clary go round. Fill me a brimmer. Here's to our forlorn hope. Courage, knight, victory attends you.

*Sir John.* And laurels shall crown mo. Drink away and be damn'd.

*Lord Rake.* Again, boys! T'other glass, and damn morality.

*Sir John. Drunk.* Ay, damn morality and damn the watch, and let the constable be married.

*All.* Huzza!

Re-enter PAGE.

*Lord Rake.* How are the streets inhabited, sirrah?

*Page.* My lord, it's Sunday night; they are full of drunken citizens.

*Lord Rake.* Along then, boys, we shall have a feast.

*Col. Bully.* Along, noble knight.

*Sir John.* Ay, along, Bully. And he that says Sir John Brute is not as drunk and as religious as the drunkest citizen of 'em all—is a liar and the son of a whore.

*Col. Bully.* Why, that was bravely spoke, and like a free-born Englishman.

*Sir John.* What's that to you, sir, whether I am an Englishman or a Frenchman?

*Col. Bully.* Zoons, you are not angry, sir?

*Sir John.* Zoons, I am angry sir. For if I am a free-born Englishman, what have you to do, even to talk of my privileges?

*Lord Rake.* Why prithee, knight, don't quarrel here. Leave private animosities to be decided by daylight. Let the night be employed against the public enemy.

*Sir John.* My lord, I respect you because you are a man of quality. But I'll make that fellow know I am within a hair's breadth as absolute by my privileges as the King of France is by his prerogative. He by his prerogative takes money where it is not his due; I by my privilege refuse paying it where I owe it. Liberty and property and old England, huzza!

Exit Sir JOHN reeling, all following him.

SCENE [III].—Lady BRUTE's bedchamber.

Enter Lady BRUTE and BELINDA.

*Lady B.* Sure, it's late, Belinda. I begin to be sleepy.

*Bel.* Yes, 'tis near twelve. Will you go to bed?

*Lady B.* To bed, my dear? And by that time I'm fallen into a sweet sleep, or perhaps a sweet dream, which is better and better, Sir John will come home, roaring drunk, and be overjoy'd he finds me in a condition to be disturb'd.

*Bel.* Oh, you need not fear him; he's in for all night. The servants say he's gone to drink with my Lord Rake.

*Lady B.* Nay, 'tis not very likely indeed such suitable company should part presently. What hogs men turn, Belinda, when they grow weary of women!

*Bel.* And what owls they are whilst they are fond of 'em!

*Lady B.* But that we may forgive well enough because they are so upon our accounts.

*Bel.* We ought to do so indeed, but 'tis a hard matter. For when a man is really in love, he looks so unsufferably silly that though a woman lik'd him well enough before, she had then much ado to endure the sight of him. And this I take to be the reason why lovers are so generally ill used.

*Lady B.* Well, I own now I'm well enough pleased to see a man look like an ass for me.

*Bel.* Ay, I'm pleas'd he should look like an ass too; that is, I'm pleased with myself for making him look so.

*Lady B.* Nay, truly, I think if he'd find some other way to express his passion 'twould be more to his advantage.

*Bel.* Yes, for then a woman might like his passion and him too.

*Lady B.* Yes, Belinda, after all, a woman's life would be but a dull business if 'twere not for men, and men that can look like asses too. We should never blame Fate for the shortness of our days; our time would hang wretchedly upon our hands.

*Bel.* Why, truly, they do help us off with a good share on't. For were there no men in the world, o' my conscience I should be no longer a-dressing than I'm a-saying my prayers. Nay, though it were Sunday; for you know that one may go to church without stays on.

*Lady B.* But don't you think emulation might do something? For every woman you see desires to be finer than her neighbour.

*Bel.* That's only that the men may like her better than her neighbour. No, if there were no men, adieu fine petticoats; we should be weary of wearing 'em.

*Lady B.* And adieu plays; we should be weary of seeing 'em.

*Bel.* Adieu Hyde Park; the dust would choke us.

*Lady B.* Adieu St. James's; walking would tire us.

*Bel.* Adieu London; the smoke would stifle us.

*Lady B.* And adieu going to church, for religion would ne'er prevail with us.

*Both.* Ha, ha, ha, ha, ha!

*Bel.* Our confession is so very hearty, sure we merit absolution.

*Lady B.* Not unless we go through with't and confess all. So prithee, for the ease of our consciences, let's hide nothing.

*Bel.* Agreed.

*Lady B.* Why then, I confess that I love to sit in the forefront of a box. For if one sits behind, there's two acts gone perhaps

before one's found out.   And when I am there, if I perceive the
men whispering and looking upon me, you must know I cannot
for my life forbear thinking they talk to my advantage.   And
that sets a thousand little tickling vanities on foot.

*Bel.* Just my case for all the world, but go on.

*Lady B.* I watch with impatience for the next jest in the play
that I may laugh and show my white teeth.   If the poet has been
dull, and the jest be long a coming, I pretend to whisper one to
my friend, and from thence fall into a short discourse in which I
take occasion to show my face in all humours:  brisk, pleas'd,
serious, melancholy, languishing.   Not that what we say to one
another causes any of these alterations, but——

*Bel.* Don't trouble yourself to explain, for if I'm not mistaken,
you and I have had some of these necessary dialogues before now,
with the same intention.

*Lady B.* Why, I'll swear, Belinda, some people do give strange
agreeable airs to their faces in speaking.   Tell me true: did you
never practise in the glass?

*Bel.* Why, did you?

*Lady B.* Yes, faith, many a time.

*Bel.* And I too, I own it.   Both how to speak myself, and how
to look when others speak.   But my glass and I could never yet
agree what face I should make when they come blurt out with a
nasty thing in a play.   For all the men presently look upon the
women, that's certain; so laugh we must not, though our stays
burst for't, because that's telling truth and owning we understand the jest.   And to look serious is so dull, when the whole
house is a-laughing.

*Lady B.* Besides, that looking serious does really betray our
knowledge in the matter as much as laughing with the company
would do.   For if we did not understand the thing we should
naturally do like other people.

*Bel.* For my part I always take that occasion to blow my nose.

*Lady B.* You must blow your nose half off then at some plays.

*Bel.* Why don't some reformer or other beat the poet for't?

*Lady B.* Because he is not so sure of our private approbation
as of our public thanks.   Well, sure there is not upon earth so
impertinent a thing as women's modesty.

*Bel.* Yes, men's fantasque, that obliges us to it.   If we quit our
modesty they say we lose our charms, and yet they know that
very modesty is affectation, and rail at our hypocrisy.

*Lady B.* Thus one would think 'twere a hard matter to please
'em, niece.   Yet our kind Mother Nature has given us something
that makes amends for all.   Let our weakness be what it will,
mankind will still be weaker, and whilst there is a world, 'tis
woman that will govern it.   But prithee, one word of poor
Constant before we go to bed, if it be but to furnish matter for
dreams.   I dare swear he's talking of me now, or thinking of me
at least, though it be in the middle of his prayers.

*Bel.* So he ought, I think, for you were pleas'd to make him a good round advance to-day, madam.

*Lady B.* Why, I have e'en plagu'd him enough to satisfy any reasonable woman; he has besieg'd me these two years to no purpose.

*Bel.* And if he besieg'd you two years more he'll be well enough paid, so he had the plundering of you at last.

*Lady B.* That may be; but I'm afraid the town won't be able to hold out much longer, for to confess the truth to you, Belinda, the garrison begins to grow mutinous.

*Bel.* Then the sooner you capitulate the better.

*Lady B.* Yet methinks I would fain stay a little longer, to see you fix'd too, that we might start together, and see who could love longest. What think you if Heartfree should have a month's mind to you?

*Bel.* Why, faith, I could almost be in love with him for despising that foolish, affected Lady Fanciful, but I'm afraid he's too cold ever to warm himself by my fire.

*Lady B.* Then he deserves to be froze to death. Would I were a man for your sake, my dear rogue.　　　*Kissing her.*

*Bel.* You'd wish yourself a woman again for your own, or the men are mistaken. But if I could make a conquest of this son of Bacchus and rival his bottle, what should I do with him? He has no fortune; I can't marry him, and sure you would not have me commit fornication.

*Lady B.* Why, if you did, child, 'twould be but a good friendly part; if 'twere only to keep me in countenance whilst I commit— you know what.

*Bel.* Well, if I can't resolve to serve you that way, I may perhaps some other, as much to your satisfaction. But, pray, how shall we contrive to see these blades again quickly?

*Lady B.* We must e'en have recourse to the old way: make 'em an appointment 'twixt jest and earnest; 'twill look like a frolic, and that, you know 's a very good thing to save a woman's blushes.

*Bel.* You advise well; but where shall it be?

*Lady B.* In Spring Garden. But they shan't know their women till their women pull off their masks, for a surprise is the most agreeable thing in the world, and I find myself in a very good humour, ready to do 'em any good turn I can think on.

*Bel.* Then pray write 'em the necessary billet, without farther delay.

*Lady B.* Let's go into your chamber then, and whilst you say your prayers I'll do it, child.　　　*Exeunt.*

## ACT IV

### SCENE [I].—*Covent Garden.*

*Enter* Lord RAKE, Sir JOHN, *etc., with swords drawn.*

*Lord Rake.* Is the dog dead?

*Col. Bully.* No, damn him, I heard him wheeze.

*Lord Rake.* How the witch his wife howl'd!

*Col. Bully.* Ay, she'll alarm the watch presently.

*Lord Rake.* Appear, knight, then. Come, you have a good cause to fight for; there's a man murder'd.

*Sir John.* Is there? Then let his ghost be satisfied; for I'll sacrifice a constable to it presently, and burn his body upon his wooden chair.

*Enter a* TAILOR, *with a bundle under his arm.*

*Col. Bully.* How now? What have we got here? A thief?

*Tailor.* No, an't please you, I'm no thief.

*Lord Rake.* That we'll see presently. Here, let the general examine him.

*Sir John.* Ay, ay, let me examine him, and I'll lay a hundred pound I find him guilty in spite of his teeth—for he looks—like a—sneaking rascal. Come, sirrah, without equivocation or mental reservation, tell me of what opinion you are and what calling, for by them—I shall guess at your morals.

*Tailor.* An't please you, I'm a dissenting journeyman tailor.

*Sir John.* Then, sirrah, you love lying by your religion and theft by your trade. And so, that your punishment may be suitable to your crimes—I'll have you first gagg'd—and then hang'd.

*Tailor.* Pray, good worthy gentlemen, don't abuse me. Indeed, I'm an honest man and a good workman, though I say it that should not say it.

*Sir John.* No words, sirrah, but attend your fate.

*Lord Rake.* Let me see what's in that bundle.

*Tailor.* An't please you, it's the doctor of the parish's gown.

*Lord Rake.* The doctor's gown! Hark you, knight, you won't stick at abusing the clergy, will you?

*Sir John.* No, I'm drunk, and I'll abuse anything—but my wife, and her I name—with reverence.

*Lord Rake.* Then you shall wear this gown whilst you charge the watch, that though the blows fall upon you, the scandal may light upon the church.

*Sir John.* A generous design—by all the gods. Give it me.
                                        *Takes the gown and puts it on.*

*Tailor.* O dear gentlemen, I shall be quite undone if you take the gown.

*Sir John.* Retire, sirrah, and since you carry off your skin—
go home and be happy.

*Tailor. Pausing.* I think I had e'en as good follow the gentleman's friendly advice, for if I dispute any longer, who knows but
the whim may take him to case me? These courtiers are fuller
of tricks than they are of money; they'll sooner cut a man's
throat than pay his bill.                                             *Exit.*

*Sir John.* So, how d'ye like my shapes now?

*Lord Rake.* This will do to a miracle. He looks like a bishop
going to the holy war. But to your arms, gentlemen, the enemy
appears.

*Enter* CONSTABLE *and* WATCH.

*Watch.* Stand! Who goes there? Come before the constable.

*Sir John.* The constable's a rascal—and you are the son of a
whore.

*Watch.* A good civil answer for a parson, truly.

*Const.* Methinks, sir, a man of your coat might set a better
example.

*Sir John.* Sirrah, I'll make you know—there are men of my
coat can set as bad examples—as you can do, you dog you.

Sir JOHN *strikes the* CONSTABLE. *They knock him down,
disarm him and seize him.* Lord RAKE, *etc., run away.*

*Const.* So, we have secur'd the parson, however.

*Sir John.* Blood and blood—and blood!

*Watch.* Lord have mercy upon us! How the wicked wretch
raves of blood. I'll warrant he has been murdering somebody
to-night.

*Sir John.* Sirrah, there's nothing got by murder but a halter.
My talent lies towards drunkenness and simony.

*Watch.* Why, that now was spoke like a man of parts, neighbour. It's pity he should be so disguis'd.

*Sir John.* You lie. I am not disguis'd, for I am drunk bare-
fac'd.

*Watch.* Look you there again. This is a mad parson, Mr.
Constable; I'll lay a pot of ale upon's head, he's a good preacher.

*Const.* Come, sir, out of respect to your calling I shan't put you
into the roundhouse, but we must secure you in our drawing-
room till morning, that you may do no mischief. So come along.

*Sir John.* You may put me where you will, sirrah, now you
have overcome me; but if I can't do mischief, I'll think of
mischief—in spite of your teeth, you dog you.          *Exeunt.*


SCENE [II].—HEARTFREE'S *bedchamber.*

*Enter* HEARTFREE, *solus.*

*Heart.* What the plague ails me? Love? No, I thank you for
that; my heart's rock still. Yet 'tis Belinda that disturbs me,

that's positive. Well, what of all that? Must I love her for being troublesome? At that rate I might love all the women I meet, egad. But hold. Though I don't love her for disturbing me, yet she may disturb me because I love her. Ay, that may be, faith. I have dreamt of her, that's certain. Well, so I have of my mother; therefore, what's that to the purpose? Ay, but Belinda runs in my mind waking. And so does many a damn'd thing that I don't care a farthing for. Methinks though, I would fain be talking to her, and yet I have no business. Well, am I the first man that has had a mind to do an impertinent thing?

*Enter* CONSTANT.

*Con.* How now, Heartfree? What makes you up and dress'd so soon? I thought none but lovers quarrell'd with their beds. I expected to have found you snoring, as I us'd to do.

*Heart.* Why, faith, friend, 'tis the care I have of your affairs that makes me so thoughtful. I have been studying all night how to bring your matter about with Belinda.

*Con.* With Belinda?

*Heart.* With my lady, I mean. And, faith, I have mighty hopes on't. Sure you must be very well satisfied with her behaviour to you yesterday.

*Con.* So well that nothing but a lover's fears can make me doubt of success. But what can this sudden change proceed from?

*Heart.* Why, you saw her husband beat her, did you not?

*Con.* That's true. A husband is scarce to be borne upon any terms, much less when he fights with his wife. Methinks she should e'en have cuckolded him upon the very spot, to show that after the battle she was master of the field.

*Heart.* A council of war of women would infallibly have advis'd her to't. But, I confess, so agreeable a woman as Belinda deserves a better usage.

*Con.* Belinda again?

*Heart.* My lady, I mean. What a pox makes me blunder so to-day? *Aside:* A plague of this treacherous tongue.

*Con.* Prithee look upon me seriously, Heartfree. Now answer me directly. Is it my lady or Belinda employs your careful thoughts thus?

*Heart.* My lady or Belinda?

*Con.* In love, by this light, in love!

*Heart.* In love?

*Con.* Nay, ne'er deny it; for thou'lt do it so awkwardly 'twill but make the jest sit heavier about thee. My dear friend, I give thee much joy.

*Heart.* Why, prithee, you won't persuade me to it, will you?

*Con.* That she's mistress of your tongue, that's plain, and I know you are so honest a fellow, your tongue and heart always go together. But how? But how the devil? Pha! Ha, ha, ha!

*Heart.* Heyday! Why sure you don't believe it in earnest?

*Con.* Yes, I do, because I see you deny it in jest.

*Heart.* Nay, but look you, Ned—a—deny in jest—a—gadzooks, you know I say—a—when a man denies a thing in jest—a——

*Con.* Pha, ha, ha, ha, ha!

*Heart.* Nay, then we shall have it. What, because a man stumbles at a word? Did you never make a blunder?

*Con.* Yes, for I am in love; I own it.

*Heart.* Then so am I. *Embracing him.* Now laugh till thy soul's glutted with mirth, but, dear Constant, don't tell the town on't.

*Con.* Nay then, 'twere almost pity to laugh at thee, after so honest a confession. But tell us a little, Jack. By what new-invented arms has this mighty stroke been given?

*Heart.* E'en by that unaccountable weapon call'd *je ne sais quoi.* For everything that can come within the verge of beauty, I have seen it with indifference.

*Con.* So in few words then: the *je ne sais quoi* has been too hard for the quilted petticoat.

*Heart.* Egad, I think the *je ne sais quoi* is in the quilted petticoat. At least 'tis certain I ne'er think on't without—a—a *je ne sais quoi* in every part about me.

*Con.* Well, but have all your remedies lost their virtue? Have you turn'd her inside out yet?

*Heart.* I dare not so much as think on't.

*Con.* But don't the two years' fatigue I have had discourage you?

*Heart.* Yes, I dread what I foresee, yet cannot quit the enterprise. Like some soldiers whose courage dwells more in their honour than in their nature, on they go, though the body trembles at what the soul makes it undertake.

*Con.* Nay, if you expect your mistress will use you as your profanations against her sex deserve, you tremble justly. But how do you intend to proceed, friend?

*Heart.* Thou know'st I'm but a novice. Be friendly and advise me.

*Con.* Why, look you then. I'd have you—serenade and a—write a song—go to church, look like a fool, be very officious, ogle, write, and lead out. And who knows but in a year or two's time, you may be—call'd a troublesome puppy and sent about your business.

*Heart.* That's hard.

*Con.* Yet thus it oft falls out with lovers, sir.

*Heart.* Pox on me for making one of the number.

*Con.* Have a care. Say no saucy things. 'Twill but augment your crime, and if your mistress hears on't, increase your punishment.

*Heart.* Prithee say something then to encourage me. You know I help'd you in your distress.

*Con.* Why then, to encourage you to perseverance, that you may be thoroughly ill us'd for your offences, I'll put you in mind that even the coyest ladies of 'em all are made up of desires as well as we, and though they do hold out a long time, they will capitulate at last. For that thundering engineer, nature, does make such havoc in the town, they must surrender at long run or perish in their own flames.

*Enter a* FOOTMAN.

*Foot.* Sir, there's a porter without with a letter. He desires to give it into your own hands.
*Con.* Call him in.                    [*Exit* FOOTMAN.]

*Enter* PORTER.

What, Jo, is it thee?
*Porter.* An't please you, sir, I was order'd to deliver this into your own hands by two well-shap'd ladies at the New Exchange. I was at your honour's lodgings, and your servants sent me hither.
*Con.* 'Tis well. Are you to carry any answer?
*Porter.* No, my noble master. They gave me my orders, and whip they were gone, like a maidenhead at fifteen.
*Con.* Very well. There.                    *Gives him money.*
*Porter.* God bless your honour.                    *Exit.*
*Con.* Now let's see what honest, trusty Jo has brought us.
*Reads:* "If you and your playfellow can spare time from your business and devotions, don't fail to be at Spring Garden about eight in the evening. You'll find nothing there but women, so you need bring no other arms than what you usually carry about you." So, playfellow, here's something to stay your stomach till your mistress's dish is ready for you.
*Heart.* Some of our old batter'd acquaintance. I won't go, not I.
*Con.* Nay, that you can't avoid. There's honour in the case. 'Tis a challenge, and I want a second.
*Heart.* I doubt I shall be but a very useless one to you, for I'm so dishearten'd by this wound Belinda has given me I don't think I shall have courage enough to draw my sword.
*Con.* Oh, if that be all, come along. I'll warrant you find sword enough for such enemies as we have to deal withal.
                                        *Exeunt.*

[SCENE III.]—*at the* JUSTICE'S *house.*

*Enter* CONSTABLE, *etc., with* Sir JOHN.

*Const.* Come along, sir. I thought to have let you slip this morning because you were a minister, but you are as drunk and as abusive as ever. We'll see what the justice of the peace will say to you.

*Sir John.* And you shall see what I'll say to the justice of the peace, sirrah.

*They knock at the door.*
*Enter* SERVANT.

*Const.* Pray acquaint his worship we have got an unruly parson here. We are unwilling to expose him, but don't know what to do with him.

*Serv.* I'll acquaint my master.                    *Exit.*

*Sir John.* You—constable—what damn'd justice is this?

*Const.* One that will take care of you, I warrant you.

*Enter* JUSTICE.

*Justice.* Well, Mr. Constable, what's the disorder here?

*Const.* An't please your worship——

*Sir John.* Let me speak and be damn'd. I'm a divine and can unfold mysteries better than you can do.

*Justice.* Sadness, sadness, a minister so overtaken! Pray, sir, give the constable leave to speak, and I'll hear you very patiently, I assure you, sir, I will.

*Sir John.* Sir—you are a very civil magistrate. Your most humble servant.

*Const.* An't please your worship then. He has attempted to beat the watch to-night, and swore——

*Sir John.* You lie.

*Justice.* Hold, pray, sir, a little.

*Sir John.* Sir, your very humble servant.

*Const.* Indeed, sir, he came at us without any provocation, call'd us whores and rogues, and laid us on with a great quarter-staff. He was in my Lord Rake's company. They have been playing the devil to-night.

*Justice.* Hem—hem—pray, sir—May you be chaplain to my lord?

*Sir John.* Sir—I presume—I may if I will.

*Justice.* My meaning, sir, is, are you so?

*Sir John.* Sir—you mean very well.

*Justice.* He, hem—hem—Under favour, sir, pray answer me directly.

*Sir John.* Under favour, sir—Do you use to answer directly when you are drunk?

*Justice.* Good lack, good lack. Here's nothing to be got from him. Pray, sir, may I crave your name?

*Sir John.* Sir—my name's— *He hiccups.* Hiccup, sir.

*Justice.* Hiccup? Doctor Hiccup. I have known a great many country parsons of that name, especially down in the fens. Pray where do you live, sir?

*Sir John.* Here—and there, sir.

*Justice.* Why, what a strange man is this? Where do you preach, sir? Have you any cure?

*Sir John.* Sir—I have—a very good cure—for a clap, at your service.

*Justice.* Lord have mercy upon us!

*Sir John. Aside.* This fellow does ask so many impertinent questions I believe, egad, 'tis the justice's wife in the justice's clothes.

*Justice.* Mr. Constable, I vow and protest I don't know what to do with him.

*Const.* Truly he has been but a troublesome guest to us all night.

*Justice.* I think I had e'en best let him go about his business, for I'm unwilling to expose him.

*Const.* E'en what your worship thinks fit.

*Sir John.* Sir—not to interrupt Mr. Constable, I have a small favour to ask.

*Justice.* Sir, I open both my ears to you.

*Sir John.* Sir, your very humble servant. I have a little urgent business calls upon me, and therefore I desire the favour of you to bring matters to a conclusion.

*Justice.* Sir, if I were sure that business were not to commit more disorders, I would release you.

*Sir John.* None—by my priesthood.

*Justice.* Then, Mr. Constable, you may discharge him.

*Sir John.* Sir, your very humble servant. If you please to accept of a bottle——

*Justice.* I thank you kindly, sir, but I never drink in a morning. Goodbye to ye, sir, goodbye to ye.

*Sir John.* Goodbye t'ye, good sir.                    *Exit* JUSTICE.
So—now, Mr. Constable, shall you and I go pick up a whore together?

*Const.* No, thank you, sir; my wife's enough to satisfy any reasonable man.

*Sir John. Aside.* He, he, he, he, he! The fool's married then. —Well, you won't go?

*Const.* Not I, truly.

*Sir John.* Then I'll go by myself, and you and your wife may be damn'd.                                   *Exit.*

*Const. Gazing after him.* Why, God-a-mercy, parson!
                                   *Exit* CONSTABLE, *etc.*


SCENE [IV].—*Spring Garden.*

CONSTANT *and* HEARTFREE *cross the stage. As they go off,
enter* Lady FANCIFUL *and* MADAMOISELLE, *mask'd and
dogging 'em.*

*Con.* So, I think we are about the time appointed. Let us walk up this way.                                   *Exeunt.*

*Lady F.* Good. Thus far I have dogg'd 'em without being

discover'd. 'Tis infallibly some intrigue that brings them to
Spring Garden. How my poor heart is torn and wrack'd with
fear and jealousy! Yet let it be anything but that flirt Belinda and
I'll try to bear it. But if it prove her, all that's woman in me
shall be employ'd to destroy her.

Exeunt after CONSTANT and HEARTFREE.

Re-enter CONSTANT and HEARTFREE. Lady FANCIFUL and<br>MADAMOISELLE still following at a distance.

*Con.* I see no females yet that have anything to say to us.
I'm afraid we are banter'd.

*Heart.* I wish we were, for I'm in no humour to make either
them or myself merry.

*Con.* Nay, I'm sure you'll make them merry enough if I tell
'em why you are dull. But prithee, why so heavy and sad
before you begin to be ill-us'd?

*Heart.* For the same reason, perhaps, that you are so brisk and
well pleas'd; because both pains and pleasures are generally
more considerable in prospect than when they come to pass.

Enter Lady BRUTE and BELINDA, mask'd and poorly dress'd.

*Con.* How now, who are these? Not our game, I hope.

*Heart.* If they are, we are e'en well enough serv'd, to come
hunting here, when we had so much better game in chase elsewhere.

*Lady F. To* MADAMOISELLE. So, those are their ladies, without
doubt. But I'm afraid that doily stuff is not worn for want of
better clothes. They are the very shape and size of Belinda and
her aunt.

*Madam.* So day be inteed, matam.

*Lady F.* We'll slip into this close arbour, where we may hear
all they say.

Exeunt Lady FANCIFUL and MADAMOISELLE.

*Lady B.* What, are you afraid of us, gentlemen?

*Heart.* Why, truly, I think we may, if appearance don't lie.

*Bel.* Do you always find women what they appear to be, sir?

*Heart.* No, forsooth, but I seldom find 'em better than they
appear to be.

*Bel.* Then the outside's best you think?

*Heart.* 'Tis the honestest.

*Con.* Have a care, Heartfree; you are relapsing again.

*Lady B.* Why, does the gentleman use to rail at women?

*Con.* He has done formerly.

*Bel.* I suppose he had very good cause for't. They did not use
you so well as you thought you deserv'd, sir?

*Lady B.* They made themselves merry at your expense, sir?

*Bel.* Laugh'd when you sigh'd?

*Lady B.* Slept while you were waking?

*Bel.* Had your porter beat?

*Lady B.* And threw your billets-doux in the fire?

*Heart.* Heyday, I shall do more than rail presently.

*Bel.* Why, you won't beat us, will you?

*Heart.* I don't know but I may.

*Con.* What the devil's coming here? Sir John in a gown? And drunk, i' faith.

*Enter* Sir JOHN.

*Sir John.* What a pox! Here's Constant, Heartfree—and two whores, egad. O you covetous rogues! What, have you never a spare punk for your friend? But I'll share with you.

*He seizes both the women.*

*Heart.* Why, what the plague have you been doing, knight?

*Sir John.* Why, I have been beating the watch and scandalizing the clergy.

*Heart.* A very good account, truly.

*Sir John.* And what do you think I'll do next?

*Con.* Nay, that no man can guess.

*Sir John.* Why, if you'll let me sup with you, I'll treat both your strumpets.

*Lady B. Aside.* Oh Lord, we are undone.

*Heart.* No, we can't sup together, because we have some affairs elsewhere. But if you'll accept of these two ladies, we'll be so complaisant to you to resign our right in 'em.

*Bel. Aside.* Lord, what shall we do?

*Sir John.* Let me see, their clothes are such damn'd clothes they won't pawn for the reckoning.

*Heart.* Sir John, your servant. Rapture attend you.

*Con.* Adieu, ladies. Make much of the gentleman.

*Lady B.* Why sure you won't leave us in the hands of a drunken fellow to abuse us?

*Sir John.* Who do you call a drunken fellow, you slut you? I'm a man of quality; the king has made me a knight.

*Heart.* Ay, ay, you are in good hands. Adieu, adieu.

*Runs off.*

*Lady B.* The devil's hands! Let me go, or I'll—For Heaven's sake, protect us!

*She breaks from him, runs to* CONSTANT, *twitching off her mask and clapping it on again.*

*Sir John.* I'll devil you, I jade you. I'll demolish your ugly face.

*Con.* Hold a little, knight; she swoons.

*Sir John.* I'll swoon her.

*Con.* Hey, Heartfree!

*Re-enter* HEARTFREE. BELINDA *runs to him and shows her face.*

*Heart.* Oh Heavens! My dear creature, stand there a little.

*Con.* Pull him off, Jack.

*Heart.* Hold, mighty man. Look you, sir, we did but jest with you. These are ladies of our acquaintance that we had a mind to frighten a little, but now you must leave us.

*Sir John.* Oons, I won't leave you, not I.

*Heart.* Nay, but you must though, and therefore make no words on't.

*Sir John.* Then you are a couple of damn'd uncivil fellows; and I hope your punks will give you sauce to your mutton. *Exit.*

*Lady B.* Oh, I shall never come to myself again, I'm so frighten'd.

*Con.* 'Twas a narrow scape indeed.

*Bel.* Women must have frolics, you see, whatever they cost 'em.

*Heart.* This might have prov'd a dear one, though.

*Lady B.* You are the more oblig'd to us for the risk we run upon your accounts.

*Con.* And I hope you'll acknowledge something due to our knight-errantry, ladies. This is the second time we have deliver'd you.

*Lady B.* 'Tis true; and since we see Fate has design'd you for our guardians, 'twill make us the more willing to trust ourselves in your hands. But you must not have the worse opinion of us for our innocent frolic.

*Heart.* Ladies, you may command our opinions in everything that is to your advantage.

*Bel.* Then, sir, I command you to be of opinion that women are sometimes better than they appear to be.

> Lady BRUTE *and* CONSTANT *talk apart.*

*Heart.* Madam, you have made a convert of me in everything. I'm grown a fool. I could be fond of a woman.

*Bel.* I thank you, sir, in the name of the whole sex.

*Heart.* Which sex nothing but yourself could ever have aton'd for.

*Bel.* Now has my vanity a devilish itch to know in what my merit consists.

*Heart.* In your humility, madam, that keeps you ignorant it consists at all.

*Bel.* One other compliment with that serious face, and I hate you for ever after.

*Heart.* Some women love to be abus'd. Is that it you would be at?

*Bel.* No, not that neither. But I'd have men talk plainly what's fit for women to hear, without putting 'em either to a real or an affected blush.

*Heart.* Why then, in as plain terms as I can find to express myself, I could love you even to—matrimony itself a'most, egad.

*Bel.* Just as Sir John did her ladyship there. What think you? Don't you believe one month's time might bring you down to the same indifference, only clad in a little better manners perhaps. Well, you men are unaccountable things: mad till you have your mistresses, and then stark mad till you are rid of 'em again. Tell me honestly, is not your patience put to a much severer trial after possession than before?

*Heart.* With a great many, I must confess, it is, to our eternal scandal; but I—Dear creature, do but try me.

*Bel.* That's the surest way indeed to know, but not the safest. *To* Lady BRUTE: Madam, are not you for taking a turn in the Great Walk? It's almost dark; nobody will know us.

*Lady B.* Really I find myself something idle, Belinda. Besides, I dote upon this little odd private corner. But don't let my lazy fancy confine you.

*Con. Aside.* So, she would be left alone with me. That's well.

*Bel.* Well, we'll take one turn and come to you again. *To* HEARTFREE: Come, sir, shall we go pry into the secrets of the garden? Who knows what discoveries we may make?

*Heart.* Madam, I'm at your service.

*Con. To* HEARTFREE *aside.* Don't make too much haste back, for—d'ye hear—I may be busy.

*Heart.* Enough. *Exeunt* BELINDA *and* HEARTFREE.

*Lady B.* Sure you think me scandalously free, Mr. Constant. I'm afraid I shall lose your good opinion of me.

*Con.* My good opinion, madam, is like your cruelty, never to be remov'd.

*Lady B.* But if I should remove my cruelty, then there's an end of your good opinion.

*Con.* There is not so strict an alliance between 'em neither. 'Tis certain I should love you then better, if that be possible, than I do now; and where I love I always esteem.

*Lady B.* Indeed, I doubt you much. Why, suppose you had a wife, and she should entertain a gallant?

*Con.* If I gave her just cause, how could I justly condemn her?

*Lady B.* Ah, but you'd differ widely about just causes.

*Con.* But blows can bear no dispute.

*Lady B.* Nor ill manners much, truly.

*Con.* Then no woman upon earth has so just a cause as you have.

*Lady B.* Oh, but a faithful wife is a beautiful character.

*Con.* To a deserving husband, I confess it is.

*Lady B.* But can his faults release my duty?

*Con.* In equity, without doubt. And where laws dispense with equity, equity should dispense with laws.

*Lady B.* Pray let's leave this dispute, for you men have as much witchcraft in your arguments as women have in their eyes.

*Con.* But whilst you attack me with your charms, 'tis but reasonable I assault you with mine.

*Lady B.* The case is not the same. What mischief we do we can't help, and therefore are to be forgiven.

*Con.* Beauty soon obtains pardon, for the pain that it gives when it applies the balm of compassion to the wound. But a fine face and a hard heart is almost as bad as an ugly face and a soft one; both very troublesome to many a poor gentleman.

*Lady B.* Yes, and to many a poor gentlewoman too, I can assure you. But, pray, which of 'em is it that most afflicts you?

*Con.* Your glass and conscience will inform you, madam. But, for Heaven's sake—for now I must be serious—if pity or gratitude can move you, *Taking her hand.* if constancy and truth have power to tempt you, if love, if adoration can affect you, give me at least some hopes that time may do what you perhaps mean never to perform. 'Twill ease my sufferings, though not quench my flame.

*Lady B.* Your sufferings eas'd, your flame would soon abate, and that I would preserve, not quench it, sir.

*Con.* Would you preserve it, nourish it with favours; for that's the food it naturally requires.

*Lady B.* Yet on that natural food 'twould surfeit soon, should I resolve to grant all that you would ask.

*Con.* And in refusing all, you starve it. Forgive me, therefore, since my hunger rages, if I at last grow wild, and in my frenzy force at least this from you. *Kissing her hand.* Or if you'd have my flame soar higher still, then grant me this and this and this and thousands more. *Kissing first her hand, then her neck. Aside:* For now's the time; she melts into compassion.

*Lady B. Aside.* Poor coward virtue, how it shuns the battle.— Oh Heavens, let me go!

*Con.* Ay, go, ay. Where shall we go, my charming angel? Into this private arbour. Nay, let's lose no time; moments are precious..

*Lady B.* And lovers wild. Pray, let us stop here, at least for this time.

*Con.* 'Tis impossible. He that has power over you can have none over himself.

*Lady B.* Ah, I'm lost.

> As he is forcing her into the arbour, Lady FANCIFUL and MADAMOISELLE bolt out upon them and run over the stage.

*Lady F.* Fie, fie, fie, fie, fie.

*Madam.* Fie, fie, fie, fie, fie.

*Con.* Death and furies, who are these?

*Lady B.* Oh Heavens, I'm out of my wits! If they knew me, I'm ruin'd.

*Con.* Don't be frightened. Ten thousand to one they are strangers to you.

*Lady B.* Whatever they are, I won't stay here a moment longer.

*Con.* Whither will you go?

*Lady B.* Home, as if the devil were in me. Lord, where's this Belinda now?

*Enter* BELINDA *and* HEARTFREE.

Oh, it's well you are come.   I'm so frightened my hair stands an end.   Let's be gone, for Heaven's sake.

*Bel.* Lord, what's the matter?

*Lady B.* The devil's the matter! We are discover'd.  Here's a couple of women have done the most impertinent thing. Away, away, away, away, away!                    *Exeunt running.*

*Re-enter* Lady FANCIFUL *and* MADAMOISELLE.

*Lady F.* Well, Madamoiselle, 'tis a prodigious thing how women can suffer filthy fellows to grow so familiar with 'em.

*Madam.* Ah, matam, *il n'y a rien de si naturel.*

*Lady F.* Fie, fie, fie.   But, oh my heart! O jealousy! O torture! I'm on the rack.   What shall I do?   My lover's lost; I ne'er shall see him mine.   *Pausing.*   But I may be reveng'd, and that's the same thing.   Ah, sweet revenge!   Thou welcome thought, thou healing balsam to my wounded soul.   Be but propitious on this one occasion, I'll place my heaven in thee for all my life to come.

> To woman, how indulgent nature's kind.
> No blast of fortune long disturbs her mind.
> Compliance to her fate supports her still;
> If love won't make her happy, mischief will.

                                   *Exeunt.*

# ACT V

### SCENE [I].—Lady FANCIFUL's *house.*

*Enter* Lady FANCIFUL *and* MADAMOISELLE.

*Lady F.* Well, madamoiselle, did you dog the filthy things?

*Madam.* Oh, *que oui,* matam.

*Lady F.* And where are they?

*Madam. Au logis.*

*Lady F.* What, men and all?

*Madam. Tous ensemble.*

*Lady F.* Oh confidence!   What, carry their fellows to their own house?

*Madam. C'est que le mari n'y est pas.*

*Lady F.* No, so I believe truly.   But he shall be there, and quickly too, if I can find him out.   Well, 'tis a prodigious thing to see, when men and women get together, how they fortify one another in their impudence.   But if that drunken fool her husband be to be found in e'er a tavern in town, I'll send him amongst 'em.   I'll spoil their sport.

*Madam. En verité,* matam *ce rait dommage.*

*Lady F.* 'Tis in vain to oppos it, Madamoiselle; therefore, never go about it.   For I am the steadiest creature in the world when I have determin'd to do mischief.   So, come along.

                                   *Exeunt.*

SCENE [II].—Sir JOHN BRUTE's *house*.

*Enter* CONSTANT, HEARTFREE, Lady BRUTE, BELINDA,
*and* LOVEWELL.

*Lady B.* But are you sure you don't mistake, Lovewell?

*Love.* Madam, I saw 'em all go into the tavern together, and
my master was so drunk he could scarce stand.      [*Exit.*]

*Lady B.* Then, gentlemen, I believe we may venture to let you
stay and play at cards with us for an hour or two, for they'll
scarce part till morning.

*Bel.* I think 'tis pity they should ever part——

*Con.* The company that's here, madam.

*Lady B.* Then, sir, the company that's here must remember to
part itself in time.

*Con.* Madam, we don't intend to forfeit your favours by an
indiscreet usage of this. The moment you give us the signal we
shan't fail to make our retreat.

*Lady B.* Upon those conditions then, let us sit down to cards.

*Enter* LOVEWELL.

*Love.* Oh Lord, madam, here's my master just staggering in
upon you. He has been quarrelsome yonder, and they have
kick'd him out of the company.

*Lady B.* Into the closet, gentlemen, for Heaven's sake. I'll
wheedle him to bed if possible.

CONSTANT *and* HEARTFREE *run into the closet.*

*Enter* Sir JOHN, *all dirt and bloody.*

Ah, ah, he's all over blood.

*Sir John.* What the plague does the woman—squall for?
Did you never see a man in pickle before?

*Lady B.* Lord, where have you been?

*Sir John.* I have been at—cuffs.

*Lady B.* I fear that is not all. I hope you are not wounded.

*Sir John.* Sound as a roach, wife.

*Lady B.* I'm mighty glad to hear it.

*Sir John.* You know—I think you lie.

*Lady B.* I know you do me wrong to think so then. For
Heaven's my witness, I had rather see my own blood trickle down
than yours.

*Sir John.* Then will I be crucified.

*Lady B.* 'Tis a hard fate, I should not be believ'd.

*Sir John.* 'Tis a damn'd atheistical age, wife.

*Lady B.* I am sure I have given you a thousand tender proofs
how great my care is of you. Nay, spite of all your cruel thoughts
I'll still persist, and at this moment, if I can, persuade you to lie
down and sleep a little.

*Sir John.* Why,—do you think I am drunk—you slut you?

*Lady B.* Heaven forbid I should! But I'm afraid you are feverish. Pray let me feel your pulse.

*Sir John.* Stand off and be damn'd.

*Lady B.* Why, I see your distemper in your very eyes. You are all on fire. Pray go to bed, let me entreat you.

*Sir John.* Come, kiss me then.

*Lady B. Kissing him.* There. Now go. *Aside:* He stinks like poison.

*Sir John.* I see it goes damnably against your stomach—and therefore—kiss me again.

*Lady B.* Nay, now you fool me.

*Sir John.* Do't, I say.

*Lady B. Aside.* Ah, Lord have mercy upon me!—Well, there. Now will you go?

*Sir John.* Now, wife, you shall see my gratitude. You give me two kisses—I'll give you—two hundred.

Kisses and tumbles her.

*Lady B.* Oh Lord! Pray, Sir John, be quiet. *Aside:* Heavens, what a pickle am I in!

*Bel. Aside.* If I were in her pickle, I'd call my gallant out of the closet, and he should cudgel him soundly.

*Sir John.* So, now, you being as dirty and as nasty as myself, we may go pig together. But first I must have a cup of your cold tea, wife. Going to the closet.

*Lady B. Aside.* Oh, I'm ruin'd!—There's none there, my dear.

*Sir John.* I'll warrant you I'll find some, my dear.

*Lady B.* You can't open the door; the lock's spoil'd. I have been turning and turning the key this half hour to no purpose. I'll send for the smith tomorrow.

*Sir John.* There's ne'er a smith in Europe can open a door with more expedition than I can do. As for example—Pou! *He bursts open the door with his foot.* How now? What the devil have we got here? Constant—Heartfree—and two whores again, egad. This is the worst cold tea—that ever I met with in my life.

Enter CONSTANT and HEARTFREE.

*Lady B. Aside.* Oh Lord, what will become of us?

*Sir John.* Gentlemen—I am your very humble servant—I give you many thanks—I see you take care of my family—I shall do all I can to return the obligation.

*Con.* Sir, how oddly soever this business may appear to you, you would have no cause to be uneasy if you knew the truth of all things. Your lady is the most virtuous woman in the world, and nothing has pass'd but an innocent frolic.

*Heart.* Nothing else, upon my honour, sir.

*Sir John.* You are both very civil gentlemen—and my wife there is a very civil gentlewoman; therefore I don't doubt but many civil things have pass'd between you. Your very humble servant.

*Lady B. Aside to* CONSTANT. Pray be gone. He's so drunk he can't hurt you to-night, and to-morrow morning you shall hear from us.

*Con.* I'll obey you, madam. Sir, when you are cool, you'll understand reason better. So then I shall take the pains to inform you. If not, I wear a sword, sir, and so goodbye to you. Come along, Heartfree.      *Exeunt* CONSTANT *and* HEARTFREE.

*Sir John.* Wear a sword, sir? And what of all that, sir? He comes to my house, eats my meat, lies with my wife, dishonours my family, gets a bastard to inherit my estate, and when I ask a civil account of all this—"Sir," says he, "I wear a sword." Wear a sword, sir? "Yes, sir," says he, "I wear a sword." It may be a good answer at cross purposes, but 'tis a damn'd one to a man in my whimsical circumstance. "Sir," says he, "I wear a sword." *To* Lady BRUTE: And what do you wear now? Ha? Tell me. *Sitting down in a great chair.* What, you are modest and can't? Why then, I'll tell you, you slut you. You wear—an impudent lewd face—a damn'd designing heart—and a tail—a tail full of—      *He falls fast asleep snoring.*

*Lady B.* So, thanks to kind Heaven, he's fast for some hours.

*Bel.* 'Tis well he is so, that we may have time to lay our story handsomely; for we must lie like the devil to bring ourselves off.

*Lady B.* What shall we say, Belinda?

*Bel. Musing.* I'll tell you. It must all light upon Heartfree and I. We'll say he has courted me some time, but for reasons unknown to us has ever been very earnest the thing might be kept from Sir John. That therefore hearing him upon the stairs, he run into the closet, though against our will, and Constant with him, to prevent jealousy. And to give this a good impudent face of truth—that I may deliver you from the trouble you are in—I'll e'en, if he pleases, marry him.

*Lady B.* I'm beholding to you, cousin; but that would be carrying the jest a little too far for your own sake. You know he's a younger brother, and has nothing.

*Bel.* 'Tis true, but I like him and have fortune enough to keep above extremity. I can't say I would live with him in a cell upon love and bread and butter, but I had rather have the man I love and a middle state of life than that gentleman in the chair there and twice your ladyship's splendour.

*Lady B.* In truth, niece, you are in the right on't, for I am very uneasy in my ambition. But perhaps, had I married as you'll do, I might have been as ill us'd.

*Bel.* Some risk, I do confess, there always is. But if a man has the least spark, either of honour or good nature, he can never use a woman ill that loves him and makes his fortune both. Yet I must own to you some little struggling I still have with this

teasing ambition of ours.   For pride, you know, is as natural to
a woman as 'tis to a saint.   I can't help being fond of this rogue,
and yet it goes to my heart to think I must never whisk to Hyde
Park with above a pair of horses, have no coronet upon my
coach, nor a page to carry up my train.   But above all, that
business of place—Well, taking place is a noble prerogative.

*Lady B.* Especially after a quarrel.

*Bel.* Or of a rival.   But pray say no more on't, for fear I
change my mind.   For o' my conscience, were't not for your
affair in the balance, I should go near to pick up some odious
man of quality yet, and only take poor Heartfree for a gallant.

*Lady B.* Then him you must have, however things go?

*Bel.* Yes.

*Lady B.* Why, we may pretend what we will, but 'tis a hard
matter to live without the man we love.

*Bel.* Especially when we are married to the man we hate.   Pray
tell me, do the men of the town ever believe us virtuous when
they see us do so?

*Lady B.* Oh no; nor indeed hardly, let us do what we will.
They most of 'em think there is no such thing as virtue, consider'd in the strictest notions of it; and therefore when you hear
'em say such a one is a woman of reputation, they only mean she's
a woman of discretion.   For they consider we have no more
religion than they have, nor so much morality.   And between
you and I, Belinda, I'm afraid the want of inclination seldom
protects any of us.

*Bel.* But what think you of the fear of being found out?

*Lady B.* I think that never kept any woman virtuous long.
We are not such cowards neither.   No, let us once pass fifteen,
and we have too good an opinion of our own cunning to believe
the world can penetrate into what we would keep a secret.   And
in short, we cannot reasonably blame the men for judging of us
by themselves.

*Bel.* But sure we are not so wicked as they are, after all.

*Lady B.* We are as wicked, child, but our vice lies another
way.   Men have more courage than we, so they commit more
bold, impudent sins.   They quarrel, fight, swear, drink, blas-
pheme, and the like.   Whereas we, being cowards, only backbite,
tell lies, cheat at cards, and so forth.   But 'tis late.   Let's end
our discourse for to-night, and, out of an excess of charity, take
a small care of that nasty drunken thing there.   Do but look at
him, Belinda.

*Bel.* Ah, 'tis a savoury dish.

*Lady B.* As savoury as 'tis, I'm cloyed with't.   Prithee call the
butler to take away.

*Bel.* Call the butler?   Call the scavenger!   *To a servant
within:* Who's there?   Call Razor.   Let him take away his
master, scour him clean with a little soap and sand, and so put
him to bed.

*Lady B.* Come, Belinda, I'll e'en lie with you to-night, and in the morning we'll send for our gentlemen to set this matter even.

*Bel.* With all my heart.

*Lady B.* [*To* Sir John.] Good night, my dear.   *Making a low curtsy.*

*Both.* Ha, ha, ha!.                                         *Exeunt.*

### *Enter* Razor.

*Razor.* My lady there's a wag, my master there's a cuckold. Marriage is a slippery thing.   Women have deprav'd appetites. My lady's a wag.   I have heard all, I have seen all, I understand all, and I'll tell all; for my little Frenchwoman loves news dearly. This story'll gain her heart or nothing will.   *To his master:* Come, sir, your head's too full of fumes at present to make room for your jealousy; but I reckon we shall have rare work with you when your pate's empty.   Come, to your kennel, you cuckoldly drunken sot you.                          *Carries him out upon his back.*

### SCENE [III].—Lady Fanciful's *house.*

#### *Enter* Lady Fanciful *and* Madamoiselle.

*Lady F.* But why did not you tell me before, Madamoiselle, that Razor and you were fond ?

*Madam.* De modesty hinder me, matam.

*Lady F.* Why truly, modesty does often hinder us from doing things we have an extravagant mind to.   But does he love you well enough yet to do anything you bid him ?   Do you think to oblige you he would speak scandal ?

*Madam.* Matam, to oblige your ladyship he shall speak blasphemy.

*Lady F.* Why then, Madamoiselle, I'll tell you what you shall do.   You shall engage him to tell his master all that pass'd at Spring Garden.   I have a mind he should know what a wife and a niece he has got.

*Madam.* Il le fera, matam.

#### *Enter a* Footman, *who speaks to* Madamoiselle *apart.*

*Foot.* Madamoiselle, yonder's Mr. Razor desires to speak with you.

*Madam.* Tell him I come presently.              *Exit* Footman. Razor be dare, matam.

*Lady F.* That's fortunate.   Well, I'll leave you together. And if you find him stubborn, Madamoiselle—hark you—don't refuse him a few reasonable liberties to put him into humour.

*Madam.* Laissez moi faire.              *Exit* Lady Fanciful.

Razor *peeps in, and seeing* Lady Fanciful *gone, runs to* Madamoiselle, *takes her about the neck and kisses her.*

How now, confidence?

*Razor.* How now, modesty?

*Madam.* Who make you so familiar, sirrah?

*Razor.* My impudence, hussy.

*Madam.* Stand off, rogue-face.

*Razor.* Ah, Madamoiselle, great news at our house.

*Madam.* Why, wat be de matter?

*Razor.* The matter? Why, uptails all's the matter.

*Madam.* *Tu te mocque de moi.*

*Razor.* Now do you long to know the particulars—the time when, the place where, the manner how, but I won't tell you a word more.

*Madam.* Nay, den dou kill me, Razor.

*Razor.* Come, kiss me then.          *Clapping his hands behind him.*

*Madam.* Nay, pridee tell me.

*Razor.* Goodbye to ye.                                        *Going.*

*Madam.* Hold, hold. I will kiss dee.                *Kissing him.*

*Razor.* So, that's civil. Why now, my pretty poll, my gold-finch, my little water wagtail, you must know that—Come, kiss me again.

*Madam.* I won't kiss dee no more.

*Razor.* Goodbye to ye.

*Madam. Doucement.* Dare. *Kissing him. Es tu content?*

*Razor.* So, now I'll tell thee all. Why, the news is that cuckoldom in folio is newly printed, and matrimony in quarto is just going into the press. Will you buy any books, Madamoiselle?

*Madam. Tu parle comme un libraire.* De devil no understand dee.

*Razor.* Why then that I may make myself intelligible to a waiting-woman, I'll speak like a valet de chambre. My lady has cuckolded my master.

*Madam. Bon.*

*Razor.* Which we take very ill from her hands, I can tell her that. We can't yet prove matter of fact upon her.

*Madam. N'importe.*

*Razor.* But we can prove that matter of fact had like to have been upon her.

*Madam. Oui da.*

*Razor.* For we have such bloody circumstances——

*Madam. Sans doute.*

*Razor.* That any man of parts may draw tickling conclusions from 'em.

*Madam. Fort bien.*

*Razor.* We have found a couple of tight, well-built gentlemen stuff'd into her ladyship's closet.

*Madam. Le diable!*

*Razor.* And I, in my particular person, have discover'd a most damnable plot how to persuade my poor master that all this hide

and seek, this will-in-the-wisp, has no other meaning than a
Christian marriage for sweet Mrs. Belinda.

*Madam. Une mariage ? Ah, les drôlesses!*

*Razor.* Don't you interrupt me, hussy. 'Tis agreed, I say.
And my innocent lady, to wriggle herself out at the back door of
the business, turns marriage-bawd to her niece, and resolves to
deliver up her fair body to be tumbled and mumbled by that
young liquorish whipster, Heartfree.  Now are you satisfied?

*Madam.* No.

*Razor.* Right woman, always gaping for more!

*Madam.* Dis be all den, dat dou know?

*Razor.* All?  And a good deal too, I think.

*Madam.* Dou be fool, dou know noting! *Écoute, mon pauvre*
Razor. Dou see des two eyes? Des two eyes have s:e de devil.

*Razor.* The woman's mad.

*Madam.* In Spring Garden dat rogue Constant meet dy lady.

*Razor. Bon.*

*Madam.* I'll tell dee no more.

*Razor.* Nay, prithee, my swan.

*Madam.* Come, kiss me den.

> *Clapping her hands behind her, as he had done before.*

*Razor.* I won't kiss you, not I.

*Madam.* Adieu.

*Razor.* Hold. *Gives her a hearty kiss.*  Now proceed.

*Madam. À ça.*  I hide myself in one cunning place, where I
hear all and see all.  First de drunken master come *mal à
propos*; but de sot no know his own dear wife, so he leave her to
her sport.  Den de game begin.  *As she speaks,* RAZOR *still acts
the man and she the woman.*  De lover say soft ting.  De lady
look upon de ground.  He take her by de hand.  She turn her
head one oder way.  Den he squeeze very hard.  Den she pull—
very softly.  Den he take her in his arm.  Den she give him leetel
pat.  Den he kiss her tetons.  Den she say, "Pish, nay, see."  Den
he tremble.  Den she—sigh.  Den he pull her into de arbour.
Den she pinch him.

*Razor.* Ay, but not so hard, you baggage you.

*Madam.* Den he grow bold.  She grow weak.  He tro her
down. *Il tombe dessus.  Le diable assiste.  Il emporte tout.*

> RAZOR *struggles with her, as if he would throw her down.*
Stand off, sirrah!

*Razor.* You have set me afire, you jade you.

*Madam.* Den go to de river and quench dyself.

*Razor.* What an unnatural harlot 'tis!

*Madam. Looking languishingly on him.* Razor.

*Razor.* Madamoiselle.

*Madam.* Dou no love me?

*Razor.* Not love thee?  More than a Frenchman does soup.

*Madam.* Den dou will refuse noting dat I bid dee?

*Razor.* Don't bid me be damn'd then.

*Madam.* No.   Only tell dy master all I have tell dee of dy laty.

*Razor.* Why, you little malicious strumpet you!   Should you like to be serv'd so?

*Madam.* Dou dispute den?   Adieu.

*Razor.* Hold.   But why wilt thou make me to be such a rogue, my dear?

*Madam. Voilà un vrai Anglais!   Il est amoureux et cependant il veut raisonner.   Va t'en au diable.*

*Razor.* Hold once more.   In hopes thou'lt give me up thy body, I resign thee up my soul.

*Madam.* Bon. *Écoute donc:* If dou fail me, I never see dee more; if dou obey me, *je m'abandonne à toi.*

> *She takes him about the neck and gives him a smacking kiss, and exit.*

*Razor. Licking his lips.* Not be a rogue? *Amor vincit omnia.*

*Exit.*

### Enter Lady FANCIFUL *and* MADAMOISELLE.

*Lady F.* Marry, say ye?   Will the two things marry?

*Madam. On le va faire*, matam.

*Lady F.* Look you, Madamoiselle, in short, I can't bear it. No, I find I can't.   If once I see 'em a-bed together, I shall have ten thousand thoughts in my head will make me run distracted. Therefore run and call Razor back immediately, for something must be done to stop this impertinent wedding.   If I can but defer it four and twenty hours, I'll make such work about town with that little pert slut's reputation, ho shall as soon marry a witch.

*Madam. Aside.   La voilà bien intentionée.*                    *Exeunt.*

### SCENE [IV].—CONSTANT'S *lodgings.*

### Enter CONSTANT *and* HEARTFREE.

*Con.* But what dost think will come of this business?

*Heart.* 'Tis easier to think what will not come on't.

*Con.* What's that?

*Heart.* A challenge.   I know the knight too well for that.   His dear body will always prevail upon his noble soul to be quiet.

*Con.* But though he dare not challenge me, perhaps he may venture to challenge his wife.

*Heart.* Not if you whisper him in the ear, you won't have him do't, and there's no other way left that I see.   For as drunk as he was, he'll remember you and I were where we should not be, and I don't think him quite blockhead enough yet to be persuaded we were got into his wife's closet only to peep in her prayer book.

### Enter SERVANT, *with a letter.*

*Serv.* Sir, here's a letter.   A porter brought it.

*Con.* Oh ho, here's instructions for us.   *Reads.*   "The accident that has happen'd has touch'd our invention to the quick.   We would fain come off without your help, but find that's impossible. In a word, the whole business must be thrown upon a matrimonial intri u e between your friend and mine.   But if the parties are not fond n ugh to go quite through with the matter, 'tis sufficient for our turn they own the design.   We'll find pretences enough to break the match. Adieu." Well, woman for invention!   How long would my blockhead have been a-producing this?   Hey, Heart-free!   What, musing, man?   Prithee be cheerful.   What say'st thou, friend, to this matrimonial remedy?

*Heart.* Why, I say it's worse than the disease.

*Con.* Here's a fellow for you!   There's beauty and money on her side, and love up to the ears on his, and yet——

*Heart.* And yet, I think I may reasonably be allow'd to boggle at marrying the niece, in the very moment that you are a-debauching the aunt.

*Con.* Why truly, there may be something in that.   But have not you a good opinion enough of your own parts to believe you could keep a wife to yourself?

*Heart.* I should have, if I had a good opinion enough of hers to believe that she could do as much by me.   For to do 'em right after all, the wife seldom rambles till the husband shows her the way.

*Con.* 'Tis true.   A man of real worth scarce ever is a cuckold but by his own fault.   Women are not naturally lewd; there must be something to urge 'em to it.   They'll cuckold a churl out of revenge, a fool because they despise him, a beast because they loath him.   But when they make bold with a man they once had a well-grounded value for, 'tis because they first see themselves neglected by him.

*Heart.* Nay, were I well assur'd that I should never grow Sir John, I ne'er should fear Belinda play'd my lady.   But our weakness, thou know'st, my friend, consists in that very change we so impudently throw upon, indeed, a steadier and more generous sex.

*Con.* Why, faith, we are a little impudent in that matter; that's the truth on't.   But this is wonderful, to see you grown so warm an advocate for those but t'other day you took so much pains to abuse.

*Heart.* All revolutions run into extremes.   The bigot makes the boldest atheist, and the coyest saint the most extravagant strumpet.   But prithee, advise me in this good and evil, this life and death, this blessing and cursing, that is set before me; shall I marry or die a maid?

*Con.* Why, faith, Heartfree, matrimony is like an army going to engage.   Love's the forlorn hope, which is soon cut off; the marriage knot is the main body, which may stand buff a long,

long time; and repentance is the rear guard, which rarely gives ground as long as the main battle has a being.

*Heart.* Conclusion then: you advise me to whore on, as you do.

*Con.* That's not concluded yet. For though marriage be a lottery in which there are a wondrous many blanks, yet there is one inestimable lot in which the only Heaven on earth is written. Would your kind fate but guide your hand to that, though I were wrapp'd in all that luxury itself could clothe me with, I still should envy you.

*Heart.* And justly too; for to be capable of loving one doubtless is better than to possess a thousand. But how far that capacity's in me, alas I know not.

*Con.* But would you know?

*Heart.* I would so.

*Con.* Matrimony will inform you. Come, one flight of resolution carries you to the land of experience, where in a very moderate time you'll know the capacity of your soul and your body both, or I'm mistaken. *Exeunt.*

SCENE [V].—Sir JOHN BRUTE'S *house.*

*Enter* Lady BRUTE *and* BELINDA.

*Bel.* Well, madam, what answer have you from 'em?

*Lady B.* That they'll be here this moment. I fancy 'twill end in a wedding. I'm sure he's a fool if it don't. Ten thousand pound and such a lass as you are is no contemptible offer to a younger brother. But are not you under strange agitations? Prithee how does your pulse beat?

*Bel.* High and low. I have much ado to be valiant. Sure it must feel very strange to go to bed to a man.

*Lady B.* Um, it does feel a little odd at first, but it will soon grow easy to you.

*Enter* CONSTANT *and* HEARTFREE.

*Lady B.* Good morrow, gentlemen. How have you slept after your adventure?

*Heart.* Some careful thoughts, ladies, on your accounts have kept us waking.

*Bel.* And some careful thoughts on your own, I believe, have hinder'd you from sleeping. Pray how does this matrimonial project relish with you?

*Heart.* Why, faith, e'en as storming towns does with soldiers, where the hopes of delicious plunder banishes the fear of being knock'd on the head.

*Bel.* Is it then possible, after all, that you dare think of downright lawful wedlock?

*Heart.* Madam, you have made me so foolhardy I dare do anything.

*Bel.* Then, sir, I challenge you, and matrimony's the spot where I expect you.

*Heart.* 'Tis enough; I'll not fail. *Aside:* So, now I am in for Hobbes's voyage, a great leap in the dark.

*Lady B.* Well, gentlemen, this matter being concluded then, have you got your lessons ready? For Sir John is grown such an atheist of late he'll believe nothing upon easy terms.

*Con.* We'll find ways to extend his faith, madam. But, pray, how do you find him this morning?

*Lady B.* Most lamentably morose, chewing the cud after last night's discovery, of which, however, he had but a confus'd notion e'en now. But I'm afraid his valet de chambre has told him all, for they are very busy together at this moment. When I told him of Belinda's marriage, I had no other answer but a grunt; from which you may draw what conclusions you think fit. But to your notes, gentlemen, he's here.

*Enter* Sir JOHN *and* RAZOR.

*Con.* Good morrow, sir.

*Heart.* Good morrow, Sir John. I'm very sorry my indiscretion should cause so much disorder in your family.

*Sir John.* Disorders generally come from indiscretions, sir; 'tis no strange thing at all.

*Lady B.* I hope, my dear, you are satisfied there was no wrong intended you.

*Sir John.* None, my dove.

*Bel.* If not, I hope my consent to marry Mr. Heartfree will convince you. For as little as I know of amours, sir, I can assure you one intrigue is enough to bring four people together, without further mischief.

*Sir John.* And I know too that intrigues tend to procreation of more kinds than one. One intrigue will beget another as soon as beget a son or a daughter.

*Con.* I am very sorry, sir, to see you still seem unsatisfied with a lady whose more than common virtue, I am sure, were she my wife, should meet a better usage.

*Sir John.* Sir, if her conduct has put a trick upon her virtue, her virtue's the bubble, but her husband's the loser.

*Con.* Sir, you have receiv'd a sufficient answer already to justify both her conduct and mine. You'll pardon me for meddling in your family affairs, but I perceive I am the man you are jealous of, and therefore it concerns me.

*Sir John.* Would it did not concern me, and then I should not care who it concern'd.

*Con.* Well, sir, if truth and reason won't content you, I know but one way more which, if you think fit, you may take.

[*Displays his sword.*]

*Sir John.* Lord, sir, you are very hasty; if I had been found at prayers in your wife's closet, I should have allow'd you twice as much time to come to yourself in.

*Con.* Nay, sir, if time be all you want, we have no quarrel.

Sir JOHN *muses.*

*Heart.* I told you how the sword would work upon him.

*Con.* Let him muse; however, I'll lay fifty pound our foreman brings us in not guilty.

*Sir John. Aside.* 'Tis well, 'tis very well. In spite of that young jade's matrimonial intrigue, I am a downrignt stinking cuckold. Here they are. *Putting his hand to his forehead.* Boo! Methinks I could butt with a bull. What the plague did I marry her for? I knew she did not like me; if she had, she would have lain with me, for I would have done so because I lik'd her. But that's past, and I have her. And now what shall I do with her? If I put my horns in my pocket, she'll grow insolent; if I don't, that goat there, that stallion, is ready to whip me through the guts. The debate then is reduc'd to this: shall I die a hero or live a rascal? Why, wiser men than I have long since concluded that a living dog is better than a dead lion. *To* CONSTANT *and* HEARTFREE: Gentlemen, now my wine and passion are governable, I must own I have never observ'd anything in my wife's course of life to back me in my jealousy of her. But jealousy's a mark of love, so she need not trouble her head about it, as long as I make no more words on't.

Lady FANCIFUL *enters disguis'd and addresses to* BELINDA *apart.*

*Con.* I am glad to see your reason rule at last. Give me your hand. I hope you'll look upon me as you are wont.

*Sir John.* Your humble servant. *Aside:* A wheedling son of a whore.

*Heart.* And that I may be sure you are friends with me too, pray give me your consent to wed your niece.

*Sir John.* Sir, you have it with all my heart, damn me if you han't. *Aside:* 'Tis time to get rid of her. A young pert pimp, she'll make an incomparable bawd in a little time.

*Enter a servant, who gives* HEARTFREE *a letter.*

*Bel.* [*To* Lady FANCIFUL.] Heartfree your husband, say you? 'Tis impossible.

*Lady F.* Would to kind Heaven it were! But 'tis too true, and in the world there lives not such a wretch. I'm young, and either I have been flatter'd by my friends as well as glass, or nature has been kind and generous to me. I had a fortune too was greater far than he could ever hope for. But with my heart, I am robb'd of all the rest. I'm slighted and I'm beggar'd both at once. I have scarce a bare subsistence from the villain, yet dare complain to none, for he has sworn if e'er 'tis known I am his wife he'll murder me.    *Weeping.*

*Bel.* The traitor!

*Lady F.* I accidentally was told he courted you. Charity soon prevail'd upon me to prevent your misery; and, as you see, I'm still so generous even to him as not to suffer he should do a thing for which the law might take away his life. *Weeping.*

*Bel.* Poor creature, how I pity her.

*They continue talking aside.*

*Heart. Aside.* Death and damnation! Let me read it again. *Reads.* "Though I have a particular reason not to let you know who I am till I see you, yet you'll easily believe 'tis a faithful friend that gives you this advice. I have lain with Belinda. (Good!) I have a child by her, (Better and better) which is now at nurse, (Heav'n be prais'd!) and I think the foundation laid for another. (Ha, old truepenny!) No rack could have tortur'd this story from me, but friendship has done it. I heard of your design to marry her, and could not see you abus'd. Make use of my advice, but keep my secret till I ask you for't again. Adieu."

*Exit* Lady FANCIFUL.

*Con. To* BELINDA. Come, madam, shall we send for the parson? I doubt here's no business for the lawyer; younger brothers have nothing to settle but their hearts, and that I believe my friend here has already done very faithfully.

*Bel. Scornfully.* Are you sure, sir, there are no old mortgages upon it?

*Heart. Coldly.* If you think there are, madam, it mayn't be amiss to defer the marriage till you are sure they are paid off.

*Bel. Aside.* How the gall'd horse kicks! *To* HEARTFREE: We'll defer it as long as you please, sir.

*Heart.* The more time we take to consider on't, madam, the less apt we shall be to commit oversights. Therefore, if you please, we'll put it off for just nine months.

*Bel.* Guilty consciences make men cowards. I don't wonder you want time to resolve.

*Heart.* And they make women desperate. I don't wonder you were so quickly determin'd.

*Bel.* What does the fellow mean?

*Heart.* What does the lady mean?

*Sir John.* Zoons, what do you both mean? HEARTFREE *and* BELINDA *walk chafing about.*

*Razor. Aside.* Here is so much sport going to be spoil'd, it makes me ready to weep again. A pox o' this impertinent Lady Fanciful and her plots, and her Frenchwoman too. She's a whimsical, ill-natur'd bitch, and when I have got my bones broke in her service, 'tis ten to one but my recompense is a clap. I hear 'em tittering without still. Ecod, I'll e'en go lug 'em both in by the ears and discover the plot, to secure my pardon.

*Exit* RAZOR.

*Con.* Prithee explain, Heartfree.

*Heart.* A fair deliverance, thank my stars and my friend.

*Bel.* 'Tis well it went no farther. A base fellow.

*Lady B.* What can be the meaning of all this?

*Bel.* What's his meaning I don't know, but mine is, that if I had married him, I had had no husband.

*Heart.* And what's her meaning I don't know, but mine is, that if I had married her, I had had wife enough.

*Sir John.* Your people of wit have got such cramp ways of expressing themselves, they seldom comprehend one another. Pox take you both, will you speak that you may be understood?

*Enter* RAZOR *in sackcloth, pulling in* Lady FANCIFUL *and* MADAMOISELLE.

*Razor.* If they won't, here comes an interpreter.

*Lady B.* Heavens, what have we here?

*Razor.* A villain, but a repenting villain. Stuff which saints in all ages have been made of.

*All.* Razor!

*Lady B.* What means this sudden metamorphose?

*Razor.* Nothing, without my pardon.

*Lady B.* What pardon do you want?

*Razor.* Imprimis, your ladyship's, for a damnable lie made upon your spotless virtue and set to the tune of Spring Garden. *To* SIR JOHN: Next, at my generous master's feet I bend, for interrupting his more noble thoughts with phantoms of disgraceful cuckoldom. *To* CONSTANT: Thirdly, I to this gentleman apply, for making him the hero of my romance. *To* HEARTFREE: Fourthly, your pardon, noble sir, I ask for clandestinely marrying you, without either bidding of banns, bishop's licence, friends' consent, or your own knowledge. *To* BELINDA: And lastly, to my good young lady's clemency I come, for pretending the corn was sow'd in the ground before ever the plough had been in the field.

*Sir John. Aside.* So that after all, 'tis a moot point whether I am a cuckold or not.

*Bel.* Well, sir, upon condition you confess all, I'll pardon you myself, and try to obtain as much from the rest of the company. But I must know then, who 'tis has put you upon all this mischief?

*Razor.* Satan and his equipage. Woman tempted me, lust weaken'd me, and so the devil overcame me. As fell Adam, so fell I.

*Bel.* Then pray, Mr. Adam, will you make us acquainted with your Eve?

*Razor. To* MADAMOISELLE. Unmask, for the honour of France.

*All.* Madamoiselle?

*Madam.* Me ask ten tousand pardon of all de good company.

*Sir John.* Why, this mystery thickens instead of clearing up. *To* RAZOR: You son of a whore you, put us out of our pain.

*Razor.* One moment brings sunshine. *Showing* MADAMOISELLE. 'Tis true, this is the woman that tempted me. But this

is the serpent that tempted the woman. And if my prayers
might be heard, her punishment for so doing should be like the
serpent's of old. *Pulls off* Lady FANCIFUL'*s mask*. She should
lie upon her face all the days of her life.

*All*. Lady Fanciful!

*Bel*. Impertinent.

*Lady B*. Ridiculous.

*All*. Ha, ha, ha, ha, ha!

*Bel*. I hope your ladyship will give me leave to wish you joy,
since you have own'd your marriage yourself. Mr. Heartfree, I
vow 'twas strangely wicked in you to think of another wife when
you had one already so charming as her ladyship.

*All*. Ha, ha, ha, ha, ha!

*Lady F. Aside*. Confusion seize 'em as it seizes me.

*Madam. Que le diable étouffe çe maraud de Razor.*

*Bel*. Your ladyship seems disorder'd. A breeding qualm perhaps. Mr. Heartfree, your bottle of Hungary water to your
lady. Why, madam, he stands as unconcern'd as if he were your
husband in earnest.

*Lady F*. Your mirth's as nauseous as yourself, Belinda. You
think you triumph o'er a rival now. *Hélas, ma pauvre fille*,
where'er I'm rival there's no cause for mirth. No, my poor
wretch, 'tis from another principle I have acted. I knew that
thing there would make so perverse a husband and you so
impertinent a wife, that lest your mutual plagues should make
you both run mad, I charitably would have broke the match.
He, he, he, he, he!

> *Exit laughing affectedly*, MADAMOISELLE *following her*.

*Madam*. He, he, he, he, he!

*All*. Ha, ha, ha, ha, ha!

*Sir John. Aside*. Why now this woman will be married to
somebody too.

*Bel*. Poor creature, what a passion she's in. But I forgive her.

*Heart*. Since you have so much goodness for her, I hope you'll
pardon my offence too, madam.

*Bel*. There will be no great difficulty in that, since I am guilty
of an equal fault.

*Heart*. Then pardons being pass'd on all sides, let's to church
to conclude the day's work.

*Con*. But before you go, let me treat you, pray, with a song a
new-married lady made within this week. It may be of use to
you both.

SONG

I

When yielding first to Damon's flame,
    I sunk into his arms
He swore he'd ever be the same,
    Then rifl'd all my charms.

But fond of what h'ad long desir'd,
  Too greedy of his prey,
My shepherd's flame, alas, expir'd
  Before the verge of day.

### II

My innocence in lovers' wars
  Reproach'd his quick defeat.
Confus'd, asham'd, and bath'd in tears,
  I mourn'd his cold retreat.
At length, "Ah, shepherdess," cried he,
  "Would you my fire renew,
Alas you must retreat like me,
  I'm lost if you pursue."

*Heart.* So, madam, now had the parson but done his business——
*Bel.* You'd be half weary of your bargain.
*Heart.* No sure, I might dispense with one night's lodging.
*Bel.* I'm ready to try, sir.
*Heart.* Then let's to church, and if it be our chance to dis-
agree——
*Bel.* Take heed, the surly husband's fate you see.    [*Exeunt.*]

# EPILOGUE

By another hand.

## SPOKEN BY LADY BRUTE AND BELINDA

*Lady B.* No epilogue?

*Bel.*                  I swear I know of none.

*Lady B.* Lord, how shall we excuse it to the town?

*Bel.* Why, we must e'en say something of our own.

*Lady B.* Our own! Ay, that must needs be precious stuff.

*Bel.* I'll lay my life they'll like it well enough.

Come, faith, begin.

*Lady B.*           Excuse me, after you.

*Bel.* Nay, pardon me for that. I know my cue.

*Lady B.* Oh, for the world, I would not have precedence.

*Bel.* Oh, Lord!

*Lady B.*       I swear——

*Bel.*               Oh, fie!

*Lady B.*                   I'm all obedience.

First then, know all, before our doom is fix'd,

The third day is for us——

*Bel.*             Nay, and the sixth.

*Lady B.* We speak not from the poet now, nor is it

His cause—I want a rhyme——

*Bel.*               That we solicit.

*Lady B.* Then sure you cannot have the hearts to be severe

And damn us——

*Bel.*       Damn us? Let 'em if they dare.

*Lady B.* Why, if they should, what punishment remains?

*Bel.* Eternal exile from behind our scenes.

*Lady B.* But if they're kind, that sentence we'll recall.

We can be grateful——

*Bel.*         And have wherewithal.

*Lady B.* But at grand treaties, hope not to be trusted

Before preliminaries are adjusted.

*Bel.* You know the time, and we appoint this place

Where, if you please, we'll meet and sign the peace.

# THE MAN OF MODE
## OR, SIR FOPLING FLUTTER
### A COMEDY

# DRAMATIS PERSONÆ

Mr. DORIMANT,
Mr. MEDLEY,
OLD BELLAIR,                    } Gentlemen.
YOUNG BELLAIR,
Sir FOPLING FLUTTER.

LADY TOWNLEY,
EMILIA,
Mrs. LOVEIT,                    } Gentlewomen.
BELINDA,
LADY WOODVIL,
HARRIET, her daughter.

PERT and BUSY, waiting-women.
A Shoemaker.
An Orange-Woman.
Three Slovenly Bullies.
Two Chairmen.
Mr. SMIRK, a parson.
HANDY, a valet-de-chambre.
Pages, Footmen, etc.

SCENE—LONDON.

## THE DUCHESS

MADAM, Poets, however they may be modest otherwise, have always too good an opinion of what they write. The world, when it sees this play dedicated to your Royal Highness, will conclude I have more than my share of that vanity. But I hope the honour I have of belonging to you will excuse my presumption. 'Tis the first thing I have produced in your service, and my duty obliges me to what my choice durst not else have aspired.

I am very sensible, madam, how much it is beholding to your indulgence for the success it had in the acting, and your protection will be no less fortunate to it in the printing; for all are so ambitious of making their court to you, that none can be severe to what you are pleased to favour.

This universal submission and respect is due to the greatness of your rank and birth; but you have other illustrious qualities which are much more engaging. Those would but dazzle, did not these really charm the eyes and understandings of all who have the happiness to approach you.

Authors, on these occasions, are never wanting to publish a particular of their patron's virtues and perfections; but your Royal Highness's are so eminently known, that, did I follow their examples, I should but paint those wonders here of which every one already has the idea in his mind. Besides, I do not think it proper to aim at that in prose which is so glorious a subject for verse; in which hereafter if I show more zeal than skill, it will not grieve me much, since I less passionately desire to be esteemed a poet than to be thought,

Madam,
> Your Royal Highness's
>> most humble, most obedient,
>>> and most faithful servant,

GEORGE ETHEREGE.

449

# PROLOGUE

## BY SIR CAR SCROOPE, BARONET

LIKE dancers on the ropes poor poets fare,
Most perish young, the rest in danger are;
This, one would think, should make our authors wary,
But, gamester like, the giddy fools miscarry.
A lucky hand or two so tempts 'em on,
They cannot leave off play till they're undone.
With modest fears a muse does first begin,
Like a young wench newly enticed to sin;
But tickled once with praise, by her good will,
The wanton fool would never more lie still.
'Tis an old mistress you 'll meet here to-night,
Whose charms you once have look'd on with delight;
But now of late such dirty drabs have known ye,
A muse o'th' better sort's ashamed to own ye.
Nature well drawn, and wit, must now give place
To gaudy nonsense and to dull grimace:
Nor is it strange that you should like so much
That kind of wit, for most of yours is such.
But I'm afraid that while to France we go,
To bring you home fine dresses, dance, and show,
The stage, like you, will but more foppish grow.
Of foreign wares why should we fetch the scum
When we can be so richly served at home?
For, Heav'n be thank'd, 'tis not so wise an age
But your own follies may supply the stage.
Though often plough'd, there's no great fear the soil
Should barren grow by the too frequent toil,
While at your doors are to be daily found
Such loads of dunghill to manure the ground.
'Tis by your follies that we players thrive,
As the physicians by diseases live;
And as each year some new distemper reigns,
Whose friendly poison helps t'increase their gains
So among you there starts up every day
Some new unheard-of fool for us to play.
Then for your own sakes be not too severe,
Nor what you all admire at home, damn here:
Since each is fond of his own ugly face,
Why should you, when we hold it, break the glass?

# THE MAN OF MODE

## OR, SIR FOPLING FLUTTER

### ACT I

SCENE I.—*A Dressing-room. A table covered with a toilet; clothes laid ready*

*Enter* DORIMANT *in his gown and slippers, with a note in his hand made up, repeating verses.*

*Dor.* Now for some ages had the pride of Spain
Made the sun shine on half the world in vain.

> [*Then looking on the note.*

[*For* Mrs. LOVEIT.] What a dull insipid thing is a *billet-doux* written in cold blood, after the heat of the business is over! It is a tax upon good-nature which I have here been labouring to pay, and have done it, but with as much regret as ever fanatic paid the Royal Aid or Church Duties. 'Twill have the same fate, I know, that all my notes to her have had of late, 'twill not be thought kind enough. Faith, women are i' the right when they jealously examine our letters, for in them we always first discover our decay of passion.——Hey! Who waits?

### *Enter* HANDY

*Handy.* Sir——

*Dor.* Call a footman.

*Handy.* None of 'em are come yet.

*Dor.* Dogs! Will they ever lie snoring a-bed till noon?

*Handy.* 'Tis all one, sir: if they're up, you indulge 'em so they're ever poaching after whores all the morning.

*Dor.* Take notice henceforward, who's wanting in his duty, the next clap he gets, he shall rot for an example. What vermin are those chattering without?

*Handy.* Foggy Nan the orange-woman and swearing Tom the shoemaker.

*Dor.* Go; call in that overgrown jade with the flasket of guts before her; fruit is refreshing in a morning.  [*Exit* HANDY.

> It is not that I love you less
> Than when before your feet I lay.

*Enter* ORANGE-WOMAN *with* HANDY.

How now, Double Tripe! what news do you bring?

*Or.-Wom.* News! Here's the best fruit has come to town
t'year; gad, I was up before four a'clock this morning, and bought
all the choice i' the market.

*Dor.* The nasty refuse of your shop.

*Or.-Wom.* You need not make mouths at it; I assure you 'tis
all culled ware.

*Dor.* The citizens buy better on a holiday in their walk to
Totnam.[1]

*Or.-Wom.* Good or bad, tis all one; I never knew you commend
anything.   Lord! would the ladies had heard you talk of 'em as
I have done.   Here, bid your man give me an angel.

[*Sets down the fruit.*

*Dor.* Give the bawd her fruit again.

*Or.-Wom.* Well, on my conscience, there never was the like
of you.   God's my life, I had almost forgot to tell you there is a
young gentlewoman lately come to town with her mother, that
is so taken with you.

*Dor.* Is she handsome?

*Or.-Wom.* Nay, gad, there are few finer women, I tell you but
so, and a hugeous fortune, they say.   Here, eat this peach, it
comes from the stone; 'tis better than any Newington y' have
tasted.

*Dor.* This fine woman, I'll lay my life,

[*Taking the peach.*

is some awkward, ill-fashioned, country toad, who, not having
above four dozen of black hairs on her head, has adorned her
baldness with a large white fruz, that she may look sparkishly
in the forefront of the King's box at an old play.

*Or.-Wom.* Gad, you'd change your note quickly if you did
but see her.

*Dor.* How came she to know me?

*Or.-Wom.* She saw you yesterday at the Change; she told me
you came and fooled with the woman at the next shop.

*Dor.* I remember there was a mask observed me indeed.
Fooled, did she say?

*Or.-Wom.* Ay, I vow she told me twenty things you said too;
and acted with her head and with her body so like you——

---

[1] Cf. *The Virtuoso* (v.): "The suburb fools trudge to Lamb's Conduit
or Totnam."   Later on the walk became more modish:

When the sweet breathing spring unfolds the buds

.      .      .      .      .      .

Then Totenham fields with roving beauty swarms.

GAY, *Epistle to Pulteney.*

*Enter* MEDLEY.

*Med.* Dorimant, my life, my joy, my darling sin, how dost thou?

*Or.-Wom.* Lord! what a filthy trick these men have got of kissing one another! 　　　　　　　　　　　　[*She spits.*

*Med.* Why do you suffer this cartload of scandal to come near you and make your neighbours think you so improvident to need a bawd?

*Or.-Wom.* Good, now we shall have it! you did but want him to help you; come, pay me for my fruit.

*Med.* Make us thankful for it, huswife; bawds are as much out of fashion as gentlemen-ushers: none but old formal ladies use the one, and none but foppish old stagers employ the other—go, you are an insignificant brandy bottle.

*Dor.* Nay, there you wrong her, three quarts of canary is her business.

*Or.-Wom.* What you please, gentlemen.

*Dor.* To him! give him as good as he brings.

*Or.-Wom.* Hang him, there is not such another heathen in the town again, except it be the shoemaker without.

*Med.* I shall see you hold up your hand at the bar next sessions for murder, huswife; that shoemaker can take his oath you are in fee with the doctor's to sell green fruit to the gentry, that the crudities may breed diseases.

*Or.-Wom.* Pray give me my money.

*Dor.* Not a penny; when you bring the gentlewoman hither you spoke of, you shall be paid.

*Or.-Wom.* The gentlewoman! the gentlewoman may be as honest as your sisters, for aught as I know. Pray pay me, Mr. Dorimant, and do not abuse me so; I have an honester way of living, you know it.

*Med.* Was there ever such a resty bawd?

*Dor.* Some jade's tricks she has, but she makes amends when she's in good-humour. Come, tell me the lady's name, and Handy shall pay you.

*Or.-Wom.* I must not, she forbid me.

*Dor.* That's a sure sign she would have you.

*Med.* Where does she live?

*Or.-Wom.* They lodge at my house.

*Med.* Nay, then she's in a hopeful way.

*Or.-Wom.* Good Mr. Medley, say your pleasure of me, but take heed how you affront my house. God's my life, in a hopeful way!

*Dor.* Prithee, peace! what kind of woman's the mother?

*Or.-Wom.* A goodly grave gentlewoman. Lord! how she talks against the wild young men o' the town! As for your part, she thinks you an arrant devil; should she see you, on my conscience she would look if you had not a cloven foot.

*Dor.* Does she know me?

*Or.-Wom.* Only by hearsay; a thousand horrid stories have been told her of you, and she believes 'em all.

*Med.* By the character, this should be the famous Lady Woodvil and her daughter Harriet.

*Or.-Wom.* The devil's in him for guessing, I think.

*Dor.* Do you know 'em?

*Med.* Both very well; the mother's a great admirer of the forms and civility of the last age.

*Dor.* An antiquated beauty may be allowed to be out of humour at the freedoms of the present. This is a good account of the mother; pray, what is the daughter?

*Med.* Why, first she's an heiress, vastly rich.

*Dor.* And handsome?

*Med.* What alteration a twelvemonth may have bred in her I know not, but a year ago she was the beautifullest creature I ever saw; a fine, easy, clean shape; light brown hair in abundance; her features regular; her complexion clear and lively; large wanton eyes; but above all, a mouth that has made me kiss it a thousand times in imagination, teeth white and even, and pretty pouting lips, with a little moisture ever hanging on them, that look like the Provence rose fresh on the bush, ere the morning sun has quite drawn up the dew.

*Dor.* Rapture, mere rapture!

*Or.-Wom.* Nay, gad, he tells you true; she's a delicate creature.

*Dor.* Has she wit?

*Med.* More than is usual in her sex, and as much malice. Then she's as wild as you would wish her, and has a demureness in her looks that makes it so surprising.

*Dor.* Flesh and blood cannot hear this, and not long to know her.

*Med.* I wonder what makes her mother bring her up to town; an old doting keeper cannot be more jealous of his mistress.

*Or.-Wom.* She made me laugh yesterday; there was a judge came to visit 'em, and the old man, she told me, did so stare upon her, and when he saluted her smacked so heartily; who would think it of 'em?

*Med.* God a mercy, a judge! [1]

*Dor.* Do 'em right, the gentlemen of the long robe have not been wanting by their good examples to countenance the crying sin o' the nation.

*Med.* Come, on with your trappings; 'tis later than you imagine.

*Dor.* Call in the shoemaker, Handy.

*Or.-Wom.* Good Mr. Dorimant, pay me; gad, I had rather give you my fruit than stay to be abused by that foul-mouthed rogue; what you gentlemen say, it matters not much, but such a dirty fellow does one more disgrace.

---

[1] The first edition (1676) has "God-a-mercy, Judge": the correction ~~ms to be necessary.

*Dor.* Give her ten shillings, and be sure you tell the young gentlewoman I must be acquainted with her.

*Or.-Wom.* Now do you long to be tempting this pretty creature. Well, heavens mend you!

*Med.* Farewell, Bog.    [*Exeunt* ORANGE-WOMAN *and* HANDY. Dorimant, when˙ did you see your *pis-aller*, as you call her Mrs. Loveit?

*Dor.* Not these two days.

*Med.* And how stand affairs between you?

*Dor.* There has been great patching of late, much ado; we make a shift to hang together.

*Med.* I wonder how her mighty spirit bears it.

*Dor.* Ill enough, on all conscience; I never knew so violent a creature.

*Med.* She's the most passionate in her love, and the most extravagant in her jealousy, of any woman I ever heard of. What note is that?

*Dor.* An excuse I am going to send her for the neglect I am guilty of.

*Med.* Prithee read it.

*Dor.* No; but if you will take the pains you may.

*Med.* [*reads*]. "I never was a lover of business, but now I have a just reason to hate it, since it has kept me these two days from seeing you. I intend to wait upon you in the afternoon, and in the pleasure of your conversation forget all I have suffered during this tedious absence." This business of yours, Dorimant, has been with a vizard at the playhouse; I have had an eye on you. If some malicious body should betray you, this kind note would hardly make your peace with her.

*Dor.* I desire no better.

*Med.* Why, would her knowledge of it oblige you?

*Dor.* Most infinitely; next to the coming to a good understanding with a new mistress, I love a quarrel with an old one; but the devil's in't, there has been such a calm in my affairs of late, I have not had the pleasure of making a woman so much as break her fan, to be sullen, or forswear herself these three days.

*Med.* A very great misfortune. Let me see, I love mischief well enough to forward this business myself; I'll about it presently and though I know the truth of what you've done will set her a-raving, I'll heighten it a little with invention, leave her in a fit o' the mother, and be here again before you're ready.

*Dor.* Pray stay; you may spare yourself the labour; the business is undertaken already by one who will manage it with as much address, and I think with a little more malice than you can.

*Med.* Who i' the devil's name can this be?

*Dor.* Why the vizard—that very vizard you saw me with.

*Med.* Does she love mischief so well as to betray herself to spite another?

*Dor.* Not so neither, Medley. I will make you comprehend the mystery: this mask, for a farther confirmation of what I have been these two days swearing to her, made me yesterday at the playhouse make her a promise before her face utterly to break off with Loveit; and because she tenders my reputation, and would not have me do a barbarous thing, has contrived a way to give me a handsome occasion.

*Med.* Very good.

*Dor.* She intends, about an hour before me, this afternoon to make Loveit a visit, and (having the privilege, by reason of a professed friendship between 'em) to talk of her concerns.

*Med.* Is she a friend?

*Dor.* Oh, an intimate friend!

*Med.* Better and better; pray proceed.

*Dor.* She means insensibly to insinuate a discourse of me, and artificially raise her jealousy to such a height, that transported with the first motions of her passion, she shall fly upon me with all the fury imaginable as soon as ever I enter; the quarrel being thus happily begun, I am to play my part, confess and justify all my roguery, swear her impertinence and ill-humour makes her intolerable, tax her with the next fop that comes into my head, and in a huff march away; slight her, and leave her to be taken by whosoever thinks it worth his time to lie down before her.

*Med.* This vizard is a spark, and has a genius that makes her worthy of yourself, Dorimant.

### Enter HANDY, *Shoemaker, and Footman.*

*Dor.* You rogue there, who sneak like a dog that has flung down a dish, if you do not mend your waiting I'll uncase you, and turn you loose to the wheel of fortune. Handy, seal this, and let him run with it presently. [*Exeunt* HANDY [1] *and Footman.*

*Med.* Since you're resolved on a quarrel, why do you send her this kind note?

*Dor.* To keep her at home in order to the business. [*To the Shoemaker.*] How now, you drunken sot?

*Shoem.* 'Zbud, you have no reason to talk; I have not had a bottle of sack of yours in my belly this fortnight.

*Med.* The orange-woman says your neighbours take notice what a heathen you are, and design to inform the bishop and have you burned for an atheist.

*Shoem.* Damn her, dunghill! if her husband does not remove her, she stinks so the parish intend to indict him for a nuisance.

*Med.* I advise you like a friend, reform your life; you have brought the envy of the world upon you by living above yourself. Whoring and swearing are vices too genteel for a shoemaker.

*Shoem.* 'Zbud, I think you men of quality will grow as un-

---

[1] Who presently returns, though the entry is not marked.

reasonable as the women; you would engross the sins o' the nation; poor folks can no sooner be wicked, but they're railed at by their betters.

*Dor.* Sirrah, I'll have you stand i' the pillory for this libel.

*Shoem.* Some of you deserve it, I'm sure; there are so many of 'em, that our journeymen nowadays, instead of harmless ballads, sing nothing but your damned lampoons.

*Dor.* Our lampoons, you rogue?

*Shoem.* Nay, good master, why should not you write your own commentaries as well as Cæsar?

*Med.* The rascal's read, I perceive.

*Shoem.* You know the old proverb—ale and history.

*Dor.* Draw on my shoes, sirrah.

*Shoem.* Here's a shoe

*Dor.* Sits with more wrinkles than there are in an angry bully's forehead.

*Shoem.* 'Zbud, as smooth as your mistress's skin does upon her; so strike your foot in home. 'Zbud, if e'er a *monsieur* of 'em all make more fashionable wear, I'll be content to have my ears whipped off with my own paring-knife.

*Med.* And served up in a *ragoût* instead of coxcombs to a company of French shoemakers for a collation.

*Shoem.* Hold, hold! damn 'em, caterpillars! let 'em feed upon cabbage. Come, master, your health this morning next my heart now.

*Dor.* Go, get you home, and govern your family better; do not let your wife follow you to the alehouse, beat your whore, and lead you home in triumph.

*Shoem.* 'Zbud, there's never a man i' the town lives more like a gentleman with his wife than I do. I never mind her motions, she never inquires into mine; we speak to one another civilly, hate one another heartily, and because 'tis vulgar to lie and soak together, we have each of us our several settle-bed.

*Dor.* Give him half-a-crown.

*Med.* Not without he will promise to be bloody drunk.

*Shoem.* Tope's the word i' the eye of the world, for my master's honour, Robin.

*Dor.* Do not debauch my servants, sirrah.

*Shoem.* I only tip him the wink; he knows an alehouse from a hovel. [*Exit Shoemaker.*

*Dor.* My clothes, quickly.

*Med.* Where shall we dine to-day?

*Enter* BELLAIR.

*Dor.* Where you will; here comes a good third man.

*Bell.* Your servant, gentlemen.

*Med.* Gentle sir, how will you answer this visit to your honourable mistress? 'Tis not her interest you should keep company with men of sense, who will be talking reason.

*Bell.* I do not fear her pardon, do you but grant me yours for my neglect of late.

*Med.* Though you've made us miserable by the want of your good company, to show you I am free from all resentment, may the beautiful cause of our misfortune give you all the joys happy lovers have shared ever since the world began.

*Bell.* You wish me in Heaven, but you believe me on my journey to Hell.

*Med.* You have a good strong faith, and that may contribute much towards your salvation.　I confess I am but of an untoward constitution, apt to have doubts and scruples, and in love they are no less distracting than in religion; were I so near marriage, I should cry out by fits as I ride in my coach, *Cuckold, Cuckold*, with no less fury than the mad fanatic does *Glory* in Bethlem.

*Bell.* Because religion makes some run mad, must I live an atheist?

*Med.* Is it not great indiscretion for a man of credit, who may have money enough on his word, to go and deal with Jews who for little sums make men enter into bonds and give judgments?

*Bell.* Preach no more on this text, I am determined, and there is no hope of my conversion.

*Dor.* [*to* HANDY, *who is fiddling about him*]. Leave your unnecessary fiddling; a wasp that's buzzing about a man's nose at dinner is not more troublesome than thou art.

*Handy.* You love to have your clothes hang just, sir.

*Dor.* I love to be well dressed, sir; and think it no scandal to my understanding.

*Handy.* Will you use the essence, or orange-flower water?

*Dor.* I will smell as I do to-day, no offence to the ladies' noses.

*Handy.* Your pleasure, sir.

*Dor.* That a man's excellency should lie in neatly tying of a ribbon or a cravat! How careful's nature in furnishing the world with necessary coxcombs?

*Bell.* That's a mighty pretty suit of yours, Dorimant.

*Dor.* I am glad't has your approbation.

*Bell.* No man in town has a better fancy in his clothes than you have.

*Dor.* You will make me have an opinion of my genius.

*Med.* There is a great critic, I hear, in these matters lately arrived piping hot from Paris.

*Bell.* Sir Fopling Flutter. you mean.

*Med.* The same.

*Bell.* He thinks himself the pattern of modern gallantry.

*Dor.* He is indeed the pattern of modern foppery.

*Med.* He was yesterday at the play, with a pair of gloves up to his elbows and a periwig more exactly curled than a lady's head newly dressed for a ball.

*Bell.* What a pretty lisp he has!

*Dor.* Ho! that he affects in imitation of the people of quality of France.

*Med.* His head stands for the most part on one side, and his looks are more languishing than a lady's when she lolls at stretch in her coach or leans her head carelessly against the side of a box i' the playhouse.

*Dor.* He is a person indeed of great acquired follies.

*Med.* He is like many others, beholding to his education for making him so eminent a coxcomb; many a fool had been lost to the world had their indulgent parents wisely bestowed neither learning nor good breeding on 'em.

*Bell.* He has been, as the sparkish word is, brisk upon the ladies already; he was yesterday at my Aunt Townley's, and gave Mrs. Loveit a catalogue of his good qualities under the character of a complete gentleman, who, according to Sir Fopling, ought to dress well, dance well, fence well, have a genius for love-letters, an agreeable voice for a chamber, be very amorous, something discreet, but not over-constant.

*Med.* Pretty ingredients to make an accomplished person.

*Dor.* I am glad he pitched upon Loveit.

*Bell.* How so?

*Dor.* I wanted a fop to lay to her charge, and this is as pat as may be.

*Bell.* I am confident she loves no man but you.

*Dor.* The good fortune were enough to make me vain, but that I am in my nature modest.

*Bell.* Hark you, Dorimant; with your leave, Mr. Medley, 'tis only a secret concerning a fair lady.

*Med.* Your good breeding, sir, gives you too much trouble; you might have whispered without all this ceremony.

*Bell.* [*to* DORIMANT]. How stand your affairs with Belinda of late?

*Dor.* She's a little jilting baggage.

*Bell.* Nay, I believe her false enough, but she's ne'er the worse for your purpose; she was with you yesterday in a disguise at the play.

*Dor.* There we fell out, and resolved never to speak to one another more.

*Bell.* The occasion?

*Dor.* Want of courage to meet me at the place appointed. These young women apprehend loving as much as the young men do fighting at first; but, once entered, like them too, they all turn bullies straight.

*Enter* HANDY [1]

*Handy* [*to* BELLAIR]. Sir, your man without desires to speak with you.

*Bell.* Gentlemen, I'll return immediately.    [*Exit* BELLAIR.

[1] Whose previous exit had not been noticed.

*Med.* A very pretty fellow this.

*Dor.* He's handsome, well-bred, and by much the most tolerable of all the young men that do not abound in wit.

*Med.* Ever well-dressed, always complaisant, and seldom impertinent; you and he are grown very intimate, I see.

*Dor.* It is our mutual interest to be so: it makes the women think the better of his understanding and judge more favourably of my reputation; it makes him pass upon some for a man of very good sense and I upon others for a very civil person.

*Med.* What was that whisper?

*Dor.* A thing which he would fain have known, but I did not think it fit to tell him; it might have frighted him from his honourable intentions of marrying.

*Med.* Emilia, give her her due, has the best reputation of any young woman about the town who has beauty enough to provoke detraction; her carriage is unaffected, her discourse modest, not at all censorious nor pretending, like the counterfeits of the age.

*Dor.* She's a discreet maid, and I believe nothing can corrupt her but a husband.

*Med.* A husband?

*Dor.* Yes, a husband; I have known many women make a difficulty of losing a maidenhead who have afterwards made none of making a cuckold.

*Med.* This prudent consideration, I am apt to think, has made you confirm poor Bellair in the desperate résolution he has taken.

*Dor.* Indeed, the little hope I found there was of her, in the state she was in, has made him by my advice contribute something towards the changing of her condition.

#### *Enter* BELLAIR.

Dear Bellair, by heavens I thought we had lost thee; men in love are never to be reckoned on when we would form a company.

*Bell.* Dorimant I am undone; my man has brought the most surprising news i' the world.

*Dor.* Some strange misfortune is befallen your love.

*Bell.* My father came to town last night, and lodges i' the very house where Emilia lies.

*Med.* Does he know it is with her you are in love?

*Bell.* He knows I love, but knows not whom, without some officious sot has betrayed me.

*Dor.* Your Aunt Townley is your confidante and favours the business.

*Bell.* I do not apprehend any ill office from her; I have received a letter, in which I am commanded by my father to meet him at my aunt's this afternoon; he tells me farther he has made a match for me, and bids me resolve to be obedient to his will or expect to be disinherited.

*Med.* Now's your time, Bellair; never had lover such an opportunity of giving a generous proof of his passion.

*Bell.* As how, I pray?

*Med.* Why, hang an estate, marry Emilia out of hand, and provoke your father to do what he threatens; 'tis but despising a coach, humbling yourself to a pair of goloshes, being out of countenance when you meet your friends, pointed at and pitied wherever you go by all the amorous fops that know you, and your fame will be immortal.

*Bell.* I could find in my heart to resolve not to marry at all.

*Dor.* Fie, fie! that would spoil a good jest and disappoint the well-natured town of an occasion of laughing at you.

*Bell.* The storm I have so long expected hangs o'er my head and begins to pour down upon me; I am on the rack, and can have no rest till I'm satisfied in what I fear; where do you dine?

*Dor.* At Long's or Locket's.[1]

*Med.* At Long's let it be.

*Bell.* I'll run and see Emilia, and inform myself how matters stand; if my misfortunes are not so great as to make me unfit for company, I'll be with you. [*Exit* BELLAIR.

*Enter a Footman with a letter.*

*Foot.* [*to* DORIMANT]. Here's a letter, sir.

*Dor.* The superscription's right: *For Mr. Dorimant.*

*Med.* Let's see: the very scrawl and spelling of a true-bred whore.

*Dor.* I know the hand; the style is admirable, I assure you.

*Med.* Prithee read it.

*Dor.* [*reads*]. "I told a you you dud not love me, if you dud, you would have seen me again e'er now; I have no money, and am very mallicolly; pray send me a guynie to see the operies. Your servant to command, Molly."

*Med.* Pray let the whore have a favourable answer, that she may spark it in a box and do honour to her profession.

*Dor.* She shall, and perk up i' the face of quality. Is the coach at door?

*Handy.* You did not bid me send for it.

*Dor.* Eternal blockhead! [HANDY *offers to go out.*] Hey, sot.

*Handy.* Did you call me, sir?

*Dor.* I hope you have no just exception to the name, sir?

*Handy.* I have sense, sir.

*Dor.* Not so much as a fly in winter.——How did you come, Medley?

*Med.* In a chair.

---

[1] Famous ordinaries; the former in the Haymarket, the latter near Charing Cross. "I'll marry a drawer," says Lady Wishfort in *The Way of the World,* iii, 1, "to have him poisoned in his wine. I'll send for Robin from Locket's immediately." Compare, too, *Love for Love,* iii, 3.

*Footman.* You may have a hackney coach if you please, sir.

*Dor.* I may ride the elephant if I please, sir; call another chair, and let my coach follow to Long's.

[*Exeunt singing, Be calm, ye great parents, etc.*

## ACT II

### SCENE I

*Enter my* Lady TOWNLEY *and* EMILIA.

*Lady Town.* I was afraid, Emilia, all had been discovered.

*Emil.* I tremble with the apprehension still.

*Lady Town.* That my brother should take lodgings i' the very house where you lie!

*Emil.* 'Twas lucky we had timely notice to warn the people to be secret; he seems to be a mighty good-humoured old man.

*Lady Town.* He ever had a notable smirking way with him.

*Emil.* He calls me rogue, tells me he can't abide me, and does so bepat me.

*Lady Town.* On my word you are much in his favour then.

*Emil.* He has been very inquisitive, I am told, about my family, my reputation, and my fortune.

*Lady Town.* I am confident he does not i' the least suspect you are the woman his son's in love with.

*Emil.* What should make him then inform himself so particularly of me?

*Lady Town.* He was always of a very loving temper himself; it may be he has a doting fit upon him; who knows?

*Emil.* It cannot be.

### Enter YOUNG BELLAIR.

*Lady Town.* Here comes my nephew. Where did you leave your father?

*Y. Bell.* Writing a note within. Emilia, this early visit looks as if some kind jealousy would not let you rest at home.

*Emil.* The knowledge I have of my rival gives me a little cause to fear your constancy.

*Y. Bell.* My constancy! I vow——

*Emil.* Do not vow——Our love is frail as is our life, and full as little in our power; and are you sure you shall outlive this day?

*Y. Bell.* I am not; but when we are in perfect health 'twere an idle thing to fright ourselves with the thoughts of sudden death.

*Lady Town.* Pray what has passed between you and your father i' the garden?

*Y. Bell.* He's firm in his resolution, tells me I must marry Mrs. Harriet, or swears he'll marry himself and disinherit me; when I saw I could not prevail with him to be more indulgent, I dissembled an obedience to his will which has composed his passion, and will give us time, and I hope opportunity, to deceive him.

*Enter* OLD BELLAIR *with a note in his hand.*

*Lady Town.* Peace, here he comes.

*O. Bell.* Harry, take this, and let your man carry it for me to Mr. Fourbes's chamber, my lawyer, i' the Temple.

　　　　　　　　　　　　　　　*Exit* YOUNG BELLAIR.

[*To* EMILIA.] Neighbour, adod, I am glad to see thee here; make much of her, sister, she's one of the best of your acquaintance; I like her countenance and her behaviour well, she has a modesty that is not common i' this age, adod, she has.

*Lady Town.* I know her value, brother, and esteem her accordingly.

*O. Bell.* Advise her to wear a little more mirth in her face, adod, she's too serious.

*Lady Town.* The fault is very excusable in a young woman.

*O. Bell.* Nay, adod, I like her ne'er the worse, a melancholy beauty has her charms; I love a pretty sadness in a face which varies now and then, like changeable colours, into a smile.

*Lady Town.* Methinks you speak very feelingly, brother.

*O. Bell.* I am but five-and-fifty, sister, you know, an age not altogether insensible! [*To* EMILIA.] Cheer up, sweetheart, I have a secret to tell thee may chance to make thee merry; we three will make collation together anon; i' the meantime mum, I can't abide you; go, I can't abide you.

*Enter* YOUNG BELLAIR.

Harry, come, you must along with me to my Lady Woodvil's. I am going to slip the boy at a mistress.

*Y. Bell.* At a wife, sir, you would say.

*O. Bell.* You need not look so glum, sir; a wife is no curse when she brings the blessings of a good estate with her; but an idle town flirt, with a painted face, a rotten reputation, and a crazy fortune, adod, is the devil and all; and such a one I hear you are in league with.

*Y. Bell.* I cannot help detraction, sir.

*O. Bell.* Out, a pise o' their breeches, there are keeping fools enough for such flaunting baggages, and they are e'en too good for 'em. [*To* EMILIA.] Remember night, go, you're a rogue, you're a rogue; fare you well, fare you well; come, come, come along, sir.　　　　　　　　　[*Exeunt* OLD *and* YOUNG BELLAIR.

*Lady Town.* On my word the old man comes on apace; I'll lay my life he's smitten.

*Emil.* This is nothing but the pleasantness of his humour.

*Lady Town.* I know him better than you; let it work, it may prove lucky.

### *Enter a Page.*

*Page.* Madam, Mr. Medley has sent to know whether a visit will not be troublesome this afternoon?

*Lady Town.* Send him word his visits never are so.

[*Exit Page.*

*Emil.* He's a very pleasant man.

*Lady Town.* He's a very necessary man among us women; he's not scandalous i' the least, perpetually contriving to bring good company together, and always ready to stop up a gap at ombre; then he knows all the little news o' the town.

*Emil.* I love to hear him talk o' the intrigues; let 'em be never so dull in themselves, he'll make 'em pleasant i' the relation.

*Lady Town.* But he improves things so much one can take no measure of the truth from him. Mr. Dorimant swears a flea or a maggot is not made more monstrous by a magnifying glass than a story is by his telling it.

*Emil.* Hold, here he comes.

### *Enter* MEDLEY.

*Lady Town.* Mr. Medley.

*Med.* Your servant, madam.

*Lady Town.* You have made yourself a stranger of late.

*Emil.* I believe you took a surfeit of ombre last time you were here.

*Med.* Indeed I had my bellyful of that termagant Lady Dealer; there never was so insatiable a carder, an old gleeker never loved to sit to't like her; I have played with her now at least a dozen times till she's worn out all her fine complexion, and her tour [1] would keep in curl no longer.

*Lady Town.* Blame her not, poor woman; she loves nothing so well as a black ace.

*Med.* The pleasure I have seen her in when she has had hope in drawing for a matadore!

*Emil.* 'Tis as pretty sport to her as persuading masks off is to you to make discoveries.

*Lady Town.* Pray, where's your friend Mr. Dorimant?

*Med.* Soliciting his affairs; he's a man of great employment has more mistresses now depending than the most eminent lawyer in England has causes.

*Emil.* Here has been Mrs. Loveit, so uneasy and out of humour these two days.

---

[1] Headdress.

*Lady Town.* How strangely love and jealousy rage in that poor woman!

*Med.* She could not have picked out a devil upon earth so proper to torment her; he has made her break a dozen or two of fans already, tear half a score points in pieces, and destroy hoods and knots without number.

*Lady Town.* We heard of a pleasant serenade he gave her t'other night.

*Med.* A Danish serenade, with kettledrums and trumpets.

*Emil.* Oh, barbarous!

*Med.* What, you are of the number of the ladies whose ears are grown so delicate since our operas,[1] you can be charmed with nothing but *flutes douces* [2] and French hautboys.

*Emil.* Leave your raillery, and tell us is there any new wit come forth, songs or novels?

*Med.* A very pretty piece of gallantry by an eminent author called *The Diversions of Brussels* [3]; very necessary to be read by all old ladies who are desirous to improve themselves at questions and commands, blindman's buff, and the like fashionable recreations.

*Emil.* Oh, ridiculous!

*Med.* Then there is *The Art of Affectation*, written by a late beauty of quality, teaching you how to draw up your breasts, stretch up your neck, to thrust out your breech, to play with your head, to toss up your nose, to bite your lips, to turn up your eyes, to speak in a silly soft tone of a voice, and use all the foolish French words that will infallibly make your person and conversation charming, with a short apology at the latter end, in the behalf of young ladies who notoriously wash and paint, though they have naturally good complexions.

*Emil.* What a deal of stuff you tell us?

*Med.* Such as the town affords, madam. The Russians hearing the great respect we have for foreign dancing have lately sent over some of their best balladines, who are now practising a famous ballet, which will be suddenly danced at the Bear Garden.

*Lady Town.* Pray forbear your idle stories, and give us an account of the state of love as it now stands.

[1] " I saw an Italian opera in music, the first that had been in England of the kind."—Evelyn, 5 Jan., 1674.

[2] Here, and later on (iv, 1), variously spelt *flute doux* and *flutes deux*. It has been suggested (*Notes and Queries*, 7th S., v, 135) that *flutes douces* is the right reading, and this has been adopted. The *flute douce* may have been something like the *flute d'amour*, or *Liebesflöte*, "an old form of flute with a narrow bore, supposed to have a smooth and fascinating quality."

[3] Medley ridicules Richard Flecknoe's *Treatise of the Sports of Wit*, 1675, a serious account of a gathering of intellectual ladies near Brussels, 1650, and their diversions during seven days of earnest debate. (R. S. Cox, Jr., 'Richard Flecknoe and *The Man of Mode*', *M.L.Q.*, XXIX (March 1968), 183-9.)

*Med.* Truly there has been some revolutions in those affairs, great chopping and changing among the old, and some new lovers, whom malice, indiscretion, and misfortune have luckily brought into play.

*Lady Town.* What think you of walking into the next room, and sitting down before you engage in this business?

*Med.* I wait upon you, and I hope (though women are commonly unreasonable) by the plenty of scandal I shall discover to give you very good content, ladies. [*Exeunt.*

## SCENE II

*Enter* Mrs. LOVEIT *and* PERT. Mrs. LOVEIT *putting up a letter, then pulling out her pocket-glass, and looking in it.*

*Lov.* Pert.

*Pert.* Madam.

*Lov.* I hate myself. I look so ill to-day.

*Pert.* Hate the wicked cause on't, that base man Mr. Dorimant, who makes you torment and vex yourself continually.

*Lov.* He is to blame, indeed.

*Pert.* To blame to be two days without sending, writing, or coming near you, contrary to his oath and covenant! 'twas to much purpose to make him swear: I'll lay my life there's not an article but he has broken——talked to the vizards i' the pit; waited upon the ladies from the boxes to their coaches; gone behind the scenes and fawned upon those little insignificant creatures the players; 'tis impossible for a man of his inconstant temper to forbear, I'm sure.

*Lov.* I know he is a devil, but he has something of the angel yet undefaced in him, which makes him so charming and agreeable that I must love him be he never so wicked.

*Pert.* I little thought, madam, to see your spirit tamed to this degree, who banished poor Mr. Lackwit but for taking up another lady's fan in your presence.

*Lov.* My knowing of such odious fools contributes to the making of me love Dorimant the better.

*Pert.* Your knowing of Mr. Dorimant, in my mind, should rather make you hate all mankind.

*Lov.* So it does, besides himself.

*Pert.* Pray, what excuse does he make in his letter?

*Lov.* He has had business.

*Pert.* Business in general terms would not have been a current excuse for another; a modish man is always very busy when he is in pursuit of a new mistress.

*Lov.* Some fop has bribed you to rail at him; he had business, I will believe it, and will forgive him.

*Pert.* You may forgive him anything, but I shall never forgive him his turning me into ridicule, as I hear he does.

*Lov.* I perceive you are of the number of those fools his wit has made his enemies.

*Pert.* I am of the number of those he's pleased to rally, madam; and if we may believe Mr. Wagfan and Mr. Caperwell, he sometimes makes merry with yourself too among his laughing companions.

*Lov.* Blockheads are as malicious to witty men as ugly women are to the handsome; 'tis their interest, and they make it their business to defame 'em.

*Pert.* I wish Mr. Dorimant would not make it his business to defame you.

*Lov.* Should he, I had rather be made infamous by him than owe my reputation to the dull discretion of those fops you talk of.

*Enter* BELINDA.

Belinda! [*Running to her.*

*Bel.* My dear.

*Lov.* You have been unkind of late.

*Bel.* Do not say unkind, say unhappy!

*Lov.* I could chide you; where have you been these two days?

*Bel.* Pity me rather, my dear, where I have been so tired with two or three country gentlewomen, whose conversation has been more insufferable than a country fiddle.

*Lov.* Are they relations?

*Bel.* No, Welsh acquaintance I made when I was last year at St. Winifred's; they have asked me a thousand questions of the modes and intrigues of the town, and I have told 'em almost as many things for news that hardly were so when their gowns were in fashion.

*Lov.* Provoking creatures, how could you endure 'em?

*Bel.* [*aside*]. Now to carry on my plot; nothing but love could make me capable of so much falsehood; 'tis time to begin, lest Dorimant should come before her jealousy has stung her.

[*Laughs, and then speaks on.*

I was yesterday at a play with 'em, where I was fain to show 'em the living, as the man at Westminster does the dead; that is Mrs. Such-a-one, admired for her beauty; this is Mr. Such-a-one, cried up for a wit; that is sparkish Mr. Such-a-one, who keeps reverend Mrs. Such-a-one, and there sits fine Mrs. Such-a-one, who was lately cast off by my Lord Such-a-one.

*Lov.* Did you see Dorimant there?

*Bel.* I did, and imagine you were there with him and have no mind to own it.

*Lov.* What should make you think so?

*Bel.* A lady masked in a pretty *déshabillé*, whom Dorimant entertained with more respect than the gallants do a common vizard.

*Lov.* [*aside.*] Dorimant at the play entertaining a mask, oh heavens!

*Bel.* [*aside*]. Good.

*Love.* Did he stay all the while?

*Bel.* Till the play was done, and then led her out, which confirms me it was you.

*Lov.* Traitor!

*Pert.* Now you may believe he had business, and you may forgive him too.

*Lov.* Ungrateful, perjured man!

*Bel.* You seem so much concerned, my dear, I fear I have told you unawares what I had better have concealed for your quiet.

*Lov.* What manner of shape had she?

*Bel.* Tall and slender, her motions were very genteel; certainly she must be some person of condition.

*Lov.* Shame and confusion be ever in her face when she shows it!

*Bel.* I should blame your discretion for loving that wild man, my dear; but they say he has a way so bewitching that few can defend their hearts who know him.

*Lov.* I will tear him from mine, or die i' the attempt.

*Bel.* Be more moderate.

*Lov.* Would I had daggers, darts, or poisoned arrows in my breast, so I could but remove the thoughts of him from thence!

*Bel.* Fie, fie! your transports are too violent, my dear.  This may be but an accidental gallantry, and 'tis likely ended at her coach.

*Pert.* Should it proceed farther, let your comfort be, the conduct Mr. Dorimant affects will quickly make you know your rival, ten to one let you see her ruined, her reputation exposed to the town; a happiness none will envy her but yourself, madam.

*Lov.* Whoe'er she be, all the harm I wish her is, may she love him as well as I do, and may he give her as much cause to hate him!

*Pert.* Never doubt the latter end of your curse, madam.

*Lov.* May all the passions that are raised by neglected love, jealousy, indignation, spite, and thirst of revenge, eternally rage in her soul as they do now in mine!

[*Walks up and down with a distracted air.*

*Enter a Page.*

*Page.* Madam, Mr. Dorimant.

*Lov.* I will not see him.

*Page.* I told him you were within, madam.

*Lov.* Say you lied, say I'm busy, shut the door; say anything.

*Page.* He's here, madam.

*Enter* DORIMANT.

*Dor.*     They taste of death who do at Heaven arrive,
        But we this paradise approach alive.

[*To* LOVEIT.] What, dancing the galloping nag without a fiddle?
        [*Offers to catch her by the hand ; she flings away and
        walks on.*

I fear this restlessness of the body, madam [*Pursuing her.*]
proceeds from an unquietness of the mind. What unlucky
accident puts you out of humour; a point ill washed, knots spoiled
i' the making up, hair shaded awry, or some other little mistake
in setting you in order?

*Pert.* A trifle, in my opinion, sir, more inconsiderable than any
you mention.

*Dor.* Oh, Mrs Pert, I never knew you sullen enough to be
silent; come, let me know the business.

*Pert.* The business, sir, is the business that has taken you up
these two days; how have I seen you laugh at men of business,
and now to become a man of business yourself!

*Dor.* We are not masters of our own affections, our inclinations
daily alter; now we love pleasure, and anon we shall dote on
business: human frailty will have it so, and who can help it?

*Lov.* Faithless, inhuman, barbarous man!——

*Dor.* Good, now the alarm strikes.——

*Lov.* Without sense of love, of honour, or of gratitude, tell me
—for I will know—what devil, masked she was, you were with at
the play yesterday?

*Dor.* Faith, I resolved as much as you. but the devil was
obstinate and would not tell me.

*Lov.* False in this as in your vows to me! you do know.

*Dor.* The truth is, I did all I could to know.

*Lov.* And dare you own it to my face? Hell and furies!
                                    [*Tears her fan in pieces.*

*Dor.* Spare your fan, madam; you are growing hot, and will
want it to cool you.

*Lov.* Horror and distraction seize you, sorrow and remorse
gnaw your soul, and punish all your perjuries to me!—— [*Weeps.*

*Dor.*        So thunder breaks the cloud in twain,
            And makes a passage for the rain.
                                    [*Turning to* BELINDA.

Belinda, you are the devil that have raised this storm; you were
at the play yesterday, and have been making discoveries to
your dear.

*Bel.* You're the most mistaken man i' the world.

*Dor.* It must be so, and here I vow revenge; resolve to pursue
and persecute you more impertinently than ever any loving fop
did his mistress, hunt you i' the Park, trace you i' the Mall, dog
you in every visit you make, haunt you at the plays and i' the

drawing room, hang my nose in your neck, and talk to you whether you will or no, and ever look upon you with such dying eyes, till your friends grow jealous of me, send you out of town, and make the world suspect your reputation. [*In a lower voice.* At my Lady Townley's when we go from hence.

[*He looks kindly on* BELINDA.

*Bel.* I'll meet you there.

*Dor.* Enough.

*Lov.* Stand off, you sha' not stare upon her so.

[*Pushing* DORIMANT *away.*

*Dor.* Good! There's one made jealous already.

*Lov.* Is this the constancy you vowed?

*Dor.* Constancy at my years! 'tis not a virtue in season; you might as well expect the fruit the autumn ripens i' the spring.

*Lov.* Monstrous principle!

*Dor.* Youth has a long journey to go, madam: should I have set up my rest at the first inn I lodged at, I should never have arrived at the happiness I now enjoy.

*Lov.* Dissembler, damned dissembler!

*Dor.* I am so, I confess; good nature and good manners corrupt me. I am honest in my inclinations, and would not, were't not to avoid offence, make a lady a little in years believe I think her young, wilfully mistake art for nature, and seem as fond of a thing I am weary of as when I doted on't in earnest.

*Lov.* False man!

*Dor.* True woman!

*Lov.* Now you begin to show yourself!

*Dor.* Love gilds us over and makes us show fine things to one another for a time, but soon the gold wears off, and then again the native brass appears.

*Lov.* Think on your oaths, your vows and protestations, perjured man.

*Dor.* I made 'em when I was in love.

*Lov.* And therefore ought they not to bind? Oh, impious!

*Dor.* What we swear at such a time may be a certain proof of a present passion; but to say truth, in love there is no security to be given for the future.

*Lov.* Horrid and ungrateful, begone, and never see me more.

*Dor.* I am not one of those troublesome coxcombs, who because they were once well received take the privilege to plague a woman with their love ever after; I shall obey you, madam, though I do myself some violence.

[*He offers to go, and* LOVEIT *pulls him back.*

*Lov.* Come back, you sha' not go. Could you have the ill-nature to offer it?

*Dor.* When love grows diseased, the best thing we can do is to put it to a violent death; I cannot endure the torture of a lingering and consumptive passion.

*Lov.* Can you think mine sickly?

*Dor.* Oh, 'tis desperately ill! What worse symptoms are there than your being always uneasy when I visit you, your picking quarrels with me on slight occasions, and in my absence kindly listening to the impertinences of every fashionable fool that talks to you?

*Lov.* What fashionable fool can you lay to my charge?

*Dor.* Why, the very cock-fool of all those fools, Sir Fopling Flutter.

*Lov.* I never saw him in my life but once.

*Dor.* The worse woman you, at first sight to put on all your charms, to entertain him with that softness in your voice and all that wanton kindness in your eyes you so notoriously affect when you design a conquest.

*Lov.* So damned a lie did never malice yet invent. Who told you this?

*Dor.* No matter; that ever I should love a woman that can dote on a senseless caper, a tawdry French ribbon, and a formal cravat.

*Lov.* You make me mad.

*Dor.* A guilty conscience may do much; go on, be the game-mistress o' the town, and enter all our young fops as fast as they come from travel.

*Lov.* Base and scurrilous!

*Dor.* A fine mortifying reputation 'twill be for a woman of your pride, wit, and quality!

*Lov.* This jealousy's a mere pretence, a cursed trick of your own devising; I know you.

*Dor.* Believe it, and all the ill of me you can: I would not have a woman have the least good thought of me that can think well of Fopling; farewell; fall to, and much good may [it] do you with your coxcomb.

*Lov.* Stay, oh! stay, and I will tell you all.

*Dor.* I have been told too much already.

[*Exit* DORIMANT.

*Lov.* Call him again.

*Pert.* E'en let him go, a fair riddance.

*Lov.* Run, I say; call him again. I will have him called.

*Pert.* The devil should carry him away first, were it my concern.

[*Exit* PERT.

*Bel.* He's frightened me from the very thoughts of loving men; for heaven's sake, my dear, do not discover what I told you; I dread his tongue as much as you ought to have done his friendship.

*Enter* PERT.

*Pert.* He's gone, madam.

*Lov.* Lightning blast him!

*Pert.* When I told him you desired him to come back, he smiled, made a mouth at me, flung into his coach, and said——

*Lov.* What did he say?

*Pert.* " *Drive away* "; and then repeated verses.

*Lov.* Would I had made a contract to be a witch, when first I entertained this greater devil, monster, barbarian; I could tear myself in pieces.    Revenge, nothing but revenge can ease me: plague, war, famine, fire, all that can bring universal ruin and misery on mankind; with joy I'd perish to have you in my power but this moment                                                [*Exit* LOVEIT.

*Pert.* Follow, madam; leave her not in this outrageous passion.
                                                [PERT *gathers up the things.*

*Bel.* He's given me the proof which I desired of his love:
    But 'tis a proof of his ill-nature too;
    I wish I had not seen him use her so.
    I sigh to think that Dorimant may be
    One day as faithless and unkind to me.                    [*Exeunt.*


# ACT III

## SCENE I.—Lady WOODVIL'S *Lodgings.*

*Enter* HARRIET *and* BUSY *her woman.*

*Busy.* Dear madam!    Let me set that curl in order.

*Har.* Let me alone, I will shake 'em all out of order.

*Busy.* Will you never leave this wildness?

*Har.* Torment me not.

*Busy.* Look! there's a knot falling off.

*Har.* Let it drop.

*Busy.* But one pin, dear madam.

*Har.* How do I daily suffer under thy officious fingers!

*Busy.* Ah, the difference that is between you and my Lady Dapper!    How uneasy she is if the least thing be amiss about her!

*Har.* She is indeed most exact; nothing is ever wanting to make her ugliness remarkable.

*Busy.* Jeering people say so.

*Har.* Her powdering, painting, and her patching never fail in public to draw the tongues and eyes of all the men upon her.

*Busy.* She is indeed a little too pretending.

*Har.* That women should set up for beauty as much in spite of nature as some men have done for wit!

*Busy.* I hope, without offence, one may endeavour to make oneself agreeable.

*Har.* Not when 'tis impossible.    Women then ought to be no more fond of dressing than fools should be of talking.    Hoods and modesty, masks and silence, things that shadow and conceal: they should think of nothing else.

*Busy.* Jesu! madam, what will your mother think is become of you? For heaven's sake, go in again.

*Har.* I won't.

*Busy.* This is the extravagant'st thing that ever you did in your life, to leave her and a gentleman who is to be your husband.

*Har.* My husband! Hast thou so little wit to think I spoke what I meant when I overjoyed her in the country with a low courtsey and *What you please, madam, I shall ever be obedient*?

*Busy.* Nay, I know not, you have so many fetches.

*Har.* And this was one to get her up to London; nothing else, I assure thee.

*Busy.* Well, the man, in my mind, is a fine man.

*Har.* The man indeed wears his clothes fashionably, and has a pretty negligent way with him, very courtly and much affected; he bows, and talks, and smiles so agreeably as he thinks.

*Busy.* I never saw anything so genteel.

*Har.* Varnished over with good breeding many a blockhead makes a tolerable show.

*Busy.* I wonder you do not like him.

*Har.* I think I might be brought to endure him, and that is all a reasonable woman should expect in a husband; but there is duty i' the case——and like the haughty Merab,

> I find much aversion in my stubborn mind,
> Which is bred by being promised and design'd.

*Busy.* I wish you do not design your own ruin! I partly guess your inclinations, madam,——that Mr. Dorimant——

*Har.* Leave your prating, and sing some foolish song or other.

*Busy.* I will; the song you love so well ever since you saw Mr. Dorimant.

#### Song

> When first Amintas charm'd my heart,
>  My heedless sheep began to stray;
> The wolves soon stole the greatest part,
>  And all will now be made a prey.
>
> Ah! let not love your thoughts possess,
>  'Tis fatal to a shepherdess;
> The dang'rous passion you must shun,
>  Or else, like me, be quite undone.

*Har.* Shall I be paid down by a covetous parent for a purchase? I need no land; no, I'll lay myself out all in love. It is decreed——

*Enter* YOUNG BELLAIR.

*Y. Bell.* What generous resolution are you making, madam?

*Har.* Only to be disobedient, sir.

*Y. Bell.* Let me join hands with you in that.

*Har.* With all my heart; I never thought I should have given you mine so willingly.   Here I, Harriet——

*Y. Bell.* And I, Harry——

*Har.* Do solemnly protest——

*Y. Bell.* And vow——

*Har.* That I with you——

*Y. Bell.* And I with you——

*Both.* Will never marry.

*Har.* A match!

*Y. Bell.* And no match!   How do you like this indifference now?

*Har.* You expect I should take it ill, I see.

*Y. Bell.* 'Tis not unnatural for you women to be a little angry [if] you miss a conquest, though you would slight the poor man were he in your power.

*Har.* There are some, it may be, have an eye like Bartholomew, big enough for the whole fair, but I am not of the number, and you may keep your gingerbread: 'twill be more acceptable to the lady whose dear image it wears, sir.

*Y. Bell.* I must confess, madam, you came a day after the fair

*Har.* You own then you are in love.

*Y. Bell.* I do.

*Har.* The confidence is generous, and in return I could almost find in my heart to let you know my inclinations.

*Y. Bell.* Are you in love?

*Har.* Yes, with this dear town, to that degree I can scarce endure the country in landscapes and in hangings.

*Y. Bell.* What a dreadful thing 'twould be to be hurried back to Hampshire?

*Har.* Ah! name it not!

*Y. Bell.* As for us, I find we shall agree well enough!   Would we could do something to deceive the grave people!

*Har.* Could we delay their quick proceeding, 'twere well; a reprieve is a good step towards the getting of a pardon.

*Y. Bell.* If we give over the game we are undone; what think you of playing it on booty?

*Har.* What do you mean?

*Y. Bell.* Pretend to be in love with one another; 'twill make some dilatory excuses we may feign pass the better.

*Har.* Let us do't, if it be but for the dear pleasure of dissembling.

*Y. Bell.* Can you play your part?

*Har.* I know not what it is to love, but I have made pretty remarks by being now and then where lovers meet.   Where did you leave their gravities?

*Y. Bell.* I' th' next room; your mother was censuring our modern gallant.

*Enter* OLD BELLAIR *and* Lady WOODVIL.

*Har.* Peace! Here they come, I will lean against this wall and look bashfully down upon my fan, while you like an amorous spark modishly entertain me.

*Lady Wood.* Never go about to excuse 'em; come, come, it was not so when I was a young woman.

*O. Bell.* Adod, they're something disrespectful.

*Lady Wood.* Quality was then considered, and not rallied by every fleering fellow.

*O. Bell.* Youth will have its jest, adod it will.

*Lady Wood.* 'Tis good breeding now to be civil to none but players and Exchange women; they are treated by 'em as much above their condition as others are below theirs.

*O. Bell.* Out, a pise on 'em! talk no more; the rogues ha got an ill habit of preferring beauty, no matter where they find it.

*Lady Wood.* See your son and my daughter, they have improved their acquaintance since they were within.

*O. Bell.* Adod, methinks they have; let's keep back and observe.

*Y. Bell.* Now for a look and gestures that may persuade 'em I am saying all the passionate things imaginable.

*Har.* Your head a little more on one side, ease yourself on your left leg, and play with your right hand.

*Y. Bell.* Thus, is it not?

*Har.* Now set your right leg firm on the ground, adjust your belt, then look about you.

*Y. Bell.* A little exercising will make me perfect.

*Har.* Smile, and turn to me again very sparkish.

*Y. Bell.* Will you take your turn and be instructed?

*Har.* With all my heart.

*Y. Bell.* At one motion play your fan, roll your eyes, and then settle a kind look upon me.

*Har.* So.

*Y. Bell.* Now spread your fan, look down upon it, and tell the sticks with a finger.

*Har.* Very modish!

*Y. Bell.* Clap your hand up to your bosom, hold down your gown; shrug a little, draw up your breasts, and let 'em fall again gently, with a sigh or two, etc.

*Har.* By the good instructions you give, I suspect you for one of those malicious observers who watch people's eyes and from innocent looks make scandalous conclusions.

*Y. Bell.* I know some, indeed, who, out of mere love to mischief, are as vigilant as jealousy itself, and will give you an account of every glance that passes at a play and i' th' circle.[1]

[1] In Hyde Park.

*Har.* 'Twill not be amiss now to seem a little pleasant.

*Y. Bell.* Clap your fan then in both your hands, snatch it to your mouth, smile, and with a lively motion fling your body a little forwards. So,——now spread it; fall back on the sudden, cover your face with it, and break out in to a loud laughter—— take up! look grave, and fall a-fanning of yourself——admirably well acted.

*Har.* I think I am pretty apt at these matters.

*O. Bell.* Adod, I like this well.

*Lady Wood.* This promises something.

*O. Bell.* Come! there is love i' th' case, adod there is, or will be; what say you, young lady?

*Har.* All in good time, sir; you expect we should fall to and love, as gamecocks fight, as soon as we are set together; adod, you're unreasonable!

*O. Bell.* Adod, sirrah, I like thy wit well.

*Enter a Servant.*

*Serv.* The coach is at the door, madam.

*O. Bell.* Go, get you and take the air together.

*Lady Wood.* Will not you go with us?

*O. Bell.* Out a pise. Adod, I ha' business and cannot. We shall meet at night at my sister Townley's.

*Y. Bell.* [*aside*]. He's going to Emilia. I overheard him talk of a collation. [*Exeunt.*

## SCENE II

*Enter* Lady Townley, Emilia, *and* Mr. Medley.

*Lady Town.* I pity the young lovers we last talked of; though, to say truth, their conduct has been so indiscreet they deserve to be unfortunate.

*Med.* You've had an exact account, from the great lady i' th' box down to the little orange-wench.

*Emil.* You're a living libel, a breathing lampoon; I wonder you are not torn in pieces.

*Med.* What think you of setting up an office of intelligence for these matters? The project may get money.

*Lady Town.* You would have great dealings with country ladies.

*Med.* More than Muddiman [1] has with their husbands.

---

[1] Henry Muddiman, 1629–92, editor of series of newsletters particularly popular in the provinces: *The Parliamentary Intelligencer*, renamed *The Kingdom's Intelligencer* (1659–63), *The Oxford Gazette* (1665–7), *The London Gazette* (1667–present).

*Enter* BELINDA.

*Lady Town.* Belinda, what has been become of you? we have not seen you here of late with your friend Mrs. Loveit.

*Bel.* Dear creature, I left her but now so sadly afflicted.

*Lady Town.* With her old distemper, jealousy?

*Med.* Dorimant has played her some new prank.

*Bel.* Well, that Dorimant is certainly the worst man breathing.

*Emil.* I once thought so.

*Bel.* And do you not think so still?

*Emil.* No, indeed!

*Bel.* Oh, Jesu!

*Emil.* The town does him a great deal of injury, and I will never believe what it says of a man I do not know again, for his sake.

*Bel.* You make me wonder!

*Lady Town.* He's a very well-bred man.

*Bel.* But strangely ill-natured.

*Emil.* Then he's a very witty man.

*Bel.* But a man of no principles.

*Med.* Your man of principles is a very fine thing indeed!

*Bel.* To be preferred to men of parts by women who have regard to their reputation and quiet. Well, were I minded to play the fool, he should be the last man I'd think of.

*Med.* He has been the first in many lady's favours, though you are so severe, madam.

*Lady Town.* What he may be for a lover I know not, but he's a very pleasant acquaintance, I am sure.

*Bel.* Had you seen him use Mrs. Loveit as I have done, you would never endure him more.

*Emil.* What, he has quarrelled with her again?

*Bel.* Upon the slightest occasion; he's jealous of Sir Fopling.

*Lady Town.* She never saw him in her life but yesterday, and that was here.

*Emil.* On my conscience, he's the only man in town that's her aversion; how horribly out of humour she was all the while he talked to her!

*Bel.* And somebody has wickedly told him——

*Emil.* Here he comes.

*Enter* DORIMANT.

*Med.* Dorimant! you are luckily come to justify yourself—— here's a lady——

*Bel.* Has a word or two to say to you from a disconsolate person.

*Dor.* You tender your reputation too much, I know, madam, to whisper with me before this good company.

*Bel.* To serve Mrs. Loveit, I'll make a bold venture.

*Dor.* Here's Medley, the very spirit of scandal.

*Bel.* No matter!

*Emil.* 'Tis something you are unwilling to hear, Mr. Dorimant.

*Lady Town.* Tell him, Belinda, whether he will or no.

*Bel.* [*aloud*]. Mrs. Loveit——

*Dor.* Softly, these are laughers, you do not know 'em.

*Bel.* [*to* DORIMANT, *apart*]. In a word, you've made me hate you, which I thought you never could have done.

*Dor.* In obeying your commands.

*Bel.* 'Twas a cruel part you played! how could you act it?

*Dor.* Nothing is cruel to a man who could kill himself to please you; remember, five o'clock to-morrow morning.

*Bel.* I tremble when you name it.

*Dor.* Be sure you come.

*Bel.* I sha' not.

*Dor.* Swear you will.

*Bel.* I dare not.

*Dor.* Swear, I say.

*Bel.* By my life! by all the happiness I hope for——

*Dor.* You will.

*Bel.* I will.

*Dor.* Kind.

*Bel.* I am glad I've sworn, I vow I think I should ha' failed you else!

*Dor.* Surprisingly kind! In what temper did you leave Loveit?

*Bel.* Her raving was prettily over, and she began to be in a brave way of defying you and all your works. Where have you been since you went from thence?

*Dor.* I looked in at the play.

*Bel.* I have promised, and must return to her again.

*Dor.* Persuade her to walk in the Mall [1] this evening.

*Bel.* She hates the place, and will not come.

*Dor.* Do all you can to prevail with her.

*Bel.* For what purpose?

*Dor.* Sir Fopling will be here anon; I'll prepare him to set upon her there before me.

*Bel.* You persecute her too much; but I'll do all you'll ha' me.

*Dor.* [*aloud*]. Tell her plainly, 'tis grown so dull a business I can drudge on no longer.

*Emil.* There are afflictions in love, Mr. Dorimant.

*Dor.* You women make 'em, who are commonly as unreasonable in that as you are at play; without the advantage be on your side a man can never quietly give over when he's weary.

*Med.* If you would play without being obliged to complaisance, Dorimant, you should play in public places.

---

[1] i.e. Pall Mall, which roused the enthusiasm of even the fastidious Gay:

> "O bear me to the paths of fair Pell Mell."
>
> *Trivia*, ii, 257.

*Dor.* Ordinaries were a very good thing for that, but gentlemen do not of late frequent 'em; the deep play is now in private houses.  [BELINDA *offering to steal away.*

*Lady Town.* Belinda, are you leaving us so soon?

*Bel.* I am to go to the Park with Mrs. Loveit, madam.

[*Exit* BELINDA.

*Lady Town.* This *confidence* will go nigh to spoil this young creature.

*Med.* 'Twill do her good, madam. Young men who are brought up under practising lawyers prove the abler counsel when they come to be called to the Bar themselves.

*Dor.* The town has been very favourable to you this afternoon, my Lady Townley; you use to have an *embarras* of chairs and coaches at your door, an uproar of footmen in your hall, and a noise of fools above here.

*Lady Town.* Indeed my house is the general *rendezvous*, and, next to the playhouse, is the common refuge of all the young idle people.

*Emil.* Company is a very good thing, madam, but I wonder you do not love it a little more chosen.

*Lady Town.* 'Tis good to have an universal taste; we should love wit, but for variety be able to divert ourselves with the extravagancies of those who want it.

*Med.* Fools will make you laugh.

*Emil.* For once or twice; but the repetition of their folly after a visit or two grows tedious and unsufferable.

*Lady Town.* You are a little too delicate, Emilia.

### *Enter a Page.*

*Page.* Sir Fopling Flutter, madam, desires to know if you are to be seen.

*Lady Town.* Here's the freshest fool in town, and one who has not cloyed you yet. Page!

*Page.* Madam!

*Lady Town.* Desire him to walk up.  [*Exit Page.*

*Dor.* Do not you fall on him, Medley, and snub him. Soothe him up in his extravagance; he will show the better.

*Med.* You know I have a natural indulgence for fools, and need not this caution, sir.

### *Enter* Sir FOPLING FLUTTER, *with his Page after him.*

*Sir Fop.* Page, wait without. Madam [*To* Lady TOWNLEY.], I kiss your hands. I see yesterday was nothing of chance; the *belles assemblées* form themselves here every day. Lady [*To* EMILIA.], your servant. Dorimant, let me embrace thee; without lying, I have not met with any of my acquaintance who retain so much of Paris as thou dost—the very air thou hadst when the

marquis mistook thee i' th' Tuileries, and cried, *Hey! Chevalier!*
and then begged thy pardon.

*Dor.* I would fain wear in fashion as long as I can, sir; 'tis a
thing to be valued in men as well as baubles.

*Sir Fop.* Thou art a man of wit, and understandest the town;
prithee let thee and I be intimate, there is no living without
making some good man the confidant of our pleasures.

*Dor.* 'Tis true! but there is no man so improper for such a
business as I am.

*Sir Fop.* Prithee, why hast thou so modest an opinion of
thyself?

*Dor.* Why, first, I could never keep a secret in my life, and then
there is no charm so infallibly makes me fall in love with a woman
as my knowing a friend loves her. I deal honestly with you.

*Sir Fop.* Thy humour's very gallant, or let me perish; I knew
a French count so like thee.

*Lady Town.* Wit, I perceive, has more power over you than
beauty, Sir Fopling, else you would not have let this lady stand
so long neglected.

*Sir Fop.* [*to* EMILIA]. A thousand pardons, madam; some
civilities due, of course, upon the meeting a long absent friend.
The *éclat* of so much beauty, I confess, ought to have charmed
me sooner.

*Emil.* The *brilliant* of so much good language, sir, has much
more power than the little beauty I can boast.

*Sir Fop.* I never saw anything prettier than this high work
on your *point d'Espagne.*——

*Emil.* 'Tis not so rich as *point de Venise.*——

*Sir Fop.* Not altogether, but looks cooler, and is more proper
for the season. Dorimant, is not that Medley?

*Dor.* The same, sir.

*Sir Fop.* Forgive me, sir; in this *embarras* of civilities I could
not come to have you in my arms sooner. You understand an
equipage the best of any man in town, I hear.

*Med.* By my own you would not guess it.

*Sir Fop.* There are critics who do not write, sir.

*Med.* Our peevish poets will scarce allow it.

*Sir Fop.* Damn 'em, they'll allow no man wit who does not
play the fool like themselves, and show it! Have you taken
notice of the *ca'èche* I brought over?

*Med.* Oh, yes! 'T has quite another air than th' English
makes.

*Sir Fop.* 'Tis as easily known from an English tumbril as an
Inns of Court man is from one of us.

*Dor.* Truly, there is a *bel-air* in *calèches* as well as men.

*Med.* But there are few so delicate to observe it.

*Sir Fop.* The world is generally very *grossier* here, indeed.

*Lady Town.* He's very fine.

*Emil.* Extreme proper.

*Sir Fop.* A slight suit I made to appear in at my first arrival, not worthy your consideration, ladies.

*Dor.* The pantaloon is very well mounted.

*Sir Fop.* The tassels are new and pretty.

*Med.* I never saw a coat better cut.

*Sir Fop.* It makes me show long-waisted, and, I think, slender.

*Dor.* That's the shape our ladies dote on.

*Med.* Your breech, though, is a handful too high in my eye, Sir Fopling.

*Sir Fop.* Peace, Medley; I have wished it lower a thousand times, but a pox on't, 'twill not be.

*Lady Town.* His gloves are well fringed, large and graceful.

*Sir Fop.* I was always eminent for being *bien-gante*.

*Emil.* He wears nothing but what are originals of the most famous hands in Paris.

*Sir Fop.* You are in the right, madam.

*Lady Town.* The suit?

*Sir Fop.* Barroy.[1]

*Emil.* The garniture?

*Sir Fop.* Le Gras.

*Med.* The shoes?

*Sir Fop.* Piccat.

*Dor.* The periwig?

*Sir Fop.* Chedreux.[2]

*Lady Town. and Emil.* The gloves?

*Sir Fop.* Orangerie: you know the smell, ladies. Dorimant, I could find in my heart for an amusement to have a gallantry with some of our English ladies.

*Dor.* 'Tis a thing no less necessary to confirm the reputation of your wit than a duel will be to satisfy the town of your courage.

*Sir Fop.* Here was a woman yesterday——

*Dor.* Mistress Loveit.

*Sir Fop.* You have named her.

*Dor.* You cannot pitch on a better for your purpose.

*Sir Fop.* Prithee, what is she?

*Dor.* A person of quality, and one who has a rest of reputation enough to make the conquest considerable. Besides, I hear she likes you too.

*Sir Fop.* Methought she seemed, though, very reserved and uneasy all the time I entertained her.

---

[1] Perhaps this should be *Barri.* The "drap du Barri" was later on extremely fashionable.

[2] A species of perruque, so called from the name of its inventor. Dryden wore a chedreux and a sword when he ate tarts with Mrs. Reeve at the Mulberry Garden, and Oldham, in his imitation of the Third Satire of Juvenal, has:

> "Their tawdry clothes, pulvilios, essences;
> Their chedreux perruques and their vanities."

*Dor.* Grimace and affectation. You will see her i' th' Mall to-night.

*Sir Fop.* Prithee let thee and I take the air together.

*Dor.* I am engaged to Medley, but I'll meet you at St. James's and give you some information upon the which you may regulate your proceedings.

*Sir Fop.* All the world will be in the Park to-night: ladies, 'twere pity to keep so much beauty longer within doors and rob the Ring of all those charms that should adorn it.——Hey, page!

*Enter Page, and goes out again.*

See that all my people be ready. Dorimant, *au revoir !*

[*Exit* Sir FOPLING.

*Med.* A fine mettled coxcomb.

*Dor.* Brisk and insipid.

*Med.* Pert and dull.

*Emil.* However you despise him, gentlemen, I'll lay my life he passes for a wit with many.

*Dor.* That may very well be; nature has her cheats, stums a brain, and puts sophisticate dulness often on the tasteless multitude for true wit and good-humour. Medley, come.

*Med.* I must go a little way, I will meet you i' the Mall.

*Dor.* I'll walk through the garden thither. [*To the Women.*] We shall meet anon and bow.

*Lady Town.* Not to-night; we are engaged about a business the knowledge of which may make you laugh hereafter.

*Med.* Your servant, ladies.

*Dor. Au revoir !* as Sir Fopling says.

[*Exeunt* MEDLEY *and* DORIMANT.

*Lady Town.* The old man will be here immediately.

*Emil.* Let's expect him i' th' garden.

*Lady Town.* Go, you are a rogue.

*Emil.* I can't abide you. [*Exeunt*

### SCENE III.—*The Mall*

*Enter* HARRIET *and* YOUNG BELLAIR, *she pulling him.*

*Har.* Come along.

*Y. Bell.* And leave your mother?

*Har.* Busy will be sent with a hue and cry after us; but that's no matter.

*Y. Bell.* 'Twill look strangely in me.

*Har.* She'll believe it a freak of mine and never blame your manners.

*Y. Bell.* What reverend acquaintance is that she has met?

*Har.* A fellow-beauty of the last King's time, though by the ruins you would hardly guess it.     [*Exeunt.*

*Enter* DORIMANT, *and crosses the stage.*

*Enter* YOUNG BELLAIR *and* HARRIET.

*Y. Bell.* By this time your mother is in a fine taking.

*Har.* If your friend Mr. Dorimant were but here now, that she might find me talking with him.

*Y. Bell.* She does not know him, but dreads him, I hear, of all mankind.

*Har.* She concludes if he does but speak to a woman she's undone; is on her knees every day to pray Heav'n defend me from him.

*Y. Bell.* You do not apprehend him so much as she does.

*Har.* I never saw anything in him that was frightful.

*Y. Bell.* On the contrary, have you not observed something extreme delightful in his wit and person?

*Har.* He's agreeable and pleasant I must own, but he does so much affect being so, he displeases me.

*Y. Bell.* Lord, madam, all he does and says is so easy and so natural.

*Har.* Some men's verses seem so to the unskilful, but labour i' the one and affectation in the other to the judicious plainly appear.

*Y. Bell.* I never heard him accused of affectation before.

*Enter* DORIMANT, *and stares upon her.*

*Har.* It passes on the easy town, who are favourably pleased in him to call it humour.

[*Exeunt* YOUNG BELLAIR *and* HARRIET.

*Dor.* 'Tis she! it must be she, that lovely hair, that easy shape, those wanton eyes, and all those melting charms about her mouth which Medley spoke of; I'll follow the lottery, and put in for a prize with my friend Bellair.     [*Exit* DORIMANT *repeating :*

In love the victors from the vanquish'd fly;
They fly that wound, and they pursue that die.

*Enter* YOUNG BELLAIR *and* HARRIET, *and after them* DORIMANT, *standing at a distance.*

*Y. Bell.* Most people prefer High Park [1] to this place.

*Har.* It has the better reputation, I confess; but I abominate the dull diversions there, the formal bows, the affected smiles, the silly by-words, and amorous tweers in passing; here one meets with a little conversation now and then.

---

[1] i.e. Hyde Park, *the* park *par excellence*; references to it are endless. The great resort there was the so-called Ring. The name *High* Park seems unusual.

*Y. Bell.* These conversations have been fatal to some of your sex, madam.

*Har.* It may be so; because some who want temper have been undone by gaming, must others who have it wholly deny themselves the pleasure of play?

*Dor.* Trust me, it were unreasonable, madam.

                         *[Coming up gently, and bowing to her.*

*Har.* Lord! who's this?        *[She starts, and looks grave.*

*Y. Bell.* Dorimant.

*Dor.* Is this the woman your father would have you marry?

*Y. Bell.* It is.

*Dor.* Her name?

*Y. Bell.* Harriet.

*Dor.* I am not mistaken, she's handsome.

*Y. Bell.* Talk to her, her wit is better than her face; we were wishing for you but now.

*Dor.* [*to* HARRIET]. Overcast with seriousness o' the sudden! A thousand smiles were shining in that face but now; I never saw so quick a change of weather.

*Har.* [*aside*]. I feel as great a change within; but he shall never know it.

*Dor.* You were talking of play, madam; pray what may be your stint?

*Har.* A little harmless discourse in public walks, or at most an appointment in a box barefaced at the playhouse; you are for masks and private meetings where women engage for all they are worth, I hear.

*Dor.* I have been used to deep play, but I can make one at small game when I like my gamester well.

*Har.* And be so unconcerned you'll ha' no pleasure in't.

*Dor.* Where there is a considerable sum to be won the hope of drawing people in makes every trifle considerable.

*Har.* The sordidness of men's natures, I know, makes 'em willing to flatter and comply with the rich, though they are sure never to be the better for 'em.

*Dor.* 'Tis in their power to do us good, and we despair not but at some time or other they may be willing.

*Har.* To men who have fared in this town like you, 'twould be a great mortification to live on hope; could you keep a Lent for a mistress?

*Dor.* In expectation of a happy Easter, and though time be very precious, think forty days well lost to gain your favour.

*Har.* Mr. Bellair! let us walk, 'tis time to leave him; men grow dull when they begin to be particular.

*Dor.* You're mistaken, flattery will not ensue, though I know you're greedy of the praises of the whole Mall.

*Har.* You do me wrong.

*Dor.* I do not; as I followed you I observed how you were pleased when the fops cried: "She's handsome, very handsome,

By God she is," and whispered aloud your name, the thousand
several forms you put your face into; then, to make yourself
more agreeable, how wantonly you played with your head, flung
back your locks, and looked smilingly over your shoulder at 'em.

*Har.* I do not go begging the men's, as you do the ladies' good
liking, with a sly softness in your looks and a gentle slowness in
your bows as you pass by 'em——as thus, sir; ——    [*Acts him.*
Is not this like you?

### Enter Lady WOODVIL *and* BUSY.

*Y. Bell.* Your mother, madam.
                              [*Pulls* HARRIET; *she composes herself.*
*Lady Wood.* Ah, my dear child Harriet!

*Busy.* Now is she so pleased with finding her again she cannot
chide her.

*Lady Wood.* Come away!

*Dor.* 'Tis now but high Mall, madam, the most entertaining
time of all the evening.

*Har.* I would fain see that Dorimant, mother, you so cry out
for a monster; he's in the Mall, I hear.

*Lady Wood.* Come away then! the plague is here, and you
should dread the infection.

*Y. Bell.* You may be misinformed of the gentleman.

*Lady Wood.* Oh, no! I hope you do not know him! He is
the prince of all the devils in the town, delights in nothing but
in rapes and riots.

*Dor.* If you did but hear him speak, madam!

*Lady Wood.* Oh! he has a tongue, they say, would tempt the
angels to a second fall.

*Enter* Sir FOPLING *with his Equipage, six Footmen and a Page.*

*Sir Fop.* Hey, Champagne, Norman, La Rose, La Fleur, La
Tour, La Verdure.  Dorimant!——

*Lady Wood.* Here, here he is among this rout, he names him;
come away, Harriet, come away.
              [*Exeunt* Lady WOODVIL, HARRIET, BUSY, *and* YOUNG
                                      BELLAIR.

*Dor.* This fool's coming has spoiled all; she's gone, but she has
left a pleasing image of herself behind that wanders in my soul
——It must not settle there.

*Sir Fop.* What reverie is this?  Speak, man.

*Dor.*          Snatch'd from myself, how far behind
                Already I behold the shore!

### Enter MEDLEY.

*Med.* Dorimant, a discovery!  I met with Bellair.

*Dor.* You can tell me no news, sir; I know all.

*Med.* How do you like the daughter?

*Dor.* You never came so near truth in your life as you did in her description.

*Med.* What think you of the mother?

*Dor.* Whatever I think of her, she thinks very well of me, I find.

*Med.* Did she know you?

*Dor.* She did not; whether she does now or no, I know not. Here was a pleasant scene towards, when in came Sir Fopling, mustering up his equipage, and at the latter end named me and frighted her away.

*Med.* Loveit and Belinda are not far off, I saw 'em alight at St. James's.

*Dor.* [*whispers*]. Sir Fopling, hark you, a word or two. Look you do not want assurance.

*Sir Fop.* I never do on these occasions.

*Dor.* Walk on, we must not be seen together; make your advantage of what I have told you; the next turn you will meet the lady.

*Sir Fop.* Hey——Follow me all.

[*Exeunt* Sir FOPLING *and his Equipage.*

*Dor.* Medley, you shall see good sport anon between Loveit and this Fopling.

*Med.* I thought there was something toward by that whisper

*Dor.* You know a worthy principle of hers?

*Med.* Not to be so much as civil to a man who speaks to her in the presence of him she professes to love.

*Dor.* I have encouraged Fopling to talk to her to-night.

*Med.* Now you are here she will go nigh to beat him.

*Dor.* In the humour she's in, her love will make her do some very extravagant thing, doubtless.

*Med.* What was Belinda's business with you at my Lady Townley's?

*Dor.* To get me to meet Loveit here in order to an *éclaircissement.* I made some difficulty of it, and have prepared this *rencontre* to make good my jealousy.

*Med.* Here they come!


### Enter LOVEIT, BELINDA, *and* PERT.

*Dor.* I'll meet her and provoke her with a deal of dumb civility in passing by, then turn short and be behind her when Sir Fopling sets upon her

> See how unregarded now
> That piece of beauty passes.

[*Exeunt* DORIMANT *and* MEDLEY.

*Bel.* How wonderful respectfully he bowed!

*Pert.* He's always over-mannerly when he has done a mischief.

*Bel.* Methought indeed at the same time he had a strange despising countenance.

*Pert.* The unlucky look, he thinks, becomes him.

*Bel.* I was afraid you would have spoke to him, my dear.

*Lov.* I would have died first; he shall no more find me the loving fool he has done.

*Bel.* You love him still!

*Lov.* No.

*Pert.* I wish you did not.

*Lov.* I do not, and I will have you think so.  What made you hale me to this odious place, Belinda?

*Bel.* I hate to be hulched up in a coach; walking is much better.

*Lov.* Would we could meet Sir Fopling now!

*Bel.* Lord! would you not avoid him?

*Lov.* I would make him all the advances that may be.

*Bel.* That would confirm Dorimant's suspicion, my dear.

*Lov.* He is not jealous, but I will make him so, and be revenged a way he little thinks on.

*Bel.* [*aside*]. If she should make him jealous, that may make him fond of her again: I must dissuade her from it.  Lord! my dear, this will certainly make him hate you.

*Lov.* 'Twill make him uneasy, though he does not care for me; I know the effects of jealousy on men of his proud temper.

*Bel.* 'Tis a fantastic remedy, its operations are dangerous and uncertain.

*Lov.* 'Tis the strongest cordial we can give to dying love, it often brings it back when there's no sign of life remaining.  But I design not so much the reviving his, as my revenge.

*Enter* Sir FOPLING *and his Equipage.*

*Sir Fop.* Hey! bid the coachman send home four of his horses, and bring the coach to Whitehall; I'll walk over the Park——Madam, the honour of kissing your fair hands is a happiness I missed this afternoon at my Lady Townley's.

*Lov.* You were very obliging, Sir Fopling, the last time I saw you there.

*Sir Fop.* The preference was due to your wit and beauty. Madam, your servant; there never was so sweet an evening.

*Bel.* 'T has drawn all the rabble of the town hither.

*Sir Fop.* 'Tis pity there's not an order made that none but the *beau monde* should walk here.

*Lov.* 'Twould add much to the beauty of the place.  See what a sort of nasty fellows are coming.

*Enter three ill-fashioned Fellows, singing,*

'Tis not for kisses alone, etc.

*Lov.* Fo! Their periwigs are scented with tobacco so strong——

*Sir Fop.* It overcomes our pulvillio [1]——Methinks I smell the coffee-house they come from.

1 *Man.* Dorimant's convenient, Madam Loveit.

2 *Man.* I like the oily buttock with her.

3 *Man.* What spruce prig is that?

1 *Man.* A caravan lately come from Paris.

2 *Man.* Peace, they smoke. [2]

> There's something else to be done, etc.
>
> *[All of them coughing; exeunt, singing.*

#### *Enter* DORIMANT *and* MEDLEY.

*Dor.* They're engaged.

*Med.* She entertains him as if she liked him.

*Dor.* Let us go forward; seem earnest in discourse, and show ourselves. Then you shall see how she'll use him.

*Bel.* Yonder's Dorimant, my dear.

*Lov.* [*aside*]. I see him, he comes insulting; but I will disappoint him in his expectation. [*To* Sir FOPLING.] I like this pretty nice humour of yours, Sir Fopling. With what a loathing eye he looked upon those fellows!

*Sir Fop.* I sat near one of 'em at a play to-day, and was almost poisoned with a pair of cordovan gloves he wears.

*Lov.* Oh! filthy cordovan, how I hate the smell!

> *[Laughs in a loud affected way.*

*Sir Fop.* Did you observe, madam, how their cravats hung oose an inch from their neck, and what a frightful air it gave 'em?

*Lov.* Oh! I took particular notice of one that is always spruced up with a deal of dirty sky-coloured ribbon.

*Bel.* That's one of the walking flageolets who haunt the Mall o' nights.

*Lov.* Oh! I remember him; he's a hollow tooth enough to spoil the sweetness of an evening.

*Sir Fop.* I have seen the tallest walk the streets with a dainty pair of boxes neatly buckled on.

*Lov.* And a little footboy at his heels pocket-high, with a flat cap——a dirty face.

*Sir Fop.* And a snotty nose.

*Lov.* Oh——odious! there's many of my own sex with that Holborn equipage trig to Gray's Inn Walks, and now and then travel hither on a Sunday.

*Med.* She takes no notice of you.

*Dor.* Damn her! I am jealous of a counterplot!

---

[1] A favourite essence.

> "The patch, the powder-box, pulville-perfumes."
> GAY, *The Fan*, i, 129.

"Have you pulvilled the coachman?"—*The Way of the World*, iv, 1.

[2] i.e. suspect that we are talking about them.

*Lov.* Your liveries are the finest, Sir Fopling.——Oh, that page! that page is the prettily'st dressed——They are all Frenchmen?

*Sir Fop.* There's one damned English blockhead among 'em, you may know him by his mien.

*Lov.* Oh! that's he, that's he! what do you call him?

*Sir Fop.* Hey!——I know not what to call him.——

*Lov.* What's your name?

*Footman.* John Trott, madam!

*Sir Fop.* Oh, unsufferable! Trott, Trott, Trott! there's nothing so barbarous as the names of our English servants. What countryman are you, sirrah?

*Footman.* Hampshire, sir.

*Sir Fop.* Then Hampshire be your name. Hey, Hampshire!

*Lov.* Oh, that sound! that sound becomes the mouth of a man of quality!

*Med.* Dorimant, you look a little bashful on the matter.

*Dor.* She dissembles better than I thought she could have done.

*Med.* You have tempted her with too luscious a bait: she bites at the coxcomb.

*Dor.* She cannot fall from loving me to that?

*Med.* You begin to be jealous in earnest.

*Dor.* Of one I do not love?

*Med.* You did love her.

*Dor.* The fit has long been over.

*Med.* But I have known men fall into dangerous relapses when they have found a woman inclining to another.

*Dor.* [*to himself*]. He guesses the secret of my heart! I am concerned, but dare not show it lest Belinda should mistrust all I have done to gain her.

*Bel.* [*aside*]. I have watched his look, and find no alteration there: did he love her, some signs of jealousy would have appeared.

*Dor.* I hope this happy evening, madam, has reconciled you to the scandalous Mall; we shall have you now hankering here again.

*Lov.* Sir Fopling, will you walk?

*Sir Fop.* I am all obedience, madam.

*Lov.* Come along then, and let's agree to be malicious on all the ill-fashioned things we meet.

*Sir Fop.* We'll make a *critique* on the whole Mall, madam.

*Lov.* Belinda, you shall engage——

*Bel.* To the reserve of our friends, my dear.

*Lov.* No, no exceptions——

*Sir Fop.* We'll sacrifice all to our diversion.

*Lov.* All—all——

*Sir Fop.* All.

*Bel.* All? Then let it be.

[*Exeunt* Sir FOPLING, LOVEIT, BELINDA, *and* PERT, *laughing.*

*Med.* Would you had brought some more of your friends, Dorimant, to have been witnesses of Sir Fopling's disgrace and your triumph.

*Dor.* 'Twere unreasonable to desire you not to laugh at me; but pray do not expose me to the town this day or two.

*Med.* By that time you hope to have regained your credit?

*Dor.* I know she hates Fopling, and only makes use of him in hope to work me on again; had it not been for some powerful considerations which will be removed to-morrow morning, I had made her pluck off this mask and show the passion that lies panting under.

*Enter a Footman.*

*Med.* Here comes a man from Bellair, with news of your last adventure.

*Dor.* I am glad he sent him. I long to know the consequence of our parting.

*Footman.* Sir, my master desires you to come to my Lady Townley's presently, and bring Mr. Medley with you. My Lady Woodvil and her daughter are there.

*Med.* Then all's well, Dorimant.

*Footman.* They have sent for the fiddles and mean to dance! He bid me tell you, sir, the old lady does not know you, and would have you own yourself to be Mr. Courtage. They are all prepared to receive you by that name.

*Dor.* That foppish admirer of quality who flatters the very meat at honourable tables, and never offers love to a woman below a lady-grandmother.

*Med.* You know the character you are to act, I see.

*Dor.* This is Harriet's contrivance——wild, witty, lovesome, beautiful and young——come along, Medley.

*Med.* This new woman would well supply the loss of Loveit.

*Dor.* That business must not end so; before to-morrow's sun is set I will revenge and clear it:

And you and Loveit to her cost shall find,
I fathom all the depths of womankind.        [*Exeunt.*

## ACT IV

SCENE I.—*The scene opens with the fiddles playing a country dance.*

*Enter* DORIMANT, Lady WOODVIL, YOUNG BELLAIR, *and* Mrs. HARRIET, OLD BELLAIR, *and* EMILIA, Mr. MEDLEY *and* Lady TOWNLEY, *as having just ended the dance.*

*O. Bell.* So, so, so, a smart bout, a very smart bout, adod!

*Lady Town.* How do you like Emilia's dancing, brother?

*O. Bell.* Not at all, not at all.

*Lady Town.* You speak not what you think, I am sure.

*O. Bell.* No matter for that; go, bid her dance no more, it don't become her, it don't become her, tell her I say so. [*Aside.*] Adod, I love her.

*Dor.* [*to* Lady WOODVIL]. All people mingle nowadays, madam, and in public places women of quality have the least respect showed 'em.

*Lady Wood.* I protest you say the truth, Mr. Courtage.

*Dor.* Forms and ceremonies, the only things that uphold quality and greatness, are now shamefully laid aside and neglected.

*Lady Wood.* Well! this is not the women's age, let 'em think what they will; lewdness is the business now, love was the business in my time.

*Dor.* The women indeed are little beholding to the young men of this age; they're generally only dull admirers of themselves, and make their court to nothing but their periwigs and their cravats, and would be more concerned for the disordering of 'em, though on a good occasion, than a young maid would be for the tumbling of her head or handkercher.

*Lady Wood.* I protest you hit 'em.

*Dor.* They are very assiduous to show themselves at Court well dressed to the women of quality, but their business is with the stale mistresses of the town, who are prepared to receive their lazy addresses by industrious old lovers who have cast 'em off and made 'em easy.

*Har.* He fits my mother's humour so well, a little more and she'll dance a kissing dance with him anon.

*Med.* Dutifully observed, madam.

*Dor.* They pretend to be great critics in beauty; by their talk you would think they liked no face, and yet can dote on an ill one if it belong to a laundress or a tailor's daughter; they cry a woman's past her prime at twenty, decayed at four-and-twenty, old and unsufferable at thirty.

*Lady Wood.* Unsufferable at thirty! That they are in the
wrong, Mr. Courtage, at five-and-thirty there are living proofs
enough to convince 'em.

*Dor.* Ay, madam, there's Mrs. Setlooks, Mrs. Droplip, and my
Lady Loud; show me among all our opening buds a face that
promises so much beauty as the remains of theirs.

*Lady Wood.* The depraved appetite of this vicious age tastes
nothing but green fruit, and loathes it when 'tis kindly ripened.

*Dor.* Else so many deserving women, madam, would not be so
untimely neglected.

*Lady Wood.* I protest, Mr. Courtage, a dozen such good men
as you would be enough to atone for that wicked Dorimant and
all the under-debauchees of the town.

[HARRIET, EMILIA, YOUNG BELLAIR, MEDLEY, *and*
Lady TOWNLEY *break out into a laughter.*

What's the matter there?

*Med.* A pleasant mistake, madam, that a lady has made,
occasions a little laughter.

*O. Bell.* Come, come, you keep 'em idle, they are impatient
till the fiddles play again.

*Dor.* You are not weary, madam?

*Lady Wood.* One dance more; I cannot refuse you, Mr.
Courtage.                                        [*They dance.*

*Emil.* You are very active, sir.

[*After the dance* OLD BELLAIR *singing and dancing up to*
EMILIA.

*O. Bell.* Adod, sirrah, when I was a young fellow I could ha'
capered up to my woman's gorget.

*Dor.* You are willing to rest yourself, madam?

*Lady Town.* We'll walk into my chamber and sit down.

*Med.* Leave us Mr. Courtage, he's a dancer, and the young
ladies are not weary yet.

*Lady Wood.* We'll send him out again.

*Har.* If you do not quickly, I know where to send for Mr.
Dorimant.

*Lady Wood.* This girl's head, Mr. Courtage, is ever running on
that wild fellow.

*Dor.* 'Tis well you have got her a good husband, madam; that
will settle it.

[*Exeunt* Lady TOWNLEY, Lady WOODVIL, *and* DORIMANT.

*O. Bell.* [*to* EMILIA]. Adod, sweetheart, be advised, and do not
throw thyself away on a young idle fellow.

*Emil.* I have no such intention, sir.

*O. Bell.* Have a little patience, thou shalt have the man I
spake of. Adod, he loves thee, and will make a good husband;
but no words.

*Emil.* But, sir.——

*O. Bell.* No answer——out a pise! peace! and think on't.

*Enter* DORIMANT.

*Dor.* Your company is desired within, sir.

*O. Bell.* I go, I go, good Mr. Courtage—— [*To* EMILIA.] Fare you well; go, I'll see you no more.

*Emil.* What have I done, sir?

*O. Bell.* You are ugly, you are ugly; is she not, Mr. Courtage?

*Emil.* Better words, or I shan't abide you.

*O. Bell.* Out a pise——adod, what does she say? Hit her a pat for me there.　　　　　　　　　　[*Exit* OLD BELLAIR.

*Med.* You have charms for the whole family.

*Dor.* You'll spoil all with some unseasonable jest, Medley.

*Med.* You see I confine my tongue and am content to be a bare spectator, much contrary to my nature.

*Emil.* Methinks, Mr. Dorimant, my Lady Woodvil is a little fond of you.

*Dor.* Would her daughter were!

*Med.* It may be you may find her so; try her, you have an opportunity.

*Dor.* And I will not lose it. Bellair, here's a lady has something to say to you.

*Y. Bell.* I wait upon her. Mr. Medley, we have both business with you.

*Dor.* Get you all together then. [*To* HARRIET.] That demure curtsey is not amiss in jest, but do not think in earnest it becomes you.

*Har.* Affectation is catching, I find; from your grave bow I got it.

*Dor.* Where had you all that scorn and coldness in your look?

*Har.* From nature, sir; pardon my want of art: I have not learnt those softnesses and languishings which now in faces are so much in fashion.

*Dor.* You need 'em not; you have a sweetness of your own, if you would but calm your frowns and let it settle.

*Har.* My eyes are wild and wandering like my passions, and cannot yet be tied to rules of charming.

*Dor.* Women, indeed, have commonly a method of managing those messengers of love; now they will look as if they would kill, and anon they will look as if they were dying. They point and rebate [1] their glances the better to invite us.

*Har.* I like this variety well enough, but hate the set face that always looks as it would say, Come, love me—a woman who at plays makes the *doux yeux* to a whole audience and at home cannot forbear 'em to her monkey.

*Dor.* Put on a gentle smile, and let me see how well it will become you.

*Har.* I am sorry my face does not please you as it is, but I shall not be complaisant and change it.

　　　　　　　[1] A fencing term: blunt.

*Dor.* Though you are obstinate, I know 'tis capable of improvement, and shall do you justice, madam, if I chance to be at Court when the critics of the circle pass their judgment; for thither you must come.

*Har.* And expect to be taken in pieces, have all my features examined, every motion censured, and on the whole be condemned to be but pretty, or a beauty of the lowest rate. What think you?

*Dor.* The women, nay, the very lovers who belong to the drawing-room, will maliciously allow you more than that; they always grant what is apparent that they may the better be believed when they name concealed faults they cannot easily be disproved in.

*Har.* Beauty runs as great a risk exposed at Court as wit does on the stage, where the ugly and the foolish all are free to censure.

*Dor.* [*aside*]. I love her, and dare not let her know it; I fear she has an ascendant o'er me, and may revenge the wrongs I have done her sex. [*To her.*] Think of making a party, madam, love will engage.

*Har.* You make me start! I did not think to have heard of love from you.

*Dor.* I never knew what 'twas to have a settled ague yet, but now and then have had irregular fits.

*Har.* Take heed! sickness after long health is commonly more violent and dangerous.

*Dor.* [*aside*]. I have took the infection from her, and feel the disease now spreading in me—— [*To her.*] Is the name of love so frightful that you dare not stand it?

*Har.* 'Twill do little execution out of your mouth on me, I am sure.

*Dor.* It has been fatal——

*Har.* To some easy women, but we are not all born to one destiny; I was informed you use to laugh at love. and not make it.

*Dor.* The time has been, but now I must speak——

*Har.* If it be on that idle subject, I will put on my serious look, turn my head carelessly from you, drop my lip, let my eyelids fall and hang half o'er my eyes—thus—while you buzz a speech of an hour long in my ear, and I answer never a word; why do you not begin?

*Dor.* That the company may take notice how passionately I make advances of love, and how disdainfully you receive 'em.

*Har.* When your love's grown strong enough to make you bear being laughed at, I'll give you leave to trouble me with it: till when, pray forbear, sir.

*Enter* Sir FOPLING *and others in masks.*

*Dor.* What's here, masquerades?

*Har.* I thought that foppery had been left off and people might have been in private with a fiddle.

*Dor.* 'Tis endeavoured to be kept on foot still by some who find themselves the more acceptable the less they are known.

*Y. Bell.* This must be Sir Fopling.

*Med.* That extraordinary habit shows it.

*Y. Bell.* What are the rest?

*Med.* A company of French rascals whom he picked up in Paris and has brought over to be his dancing equipage on these occasions. Make him own himself; a fool is very troublesome when he presumes he is incognito.

*Sir Fop. [to* HARRIET]. Do you know me?

*Har.* Ten to one but I guess at you.

*Sir Fop.* Are you women as fond of a vizard as we men are?

*Har.* I am very fond of a vizard that covers a face I do not like, sir.

*Y. Bell.* Here are no masks, you see, sir, but those which came with you; this was intended a private meeting, but because you look like a gentleman, if you will discover yourself, and we know you to be such, you shall be welcome.

*Sir Fop. [pulling off his mask].* Dear Bellair.

*Med.* Sir Fopling! how came you hither?

*Sir Fop.* Faith, as I was coming late from Whitehall, after the King's *couchée*, one of my people told me he had heard fiddles at my Lady Townley's, and——

*Dor.* You need not say any more, sir.

*Sir Fop.* Dorimant, let me kiss thee.

*Dor. [whispers].* Hark you, Sir Fopling.

*Sir Fop.* Enough, enough——Courtage. A pretty kind of young woman that, Medley; I observed her in the Mall; more *éveillée* [1] than our English women commonly are; prithee, what is she?

*Med.* The most noted *coquette* in town; beware of her.

*Sir Fop.* Let her be what she will, I know how to take my measures; in Paris the *mode* is to flatter the *prude*, laugh at the *faux-prude*, make serious love to the *demi-prude*, and only rally with the *coquette*. Medley, what think you?

*Med.* That for all this smattering of the mathematics, you may be out in your judgment at tennis.

*Sir Fop.* What a *coq-à-l'âne* is this! I talk of women, and thou answer'st tennis.

*Med.* Mistakes will be for want of apprehension.

*Sir Fop.* I am very glad of the acquaintance I have with this family.

*Med.* My lady truly is a good woman.

*Sir Fop.* Ah! Dorimant——Courtage I would say——would thou hadst spent the last winter in Paris with me. When thou wert

---

[1] Cf. the *Spectator*, No. 45, on the "Invasion of French Manners": "The whole behaviour of the French is to make the sex (women) more fantastical, or (as they are pleased to call it) more *awakened*."

there La Corneus and Sallyes [1] were the only habitudes we had; a comedian would have been a *bonne fortune*. No stranger ever passed his time so well as I did some months before I came over. I was well received in a dozen families where all the women of quality used to visit; I have intrigues to tell thee more pleasant than ever thou read'st in a novel.

*Har.* Write 'em, sir, and oblige us women; our language wants such little stories.

*Sir Fop.* Writing, madam, 's a mechanic part of wit; a gentleman should never go beyond a song or a billet.

*Har.* Bussy was a gentleman.

*Sir Fop.* Who, d'Ambois? [2]

*Med.* Was there ever such a brisk blockhead?

*Har.* Not d'Ambois, sir, but Rabutin [3]—he who writ *The Loves of France*.

*Sir Fop.* That may be madam: many gentlemen do things that are below 'em. Damn your authors, Courtage; women are the prettiest things we can fool away our time with.

*Har.* I hope ye have wearied yourself to-night at Court sir, and will not think of fooling with anybody here.

*Sir Fop.* I cannot complain of my fortune there, madam—— Dorimant——

*Dor.* Again!

*Sir Fop.* Courtage, a pox on't! I have something to tell thee.

---

[1] So the old editions. Possibly Etherege wrote *Cornuel* and *Selles*. Readers of Madame de Sévigné will remember allusions to a Madame Cornuel whose epigrams were deservedly admired. She is mentioned in Bussy's letters, plays some part in the *Histoire Amoureuse* (*Memoires*, vol. ii, pp. 350–8), and altogether seems to have been a distinguished figure in French society. Very probably Etherege knew her, at least by fame, and may be referring to her here. Madame Selles is less tangible. Bussy, however, mentions a lady of that name who had attracted some attention by "une petite histoire de ses amours." This *histoire* is spoken of several times in the *Correspondance* (vol. ii, pp. 134-7), and its author may have presided over one of the fashionable *salons* of the time. At any rate, it should be noticed that all the names which occur in the play—Candale, Merille, Lambert, etc.—are those of contemporaries, and all through Etherege is bent on showing his close familiarity with the great world of Paris.

[2] To whom is Etherege referring?—the great French cardinal and minister, or the nobleman whose adventures are chronicled in Dumas' *La Dame de Monsoreau*?

[3] Bussy-Rabutin, Roger, Comte de; born 1618, died 1693; a cousin of Madame de Sévigné, with whom he corresponded. A complete edition of his *Memoires* and *Correspondance* was published at Paris, 1857-9. Etherege speaks so familiarly of him that one is tempted to think he knew the author of the *Histoire Amoureuse*, and I hoped— vainly, however—to find some reference in the letters to the English dramatist. Of Bussy's numerous works the fame of the *Histoire Amoureuse des Gaules* alone has survived. It appears to have been extremely popular, possessing "a thousand irresistible graces," according to the dictum of that politest of eighteenth-century critics, the ingenious and courtly Major Pack (*Works*, ed. 1729).

When I had made my court within, I came out and flung myself upon the mat under the state i' th' outward room i' th' midst of half a dozen beauties who were withdrawn to jeer among themselves, as they called it.

*Dor.* Did you know 'em?

*Sir Fop.* Not one of 'em by heavens! not I. But they were all your friends.

*Dor.* How are you sure of that?

*Sir Fop.* Why we laughed at all the town; spared nobody but yourself; they found me a man for their purpose.

*Dor.* I know you are malicious to your power.

*Sir Fop.* And faith I had occasion to show it for I never saw more gaping fools at a ball or on a Birthday.

*Dor.* You learned who the women were?

*Sir Fop.* No matter; they frequent the drawing-room.

*Dor.* And entertain themselves pleasantly at the expense of all the fops who come there.

*Sir Fop.* That's their business; faith, I sifted 'em, and find they have a sort of wit among them——Ah! filthy.

　　　　　　　　　　　　　　*[Pinches a tallow candle.*

*Dor.* Look, he has been pinching the tallow candle.

*Sir Fop.* How can you breathe in a room where there's grease frying? Dorimant, thou art intimate with my lady, advise her for her own sake, and the good company that comes hither, to burn wax lights.

*Har.* What are these masquerades who stand so obsequiously at a distance?

*Sir Fop.* A set of *balladins* whom I picked out of the best in France, and brought over with a *flutes douces* or two, my servants; they shall entertain you.

*Har.* I had rather see you dance yourself, Sir Fopling.

*Sir Fop.* And I had rather do it—all the company knows it —but, madam——

*Med.* Come, come, no excuses, Sir Fopling.

*Sir Fop.* By heavens, Medley!

*Med.* Like a woman, I find you must be struggled with before one brings you to what you desire.

*Har.* [*aside*]. Can he dance?

*Emil.* And fence and sing too, if you'll believe him.

*Dor.* He has no more excellence in his heels than in his head. He went to Paris a plain bashful English blockhead, and is returned a fine undertaking French fop.

*Med.* I cannot prevail.

*Sir Fop.* Do not think it want of complaisance, madam.

*Har.* You are too well bred to want that, Sir Fopling. I believe it want of power.

*Sir Fop.* By heavens! and so it is. I have sat up so damned late and drunk so cursed hard since I came to this lewd town, that

I am fit for nothing but low dancing now, a *corant*, *bourée*,[1] or a *menuet*; but St. André tells me, if I will but be regular, in one month I shall rise again. Pox on this debauchery!

[*Endeavours at a caper.*

*Emil.* I have heard your dancing much commended.

*Sir Fop.* It had the good fortune to please in Paris. I was judged to rise within an inch as high as the *basque*, in an entry I danced there.

*Har.* I am mightily taken with this fool; let us sit. Here's a seat, Sir Fopling.

*Sir Fop.* At your feet, madam; I can be nowhere so much at ease: by your leave, gown.

*Har. and Emil.* Ah! you'll spoil it.

*Sir Fop.* No matter, my clothes are my creatures; I make 'em to make my court to you ladies. Hey,—— [TROTT *dances.* *qu'on commence!* To an English dancer English motions. I was forced to entertain this fellow, one of my set miscarrying—— Oh, horrid! leave your damned manner of dancing, and put on the French air; have you not a pattern before you——pretty well! Imitation in time may bring him to something.

*After the dance enter* OLD BELLAIR, Lady WOODVIL, *and* Lady TOWNLEY.

*O. Bell.* Hey, adod! what have we here, a mumming?

*Lady Wood.* Where's my daughter——Harriet?

*Dor.* Here, here, madam. I know not but under these disguises there may be dangerous sparks; I gave the young lady warning.

*Lady Wood.* Lord! I am so obliged to you, Mr. Courtage.

*Har.* Lord! how you admire this man.

*Lady Wood.* What have you to except against him?

*Har.* He's a fop.

*Lady Wood.* He's not a Dorimant, a wild extravagant fellow of the times.

*Har.* He's a man made up of forms and commonplaces sucked out of the remaining lees of the last age.

*Lady Wood.* He's so good a man, that were you not engaged——

*Lady Town* You'll have but little night to sleep in.

*Lady Wood.* Lord! 'tis perfect day——

*Dor.* [*aside*]. The hour is almost come I appointed Belinda, and I am not so foppishly in love here to forget: I am flesh and blood yet.

*Lady Town.* I am very sensible, madam.

---

[1] For the former, cf. *Henry V*, iii, 5, 33:

"And teach lavoltas high and swift corantos."

For a note on the *bourée* Ashton's *Social Life in the Reign of Queen Anne* (i, 100) may be consulted.

*Lady Wood.* Lord, madam!

*Har.* Look, in what a struggle is my poor mother yonder?

*Y. Bell.* She has much ado to bring out the compliment.

*Dor.* She strains hard for it.

*Har.* See, see! her head tottering, her eyes staring, and her under lip trembling.

*Dor.* [*aside*]. Now, now she's in the very convulsions of her civility. 'Sdeath, I shall lose Belinda. I must fright her hence; she'll be an hour in this fit of good manners else. [*To* Lady Woodvil..] Do you not know Sir Fopling, madam?

*Lady Wood.* I have seen that face. Oh, Heav'n! 'tis the same we met in the Mall; how came he here?

*Dor.* A fiddle in this town is a kind of fop-call; no sooner it strikes up but the house is besieged with an army of masquerades straight.

*Lady Wood.* Lord! I tremble, Mr. Courtage; for certain Dorimant is in the company.

*Dor.* I cannot confidently say he is not; you had best begone. I will wait upon you; your daughter is in the hands of Mr. Bellair.

*Lady Wood.* I'll see her before me. Harriet, come away.

*Y. Bell.* Lights! lights!

*Lady Town.* Light down there.

*O. Bell.* Adod, it needs not——

*Dor.* Call my Lady Woodvil's coach to the door quickly.

[*Exeunt* DORIMANT *and* YOUNG BELLAIR, *with the Ladies.*

*O. Bell.* Stay, Mr. Medley, let the young fellows do that duty; we will drink a glass of wine together. 'Tis good after dancing; what mumming spark is that?

*Med.* He is not to be comprehended in few words.

*Sir Fop.* Hey! La Tour.

*Med.* Whither away, Sir Fopling?

*Sir Fop.* I have business with Courtage——

*Med.* He'll but put the ladies into their coach, and come up again.

*O. Bell.* In the meantime I'll call for a bottle.

[*Exit* OLD BELLAIR.

*Enter* YOUNG BELLAIR.

*Med.* Where's Dorimant?

*Y. Bell.* Stolen home; he has had business waiting for him there all this night, I believe, by an impatience I observed in him.

*Med.* Very likely; 'tis but dissembling drunkenness, railing at his friends, and the kind soul will embrace the blessing and forget the tedious expectation.

*Sir Fop.* I must speak with him before I sleep.

*Y. Bell.* Emilia and I are resolved on that business.

*Med.* Peace, here's your father.

*Enter* OLD BELLAIR *and Butler, with a bottle of wine.*

*O. Bell.* The women are all gone to bed. Fill, boy; Mr. Medley, begin a health.

*Med.* [*whispers*]. To Emilia.

*O. Bell.* Out, a pise! she's a rogue, and I'll not pledge you.

*Med.* I know you will.

*O. Bell.* Adod, drink it then.

*Sir Fop.* Let us have the new *bachique.*

*O. Bell.* Adod, that is a hard word; what does it mean, sir?

*Med.* A catch or drinking song.

*O. Bell.* Let us have it then.

*Sir Fop.* Fill the glasses round, and draw up in a body. Hey! music!

### THEY SING

> The pleasures of love and the joys of good wine
> To perfect our happiness wisely we join.
> We to beauty all day
> Give the sovereign sway,
> And her favourite nymphs devoutly obey.
> At the plays we are constantly making our court,
> And when they are ended we follow the sport,
> To the Mall and the Park,
> Where we love till 'tis dark;
> Then sparkling champagne
> Puts an end to their reign;
> It quickly recovers
> Poor languishing lovers,
> Makes us frolic and gay, and drowns all our sorrow;
> But, alas! we relapse again on the morrow.
> Let ev'ry man stand
> With his glass in his hand,
> And briskly discharge at the word of command.
> Here's a health to all those
> Whom to-night we depose:
> Wine and beauty by turns great souls should inspire.
> Present altogether, and now, boys, give fire!

*O. Bell.* Adod, a pretty business, and very merry.

*Sir Fop.* Hark you, Medley, let you and I take the fiddles, and go waken Dorimant.

*Med.* We shall do him a courtesy, if it be as I guess. For after the fatigue of this night, he'll quickly have his bellyful, and be glad of an occasion to cry: Take away, Handy.

*Y. Bell.* I'll go with you, and there we'll consult about affairs, Medley.

*O. Bell.* [*looks at his watch*]. Adod, 'tis six o'clock.

*Sir Fop.* Let's away then.

*O. Bell.* Mr. Medley, my sister tells me you are an honest man, and, adod, I love you. Few words and hearty—that's the way with old Harry, old Harry.

*Sir Fop.* Light your *flambeaux*. Hey!

*O. Bell.* What does the man mean?

*Med.* 'Tis day, Sir Fopling.

*Sir Fop.* No matter. Our serenade will look the greater.

*[Exeunt omnes.*

SCENE II.—DORIMANT'S *Lodging.   A table, a candle, a toilet, etc.* HANDY *tying up linen*

*Enter* DORIMANT *in his gown, and* BELINDA.

*Dor.* Why will you be gone so soon?

*Bel.* Why did you stay out so late?

*Dor.* Call a chair, Handy.                    *[Exit* HANDY. What makes you tremble so?

*Bel.* I have a thousand fears about me. Have I not been seen, think you?

*Dor.* By nobody but myself and trusty Handy.

*Bel.* Where are all your people?

*Dor.* I have dispersed 'em on sleeveless [1] errands. What does that sigh mean?

*Bel.* Can you be so unkind to ask me?—Well—*[Sighs.]* were it to do again——

*Dor.* We should do it, should we not?

*Bel.* I think we should; the wickeder man you to make me love so well. Will you be discreet now?

*Dor.* I will.

*Bel.* You cannot.

*Dor.* Never doubt it.

*Bel.* I will not expect it.

*Dor.* You do me wrong.

*Bel.* You have no more power to keep the secret than I had not to trust you with it.

*Dor.* By all the joys I have had, and those you keep in store——

*Bel.* You'll do for my sake what you never did before——

*Dor.* By that truth thou hast spoken, a wife shall sooner betray herself to her husband——

*Bel.* Yet I had rather you should be false in this, than in another thing you promised me.

*Dor.* What's that?

*Bel.* That you would never see Loveit more but in public places, in the Park, at Court, and plays.

*Dor.* 'Tis not likely a man should be fond of seeing a damned old play when there is a new one acted.

*Bel.* I dare not trust your promise.

[1] i.e. fruitless: "on a sleeveless errand."—*Troilus and Cressida*, v, 4.

*Dor.* You may.

*Bel.* This does not satisfy me. You shall swear you never will see her more.

*Dor.* I will! A thousand oaths——By all——

*Bel.* Hold——You shall not, now I think on't better.

*Dor.* I will swear.

*Bel.* I shall grow jealous of the oath, and think I owe your truth to that, not to your love.

*Dor.* Then, by my love, no other oath I'll swear.

### *Enter* HANDY.

*Handy.* Here's a chair.

*Bel.* Let me go.

*Dor.* I cannot

*Bel.* Too willingly, I fear.

*Dor.* Too unkindly feared. When will you promise me again?

*Bel.* Not this fortnight.

*Dor.* You will be better than your word.

*Bel.* I think I shall. Will it not make you love me less? [*Starting.*] Hark! what fiddles are these? [*Fiddles without.*

*Dor.* Look out Handy. [*Exit* HANDY *and returns.*

*Handy.* Mr. Medley, Mr. Bellair, and Sir Fopling; they are coming up.

*Dor.* How got they in?

*Handy.* The door was open for the chair.

*Bel.* Lord! let me fly——

*Dor.* Here, here, down the back stairs. I'll see you into your chair.

*Bel.* No, no, stay and receive 'em, and be sure you keep your word and never see Loveit more: let it be a proof of your kindness.

*Dor.* It shall——Handy, direct, her. Everlasting love go along with thee. [*Kissing her hand.*

[*Exeunt* BELINDA *and* HANDY.

### *Enter* YOUNG BELLAIR, MEDLEY, *and* Sir FOPLING.

*Y. Bell.* Not a-bed yet!

*Med.* You have had an irregular fit, Dorimant.

*Dor.* I have.

*Y. Bell.* And is it off already?

*Dor.* Nature has done her part, gentlemen; when she falls kindly to work, great cures are effected in little time, you know.

*Sir Fop.* We thought there was a wench in the case by the chair that waited. Prithee make us a *confidence.*

*Dor.* Excuse me.

*Sir Fop. Le sage* Dorimant! was she pretty?

*Dor.* So pretty she may come to keep her coach and pay parish duties if the good humour of the age continue.

*Med.* And be of the number of the ladies kept by public-spirited men for the good of the whole town.

*Sir Fop.* Well said, Medley.

[Sir FOPLING *dancing by himself.*

*Y. Bell.* See, Sir Fopling dancing.

*Dor.* You are practising and have a mind to recover, I see.

*Sir Fop.* Prithee, Dorimant, why hast not thou a glass hung up here? A room is the dullest thing without one.

*Y. Bell.* Here is company to entertain you.

*Sir Fop.* But I mean in case of being alone. In a glass a man may entertain himself

*Dor.* The shadow of himself indeed.

*Sir Fop.* Correct the errors of his motions and his dress.

*Med.* I find, Sir Fopling, in your solitude you remember the saying of the wise man, and study yourself.

*Sir Fop.* 'Tis the best diversion in our retirements. Dorimant, thou art a pretty fellow, and wear'st thy clothes well, but I never saw thee have a handsome cravat. Were they made up like mine, they'd give another air to thy face. Prithee let me send my man to dress thee but one day. By heavens! an Englishman cannot tie a ribbon.

*Dor.* They are something clumsy-fisted

*Sir Fop.* I have brought over the prettiest fellow that ever spread a toilet; he served some time under Merille,[1] the greatest *genie* in the world for a *valet-de-chambre.*

*Dor.* What, he who formerly belonged to the Duke of Candale?[2]

*Sir Fop.* The same, and got him his immortal reputation.

*Dor.* You've a very fine *brandenburgh* on, Sir Fopling.

*Sir Fop.* It serves to wrap me up after the fatigue of a ball.

*Med.* I see you often in it, with your periwig tied up.

*Sir Fop.* We should not always be in a set dress; 'tis more *en cavalier* to appear now and then in a *déshabillé.*

*Med.* Pray how goes your business with Loveit?

*Sir Fop.* You might have answered yourself in the Mall last night. Dorimant! did you not see the advances she made me? I have been endeavouring at a song.

---

[1] Mentioned in the *Histoire Amoureuse* as "le prinicpal confident du duc" (i.e. Candale).—Bussy's *Mémoires,* vol. ii, p. 322. Subsequently he passed into the service of the Duke of Orleans; cf. the *Correspondance* vol. ii, p. 313 ("valet de chambre de M. le duc d'Orléans"), and vol. iii, p. 240, where he has risen to the dignity of "premier valet de chambre de Monsieur."

[2] Often referred to in Bussy's *Mémoires.* The allusion to his "immortal reputation" is explained by a passage in the *Histoire Amoureuse:* "Le duc de Candale avait les yeux bleus, le nez bien fait, les traits irreguliers, la bouche grande et désagréable mais de fort belles dents, les cheveux blonds-dorés, en la plus grande quantité du monde. Sa taille était admirable et s'habillait bien, et les plus propres tâchaient de l'imiter. Il avait l'air d'un homme de grande qualité, il tenait un des premiers rangs en France." Doubtless the duke's love-affair with Madame Olonne served as a title to distinction.

*Dor.* Already!

*Sir Fop.* 'Tis my *coup d'essai* in English; I would fain have thy opinion of it.

*Dor.* Let's see it.

*Sir Fop.* Hey, page! give me my song——Bellair, here, thou hast a pretty voice, sing it.

*Y. Bell.* Sing it yourself, Sir Fopling.

*Sir Fop.* Excuse me.

*Y. Bell.* You learnt to sing in Paris.

*Sir Fop.* I did, of Lambert,[1] the greatest master in the world; but I have his own fault, a weak voice, and care not to sing out of a *ruelle*.[2]

*Dor.* A *ruelle* is a pretty cage for a singing fop, indeed.

YOUNG BELLAIR *reads the song.*

> How charming Phyllis is! how fair!
>     Ah, that she were as willing
> To ease my wounded heart of care,
>     And make her eyes less killing!
> I sigh! I sigh! I languish now,
>     And love will not let me rest;
> I drive about the Park, and bow
>     Still as I meet my dearest.

*Sir Fop.* Sing it, sing it, man; it goes to a pretty new tune, which I am confident was made by Baptiste.[3]

*Med.* Sing it yourself, Sir Fopling; he does not know the tune.

*Sir Fop.* I'll venture.                    [Sir FOPLING *sings.*

*Dor.* Ay, marry, now 'tis something. I shall not flatter you, Sir Fopling; there is not much thought in 't, but 'tis passionate, and well turned.

*Med.* After the French way.

*Sir Fop.* That I aimed at. Does it not give you a lively image of the thing? Slap down goes the glass, and thus we are at it.

*Dor.* It does indeed. I perceive, Sir Fopling, you'll be the

---

[1] Michel Lambert, "maître de la musique de la chambre du roi"; born 1610, died July 1696.

[2] Properly the *ruelle* was the space in a bedroom between the bed and the wall: "Se disait particulièrement des chambres à coucher sous Louis XIV, des alcôves de certaines dames de qualité, servant de salon de conversation et où régnait souvent le ton précieux."—Littré. Turning to *Les Précieuses* (scene ix), we find Mascarille saying: "Et vous verrez courir de ma façon, dans les belles ruelles de Paris, deux cents chansons, autant de sonnets." The use of the word here is one of those intimate touches in which Etherege delights.

[3] "The present great composer," says Pepys, 18th June, 1666. Baptiste—his real name was Baptiste Anet—was a pupil of Corelli: as a violinist he had a great reputation. He settled in Paris, but being badly received by Louis XIV eventually retired into Poland, where he died.

very head of the sparks who are lucky in compositions of this nature.

*Enter* Sir FOPLING's *Footman.*

*Sir Fop.* La Tour, is the bath ready?

*Footman.* Yes, sir.

*Sir Fop. Adieu donc, mes chers.* [*Exit* Sir FOPLING.

*Med.* When have you your revenge on Loveit, Dorimant?

*Dor.* I will but change my linen, and about it.

*Med.* The powerful considerations which hindered have been removed then?

*Dor.* Most luckily this morning; you must along with me, my reputation lies at stake there.

*Med.* I am engaged to Bellair.

*Dor.* What's your business?

*Med.* Ma-tri-mony, an't like you.

*Dor.* It does not, sir.

*Y. Bell.* It may in time, Dorimant; what think you of Mrs. Harriet?

*Dor.* What does she think of me?

*Y. Bell.* I am confident she loves you.

*Dor.* How does it appear?

*Y. Bell.* Why, she's never well but when she's talking of you; but then she finds all the faults in you she can. She laughs at all who commend you; but then she speaks ill of all who do not.

*Dor.* Women of her temper betray themselves by their over-cunning. I had once a growing love with a lady who would always quarrel with me when I came to see her, and yet was never quiet if I stayed a day from her.

*Y. Bell.* My father is in love with Emilia.

*Dor.* That is a good warrant for your proceedings: go on and prosper; I must to Loveit. Medley, I am sorry you cannot be a witness.

*Med.* Make her meet Sir Fopling again in the same place, and use him ill before me.

*Dor.* That may be brought about, I think. I'll be at your aunt's anon, and give you joy, Mr. Bellair.

*Y. Bell.* You had not best think of Mrs. Harriet too much; without church security there's no taking up there.

*Dor.* I may fall into the snare too. But

The wise will find a difference in our fate;
You wed a woman, I a good estate. [*Exeunt.*

### SCENE III

*Enter the Chair with* BELINDA; *the Men set it down and open it.*
BELINDA *starting.*

*Bel.* [*surprised*]. Lord! where am I? in the Mall? Whither
have you brought me?

1 *Chairman.* You gave us no directions, madam.

*Bel.* [*aside*]. The fright I was in made me forget it.

1 *Chairman.* We use to carry a lady from the squire's hither.

*Bel.* [*aside*]. This is Loveit; I am undone if she sees me.
Quickly carry me away.

1 *Chairman.* Whither, an't like your honour?

*Bel.* Ask no questions.

### *Enter* LOVEIT's *Footman.*

*Footman.* Have you seen my lady, madam?

*Bel.* I am just come to wait upon her.

*Footman.* She will be glad to see you, madam. She sent me
to you this morning to desire your company, and I was told you
went out by five o'clock.

*Bel.* [*aside*]. More and more unlucky!

*Footman.* Will you walk in, madam?

*Bel.* I'll discharge my chair and follow. Tell your mistress
I am here.                                        [*Exit Footman.*
                                    [*Gives the Chairmen money.*
Take this, and if ever you should be examined, be sure you say
you took me up in the Strand, over against the Exchange, as
you will answer it to Mr. Dorimant.

*Chairmen.* We will, an't like your honour.

                                        [*Exeunt Chairmen.*

*Bel.* Now to come off, I must on——

In confidence and lies some hope is left;
'Twere hard to be found out in the first theft. [*Exit*

## ACT V

### SCENE I

*Enter* Mistress LOVEIT *and* PERT, *her woman.*

*Pert.* Well, in my eyes Sir Fopling is no such despicable person.
*Lov.* You are an excellent judge!
*Pert.* He's as handsome a man as Mr. Dorimant, and as great a gallant.
*Lov.* Intolerable! is't not enough I submit to his impertinences, but I must be plagued with yours too?
*Pert.* Indeed, madam——
*Lov.* 'Tis false, mercenary malice——

*Enter her Footman.*

*Footman.* Mrs. Belinda, madam——
*Lov.* What of her?
*Footman.* She's below.
*Lov.* How came she?
*Footman.* In a chair; ambling Harry brought her.
*Lov.* He bring her! His chair stands near Dorimant's door, and always brings me from thence——Run and ask him where he took her up; go, there is no truth in friendship neither. Women as well as men—all are false, or all are so to me at least.
*Pert.* You are jealous of her too?
*Lov.* You had best tell her I am. 'Twill become the liberty you take of late. This fellow's bringing of her, her going out by five o'clock——I know not what to think.

*Enter* BELINDA.

Belinda, you are grown an early riser, I hear.
*Bel.* Do you not wonder, my dear, what made me abroad so soon?
*Lov.* You do not use to be so.
*Bel.* The country gentlewomen I told you of (Lord! they have the oddest diversions!) would never let me rest till I promised to go with them to the markets this morning to eat fruit and buy nosegays.
*Lov.* Are they so fond of a filthy nosegay?
*Bel.* They complain of the stinks of the town, and are never well but when they have their noses in one.
*Lov.* There are essences and sweet waters.
*Bel.* Oh! they cry out upon perfumes they are unwholesome; one of 'em was falling into a fit with the smell of these *narolii*.

*Lov.* Methinks, in complaisance you should have had a nosegay too.

*Bel.* Do you think, my dear, I could be so loathsome to trick myself up with carnations and stock gillyflowers? I begged their pardon, and told them I never wore anything but orange flowers and tuberose. That which made me willing to go was a strange desire I had to eat some fresh nectarines.

*Lov.* And had you any?

*Bel.* The best I ever tasted.

*Lov.* Whence came you now?

*Bel.* From their lodgings, where I crowded out of a coach, and took a chair to come and see you, my dear.

*Lov.* Whither did you send for that chair?

*Bel.* 'Twas going by empty.

*Lov.* Where do these country gentlewomen lodge, I pray?

*Bel.* In the Strand, over against the Exchange.

*Pert.* That place is never without a nest of 'em; they are always as one goes by fleering in balconies or staring out of windows.

### Enter Footman.

*Lov.* [*whispers to the Footman*]. Come hither.

*Bel.* [*aside*]. This fellow by her order has been questioning the chairmen—I threatened 'em with the name of Dorimant; if they should have told truth I am lost for ever.

*Lov.* In the Strand, said you?

*Footman.* Yes, madam, over against the Exchange.

[*Exit Footman.*

*Lov.* She's innocent, and I am much to blame.

*Bel.* [*aside*]. I am so frighted my countenance will betray me.

*Lov.* Belinda! what makes you look so pale?

*Bel.* Want of my usual rest, and jolting up and down so long in an odious hackney.

### Enter Footman.

*Footman.* Madam, Mr. Dorimant!

*Lov.* What makes him here?

*Bel.* [*aside*]. Then I am betrayed indeed; he's broke his word, and I love a man that does not care for me.

*Lov.* Lord! you faint, Belinda.

*Bel.* I think I shall; such an oppression here on the sudden.

*Pert.* She has eaten too much fruit, I warrant you.

*Lov.* Not unlikely!

*Pert.* 'Tis that lies heavy on her stomach.

*Lov.* Have her into my chamber, give her some surfeit water, and let her lie down a little.

*Pert.* Come, madam, I was a strange devourer of fruit when I was young, so ravenous——

[*Exit* BELINDA, PERT *leading her off.*

*Lov.* Oh, that my love would be but calm awhile! that I might receive this man with all the scorn and indignation he deserves.

*Enter* DORIMANT.

*Dor.* Now for a touch of Sir Fopling to begin with. Hey—— page——give positive order that none of my people stir—— let the *canaille* wait as they should do: since noise and nonsense have such powerful charms,

> I, that I may successful prove,
> Transform myself to what you love.

*Lov.* If that would do, you need not change from what you are; you can be vain and loud enough.

*Dor.* But not with so good a grace as Sir Fopling. Hey, Hampshire! ——Oh! that sound! that sound becomes the mouth of a man of quality.

*Lov.* Is there a thing so hateful as a senseless mimic?

*Dor.* He's a great grievance indeed to all who like yourself, madam, love to play the fool in quiet.

*Lov.* A ridiculous animal who has more of the ape than the ape has of the man in him.

*Dor.* I have as mean an opinion of a sheer mimic as yourself; yet were he all ape I should prefer him to the gay, the giddy, brisk, insipid, noisy fool you dote on.

*Lov.* Those noisy fools, however you despise 'em, have good qualities, which weigh more (or ought at least) with us women than all the pernicious wit you have to boast of.

*Dor.* That I may hereafter have a just value for their merit, pray do me the favour to name 'em.

*Lov.* You'll despise 'em as the dull effects of ignorance and vanity, yet I care not if I mention some. First, they really admire us, while you at best but flatter us well.

*Dor.* Take heed! fools can dissemble too——

*Lov.* They may, but not so artificially as you: there is no fear they should deceive us. Then they are assiduous, sir; they are ever offering us their service, and always waiting on our will.

*Dor.* You owe that to their excessive idleness; they know not how to entertain themselves at home, and find so little welcome abroad, they are fain to fly to you who countenance 'em as a refuge against the solitude they would be otherwise condemned to.

*Lov.* Their conversation too diverts us better.

*Dor.* Playing with your fan, smelling to your gloves, commending your hair, and taking notice how 'tis cut and shaded after the new way.

*Lov.* Were it sillier than you can make it, you must allow 'tis pleasanter to laugh at others than to be laughed at ourselves, though never so wittily. Then though they want skill to flatter us, they flatter themselves so well they save us the labour; we need not take that care and pains to satisfy 'em of our love, which we so often lose on you.

*Dor.* They commonly indeed believe too well of themselves, and always better of you than you deserve.

*Lov.* You are in the right; they have an implicit faith in us which keeps 'em from prying narrowly into our secrets, and saves us the vexatious trouble of clearing doubts which your subtle and causeless jealousies every moment raise.

*Dor.* There is an inbred falsehood in women which inclines 'em still to them whom they may most easily deceive.

*Lov.* The man who loves above his quality does not suffer more from the insolent impertinence of his mistress than the woman who loves above her understanding does from the arrogant presumptions of her friend.

*Dor.* You mistake the use of fools: they are designed for properties, and not for friends. You have an indifferent stock of reputation left yet. Lose it all like a frank gamester on the square; 'twill then be time enough to turn rook and cheat it up again on a good substantial bubble.

*Lov.* The old and the ill-favoured are only fit for properties indeed, but young and handsome fools have met with kinder fortunes.

*Dor.* They have, to the shame of your sex be it spoken; 'twas this, the thought of this, made me, by a timely jealousy, endeavour to prevent the good fortune you are providing for Sir Fopling——but against a woman's frailty all our care is vain.

*Lov.* Had I not with a dear experience bought the knowledge of your falsehood, you might have fooled me yet. This is not the first jealousy you have feigned to make a quarrel with me and get a week to throw away on some such unknown inconsiderable slut as you have been lately lurking with at plays.

*Dor.* Women, when they would break off with a man, never want th' address to turn the fault on him.

*Lov.* You take a pride of late in using of me ill, that the town may know the power you have over me, which now (as unreasonably as yourself) expects that I (do me all the injuries you can) must love you still.

*Dor.* I am so far from expecting that you should, I begin to think you never did love me.

*Lov.* Would the memory of it were so wholly worn out in me that I did doubt it too! What made you come to disturb my growing quiet?

*Dor.* To give you joy of your growing infamy.

*Lov.* Insupportable! insulting devil! this from you, the only author of my shame! This from another had been but justice, but from you 'tis a hellish and inhuman outrage. What have I done?

*Dor.* A thing that puts you below my scorn and makes my anger as ridiculous as you have made my love.

*Lov.* I walked last night with Sir Fopling.

*Dor.* You did, madam, and you talked and laughed aloud, ha, ha, ha!——Oh! that laugh! that laugh becomes the confidence of a woman of quality.

*Lov.* You, who have more pleasure in the ruin of a woman's reputation than in the endearments of her love, reproach me not with yourself, and I defy you to name the man can lay a blemish on my fame.

*Dor.* To be seen publicly so transported with the vain follies of that notorious fop, to me is an infamy below the sin of prostitution with another man.

*Lov.* Rail on, I am satisfied in the justice of what I did; you had provoked me to't.

*Dor.* What I did was the effect of a passion whose extravagances you have been willing to forgive.

*Lov.* And what I did was the effect of a passion you may forgive if you think fit.

*Dor.* Are you so indifferent grown?

*Lov.* I am.

*Dor.* Nay! then 'tis time to part. I'll send you back your letters you have so often asked for. I have two or three of 'em about me.

*Lov.* Give 'em me.

*Dor.* You snatch as if you thought I would not——there—— and may the perjuries in 'em be mine if e'er I see you more.

[*Offers to go, she catches him.*

*Lov.* Stay!

*Dor.* I will not.

*Lov.* You shall.

*Dor.* What have you to say?

*Lov.* I cannot speak it yet.

*Dor.* Something more in commendation of the fool. Death! I want patience, let me go.

*Lov.* [*aside*]. I cannot. I can sooner part with the limbs that hold him. I hate that nauseous fool, you know I do.

*Dor.* Was it the scandal you were fond of then?

*Lov.* You'd raised my anger equal to my love, a thing you ne'er could do before, and in revenge I did——I know not what I did.—— Would you not think on't any more!

*Dor.* Should I be willing to forget it, I shall be daily minded of it, 'twill be a commonplace for all the town to laugh at me; and Medley, when he is rhetorically drunk, will ever be declaiming on it in my ears.

*Lov.* 'Twill be believed a jealous spite! Come, forget it.

*Dor.* Let me consult my reputation; you are too careless of it [*pauses*]. You shall meet Sir Fopling in the Mall again to-night.

*Lov.* What mean you?

*Dor.* I have thought on it, and you must: 'tis necessary to

justify my love to the world; you can handle a coxcomb as he
deserves when you are not out of humour, madam.

*Lov.* Public satisfaction for the wrong I have done you! This
is some new device to make me more ridiculous.

*Dor.* Hear me.

*Lov.* I will not.

*Dor.* You will be persuaded.

*Lov.* Never.

*Dor.* Are you so obstinate?

*Lov.* Are you so base?

*Dor.* You will not satisfy my love?

*Lov.* I would die to satisfy that, but I will not to save you from
a thousand racks do a shameless thing to please your vanity.

*Dor.* Farewell, false woman!

*Lov.* Do! go!

*Dor.* You will call me back again.

*Lov.* Exquisite fiend! I knew you came but to torment me.

*Enter* BELINDA *and* PERT.

*Dor.* [*surprised*]. Belinda here!

*Bel.* [*aside*]. He starts and looks pale; the sight of me has
touched his guilty soul.

*Pert.* 'Twas but a qualm, as I said, a little indigestion; the
surfeit water did it, madam, mixed with a little *mirabilis.*

*Dor.* I am confounded, and cannot guess how she came hither!

*Lov.* 'Tis your fortune, Belinda, ever to be here when I am
abused by this prodigy of ill-nature.

*Bel.* I am amazed to find him here! How has he the face to
come near you?

*Dor.* [*aside*]. Here is fine work towards! I never was at such
a loss before.

*Bel.* One who makes a public profession of breach of faith
and ingratitude; I loathe the sight of him.

*Dor.* [*aside*]. There is no remedy; I must submit to their
tongues now, and some other time bring myself off as well as I can.

*Bel.* Other men are wicked, but then they have some sense of
shame: he is never well but when he triumphs, nay, glories to a
woman's face in his villainies.

*Lov.* You are in the right, Belinda; but methinks your kindness
for me makes you concern yourself too much with him.

*Bel.* It does indeed, my dear; his barbarous carriage to you
yesterday made me hope you ne'er would see him more, and the
very next day to find him here again provokes me strangely; but,
because I know you love him, I have done.

*Dor.* You have reproached me handsomely, and I deserve it
for coming hither; but——

*Pert.* You must expect it, sir; all women will hate you for my
lady's sake.

*Dor.* [*aside to* BELINDA]. Nay, if she begins too, 'tis time to fly; I shall be scolded to death else.  I am to blame in some circumstances, I confess; but as to the main, I am not so guilty as you imagine.  I shall seek a more convenient time to clear myself.

*Lov.* Do it now! what impediments are here?

*Dor.* I want time, and you want temper.

*Lov.* These are weak pretences!

*Dor.* You were never more mistaken in your life, and so farewell.                                        [DORIMANT *flings off.*

*Lov.* Call a footman, Pert, quickly; I will have him dogged.

*Pert.* I wish you would not for my quiet and your own.

*Lov.* I'll find out the infamous cause of all our quarrels, pluck her mask off, and expose her barefaced to the world.

*Bel.* [*aside*]. Let me but escape this time I'll never venture more.

*Lov.* Belinda! you shall go with me.

*Bel.* I have such a heaviness hangs on me with what I did this morning, I would fain go home and sleep, my dear.

*Lov.* Death and eternal darkness! I shall never sleep again. Raging fevers seize the world, and make mankind as restless all as I am!                                        [*Exit* LOVEIT.

*Bel.* I knew him false, and helped to make him so.  Was not her ruin enough to fright me from the danger?  It should have been, but love can take no warning.            [*Exit* BELINDA.


### SCENE II.——Lady TOWNLEY's *house*

*Enter* MEDLEY, YOUNG BELLAIR, Lady TOWNLEY. EMILIA, *and Chaplain.*

*Med.* Bear up, Bellair, and do not let us see that repentance in thine we daily do in married faces.

*Lady Town.* This wedding will strangely surprise my brother when he knows it.

*Med.* Your nephew ought to conceal it for a time, madam, since marriage has lost its good name; prudent men seldom expose their own reputations till 'tis convenient to justify their wives.

*O. Bell.* [*without*]. Where are you all there?  Out, adod, will nobody hear?

*Lady Town.* My brother! quickly, Mr. Smirk, into this closet; you must not be seen yet.                  [*He goes into the closet.*

#### *Enter* OLD BELLAIR *and* Lady TOWNLEY's *Page.*

*O. Bell.* Desire Mr. Fourbes to walk into the lower parlour, I will be with him presently. [*To* YOUNG BELLAIR.] Where have you been, sir, you could not wait on me to-day?

*Y. Bell.* About a business.

*O. Bell.* Are you so good at business? Adod, I have a business too you shall despatch out of hand, sir. Send for a parson, sister; my Lady Woodvil and her daughter are coming.

*Lady Town.* What need you huddle up things thus!

*O. Bell.* Out a pise! youth is apt to play the fool, and 'tis not good it should be in their power.

*Lady Town.* You need not fear your son.

*O. Bell.* He's been idling this morning, and, adod, I do not like him. [*To* EMILIA.] How dost thou do, sweetheart?

*Emil.* You are very severe, sir; married in such haste.

*O. Bell.* Go to, thou'rt a rogue, and I will talk with thee anon. Here's my Lady Woodvil come.

### *Enter* Lady WOODVIL, HARRIET, *and* BUSY.

Welcome, madam; Mr. Fourbes is below with the writings.

*Lady Wood.* Let us down, and make an end then.

*O. Bell.* Sister, show the way. [*To* YOUNG BELLAIR, *who is talking to* HARRIET.] Harry, your business lies not there yet; excuse him till we have done, lady, and then, adod, he shall be for thee. Mr. Medley, we must trouble you to be a witness.

*Med.* I luckily came for that purpose, sir.

[*Exeunt* OLD BELLAIR, MEDLEY, YOUNG BELLAIR, Lady
        TOWNLEY, *and* Lady WOODVIL.

*Busy.* What will you do, madam?

*Har.* Be carried back and mewed up in the country again, run away here, anything rather than be married to a man I do not care for——Dear Emilia, do thou advise me.

*Emil.* Mr. Bellair is engaged, you know.

*Har.* I do; but know not what the fear of losing an estate may fright him to.

*Emil.* In the desperate condition you are in you should consult with some judicious man; what think you of Mr. Dorimant?

*Har.* I do not think of him at all.

*Busy.* She thinks of nothing else, I am sure.

*Emil.* How fond your mother was of Mr. Courtage!

*Har.* Because I contrived the mistake to make a little mirth you believe I like the man.

*Emil.* Mr. Bellair believes you love him.

*Har.* Men are seldom in the right when they guess at a woman's mind; would she whom he loves loved him no better!

*Busy* [*aside*]. That's e'en well enough, on all conscience.

*Emil.* Mr. Dorimant has a great deal of wit.

*Har.* And takes a great deal of pains to show it.

*Emil.* He's extremely well-fashioned.

*Har.* Affectedly grave or ridiculously wild and apish.

*Busy.* You defend him still against your mother.

*Har.* I would not were he justly rallied, but I cannot hear any one undeservedly railed at.

*Emil.* Has your woman learnt the song you were so taken
with?

*Har.* I was fond of a new thing; 'tis dull at second hearing.

*Emil.* Mr. Dorimant made it.

*Busy.* She knows it, madam, and has made me sing it at least
a dozen times this morning.

*Har.* Thy tongue is as impertinent as thy fingers.

*Emil.* You have provoked her.

*Busy.* 'Tis but singing the song,[1] and I shall appease her.

*Emil.* Prithee do.

*Har.* She has a voice will grate your ears worse than a cat-call,
and dresses so ill she's scarce fit to trick up a yeoman's daughter
on a holiday.

*Busy* [*sings*].

> As Amoret with Phyllis sat
>   One evening on the plain,
> And saw the charming Strephon wait
>   To tell the nymph his pain,
>
> The threat'ning danger to remove
>   She whisper'd in her ear,
> Ah, Phyllis! if you would not love,
>   This shepherd do not hear.
>
> None ever had so strange an art
>   His passion to convey
> Into a list'ning virgin's heart,
>   And steal her soul away.
>
> Fly, fly betimes, for fear you give
>   Occasion for your fate.
> In vain, said she, in vain I strive,
>   Alas! 'tis now too late.

*Enter* DORIMANT.

*Dor.* Music so softens and disarms the mind——

*Har.* That not one arrow does resistance find.

*Dor.* Let us make use of the lucky minute then.

*Har.* [*aside, turning from* DORIMANT]. My love springs with
my blood into my face, I dare not look upon him yet.

*Dor.* What have we here, the picture of celebrated beauty
giving audience in public to a declared lover?

*Har.* Play the dying fop and make the piece complete, sir.

---

[1] "A translation," says Coxeter (MS. note in his copy of Gildon's
*Lives*), "from the French of Madame la Comtesse de la Suze in Le
Recüeil des Pièces Gallantes." The version was by Sir Car Scroope;
indeed all the old editions prefix to the verses a note—"Song by
Sir C. S."

*Dor.* What think you if the hint were well improved—the whole mystery of making love pleasantly designed and wrought in a suit of hangings?

*Har.* 'Twere needless to execute fools in effigy who suffer daily in their own persons.

*Dor.* [*aside to* EMILIA]. Mrs. Bride, for such I know this happy day has made you.

*Emil.* Defer the formal joy you are to give me and mind your business with her. [*Aloud.*] Here are dreadful preparations, Mr. Dorimant, writings sealing, and a parson sent for.

*Dor.* To marry this lady?

*Busy.* Condemned she is, and what will become of her I know not, without you generously engage in a rescue.

*Dor.* In this sad condition, madam, I can do no less than offer you my service.

*Har.* The obligation is not great; you are the common sanctuary for all young women who run from their relations.

*Dor.* I have always my arms open to receive the distressed. But I will open my heart, and receive you where none yet did ever enter: you have filled it with a secret, might I but let you know it——

*Har.* Do not speak it if you would have me believe it; your tongue is so famed for falsehood 'twill do the truth an injury.
[*Turns away her head.*

*Dor.* Turn not away then; but look on me and guess it.

*Har.* Did you not tell me there was no credit to be given to faces? that women nowadays have their passions as much at will as they have their complexions, and put on joy and sadness, scorn and kindness, with the same ease they do their paint and patches [1]——Are they the only counterfeits?

*Dor.* You wrong your own while you suspect my eyes; by all the hope I have in you, the inimitable colour in your cheeks is not more free from art than are the sighs I offer.

*Har.* In men who have been long hardened in sin we have reason to mistrust the first signs of repentance.

*Dor.* The prospect of such a heaven will make me persevere and give you marks that are infallible.

*Har.* What are those?

*Dor.* I will renounce all the joys I have in friendship and in wine, sacrifice to you all the interest I have in other women——

*Har.* Hold!—though I wish you devout I would not have you turn fanatic—Could you neglect these awhile and make a journey into the country?

*Dor.* To be with you I could live there and never send one thought to London.

---

[1] When the custom of patching (to which the *Spectator* objected so strongly, No. 81) first became fashionable is not quite clear. Shadwell, however, in *The Virtuoso*, writes: "They have so many tricks to disguise themselves, washing, painting, patching."

*Har.* Whate'er you say, I know all beyond High Park's a desert to you, and that no gallantry can draw you farther.

*Dor.* That has been the utmost limit of my love, but now my passion knows no bounds, and there's no measure to be taken of what I'll do for you from anything I ever did before.

*Har.* When I hear you talk thus in Hampshire I shall begin to think there may be some truth enlarged upon.

*Dor.* Is this all?——will you not promise me?——

*Har.* I hate to promise! What we do then is expected from us, and wants much of the welcome it finds when it surprises.

*Dor.* May I not hope?

*Har.* That depends on you and not on me; and 'tis to no purpose to forbid it.                         [*Turns to* BUSY.

*Busy.* Faith, madam, now I perceive the gentleman loves you too; e'en let him know your mind, and torment yourselves no longer.

*Har.* Dost think I have no sense of modesty?

*Busy.* Think, if you lose this you may never have another opportunity.

*Har.* May he hate me—a curse that frights me when I speak it—if ever I do a thing against the rules of decency and honour!

*Dor.* [*to* EMILIA]. I am beholding to you for your good intentions, madam.

*Emil.* I thought the concealing of our marriage from her might have done you better service.

*Dor.* Try her again.

*Emil.* What have you resolved, madam? The time draws near.

*Har.* To be obstinate, and protest against this marriage.

*Enter* Lady TOWNLEY *in haste.*

*Lady Town.* [*To* EMILIA]. Quickly, quickly, let Mr. Smirk out of the closet.                    [SMIRK *comes out of the closet.*

*Har.* A parson! had you laid him in here?

*Dor.* I knew nothing of him.

*Har.* Should it appear you did, your opinion of my easiness may cost you dear.

*Enter* OLD BELLAIR, YOUNG BELLAIR, MEDLEY, *and*
Lady WOODVIL.

*O. Bell.* Out a pise! the canonical hour is almost past. Sister, is the man of God come?

*Lady Town.* He waits your leisure.

*O. Bell.* By your favour, sir. Adod, a pretty spruce fellow! what may we call him?

*Lady Town.* Mr. Smirk, my Lady Biggot's chaplain.

*O. Bell.* A wise woman! adod, she is. The man will serve for the flesh as well as the spirit. Please you, sir, to commission a young couple to go to bed together i' God's name? Harry.

*Y. Bell.* Here, sir.

*O. Bell.* Out a pise! without your mistress in your hand!

*Smirk.* Is this the gentleman?

*O. Bell.* Yes, sir.

*Smirk.* Are you not mistaken, sir?

*O. Bell.* Adod, I think not, sir.

*Smirk.* Sure you are, sir.

*O. Bell.* You look as if you would forbid the banns; Mr. Smirk, I hope you have no pretension to the lady?

*Smirk.* Wish him joy, sir! I have done him the good office to-day already.

*O. Bell.* Out a pise! what do I hear?

*Lady Town.* Never storm, brother, the truth is out.

*O. Bell.* How say you, sir? is this your wedding-day?

*Y. Bell.* It is, sir.

*O. Bell.* And, adod, it shall be mine too; give me thy hand, sweetheart. [*To* EMILIA.] What dost thou mean? give me thy hand, I say.          [EMILIA *kneels, and* YOUNG BELLAIR.

*Lady Town.* Come, come, give her your blessing; this is the woman your son loved and is married to.

*O. Bell.* Ha! cheated! cozened! and by your contrivance, sister!

*Lady Town.* What would you do with her? She's a rogue, and you can't abide her.

*Med.* Shall I hit her a pat for you, sir?

*O. Bell.* Adod, you are all rogues, and I never will forgive you.

*Lady Town.* Whither! whither away?

*Med.* Let him go and cool awhile.

*Lady Wood.* [*to* DORIMANT]. Here's a business broke out now; Mr. Courtage, I am made a fine fool of.

*Dor.* You see the old gentleman knew nothing of it.

*Lady Wood.* I find he did not. I shall have some trick put upon me if I stay in this wicked town any longer. Harriet! dear child! where art thou? I'll into the country straight.

*O. Bell.* Adod, madam, you shall hear me first.

#### *Enter* LOVEIT *and* BELINDA.

*Lov.* Hither my man dogged him.

*Bel.* Yonder he stands, my dear.

*Lov.* I see him. [*Aside.*] And with him the face that has undone me! Oh, that I were but where I might throw out the anguish of my heart! here it must rage within and break it.

*Lady Town.* Mrs. Loveit, are you afraid to come forward?

*Lov.* I was amazed to see so much company here in a morning, the occasion sure is extraordinary.

*Dor.* [*aside*]. Loveit and Belinda! the devil owes me a shame to-day, and I think never will have done paying it.

*Lov.* Married! dear Emilia! how am I transported with the news?

*Har.* [*to* DORIMANT]. I little thought Emilia was the woman Mr. Bellair was in love with; I'll chide her for not trusting me with the secret.

*Dor.* How do you like Mrs. Loveit?

*Har.* She's a famed mistress of yours, I hear.

*Dor.* She has been on occasion.

*O. Bell.* [*to* Lady WOODVIL]. Adod, madam, I cannot help it.

*Lady Wood.* You need make no more apologies, sir.

*Emil.* [*to* LOVEIT]. The old gentleman's excusing himself to my Lady Woodvil.

*Lov.* Ha, ha, ha! I never heard of anything so pleasant.

*Har.* [*to* DORIMANT]. She's extremely overjoyed at something.

*Dor.* At nothing; she is one of those hoiting ladies who gaily fling themselves about and force a laugh when their aching hearts are full of discontent and malice.

*Lov.* Oh, Heav'n! I was never so near killing myself with aughing. Mr. Dorimant, are you a brideman?

*Lady Wood.* Mr. Dorimant! Is this Mr. Dorimant, madam?

*Lov.* If you doubt it, your daughter can resolve you, I suppose.

*Lady Wood.* I am cheated too, basely cheated.

*O. Bell.* Out a pise! what's here? more knavery yet?

*Lady Wood.* Harriet! on my blessing, come away, I charge you.

*Har.* Dear mother, do but stay and hear me.

*Lady Wood.* I am betrayed, and thou art undone, I fear.

*Har.* Do not fear it. I have not, nor never will do anything against my duty; believe me, dear mother, do.

*Dor.* [*to* LOVEIT]. I had trusted you with this secret, but that I knew the violence of your nature would ruin my fortune, as now unluckily it has. I thank you, madam.

*Lov.* She's an heiress, I know, and very rich.

*Dor.* To satisfy you I must give up my interest wholly to my love; had you been a reasonable woman, I might have secured 'em both and been happy.

*Lov.* You might have trusted me with anything of this kind, you know you might. Why did you go under a wrong name?

*Dor.* The story is too long to tell you now—be satisfied, this is the business, this is the mask has kept me from you.

*Bel.* [*aside*]. He's tender of my honour, though he's cruel to my love.

*Lov.* Was it no idle mistress then?

*Dor.* Believe me, a wife, to repair the ruins of my estate that needs it.

*Lov.* The knowledge of this makes my grief hang lighter on my soul; but I shall never more be happy.

*Dor.* Belinda!

*Bel.* Do not think of clearing yourself with me, it is impossible. Do all men break their words thus?

*Dor.* Th' extravagant words they speak in love; 'tis as unreasonable to expect we should perform all we promise then, as do all we threaten when we are angry. When I see you next——

*Bel.* Take no notice of me, and I shall not hate you.

*Dor.* How came you to Mrs. Loveit?

*Bel.* By a mistake the chairmen made for want of my giving them directions.

*Dor.* 'Twas a pleasant one. We must meet again.

*Bel.* Never.

*Dor.* Never?

*Bel.* When we do, may I be as infamous as you are false

*Lady Town.* Men of Mr. Dorimant's character always suffer in the general opinion of the world.

*Med.* You can make no judgment of a witty man from common fame, considering the prevailing faction, madam.

*O. Bell.* Adod, he's in the right.

*Med* Besides, 'tis a common error among women to believe too well of them they know and too ill of them they don't.

*O. Bell.* Adod, he observes well.

*Lady Town.* Believe me, madam, you will find Mr. Dorimant as civil a gentleman as you thought Mr. Courtage.

*Har.* If you would but know him better——

*Lady Wood.* You have a mind to know him better; come away! You shall never see him more.

*Har.* Dear mother, stay!

*Lady Wood.* I wo' not be consenting to your ruin.

*Har.* Were my fortune in your power——

*Lady Wood.* Your person is.

*Har.* Could I be disobedient I might take it out of yours, and put it into his.

*Lady Wood.* 'Tis that you would be at; you would marry this Dorimant?

*Har.* I cannot deny it; I would, and never will marry any other man.

*Lady Wood.* Is this the duty that you promised?

*Har.* But I will never marry him against your will——

*Lady Wood.* [*aside*]. She knows the way to melt my heart. [*To* HARRIET.] Upon yourself light your undoing.

*Med.* [*to* OLD BELLAIR]. Come, sir, you have not the heart any longer to refuse your blessing.

*O. Bell.* Adod, I ha' not——Rise, and God bless you both! Make much of her, Harry, she deserves thy kindness. [*To* EMILIA.] Adod, sirrah, I did not think it had been in thee.

*Enter* Sir FOPLING *and his Page.*

*Sir Fop.* 'Tis a damned windy day; hey, page? Is my periwig right?

*Page.* A little out of order, sir.

*Sir Fop.* Pox o' this apartment! it wants an antechamber to adjust oneself in. [*To* LOVEIT.] Madam, I came from your house, and your servants directed me hither.

*Lov.* I will give order hereafter they shall direct you better.

*Sir Fop.* The great satisfaction I had in the Mall last night has given me much disquiet since.

*Lov.* 'Tis likely to give me more than I desire.

*Sir Fop.* What the devil makes her so reserved? Am I guilty of an indiscretion, madam?

*Lov.* You will be of a great one if you continue your mistake, sir.

*Sir Fop.* Something puts you out of humour.

*Lov.* The most foolish inconsiderable thing that ever did.

*Sir Fop.* Is it in my power?

*Lov.* To hang or drown it; do one of 'em, and trouble me no more.

*Sir Fop.* So *fière*? *Serviteur, madame.* Medley, where's Dorimant?

*Med.* Methinks the lady has not made you those advances to-day she did last night, Sir Fopling.

*Sir Fop.* Prithee do not talk of her.

*Med.* She would be a *bonne fortune.*

*Sir Fop.* Not to me, at present.

*Med.* How so?

*Sir Fop.* An intrigue now would be but a temptation to me to throw away that vigour on one which I mean shall shortly make my court to the whole sex in a *ballet.*

*Med.* Wisely considered, Sir Fopling.

*Sir Fop.* No one woman is worth the loss of a cut in a caper.

*Med.* Not when 'tis so universally designed.

*Lady Wood.* Mr. Dorimant, every one has spoke so much in your behalf that I can no longer doubt but I was in the wrong.

*Lov.* There's nothing but falsehood and impertinence in this world; all men are villains or fools. Take example from my misfortunes, Belinda; if thou wouldst be happy, give thyself wholly up to goodness.

*Har.* [*To* LOVEIT]. Mr. Dorimant has been your God Almighty long enough; 'tis time to think of another.

*Lov.* Jeered by her! I will lock myself up in my house, and never see the world again.

*Har.* A nunnery is the more fashionable place for such a retreat, and has been the fatal consequence of many a *belle passion.*

*Lov.* Hold, heart! till I get home; should I answer 'twould make her triumph greater. [*Is going out.*

*Dor.* Your hand, Sir Fopling.

*Sir Fop.* Shall I wait upon you, madam?

*Lov.* Legion of fools, as many devils take thee!

[*Exit* LOVEIT.

*Med.* Dorimant! I pronounce thy reputation clear and

henceforward when I would know anything of woman, I will consult no other oracle.

*Sir Fop.* Stark mad, by all that's handsome! Dorimant, thou hast engaged me in a pretty business.

*Dor.* I have not leisure now to talk about it.

*O. Bell.* Out a pise! what does this Man of Mode do here again?

*Lady Town.* He'll be an excellent entertainment within, brother, and is luckily come to raise the mirth of the company.

*Lady Wood.* Madam, I take my leave of you.

*Lady Town.* What do you mean, madam?

*Lady Wood.* To go this afternoon part of my way to Hartley.

*O. Bell.* Adod, you shall stay and dine first; come, we will all be good friends, and you shall give Mr. Dorimant leave to wait upon you and your daughter in the country.

*Lady Wood.* If his occasions bring him that way, I have now so good an opinion of him he shall be welcome.

*Har.* To a great rambling lone house that looks as it were not inhabited, the family's so small; there you'll find my mother, an old lame aunt, and myself, sir, perched up on chairs at a distance in a large parlour, sitting moping like three or four melancholy birds in a spacious volery. Does not this stagger your resolution?

*Dor.* Not at all, madam. The first time I saw you you left me with the pangs of love upon me, and this day my soul has quite given up her liberty.

*Har.* This is more dismal than the country, Emilia; pity me who am going to that sad place. Methinks I hear the hateful noise of rooks already—kaw, kaw, kaw. There's music in the worst cry in London, *My dill and cucumbers to pickle.*[1]

*O. Bell.* Sister, knowing of this matter, I hope you have provided us some good cheer.

*Lady Town.* I have, brother, and the fiddles too.

*O. Bell.* Let 'em strike up then; the young lady shall have a dance before she departs. [*Dance.*

[*After the dance.*] So, now we'll in and make this an arrant wedding-day.

[*To the pit.*] And if these honest gentlemen rejoice,

Adod, the boy has made a happy choice.

[*Exeunt omnes.*

---

[1] Addison thought differently: "I am always pleased with that particular time of the year which is proper for the pickling of dill and cucumbers; but, alas! this cry, like the song of the nightingale, is not heard above two months. It would therefore be worth while to consider whether the same air might not in some cases be adapted to other words."—In the classic dissertation on London "Cries," *Spectator,* No. 251.

# THE EPILOGUE

## BY MR. DRYDEN

Most modern wits such monstrous fools have shown,
They seem'd not of heaven's making, but their own.
Those nauseous harlequins in farce may pass,
But there goes more to a substantial ass;
Something of man must be exposed to view,
That, gallants, they may more resemble you:
Sir Fopling is a fool so nicely writ,
The ladies would mistake him for a wit,
And when he sings, talks loud, and cocks, would cry,
*I vow, methinks he's pretty company !* [1]
So brisk, so gay, so travell'd, so refined,
As he took pains to graft upon his kind.
True fops help nature's work, and go to school
To file and finish God Almighty's fool.
Yet none Sir Fopling him, or him, can call [1];
He's knight o' th' shire, and represents ye all.
From each he meets he culls whate'er he can,
Legion's his name, a people in a man:
His bulky folly gathers as it goes,
And, rolling o'er you, like a snowball grows.
His various modes from various fathers follow;
One taught the toss, and one the new French wallow
His sword-knot this, his cravat this design'd,
And this the yard-long snake he twirls behind.
From one the sacred periwig he gain'd,
Which wind ne'er blew, nor touch of hat profaned
Another's diving bow he did adore,
Which with a shog casts all the hair before;
Till he, with full decorum, brings it back,
And rises with a water-spaniel shake.
As for his songs (the ladies' dear delight)
Those sure he took from most of you who write.
Yet every man is safe from what he fear'd,
For no one fool is hunted from the herd.

---

[1] This, with what follows, is not unsuggestive of Shadwell's prologue
to *The Virtuoso*:

> Yet no one coxcomb in this play is shown,
> No one man's humour makes a part alone,
> But scatter'd follies gather'd into one.

# APPENDIX A

*Variant Scene in 'The Beaux Stratagem'*
*from the Edition of 1728*

The scene begins with Count Bellair's entrance in the 1707 edition, p. 374 above. Speeches of characters other than Foigard are included below only if they differ from the 1707 version.

*Enter* FOIGARD.

| | | |
|---|---|---|
| 374. 8 | *Foig.* | Arra, fait, de people do say you be all robb'd, joy. |
| 10 | *Aim.* | The ladies have been in some danger, sir, as you was. |
| 11 | *Foig.* | Upon my shoul, our inn be rob too. |
| 13 | *Foig.* | Upon my shalwation, our landlord has robb'd him- |
| 14 | | self and run away wid da money. |
| 16 | *Foig.* | Ay fait! And me too of a hundred pounds. |
| 17 | *Arch.* | Robb'd you of a hundred pound! |
| 18 | *Foig.* | Yes, fait, honny, that I did owe to him. |
| 375. 5 | *Foig.* | Ay, upon my shoul, we'll all asshist. |
| 13 | *Foig.* | Ay, but upon my conshience, de question be apropro, for all dat. |
| 22 | *Foig.* | Arra, not part wid your wife! Upon my shoul, de man dosh not understand common shivility. |
| 46 | *Foig.* | Upon my conshience, dere accounts vil agree. |
| 376. 9 | *Foig.* | Arra, honeys, a clear caase, a clear caase! |
| 35 | *Foig.* | Upon my shoul, a very pretty sheremony. |
| 42 | *Arch.* | What is her portion? |

Foigard does not speak again. Some of Count Bellair's words, l. 46, are transferred to Archer, and the reviser has given this phase of the play an ending quite different from the original:

| | | |
|---|---|---|
| 46 | *Arch.* | I'll pay it. My Lord, I thank him, has enabled me, and if the lady pleases, she shall go home with me. This night's adventure . . . |

# APPENDIX B

*Vanbrugh, 'The Provok'd Wife'. Lines revised in Edition of 1743 (published in Dublin)*

## ACT IV. SCENE I (p. 417. 33 ff.)

*Tailor.* An't please you, it is my lady's short cloak and wrapping gown.

*Sir John.* What lady, you reptile you?

*Tailor.* My Lady Brute, your honour.

*Sir John.* My Lady Brute! My wife! The robe of my wife! With reverence let me approach it. The dear angel is always taking care of me in danger, and has sent me this suit of armour to protect me in this day of battle. On they go.

*All.* O brave knight!

*Lord Rake.* Live Don Quixote the Second!

*Sir John.* Sancho, my squire, help me on with my armour.

*Tailor.* O dear gentlemen, I shall be quite undone if you take the gown.

*Sir John.* Retire, sirrah, and since you carry off your skin, go home and be happy.

*Tailor.* [*Aside.*] I think I'd e'en as good follow the gentleman's friendly advice, for if I dispute any longer, who knows but the whim may take 'em to case me? These courtiers are fuller of tricks than they are of money. They'll sooner break a man's bones than pay his bill.

*Exit.*

*Sir John.* So, how do you like my shapes now?

*Lord Rake.* To a miracle! He looks like a queen of the Amazons. But to your arms, gentlemen! The enemy's upon their march. Here's the watch.

*Sir John.* Oons, if it were Alexander the Great at the head of his army, I would drive him into a horse pond.

*All.* Huzza! O brave knight!

*Sir John.* See, here he comes with all his Greeks about him. Follow me, boys.

### Enter WATCH.

*1 Watch.* Heyday! Who have we got here? Stand!

*Sir John.* Mayhap not.

*1 Watch.* What are you all doing here in the street at this time of night? And who are you, madam, that seem to be at the head of this noble crew?

*Sir John.* Sirrah, I am Bonduca, Queen of the Welshmen, and with a leek as long as my pedigree I will destroy your Roman legion in an instant. Britons, strike home!

*Fights [with the* WATCHMEN. *The others run away*].

1 *Watch.* So, we have got the queen, however. We'll make her pay well for her ransom. Come, madam, will your majesty please to walk before the constable?

*Sir John.* The constable's a rascal, and you are a son of a whore.

1 *Watch.* A most princely reply, truly. If this be her royal style, I'll warrant her maids of honour prattle prettily. But we'll teach you a little of our court dialect before we part with you, princess. Away with her to the roundhouse.

*Sir John.* Hands off, you ruffians! My honour's dearer to me than my life. I hope you won't be uncivil.

1 *Watch.* Away with her.

*Sir John.* Oh, my honour, my honour!        *Exeunt.*

## ACT. IV. SCENE III (p. 421. 40 ff.)

*Enter* CONSTABLE *and* WATCH *with* SIR JOHN.

*Const.* Come, forsooth, come along, if you please. I once in compassion thought to have seen you safe home this morning, but you have been so rampant and abusive all night I shall see what the justice of peace will say to you.

*Sir John.* And you shall see what I'll say to the justice of peace.

WATCH *knocks. A* SERVANT *enters.*

*Const.* Is Mr. Justice at home?

*Serv.* Yes.

*Const.* Pray acquaint his worship we have got an unruly woman here, and desire to know what he'll please to have done with her.

*Serv.* I'll acquaint my master.        *Exit.*

*Sir John.* Hark you, constable, what cuckoldly justice is this?

*Const.* One that will know how to deal with such romps as you are, I warrant you.

*Enter* JUSTICE.

*Justice.* Well, Mr. Constable, what's the matter here?

*Const.* An't please your worship, this here comical sort of a gentlewoman has committed great outrages tonight. She has been frolicking with my Lord Rake and his gang. They have attack'd the watch, and I hear there has been a gentleman kill'd. I believe 'tis they have done't.

*Sir John.* There may have been murder for aught I know, and 'tis a great mercy there has not been a rape too, for this fellow would have ravish'd me.

1 *Watch.* Ravish? I ravish? Oh lud! Oh lud! Oh lud' I ravish her? Why, please your honour, I heard Mr. Constable say he believ'd she was little better than a mophrodite.

*Justice.* Why truly, she does seem to be a little masculine about the mouth.

1 *Watch.* Yes, and about the hands too, an't please your worship. I did but offer in mere civility to help her up the steps into our apartment, and with her grippen fist— SIR JOHN *knocks him down.* Ay, just so, sir.

*Sir John.* I fell'd him to the ground like an ox.

*Justice.* Out upon this boisterous woman! Out upon her!

*Sir John.* Mr. Justice, he would have been uncivil. It was in defence of my honour, and I demand satisfaction.

1 *Watch.* I hope your worship will satisfy her honour in Bridewell. That fist of hers will make an admirable hemp-beater.

*Sir John.* Sir, I hope you will protect me against that libidinous rascal. I am a woman of quality, and virtue too, for all I am in a sort of an undress this morning.

*Justice.* Why, she really has the air of a sort of a woman a little somethingish out of the common. Madam, if you expect I should be favourable to you, I desire I may know who you are.

*Sir John.* Sir, I am anybody, at your service.

*Justice.* Lady, I desire to know your name.

*Sir John.* Sir, my name's Mary.

*Justice.* Ay, but your surname, madam.

*Sir John.* Sir, my surname's the very same as my husband's.

*Justice.* A strange woman, this. Who is your husband, pray?

*Sir John.* Why, Sir John.

*Justice.* Sir John who?

*Sir John.* Why, Sir John Brute.

*Justice.* Is it possible, madam, you can be my Lady Brute?

*Sir John.* That happy woman, sir, am I. Only a little in my merriment tonight.

*Justice.* I'm concern'd for Sir John.

*Sir John.* Truly, so am I.

*Justice.* I've heard he's an honest gentleman.

*Sir John.* As ever drank.

*Justice.* Good lack! Indeed, lady, I am sorry he should have such a wife.

*Sir John.* Sir, I am sorry he has any wife at all.

*Justice.* And so perhaps may he. I doubt you have not given him a very good taste of matrimony.

*Sir John.* Taste, sir? I have scorn'd to stint him to a taste; I have given him a full meal of it.

*Justice.* Indeed, I believe so. But pray, fair lady, may he have given you any occasion for this extraordinary conduct? Does he not use you well?

*Sir John.* A little upon the rough sometimes.

*Justice.* Ay, any man may be out of humour now and then.

*Sir John.* Sir, I love peace and quiet, and when a woman don't find that at home, she's apt sometimes to comfort herself with a few innocent diversions abroad.

*Justice.* I doubt he uses you but too well. Pray, how does he as to that weighty thing, money? Does he allow you what's proper of that?

*Sir John.* Sir, I generally have enough to pay the reckoning, if this son of a whore the drawer would bring his bill.

*Justice.* A strange woman, this. Does he spend a reasonable portion of his time at home, to the comfort of his wife and children?

*Sir John.* Never gave his wife cause to repine at his being abroad in his life.

*Justice.* Pray, madam, how may he be in the grand matrimonial point? Is he true to your bed?

*Sir John.* Chaste?—*Aside*: Oons, this fellow asks so many impertinent questions, egad, I believe it is the justice's wife in the justice's clothes.

*Justice.* 'Tis a great pity he should have been thus dispos'd of. Pray, madam, and then I have done, what may be your ladyship's common method of life, if I may presume so far?

*Sir John.* Why, sir, much like that of a woman of quality.

*Justice.* Pray, how may you generally pass your time, madam? Your morning, for example.

*Sir John.* Sir, like a woman of quality: I wake about two a'clock in the afternoon, I stretch, and then make a sign for my chocolate. When I have drank three cups, I slide down again upon my back, with my arms over my head, while two maids puts on my stockings; then, hanging upon their shoulders, I am trail'd to my great chair, where I sit and yawn for my breakfast. If it don't come presently, I lie down upon my couch to say my prayers, while my maid reads me the playbills.

*Justice.* Very well, madam.

*Sir John.* When the tea is brought in I drink twelve regular dishes, with eight slices of bread and butter, and half an hour after, I send to the cook to know if the dinner is almost ready.

*Justice.* Soh, madam.

*Sir John.* By that time my head's half dress'd, I hear my husband swearing himself into a state of perdition that the meat's all cold upon the table; to mend which I come down in an hour more, and have it sent back to the kitchen to be all dress'd over again.

*Justice.* Poor man.

*Sir John.* When I have din'd, and my idle servants are presumptuously set down at their ease to do so too, I call for my coach, go to visit fifty dear friends, of whom I hope I never shall find one at home while I shall live.

*Justice.* So there's the morning and afternoon pretty well disposed of. Pray, madam, how do you pass your evenings?

*Sir John.* Like a woman of spirit, sir, a great spirit. Give me a box and dice: seven's the main. Oons, sir, I set you a hundred pounds. Why, do you think women are married nowadays to sit at home and mend napkins? Sir, we have nobler ways of passing time.

*Justice.* Mercy upon us, Mr. Constable, what will this age come to?

*Const.* What will it come to indeed, if such women as these are not set in the stocks?

*Sir John.* I have a little urgent business calls upon me, and therefore I desire the favour of you to bring matters to a conclusion.

*Justice.* Madam, if I were sure that business were not to commit more disorders, I would release you.

*Sir John.* None, by my virtue.

*Justice.* Then, Mr. Constable, you may discharge her.

*Sir John.* Sir, your very humble servant. If you please to accept of a bottle—

*Justice.* I thank you kindly, madam, but I never drink in a morning. Goodbye, madam, goodbye to ye.

*Sir John.* Goodbye t'ye, good sir. *Exit* JUSTICE. So now, Mr. Constable, shall you and I go pick up a whore together?

*Const.* No, thank you, madam; my wife's enough to satisfy any reasonable man.

*Sir John. Aside.* He, he, he, he, he! The fool is married then. —Well, you won't go?

*Const.* Not I, truly.

*Sir John.* Then I'll go by myself, and you and your wife may be damn'd. *Exit.*

*Const. Gazing after him.* Why, God a mercy, my lady. *Exeunt.*

## ACT IV. SCENE IV (p. 425. 13–14)

*Sir John.* Why, I have been beating the watch and scandalizing the women.

# NOTES

[Line numbering in notes includes all material supplementary to text (except head titles), i.e. act and scene indications, stage directions, and half lines.]

## ALL FOR LOVE

**Page 1. Line 5.** *Danby* 1631–1712, first Earl, Charles II's chief minister 1673 1679, when he was impeached and imprisoned.

**4.11.** *pretend* claim.

**4.22.** *He who* . . . Doubtless the first Earl of Shaftesbury.

**4.46.** *your father* Sir Edward Osborne, 1596–1647, deputy lieutenant-general under Charles I.

**5.6.** *noble family of your lady* Danby was married to Bridget, grand-daughter of the first Earl of Lindsey, 1582–1642, general-in-chief of royalist forces, killed at Battle of Edgehill; daughter of the second Earl of Lindsey, c. 1608–66, important royalist leader.

**7.16.** *Appian and Dion Cassius* authors of histories of Rome.

**7.38.** *machine* device.

**9.5.** *Hippolytus* hero of Euripides' *Hippolytus*, 428 B.C.; Racine's *Phaedra*, 1677, is a simplified and sentimental adaptation of the story.

**9.26.** *Chedreux* fashionable. Chedreux was a popular French wig-maker.

**10.12.** *satires* Here and below Dryden hits at John Wilmot, second Earl of Rochester, 1647–80, who had criticized him in print.

**10.46.** *Dionysius c.* 431–367 B.C., Tyrant of Syracuse, would-be playwright; as a matter of diplomacy he was once awarded a first prize. *Nero* A.D. 37–68, Roman emperor, vain and dissolute, ambitious to be actor, painter and poet.

**11.17.** *Lucan c.* A.D. 39–65. Dryden alludes to legend that Lucan bested Emperor Nero in a poetry competition, and was later executed for supposed treason.

**11.21.** *grinning honour* echo of Falstaff's words, *1 Henry IV*, V, iii, 62.

**11.23.** *but one way with him* a reference to Falstaff, *Henry V*, II, iii, 15–16. *Maecenas c.* 70–8 B.C., poet, patron of literature; colleague of Antony until c. 36 B.C., when he allied himself to Octavius as general and administrator.

**11.35.** *zanies* and *ad Aethiopem cygnum* (12.41) Allusions to

Rochester's having posed as a mountebank near the Black Swan Inn, c. 1675.

11.41. *Crispinus* prototype of a bore; Horace, *Satires*, I, i, 120.

12.13. [Thomas] *Sternhold* 1500–49, popular but undistinguished poet, author of metrical version of *Psalms*, c. 1547, with subsequent revisions.

12.16. *lion's skin* Aesop fable; an ass disguised himself as a lion, but was detected by his bray.

13.2. [Thomas] *Rymer* 1641–1713, literary critic; *Tragedies of the Late Age*, 1678, etc.

15.10. *Dido* legendary foundress of Carthage, c. 8th century B.C.; she killed herself rather than marry the King of Libya.

15.12. *Bates of* decreases.

15.16. *keeping Tonies* i.e. kept, supported simpletons (punning on 'Antony'), in same sense as 'kept woman' or 'kept player' (*Country Wife*, IV, iii, p. 132).

15.23. *Hectors* bullies.

17.14. *phocae* seals.

17.17. *Sea horses* hippopotami.

17.29. *boy-king* Ptolemy XIV, co-ruler of Egypt with Cleopatra, who is thought to have had him poisoned in 44 B.C.

18.22. *Agrippa* commander of the fleet under Octavius, responsible for defeat of Antony at Actium.

18.30. *Isis* Egyptian moon-goddess.

19.19. *Parthia* part of modern Iran.

19.23. *Cilicia* in S. Turkey.

22.33. *soothe* encourage.

25.3. *officious* zealous.

25.16. *Tully* Marcus Tullius Cicero, 106–43 B.C., orator, writer, administrator, supporter of Octavius; ordered to be executed by Antony, he invited pursuing soldiers to behead him.

25.30. *chopt* chapped.

28.12. *planted* hid.

31.15. *Lictors with Fasces* attendants carrying symbols of authority, bound bundles of rods, each bundle including an axe.

31.23. *Illyria* modern Albania and part of N. Greece.

32.4. *wren* allusion to medieval tale of a competition amongst birds; a wren hid in the feathers of an eagle, enabling the wren to fly slightly higher.

33.35. *aconite* a poison derived from monkshood or wolfsbane.

34.11. *washed an Aethiop* laboured in vain.

38.11. *proscribing hand* Octavius Caesar, Lepidus and Antony drew up a list of political enemies, many of whom were excuted after the assassination of Julius Caesar, 44 B.C.

40.23. *Phlegraean plains* in Macedonia, where Hercules and other gods overwhelmed the Gigantes.

40.25. *pared* i.e. sliced off in alternate blows.

41.14. *Hercules' father* i.e. Jupiter.

42.2. *Thank thy love* i.e. I thank thy love.

45.40. *grudgings* slight symptoms.

48.35. *His children* Antony had three children by Cleopatra; in Roman eyes, illegitimate.

50.16. *sister of the thunderer Jove* i.e. Juno.

50.31. *my lover's Juno* she regards Octavia as the consort of her lover Jupiter, i.e. Antony.

53.39. *porc' pisce porcus piscis*, porpoise.

54.3. *puts out* brings out.

54.39. *Gallus and Tibullus* Roman poets, 1st century B.C., who wrote about their mistresses, Cytheris and Delia.

58.1. *Thessalian charms* Thessaly, Greece, was reputed to be a centre of witchcraft.

60.48. *Ind and Meroe* India and an ancient city, now ruined, in N. Sudan.

64.2. *rolling stone, and gnawing vulture* Sisyphus's punishment in Hades was rolling a stone uphill, which immediately rolled down again; Tityus had vultures gnawing eternally at his liver.

64.6. *pose* puzzle.

67.12. *imprecating* imploring.

67.16. *keep my breath* i.e. hold my breath, until my life ends.

68.25. *Pharos* the lighthouse at Alexandria, built *c.* 280 B.C., reputed to have been 800 ft high.

68.35. *Osiris* Egyptian divinity, husband of Isis.

69.22. *in few* in brief.

70.47. *Nile* legend had it that living creatures were generated by Nile mud.

71.23. *emulous* in rivalry.

72.36. *Lucrece* Roman noblewoman, 6th century B.C.; according to legend, after being raped by Tarquinius Sextus, she took her life.

73.20. *double* doubling back.

75.37. *played booty* deliberately to lose in a game in order to trick a victim later.

80.18. *Mr. Bayes* satiric portrait of Dryden in a popular comedy *The Rehearsal* (performed 1671) by George Villiers, second Duke of Buckingham (1628–87) and others. Dryden later satirized Buckingham as Zimri in *Absalom and Achitophel*, 1681.

80.20. *sue out* put in suit.   *writ of ease* certificate of discharge from employment.


## THE COUNTRY WIFE

83.12. *Castril* 'The Angry Boy', Jonson, *The Alchemist*, 1610.

83.13. *Bayes's* name for any playwright, deriving from 'Bayes' as a nickname for Dryden; see note for 80.18 above.

85.15. *tire-women* ladies' maids.

**85.20.** *aniseed Robin* notorious London hermaphrodite; lived during first half of 17th century.

**85.29.** *English-French disaster* a venereal disease, the pox. 'French', as used later in the play, generally has such a connotation.

**86.26.** *occasional* timely.

**87.4.** *Mercury!* quicksilver; then used in the treatment of venereal diseases.

**87.15.** *new postures* probable allusions to an edition of Pietro Aretino's *Sonetti Lussuriosi*, 1524, with engravings of Marc Raimondi, based on indecent drawings of Giulo Romano (Jules Romain).

**87.16.** *École des Filles* a pornographic book by Michel Mililot or Millot, 1655 or a later edition. Pepys was familiar with it (*Diary*, 13 January and 8 February 1668).

**87.32.** *chairs* sedan chairs.

**88.29.** *chemist* i.e. alchemist.

**88.37.** *right* promiscuous.

**89.7.** *vizard-mask* prostitute.

**89.9.** *ill* inferior.

**89.34.** *doze* confuse.

**90.27.** *Sir Martin Mar-all* in Dryden's *Sir Martin Mar-all* (1667) he serenades his mistress in mime whilst his hidden servant plays and sings (V). Sir Martin fails to stop when Warner does.

**91.27.** *crowd* fiddle.

**92.16ff.** *Chateline's, Cock, Dog and Partridge* well-known London restaurant and taverns.

**93.6.** *Smithfield jade* from the tradition that a horse bought in Smithfield Market, London, would likely be of dubious quality.

**93.9.** *foiled* injured.

**94.40.** *eighteenpenny place* middle gallery of a theatre.

**95.19.** *Cheapside husband of a Covent Garden wife* i.e. as a business man of a sophisticated, fashionable wife.

**95.33.** *Mulberry Garden* fashionable park where Buckingham Palace now stands.

**95.35.** *New Exchange* large building in the Strand, with an arcade and shops.

**96.24.** *fropish* peevish.    *nangered* angered.

**97.4.** *place-house* country house.

**99.45.** *stock blind* as blind as a block of wood, etc.

**100.47.** *cit* i.e. citizen, a tradesman.

**101.4.** *bubble* dupe, fool.

**105.48.** *drolling* comical.    *ombre* card game for three people, very popular from *c.* 1660 to 1726.

**106.4.** *crazy* infirm.

**106.12.** *make fine* exempt by means of a payment of money.

**106.20.** *shocks* poodles.

**108.26.** *pure* splendid.

**111.19.** *tosses with a marker* throws dice with a scorekeeper.

111.20. *ure* practice.

112.9. *snack* share.

112.49. *Phillis* conventional name for lover in pastoral poetry and drinking songs.

113.6. *Hictius doctius topsy turvy* jugglers' jargon.

114.27. *stir* be upset.

114.30. *she nor her brother* Alithea nor, in fact, Mrs Pinchwife.

116.8. *jealous* vehement.

116.32. *carelessly* casually.

118.13. *frank* generous (used ironically here and below).

123.23. *strapper* a robust person.

124.24. *megrim* migraine.

124.35. *natural* simpleton.

126.49. *die* engage in sexual intercourse.

130.46. *evads* i.e. i'vads, i' faith.

131.35. *curiously* skilfully.

132.7. *fadges* prospers.

132.23. *squab* squat and plump.

134.7. *pies* magpies.

135.32. *tomrigg* tomboy or strumpet.

136.35. *roll-waggon* lit. a blue and white cylindrical vase of Transitional or K'ang Hsi period; it is related to the sexual innuendo of 'china' (Wycherley, *Complete Plays*, ed. G. Weales, N.Y., 1967, p. 369).

137.44. *diffide* distrust.

138.13. *Locket's* a fashionable, expensive restaurant at Charing Cross.

140.21. *Piazza* fashionable residential area, an arcade on north and east sides of the square of Covent Garden, designed by Inigo Jones, *c.* 1634.

142.42. *sensible* acutely felt.

143.3. *shy* suspicious.

145.42. *night-gown* dressing gown.

147.13. *paw* improper.

147.48. *their writings* usurers' documents.

150.32. *Lanterlu* from the card game, usually called 'loo'.

151.28. *these arms* the wine glasses.

152.21. *druggets* cheap woollen materials.

153.39. *pass your grants* accept your favours.

158.43. *wounds* received in a duel, then illegal.

159.27. *fancying* imagining.

159.39. *country murrain* cattle plague.

161.20. *essenced* perfumed.

## THE WAY OF THE WORLD

**165.2.** *Montague* diplomat, ambassador, politician under Charles II, James II, William III. Reputed to be unscrupulous.

**165.38.** *Truewit* perceptive, unquestionably witty; major character in Jonson's *Epicoene*, 1609.

**168.17.** *buttered* to gamble with a repeatedly doubled stake; i.e. to depend over-heavily on one patron. *O.E.D.* gives 'flattered lavishly'.

**170.23.** *ratafia* a fruit-flavoured liqueur.

**171.19.** *Pancras* St Pancras Church, then located in Pancras Road outside the city; notable for irregular marriages.

**171.24.** *Duke's Place* i.e. at St James's Church, Duke's Place, Aldgate; marriages were performed without a licence.

**171.34.** *Dame Partlet* i.e. Foible. The reference is to Pertelote, wife of the cock Chauntecleer in Chaucer, 'The Nun's Priest's Tale'.

**171.35.** *Rosamond's Pond* a small lake in St James's Park, later filled in, a trysting place.

**173.24.** *medlar . . . crab* a fruit eaten when over-ripe; crab apples are hard and tart.

**173.31.** *'Tempest'* probably an allusion to Thomas Shadwell's popular opera (1674 and frequently revived) based on Shakespeare's *Tempest*, as revised by D'Avenant and Dryden, 1667.

**177.18.** *sultana queens* mistresses.

**177.19.** *Roxolana* former concubine, later wife of Solyman the Magnificent, D'Avenant's *Siege of Rhodes*, 1661.

**180.31.** *free* frank.

**181.16.** *Penthesilea* queen of the Amazons; aided Trojans and slain by Achilles.

**183.21.** *oversee* overlook.

**186.15.** *servant* suitor.

**186.23.** *Mosca . . . terms* i.e. bargain like Mosca, the parasite, in Jonson's *Volpone* (1606), V, iii, vii, viii.

**188.35.** *card-matches* matches made of strips of cardboard dipped in melted sulphur.

**189.22.** *assa-foetida* a resinous gum, an antispasmodic.

**189.23.** *You . . . fools?* i.e. are you taking a cure consisting of association with fools?

**192.14.** *person* someone of consequence.

**192.15.** *mopus* stupid.

**192.19.** *Spanish paper* paper impregnated with rouge, made in Spain.

**193.8.** *Maritornes the Asturian* a homely chambermaid, from Asturias, north-west Spain (I, xvi). Thomas D'Urfey's play *The History of Don Quixote*, 1694, was popular. See Part I; II, i.

**193.34.** *Quarles* Francis Quarles, religious poetry and narratives; *Emblemes*, 1696. *Prynne* William Prynne. *Historio-Mastix*.

*The Players Scourge* ..., 1633 and many later editions; 1006-page Puritan attack on the stage.

193.35. *The Short View of the Stage* i.e. *A Short View of the Immorality and Profaneness of the English Stage*, 1698, by Jeremy Collier. He attacked Congreve's earlier plays, Chapter II, pp. 63–74.

194.3. *like* i.e. a good likeness.

194.42. *Incontinently* immediately.

194.48. *Long-Lane penthouse* a covered stall in Long Lane, between West Smithfield and Barbican, where old clothes were sold.

195.1. *million lottery* a government scheme to raise £1,000,000 in 1694 by means of lottery tickets at £10 each. This sum was paid back, in instalments, over several years, and certain tickets won valuable cash prizes.

195.4. *Ludgate* from Ludgate Prison prisoners lowered mittens on a string to beg for contributions from passersby.

196.29. *month's mind* strong inclination.

197.2. *horns* i.e. the traditional horns of a cuckold.

197.10. *day of projection* the climax of an alchemist's attempt to transmute base metals into gold.

197.18. *olio* hotchpotch.

198.23. *doily stuff* a light, inexpensive woollen cloth, invented by Thomas Doyley, a late 17th-century linen-draper in the Strand.

198.26. *drap-de-berry* a coarse woollen cloth originating in the province of Berry, France.

198.41. *Rhenish wine tea* used as a substitute for tea, Rhenish wine was believed to cure obesity.

204.3. *Dawks's Letter* a popular thrice-weekly newsletter, 1696–1716, printed with manuscript type.

204.4. *Weekly Bill* The Weekly Bills of Mortality for London, published, 1538–1837, by the Parish Clerks Company.

204.25. *peace* The Peace of Ryswick (1697) ended the War of the League of Augsburg between France and England. The War of the Spanish Succession began in 1701.

206.8. *cap of maintenance* a cap with two horn-like points, a symbol of rank or importance.

206.9. *away with* endure.

208.36–7. *There ... cursed* first lines of Suckling, Poem 63, *Poems*, in *Non-Dramatic Works*, ed. T. Clayton (Oxford, 1971).

209.4. *Thyrsis ...* first line of Edmund Waller's 'The Story of Phoebus and Daphne, Applied', *Works*, 1645, p. 32.

209.38, 39, 41; 210.3, 4. *I prithee ... art* stanza 1, Suckling, Poem 54, *Poems*, in *Non-Dramatic Works*, ed. T. Clayton (Oxford, 1971).

210.6. *Anan?* a rural expression, 'How's that?'

210.15. *fought* taken.

210.23. *Ah l'étourdie* i.e. fool. Millamant was modelled in part on

Melantha, in Dryden's *Marriage à la Mode* (1673), who uses the phrase *étourdi bête* ('thoughtless fool').

210.33. *spare . . . speed* 'those frugal of speech don't get very far' (proverbial).

210.47 and 211.3. *Like Phoebus . . . coy* The third and fourth lines of Waller's poem referred to at 209.4.

211.5. *curious* careful.

212.5. *strange* reserved.

212.48. *atlasses* an Oriental satin.

213.17. *Barbados waters* a cordial flavoured with orange and lemon peel.

213.19. *dormitives* potions to encourage sleep.

214.22. *unsized camlet* an unstiffened wool and silk Oriental fabric.

214.23. *noli prosequi* the giving up of a law suit before its conclusion.

214.32. *whim* spin.

215.1. *Lacedemonian* i.e. laconic.

215.8. *Baldwin* i.e. Boudewyn, the ass who, in the medieval story, climbed on his master's shoulders as his hound did and was beaten.

215.10. *mustard-seed* a sharp seasoning; a fairy in *A Midsummer Night's Dream*, III, i; IV, i.

215.38. *rantipole* disorderly.

215.42. *borachio* drunkard; a character in *Much Ado about Nothing*.

216.26. *pimple* boon companion.

217.8. *mufti* a Mohammedan priest.

217.30. *shake-bag* lit., a fighting cock; i.e. lively.

217.35. *Tantony* St Anthony, A.D. 251–356, ascetic, hermit, patron saint of domestic animals, depicted as followed by a pig.

218.1. *year of jubilee* a year, like 1700, in which the Pope granted a general remission of the punishments already imposed for sins.

218.20. *respect* consider.

218.36. *save-all* a dish with a central spike, designed to use up candle ends.

219.6. *camphire* i.e. camphor, reputed to be an anaphrodisiac; Dryden, *The Spanish Friar* (1681), Act I, p. 14.

219.16. *incessantly* immediately.

219.26. *chairman in the dog-days* a bearer of a sedan chair in the heat of summer.

221.29. *traverse rag* a curtain on a cord across the back of the shop, intended to give privacy.

221.34. *bulk* stall.

221.35. *frisoneer gorget* a neckpiece made of coarse woollen material.

221.36. *colberteen* a cheap kind of lace.

222.2. *governante* housekeeper.

222.15. *frontless* shameless.

222.22. *put upon his clergy* compelled to plead 'benefit of clergy', i.e. to claim the ability to read and write as a means o escaping punishment.

222.28. *botcher* lit., a mender of old clothes.

222.29. *Abigails and Andrews* comprehensive terms for maids and menservants.

224.31. *naught* immoral.

224.32. *sophisticated* corrupted.

224.44. *temper* composure, restraint.

225.26. *babies* dolls.

226.2. *quoif* the white cap of a lawyer.

226.10. *cantharides* Spanish fly, a dried beetle used as diuretic, aphrodisiac, etc.

226.14. *prentices at a conventicle* apprentices of nonconformist merchants were obliged to attend Sunday services and write précis.

226.22. *flounder-man* London fish-vendor notable for his manner of calling his wares.

227.16. *czarish majesty* Peter the Great of Russia visited England in 1698.

227.44. *her year* i.e. a year of mourning.

228.1. *my son Languish* i.e. son-in-law.

228.43. *Pylades and Orestes* i.e. devoted friends. Pylades assisted Orestes in avenging the death of Agamemnon and, in some versions of the story, later married Orestes' sister Electra.

229.41. *quorum* one of a group of justices.

231.43. *Messalina's* the word was probably 'Miscellaneous'.

232.29. *Whose hand's out?* What's the trouble?

# VENICE PRESERV'D

239.3. *Duchess of Portsmouth* Louise Renée de Kéroualle, 1649–1734, French mistress of Charles II, privately working with the Whigs in the hope that her child by the king, Charles Lennox, might succeed to the throne. Lennox is the young prince referred to at line 37.

239.13. *a poor peasant* i.e. an innocent cause of trouble. The emperor, Theodosius II, of the eastern Roman empire, gave the apple to his wife; she made a gift of it to her lover, who later offered the same apple to the emperor.

241.4. *three years* The Popish Plot, instigated by Titus Oates, began in 1678; reverberations continued until his imprisonment, 1685. (*Venice Preserv'd* was first produced early in 1682.)

241.8. *take* be popular.

241.9. *inch-board* i.e. solid, tangible. (The allusion is to a board one inch thick.)

241.16. *black bills* battle weapons, like halberds or pikes.

241.17. *Spanish pilgrims* A false rumour claimed that Jesuits intended to invade England via Wales with an Irish army disguised as pilgrims.

241.18. *murther'd magistrate* Sir Edmund Berry Godfrey, 1621–1678, was murdered, apparently by followers of Titus Oates, at Somerset House, London; the culprits removed his body a few days later in a sedan chair.

241.23. *commission* Pope Innocent XI was reputed to have sent commissions to England to raise a rebel army.

241.34. *Mother Creswold* or Creswell, a well-known procuress of London.

241.35. *Poland* Shaftesbury was said to have sought the throne of Poland in 1675.

244.3. *Adriatic . . . Duke* the Ascension Day ceremony during which the Doge threw a ring into the sea to symbolize the union of Venice and the Adriatic. See IV, ii, p. 283, ll. 28–30.

244.36. *bait* harass.

247.31. *Hirco* goat.

252.33. *foil* defile.

253.13. *Ephesian matron* the widow of Ephesus who, in Petronius' *Satyricon* (sections 111 and 112), weeps at her husband's tomb until a young soldier persuades her that living is better than mourning.

253.21. *mumping* munching.

255.39. *counters* tokens, i.e. substitutes for real coins.

257.31. *sea-coal* coal carried by or found at the edge of the sea, as distinct from charcoal.

258.22. *feigned* invented.

258.28. *Catiline* Lucius Sergius Catilina, unsuccessful politician, demagogue, executed for conspiracy 62 B.C.

258.33. *Cethegus* conspirator, with Catiline. in an unsuccessful scheme to murder Cicero and other notables; executed 63 B.C.

258.34. *Cassius* Gaius Cassius Longinus, military leader, statesman; with Brutus and others stabbed Julius Caesar 44 B.C.; among the conspirators defeated by Antony and Octavius 42 B.C.; committed suicide.

262.46. *ambo* both.

263.20. *Fubbs, Pugg* terms of endearment; chubby person, doll, etc.

263.24. *game at rump* frolic.

264.34. *basan-bull* notable for strength and ferocity; Psalms 22:12.

266.9. *Tarquin* Tarquinius Sextus, 6th century B.C., raped Lucrece, a Roman noblewoman.

267.21. *Portia* wife of Marcus Junius Brutus (85–42 B.C.): said to have wounded herself to prove that she was worthy to share her husband's secrets.

271.2. *foil* the track of a hunted animal.

271.4. *caudles* warm, medicinal drinks.

271.41. *monster* cuckold.

273.35. *Secque* i.e. the Mint.

**273.36.** *Procuralle* a residence for procurators, high-ranking Venetian officials.

**280.30.** *from unknown hands* ... This statement, if true, strengthens Priuli's justification for calling up the Senate in the night, but weakens Jaffeir's value as an informant.

**304.12.** *smuggle* cuddle, caress.

**305.21.** *Rose-Alley* John Dryden was beaten up in Rose Alley in 1679 by thugs said to have been hired by John Wilmot, second Earl of Rochester.

**305.25.** *picture mangler* 'The Rascal that cut the Duke of York's picture.'—Q note. The culprit was never apprehended, although a large reward was offered. This portrait of James, Duke of York, does not now exist.

**305.33.** *great Martyr* King Charles I, executed 1649.

**308.7.** *blains* inflammations.

**308.13.** *whence before one sickness* ... i.e. a rebellion in Scotland. James, Duke of York, was there as a military commander 1680–2.

**308.35.** *Bout'feus* troublemakers, incendiaries (lit., devices for setting off cannon).

**309.5.** *Priests of Baal* i.e. sanctimonious priests of false deities.

**309.6.** *Wapping* ... *Mile End* in east London, the former notorious for pirates, the latter a militia training ground. The line hints at Whig bribery, since Shaftesbury derived much support from this area.

**309.** A third prologue (by Dryden) and a third epilogue (by Otway) were written for the visit of Mary, Duchess of York, to the play 31 May 1682; the former was published as a broadside in 1682, the latter in Otway's 'Poems upon Several Occasions', *Works*, 1712, vol. ii, pp. 389–90.

# BEAUX STRATAGEM

**314.2.** *Wilks* Robert Wilks acted the part of Archer regularly at Drury Lane Theatre from the opening of the play (1707) to the year of his death, 1732. Wilks had urged the ill and impoverished Farquhar to write *The Beaux Stratagem*.

**314.5.** *Plain-Dealer* i.e. Wycherley, author of play of this name, 1677.

**314.10.** *Union* the Act of Union of the Parliaments of England and Scotland, 6 March 1707; this play was first produced 8 March 1707.

**314.11.** *Anna's sceptre* Queen Anne reigned 1702–14.

**314.21.** *simpling* gathering medicinal herbs.

**315.11.** *Warrington* a town sixty-five miles N.W. of Lichfield.

**315.23.** *Lion and the Rose* the names of rooms at the inn.

**316.3.** *tun* casks each holding about 250 gallons.

316.6. *old style* England did not adopt the Gregorian calendar, with a new year beginning on 1 January, until 1752; on the Continent on 5 March it was already 1707, but it was 1706 in England until 25 March.

316.10. *1706* i.e. this year's ale.

316.31. *dram* a small quantity of spirits.

316.37. *tympanies* tumours.

316.47. *king's evil* scrofula. The custom of the ruler touching a victim to cure the disease died out only with the reign of Queen Anne. *chincough* whooping cough.

317.16. *whisk* i.e. whist.

317.19. *curious* clever.

317.21. *He has it there* the sign of a cuckold, a pair of horns.

317.30. *French officers* prisoners of war on parole.

318.43. *tits* small horses.

319.13. *venturing one of the hundreds* attempting to carry out their scheme in a county subdivision.

319.15. *counterscarp* a part of a fortification.

319.36. *kind keepers* men who support mistresses. See Dryden, *The Kind Keeper or Mr Limberham*, 1680.

320.5. *Actacon* As punishment for watching Artemis and attendants bathing, he was turned into a stag and killed by his dogs.

321.26. *new-purchased* newly obtained.

322.30–40. *But you look so bright* . . . Only the first two lines appear in the 1707 quarto. The remainder is supplied from the fifth edition, vol. ii, 1728.

323.39. *Doctors-Commons* the College of Doctors of Civil Law, London.

324.13. *hospital child* foundling.

324.22. *fat* strong.

324.24. *stilling* distilling.

324.37. *weekly bills* i.e. dead. See note to *Way of the World*, III, 15, p. 204. 4.

328.8. *coronation* Queen Anne was crowned 23 April 1702.

329.23. *Old Brentford* a town 8 miles west of London, reputedly muddy.

329.44. *a contrary way* i.e. to be hanged.

331.21. *make the bed* so Q: 'make my master's bed' 1728.

333.3. *cephalic plaster* a remedy for headache.

334.4. *bag* a pouch to contain the back hair of a wig.

334.39. *Oroondates* hero of La Calprenède's *Cassandra*, a romance published in France 1642–5 (10 vols), in England 1652. *Cesario* In *Twelfth Night* Viola disguises herself as Cesario. *Amadis* Amadis de Gaul, hero of a popular fourteenth-century Spanish romance, first published in Spain in 1508, in England in 1567.

334.41. *Ceres* Roman corn-goddess.

335.14. *brazen engine* warming pan.

335.29. *Orpheus* In classical legend, the music of Orpheus' lyre made trees and rocks follow him. *Toftida* Mrs Katherine Tofts, *c.* 1680–1760; notable soprano 1703–9, performed in many popular operas.

335.36. *bill* promissory note.

335.37. *ingrossed* monopolized.

336.30. *plantations* i.e. as a transported criminal.

336.34. *Roman* a pseudo-virtuous claim that he was, like a true Roman, serving in the army, without pay, for the good of his country.

337.10. *charge* a sum of money or a quantity of powder and shot.

338.10. *joy* darling (Irish).

338.17. *Teague* Irishman; Teague is an Irish servant in Farquhar's *Twin Rivals*, 1703.

338.20. *King of Spain* A 1707 truce in the War of the Austrian Succession left the rule of Spain still in doubt; the matter was not settled until 1713, when the Treaty of Utrecht gave the throne to Philip V.

339.47. *put it upon that lay* take that tack.

339.49. *Pressing Act* An impressment act was passed in 1703.

340.15. *whore of Babylon* the Roman Catholic Church; from Rev. 17:5.

342.26. *incapable* disqualified.

342.49. *Sir Simon the King* first published as 'Old Simon the King' in John Playford, *Musick's Recreation* . . ., 1652.

343.1ff. *A trifling song* . . . Only the first two lines appear in the 1707 quarto. The remainder is supplied from the fifth edition, vol. ii, 1728 (following Act V).

343.22. *Gold keys* symbols of the Lord Chamberlain.

343.23. *White rods* symbols of high office, such as Lord High Treasurer, etc.

343.27. *levee* morning reception. *His Grace* . . . probably a hit at the Duke of Ormond, Lord Lieutenant of Ireland, who apparently promised aid to Farquhar in 1706, but forgot or ignored him.

344.32. *tapis* table-cloth; i.e. to be debated.

346.14. *bully* a protector of prostitutes.

347.20. *Fair Dorinda* a song in Owen Swiney's (or Mac Swiney's) opera, *Camilla* (I, ix), published 1707. Farquhar referred slightingly to *Camilla* in his prose Epilogue to *The Recruiting Officer*, 1706.

349.36. *receipts* prescriptions.

351.37. *Hungary water* used as a lotion or drunk as a restorative; made from rosemary flowers and spirit of wine. Reputed to have been first prepared for an unidentified queen of Hungary.

351.46. *Proserpine* or Persephone, queen of the underworld.

352.1. *Eurydice* Pluto permitted Orpheus to lead his wife, Eurydice, out of Hades, provided that he did not look back at her; he did so and lost her.

352.46. *originals* eccentrics.

353.24. *Cedunt arma togae* Arms give precedence to the gown—
Cicero, *Officia*, I, 22.

353.31. *gra* dear (Irish).

353.42. *louis d'ors* French gold coins, each worth approximately
85p.

353.47. *gratification* gratuity.

354.30. *Leda* Jupiter seduced Leda disguised as a swan.

354.33. *Le Brun* Charles Le Brun, 1619–90, distinguished French
painter of scenes based on battles of Alexander the Great.

354.34. *Danube . . . Granicus* The Duke of Marlborough defeated
a French and Bavarian army at the Battle of Blenheim, 1704,
in Bavaria; Alexander overcame the Persians by the river
Granicus in 334 B.C.

354.36. *Ramillies . . . Arbela* In 1706 Marlborough defeated the
French at Ramillies, Belgium; Alexander overwhelmed the
Persians at Arbela, N.E. Iraq, in 331 B.C.

354.38. *Ovid* Publius Ovidius Naso, 43 B.C.–A.D. 18, Roman poet
(wrote, *inter alia*, *Ars Amatoria*) banished in A.D. 1 as the result
of some obscure scandal.

355.33. *offer* attempt.

356.35. *beg . . . gallows-foot* to beg a person was to appeal in court
for his/her custody; it was possible for a criminal to escape
hanging if a woman volunteered to marry him.

358.37. *club* proportion.

358.39. *bohea* black China tea, introduced *c.* 1700; tea drinking
in England was first referred to in 1658. *scored* kept account
of by chalk marks behind the door of an inn or coffee-house.

358.42. *between both houses* i.e. at one or the other of the licenced
theatres.

358.43. *steal two acts* It was then possible to see part of a play
before payment was demanded. See Farquhar, 'A Discourse
upon Comedy in Reference to the English Stage', *Love and
Business* (1702), p. 147.

360.37. *too much upon the brogue* too much of a trick.

361.13. *entered him* introduced him (to drinking).

361.29. *Vigo* At the Battle of Vigo (off the N.W. coast of Spain),
1702, the English and Dutch fleets captured many French
warships and several rich Spanish treasure ships.

361.32. *Tyburn* the usual place for public executions until 1783,
near Marble Arch, London.

361.34. *household* i.e. the royal household.

363.49. *all-fours* a game of cards played by two people.

364.31. *executed* inflicted.

365.18. *Alcmena* wife of Amphitrion, whose features Jupiter
adopted in order to seduce her. (Hercules was the son of Jupiter
and Alcmena.)

365.41. *engineer* plotter.

369.26. *Tartar* thief.

370.34. *Swiss* Swiss soldiers sold their services as bodyguards, etc.

**371.6.** *Eddystone* lighthouse 13 miles off coast of south Devon; built of wood 1699, destroyed by storm 1703.

**371.13.** *Hybla* a town in Sicily, noted for its honey.

**371.16.** *boat* i.e. both.

**373.39.** *airy* gay.

**375.41.** *Rib* scold.

**376 41.** *stiver* a small Dutch coin, worth about ½p.

**377.1.** *livres* French money of account; a livre was then equivalent to approximately 9d.

**378.1.** *Epilogue* The edition of 1733 describes this Epilogue as written 'by Mr Smith, the Author of *Phaedra und Hypolitis* [1707].' This is the only play by Edmund Smith, 1672–1710, dilettante poet and scholar.

**378.11.** *Leuctra* in Boeotia, Greece, where Epaminondas and his Theban army defeated the Spartans, 371 B.C., but he did not in fact die here.

**378.16.** *Serjeant Kite* the principal comic character in Farquhar's *Recruiting Officer*, 1706.

## THE PROVOK'D WIFE

**381.2.** *Mistress Bracegirdle* Anne Bracegirdle, *c.* 1663–1748, very popular London actress from *c.* 1688 to her retirement, 1707.

**381.14.** *Three plays at once* Vanbrugh's *Relapse* and *Aesop* (an adaptation) had been staged earlier in the 1696–7 season.

**384.20.** *maintenance* i.e. an allowance from an estranged husband.

**384.22.** *monster* cuckold.

**384.45.** *cousin* in fact, niece. 'Cousin' was then more casually used than now.

**385.13–14.** *Court of Chancery* a court of equity.

**385.15.** *House of Lords* the only possible earthly source of a divorce; in rare instances it could be obtained by means of a private bill in the Lords.

**387.1–2.** *our neighbour* i.e. Lady Fanciful.

**387.4.** *original* an eccentric.

**388.8.** *dementi* lie.

**389.5.** *Park* i.e. St James's Park, the most fashionable promenade.

**389.40.** *accablées* overburdened.

**391.27.** *da* indeed.

**392.39.** *Quaker's bargain* giving no alternatives.

**393.16.** *raree-show* a peep-show carried in a box.

**393.40.** *clapper* tongue.

**394.18.** *jack pudding* buffoon.

**395.7–8.** *tire-woman* lady's maid.

**396.40.** *conjunction* a term from astrology; two planets seeming

to come close to one another could be a force for good or ill,
here the latter.

398.3. *daggles* trails through mud, etc.

398.4. *Betty Sands* 1667–99, prostitute, orange-seller at Drury
Lane Theatre, mistress of Peter the Great during his visit to
England (1698). See Alexander Smith, 'Betty Sands and the
C——— of Muscovy', *The School of Venus*, 1716, vol. i, pp.
185–92. (A. Coleman, 'Five Notes on *Provok'd Wife*', *Notes
and Queries*, XVI (August 1969), pp. 298–300.)

400.25. '*Chevy Chase*' a famous, but by 1697 old-fashioned, 16th-
century ballad about the fatal rivalry and battle between the
Earl of Northumberland and Earl Douglas with their forces.

400.27. *levee* morning reception.

402.9. *paper mill* i.e. a very noisy place.

403.19. *split* tear apart.

404.11. *Blue Posts* an inn in the Haymarket.

405.27. *cry roast meat* boast about good fortune (proverbial).

411.42. *peace* The Treaty of Ryswick was not in fact signed until
20 September 1697; *The Provok'd Wife* first reached the stage
in mid April 1697.   *Bank of England* founded 1694, still (in
1697) somewhat suspect, partly because of a run on it in
1696.

412.16. *consciences* The Tolerance Act of 1689 allowed noncon-
formists a greater freedom to worship according to their consciences.

412.18. *dispensation* a power to dispense with the established
laws, claimed by both Charles II and James II.

412.23. *penal laws* restrictions on the activities of Roman Catho-
lics.

413.5. *clary* a sweet liquor made from wine, clarified honey, etc.

415.39. *fantasque* whim.

416.15. *month's mind* strong inclination.

416.37. *Spring Garden* the new pleasure gardens established
c. 1661 at Vauxhall.

418.5. *case* skin.

418.37. *roundhouse* lockup.

420.39. *lead out* dance.

421.15. *New Exchange* a large building in the Strand, with an
arcade and shops.

422.47. *cure* parish.

424.25. *doily stuff* see note to *Way of the World*, III, x, 198.23.

426.8. *give you sauce* will make you pay a high price, i.e. give you
a venereal disease.

431.24–5. *cold tea* a contemporary euphemism for brandy. See
Pope, *The Rape of the Lock*, III, 8.

433.6. *place* rank.

435.8. *uptails all* great confusion; the name of an old song
(c. 1610).

435.18. *poll* parrot.

**440.6.** *Hobbes's voyage* Thomas Hobbes translated Books IX–XII of Homer's *Odyssey* as *The Travels of Ulysses*, 1673 and several later editions.

**442.5.** *law* . . . Bigamy was punishable by death.

**442.13.** *old truepenny* 'good fellow' (*Hamlet*, I, v, 150).

**443.23.** *romance* fiction.

**444.15.** *Hungary water* see note to *The Beaux Stratagem*, IV, i, 351.37.

**445.16.** *dispense with* abstain from.

**446.19.** *third day* The profits from the third (and sometimes the sixth) performance of a play were usually the perquisite of the author. Occasionally a day's profits were assigned to the actors; there is a record of Settle's having contributed his third day's rights to the actresses (*The London Stage*, Part 1, vol. i, p. lxxix).

**APPENDIX B 527.1.** *Bonduca* or Boadicea, queen of the Iceni (Norfolk and Suffolk), who fought vigorously but unsuccessfully against the Romans *c.* A.D. 60. She has no known associations with Wales. Purcell's opera *Bonduca* was produced in 1696.

**528.10.** *grippen* clenched.

**528.16–17.** *Bridewell* a London prison near Fleet St; *beating hemp* a frequent punishment for female prisoners.

## THE MAN OF MODE

**449.2.** *Duchess* Mary of Modena, 1658–1718, Duchess of York, married 1673, later queen-consort when the Duke became King James II.

**450.2.** *Scroope* 1649–80; poet, courtier in court of Charles II.

**451.8–9.** *Now for . . . in vain* Edmund Waller, 'Of a War with Spain, and a Fight at Sea', *Poems*, 1905. Etherege was evidently partial to the work of this poet. Several excerpts appear below.

**451.14.** *fanatic* dissenter, nonconformist.

**451.15.** *Royal Aid* a tax for the benefit of royalty.  *Church Duties* fees charged for various services rendered by the church.

**451.30.** *Foggy* fat.

**451.34–5.** *It is . . . I lay* Waller, 'The Self-Banished'.

**452.13.** *angel* a gold coin worth 50p.

**452.23.** *Newington* a variety of peach, from Kent.

**452.34.** *Change* i.e. the New Exchange, an arcade with shops in the Strand.

**453.11.** *Make us . . .* i.e. God make us . . .

**453.13.** *stagers* veterans.

**453.15.** *canary* a light sweet wine from the Canary Islands; *mistress*, whore.

**453.24.** *crudities* undigested matter in the stomach.

454.21. *Provence* more correctly Provins, a town in N.E. France noted for roses.

455.5. *Bog* corpulent person.

455.6. *pis-aller* last resource.

455.27. *vizard* mask, with the implication of 'prostitute'.

456.15. *insensibly* gradually.

456.16. *artificially* skilfully.

456.29. *uncase* strip you (of livery).

457.1. *engross* monopolize.

457.12. *ale and history* 'Truth is in ale as in history'.

457.23. *caterpillars* parasites.

457.24. *your health . . . now* He asks for a gratuity in order sincerely to drink Dorimant's health.

457.30. *motions* activities.

457.32. *soak* drink.

457.33. *several* separate.  *settle-bed* a bench that may be converted into a bed.

458.14. *fanatic . . . Bethlem* an allusion to Oliver Cromwell's servant who was put in Bethlem, the lunatic asylum *c.* 1650. See M. Prior, 'A Dialogue Between Oliver Cromwell and his Porter', *Literary Works* (Oxford, 1959), vol. i, pp. 655–63.

458.34. *necessary* predestined.

461.4. *goloshes* originally a country shoe with leather uppers and wooden sole.

463.12. *Mr. Fourbes* to fourbe means to cheat.

463.42. *a pise o'* Old Bellair's usual imprecation; perhaps 'a pox on'.  *keeping fools* i.e. fools who keep mistresses.

464.30. *gleeker* player of gleek, a card game for three persons.

464.37. *matadore* one of the winning cards in ombre; they included the two black aces.

465.5. *points* pieces of lace.

465.6. *knots* bows of ribbon.

465.9. *Danish serenade* See *Hamlet*, I, iv, 11.

465.18. *questions and commands* a game involving ridiculous questions and commands.

465.29. *wash* use cosmetic washes.

465.35. *suddenly* soon.  *Bear Garden* Bear baiting was popular here from 1617 to Restoration times. Medley's comment is facetious.

466.40. *current* acceptable.

467.27. *St. Winifred's* a miraculous shrine and well at Holywell, Wales.

469.2–3. *They taste . . . alive* Waller, 'Of her Chamber'.

469.4. *galloping nag* a lively country dance.

469.37–8. *So thunder . . . rain* Matthew Roydon, 'An Elegy, or Friend's Passion, for his Astrophell' (a tribute to Sidney) in *The Phoenix Nest*, 1593. (R. Howarth, 'Untraced Quotations in Etherege', *Notes and Queries*, CLXXXVIII, 30 June 1945, p. 281.)

**471.21.** *enter* initiate.

**472.32.** *patching* Wearing small patches (usually of black silk) on the face was a contemporary fad.

**473.12.** *fetches* tricks.

**473.26–7.** *I find . . . design'd* paraphrase of lines about Merab, eldest daughter of Saul, in A. Cowley, *Davideis*, Book III, lines 625–6, in *Poems* (Cambridge, 1905), 341.

**473.43.** *lay myself out* exert myself.

**474.20.** *Bartholomew* i.e. Bartholomew Cokes, of Jonson's *Bartholomew Fair* (1614); he was carried away by enthusiasm for gingerbread and other gewgaws of the Fair.

**474.31.** *hangings* tapestries, etc.

**474.40.** *playing it on booty* deliberately to lose in a game in order to trick a victim later.

**474.48.** *remarks* observations.

**475.11.** *fleering* impudent.

**479.1.** *ordinaries* taverns or eating houses.

**479.7.** *confidence* intimacy.

**480.27.** *point d'Espagne* Spanish lace.

**480.40.** *calèche* a light carriage with collapsible top.

**480.43.** *tumbril* dung cart.

**481.20.** *garniture* trimmings.

**481.37.** *rest* remnant.

**482.18.** *stums* to renew fermentation temporarily in dull wine by adding must (unfermented or partly fermented grape juice).

**482.19.** *sophisticate* adulterated.

**483.1.** *the last king's time* i.e. the period of Charles I, who died in 1649.

**483.5.** *taking* state.

**483.33–4.** *In love . . . die* Waller, 'To a Friend, of the Different Success of their Loves'.

**483.40.** *tweers* covert glances.

**484.3.** *temper* moderation.

**485.40–1.** *Snatch'd . . . shore* Waller, 'Of Loving at First Sight'.

**486.8.** *towards* in prospect.

**486.12.** *St. James's* St James's Palace, near the west end of the Mall.

**486.41–2.** *See how . . . passes* Suckling, Sonnet I, *Fragmenta Aurea*, 1646, p. 14.

**487.1.** *unlucky* mischievous.

**487.42.** *sort* crowd.

**488.3.** *convenient* mistress.

**488.4.** *oily* fat.

**488.6.** *caravan* an object for plunder.

**488.16.** *insulting* triumphant.

**488.21.** *cordovan* leather, made in Cordova, Spain, from horsehide.

**488.38.** *trig* trip.

**489.34.** *hankering* loitering.

**489.42.** *reserve* exception.

**491.29.** *handkercher* head or neck covering.

492.8. *kindly* naturally.

495.23. *couchée* evening reception.

495.38. *coq-à-l'âne* piece of nonsense.

496.1. *habitudes* acquaintances.

496.12. *d'Ambois* Sir Fopling naïvely identifies 'Bussy' as Bussy d'Ambois, the hero of George Chapman's play of this title (1607), revived in London 1661 and *c*. 1675.

497.2. *state* canopy.

497.11. *to your power* to the limits of your ability.

497.13. *Birthday* the celebration of King Charles II's birthday (29 May).

497.42. *undertaking* bold.

498.1. *corant* a running or gliding dance, without capers. *bourée* a rustic dance.

498.2. *menuet* a slow, stately dance. *St. André* a French dancer (Crowne's *Calisto*, 1675) and choreographer (Shadwell's *Psyche*, 1675).

498.7. *basque* a waist-length skirt of a doublet. *entry* interlude.

498.17. *entertain* hire.

498.23. *mumming* a performance of a mummers' play.

498.43. *sensible* capable of delicate feeling.

500.8. *bachique* drinking song.

500.15ff. *The pleasures* . . . adapted from Thomas Shadwell, *Psyche*, 1675, V, p. 70.

503.26. *Candale* 1627–58, notably brave general in the French army.

503.28. *brandenburgh* woollen morning gown.

504.2. *coup d'essai* first attempt.

504.24. *Baptiste* Etherege may have had in mind Jean Baptiste Lully, 1633–87, composer and director of music and opera in the court of Louis XIV.

505.38. *taking up* taking possession.

507.40. *narolii* perfumes based on essence of leaves of orange trees.

508.7. *nectarines* Such a wish was reputed to be an indication of pregnancy. See the innuendos below and Webster, *The Duchess of Malfi*, II, i, 132–77 and Ford, *'Tis Pity She's a Whore*, III, iv, 3–9.

508.43. *surfeit water* a medicinal drink.

509.7. *canaille* rabble.

509.9–10. *I, that . . . love* Waller, 'To the Mutable Fair'.

510.16. *properties* instruments. *indifferent* moderate.

510.18. *square* gaming board. *rook* swindler.

510.19. *bubble* dupe.

512.23. *mirabilis aqua mirabilis*, a medicinal drink made from wine and spices.

513.38. *closet* private room.

514.47. *rallied* ridiculed.

515.27. *betimes* speedily.

515.32–3. *Music . . . find* Waller, 'Of my Lady Isabella, Playing the Lute'.
519.15. *hoiting* noisy.
521.16. *fière* haughty.
521.28. *cut* a leap in a dance, with feet twiddling.
522.11. *Hartley* probably Hartley Row, near Basingstoke, Hants.
522.21. *volery* aviary.
523.11. *cocks* struts.
523.18. *knight o' th' shire* a member of parliament.
523.24. *wallow* rolling way of walking.
523.25. *sword-knot* ribbon tied on the hilt of a sword.
523.26. *snake* a tail attached to a wig.
523.30. *shog* shake.

# GLOSSARY

Frequently used words whose seventeenth-century meanings may not be immediately clear in their dramatic contexts are explained below. Words readily found in a modern dictionary are not included. In the interests of space, neither the Notes nor the Glossary makes reference to several oaths or expletives often used in the plays. Most are self-evidently modifications (Ods, 'Sbud, 'Sdeath, Oons, Zoons, etc.) of stronger oaths beginning By God, By God's blood, death, wounds, and so forth.

*'a* he, she, it
*an* if
*canonical hour* marriages might then be legally performed between 8.00 a.m. and noon
*close* secret
*discover* reveal
*doubts* fears
*event* outcome
*expect* wait
*fond* foolish
*gazettes* news sheets
*honest* chaste
*How!* Indeed!
*just* exact
*Marry!* Indeed!
*mere* absolute
*mother* hysteria

*or . . . or* either . . . or
*own* acknowledge
*parts* talents
*present* immediate
*prevent* anticipate
*proper* handsome
*pulvillio* scented powder
*quoif* coif, close-fitting cap
*salutes* kisses
*silly* ignorant
*still* always
*turtles* turtle doves
*used* accustomed
*vapours* fashionable ailment; emotional depression
*want* lack
*whispers* addresses
*without* unless
*writings* documents